D1605062

Parthenope

Tomas Hägg

PARTHENOPE

Selected Studies in Ancient Greek Fiction
(1969–2004)

Edited by
Lars Boje Mortensen & Tormod Eide

MUSEUM TUSCULANUM PRESS
UNIVERSITY OF COPENHAGEN
2004

Parthenope — Selected Studies in Ancient Greek Fiction (1969-2004)

© 2004 Museum Tusculanum Press and the Author
Edited by: Lars Boje Mortensen & Tormod Eide

Cover design: Pernille Sys Hansen
Set and printed in Denmark by Narayana Press
ISBN 87 7289 907 7

Cover illustration: "Parthenope", detail of Roman floor mosaic
from Zeugma-Belkis, Turkey (ca. AD 200), now in Gaziantep
Museum. Photo: Suat Eman. Reproduced with the permission
of A Turizm Yayınları & Friends of Gaziantep Museum.

Published with support from

The Research Council of Norway/Programme for Classical
Studies/Project: The Construction of Christian Identity in Antiquity
and
University of Bergen, The Faculty of Arts
Nordea Danmark Fonden

Museum Tusculanum Press
Njalsgade 94
DK – 2300 Copenhagen S

www.mtp.dk

Contents

A Memoir

Forty Years in and out of the Greek Novel
– A Memoir

"What about narrative technique in the Greek novels, then?" It must have been in the early autumn of 1963, in Jonas Palm's office at Uppsala University. The Professor had been turning over the leaves of the black notebook in which he had the habit of entering suitable topics of research, originally for future work of his own, later also for the theses of his prospective students. True to the tradition that he brought with him from Lund to his Chair of Greek language and literature in Uppsala, most of the suggestions began "Zur Sprache und Stil des ..." and concerned Greek authors of the Roman Imperial period. I had remained politely unenthusiastic until the one literary topic finally came up. Not that I had by then read any of the Greek novels — they had not been on our Uppsala curriculum — but I had a couple of years earlier heard Ebbe Vilborg giving a stimulating paper on them; and, more importantly, a book by Staffan Björck (the younger brother of the Uppsala Grecist Gudmund Björck) about narrative technique in modern Swedish novels had made a deep impression on me in my schooldays.[1] I had been an avid novel reader and Björck's elegant unmasking of the tricks of the trade, taking his examples from books I knew, gave many aha experiences and made me aware that there were other ways of illuminating literary works than the biographical approach that still dominated school teaching. It turned out that it was the same book that had originally inspired Jonas Palm to formulate his topic for a potential study of the Greek novels. We now had a short discussion about the possibilities to use some of the same, mainly Anglo-American methods on these ancient texts, and I decided to give it a try.

In spite of these intentions, what I presented four years later as my thesis for the degree of Licentiate of Philosophy (A0)[2] bore very few marks

---

[1] Staffan Björck, *Romanens formvärld: Studier i prosaberättarens teknik*, Stockholm 1953.

[2] I refer to titles in the "Bibliography" (below, pp. 29–37) by capital letter and number, to articles reprinted in the present volume also by their number in boldface.

of modern literary criticism. It was all about the narrative technique of one author, Xenophon of Ephesos, but based on close observation of distinctive traits of the text itself — parallel action and alternation technique, recapitulations, and the introduction and naming of the characters — rather than on the imposition of any external model. My reading of secondary literature had been focussed mainly on works of classical philology, and my first published article (A1=6) — based on an appendix to my unpublished thesis — was devoted to a typically philological problem: is the version of Xenophon's *Ephesiaka* that has come down to us (in one sole manuscript) really an abbreviation of the original, as most scholars have believed? It was Erwin Rohde who had first, in noncommittal casualness, put forward this idea in his *Der griechische Roman* (1876), a book as full of remarkable insights and accurate formulations as of prejudice typical of the period. The belief that the *Ephesiaka* was an epitome had led to some contradictory studies of the novel or, more often, to its neglect (true to the maxim that only an Original work is worth studying). My own conclusion was that the German article of 1892 to which everyone referred did not prove its case;[3] in all its apparent *Wissenschaftlichkeit* it was highly subjective and illogical. My studies of the recapitulations had not revealed any lacunas in the plot or any differences of emphasis between primary narrative and recapitulation, nor could I find any close parallels or good reasons for manufacturing an epitome of a simple novel of adventure.[4] In a much later conference paper (1990, published in 1994 as A28=4), I tried to supplement this mainly negative demonstration by placing Xenophon's narrative technique in an oral/aural context. The (to my mind) definitive vindication of the *Ephesiaka* as an original work came in 1995 when James O'Sullivan presented his detailed analysis of its oral compositional technique.[5]

The next step in my academic career, a dissertation for the degree of Doctor of Philosophy, was to build on the former thesis but clearly demanded an extension of both corpus and theoretical basis. French "nar-

---

[3] K. Bürger, "Zu Xenophon von Ephesus", *Hermes* 27, 1892, 36–67. For a critical examination of the controversy, see C. Ruiz-Montero, "Xenophon von Ephesos: Ein Überblick", in: *ANRW* II.34.2, 1088–1138, at 1094–1096.

[4] Since my article has perhaps been more frequently cited than actually read, it appears in the present collection translated from German into English.

[5] James N. O'Sullivan, *Xenophon of Ephesus: His compositional technique and the birth of the novel*, Berlin & New York 1995. Cf. further my essay A35, pp. 22–25, to appear in English as A37.

ratology" was not yet (quite) born, and what I read of pre-Genette French literary theory never appealed to me. I found the British and American discussions of narrative technique, from Henry James and E.M. Forster to Wayne Booth, more congenial; and the taxonomic approach of German-language scholars like Günther Müller, Eberhart Lämmert and Franz Stanzel proved still more easily applicable to my ancient narrative texts. At that time, there was little written in this vein about the Greek and Latin novels themselves (more, of course, about ancient epic) and nothing that could serve as inspiration or model. For better or for worse, I had to work out my own investigative tools — a deliberately eclectic set — for my comparative study of Chariton, Xenophon and Achilleus Tatios. Starting with a very concrete mapping of the tempo and phases of the narrative, with diagrams and all, I went on to types of narrative (scene and summary, description and commentary), point of view, and time and action, and subsequently to what I called the internal reference system, anticipations and recapitulations. All was strictly text-internal, only a concluding chapter tried to sketch an historical framework.

Narrative technique in ancient Greek romances appeared in 1971 (A2). In the last section of the last chapter I payed hommage to two seminal studies that had appeared while I was working, but too late to have had any impact on the direction of my studies: Ben Edwin Perry's monograph *The ancient romances: A literary-historical account of their origins* and Bryan Reardon's magisterial article "The Greek novel".[6] My own investigation was later characterized by Gerry Sandy as conducted "[i]n almost clinically abstract fashion", not necessarily intended as a compliment,[7] and by Brian Vickers (in a *TLS* review of my later book, *The novel in antiquity*) as "a rigorous but 'pre-modern' study".[8] I can see their point (though I am not quite sure what Vickers' "but" implies). In fact, there appeared at the time a fair number of positively appreciative re-

[6] B.E. Perry, *The ancient romances: A literary-historical account of their origins*, Berkeley & Los Angeles 1967; B.P. Reardon, "The Greek novel", *Phoenix* 23, 1969, 291–309.

[7] G.N. Sandy, "Recent scholarship on the prose fiction of Classical Antiquity", *Classical World* 67, 1974, 321–359, at 335. Bryan Reardon has in a couple of articles, explicitly basing himself on my findings, demonstrated what I could have done if I had only dared to take a step further in my analysis from form to meaning: "Theme, structure and narrative in Chariton", *Yale Classical Studies* 27, 1982, 1–27, and "Achilles Tatius and ego-narrative", in J.R. Morgan & R. Stoneman (eds.), *Greek fiction: The Greek novel in context*, London & New York 1994, 80–96.

[8] *The Times Literary Supplement* April 20 1984, 427.

views, and I have the impression that the book has later proved useful. Some reviewers, however, gave expression to the same sort of misgivings as I had encountered through the years from my own philological environment in Uppsala (with Jonas Palm as an important exception): do these simple texts really deserve all this attention, and what is the point in scholarship that does not solve problems, "crack nuts"?[9] The distinguished Swiss philologist Fritz Wehrli, in a rather devastating twenty-liner in *Museum Helveticum*, ended by graciously suggesting that maybe my "laborious" study was in fact just intended as *Vorarbeit* to something really worthwhile.[10]

Reactions of that kind were part of the background for my decision to leave the novels and literary criticism, and do something truly "philological" (in the Germanic sense of the word) — especially since "philology" and textual criticism had always appealed to me, and was what I was really trained for. Another reason, of course, was a certain saturation, not to say satiety, after eight years' immersion in these "simple" texts. Career considerations were also present in my mind: for a professorship, one was expected to show several different skills.

I had by this time my own black notebook (or was mine yellow?) in which "Fact and Fiction in the Greek Novels" would under other circumstances have been a serious option. My article, "The naming of the characters in the romance of Xenophon Ephesius" (A3=7), written in tandem with the dissertation, may be regarded as a first instalment in that intended (but never fulfilled) project. To establish a factual foil to the novelist's choice of names — this was before the *Lexicon of Greek personal names* (to which I later made a modest contribution) — I was happy to revisit epigraphy, a discipline I had first encountered actively

---

[9] A civilized version of this kind of criticism is found in Lennart Rydén's review in *Gnomon* 45, 1973, 442–447, based on his opposition at the public defense of the dissertation at Uppsala University (April 17, 1971).

[10] *Museum Helveticum* 28, 1971, 238. His review began "Der Vf. ist der strukturalistischen Betrachtungsweise verpflichtet" — apparently as much an insult in Zürich as in Uppsala of the sixties — and ended: "Dass es dem Vf. nicht gelingt, eine Vorstellung von der Gesamtstruktur der drei behandelten Romane zu vermitteln, liegt zunächst an seiner isolierenden, mit Vorliebe auf die Häufigkeit der einzelnen Formenelemente gerichteten Betrachtungsweise. Es mag sein, dass er seine mühevollen Untersuchungen als blosse Vorarbeit für spätere Studien betrachtet, welchen er vorbehält, den Blick von den Teilen aufs Ganze zu richten." The leading English review journals, *Classical Review* and *Journal of Hellenic Studies*, never published a review of the book (while nearly 20 others around the world did), probably an eloquent silence.

when collecting material for my Master's thesis in Ancient history on *damnatio memoriae* (Fo).[11]

Instead, however, my need for a real contrast led to an investigation of the *Bibliotheca* of the Byzantine scholar Photios (9th century) and its treatment of postclassical Greek literature. This involved manuscript studies (cf. B3, B9), textual criticism and much strictly philological analysis. Almost as a natural consequence, I wrote the book in German, mostly during my periods as a Humboldt scholar at the University of Cologne (*Photios als Vermittler antiker Literatur*, 1975, B2). Yet there were a couple of organic links to my study of ancient fiction. My interest in Photios' methods and reliability had first been awakened by his analytical epitomes of a couple of lost novels, Iamblichos' *Babyloniaka* and Antonios Diogenes' *Marvels beyond Thule*, and by his strange review of Heliodoros' *Aithiopika*, ignoring completely this novel's complex narrative structure. In addition, as my prime test case — which had to be a work extant today in its original form to permit the exact diagnosis of the Patriarch's methods of abbreviation — I chose his double readings of Philostratos' biographical novel *Life of Apollonios of Tyana* (cf. B1=15). This manifold text, until quite recently neglected by historians of ancient literature, has remained a companion through the years, as can be seen from a number of studies of its *Nachleben* included in the present volume (13-16). Yet the critical edition for Teubner for which I did extensive preliminary work in various manuscript collections, never materialized. The lustful experience of touching and smelling the medieval manuscripts and extracting their hidden inky secrets with the help of a strong magnifying glass was not easily transferable to months and years before a microfilm reader at home.

Speaking of projects unfulfilled or redirected, pure chance led me to one of the true outposts of classical studies, the study of the remarkable, if narrow, survival of the Greek language in Christian Nubia through much of the Byzantine period. It all started when I was invited to take

[11] It may be noted at this point that it was the Uppsala Seminar in Classical Archaeology and Ancient History, directed by Arne Furumark and his successor Sture Brunnsåker, that provided me with the main intellectual stimulation in my student years. I found there an openness and a curiosity about new ideas — and a critical (often, it is true, deadly hypercritical) examination of them — that I missed in the philological milieu, with its emphasis on the accumulation of learning and gradual refinement of traditional methods. Also, it was not through my teachers in Greek that my interest in textual criticism developed, but in the inspiring lectures of the Latinist Alf Önnerfors.

part in an excursion, arranged in the winter of 1972/73 by the Finnish Egyptological Society and led by Rostislav Holthoer, through the non-flooded parts of Nubia. From Khartoum we took the route through the Bayuda desert to Dongola, then along the Nile down to (new) Wadi Halfa. We visited the principal sites on both sides of the river and were guided and entertained by several of the excavation or survey teams. Finally, we crossed Lake Nasser and arrived at Assuan via Abu Simbel and Philae. The scholarly object had been to document a monastery in the desert, my assigned role being to trace Greek graffiti on its walls. Though we never managed to reach that particular monastery (and my qualifications for the job luckily did not have to be tested), the outcome for my part was a lasting fascination with the area and period.

It also meant my admission to the intense interdisciplinary research milieu of "Nubiology" emerging in the wake of the UNESCO campaign of the early sixties to save Nubian antiquities. Torgny Säve-Söderbergh, head of the Scandinavian Joint Expedition to Sudanese Nubia, subsequently entrusted me with the publication of a couple of major inscriptions in Greek (C5), other similar commissions followed (C7, 17), and for many years I was assiduously collecting material for a linguistic study of the Greek language in Christian Nubia (cf. C4, 6, 12, 16, 22, 27). Though probably the most time-consuming of my research activities after the doctorate — and in many ways the most inspiring one through the access to virgin textual material — this project never resulted in a major synthetic study. Too much epigraphical and philological groundwork would have been needed in order properly to establish all the documentary texts (cf. C9), too diverse and profound a linguistic knowledge (in Coptic and Old Nubian in addition to Greek of various species) to be able to interpret the data in a satisfactory manner.

Gradually, however, my Nubian efforts were redirected from the Byzantine to the ancient period and to encompass all the Greek and Latin textual sources for Nubian history, literary as well as documentary. This had to do with my move, in 1977, from Uppsala to the University of Bergen and its Chair of Classical Philology. By a remarkable coincidence, two of my new colleagues at the Department of Classics, the Egyptologist Richard Holton Pierce and the Classicist Tormod Eide, were already engaged in Nubian studies, though from a different angle than mine. They had started, on a rather small scale, to translate Late Antique historical sources to make them available in reliable versions to the rapidly growing community of scholars engaged in Egyptology/Nubiology without knowledge of the old languages: archaeologists, anthropologists, and, in particular, new generations of Sudanese students eager to explore their own heritage (Pierce was in 1977 just back in Bergen from a year in Khartoum as visiting professor at the Department of Archaeology). This was a way Classics and Egyptology could be made immediately useful, we felt. Our modest project (cf. C2, 3, 11) took a giant leap forward, in scope and ambition, through the influence of that complete Nubiologist, László Török of the Hungarian Academy of Sciences, who for several extended periods since 1980 had been a visiting scholar at our department. He managed to persuade us to work together towards a commented collection and translation of all the historically relevant texts on the Middle Nile Region, whether in Egyptian (including Demotic and Coptic) or one of the Classical languages, from the eighth century BC to the sixth century AD–the *Fontes Historiae Nubiorum*. Throughout the nineties, we published one large volume of texts, translations, comments and bibliography every second year, ending up with page 1375 in the year 2000 (C18, 20, 21, 24). For my part, this may be said to have created a certain balance, after all, between time spent in Nubian Greek studies and actual output. But, more importantly, I remember the many morning hours we spent together in our small translation group, intensely discussing niceties of the Greek, Latin and English languages as well as Classical historiographic conventions and Nubian *realia*, as something of the most stimulating I have experienced as a classical scholar.

Those who have expected this memoir, true to its title, to be more consistently focussed on the Greek novel, need not despair: I shall soon be back on track, after these digressions into Byzantine humanism and Nubian exotica. Without them, however, my way in and out of novel studies during these forty years would hardly be understandable. Concentration on one line of research, besides all the other obligations that go with a university professorship, would no doubt have resulted in a more coherent and satisfying scholarly output. Only following up the bibliography of two or three completely separate fields of research consumes a lot of time and energy. But I do not think I could have chosen otherwise. Among other things, the positivist within me has needed the concrete philological labour with manuscripts and inscriptions, with editorial work and corpus building, producing results that one imagines are definitive in one sense or other, in contrast to the exciting but precarious and largely ephemeral occupation with literary questions. Yet, one never feels as familiar with any material, I think, as with the primary

sources and previous scholarship one toiled to master for one's dissertation, and I have tended always to return to the novels. Sometimes I
have done so following external calls to order, sometimes — as I like to
construe it — by pure chance. Yet, I believe, each time with a sense of
relief, as coming home.

The first return was definitely caused by outside forces. Classicists in
Copenhagen had come across my dissertation and apparently found it
interesting enough to invite me for a series of lectures. Since no similar interest had ever been noticeable in Swedish classical departments, I
had no experience of lecturing on the novels. Now I was forced, for the
first time, to look at them and my dissertation from outside, in order
to make the genre and my findings accessible to a wider audience. In
the early spring of 1974, on my way to Venice for two months with the
venerable *Bibliotheca* manuscripts in the Biblioteca Marciana (cf. B3),
I stopped for a week to deliver my lectures in Copenhagen (and one
in Aarhus as well). My first lecture, a general introduction to the genre
and its modern exploration "from Rohde to Perry", which had cost me
most sweat and most compromises with my inherited ideals of original
scholarship — the art of popularization was not yet on the university
curriculum — was later to appear as the postscript to a Danish translation of Heliodoros' *Aithiopika* (A8). This was the first step towards what
was to become, almost a decade later, *The novel in antiquity*.

My move to Bergen in 1977 entailed further lecture writing on both
Greek and Roman novels, with students and teachers of comparative
literature as the target group. So when I met with an enterprising and
enthusiastic Swedish publisher (and former Latinist), Jörn Johanson of
Carmina publishing house, I was easily persuaded into trying to write
a popular book on the subject — and a book with many pictures, since
this was part of the publisher's general policy. I could hardly have moved
further away from the expectations I had once tried to meet with my
dissertation. The whole process was immensely instructive. No pictures
of bodies without heads, or faces without noses (also transferable, I
gathered, to the textual material)! No portrait gallery (I had, in all in-
nocence, suggested photos of Rohde and Perry). No detailed accounts
of research which is afterwards declared wrong-headed, abortive and a
thing of the past: you just make the reader regret s/he ever started reading it. The telling detail rather than exhaustiveness. Generous extracts in
translation from the novels themselves — showing and telling, in that
order. No references to footnotes or endnotes that detract attention from

the reading. Informative index (added information about people, places and dates, so that it need not encumber the text). Captions to the pictures that both summarize part of your text and give new details: looking at the pictures and reading the captions should provide appetizing glimpses of what the book has to offer. And, of course, the golden rule of all popularization: never overestimate your readers' knowledge, never underestimate their intelligence.

Den antika romanen (A10), issued in 1980, proved a success with Swedish critics and public. Still, I never dreamed of having it translated into any of the international languages. This perhaps needs some explanation. As a Swedish classicist, I was wont always to publish the results of my own research in an international language (since the prospective readership in Swedish would anyway be minimal). Only more popular or derivative things would appear in Swedish. Thereby, the two "genres" of scholarship were (and are) kept rigorously apart, in a way they are not for native writers of English, French etc. Moreover, I had the impression that English (etc.) writers of similarly introductory books on classical literary subjects could (and would) demand much more previous knowledge about antiquity from their readers than I (and my publisher) expected from a Swedish general audience. My book would thus be too elementary and boring for those (educated) readers who would at all aspire to reading a work on this topic in English.

Well, Chance entered the scene again. Carmina had a stand at the Frankfurter Buchmesse which was visited by a representative for Blackwells. Presented with my book, he at once realized that, whatever his own interest in publishing it, his principal would want him to do so, for sentimental reasons: Sir Basil had early in his publishing career taken on Martin Braun's *History and romance in Graeco-Oriental literature* (1938) and would now, in his early nineties, be pleased to follow that up. Readers' reports proved favourable and I was asked to be my own translator. Though quite time-consuming, this gave me the chance to scrutinize my formulations throughout, take advantage of some new research, and revise more substantially some parts that seemed either too evasive (especially about the first readership of the novels) or too provincially Swedish. I also equipped the book with a systematic "Further Reading" section that the first edition had lacked. The number of illustrations had to be somewhat reduced and the colour plates sacrificed. Richard Holton Pierce and Bryan Reardon helped all along improving my English style (and sharpening my argument). Thus, *The novel in antiquity*, as it appeared in 1983 (A15), was not a very different, but still a better book, and the English edition later became the starting-point for up-dated translations into German and Greek as well (A19, 27). Just for the record, the German edition was provided with numbered endnotes, since German readers were expected to take offence at unassigned references to previous scholarship; and a negotiated French edition never materialized, apparently because a scholarly book on a literary topic profusely illustrated was conceived of as something of a bastard.

The recipe thought out for the Swedish public proved successful internationally as well. My apprehensions had obviously been groundless. Reviews were favourable, the book found readers even among classical scholars (for whom it was not primarily intended) and has since been used as an academic textbook, especially in American universities. To my great astonishment, when I happened to spend a sabbatical at Oxford in the spring of 1986, it functioned as an open sesame, generating coffee-shop interviews as well as high-table invitations. I was referred to as "the novel man" — a label that would have fitted me better fifteen years earlier. Obviously, it had come as something of a shock when suddenly one morning Blackwell's show-window, at the very heart of that bastion of classical studies, was filled with copies of a classical book — even a readable one — whose author nobody had heard of before. Understandably so: for since the publication of my dissertation in 1971 (which was not reviewed in England) and of the two major articles accompanying it (in Scandinavian journals), I had done no more research on the novel and by 1983, apart from a few reviews (A6, 11, 12=**17–19**), had published nothing in the field. I had been fully occupied with Byzantium and Nubia.

I had also missed being part of the revival of novel studies as manifested in the first international conference on the ancient novel (ICAN), convened by Bryan Reardon at Bangor in 1976, on the hundredth anniversary of Rohde's *Der griechische Roman*.[12] (I vaguely recollect having seen a notice of it in a journal, but rejecting the idea to take part, thinking that Bangor was a place in India. Uppsala could not be expected to provide that kind of travelling money. Bryan Reardon kindly invited me to Wales a couple of years later to inspect the venue and learn some geography.) While I had been a fairly regular participant in the confer-

---

[12] The rare book, *Erotica antiqua* (1977, ed. B.P. Reardon), which resulted from that occasion, contains the names of most of the (young) people who were to embody the revival of the late seventies and eighties.

ences of Nubian and Meroitic studies that took place every second year, I first met with international colleagues in the ancient-novel field as late as 1986 when — again with *The novel in antiquity* as my credentials — I was invited by Roderick Beaton to contribute to "The Greek Novel AD 1–1985" at King's College London, with a paper on "The beginnings of the historical novel" (A18=**2**, 21, 31). As it happened, I could not attend the next ICAN either, arranged in July 1989 at Dartmouth College in New Hampshire, since my wife was expected to give birth to our twin daughters only a couple of weeks later (evoking the twin motif was considered, I was told, a suitable excuse among the ancient-fiction people assembled there); my participation was limited to an abstract (A25).

My point in dwelling on these mundane matters is simply that, whether one likes it or not, such external factors as conferences and invitations have come to decide more and more about the direction of one's research, even as a humanist. Accepting an invitation (or applying for money to participate on one's own initiative) means having to write a paper, more or less genuinely adjusted to the specific topic of the conference, and later to prepare it for publication in the conference acts. On the positive side, it may mean an impetus to write at all, and perhaps to think along new lines about one's speciality, and it of course means exchange of ideas (and academic gossip) with colleagues in agreeable circumstances; on the negative side, it disturbs the natural rhythm of humanistic scholarship, atomizes the little time available for research, and all but prevents the *longue durée* projects grown from one's own inclinations. To be less general and more personal, my membership in the Nubian-studies community and my outsider position in novel studies no doubt influenced my productivity in those fields. Yet, in the early and mid-eighties, "the novel man" again got more living-space, if only for a while.

I guess my work on *The novel in antiquity* and its positive reception had made me mentally prepared for a return to research in that area. But the fact that novel studies had become fashionable in the meantime, with a rapidly increasing output of articles of varying quality, and even some books, meant no enticement to me, rather the opposite. I have always been more attracted to areas and topics where there is ample room for basic work and one is not forced to choose a very narrow problem or apply an eccentric theoretical model to be able to do something that has not been done before, nor may simultaneously be attempted by someone else as well. The corpus of Greek novels is small and does not deserve to be to classicists what the New Testament is to exegetes; nor does it have hidden qualities sufficient to repay infinite recycling on a par with Homer or Attic drama. But, to be sure, we are not there yet. The novel was neglected for so long as a serious object of study that even some basic work remains to be done: textual editions, commentaries, reception studies. In addition, general trends in modern literary and cultural studies — gender issues, history of sexuality, cultural myths — have made these texts a more central concern than much other ancient literature. So, the idea to engage in novel studies again was not alien to me.

Yet, that it should be precisely the fragments of Greek novels that I should choose for my comeback, was no obvious thing. I had necessarily left them out in my study of narrative technique (which had to build on complete works) and deliberately kept them in the background in my introduction to the genre too (no bodies without heads). Furthermore, I am not a papyrologist, nor naturally inclined to much speculation on a minimal basis. So again I have no better explanation than pure chance, even in repeated appearance.

One day, probably early in 1982, my colleague Pierce brought to my office an article published in a supplementary volume to the Bulletin of the French Institute of Oriental Archaeology at Cairo — not the type of publication a classicist would normally browse through. It had the title "Le roman de Παρθενόπη/Bartânûbâ"[13] and presented the story of a young Christian girl in the time of Constantine who died a virgin martyr, extant in several Arabic manuscripts and now also identified in a Coptic manuscript fragment. Reading the French translation I was immediately struck by the similarities in motifs and intrigue with the Greek novels, particularly those of the early "non-sophistic" type. Could it be just a coincidence that the girl also had the same name as the heroine of the novel of *Metiochos and Parthenope*, recently reconstructed by Herwig Maehler? I argued the case, put into the larger framework of novelistic material in Christian hagiography overall, in my article "The Parthenope Romance decapitated?" (A14=8). But meanwhile, before that article was printed in 1984, another strange chain of coincidences had led to a discovery that determined the direction of practically all my subsequent research on the novels. Time for another anecdote.

To be able to launch *The novel in antiquity* in the United States as well, Blackwells had turned to the University of California Press which had

---

[13] R.-G. Coquin, "Le roman de Παρθενόπη/Bartânûbâ (ms. *IFAO, Copte* 22, ffo 1r–v 2r), *Bulletin de Centenaire*, Suppl. au *BIFAO* 81, 1981, 343–58 + Pl. XLII.

already commissioned Bryan Reardon to edit a collection of all the extant Greek novels in English translation (it finally appeared in 1989); the two books were supposed to make a nice couple in marketing. Though already accepted by Blackwells, my manuscript had to be submitted to the Advisory Board of UCP as well. The experts on that board, it appeared, had a problem, mediated to me by the administration: Why did I not discuss in my book the fact that many of the Greek novels were translated into Arabic and then from Arabic into Latin in the Middle Ages? I was taken aback by the professional ignorance reflected in the question: we do not by any means have "many" Greek novels, and none was transmitted via the Arabs to the Latin West. Bryan Reardon intervened and the book was accepted without further ado. But the problem raised indirectly by the question kept lingering in my mind, and eventually proved to be productive. Even if we have no traces of Greek novels in Arabic versions, I asked myself, can we be sure that there never were any, and if so, why, seeing all the Greek literature received by the Abbasids in the Golden Age of Arabic culture of the ninth and tenth centuries?

So when I was invited to contribute to a Festschrift to the distinguished Uppsala Semitist Frithiof Rundgren, who had himself written about Greek influence on Arabic literature, I thought it might be a good idea to write a short piece discussing why there was no Arabic reception of the Greek novels. I worked for a while on the topic, arriving at the conclusion that probably the utility aspect behind the great translation movement hindered such popular fiction to come through. I was happy to come across an authoritative statement by Richard Walzer: "neither Greek poetry nor artistic prose was ever translated into Classical Arabic".[14] Yet, I pondered, maybe there were other routes from Greece to Baghdad than through Christian Syria, the needle's eye through which the philosophy, science and medicine usually had to pass? From my Photios studies I was aware that there were close connections between Constantinople and Baghdad in the ninth century, that there existed Greek novels in the former metropolis that are lost to us, and that there was a collection of Greek manuscripts in the latter's "House of Wisdom". Could there still be a chance? Was there a realistic hope that one day an Arabic translation of a lost Greek novel would emerge in some collection of Oriental manuscripts?

[14] R. Walzer, "Arabic transmission of Greek thought to Medieval Europe", *Bulletin of the John Rylands Library* 29, 1945–46, 160–83, at 162.

Having arrived that far in my speculations, on a visit to Uppsala in the autumn of 1983, I went to see an old schoolmate, Bo Utas, who had specialized in Oriental studies and was now professor of Iranian languages. I aired these questions and asked him for suggestions. He recalled that he had in his possession the edition of a fragmentary Persian epic poem, published in Pakistan in the 1960s, which had inside its covers a map of the Aegean Sea in antiquity. He lent it to me and in a few minutes, leafing through its English introduction, I arrived at a thrilling conclusion: this 11th-century epic poem on "The Lover and the Virgin" not only had a Greek background, as its Pakistani editor was aware, but built precisely on *Metiochos and Parthenope*, the very text I had been working on during the last year. There was still time to add a postscript to that effect to my article on the decapitated Parthenope, which was now in proof. Here she was again, head intact and revealing at least part of her body.

My "survey with some preliminary considerations" about the Oriental reception of Greek novels developed into something too voluminous to be housed in the Festschrift, but appeared elsewhere (A17=10). It discussed, among other things, the possible route this story had taken from Greek novel to Persian epic poem — a journey of a thousand years — and the potential intermediary versions, Arabic or other. I had now my own preserves within the territory of novel studies.

Bo Utas and I had immediately agreed to collaborate with a view to publishing a book presenting all the textual material, Greek as well as Persian, in critical editions, with an English translation and comments. Waiting for this joint enterprise to start in full measure — among other things, Utas wanted first to inspect for himself, if possible, the Persian manuscript fragment to be certain of the order of the leaves and check uncertain readings — we each published articles discussing selected problems actualized by the juxtaposition of the Greek and Persian fragments and testimonia. The historicity of the novel could be further illuminated by the additional identification of names of historical persons taking part in the novel, such as Ibykos the poet and Syloson the brother of Polykrates of Samos (A16=9). A further remarkable component of the story, surviving only in the Persian fragment, was an unorthodox version of the story of Hermes' invention of the lyre, echoed, it transpired, in some later Greek and Latin texts but not known in its narrative form until now (A23=11, A30). This article, starting with the *Homeric Hymn to Hermes* and Sophokles' satyr play *Ichneutai*, is perhaps the closest I have come in my research to the core areas and traditional concerns of classical philology and to the display of "learning" that only a well-supplied open-stack library and undisturbed time might allow (I wrote it in 1987 during a period as visiting professor at the Memorial University of Newfoundland at St. John's).

The actual monograph on the Parthenope fragments, *The virgin and her lover* (A36), was not to be brought to completion and published until the autumn of 2003 — exactly twenty years after our joint discovery and forty years after I started my novel studies. (I had not observed the wonderfully symmetrical structure of this time span, with the Discovery as the peak of the curve, until I wrote these words.) Work on this book finally allowed me to combine, in a way that gave me great personal satisfaction, my interest in the novel with editorial and interpretive work of the kind I have always tended to appreciate. The reconstruction of the plot of the novel/epic poem, also making full use of the many quotations from the poem found in various Persian lexica, was a rare instance of interdisciplinary cooperation that really functioned. It produced results that neither of us, though familiar with the material for almost twenty years, had anticipated before the chapter was actually written. Or perhaps this aspect was not so remarkable after all; humanistic research, at least of the type I know from my own experience, is special in producing its most important results in the very course of the writing process. Naturally, you have done your reading, of sources as well as some secondary literature; you have "collected material" and (in a preliminary way) analysed it; but you cannot say, as in most natural and social sciences, that you are now in possession of your results and just have to put them down in writing. Only in the most trivial sense, do you "know" at that point what will come out of your studies; what is really worthwhile saying, is mostly created only in the moment you are formulating it (if at all).

Since this is an essay in self-contemplation, not to say self-promotion, I may be allowed to exemplify this (as I believe) general function from my own recent experience. A few years ago, I was asked by the Stanford Anglist Franco Moretti to contribute to his five-volume Einaudi production, *Il romanzo*, writing the main piece — some 14,000 words — on the ancient novel. The essay should introduce the genre to those unfamiliar with it, but combine presentation with some captivating thesis. I had free hands, but to fit the project — a demonstration that the novel is a universal phenomenon that has "risen" at many places and in many periods apart from eighteenth-century England — a topic like "The ancient novel: A single model or a plurality of forms?" would be ideal. Since I had no better idea myself, I chose that title (though restricting myself to the Greek novel), and just started writing when the deadline had come threateningly close. Except for intending to stress variety rather than uniformity in the genre (something I had already done in my dissertation), I only had the vague idea that my "own" novel, *Parthenope*, should be utilized to show the beginnings of the genre. The rest just came during the rather intense writing process. Though I had earlier declined to write about "the origins of the Greek novel", a favourite topic of the past, I now found myself formulating a new hypothesis, based, on the one hand, on the different character of the surviving early specimens (besides the reconstructed *Parthenope*, in particular Chariton's *Kallirhoe* and Xenophon's *Ephesiaka*), on the other, on the hitherto unused evidence of the different types of title: heroine's name, hero-and-heroine's names, ethnicon in the collective neuter plural. Instead of a single model — Perry's famous author-inventor who deliberately sat down to write his novel, the first in history, on a Tuesday afternoon in July — I envisaged an initial plurality of forms and the successive convergence of two main strands, a popular one with an oral prehistory (as demonstrated by O'Sullivan) and having the ethnic title (cf. the popular *Milesiaka*), and a more "bookish" one, from the beginning with a strong attachment to history (like *Parthenope*) and named after the female protagonist only (like Hellenistic erotic poems). The double title, I contended, became standard only later, intruding on the two original forms, at the height of the Imperial period when the genre was consolidated; hence forms such as the expanded *Chaireas and Kallirhoe* and the contaminated *Ephesian tales about Habrokomes and Antheia*.

This will suffice as an indication of what lines of thought I came to follow; for the details, and how types other than the "ideal" novel were accomodated in the scheme (the nationalistic *Ninos* of Oriental origin, the explicitly erotic *Phoinikika* etc.), readers are referred to the essay (A35, to appear in English, slightly revised, as A37).[15] The point here is not the construction itself, but how it came about, almost like an extempore exercise on a set topic. I would like to think that the absence of any rigid hypothesis of my own making, and the pure delight in writing, liberated

---

[15] For copyright reasons, this article could not be reprinted in the present volume.

my thought and made me see interrelationships that would otherwise have eluded me. Whether my view of the origins will command assent among colleagues, is another matter; no earlier hypothesis has won anything like common acceptance, and there are certainly some weak links in mine too. Still I have, at long last, arrived at the kind of confident pronouncements on general issues that some critics would have liked to see already in my dissertation and that many in the field have always been better at.

The plurality-of-forms essay is not, of course, unique in my output as written to order, though the set title, I admit, was a novelty. The invitation to a midnight-sun conference at the University of Tromsø on "early narrative" made me work again on the elusive question of the novel's first readership, its number and composition in terms of age, sex, education and (in particular) degree of literacy (A28=4).[16] A seminar at Karen Blixen's Rungstedlund north of Copenhagen on "conventional values of the Hellenistic Greeks" provided the opportunity to present a reading of the *Life of Aesop*, alias the *Aesop Romance*, and argue that the core of it — philosopher and slave on Samos — belongs to the Hellenistic period (E6=1). Invitations to lecture in Athens and later at the J. Paul Getty Museum in California obliged me to rework for an international audience an older well-worn lecture on "the novel in art and art in the novel" (A22). A colloquium of Graeco-Oriental and African studies at Neapoli in Laconia, convened by Vassily Christides, gave me the impetus needed for combining at long last my interest in Nubian history with the *Aithiopika*, using the texts translated and analysed in *Fontes Historiae Nubiorum* as a foil to Heliodoros' fictitious Meroe (A33=12); for, as I explained above, my occupation with Meroitic culture had originally nothing to do with Heliodoros. A conference at Rhethymnon with "epiphanies" as its topic, arranged in the honour of my brother Robin Hägg, classical archaeologist and explorer of prehistoric Greek religion, induced me to revisit Chariton, Longos and the other novelists to see if and how they used the epiphany motif in the construction of their plots (A34=5). Presently

---

[16] This paper took issue with some, in my view, all too reductionist views of the novel's early history and readership, as expressed by Ewen Bowie and Susan Stephens in the published acts from ICAN II. It later received a balanced reply in Ewen Bowie's chapter "The ancient readers of the Greek novels" in the handbook edited by Gareth Schmeling, *The novel in the ancient world*, Leiden 1996, 87–106, and now an ingenious follow-up by Stephanie West, "ΚΕΡΚΙΔΟΣ ΠΑΡΑΜΥΘΙΑ? For whom did Chariton write?", *Zeitschrift für Papyrologie und Epigraphik* 143, 2003, 63–69.

I am preparing a contribution to a symposium on "the epic journey" at Odense, predictably dealing with the quest structure in the Greek novels. That kind of trade seemingly never ends; everyone who takes an active part in today's academic life will recognize the pattern.

"A life is not what has happened to a person, but what one remembers and how one remembers it." Thus the motto of Gabriel García Márquez' recent autobiographical work, *Vivir para contarla* (2002) or *Living to tell the tale*. This also applies — *si parva licet componere magnis* — to this philologist's life with the novel. Arriving at the last ten or fifteen years, however, I find that the task of sorting the memories meaningfully gets more difficult. The lines of development and causal connections are less easy to identify with any degree of confidence. No doubt, the early years emerge in a clearer light simply because I have forgotten more of the complex reality, and already shaped the extant memories for myself and arranged them in a neat sequence. Not so with the more recent past. Between the alternatives to be boringly detailed or quite brief, I choose the latter.

Besides the final massive work on *The virgin and her lover* in the last few years and the concentrated efforts to produce the conference papers just referred to (and then, again, to prepare each of them for printing), I have not devoted much time or continuous thought to the Greek novel since the late eighties. I have to a certain extent followed what has appeared in the form of books or articles; my reviews from the period sometimes give discreet expression to the alienation I have felt when encountering the more extreme cases of sophisticated interpretive play with the novels (A26, E2, A29, A32=**20–23**). I have felt no temptation to take part in that particular game, nor, for that matter, to embark on any major study of my own choice. There is indeed no lack of fruitful topics for those equipped to tackle them, as some recent brilliant studies have shown. The most promising development, to my mind, has been the new keen interest internationally in the Greek literature of the Imperial period as a whole, in authors like Plutarch, Dio Chrysosthomos, Lucian, Ailios Aristeides, Pausanias and Philostratos, and in the Hellenism of the period. For one fostered in Jonas Palm's seminar (and his private reading group), where these Imperial authors were the constant focus of attention and discussion, a certain sense of *déjà vu* is unavoidable. But my main response is one of satisfaction that these texts are now being studied using such a wide spectrum of approaches and perspectives, and that future study of the novels can thus be pursued within that context.

An obvious lack of a wider reading in the literature of the period has sometimes in the recent past produced studies that make the novels seem a more isolated phenomenon than they were. Now they are central in the rediscovery of the Second Sophistic as a creative cultural movement and instrumental in the obliteration of false divides between works of "fact" and works of "fiction", between history, ethnography, philosophy, rhetoric etc. on the one hand, the novel on the other. The novel partakes in all these kinds, and they share its literariness. Ancient novel studies will no doubt also benefit, in the context of university politics, from the increased prestige automatically bestowed on the arena when the big elephants decide to dance there. For myself, I prefer to watch.

Instead, my literary interests have turned to a cognate but (so far) more desolate genre, Greek and Roman biographical writings, including the specimens that are sometimes also called novels (from the *Cyropaedia* to the *Life of Apollonios*). A year as a member of the Institute for Advanced Study in Princeton (1992–93) gave the necessary peace and inspiration to plan the project in detail, work through the bibliography and write a theoretical chapter. I also completed a comprehensive analysis of my key text, the *Life of Antony* — no, not that of Plutarch, but Athanasios' ideal life of the great desert father. Some more chapters, covering the fourth century BC, the Hellenistic period and the Gospels, have been composed in occasional stolen weeks in the years since, in secluded places like the Fondation Hardt and the Ashmolean/Sackler libraries. The idea informing my prospective *The art of biography in antiquity* is to analyse the surviving texts, not so much to speculate about the lost ones, and to treat them as literary rather than (failed) historical works. The key concept in this context, rather than fiction or fact, is the workings of "creative imagination" (on some sort of historical basis). To write a book similar to *The novel in antiquity* proved impracticable, at least for me; this "genre" is more diverse, and there is (with the exception of Plutarch) comparatively little literary analysis to build on.[17]

In addition, the time available for individual research has been still more reduced in the last decade, due to the new trend in universities and research councils to give priority to larger collective projects, draining other activities for money. If you are not in, you are out (and so, presumably, are your advanced students). In the four interdisciplinary projects with external funding that I have codirected or been part of in

---

[17] Cf. further the *Vorarbeiten* under the heading E in the Bibliography.

the last ten years, my own work has mostly been concerned with late antique biographical and panegyrical texts. A particular stimulus all along
in these common enterprises has been the close cooperation with my
colleague Jostein Børtnes, whose research interests have moved from
Old Slavonic hagiography and classical Russian literature to the Late
Antique sources of Orthodoxy;[18] his constant impetus towards new ho-
rizons in scholarship has, I think, in a fruitful way counterbalanced my
own innate scepticism toward trends and fashions. (Well, perhaps not as
much innate as implanted, a part of my Uppsala inheritance.) Among
the literary works actualised in the projects were the various Pythagorean
and Neo-Platonic lives, including — again — the *Life of Apollonios of
Tyana*; but we have mostly studied Christian texts, by the Cappadocian
Fathers in particular, quite a new and enriching experience. Classicists
have all too willingly left the treasures of Patristic Greek literature to
be explored by historians and theologians. When the present book appears, I shall be immersed in a new project of similar orientation. The
novel will have to yield, as always — but will no doubt reappear again
when I least expect it.

---

[18] Tracing Jostein Børtnes' scholarly profile in F29 was my first attempt at putting into
practice my interest in biography, this memoir being the second. I thank the editors of
the book for giving me the opportunity.

Bibliography of the Writings of Tomas Hägg

A. The Greek Novel

0   *Berättartekniska studier till Xenophon Ephesios.* Unpublished thesis for the degree of Licentiate of Philosophy, Uppsala University, 1967. VIII + 167 pp., 12 figs.

1   "Die Ephesiaka des Xenophon Ephesios — Original oder Epitome?", *Classica et Mediaevalia* 27, 1966 (pr. 1969), 118–161. [Printed here in an English translation by the author as no. **6**]

2   *Narrative Technique in Ancient Greek Romances: Studies of Chariton, Xenophon Ephesius, and Achilles Tatius* (Acta Instituti Atheniensis Regni Sueciae 8°, 8), Stockholm 1971. 376 pp. [Diss. Uppsala.]

3   "The Naming of the Characters in the Romance of Xenophon Ephesius", *Eranos* 69, 1971, 25–59. [Printed here as no. **7**]

4   "Some Technical Aspects of the Characterization in Chariton's Romance", in: *Studi classici in onore di Q. Cataudella*, Vol. 2, Catania 1972 (pr. 1975), 545–556. [Printed here as no. **3**]

5   "Aristoteles och den grekiska romanen", *Kungl. Vetenskaps-Societeten i Uppsala, Årsbok* 1974, 46–52.

6   [Rev.] A.D. Papanikolaou (ed.), Xenophontis Ephesii Ephesiacorum libri V de amoribus Anthiae et Abrocomae (1973), *Gnomon* 49, 1977, 457–462. [Printed here as no. **17**]

7   "Den antika romanen från Chariton till Heliodoros", *Museum Tusculanum* 30–31, 1977, 39–55. [Preprint of A8.]

8   "Efterskrift", in: Heliodor, *Fortællingen om Theagenes og Charikleia (Aithiopika)*, overs. af E. Harsberg, København 1978, 271–304.

9   "På offerfest i Delfi", *Hellenika* 5, 1978, 6–10.

10   *Den antika romanen*, Uppsala 1980. 367 pp.

11   [Rev.] R. Merkelbach, Die Quellen des griechischen Alexanderromans, 2. Aufl. (1977), and J. Trumpf (ed.), Vita Alexandri regis Macedonum (1974), *Byzantinische Zeitschrift* 73, 1980, 54–57. [Printed here as no. **18**]

12   [Rev.] G. Molinié (ed.), Chariton, Le roman de Chairéas et Callirhoé (1979), *Gnomon* 53, 1981, 698–700. [Printed here as no. **19**]

13   *The Novel in Antiquity*, Oxford & Berkeley 1983. 264 pp. [Revised 2nd ed. of A10, translated by TH.]

14   "The *Parthenope Romance* Decapitated?", *Symbolae Osloenses* 59, 1984, 61–91. [Printed here as no. **8**]

15 "Grekiska romaner och egyptiska martyrakter", in: *Idékonfrontation under senantiken*, København 1985, 147–161.

16 "Metiochus at Polycrates' Court", *Eranos* 83, 1985, 92–102. [Printed here as no. 9]

17 "The Oriental Reception of Greek Novels: A Survey with Some Preliminary Considerations", *Symbolae Osloenses* 61, 1986, 99–131. [Printed here as no. 10]

18 "*Callirhoe* and *Parthenope*: The Beginnings of the Historical Novel", *Classical Antiquity* 6, 1987, 184–204. [Printed here as no. 2]

19 *Eros und Tyche. Der Roman in der antiken Welt* (Kulturgeschichte der antiken Welt, 36), Mainz am Rhein 1987. 311 pp. [Updated 3rd. ed. of A10, translated by K. Brodersen.]

20 "La rinascita del romanzo greco", in: P. Janni (ed.), *Il romanzo greco. Guida storica e critica*, Roma & Bari 1987, 179–204. [Translation of A13, Ch. 8.]

21 "The Beginnings of the Historical Novel", in: R. Beaton (ed.), *The Greek Novel AD 1–1985*, London 1988, 169–181. [Short version of A18.]

22 "Romanen i konsten och konsten i romanen", *Klassisk Forum* 1988:2, 7–21.

23 "Hermes and the Invention of the Lyre: An Unorthodox Version", *Symbolae Osloenses* 64, 1989, 36–73. [Printed here as no. 11]

24 "Hermes og lyren. En myte og dens forvandlinger", in: F11, 167–180. [Popular version of A23.]

25 "Parthenope Persica: On Reconstructing *Metiochus and Parthenope* from the Greek and Persian Fragments", in: J. Tatum & G.M. Vernazza, *The Ancient Novel: Classical Paradigms and Modern Perspectives*, Hanover, N.H. 1990, 155–156. [Description of the research project published as A36.]

26 [Rev.] S. Bartsch, Decoding the Ancient Novel: The Reader and the Role of Description in Heliodorus and Achilles Tatius (1989), *Journal of Hellenic Studies* 112, 1992, 192–193. [Printed here as no. 20]

27 Τὸ ἀρχαῖο μυθιστόρημα, Athens 1992. 300 pp. [Bibliographically updated 4th ed. of A10, translated by T. Mastorake.]

28 "Orality, Literacy, and the 'Readership' of the Early Greek Novel", in: R. Eriksen (ed.), *Contexts of Pre-Novel Narrative: The European Tradition*, Berlin & New York 1994, 47–81. [Printed here as no. 4]

29 [Rev.] J. Tatum (ed.), The Search for the Ancient Novel (1994) and J.R. Morgan & R. Stoneman (eds.), Greek Fiction: the Greek Novel in Context, *Journal of Hellenic Studies* 115, 1995, 201–202. [Printed here as no. 22]

30 "Hermes e l'invenzione della lyra: una versione non ortodossa", in: D. Restani (ed.), *Musica e mito nella Grecia antica*, Bologna 1995, 209–234. [Partial translation of A23.]

31 "*Callirhoe* and *Parthenope*: The Beginnings of the Historical Novel", in: S. Swain (ed.), *Oxford Readings in the Greek Novel*, Oxford 1999, 137–160. [Republication of A18.]

32 [Rev.] R. Hunter (ed.), Studies in Heliodorus (1998), *The Classical Review* N.S. 49, 1999, 380–381. [Printed here as no. 23]

33 "The Black Land of the Sun: Meroe in Heliodoros's Romantic Fiction", in: V. Christides & Th. Papadopoullos (eds.), *Proceedings of the Sixth International Congress of Graeco-Oriental and African Studies, Nicosia 30 April – 5 May 1996*, Nicosia 2000 (= *Graeco-Arabica* 7-8, 2000), 195-220. [Printed here as no. **12**]

34 "Epiphany in the Greek Novels: The Emplotment of a Metaphor", *Eranos* 100, 2002, 51-61. [Printed here as no. **5**]

35 "Il romanzo greco: modello unico o pluralità di forme?", in: F. Moretti (ed.), *Il romanzo*, III: *Storia e geografia*, Torino 2002, 5-32.

36 [With B. Utas] *The Virgin and her Lover: Fragments of an Ancient Greek Novel and a Persian Epic Poem* (Brill Studies in Middle Eastern Literatures, 30), Leiden 2003. 278 pp.

37 "The Ancient Greek Novel: a Single Model or a Plurality of Forms?", in: F. Moretti (ed.), *The Novel*, I, Princeton University Press, 2004 (forthcoming). [Revised English version of A35.]

B. On Photius, Bibliotheca (and related topics)

1 "Photius at Work: Evidence from the Text of the *Bibliotheca*", *Greek, Roman, and Byzantine Studies* 14, 1973, 213-222. [Printed here as no. **15**]

2 *Photios als Vermittler antiker Literatur. Untersuchungen zur Technik des Referierens und Exzerpierens in der Bibliotheke* (Acta Universitatis Upsaliensis, Studia Graeca Upsaliensia, 8), Uppsala 1975. 218 pp.

3 [Rev.] R. Henry (ed.), Photius, Bibliothèque, Tome I–VII (1959-74), *Göttingische Gelehrte Anzeigen* 228, 1976, 32-60.

4 "Photios — biblioman i Bysans", *Svenska Forskningsinstitutet i Istanbul, Meddelanden* 2, 1977, 30-43.

5 "Böcker och bokläsare i 800-talets Bysans", *Artes* 3:6, 1977, 35-43.

6 "Rhos ante portas! Grekiska källor om rusernas angrepp på Konstantinopel 860", *Svenska Forskningsinstitutet i Istanbul, Meddelanden* 4, 1979, 27-49.

7 [Rev.] W.T. Treadgold, The Nature of the *Bibliotheca* of Photius (1980), *Byzantinische Zeitschrift* 76, 1983, 28-31.

8 [Rev.] N.G. Wilson, Scholars of Byzantium (1983), *Journal of Hellenic Studies* 105, 1985, 249-250.

9 [With W. Treadgold] "The Preface of the *Bibliotheca* of Photius Once More", *Symbolae Osloenses* 61, 1986, 133-138.

10 [Rev.] N.G. Wilson (ed.), Photius, The Bibliotheca (1994), *Byzantinische Zeitschrift* 88, 1995, 484-485.

11 "Photius as a Reader of Hagiography: Selection and Criticism", *Dumbarton Oaks Papers* 53, 1999, 43-58.

C. Greek in Nubia

1   [Rev.] J. Kubińska, Faras IV. Inscriptions grecques chrétiennes (1974), *Orientalia Suecana* 25-26, 1976-77, 144-150.

2   [With T. Eide and R.H. Pierce] "Greek, Latin, and Coptic Sources for Nubian History (I)", *Sudan Texts Bulletin* 1, 1979, 3-12.

3   [With T. Eide and R.H. Pierce] "Greek, Latin, and Coptic Sources for Nubian History (II)", *Sudan Texts Bulletin* 2, 1980, 2-15.

4   "Griechisch im christlichen Nubien", *Jahrbuch der Österreichischen Byzantinistik* 31/Beiheft, 1981, 2.1.

5   "Two Christian Epitaphs in Greek of the 'Euchologion Mega' Type", in: T. Säve-Söderbergh (ed.), *Late Nubian Cemeteries* (Scandinavian Joint Expedition to Sudanese Nubia, 6), Solna 1981 (pr. 1982), 55-62 + Pl. 105-106.

6   "Some Remarks on the Use of Greek in Nubia", in: J.M. Plumley (ed.), *Nubian Studies*, Warminster 1982, 103-107.

7   "A New Axumite Inscription in Greek from Meroe", *Meroitica* 7, 1984, 436-441 + Pl. V.

8   "Nubien och Bysans", *Svenska kommittén för bysantinska studier, Bulletin* 2, 1984, 19-22. [Short version of C10.]

9   "Nubicograeca I–III", *Zeitschrift für Papyrologie und Epigraphik* 54, 1984, 101-112.

10 "Nubien och Bysans", *Svenska Forskningsinstitutet i Istanbul, Meddelanden* 9, 1984 (pr. 1985), 5-31.

11 [With T. Eide and R.H. Pierce] "Greek, Latin, and Coptic Sources for Nubian History (III)", *Sudan Texts Bulletin* 6, 1984, 1-25.

12 "'Blemmyan Greek' and the Letter of Phonen", in: M. Krause (ed.), *Nubische Studien*, Mainz 1986, 281-286.

13 "Grekiskan i Nubien", *Museum Tusculanum* 52-55, 1983 (pr. 1986), 127-156.

14 [Ed.] *Nubian Culture: Past and Present* (Konferenser, 17), Stockholm 1987. 438 pp.

15 "Titles and Honorific Epithets in Nubian Greek Texts", *Symbolae Osloenses* 65, 1990, 147-177.

16 "Greek Language in Christian Nubia", in: A.S. Atiya (ed.), *The Coptic Encyclopedia*, Vol. 4, New York 1991, 1170-1174.

17 "Magic Bowls Inscribed with an Apostles-and-Disciples Catalogue from the Christian Settlement of Hambukol (Upper Nubia)", *Orientalia* 62, 1993, 376-399 + Tab. LVIII–LX.

18 [With T. Eide, R.H. Pierce & L. Török] *Fontes Historiae Nubiorum: Textual Sources for the History of the Middle Nile Region between the Eighth Century BC and the Sixth Century AD.* Vol. 1: *From the Eighth to the Mid-Fifth Century BC*, Bergen 1994. 343 pp.

19 "Sayce's Axumite Inscription from Meroe — Again", *Meroitic Newsletter* (Paris) 25, 1994, 45-48.

20 [With T. Eide, R.H. Pierce & L. Török] *Fontes Historiae Nubiorum: Textual Sources for the History of the Middle Nile Region between the Eighth Century BC and*

the Sixth Century AD. Vol. 2: *From the Mid-Fifth to the First Century BC*, Bergen 1996. 403 pp.

21 [With T. Eide, R.H. Pierce & L. Török] *Fontes Historiae Nubiorum: Textual Sources for the History of the Middle Nile Region between the Eighth Century BC and the Sixth Century AD*. Vol. 3: *From the First to the Sixth Century AD*, Bergen 1998. 470 pp.

22 "Greek in Upper Nubia: An Assessment of the New Material", in: *Actes de la VIIIᵉ Conférence internationale des études Nubiennes, Lille 11–17 Septembre 1994*, Vol. 3: *Études* (Cahiers de Recherches de l'Institut de Papyrologie et d'Égyptologie de Lille, 17), Lille 1998, 113–119.

23 "Nubia", in: G.W. Bowersock, P. Brown and O. Grabar (eds.), *Late Antiquity: A Guide to the Postclassical World*, Harvard University Press: Cambridge, MA 1999, 613–614.

24 [With T. Eide, R.H. Pierce & L. Török] *Fontes Historiae Nubiorum: Textual Sources for the History of the Middle Nile Region between the Eighth Century BC and the Sixth Century AD*. Vol. 4: *Corrigenda and Indices*, Bergen 2000. 160 pp.

25 [Ed., with L. Török & D.A. Welsby] Sir Laurence Kirwan, *Studies on the History of Late Antique and Christian Nubia* (Variorum Collected Studies Series: CS748), Aldershot 2002. xii+262 pp.

26 [With L. Török & D.A. Welsby] "Preface", in C26, ix–xxi.

27 "Silko's Language: a Retrospect", in: T.A. Bács (ed.), *A Tribute to Excellence: Studies Offered in Honour of Ernö Gaál, Ulrich Luft, László Török* (Studia Aegyptiaca, 17), Budapest 2002, 289–300.

28 "Axumite Inscription in Greek 6164 (SNM 24841)", in: P.L. Shinnie & J.R. Anderson (eds.), *The Capital of Kush*, Vol. II (Meroitica, 30), Berlin 2004, 106–108.

29 "Greek Inscription of a King of Aksum", in: D.A. Welsby & J.R. Anderson (eds.), *Kingdoms of the Nile: Archaeological Treasures from the National Museum, Sudan*, The British Museum Press: London 2004 (forthcoming).

30 [Rev.] S.G. Richter, Studien zur Christianisierung Nubiens (2002), *Byzantinische Zeitschrift* (forthcoming).

D. On Philostratus, Vita Apollonii (and related topics)

1 "Bentley, Philostratus, and the German Printers", *Journal of Hellenic Studies* 102, 1982, 214–216. [Printed here as no. **16**]

2 "Eusebios vs. Hierokles. En senantik polemik kring Apollonios från Tyana och Jesus från Nasaret", *Religion och Bibel* 44, 1985 (pr. 1987), 25–35.

3 "Hierocles the Lover of Truth and Eusebius the Sophist", *Symbolae Osloenses* 67, 1992, 138–150. [Printed here as no. **14**]

4 "Apollonios of Tyana — Magician, Philosopher, Counter-Christ: The Metamorphoses of a Life", paper given at the conference "The Use and Abuse of the Past: Writers, Historiographers, Holy Men and Women in the Eastern Mediterranean World", Swedish Research Institute in Istanbul, November 26–28, 1998. [Previously unpublished; printed in this volume as no. **13**]

5   "Kan en helig man dö? Glimtar av kroppslig uppståndelse i icke-kristna texter",
     in: T. Engberg-Pedersen & I.S. Gilhus (eds.), *Kropp og oppstandelse*, Oslo 2001,
     99–111.

E. Biography in Antiquity

1   "Socrates and St. Antony: A Short Cut Through Ancient Biography", in: R.
     Skarsten, E.J. Kleppe & R.B. Finnestad (eds.), *Understanding and History in Arts
     and Sciences* (Acta Humaniora Universitatis Bergensis, 1), Oslo 1991, 81–87.

2   [Rev.] J. Tatum, Xenophon's Imperial Fiction: On "The Education of Cyrus"
     (1989), and B. Due, The "Cyropaedia": Xenophon's Aims and Methods (1989),
     Classical Philology 86, 1991, 147–152. [Printed here as no. **21**]

3   [With S. Rubenson] Athanasios av Alexandria, *Antonios' liv*. I översättning och
     med inledning och kommentar, Skellefteå 1991. 144 pp.

4   "From Ancient Biography to Byzantine Hagiography" (in Russian), *Vestnik
     Drevnej Istorii* 206, 1993, 136–140.

5   "Den opopulära populärlitteraturen — romantiserad biografi och historisk ro-
     man", in: Ø. Andersen & T. Hägg (eds.), *I skyggen av Akropolis*, Bergen 1994,
     307–334.

6   "A Professor and his Slave: Conventions and Values in the *Life of Aesop*", in: P. Bil-
     de et al. (eds.), *Conventional Values of the Hellenistic Greeks* (Studies in Hellenistic
     Civilization, 8), Aarhus 1997, 177–203. [Printed here as no. **1**]

7   "After 300 Years: A New, Critical Edition of the Greek *Life of St. Antony*. Review
     Article", *Classica et Mediaevalia* 48, 1997, 267–281.

8   "På spaning efter biografins rötter i antiken", I–III, *Phania* 1998:2, 12–14; 3, 4–7;
     4, 4–8.

9   "Hagiografi och konstruktion av kristen identitet", in: D.Ø. Endsjø (ed.), *Det
     kristne menneske: Konstruksjon av ny identitet i antikken* (Antikkprogrammets
     småskrifter, 4), Oslo 1998, 84–96.

10   [Trans.] "Pionios' och hans följes martyrium", "Utdrag ur berättelsen om munkar-
     na i Egypten", "Den helige Symeons liv", in: S. Rubenson (ed.), *Martyrer och
     helgon* (Svenskt patristiskt bibliotek, 2), Skellefteå 2000, 59–82, 162–180, 237–255.

11   [Ed., with Ph. Rousseau] *Greek Biography and Panegyric in Late Antiquity* (The
     Transformation of the Classical Heritage, 31), Berkeley, Los Angeles & London
     2000.

12   [With Ph. Rousseau] "Introduction: Biography and Panegyric", in E11, 1–28.

13   "Liv och lära — Filosofbiografin som förmedlingsform i senantiken", in: Maarit
     Kaimio (ed.), *Filosofen och publiken. Rapport från Platonsällskapets femtonde sympo-
     sium Helsingfors 3-6 juni 1999*, Helsingfors 2000, 153–165.

14   "Recent Work on Ancient Biography, I. Review article", *Symbolae Osloenses* 76,
     2001, 191–200.

15   "Indledning", "Litteratur", in: C. Weber-Nielsen (trans.), *Æsopromanen*, Copen-
     hagen 2003, 9–21, 117–121.

16 "The *Life of Mani* in the Context of Graeco-Roman Spiritual Biography", in: A. Piltz et al. (eds.), *For Particular Reasons: Studies in Honour of Jerker Blomqvist*, Lund 2003, 149–163.

17 "Att plåga sin kropp för att frälsa sin själ? Motstridiga tendenser i senantikens asketiska praxis", in: J. Børtnes, S.-E. Kraft & L. Mikaelsson (eds.), *Kampen om kroppen: Kulturanalytiske blikk på kropp, helse, kjønn og seksualitet*, Kristiansand 2004, 31-48.

18 "Biografins första guldålder? Om hellenistiska biografer och deras moderna uttolkare", in: *Det Norske Videnskaps-Akademi. Årbok 2003*, Oslo (forthcoming).

19 [Ed., with J. Børtnes] *Gregory of Nazianzus: Images and Reflections*, Museum Tusculanum Press: Copenhagen (forthcoming).

20 "Playing with the Expectations: Gregory's Funeral Orations on his Brother, Sister and Father", in: E19 (forthcoming).

F. Varia

0 Ett fall av damnatio memoriae: Hur senatens hostis-förklaring av kejsar Commodus avspeglar sig i det litterära och arkeologiska materialet. Unpublished Master's Thesis in Ancient History at Uppsala University, 1963. 54 pp.

1 [Rev.] H. Görgemanns, Untersuchungen zu Plutarchs Dialog De facie in orbe lunae (1970), *Lychnos* 1971-72, 366–369.

2 [Revised ed.] G. Björck, *Djäknar och astronauter. Grekiska lånord i svenskan*, 2. uppl. av Djäknar och helikoptrar, bearb. av T. Hägg, Lund 1972. 98 pp.

3 [Rev.] J.F. Kindstrand, Homer in der zweiten Sophistik (1973), *Lychnos* 1973-74, 361–364.

4 "Hermeneutik (?) och filologi. Kring ett par nya svenska doktorsavhandlingar", *Museum Tusculanum* 32-33, 1978, 15-30. [Review article.]

5 "Vem var Medea?", *Hellenika* 12, 1980, 8-12.

6 "Internationalisering och popularisering", *Tvärsnitt* 1981:2, 60-64.

7 "Weiterleben und Neubelebung sozialer Typenbegriffe (von Homer bis Aristoteles) in der schwedischen Sprache", in: E.Ch. Welskopf (ed.), *Soziale Typenbegriffe im alten Griechenland*, Vol. 7, Berlin 1982, 395-412.

8 "Klassikernes klassiker på norsk", *Bergens Tidende* 14 Nov. 1983. [Review article.]

9 "Legers kår i Pompeii", *Bergens Tidende* 2 March 1985.

10 "Klassiskt och klassiker på norsk", *Medusa* 8, 1987:3, 37-39. [Review article.]

11 [Ed., with T. Eide] *Dionysos og Apollon. Religion og samfunn i antikkens Hellas* (Skrifter utgitt av Det norske institutt i Athen, 1), Bergen 1989. 288 pp.

12 "Konstverksekfrasen som litterär genre och konstvetenskaplig källa", in: E. Piltz (ed.), *Bysans och Norden*, Uppsala 1989, 37-50.

13 "Arethas", in: E.A. Wyller (ed.), *Platonisme i antikk og middelalder*, Vol. 2, Oslo 1989, 144-147. [Translations.]

14 "Antigone och hennes dramatiska systrar ur antropologiskt perspektiv", *Hellenika* 48, 1989, 4-8. [Review article.]

15 Articles on Greek literature in *Nationalencyklopedin*, Vol. 1-20, Höganäs 1989-96.

16 [Ed., with Ø. Andersen] *Hellas og Norge. Kontakt, komparasjon, kontrast* (Skrifter utgitt av Det norske institutt i Athen, 2), Bergen 1990. 280 pp.

17 "En bysantiner besøker Bergen", in: F16, 221-228.

18 "Klassisk filologi", in: O.E. Haugen & E. Thomassen (eds.), *Den filologiske vitenskap*, Oslo 1990, 227-252, 262-264.

19 [Rev.] S. des Bouvrie, Women in Greek Tragedy: An Anthropological Approach (1990), *Klassisk Forum* 1991:1, 79-80. [Short version of F14.]

20 "Boreas", *Boreas: Medlemsblad for Athen-instituttets Venner* 1, 1992, 3.

21 "Pausanias' stilistiska egenart", in: Ø. Andersen & T. Eide (eds.), *I Hellas med Pausanias* (Skrifter utgitt av Det norske institutt i Athen, 3), Bergen 1992, 33-49.

22 "Classica Americana 92/93: En situationsrapport från Princeton och New Orleans", *Klassisk Forum* 1993:1, 73-82.

23 [Ed., with Ø. Andersen] *I skyggen av Akropolis* (Skrifter utgitt av Det norske institutt i Athen, 5), Bergen 1994. 416 pp.

24 [Ed.] *Symbolae Osloenses*, Vol. 70, Scandinavian University Press: Oslo 1995. 261 pp.

25 [Rev.] T. Göransson, Albinus, Alcinous, Arius Didymus (1995), *Meddelanden från Collegium Patristicum Lundense* 10, 1995, 42-46.

26 "Med Aisopos till Bayern och Costa Blanca", *Klassisk Forum* 1995:2, 35-38.

27 "Forskningsrådet satsar på antiken", *Phania* 96:2, 10-13.

28 [Ed.] *Symbolae Osloenses*, Vol. 71, Scandinavian University Press: Oslo 1996. 246 pp.

29 "Jostein Børtnes: Tracing a Scholarly Profile", in: K.A. Grimstad & I. Lunde (eds.), *Celebrating Creativity: Essays in Honour of Jostein Børtnes*, Bergen 1997, 1-9.

30 [Ed.] *Symbolae Osloenses: Norwegian Journal of Greek and Latin Studies*, Vol. 72, Scandinavian University Press: Oslo 1997. 199 pp.

31 [Ed.] *Symbolae Osloenses: Norwegian Journal of Greek and Latin Studies*, Vol. 73, Scandinavian University Press: Oslo 1998. 240 pp.

32 [With J. Børtnes] "Kappadokisk *paideia*", in: Ø. Andersen (ed.), *Dannelse Humanitas Paideia*, Oslo 1999, 139-149.

33 "Pornography", in: G.W. Bowersock, P. Brown and O. Grabar (eds.), *Late Antiquity: A Guide to the Postclassical World*, Harvard University Press: Cambridge, MA 1999, 648.

34 [Ed.] *Symbolae Osloenses: Norwegian Journal of Greek and Latin Studies*, Vol. 74, Scandinavian University Press: Oslo 1999. 219 pp.

35 "FIEC, vad är det? — eller: Vi ses i Ouro Preto år 2004", *Klassisk Forum* 1999:2, 50-54.

36 [Ed., with L.B. Mortensen] *Symbolae Osloenses: Norwegian Journal of Greek and Latin Studies*, Vol. 75, Taylor & Francis: Oslo 2000. 204 pp.

37 [Rev.] Kyrre Vatsend, Die Rede Julians auf Kaiserin Eusebia (2000), *Meddelanden från Collegium Patristicum Lundense* 15, 2000, 12-13.

38   [Ed., with L.B. Mortensen] *Symbolae Osloenses: Norwegian Journal of Greek and Latin Studies*, Vol. 76, Taylor & Francis: Oslo 2001. 221 pp.

39   [Ed., with L.B. Mortensen] *Symbolae Osloenses: Norwegian Journal of Greek and Latin Studies*, Vol. 77, Taylor & Francis: Oslo 2002. 219 pp.

40   [Ed., with L.B. Mortensen] *Symbolae Osloenses: Norwegian Journal of Greek and Latin Studies*, Vol. 78, Taylor & Francis: Oslo 2003. 206 pp.

41   "A Byzantine Visit to Bergen: Laskaris Kananos and his Description of the Baltic and North Sea Region", *Graeco-Arabica* 9–10, 2002–03 (forthcoming). [Expanded version of F17.]

42   [Ed., with L.B. Mortensen] *Symbolae Osloenses: Norwegian Journal of Greek and Latin Studies*, Vol. 79, Taylor & Francis: Oslo 2004 (forthcoming).

A Hellenistic Philosophical Novel?

I

A Professor and his Slave:
Conventions and Values in the *Life of Aesop*

[originally published in P. Bilde et al. (eds.), *Conventional Values of the Hellenistic Greeks* (Studies in Hellenistic Civilization, 8), Aarhus 1997, 177–203]

The text I propose to investigate in search of Hellenistic conventional values is one that almost never appears in the source indices of scholarly works on the Hellenistic period: the anonymous *Life of Aesop*.[1] There are several reasons for this: the subliterate genre to which the text seems to belong, its composite character, the difficulties in dating it (or its composite parts), and the fact that the *editio princeps* of the earliest version we possess was issued as late as 1952.[2] The *Life of Aesop* — alias the *Aesop Romance* — has simply not belonged to the established corpus of ancient texts to which historians and others turn for information (and certainly not in regard to the Hellenistic period). It is indicative of the state of things that Keith Hopkins, in a stimulating article of 1993, could claim that he is the first to use this text — the biography of a slave — to illuminate ancient slavery (Hopkins 1993, 3).[3]

---

[1] The paper on which the present article is based was first read in the Petronian Society, Munich Section; I wish to thank Niklas Holzberg and the other participants in the discussion for valuable criticism. The final version also profited from comments of the participants in the Conventional Values conference at Rungstedgaard; the more specific of these debts are acknowledged in the notes. Finally, I thank David Konstan for correcting my English and contributing insightful comments on the subject matter as well.

[2] For a succinct and up-to-date presentation of the text and the *Stand der Forschung*, see Holzberg 1993, 84–93; for an extensive bibliography, see Beschorner and Holzberg 1992. Holzberg, having analysed the narrative structure, ends by remarking that the social and moral message of the text still remains to be investigated: "Denn Textanalyse, die nach der geistigen Aussage und dem Zeitbezug von Literatur fragt, gibt es im Bereich der Erforschung des Äsop-Romans noch nicht…" (Holzberg 1993, 93). I hope the present contribution may be regarded as a beginning.

[3] Hopkins 1993, 11 n. 14 notes that there is "mercifully little written in modern times about the *Life of Aesop*", but still seems to have missed some of the more important contributions, which makes his handling of the text as a source somewhat shaky. E.g., quoting (12 n. 15) from ch. 109, he seems unaware of the background provided by the Oriental *Life of Ahiqar*, and consequently finds Aesop "the surprising mouthpiece of

I shall therefore start with a presentation of the text and a fairly detailed discussion of its date and composition, seeking to justify its inclusion among the few literary witnesses to Hellenistic popular thought.

The version I shall deal with is transmitted in one medieval manuscript only, a codex of the 10th century labelled G after its original location in the monastery of Grottaferrata, and now preserved in the Pierpont Morgan Library, New York (MS 397). It was first published by Ben Edwin Perry in 1952 (Perry 1952), and is since 1990 available in a new critical edition by Manolis Papathomopoulos.[4] Perry's text was translated by Lloyd W. Daly (Daly 1961); I quote from his translation, with occasional minor modifications intended partly to adapt it to the new critical text.

Before the Greek text of G was published, the *Life of Aesop* had for a century been available in a shortened, less colourful version of late antique or early medieval origin, transmitted in several manuscripts and styled W after its first editor, Anton Westermann (1845). And long before that it had been known in a derivative Byzantine version, conventionally ascribed to Maximos Planudes (13th cent.),[5] printed as early as circa 1479. In addition, there are now a fair number of papyrus fragments,[6] testifying to the Life's considerable popularity in antiquity, in various versions. The oldest papyrus, the *Berolinensis* 11628, dates in the late second or early third century AD, thus constituting the most solid *terminus ante quem* for the composition of the Life.[7]

The story begins with a vivid and concrete description of the main character (1):

almost conventional wisdom". Cf. also below, n. 22 and n. 41. My observation that the *Life of Aesop* still remains outside the conventional canon of Classical literature is now confirmed by its conspicuous omission in Paul Zanker's brilliant study of "the image of the intellectual in Antiquity" (Zanker 1995).

[4] I quote from the second corrected edition (Papathomopoulos 1991). Papathomopoulos's edition corrects a number of Perry's mistakes, but it is still far from being the definitive critical edition of this manuscript; cf. the reviews by Haslam 1992, Adrados 1993 and Dijk 1994b.

[5] The ascription, though questioned by some (cf. Hausrath 1937, 774–76), is upheld by Perry 1936, 217–28; 1965, xvii; but cf. Dölger 1953, 375.

[6] Among them, notably *POxy.* 3331 + 3720, published with important commentary by Haslam 1980 and 1986.

[7] On the text of the papyri, see Perry (1936, 39–70), and, for later additions, Haslam 1980 and 1986.

The fabulist Aesop, the great benefactor of mankind, was by chance a slave but by origin a Phrygian from Amorion in Phrygia, of exceedingly loathsome aspect, decayed, potbellied, misshapen of head, snub-nosed, saddle-backed, swarthy, dwarfish, bandy-legged, shortarmed, squint-eyed, liver-lipped — a pure mistake of nature. In addition to this he had a defect more serious than his unsightliness in being speechless, for he was dumb and could not talk.

After this description,[8] we are immediately brought *in medias res.* Aesop, it appears, is the slave of an unnamed master on a farm somewhere in Asia Minor. Already the first scene shows his inventiveness: in spite of his dumbness, he manages to escape from an intrigue staged by malicious fellow slaves. He also manages to help a woman who has lost her way; she turns out to be a priestess of Isis, and as a reward the goddess herself relieves Aesop of his dumbness and persuades the Muses to confer on him "the power to devise stories and the ability to conceive and elaborate tales in Greek" (7). Aesop's newly acquired capacity to speak turns out to be a mixed blessing to fellow slaves and master alike, so he is promptly handed over to a slave dealer and brought to Ephesus to be sold.

Unable to sell the ugly slave in Ephesus, the slave dealer crosses over to Samos, where Aesop is sold to the philosopher Xanthus. A substantial part of the Life (20–91) is then taken up by the description of the relationship between Xanthus and his new slave; in fact, the title of the whole work in MS. G is: "The Book of Xanthus the Philosopher and Aesop his Slave, on the Career of Aesop" *(Biblos Xanthou philosophou kai Aisôpou doulou autou peri anastrophês Aisôpou). Anastrophê,* by the way, is perhaps better rendered as "way of life" than by Daly's "career": it is the moral side of Aesop's life, his "behaviour" *(Wandel),* that is in focus. Anyway, in a series of lively and humorous scenes, the slave's dealings with his master, his master's wife and his master's students are described. As Niklas Holzberg has recently shown (Holzberg 1992a),[9] the structuring of this part of the Life is more elaborate than was earlier supposed. It is not just a string of anecdotes — as Hopkins (1993, 11f.) still thinks — but a deliberate literary composition. Different kinds of Aesopic *logoi* are used in the different parts of the story, and each series is arranged so as to achieve an effect of *Steigerung.*

179

---

[8] There is a remarkably similar description of the slave Pseudolus in Plaut. *Pseud.* 1218–20. (I owe this reference to Ole Thomsen.) In the comedy, the description has a dramatic function, which it lacks in the Life.

[9] Cf. the review by Dijk 1994a.

After an expository section (20–33), the action begins. Aesop first (34–64) plays a number of practical jokes on Xanthus, trying to teach the professor to use words exactly. So, if the master orders: "Pick up the oil flask and the towels, and let's go to the bath!" (38), the slave does exactly that, but no more — and having arrived in the bath Xanthus discovers to his astonishment and anger that there is no oil in the flask. Again and again the same pattern is repeated, with more and more serious consequences; but Xanthus never gets the opportunity he longs for to punish his slave. Aesop is the better sophist of the two and always provides a watertight defence for his actions.

At last, Xanthus has learnt his lesson and Aesop achieves his first goal, to be treated as a thinking person. He is now given tasks to accomplish, rather than orders to obey. The next group of scenes (65–91) shows how Aesop, with a typical combination of intelligence and sophistic quibbling, manages to rescue his master from various difficulties, saving his property, his reputation, even his life. His constant aim now is to gain his freedom as a reward for his services to his master; but each time Xanthus goes back on his word. At last, it is the Samian people's assembly that enforces Aesop's emancipation, after he has helped them interpret an omen that had defied Xanthus's own attempts.

Thus a new stage in Aesop's career begins (92–100): he acts as a political counsellor to Samos in its dealings with King Croesus of Lydia. Aesop himself visits Croesus and succeeds in preventing a war between Lydia and Samos. In this section, as well as in the Delphi section at the end of the Life, the author has recourse to a third type of Aesopic *logos*, namely, the fable. Instead of letting his hero give direct advice or instruction, he presents him telling fables to achieve his purpose. On Samos — in contrast to Delphi — he is successful in this activity and spends many years there as a respected man.

Aesop then decides to make a lecture-tour around the world, and finally arrives in Babylon. He wins a reputation for wisdom there too and becomes a counsellor to King Lycorus. Since he is childless, he adopts a young man to make him "the heir to his own wisdom" (103). The adopted son, however, brings false accusations against Aesop, who is condemned to death. But he is spared and hidden away by a disloyal servant of the king, and is later rehabilitated and employed by the king for an important mission to King Nectanebo of Egypt. Again showing his resourcefulness and cleverness, he outwits the Egyptians and returns to Babylon in triumph. This whole Babylon-Memphis section of the work (101–23) is closely modelled on the Assyrian *Book of Ahiqar*, a work which circulated in a variety of languages (the earliest version surviving is in Aramaic); Ahiqar as a wise man was already known to the Greeks in the classical period (see Haslam 1986, 150f., with further refs.).

180

From Babylon Aesop travels to Delphi, where he meets his fate (124–42). Addressing the people of Delphi, he offends them by claiming that they are all descendants of slaves, namely, of prisoners of war sent to Apollo by victors as a tenth of their spoils. The officials of Delphi, afraid that Aesop will destroy the city's reputation on his continued travels, have a golden cup placed in his luggage and then accuse him of having stolen it from the temple. He is put in prison, and this time all his telling of fables cannot save him. He is sentenced to death for sacrilege, is dragged off from the shrine of the Muses where he has taken refuge, and finally throws himself off the cliff.

The composite character of this text is obvious, and has been stressed, often indeed exaggerated. But there is also a unity, as shown by Holzberg: the hand of an author, rather than just a compiler, may be perceived. Leitmotifs can be found all through the work, and there is, as we have seen, an artistic structuring of the narrative that prevents it from being just a random collection of episodes. But at what date did this anonymous author put his stamp on the *Life of Aesop?* And in what sense — or in what parts — may the work be described and used as a Hellenistic work?

The date commonly ascribed to the archetype of the surviving versions of the Life is the first century AD. The arguments were brought forward by Ben Edwin Perry in 1936; nothing of importance seems to have been added to them since, nor have their validity been seriously questioned. But Perry's cautious conclusion in his first major study was the following: "the most that one may say with certainty is that the *Life of Aesop,* in the oldest form that we know it (i.e. in G), must have been composed, or rewritten, at some time between 100 BC and 200 AD" (Perry 1936, 26). The *terminus ante quem* is the Berlin papyrus fragment dated in the late second or early third century; at the other end, the numerous Latin words and the appearance of Isis in the story are said to exclude a date before the first century BC. Perry himself in 1936 favoured a date in the second century AD, rather in the early than in the later part of that century. In 1952, however, because he was convinced there must have been an intermediate copy between the archetype and the Berlin papyrus, he opted for the first century AD.[10] In later writings, he constantly refers to the Life as a first-century text, presumably composed in Egypt; and so do practically all others, mostly without any specific comments of their own.[11] Only Francisco Adrados favours an earlier date, reaffirming his view as late as 1993: "And I still think that the prototype of recensions G and W, pace Perry, is from the Hellenistic epoch".[12]

What we learn from this retrospect is that the conventional dating "first century AD" is just a convenient shorthand for "first century BC *or* first century AD *or* second century AD". For all we know, then, the surviving Life may well have been composed in late Hellenistic times; but it may also be post-Hadrianic. It may fall as a whole well within the stricter definition of "the Hellenistic period" suggested by the convenors of the conference on which the present book is based, namely from Alexander to Augustus; or it may as a whole belong outside even their more liberal chronological framework of Alexander to Hadrian.

Now, we do not necessarily have to deal with the Life *as a whole,* nor would that actually be desirable. Few will believe that our late Hellenistic or early imperial author created his work relying only on oral sources and his own imagination: there will already have existed a biographical tradition codified in one or several written Lives, which he could use as a framework for the inclusion of other legendary material as well as inventions of his own. And for some of the constituent parts of his work it is possible to discern the approximate date, or at least some *termini ante* or *post quos.*

---

[10] Perry 1952, 5 n. 16. In the table (22) the date is specified as between *c.* 30 BC and AD 100. However, this specific-looking date, quoted e.g. by Papathomopoulos 1991, 22, is no more than a translation into figures of Perry's ascription of the *Life* to a writer living in Roman Egypt.

[11] But cf. Shipp 1983, 96: "The manuscript [sc. G] has many koine features that agree with Perry's dating [sc. in the first century AD]." Hopkins 1993, 11 n. 14 finds the date "plausible", but (rightly) suspects that "it involves simply working back from the earliest known papyrus fragment". The potentially most promising way of dating the prototype of G and W would be through an analysis of the language; but the most detailed study so far of this kind, Hostetter 1955, is inconclusive, ending (p. 129) by declaring the "unclassical forms and constructions" in G "in accord with Hellenistic literary usage", evidently defining "Hellenistic" very widely (including, i.e., "early church literature"). Cf. also Adrados 1981, 326, recognizing, with reference to Kindstrand 1976, 25–49, "Cynic" language and style in the *Vita Aesopi.*

[12] Adrados 1993, 664. Cf. Adrados 1979a, 664, and 1979b, 112 n. 16. A thorough and circumspect investigation of the Life's language and style is evidently a desideratum.

It was once fashionable to speak of a *Volksbuch* on Aesop which circulated in Ionic prose already in the sixth century BC. Chambry, Perry, Adrados, West and others have effectively dispensed with that notion.[13] But Martin West, to whom we owe the most lucid and closely argued discussion of the early stages of the *Life of Aesop,* makes a good case for the existence of a written Life as early as the middle of the fifth century BC (West 1984, 116–28).[14] The key passage is a brief reference in Aristophanes *(Av.* 471f.): "You are ignorant and incurious, and *have never explored Aesop (oud'Aisôpon pepatêkas),* who used to tell that the lark existed before everything else" (trans. West 1984, 121). The Greek word which West translates with "explore", is *pateô,* which, as he shows, can hardly refer to anything other than reading. If we combine this fact with various other references in Aristophanes and Herodotus and some further testimonia,[15] it appears that there probably existed in the fifth century BC a written book containing various fables of Aesop, set in a biographical framework. In that book, Aesop's servitude is already located in Samos, and a man named Xanthos or Xanthes appears (though a certain Iadmon is mentioned as Aesop's master). Its author was probably a Samian, or used Samian sources. The book certainly also included the story of Aesop's violent death in Delphi, perhaps the oldest part of the Aesop legend, evidently modelled on the old *pharmakos* ritual, the killing (or expulsion) of the ugly scapegoat (Wiechers 1961, 31–42; Adrados 1979b, 105–8).[16] It is possible that certain elements of the introductory part of the surviving Life as well were prefigured in the fifth-century book, since there may be traces of the *pharmakos* rite there too.[17]

The next potential Life of Aesop we know of is the *Aesopica (Aisôpeia)* of Demetrius of Phalerum, composed in the late fourth century BC. Perry argues that this was not just a collection of fables, but that it also included, "by way of introduction …, some account of Aesop

182

---

[13] Bibliographical refs. in Beschorner and Holzberg 1992b, 173. Cf. also Nøjgaard 1964, 469–70 and La Penna 1962, 282–84.

[14] Adrados 1979b discusses some of the same material, though in a more unfocussed manner and with less convincing conclusions.

[15] The testimonia are collected in Perry 1952, 211–29 and interpreted in Perry 1965, xxxv–xlvi.

[16] On this rite, cf. Burkert 1985, 82–84.

[17] Cf. Adrados 1979b, 107f.: the role played by figs in the first episode.

personally and a few anecdotes about his clever actions".[18] Demetrius' work, Perry maintains, "must have been a principal source-book ... for the author of the *Vita*" (Perry 1966, 287 n. 2). He specifically mentions the breadbasket episode narrated in ch. 18–19 of the surviving Life as probably taken over from Demetrius.[19] It is not unlikely that Perry is right about the nature of the *Aesopica;* but, as he himself admits, it cannot be proved.[20]

Another early source for our *Life of Aesop* has already been mentioned: the Assyrian *Book of Ahiqar,* which was adapted to fit in between Aesop's interference in Samian-Lydian politics and his fatal visit to Delphi. Aesop assumes the rôle of the wise Ahiqar, the King of Babylon is identified as Lycorus[21] and the King of Egypt appears as Nectanebo; but the general intrigue and the display of conventional wisdom are common to both. It should be noted, however, that the content of Aesop's hortatory speech to his adopted son is quite different from that of Ahiqar's corresponding speeches in the surviving versions (Haslam 1986, 152–55). Yet the fact that the precepts are almost wholly irrelevant to their context indicates that Aesop's speech was not invented by the author of the Life, but taken over more or less *en bloc* from some unknown source, whether another version of the *Book of Ahiqar* or some Greek ethical treatise.[22] Whatever their source — and it is not inconceivable that it was Hellenistic Greek — these precepts obviously represent a kind of conservative morality quite alien to the spirit of the rest of the Life (cf. Oettinger 1992, 21f.).

We can now see that, for our purposes, some parts at least of the present *Life of Aesop* should be set aside, or treated with extra caution, because they originate in substance before the Hellenistic period. This is true, first and foremost, for the Babylon-Memphis section, which is

---

[18] Argued in Perry 1962a; the quotation is from Perry 1966, 286 n. 2.

[19] Perry 1966, 286f. n. 2. However, his reference to Hor. *Sat.* 1.1.46–49, to support the existence of a biographical introduction in Demetrius' work, begs the question: "Horace could not have read the story about Aesop in the Vita as we have it, because that book was not yet written in his time, before 31 BC".

[20] Perry's theory is conditionally approved by Adrados 1979a, 665.

[21] *Lykoros* is the form of the name in the Berlin and Oxyrhynchus papyri and should be preferred to the trivialized *Lykourgos* of the manuscript tradition; see Haslam 1986, 149 n. 2, 164.

[22] Haslam 1986, 154f. points to similarities with the precepts of the Seven Wise Men in the collection attributed to Sosiades. Oettinger 1992, 20–22 traces a connection with a North Syrian type of *Weisheitssprüche,* subjected to occasional *Entorientalisierung.*

the most palpable *Fremdkörper* in the Life.[23] It also goes for the Delphi part, though it is obvious that much younger material has been added there to the original framework. Aesop's telling of fables in this part is probably part of an old narrative, but we cannot be sure that it contained all or the same fables as the surviving Life.[24]

It is true that Samos as the locality of Aesop's servitude and also a person named Xanthus belong, like Delphi, to the traditional, pre-Hellenistic story. Perhaps the contrast between the clever slave and his stupid master was already worked out at that early stage. But the episodes actually narrated in this part of the Life to illustrate that contrast are almost certainly not of classical origin. Some assorted indications of a post-classical date may briefly be mentioned. Most importantly, much of intrigue and characterization is similar to New Comedy, as demonstrated by Holzberg (1992a, 47–63, 72). The direction of the influence cannot be in doubt: it must have flowed from Comedy to Life.[25] There are traces of popular Cynic philosophy, especially in the rude behaviour of Aesop himself towards his master and mistress. In fact, some of the episodes told about Aesop are very similar to anecdotes told about Diogenes of Sinope.[26] The figure of Socrates, too, lies behind some traits in the characterization of Aesop; and his dealings with the sophists, as described by Plato, have perhaps influenced the description of Aesop's discussions with the professor and his students.[27] The emphasis on Aesop's deformed body, not only in the initial description, recalls Hellenistic art and its obsession with human deformity.[28]

[23] Holzberg 1992a, 65–69 demonstrates how the Ahiqar story is structurally integrated in the Life, but does not deny its role as *Vorlage*.

[24] See Merkle 1992 with refs. to earlier discussion.

[25] It should be noted that Alexis, the poet of Middle and New Comedy, wrote a piece called *Aesop*. The only fragment (Ath. 10.38.431d-f; test. 33 in Perry 1952, 223; fr. 9 PCG), however, quotes a conversation between Aesop and Solon, a topic *not* included in the *Life*.

[26] Cf. Rose 1953, La Penna 1962, 306–9, Adrados 1978; 1979b, 112 n. 16; 1981, 326–28 and the judicious discussion in Jedrkiewicz 1989, 116–27.

[27] Cf. Compton 1990, Jedrkiewicz 1989, 111–15 and Schauer and Merkle 1992.

[28] Although there is an Attic cup of the mid fifth century which depicts a dwarfish Aesop (cf. Zanker 1995, 33f., 348), the literary testimonia of the classical period do not emphasize his ugliness or deformity the way the Life does. Wiechers 1961, 32, however, connects Aesop's ugliness with the *pharmakos* figure. La Penna 1962, 280f. likewise prefers to locate Aesop's deformity among the oldest material in the Aesop legend.

These observations, though of different weight and clarity, together establish the late fourth century BC as a *terminus post quem* for the Xanthus part of the Life. We may now view the matter from the other side. There are reasons to believe that the surviving Life was composed in Egypt, although the case is not quite as clear as Perry maintains.[29] The adaptation of the Ahiqar material to fit the context appears to have been made in Egypt.[30] The role of Isis as the leader of the Muses suggests Egyptian religious syncretism.[31] The large Xanthus part, on the other hand, seems to be free of specifically Egyptian traits and may thus have been taken over by the author from a Hellenistic source without substantial modifications or additions.[32]

The same is possibly true for the Samos-Lydia part; at least, there are no references to a connection between Aesop and Croesus before the fourth century.[33] Holzberg (1992a, 64, 66f.), however, suggests that the narrative of this part of Aesop's career was deliberately structured so as to make it a counterpart to the Babylon-Memphis part, in turn closely modelled on the story of Ahiqar. It may then, in its developed form, be the creation of the author of the Life himself.

To sum up, following the order of the present text of the Life: The introductory part is a mixture of old *(pharmakos* rite) and new (Isis); the Xanthus part, which takes up half the text, is probably Hellenistic in substance; the Samos-Lydia part may be mostly a new invention; the

---

[29] The arguments of La Penna 1962, 268–73 against an Egyptian origin deserve consideration. La Penna himself, referring to the textual variants in *Vita Aesopi* 141, tentatively suggests that version G was composed for people in Syria and Palestine, version W for Sicily.

[30] See Perry 1952, 4–10 and Haslam 1986, 150. La Penna 1962, 271, however, rightly points to the curious fact that the role which King Nectanebo plays here is less glorious than one would have believed from a nationalistic Egyptian writer (cf. his role in the *Alexander Romance*).

[31] For Isis *Mousanagôgos*, see *POxy*. 1380.62 (2nd cent. AD), and cf. Plut. *De Is. et Os.* 3.352b. But, of course, the cult of Isis was widespread by the end of the Hellenistic period.

[32] Minor points of language and terminology may of course have been changed in the redactional process. For instance, Hopkins 1993, 15 n. 22, and 25 points to the term *stratêgos* employed in ch. 65 for a "local district magistrate", "a term used in this sense as far as I know only in Egypt under Greek and Roman rule".

[33] Cf. Perry 1962a, 313 n. 27, 332–34 who thinks the bringing together of Aesop and Croesus is "a dramatic literary invention of the fourth century", further propagated by Demetrius in his *Aesopica.* Cf. the comedy of Alexis (4th/3rd cent. BC; above, n. 25) which makes Aesop meet Solon.

Babylon-Memphis part has an old oriental model; the Delphi part is again a mixture of old and new.

Thus, for an investigation with the present aim, it seems wisest to concentrate on the Xanthus part, which may well go back on a separate Hellenistic work under the title "The Book of Xanthus the Philosopher and Aesop his Slave", the first part of the title transmitted in G (cf. above); for a whole life, this is a curious title, even with the addition "on Aesop's Way of Life".[34] The most reasonable explanation is that this title was originally attached to a work which covered precisely Aesop's life as a slave on Samos, and that it was mechanically taken over when that story was extended to form the surviving *Life of Aesop* (which actually covers his life, except for childhood/youth).[35] No doubt there are both pre-Hellenistic or post-Hellenistic elements in the Xanthus part as well; but we may be fairly confident, I believe, that in the main it mirrors values and beliefs current in the Hellenistic period. But current where, or with whom?

This brings us to the problem of genre, readership and tendency. To a large extent, these are questions which have to be addressed after the analysis of the values propagated by the text. The identification of these values should help situate the work, rather than the reverse. But some indications of earlier efforts to define its nature may be given at this point.

Michael Haslam's (1980, 54) characterization of the *Life of Aesop* as a "quasi-biographical specimen[s] of folk-literature" well represents the *communis opinio*. Perry, as usual, provides the most articulate characterization of the work and the most specific definition of its cultural context. Inevitably, by being so explicit he also reveals the risks one takes in using the label "folk-literature" in relation to antiquity.

---

[34] There is also the possibility (as David Konstan points out to me) that the whole title is original, then with *anastrophê* used in its earlier sense "reversal", which would fit well with the Xanthus part of the Life, culminating with Aesop's emancipation. The sense "way of life" is attested from Polybius onwards (LSJ s.v. II.3), and will anyway be how the title was understood in the Imperial period (cf. the New Testament usage).

[35] The subscription of G, on the other hand, is formulated as if we had read a full biography: *Aisôpou genna, anastrophê, prokopê kai apobiôsis*. In Rec. W, two of the best manuscripts (followed by Perry in his text) have the title *Bios Aisôpou tou philosophou*, and the others, too, display various phrases containing *bios* and/or *diêgêsis* (see Perry 1952, 81, 133).

The *Life of Aesop* belongs to a species of ancient folk-literature of which very little has survived. Like the fabulous history of Alexander, it is a naïve, popular, and anonymous book, composed for the entertainment and edification of the common people rather than for educated men, and making little or no pretense to historical accuracy or literary elegance ...

But unlike the romance of Alexander, the biography of Aesop is concerned with a cultural, not a military hero, and in this respect it is almost without parallel among the ancient Greek texts that have come down to us. ...

[The *Life of Aesop*] gives us the portrait of a wise man as seen through the eyes of the poor in spirit, at the same time enlivened by a spontaneous and vigorous, if somewhat homely, wit ...

... for us the *Life of Aesop* is interesting not for such artistic value as it may possess — though that too, I suspect, has been unduly disparaged — but because it is one of the few genuinely popular books that have come down from ancient times.[36]

In another place, Perry speaks of "Aesop as the exponent of the common man's wit and wisdom in the form of fable-lore, in conflict with the aristocratic Apollo as leader of the Muses and the patron of Greek poetry and art on the intellectual plane of fashion" (Perry 1962b, 633). The authentic biographical tradition concerning Aesop ends already with Demetrius of Phalerum, Perry explains; from now on, it is a matter of "framing Aesop in the (fanciful) history of ideas and cultural values" (Perry 1962a, 334, repeated 1965, xlii). Francisco Adrados (1979b, 102) adds: Aesop of the Life "is a man of the people who triumphs over cities and kings and confronts the powerful Delphic priesthood. He is a person who acts in opposition to the conventional values ..."

This all, at first sight, looks promising for our purpose. But what, exactly, is "a genuinely popular book" of antiquity? Considering how small the proportion of genuinely literate people was even among the Greeks of the late Hellenistic period, one may wonder who the prospective readers of such a product were, and who the author.[37] Are unedu-

---

[36] Perry 1936, 1f.; cf. Perry 1952, 3f.

[37] Cf. Harris 1989, 116–47 for a low estimate of Hellenistic literacy in general, and esp. p. 126 touching on our question (but not mentioning the *Life of Aesop*): "Any assumption that the intellectually less demanding genres of Hellenistic literature aimed at, or reached, a truly popular audience of readers should be resisted. The papyri show conclusively that popular literature did not exist in any ordinary sense of that expression ..." Cf. also p. 227–28 and my comments in Hägg 1994.

cated writers possible at all among the Hellenistic Greeks? Is this really a book of the people and for the people, or is it something that only masquerades as such?

Perry's characterization provoked doubts immediately in some of the reviews of his two books. He exaggerated, some felt, the popular character of the language of G: some vulgarisms should rather be ascribed to the Byzantine tradition of the text (Hausrath 1937, 771; Dölger 1953);[38] on the other hand, the text was said to contain more elements characteristic of a studied rhetorical style than Perry would admit (Adrados 1953, 324f.). The anti-intellectualist — or, more specifically, anti-Apollinian — tendency was considered overstated by some (Rose 1953; Blake 1954, 80–82). And Keith Hopkins (1993, 11 n. 15) now finds Perry's "assumptions about the sophisticated tastes of the educated in the Roman world and the reading capacity of the common people ... questionable". But, on the whole, there seems to have been little opposition to the description of the *Life of Aesop* as a genuine piece of folk-literature, as the quotation from Haslam shows.

I shall return to these questions at the end of my paper. Now it is high time to turn to the analysis proper of the conventional values which our text may mirror or propagate. I shall analyse its picture of two social groups, the slaves (as represented by Aesop and his fellow slaves) and the intellectuals (the professor and his students), and also its representation of gender rôles (the professor's wife in relation to her husband and to their slave).

First, the slaves. As will have become evident, my approach is different from that of Keith Hopkins in his recent article "Novel Evidence for Roman Slavery", though we happen to use the same source. His purpose, like mine, is "not to squeeze fiction for facts, but to interpret fiction as a mirror of Roman [in my case, Hellenistic] thinking and feeling" (Hopkins 1993, 4 n. 3). But Hopkins chooses to ignore the composite character of the work — the "multiple sites, origins and fantasies" (Hopkins 1993, 11 n. 14) from which it stems — and seems to regard its very anonymity and popularity as a kind of guarantee for its general trustworthiness as a witness to Roman slavery:

> The multiple versions and surviving copies of the *Life of Aesop* ... indicate its forgotten popularity, and dramatically increase its utility for us;

186

---

[38] Hostetter 1955, a dissertation supervised by Perry, reaffirms the latter's view.

what we have is not a single author's idiosyncratic vision, but a collective, composite work incorporating many different stories told about slaves … Its survival in Egypt and the occasional adaptation of the text to Egyptian conditions should not mislead us into thinking that it relates primarily to Egypt, any more than its being written first in Greek should make us think that it related primarily to Greek slavery. In my view, the *Life of Aesop is* a generic work, related generally, but not specifically, to slavery in the whole Roman world.[39]

This is, to put it mildly, an optimistic point of view. The notion of a "collective" work brings us back to the old romantic myth of the "folk-book", which modern literary research has exposed.[40] My analytical approach, in contrast, by focussing on a relatively uniform and apparently non-Egyptian part of the Life, permits us to operate within a more limited chronological and ethnic framework: Hellenistic Greek rather than generally "Roman".[41] And my concern, of course, is not with slavery generally, but, in particular, with people's attitude towards slaves.

Aesop himself is no doubt an atypical slave. But this does not mean that the Life necessarily depicts an atypical condition for a slave. On the contrary, the point of the story is often that his surroundings — his owner, his owner's friends, his fellow slaves — treat him as if he were an ordinary slave, with surprising and comical effects. Aesop constantly

---

[39] Hopkins 1993, 11. Hopkins (6 n. 6) also remarks: "I use the term 'Roman slavery' rather crudely to refer to slavery in the Roman empire, without implying either uniformity or consistency — just as one might use the term 'bread' to cover bread in France, England, Russia and the USA, in spite of the known variations". Very well; but as soon as one proceeds from basic definition to actual description, one has to choose what bread to describe.

[40] Jack Winkler 1991, 279, too, in his chapter on the *Life of Aesop,* calls it a "genuine folk-book", envisaging a kind of collective authorship. It is important, I think, to distinguish between, on the one hand, the various anecdotes and other legendary material circulating through the centuries about a figure like Aesop, and, on the other, the existence of a written story based on such material. The former stage is "collective" in the sense that many people tell and develop these anecdotes, each with his own selection and adaptation; but as soon as it comes to collecting them in a book with a continuous story, the choice and framework are due to one person, and the designation "folk-book" misleading.

[41] The fact that Aesop is a slave only in the first 90 chapters saves Hopkins from more serious consequences of his unitarian view. But on p. 25 he declares that "the murder of the scapegoat", i.e. the execution of Aesop in Delphi (132–42), "reflects … the endemic hostility to the clever slave in Roman society". Aesop's death, however, is one of the really ancient elements of the legend, already known to Herodotus (2.134). Cf. also above, n. 3.

encounters people's conventional attitudes toward a house slave, and each time he has to assert his otherness. So let us look at these conventional attitudes.

The first confrontation between Xanthus and Aesop takes place in the Samian agora, where Aesop and two other slaves are put up for sale (20–27). The most important quality in a slave, it becomes clear, is his outward appearance. Aesop's two fellow slaves on this occasion are a teacher *(grammatikos)* and a harpist *(psaltês),* and the slave dealer has brought them precisely to Samos because there should be a demand for intellectual slaves there, considering all the students Xanthus's celebrated school of philosophy attracts. Still, when it comes to having them sold at a good price, the slave dealer exerts himself in dressing them up beautifully and in hiding the young teacher's only physical defect, his thin legs. Aesop's deformity, in contrast, cannot be hidden, and the slave dealer consequently does not expect to get him sold at all. Xanthus, the philosopher, at first totally embraces this conventional estimate of a slave's worth, praising before his students the slave dealer for his commercial genius: he has put the two young and handsome slaves up for sale together with the ugly one, to emphasize their beauty.

When the beautiful slaves turn out to be too expensive for Xanthus, and his students suggest that he should buy Aesop instead, Xanthus still clings to appearance only, protesting that his wife at all events would not tolerate an ugly slave. By chance a conversation begins between Aesop, the students and Xanthus, and Aesop's wit and cleverness are demonstrated in full; and so Xanthus is persuaded to buy the ugly slave after all. He gets him at cost price, 75 denarii, whereas the *grammatikos* would have cost him 3000. It is Aesop himself, not the philosopher, who formulates the moral of the whole scene, by using a parable (26):

187

> *Aesop:*   Don't look at my appearance *(to eidos),* but examine my soul.
>
> *Xanthus:* What is appearance?
>
> *Aesop:*   It's like what often happens when we go to a wine shop to buy wine. The jars we see are ugly, but the wine tastes good.[42]

One might compare Alcibiades in Plato's *Symposium* (215a-b) who likens Socrates to a Silenus statue hiding the effigy of a god. Aesop, like Socrates, is ugly in appearance, but appearance deceives. True value is to

---

[42] Aesop again elaborates this topic in ch. 88.

be found inside the person, even inside a slave. Thus, Socratic insight is used in the *Life of Aesop* to expose a conventional assumption which even a celebrated philosopher like Xanthus is shown to share.

Outer appearance as the popular index of a slave's value continues to be illustrated in the narrative: the tax collectors remit the sales tax out of pity for the buyer (27), Xanthus's wife on seeing the new slave threatens to leave the house (31), the gardener refuses to believe that one so ugly can read (37), and the people of Samos at first refuse to listen to his interpretation of an omen for the same reason (87). Yet, both Xanthus and his wife quickly come to appreciate and make use of Aesop's cleverness. There is now, in the next series of episodes, another conventional attitude towards slaves that is again and again unwittingly demonstrated by Xanthus, to his own detriment.

In the episode with the empty oil flask (38) referred to above, Xanthus makes the mistake of not simply ordering his slave to accompany him to the bath, but of specifying what things he should bring: the oil flask and the towels. Aesop takes his revenge by not bringing what the master has not specified, namely, the oil. This, I presume, is an authentic representation of a normal attitude towards slaves, to treat and address them as infants, as people totally devoid of experience, ambition, and initiative of their own.[43] A slave is by definition an unthinking creature, he has to be programmed to perform even daily tasks. Aesop has already shown that he is a thinking being, but still Xanthus automatically assumes the conventional attitude towards him.

Xanthus, of course, fails to catch the point and changes his behaviour in the wrong direction. He takes pains to specify his orders in still greater detail, but always happens to leave some gap which allows Aesop to act in absurd ways, while taking his master literally and obeying his words rather than his intent. The authentic glimpse in the flask episode thus gives way to caricature and literary exaggeration in the following episodes. Not until the game has developed in absurdum does Xanthus finally learn his lesson and starts treating Aesop as a thinking human being, rather than as a slave.

A couple of other typical attitudes towards slaves are much emphasized throughout the narrative. Aesop's master, the philosopher, is always

188

---

[43] The same attitude, as Hopkins 1993, 19 n. 31 notes, is witnessed by Plut. *De garr.* 18.511d–e.

looking for an opportunity to beat him; but his philosophical disposition mostly prevents him from doing so, since he must have a rational cause for punishment, not only an emotional one. Aesop's mistress, on the other hand, comes to regard Aesop, in spite of his ugliness, as an attractive sexual partner, and after watching him masturbating one morning, forces him to satisfy her desires to the extreme (75). These are topics we recognize from comedy, the beating syndrome from (Roman) New Comedy, the sexual potency of slaves especially from Aristophanes (cf. Goins 1989, 28f.); and there is a combination of both in Herodas's Mime 5, "The Jealous Mistress".[44] Does that mean that they are literary conventions rather than mirroring authentic behaviour?

Probably they are both. Their topicalization no doubt reflects the literary conventions of comedy, but there is some reality to which the topoi correspond that is common to the classical and Hellenistic periods. As always in the interpretation of literary sources, we have to consider the condensation typical of the medium: the frequency with which the heroes of the ideal novels are shipwrecked or slaves are beaten in New Comedy is of course "unrealistic", but the events in themselves are taken from real life. No doubt, as documentary sources demonstrate, many households could boast of well functioning relationships between masters and slaves.[45] Still, literature shows us, in artistic articulation and enlargement, the tensions that were also there.

So, Keith Hopkins (1993, 14f., 22f.) is probably right in interpreting the topos of the virile slave who tempts and seduces his mistress as the expression of a constant underlying fear in slave masters that such things could happen. Inevitably, male domestic slaves would sometimes be left alone with the mistress in the house, they would follow her to the bath, etc. Slaves of both sexes were in fact witness to the most private life of their master and mistress, being ever-present in the house, in the bed-chamber, even in the toilet, attending "with a towel and a pitcher of water", as the *Life of Aesop* demonstrates (67). No weakness could be concealed.[46] Such a system can function psychologically only on the as-

189

---

[44] There is ample comparative material in Headlam's notes to Herod. 5. (David Konstan kindly turned my attention to this text).

[45] I owe this point to Sarah Pomeroy.

[46] See now also Hunter 1994, 70–95 (Ch. 3, "Slaves in the Household: Was Privacy Possible?"), with illustrative material both from Classical literary and archaeological sources and from records of the plantation households of the American South.

sumption that the slave is an inanimate object, like a piece of furniture, or perhaps an animal. But however much the master tried to regard his slave as of another order, as non-human, as a *thing,* the anxiety would always be there that he was in fact his equal or even superior, a human being with intelligence and attractiveness, his rival rather than his tool.

The beating topos, in turn, testifies to the persistent and enforced tendency to regard the slave as, precisely, a tool. When a tool does not function the way it is supposed to, a reaction of irrational anger lies close at hand, a wish to throw it away or destroy it. Hopkins (1993, 18) aptly compares this response, in a slightly different context, with the modern consumer's "frustration or fury at not being able to understand or follow the instructions which accompany a self-assembly kit for a piece of household equipment". Rational behaviour towards a slave is something unnatural and out-of-place, since by definition the slave himself is not a rational being. The irony in the case of Xanthus, the philosopher, is that he cannot overcome his professional commitment to reason, and thus only exceptionally (58; 77) has the satisfaction of actually laying hands on his slave. He is constantly frustrated, lacking the slave-owner's normal outlet for his aggressions.

We turn now to gender rôles. To a large extent, the *Life of Aesop* gives voice to a blatant misogyny. We have already seen the depiction of Xanthus's wife as lecherous and unfaithful. She is also described as quarrelsome and wasteful. Aesop himself, in his conversations with Xanthus and his wife, eloquently represents the misogynistic viewpoint. But these traits again have the character of literary convention derived from Old Comedy and other Greek literature, and they are anyway too common and stereotyped to be of major interest. What deserves greater attention is the attitude of Xanthus himself towards his wife.

Now, on a closer look, Xanthus is not quite the unsympathetic or ridiculous character that his rôle vis-à-vis Aesop, the hero, has made most critics assume. Despite his many stupid acts and utterances, he is also described as a rather decent man, even with a touch of self-irony (28; 40). He is, of course, inferior to Aesop in intelligence and wit, but no doubt a reflective person — and an unusually humane slave owner. His wife even rebukes him for being a *doulokoitês,* a "slave-lover" (49). Aesop's chief complaint with Xanthus is not that he treats him badly — then he would simply run away (26) — but that he refuses to set him free, in spite of the outstanding services Aesop performs for him. True, Xanthus again and again goes back on his promises to free Aesop (74; 79; 80; 90)

190

— but the conventional attitude towards slaves obviously allows him to do so without breaking any moral code or feeling any kind of remorse; and Aesop knows he has nobody to appeal to, no "right" that is his. His emotional response may be revenge (74W, implemented in 75W), but he soon returns to his rational tactic of performing services.

In his relationship to his wife, Xanthus differs markedly from the misogyny which is so characteristic of other males in the story: of Aesop, in the first place (32; 49; 50), but also of Xanthus's students (24) and of a countryman who is accidentally brought into the action (64). Officially, it is true, Xanthus teaches that one "should not listen to a woman" *(mê peithesthai gunaiki)*, as his students are eager to point out (24W). And when there is risk that his wife will leave him, he tries to give the impression that it is the dowry he is afraid of losing (29). But behind this façade the author permits us to see small glimpses of Xanthus's personal affection for his wife. The first comes when Xanthus has just brought home his new slave and presents him to his wife. She finds Aesop repulsive and says she will leave the house. Xanthus wants Aesop to use his verbal skills to prevent this, but Aesop just comes out with (31):

> *Aesop:* Well, let her go her way and be damned.
> *Xanthus:* Shut up, you trash. Don't you realize that I love her more than my life *(philô autên huper emauton)*?
> *Aesop:* You love the woman *(phileis to gunaion)*?
> *Xanthus:* I certainly do.
> *Aesop:* You want her to stay?
> *Xanthus:* I do, you contemptible fool.

This declaration of love only meets with contempt in Aesop. His diagnosis is ready: his master *gunaikokrateitai,* he is ruled by his wife, he is "hen-pecked" (31, also 29) — the typical male comment in such a situation. Later in the narrative, it is mentioned incidentally that Xanthus saves a special pig for the celebration of his wife's birthday (42). And when Xanthus himself is invited to a party by one of his students, he takes extra portions of each course that is served and has Aesop put them in a basket. He says (44): "Then take them to her who cares for me *(têi eunoousêi)*." Xanthus's charming periphrasis for "wife", *hê eunoousa*, becomes the point of departure for one of Aesop's sophistic tricks against him. He brings the food home and shows it to Xanthus's wife, who naturally assumes that it is meant for her (45):

Xanthus's wife:	Did your master send this to me?	
Aesop:	No.	
Xanthus's wife:	And to whom did he send it?	
Aesop:	To her who cares for him *(têi eunoousêi).*	
Xanthus's wife:	And who cares for him *(autôi eunoei),* you runaway?	
Aesop:	Just wait a little, and you'll see who cares for him.	

So he brings the house dog who devours the food, and Aesop returns
to Xanthus to report that his command has been executed. Xanthus's
wife, for her part, decides again to leave their house (46): "For when he
prefers *(proekrinen)* the bitch to me, how can I live with *(sunoikêsô)* him
any longer?" Here we catch a rare glimpse of the reciprocity in this marriage:[47] to the wife, too, it is evidently a question of more than a formal
economic arrangement.

Unsuspectingly, Xanthus returns home from the party in his best
mood, only to find his wife totally unresponsive (49):

> [He] went to the bedroom, where he began to talk sweet talk *(kolakeu-
> ein)* to his wife and shower her with kisses *(kataphilein).* But she turned
> her back on Xanthus and said: "Don't come near me, you slave-lover
> *(doulokoita),* or rather you dog-lover *(kunokoita).* Give me back my
> dowry."

So she again assumes the conventional Xanthippe rôle. She moves home
to her parents, and Aesop can triumphantly demonstrate to Xanthus that
"the one who cares for you" is *not* synonymous with "wife" (50).

There is reason, I think, to emphasize these unexpected expressions
of love and affection between Xanthus and his wife. They do not conform to the literary-conventional rôles played by the philosopher and
his wife, and they are not necessary for the plot (as romantic love is in
the ideal Greek novel). They are therefore all the more worth attention
as potential testimony to actual gender rôles among Hellenistic Greeks.
For there is no sign, as far as I can see, that they are meant to contribute to characterizing Xanthus as a ridiculous or stupid person; they are
rather part of the set of traits which make him, for all his snobbery and
dumbness, a surprisingly sympathetic character.

It should also be noted that there is no mention of Xanthus having
any sexual aspirations for or relations with the young female slaves of the

---

[47] Cf. also her acute description (in a negative context) of her husband's character in
the beginning of ch. 31.

household (30: *paidiskaria, korasia),* corresponding to his wife's dreams
of a handsome new slave (32–33) or her subsequent affair with Aesop
(75). In the symposia, he sometimes drinks too much, as Aesop observes
(68), but there is no hint at sexual orgies with harp players or dancers,
as in other anecdotes of philosophers' way of life:[48] no, Xanthus, as we   192
have seen, simply goes home to his wife, hoping to find her responsive
to his drunken advances (49).

We shall now turn to the third and last set of values, those concerned with intellectuals and the philosophical life, and the way these
were viewed from outside, perhaps from below. One might say that the
Xanthus part of the *Life of Aesop* bridges the gap between, on the one
side, the caricatures of classical sophists provided, in their different ways,
by Aristophanes[49] and Plato, and, on the other, Lucian's satirical works
portraying philosophers of the imperial period and such anecdotes as are
collected by Diogenes Laertius, Athenaeus and others.[50]

Xanthus, it is emphasized in the Life, was a distinguished philosopher who had studied in Athens "under philosophers, rhetoricians, and
philologists (*grammatikois)*" (36) and now attracted to his island many
students from Greece and Asia Minor (20). We may perhaps venture to
compare Xanthus's imagined position on Samos with that of Posidonius
on Rhodes. In that way, we will be able to see in a popular mirror the
activities and reputation of such Hellenistic philosophers, whom we are
otherwise accustomed to regard with the admiring eyes of a Cicero. What
impression did they and their students make on their non-intellectual
fellow citizens? Were learning and a philosophical way of life met with
sympathy and respect? If not, what particular aspects of their pursuits
did arouse resentment or ridicule?

To judge from the *Life of Aesop,* there was little understanding among
ordinary people of the more central tenets of the Hellenistic schools of
philosophy. Xanthus, we are shown, resorts to philosophical jargon simply

---

[48] See, e.g., Alciphron 3.19, on the behaviour of the Epicurean and the Cynic, quoted
in Decleva Caizzi 1993, 303f.

[49] On the function of intellectuals in Aristophanes's plays, see the illuminating discussion in Zimmermann 1993.

[50] For an interpretation of these anecdotes, see Decleva Caizzi 1993. The original and
thought-provoking introductory parts of her article (303–7), sketching a programme
for the investigation of contemporary popular views of Hellenistic philosophers, are
not pursued further in the rest of her article, which is a more historically orientated
study of Zeno.

to avoid giving straight answers to common people's questions, as when the gardener asks why weeds grow up much quicker than the plants that he waters and to which he gives all kinds of attention (35):

> When Xanthus heard this philosophical question *(zêtêma)* and couldn't, on the spur of the moment, think of an answer to it, he said: "All things are subject to the stewardship of divine providence *(panta têi theiai pronoiai dioikeitai)*".

Aesop, as usual, sees right through him and begins to laugh. Xanthus gets angry, but has to put up with the retort (36): "If you talk nonsense *(mêden legêis)*, you'll have to expect to be jeered at". Xanthus weakly objects: "Things that are at the disposal of the divine order of nature are not subject to inquiry by philosophers *(ta gar hupo theias phuseôs dioikoumena hupo philosophôn zêteisthai ou dunatai)*", whereupon Aesop, the slave, solves the problem to the gardener's full satisfaction (37).[51]

Once only does Aesop allude with something like respect to formal education and philosophy, namely, when he rebukes Xanthus for forgetting precisely these values in his attempt to commit suicide (85):

> "Master, where is your philosophy? Where is your boasted education *(to tês paideias phruagma)?* Where is your doctrine of self-control *(to tês enkrateias dogma)?* Come now master, are you in such an ill-considered and cowardly rush to die that you would throw away the pleasure of life *(to hêdu zên)* by hanging yourself? Think it over *(metanoêson),* master."

Otherwise, of course, the point steadily driven home is that the slave Aesop, without any formal education but with his inborn intelligence, defeats the philosopher and his students in every test and discussion. This is innate in the comic genre and essential to the plot; and it may be that an utterance like the one just quoted better indicates what common people would actually expect from those with a philosophical education: a greater capability to deal with crises in life, to let reason prevail over emotions.

This is, in fact, visible also in the way Xanthus is depicted earlier in the narrative. We have already seen how his philosophical disposition hinders him from finding a physical outlet for his aggression against his clever slave. Another character trait should probably also be seen in

---

[51] On this scene, cf. La Penna 1962a, 302f., who sees in Aesop's solution (37) the victory of science over a philosophical-religious attempt at explanation (Xanthus's Providence).

connection with his profession: he is ostentatiously economical. He is obviously rich — in addition to Aesop, he owns a number of slave girls (30) as well as (at least) enough male slaves to carry his wife around in a litter (22).[52] Still, when he hears the price of the two attractive slaves put up for sale together with Aesop, the *grammatikos* and the *psaltês*, he at once looses interest, saying to his students (24W): "it's a principle *(dogma)* with me not to buy high-priced slaves but to be served by cheap ones". On another occasion, he invites his friends to lunch with the following words (39):

> "Gentlemen, will you share my simple fare *(eutelôs aristêsai)?* There will be lentil *(phakon).* We ought to judge our friends by their good will *(têi prothumiai)* and not by the elegance of their food. On occasion the humblest dishes afford a more genial pleasure than more pretentious ones if the host serves them with a gracious welcome *(met' eunoias pro-trepetai)."*

The lunch turns out to be even more frugal than the host had intended, since Aesop chooses to take Xanthus at his word and cooks only one lentil! So frugality as such comes under a bright comical light through this practical joke; but the pompous way in which the philosopher announces his intention of serving good will *(prothumia, eunoia)* rather than good food has already shown us that an outside onlooker would hardly accept that greed is paraded as philosophical moderation. We may assume that among common people it was considered perverse not to display and enjoy one's wealth (cf. Petronius's Trimalchio, with satire from the reverse viewpoint), and that there was little understanding for purely ethical restraints on consumption.

194

The philosophical debates and discourses that we are invited to listen to in the Life are of course caricatures in both form and content. The formal traits that are ridiculed are easiest to come to terms with. We have already seen something of Xanthus's pompous style in his invitation to lunch. But another example will more clearly display the kind of inflated intellectual discourse that people obviously reacted against. Xanthus arrives with his students *(scholastikoi)* in the slave market and discovers Aesop placed between the two handsome young slaves. He exclaims (23):

[52] Pointed out by Hopkins 1993, 17 n. 26.

Xanthus:	Bravo! Well done, by Hera! An acute and philosophical, indeed a marvellously, a perfectly experienced man!
The students:	What are you praising, professor *(kathêgêta)?* What is worthy of your admiration? Let us in on it, too. Don't begrudge us a share of the beautiful *(metaschein tou kalou).*
Xanthus:	Gentlemen and scholars *(andres philologoi)*, you must not think that philosophy consists only in what can be put in words, but also in acts. Indeed, unspoken philosophy *(hê sigômenê philosophia)* often surpasses beyond expectation that which is expressed in words. You can observe this in the case of dancers, how by the movement of their hands they surpass that which is communicated by many words. Just as philosophy can very well consist in acts, in the same way this display too expresses an unspoken philosophy. You see, this man had two handsome slaves and one ugly. He put the ugly one between the handsome ones in order that his ugliness should make their beauty noticeable, for if the ugliness were not set in contrast to that which is superior to it, the appearance of the handsome ones would not have been put to the test.
The students:	You are marvellous, professor. How fine of you to perceive so clearly his purpose!

This excellent parody of academic vices needs little comment. The stuffy atmosphere of the classroom is well captured, with the students flattering their professor and the professor delighting in his own instruction and in the admiration he earns. A question which might have been answered in a few simple words is taken as a pretext for the delivery of a small lecture on spoken and silent philosophy, only marginally relevant to the topic. When the real answer comes, it is drowned in fine words and empty philosophemes. And the author has already shown us how ordinary customers at the sale *actually* reacted to the display: contrary to the philosopher's theory, they turned their backs on all three slaves, because "that one spoils their appearance, too!" (21).

195   What we have been presented with is, no doubt, a lifelike picture of how people in general would regard the groups of students, with their professor in the middle, whom they would encounter in the streets and stoas, and parts of whose conversation they could sometimes overhear.

If the parody of philosophical form and pretence is clear enough, the actual contents of some of the discussions between Xanthus, his students and Aesop are more difficult to come to grips with. What is the relation here between fiction and reality? There are topics like: "What circumstance will produce great consternation among men?" (47), "Why is it that a sheep being led to the slaughter doesn't make a sound, but a pig squeals loudly?" (48), "Why is it that when we defecate, we often look down at our own droppings?" (67), or, as in the very first discussion between Aesop and Xanthus, why does the philosopher urinate while walking along instead of taking "a little time off for the physical necessities?" (28). There is little of what is discussed in the Xanthus part of the Life that comes closer to philosophy than these topics.

Is this really the kind of topic that people imagined intellectuals as discussing? Or is the choice of topics on the author's part perhaps merely a way of placing the pretentious form of the discussions more in focus through the contrast between an academic form and a trivial or low subject? The comic effect of the contrast between form and content may be exemplified by the conclusion of the urination debate (28):

Xanthus:	I urinated as I walked along (*peripatôn ourêsa*) to avoid three unpleasant consequences.
Aesop:	What are they?
Xanthus:	The heat of the earth, the acrid smell of the urine, and the burning of the sun.
Aesop:	How's that?
Xanthus:	You see that the sun is directly overhead (*mesouranei*) and has scorched the earth with its heat, and when I stand still to urinate, the hot ground burns my feet, the acrid smell of the urine invades my nostrils and blocks my outlets (*ekroas*)[53] and the sun burns my head. It was because I wanted to avoid these three consequences that I urinated as I walked along.
Aesop:	You've convinced me. Well invented (*sophôs epenoêsas*). Walk on.

On the other hand, the choice of topic, while naturally a caricature, is perhaps not so far from what people actually thought philosophers or sophists might discuss in all seriousness. One may compare the kind of topics we know were given for exercise to the students in the imperial schools of rhetoric and which prominent sophists excelled in too — Dio's encomium of a parrot and Lucian's of a fly, etc. (cf. Anderson 1993, 171-99). The writing and performance of such *adoxa* will have looked

[53] Adopting Papathomopoulos's plausible conjecture for *akoas* (G). Perry deletes the whole phrase.

as ridiculous to a contemporary outsider, who could not appreciate the professional virtuosity displayed, as it does to many of us today.[54]

In the case of the conversations about urination and excretion, the obvious affinity with topics occurring in Old Comedy must be taken into account as well. As in comedy, these discussions will also have been included and elaborated for the simple reason that they were supposed to have an immediate appeal to the intended audience.[55]

This leads us to the last consideration: What kind of audience is the *Life of Aesop* addressing? Are we entitled to characterize it as a specimen of popular literature? If it mirrors attitudes and values of the Hellenistic Greeks, at what level of society are they? My attempt to answer these questions must obviously be provisional — these are complex matters, and we lack much of the comparative material that would permit one to formulate conclusions with any degree of confidence.

First, the author. I am still referring, in the first place, to the Xanthus part of the Life, considering it as a unity in two respects: as an autonomous, probably Hellenistic work incorporated, more or less unaltered, into the extant Life, and as a structured whole rather than a collection of anecdotes. Whoever put this together must have been a man of some education. The parodies of intellectual rhetoric must have been composed by someone with a formal schooling. We should not let the instances of vulgar vocabulary and vulgar topics mislead us into assuming that the author too was "vulgar", in the sense that he belonged to the lower strata of society. Such a person could not have written the intellectual parts, supposing he could write at all, while an educated man of course could use vulgarisms if it happened to suit his purpose. In addition, we may note that some of the vulgar words in the Life, like some of the topics, may have a literary pedigree, deriving from Aristophanes and other Attic comedians,[56] while others may simply reflect contemporary daily language.

Thus, the author cannot, as far as I can see, be used to justify the label "popular literature" for the work. Given the restriction of literacy to

---

[54] I owe this point to Johnny Christensen.

[55] On "scatological humour" in Attic comedy, see Henderson 1975, 187–203.

[56] Cf. Hostetter 1955, 124f., who, however, prefers to regard these words as belonging to the "vernacular" in both classical and Hellenistic times and surfacing in works like comedy and the *Life of Aesop*, while they were taboo in most other literature.

the very highest levels of Hellenistic society,[57] it would indeed be strange if he could be. But his intended audience, or part of it, may well be a different matter.

Just as many of Aristophanes's jokes will have had a special appeal to the more simple-minded among his Athenian audience, it seems likely that our story, with its simple jokes, its daily-life situations, and not least its insistent mockery of intellectuals and their pretensions, was primarily directed to a popular audience. This does not preclude, of course, that intellectual readers too might have enjoyed the story and the jokes. But we should note, for instance, that the caricature of the philosophical life it provides is not distinct enough, as far as I can judge, to allow us to identify what particular philosophical sect the author is ridiculing.[58] It is not the kind of refined satire that would have appealed to people with a more intimate knowledge of the different schools of Hellenistic philosophy, and which has survived in other anecdotal material (cf. Decleva Caizzi 1993).

197

On the other hand, the fact that the hero of the story is a slave should not lead us to believe that the author had slaves, in particular, in mind as his audience. This is not a revolutionary text, in my opinion, any more than Greek and Roman New Comedy is. There is, no doubt, an element of inversion of the normal social order involved, but that is another matter. Thus, I disagree with Keith Hopkins (1993, 19) who writes:

> What is so remarkable surely about this story, designed I must stress to be read in a slave society (and perhaps even, as often happened, designed to be read aloud by a slave reader to his listening master and family), is that we are asked and expected in a slave society to side with the slave against the master.

Now, I have no quarrel with the imagined scene itself: such reading aloud within the household, whether by master or slave, is probably how we

---

[57] Cf. the references above, n. 37.

[58] Rather, there seems to be a mixture of the various special vocabularies and other characteristics of the schools: Platonism (26 *to eidos*, 35 *pronoia*, 23 *metaschein tou kalou* and *hê sigômenê philosophia*), Stoicism (36 *ta … hupo theias phuseôs dioikoumena*, 85 *enkrateia*), Epicureanism (85 *to hêdu zên*). The discourse on "peripatetic" urination may parody Aristotle and other scientific writings (Hippocrates?), the obsession with excrement and other bodily functions may be modelled on Cynicism (on Aesop himself as a Cynic type, see the references above, n. 26). These are only scattered observations, and the topic evidently needs a closer study.

should envisage much of the consumption of the entertainment literatures of Hellenistic and Roman times (cf. Hägg 1994, 58). But this text does not expect us to "side with the slave against the master". Aesop is a totally atypical slave. There is no loyalty described between him and his fellow-slaves; quite the contrary.[59] The proper resolution of the tension underlying the story is not that slaves in general are to be more respected or given power, but that Aesop, the fabulist, should be set free — be relieved from the servitude which is entirely unfitting for his genius.

The values and attitudes, then, which the story of "Xanthus the Philosopher and Aesop his Slave" demonstrates or implies, are to my mind likely to have been common among people in the Greek Hellenistic world. There is indeed nothing very surprising in the values as such, as we have seen; but that, after all, presumably lies in the very nature of "conventional values". The importance of this work, in our context, is that it gives us a contemporary confirmation of constants and developments which, with our better knowledge of the fourth century BC and of the early imperial period, we might well conjecture for the Hellenistic age, but for which we to a large extent lack the documentation.

Bibliography

Adrados, F.R. 1953. Review of Perry 1952, *Gnomon* 25, 323-28.

Adrados, F.R. 1978. "Elementos cinicos en las 'Vidas' de Esopo y Secundo y en el 'Diálogo' de Alejandro y los gimnosofistas", in: S.J. Bilbao, *Homenaje a Eleuterio Elorduy, S.J.,* 309-28.

Adrados, F.R. 1979a. *Historia de la fábula greco-latina, 1: Introducción y de los origines a la edad helenística.* Madrid.

Adrados, F.R. 1979b. "The 'Life of Aesop' and the Origins of Novel in Antiquity", *QuadUrbin* 30, 93-112.

Adrados, F.R. 1981. "Sociolingüística y griego antiguo", *RevEspLing* 11, 311-29.

Adrados, F.R. 1993. Review of Papathomopoulos 1990, *Gnomon* 65, 660-64.

Adrados, F.R. & Reverdin, O. (eds.) 1984. *La Fable.* (EntrHardt 30). Vandoeuvres.

Anderson, G. 1993. *The Second Sophistic: A Cultural Phenomenon in the Roman Empire.* London/New York.

---

[59] The clearest instances of a failure of loyalty are in the initial part of the *Life* (2-19), i.e., outside my selected part of the story, but inside that of Hopkins. Note that the other slaves mostly operate *as a group,* against Aesop.

Beschorner, A. & Holzberg, N. 1992. "A Bibliography of the Aesop Romance", in: Holzberg (ed.) 1992b, 165–87.

Blake, W.E. 1954. Review of Perry 1952, *AJPh* 75, 79–84.

Bremer, J.M. & Handley, E.W. (eds.) 1993. *Aristophane.* (EntrHardt 38). Vandoeuvres.

Bulloch, A., Gruen, E.S., Long, A.A. & Stewart, A. (eds.) 1993. *Images and Ideologies: Self-Definition in the Hellenistic World.* Berkeley/Los Angeles.

Burkert, W. 1985. *Greek Religion: Archaic and Classical.* Trans. by J. Raffan. Oxford.

Compton, T. 1990. "The Trial of the Satirist: Poetic *Vitae* (Aesop, Archilochus, Homer) as Background for Plato's *Apology*", *AJPh* 111, 330–47.

Daly, L.W. (ed.) 1961. *Aesop Without Morals: The Famous Fables, and a Life of Aesop.* New York/London.

Decleva Caizzi, F. 1993. "The Porch and the Garden: Early Hellenistic Images of the Philosophical Life", in: Bulloch, Gruen, Long & Stewart (eds.) 1993, 303–29.

Dijk, G.-J. van 1994a. Review of Holzberg 1992b, *Mnemosyne* 47, 384–89.

Dijk, G.-J. van 1994b. Review of Papathomopoulos 1990, *Mnemosyne* 47, 550–55.

Dölger, F. 1953. Review of Perry 1952, *ByzZ* 46, 373–78.

Eriksen, R. (ed.) 1994. *Contexts of Pre-Novel Narrative: The European Tradition.* Berlin/ New York.

Goins, S.E. 1989. "The Influence of Old Comedy on the *Vita Aesopis* (sic)", *ClW* 83, 28–30.

Hägg, T. 1994. "Orality, Literacy, and the 'Readership' of the Early Greek Novel", in: Eriksen (ed.) 1994, 47–81 [No. 4 in this volume].

Harris, W.V. 1989. *Ancient Literacy.* Cambridge, Mass./London.

Haslam, M.W. 1980. "3331. *Life of Aesop*", in: R.A. Coles & M.W. Haslam (eds.) *The Oxyrhynchus Papyri*, vol. 47, London, 53–56.

Haslam, M.W. 1986. "3720. *Life of Aesop* (Addendum to 3331)", in: M.W. Haslam (ed.) *The Oxyrhynchus Papyri*, vol. 53, London, 149–72.

Haslam, M.W. 1992. Review of Papathomopoulos 1990, *ClR* 42, 188–89.

Hausrath, A. 1937. Review of Perry 1936, *PhilWoch* 57, 770–77.

Henderson, J. 1975 *The Maculate Muse: Obscene Language in Attic Comedy.* New Haven/London.

Holzberg, N. 1992a. "Der Äsop-Roman. Eine strukturanalytische Interpretation", in: Holzberg (ed.) 1992b, 33–75.

Holzberg, N. (ed.) 1992b. *Der Äsop-Roman. Motivgeschichte und Erzählstruktur.* Tübingen.

Holzberg, N. 1993. *Die antike Fabel. Eine Einführung.* Darmstadt.

Hopkins, K. 1993. "Novel Evidence for Roman Slavery", *PastPres* 138, 3–27.

Hostetter, W.H. 1955. *A Linguistic Study of the Vulgar Greek Life of Aesop.* Diss. University of Illinois. Urbana.

Hunter, V.J. 1994. *Policing Athens: Social Control in the Attic Lawsuits, 420–320 B.C.* Princeton.

Jedrkiewicz, S. 1989. *Sapere e paradosso nell' antichità: Esopo e la favola.* (Filologia e critica 60). Rome.

Kindstrand, J.F. 1976. *Bion of Borysthenes: A Collection of the Fragments with Introduction and Commentary.* (Acta Universitatis Upsaliensis. Studia Graeca Upsaliensia 11). Uppsala.

La Penna, A. 1962. "Il romanzo di Esopo", *Athenaeum* 40, 264–314.

Merkle, S. 1992. "Die Fabel von Frosch und Maus. Zur Funktion der *logoi* im Delphi-Teil des Äsop-Romans", in: Holzberg (ed.) 1992b, 110–27.

Nøjgaard, M. 1964. *La fable antique*, vol. 1: *La fable grecque avant Phèdre.* Copenhagen.

Oettinger, N. 1992. "Achikars Weisheitssprüche im Licht älterer Fabeldichtung", in: Holzberg (ed.) 1992b, 3–22.

Papathomopoulos, M. (ed.) 1990. *Ho bios tou Aisôpou. Hê parallagê G. Kritikê ekdosê me eisagôgê kai metaphrasê.* Ioannina.

Papathomopoulos, M. (ed.) 1991. *Ho bios tou Aisôpou. Hê parallage G. Kritikê ekdosê me eisagôgê kai metaphrasê* (2nd ed). Ioannina.

Perry, B.E. 1936. *Studies in the Text History of the Life and Fables of Aesop.* Philological Monographs published by the American Philological Association 7). Haverford, Pa. (Repr. Chico, Cal. 1981).

Perry, B.E. 1952. *Aesopica: A Series of Texts Relating to Aesop or Ascribed to him or Closely Connected with the Literary Tradition that Bears his Name.* Urbana. (Repr. New York 1980).

Perry, B.E. 1962a. "Demetrius of Phalerum and the Aesopic Fables", *TAPhA* 93, 287–346.

Perry, B.E. 1962b. Review of Wiechers 1961, *Gnomon* 34, 620–22.

Perry, B.E. (ed.) 1965. *Babrius and Phaedrus Newly Edited and Translated into English, together with an Historical Introduction and a Comprehensive Survey of Greek and Latin Fables in the Aesopic Tradition,* The Loeb Classical Library, vol. 436. London/ Cambridge, Mass.

Perry, B.E. 1966. "Some Addenda to the Life of Aesop", *ByzZ* 59, 285–304.

Rose, H.J. 1953. Review of Perry 1952, *ClR* 67, 154–55.

Schauer, M. & Merkle, S. 1992. "Äsop und Sokrates", in: Holzberg (ed.) 1992b, 85–96.

Shipp, G.P. 1983. "Notes on the Language of *Vita Aesopi* G", *Antichthon* 17, 96–106.

West, M.L. 1984. "The Ascription of Fables to Aesop in Archaic and Classical Greece", in: Adrados & Reverdin (eds.) 1984, 105–36.

Wiechers, A. 1961. *Aesop in Delphi.* (Beiträge zur klassischen Philologie 2). Meisenheim.

Winkler, J.J. 1991. *Auctor & Actor: A Narratological Reading of Apuleius's Golden Ass.* Berkeley.

Zanker, P. 1995. *The Mask of Socrates: The Image of the Intellectual in Antiquity.* Trans. A. Shapiro. (Sather Classical Lectures 59). Berkeley.

Zimmermann, B. 1993. "Aristophanes und die Intellektuellen", in: Bremer & Handley (eds.) 1993, 255–86.

Chariton and the Early Ideal Novel

Callirhoe and *Parthenope*:
The Beginnings of the Historical Novel

[originally published in *Classical Antiquity* 6, 1987, 184–204]

The aim of the present paper is to discuss whether, or in what sense, we are entitled to describe as historical novels two of the Greek novels of antiquity, Chariton's *Chaereas and Callirhoe,* which survives in full, and the only fragmentarily (and anonymously) preserved novel of *Metiochus and Parthenope*, both possibly to be placed as early as the first century B.C. (hereafter *Callirhoe* and *Parthenope,* respectively).[1] Applying the term *historical novel* to these two works means questioning two common assumptions, one generally held by historians of modern literature and the other by classical scholars. Literary historians almost unanimously state that the historical novel is a creation of the early nineteenth century, or, more precisely, of Sir Walter Scott, whose *Waverley* was first published in 1814.[2] Classicists, on the other hand, do sometimes use

A shorter version of this paper was presented at a King's College London (KCL) symposium on "The Greek Novel, A.D. 1–1985," 24–26 March 1986, and will appear in a book by that title (ed. R. Beaton) published by Croom Helm (London) [published in 1988, pp. 169–181]. My thanks are due to the organizers and participants of the symposium; to Bryan Reardon, who was unable to take part in person in the symposium, for reading and commenting on the paper afterward; and to the anonymous referees of this journal.

[1] *Callirhoe,* simply, may in fact have been the original title of Chariton's novel (see Chariton von Aphrodisias, *Kallirhoe,* trans. K. Plepelits [Stuttgart 1976] 28f., and Chariton, *Kallirhoe,* trans. C. Lucke and K.-H. Schäfer [Leipzig 1985] 181; cf. Reardon [infra n. 54] 13 n. 22), and the analogous title *Parthenope* would well suit the anonymous novel with its apparent emphasis on the heroine and obvious play on her "speaking name." There is at least — *pace* Weinreich (infra n. 91) 28 and Treu (infra n. 5) 457f. — no evidence for these two "historical" novels having originally had titles like historical or geographical works, such as *Sicelica, Samiaca.* This type was probably introduced later *(Ephesiaca, Aethiopica),* as were the double names *(Leucippe and Clitophon,* etc.). Cf. infra n. 60.

[2] "To all intents and purposes the historical novel sprang to life, fully accoutred and mature, with the appearance of *Waverley* in 1814": thus Sanders (infra n. 12) ix, expressing the *communis opinio;* already Manzoni (infra n. 15) 1061 called Scott "l'Omero del romanzo storico." Cf., for the same sentiment, Lukács (infra n. 9) 19 and passim, Fleishman (infra n. 6) 25 (cf. 23), and A. Hook in the Penguin Classics ed. of *Waverley* (Harmondsworth 1985) 9f; less categorically, Shaw (infra n. 11) 31. See also the illuminating remarks of C. Lamont in her World's Classics ed. of *Waverley* (Oxford 1986, in substance identical with Lamont's large ed., Oxford 1981) xivf. (1981: xvif.); my references to *Waverley* will be to this edition, which reproduces the 1814 text of the novel but also appends Scott's later prefaces and notes.

the term *historical novel/romance (historischer Roman, roman historique,* etc.) for ancient literary compositions, but then mostly with reference to such works as Xenophon's *Cyropaedia* or the *Alexander Romance* of Pseudo-Callisthenes, so calling them in order to distinguish them from the so-called ideal Greek novel; I have followed that practice myself earlier.[3] My present contention, however, is that, if we speak at all of historical novels in antiquity, the ones that best qualify for that description are *Callirhoe* and *Parthenope.*[4] To demonstrate this, I will first discuss terminology, definitions, and criteria for the historical novel, as the term is used today. However, I hope it will be clear that this is not just a theoretical exercise — nor, for that matter, a naive attempt to vindicate another literary genre or subgenre for antiquity — but that the discussion is meant to shed some light on the character and purpose of the two ancient works themselves.

Now, what *is* a historical novel? How is the term generally defined by modern theorists and historians of literature, and what criteria can we employ to decide whether a given novel is also a historical novel? My concern is not, primarily, to distinguish between *historical novel* and *historiography,* though that much-debated question cannot be eschewed altogether,[5] but precisely to distinguish between *novel* in general and *historical novel* in particular. Unfortunately, a look through the standard works on literary theory and genre theory yields surprisingly few and disappointingly vague answers to these questions. The term *historical novel* (etc.) is used not infrequently, but is almost never defined — except implicitly, in that it is mostly made to refer to works by Scott himself or some of

---

[3] T. Hägg, *The Novel in Antiquity* (Oxford 1983) 125.

[4] I find this view expressed earlier only by H. Maehler, "Der Metiochos-Parthenope-Roman," *ZPE* 23 (1976) 19 (similarly Maehler in B. P. Reardon, ed., *Erotica antiqua* [Bangor 1977] 50f.), and by A. Dihle, "Zur Datierung des Metiochos-Romans," *WürzJbb* N.F. 4 (1978) 54f.

[5] See, with regard to ancient literature, in particular B. E. Perry, *The Ancient Romances: A Literary-Historical Account of Their Origins* (Berkeley and Los Angeles 1967) 32ff., and the penetrating remarks of Morgan (infra n. 90) 223–25. Cf. also B. P. Reardon, "The Greek Novel," *Phoenix* 23 (1969) 295 with n. 12, idem, *Courants littéraires grecs des IIe et IIIe siècles après J.-C.* (Paris 1971) 315, and K. Treu, "Roman und Geschichtsschreibung," *Klio* 66 (1984) 456–59. For a professional historian's mixed feelings towards the genre "historical fiction", exemplified by the *Historia Augusta*, Yourcenar's *Mémoires d'Hadrien* and some modern historians (!), see now Sir Ronald Syme's amusing essay *Fictional History Old and New: Hadrian* (Somerville College, Oxford 1986); cf. also, in quite another spirit, Helen Cam's pamphlet *Historical Novels* (Historical Association, London 1961).

his nineteenth-century followers: to Manzoni's *I promessi sposi* or Hugo's *Notre-Dame de Paris,* to Dickens' *A Tale of Two Cities,* Tolstoi's *War and Peace,* Sienkiewicz's *Quo Vadis?* and so on. As Avrom Fleishman remarks: "Everyone knows what a historical novel is; perhaps that is why few have volunteered to define it in print."[6] Joseph Turner speaks of "the morass of defining historical fiction"; his own contribution, an article with the promising title "The Kinds of Historical Fiction: An Essay in Definition and Methodology" (1979), is successful in criticizing others but unfortunately not of much help for our present purpose, his attempt at classification being based only on a handful of twentieth-century American novels.[7] A recent authoritative study by Alastair Fowler, which heralds a renaissance of critical interest in literary genres, acknowledges the historical novel as a distinct and "true" subgenre of the novel but still does not attempt any definition of the term.[8]

In the absence of an authoritative definition, the best procedure will be first to assemble a number of criteria for the typical (modern) historical novel, by looking at the novels commonly and intuitively so called and drawing on the critical work done on them. Besides Georg Lukács' seminal but rather idiosyncratic monograph of 1937, *The Historical Novel,*[9] the critical studies that I have found most useful are the book

[6] A. Fleishman, *The English Historical Novel: Walter Scott to Virginia Woolf* (Baltimore 1971) 3.

[7] W. Turner, *Genre* 12 (1979) 333. Turner distinguishes between "documented," "disguised," and "invented" historical novels, the three representing "distinct stages along the continuum" (341). A kindred tripartition was attempted by M. Wehrli, "Der historische Roman: Versuch einer Übersicht," *Helicon* 3 (1942) 89–109: "historische Belletristik (Reportage), kulturhistorischer Roman, sittlich-religiöse Geschichtsdichtung" (108), a typology based on and as much determined by *his* particular material, the German "historical novel" of the last 150 years, as Turner's by his. Green (infra n. 13), in turn, suggests the categories "Propaganda, Education, and Escapism" (37).

[8] A. Fowler, *Kinds of Literature: An Introduction to the Theory of Genres and Modes* (Oxford 1982), esp. 121f., 153f., 168. The important point is that Fowler admits of the historical novel as a more distinct "kind" than others, such as factory novel or university novel, which are grouped together exclusively according to subject matter and setting (122); cf. Shaw (infra n. 11) 20. R. Wellek and A. Warren, *Theory of Literature,* 3d ed. (Harmondsworth 1963) 232f. also dismiss "a grouping based only on subject-matter, a purely sociological classification" (e.g., the ecclesiastical novel), but admit the historical novel "because of [its] ties to the Romantic movement and to nationalism — because of the new feeling about, attitude towards, the past which it implies."

[9] G. Lukács, *The Historical Novel,* trans. H. Mitchell and S. Mitchell (London 1962).

by Avrom Fleishman already mentioned[10] and Harry Shaw's *The Forms of Historical Fiction*.[11] I have also profited from the more general reflections on the genre in Harry Henderson's and Andrew Sanders' works on the American and the Victorian historical novel, respectively.[12] The highly readable essay by Herbert Butterfield, *The Historical Novel*, has less to offer in this connection, since its main concern is the relation between the historical novel and history proper.[13] Something can also be gathered from prefaces or postscripts to historical novels, in which their authors, from Scott to Mary Renault,[14] have contributed to the critical elucidation of the genre; special mention should be made of Alessandro Manzoni's essay "Del romanzo storico e, in genere, de' componimenti misti di storia e d'invenzione."[15] Finally, it is possible to check the more popular or intuitive concept of the historical novel in a work like Daniel McGarry and Sarah Harriman White's *Historical Fiction Guide,* an "annotated chronological, geographical and topical list of five thousand selected historical novels," compiled to meet the needs of librarians, teachers, and readers of this vast popular literature.[16] It provides a healthy counterbalance to the severe exclusiveness of a Lukács, in whose eyes not many novels qualify as truly historical, whatever their authors may have intended or the general reader may think he is reading.

187

[10] Supra n. 6. Esp. chapter 1, "Towards a Theory of Historical Fiction" and chapter 2, "Origins: The Historical Novel in the Age of History." Cf. also Fleishman's work of 1978 (infra n. 29).

[11] H. E. Shaw, *The Forms of Historical Fiction: Sir Walter Scott and His Successors* (Ithaca 1983), esp. chapter 1, "An Approach to the Historical Novel."

[12] H. B. Henderson, III, *Versions of the Past: The Historical Imagination in American Fiction* (New York 1974); A. Sanders, *The Victorian Historical Novel 1840–1880* (London 1978).

[13] H. Butterfield, *The Historical Novel: An Essay* (Cambridge, England 1924). P. Green, "Aspects of the Historical Novel," *Essays by Divers Hands* n.s. 31 (Transactions of the Royal Society of Literature) (London 1962) 35–60, is another stimulating, but not too systematic, discussion of the subject.

[14] For Mary Renault's "Notes on *The King Must Die,*" see T. McCormack, ed., *Afterwords: Novelists on Their Novels* (Evanston 1969) 80–87.

[15] Ca. 1851; reprinted in A. Manzoni, *Opere,* ed. R. Bacchelli (Milan 1953) 1055–1114; now also in Eng. trans., with a useful introduction, by S. Bermann: *On the Historical Novel* (Lincoln, Nebr. 1984). The most recent detailed statement is that of Umberto Eco, *Postille a Il nome della rosa* (Milan 1983), Eng. trans. by W. Weaver: *Postscript to The Name of the Rose* (San Diego and New York 1984), see esp. 73–77.

[16] D. D. McGarry and S. Harriman White, *Historical Fiction Guide* (New York 1963) (quotation is the subtitle).

Time. Though it may be argued, and indeed not seldom is argued, that "all novels are historical novels, since they are set in historical time and social reality,"[17] normal usage reserves the term for novels set at least one or two generations back; it is customary to refer to Scott's sub-title to *Waverley*, "'Tis Sixty Years Since," as indicating something of an ideal, or of a minimum.[18] Others, then, are "novels of the recent past"[19] or "contemporary novels." Another essential criterion would be that the historical constituents of the novel are "researched rather than remembered,"[20] i.e., that the author has not himself experienced them but has had to rely mostly on written or oral sources.[21] There is, in principle, no corresponding limit backwards in time, although novels set in a dim prehistoric or mythological past may have difficulties with one or two other criteria to be mentioned below.

What matters, apparently, is only the span of time between the events narrated and the composition of the novel, not that between the events and the *reading*. A contemporary novel does not, technically, become a historical novel with the passage of time, even if it is true, for instance, that "the novels of Trollope were read primarily as romances [i.e., historical novels] during the Second World War," as Northrop Frye notes.[22] The convention may be studied in applied form in McGarry and White's selection of 5,000 historical novels. According to their definition, "fiction is historical if it includes reference to customs, conditions, identifiable persons, or events *in the past*" (my italics).[23] In spite of the book's practical and pedagogical purpose of listing works from which the reader

188

---

[17] Quoted from Fleishman (supra n. 6) 15 n. 9, who does not himself accept this view. Cf. also Henderson (supra n. 12) xvif., Turner (supra n. 7) 339f. and Shaw (supra n. 11) 29 with n. 16, who advances as a criterion the "desire to depict history."

[18] For Scott's own comment, see *Waverley* 1.1 (p. 4 Lamont). Cf. Fleishman (supra n. 6) 3, 24, and Sanders (supra n. 12) x, 11.

[19] Cf. Fleishman (supra n. 6) 3, 146, and Shaw (supra n. 11) 38, both referring for the term to K. Tillotson, *Novels of the Eighteen–Forties* (Oxford 1954) 92f. An example is Thackeray's *Vanity Fair.*

[20] Sanders (supra n. 12) 11 (cf. ix); cf. Henderson (supra n. 12) xvi: "'set' in the unexperienced past, in the world that existed before the author was born."

[21] On Scott's mixture of oral and written sources, see Lamont (supra n. 2) xv–xix (1981: xvii–xxi) and cf. Scott's own comments in the last chapter of *Waverley* (pp. 340f. Lamont) and in the various prefatory materials added in 1829 (pp. 348, 352f., 388).

[22] N. Frye, *Anatomy of Criticism: Four Essays* (Princeton 1957) 307.

[23] McGarry and White (supra n. 16) [4].

can learn about different periods of history, "in the past" is obviously seen just in relation to the author. For instance, among the books listed as illustrating the history of the United States 1865-1900,[24] the vast majority were written in the twentieth century; a contemporary novel of the period does not qualify, however much history it may teach us. In Herbert Butterfield's words, "a true 'historical novel' is one that is historical in its intention and not simply by accident, one that comes from a mind steeped in the past."[25]

Characters. The typical historical novel deals with fictitious characters — that is, after all, what makes it a novel — in a historical setting: the focus of attention is the personal experiences and concerns of private individuals.[26] As Wolfgang Kayser observes, while the epic has Odysseus as the main character, the novel features a certain Tom Jones or Ivanhoe.[27] But to make the novel historical, we expect real historical figures to appear as well,[28] ideally mixing with the fictitious ones so as to create a "mixture of the real and the imaginary on the same plane of representation."[29] For instance, in *Waverley* Prince Charles Edward and Colonel Gardiner are historical, but all the main characters fictitious.[30] The depth of characterization of the historical and fictional characters alike

---

[24] Ibid. 417-45.

[25] Butterfield (supra n. 13) 4f.; cf. Shaw (supra n. 11) 30: "they [*sc.* standard historical novels] are also united, in a minimal way, by incorporating within their systems of fictional probability *a sense of the past as past*" (my italics).

[26] Cf. Butterfield (supra n. 13) 67, 79, and Shaw (supra n. 11) 49. Scott says in *Waverley* 1.1 (pp. 4f. Lamont): "my tale is more a description of men than manners," and speaks of "throwing the force of my narrative upon the characters and passions of the actors."

[27] W. Kayser, *Das sprachliche Kunstwerk: Eine Einführung in die Literaturwissenschaft* (Bern 1948) 360f.

[28] Cf. Fleishman (supra n. 6) 3: "it is necessary to include at least one such figure in a novel if it is to qualify as historical"; Turner (supra n. 7) 336 rightly modifies this, saying that it "may not be a necessary condition …, but it comes very close to being a sufficient one." To McGarry and White (supra n. 16) [4], depiction of "the everyday way of life, outlook, mores, and living conditions" is enough.

[29] A. Fleishman, *Fiction and the Ways of Knowing: Essays on British Novels* (Austin 1978) 53. For the problems involved, cf. Manzoni (supra n. 15) 1061f. and Riikonen (infra n. 102) 24f.

[30] See Lamont (supra n. 2) xif. (1981: xiiif.), who adds: "This is a formula for characterization which has proved favourable to the historical novel." Similarly, but with reference already to the Greek novels, Treu (supra n. 5) 458: "Das Rezept war von überzeitlicher Effizienz."

— whether historical verisimilitude is achieved, individually or generally — is another matter, to be dealt with under "Truth," below.

Setting. According to Avrom Fleishman, "there is an unspoken assumption that the plot must include a number of 'historical' events, particularly those in the public sphere (war, politics, economic change, etc.), mingled with and affecting the personal fortunes of the characters."[31] Thus, a general historical background is not enough, unless specific events and figures are identified and brought into relationship with the fictitious characters. This is what makes novels set in a prehistoric milieu, or whenever written documentation of persons and events is lacking, less typically historical: they lack the peculiar appeal deriving from the juxtaposition of the real and the imaginary. At the other end of the scale we meet works that are too seriously documentary to allow the fictitious elements really to mingle with the historical ones: while *War and Peace* of course admirably mixes fact with fiction, Solzhenitsyn's *August 1914* would probably not qualify as a typical historical novel for this very reason.[32]

The setting necessarily includes not only a certain period and certain historical events, but also the physical milieu. "History is rooted in geography," says Herbert Butterfield, "and the historical novel, which is a novel that seeks to be rooted in some ways in actuality, finds one of its roots in geography."[33] The author's research, mentioned above under "Time," thus applies to both history and geography (topography, ethnography, etc.), and so does the issue of accuracy, or "Truth," to be discussed next.

"Truth," or historical probability. In one way or another, the reader of a historical novel is apt to demand some kind of truth, as far as the historical (or geographical, etc.) elements are concerned.[34] The naive reader expects that the dates will be correct, the important historical events correctly described, the historical places and figures depicted true to life. The sophisticated reader may look for a deeper kind of truth, "an artistically

[31] Fleishman (supra n. 6) 3; cf. his application of this criterion to novels by Hardy, Golding and Thackeray ibid. (179 and 257 with n. 18) and in idem (supra n. 29) 53.

[32] I owe the example of *August 1914* to Jonas Palm. Cf. C. Moody, *Solzhenitsyn* (Edinburgh 1976) 172ff., developing the comparison with *War and Peace* (and noting that Solzhenitsyn himself is anxious not to call *August 1914* a novel).

[33] Butterfield (supra n. 13) 41; cf. Fleishman (supra n. 6) xv and Shaw (supra n. 11) 25f.

[34] Cf. Fleishman (supra n. 6) 4.

faithful image of a concrete historical epoch," to quote Georg Lukács.[35] He distinguishes between "novels with historical themes," of which there are many, and the genuinely historical novel, created by Scott but not achieved by many of his followers. Whereas the naive reader expects the historical figures to be "true," a Lukács lets this demand apply as much to the purely fictitious ones: a crucial criterion for the historical novel is the "derivation of the individuality of characters from the historical peculiarity of their age."[36] "What makes a historical novel historical is the active presence of a concept of history as a shaping force," says Fleishman.[37] To these critics, history as costume or masquerade is not enough to make a novel historical, however accurate the costume may be; the characters behind the masks must not be the contemporaries of the author but should as far as possible appear as being historically true. On the other hand, the propagators of this sophisticated approach tend to pay less attention to mistakes in the external historical frame — anachronisms — so long as the historical verisimilitude is preserved. Few would deny that Scott's *Redgauntlet,* though describing a third, purely imaginary Jacobite rebellion and combining historical facts from three different decades of the eighteenth century, nevertheless is a historical novel.[38]

190

As far as "truth" is concerned, it is evident that no single, generally applicable criterion can be formulated; there is too great a gap between the popular, or intuitive, and the sophisticated, or scholarly, view. An interesting middle way, however, is indicated by Harry Shaw, who (against Lukács, Fleishman, and others) argues that "no single quality of historical insight defines historical fiction," merely demanding from the author "the recognition of 'the past as past,'" "the realization that history is comprised of ages and societies that are significantly different from our own."[39] (There will be occasion to return to this discussion below in

---

[35] Lukács (supra n. 9) 19.

[36] Ibid.; similarly Fleishman (supra n. 6) 10–12. Contrast Mary Renault's penetrating remarks (supra n. 14) 84f.

[37] Fleishman (supra n. 6) 15, and cf. 25.

[38] See K. Sutherland in her World's Classics ed. of *Redgauntlet* (Oxford 1985) vii–ix, and cf. M. Lascelles, *The Story-Teller Retrieves the Past* (Oxford 1980) 114–19 (in the chapter called "The Historical Event That Never Happened"). On historical accuracy and historical probability in Scott generally, see J. Anderson, *Sir Walter Scott and History* (Edinburgh 1981) 89–92, cf. 33–35, and, starting from the problems raised by *Redgauntlet,* D. Brown, *Walter Scott and the Historical Imagination* (London 1979) 151–94.

[39] Shaw (supra n. 11) 24, 26.

dealing with the Greek potentially historical novels.) In the end, how-ever, the lack of agreement on this crucial point, which of course affects the other groups of criteria as well, is just a reflection of the more gen-eral issue of how to define or delimit literature as an object of scholarly study. When distinguishing between genres, for instance, are we then concerned only with "serious" literature, perhaps only with acknowl-edged works of art, or with the whole spectrum of literature? Probably most of the 5,000 historical novels of the list referred to above, though still constituting a selection according to quality,[40] do not belong within the domains of traditional history or theory of literature. Harry Hen-derson symptomatically speaks of "the vulgarity of the genre," branding it as (periodically at least) "the dominant middle-brow reading enter-tainment."[41] Thus a definition of the historical novel based on "serious" literature only is bound to leave homeless the largest part of the fiction generally referred to as historical.

One way to avoid this difficulty is to take as the starting point a definition of the novel itself which largely evades the question of artis-tic quality. The *Concise Oxford Dictionary* (7th ed., 1982) defines a *novel* as a "fictitious prose narrative of book length portraying characters and actions credibly representative of real life in continuous plot." Add, after "life," "of a certain historical period," and we have a general definition of our object of study, "credibly" smoothing over the difference between the naive and the sophisticated reader, or between the inclusive and the exclusive attitude. For the present purpose, however, and on the basis of the groups of criteria discussed above, I would venture a more elabor-ate (and admittedly more arbitrary) definition of what I would call the "typical historical novel": it is set in a period at least one or two genera-tions anterior to that of the author, communicating a sense of the past as past; it is centered on fictitious characters, but puts on stage as well, mingling with these, one or several figures known from history; enacted in a realistic geographical setting, it describes the effects upon the fortunes of the characters of (a succession of) real historical events; it is — or gives the impression of being — true, as far as the historical framework is concerned. It may also aim at achieving an artistically true reconstruc-tion of the historical period in question and its way of life, making the

191

---

[40] McGarry and White (supra n. 16) [4]: "only *better* works of historical fiction."

[41] Henderson (supra n. 12) xv. Cf., on contempt for the genre, Fleishman (supra n. 6) xivf., 36, and Shaw (supra n. 11) 9.

characters typical representatives of their age and social milieu. Such an aim, or success in achieving it, is not a prerequisite, however, for the classification; as Harry Shaw pertinently remarks, "it is more useful to discriminate between great and mediocre historical novels than to exclude imperfect works from the group.[42]

With this tentative definition in mind we proceed to the ancient works which classical scholars are wont to call historical novels: Xenophon's *Cyropaedia,* the *Alexander Romance,* Philostratus's *Life of Apollonius,* to mention just the most obvious candidates. It is true that there is no consensus regarding which works to include under the generic heading *novel,* or how to divide the genre into subgenres; Heinrich Kuch in a recent article clearly demonstrates the prevailing diversity of classification.[43] Some, like Ben Edwin Perry, prefer to reserve the term *novel* (or *romance)* for the Roman "comic" and Greek "ideal" types.[44] But insofar as the term *historical novel* is used at all, it constantly refers to one or other of the works mentioned, and in particular to the *Alexander Romance.*[45] Kuch himself is more cautious than most, as regards the appropriateness of the designation: he regularly speaks of "der sog. 'historische' Roman"; while admitting it (under this name) as a subgenre, he notes that every ancient novel refers, more or less, to historical conditions and events; and he remarks that it was no genuine (*echt*) historical novel in the modern

192

---

[42] Shaw (supra n. 11) 28. Cf. 49: "*In the greatest historical fiction,* characters and narrative sequences elucidate historical process" (my italics).

[43] H. Kuch, "Gattungstheoretische Überlegungen zum antiken Roman," *Philologus* 129 (1985) 3–19. See also A. M. Scarcella, "Metastasi narratologica del dato storico nel romanzo erotico greco," *Atti del convegno internazionale 'Letterature classiche e narratologia,'* Materiali e Contributi per la Storia della Narrativa Greco-Latina 3 (Perugia 1981) 342 n. 4.

[44] Perry (supra n. 5) 34f., 40f., 84–87, 168; similarly C. W. Müller, "Der griechische Roman," in E. Vogt, ed., *Neues Handbuch der Literaturwissenschaft.* Vol. 2: *Griechische Literatur* (Wiesbaden 1981) 392, and, in practice, E. L. Bowie, "The Greek Novel," in P. E. Easterling and B. M. W. Knox, eds., *The Cambridge History of Classical Literature.* Vol. 1: *Greek Literature* (Cambridge England 1985) 683–99, 877–86. A. Scobie, *More Essays on the Ancient Romance and Its Heritage* (Meisenheim am Glan 1973) 84 f. likewise excludes from his classification of the various types of romance "fiction masquerading as history or biography"; and so does N. Holzberg in his recent survey, *Der antike Roman,* Artemis Einführungen 25 (Munich 1986) 22–26, "Romanhaft-fiktionale Biographie."

[45] See, e.g., R. Helm, *Der antike Roman,* 2. Aufl. (Göttingen 1956) 8–19, "Historische Romane" (e.g., Cyr., Alex., Ninus); O. Mazal, *JÖByz* 11/12 (1962/63) 26–55, "Der historische Roman" (e.g., Cyr., Alex., Vita Ap.); M. E. Grabar'-Passek, ed., *Anticnyj roman* (Moscow 1969, quoted from Kuch [supra n. 43] 3f.) "der historische Roman" (e.g., Alex.); and M.-P. Loicq-Berger, *EtCl* 48 (1980) 26, "le roman 'historique'" (e.g., Alex., Vita Ap.).

sense.[46] But he gives no explanation for this verdict, nor does he present any alternative, better-qualified candidates for the designation.

The *Alexander Romance* of Pseudo-Callisthenes easily qualifies according to our "Time" and "Setting" criteria. Irrespective of which stage we choose, the postulated Hellenistic sources or the final late-antique compilation, the action is firmly placed in the past. I pick out just one detail in the last chapter of the oldest extant version (Rec. A, 3.35):[47] it is stated there that the thirteen cities founded by Alexander "are still [μέχρι τοῦ νῦν] inhabited and peaceful," which implies a distant past. The basis is not, even fictitiously (as in the *Troy Romances* of Dictys and Dares), the author's own recollections, but, apparently, mostly written sources of a legendary character. The setting is historical, no matter how fancifully transformed: we are made to follow a succession of historical events, though in a peculiar order and freely mingled with purely imaginary (or legendary) ones, and all is set in a factual Mediterranean and Oriental milieu, with the important exception of the fantastic travel adventures in the Far East. The main characters are all historical: Alexander the Great, King Philip of Macedon and Queen Olympias, King Darius of Persia, Alexander's teacher Aristotle, his friends and generals, and so on. The "Truth" criterion causes greater difficulties, even in its crudest sense. The overtly and topically fantastic ingredients apart, there are in the more strictly historical parts gross anachronisms and geographical blunders; but it is uncertain to what extent the author himself or the popular audience to whom he obviously addressed himself noticed or cared about them. The unequivocal historicity of the central figure and his overall achievement probably satisfied most readers' demands in this respect, securing a kind of historical probability for the story at large.

The point at which the *Alexander Romance* clearly fails to be a typical historical novel belongs under "Characters": this is not about the private experiences of fictitious characters in a historical setting, but the account, however romanticized, of the public life and exploits of a world-historical figure himself.[48] As Avrom Fleishman remarks, such

193

---

[46] Kuch (supra n. 43) 8, 16.

[47] W. Kroll, ed., *Historia Alexandri Magni* (Berlin 1926); E. H. Haight, trans., *The Life of Alexander of Macedon* (New York 1955).

[48] A similar remark is to be found in E. Schwartz, *Fünf Vorträge über den griechischen Roman* (1896; 2. Aufl. Berlin 1943) 83 (cf. 26), explicitly referring to Scott for the modern historical novel. Cf. Reardon, *Courants littéraires* (supra n. 5) 329 on *Nectanebus* and *Alex.*

figures are not generally likely to be selected by a novelist, being "by definition exceptional," while the novelist seeks "the typical man … whose life is shaped by world-historical figures."[49] Even if Fleishman, following Lukács, naturally refers to literary works on quite a different level of intention from the *Alexander Romance,* nevertheless the private individual as protagonist seems to be the normal choice for a historical novelist, at any level. Of course there are exceptions — one need only mention, among more recent works, Marguerite Yourcenar's *Memoires d'Hadrien* and Robert Graves' *Claudius* books — but then the emphasis is still on the private or inner life of the world-historical figure. In the *Romance,* Alexander speaks much and writes letters, but mostly in direct relation to his official activities; his inner life is scarcely revealed (nor is he granted any sex life).

Yet the main generic problem with the *Alexander Romance* is not whether it should be classified as a historical novel, but whether it is a novel at all. Once we admit it as a novel, by necessity we have to call it historical, however untypical it may be for this subgenre. The same is true for the *Cyropaedia,* Xenophon's ideal image of a ruler, and, if we quickly move some six hundred years forward, for the *Life of Apollonius of Tyana* by Philostratus who, much more soberly than Pseudo-Callisthenes, draws up the historical framework for his story and even ostentatiously refers to written documentary sources.[50] The easiest way out, no doubt, is to refer to all three and their cognates as *lives* (βίοι, vitae)[51] or, rather, as *romanticized biographies,* to mark the difference from the Plutarchian *life.* These works are highly relevant in any discussion of the borderline between historiography and historical fiction; but for the present purpose it will be enough just to state that the term *historical novel* does not very adequately cover the nature of any of them.

---

[49] Fleishman (supra n. 6) 10f.

[50] G. Anderson, *Philostratus: Biography and Belles Lettres in the Third Century A.D.* (Dover, N.H. 1986) 232 characterizes the *Vita Ap.* as "a sort of Alexander-romance with the elegance of the *Cyropaedia.*" He addresses the issue of novel versus romanticized biography on 229–32. J. Palm, *Om Filostratos och hans Apollonios-biografi* (Uppsala 1976) 40 aptly suggests the modern designation *documentary novel*; according to one's assessment of the authenticity of the documents cited by Philostratus, one may prefer *pseudo-documentary.*

[51] There is ms. authority for the term βίος only in the case of the *Alexander Romance,* however; the so-called *"Vita" Apollonii* goes under the Greek title τὰ εἰς τὸν Τυανέα Ἀπολλώνιον.

As is already foreshadowed in the title and introduction of the paper, a couple of the "ideal" Greek novels are in my view better candidates for that label. It should at once be made clear, however, that it is not a question of substituting *historical* for *ideal*. A classification into genres, or subgenres, can be made from several different perspectives, such as outer form (prose, prosimetrum, verse; different kinds of verse), subject matter (historical, contemporary; love, adventure, travels, politics, etc.), attitude (ideal, sentimental, comic, realistic), and so on. The failure to realize this elementary truth has marred some of the earlier attempts to define subgenres of the Greek novel.[52] Now, from one point of view, the five extant "ideal" novels and a number of fragments form a coherent group; from another, it is more meaningful to group at least one of them, Achilles Tatius's *Leucippe and Clitophon,* together with the Roman novels of Petronius and Apuleius as being contemporary, while Chariton's *Callirhoe* and the *Parthenope* are historical. Again, in that respect, though not in others, these two go together with the *Chion Novel,* which is a political and philosophical novel-in-letters.[53] All three do so, but less closely, with the group of romanticized biographies, if we allow them novel status, and with the pseudo-documentary war chronicles of Dictys and Dares.

Chariton's attachment to history is well known and has been the subject of much comment, though mostly regarding either his relation to historiography[54] or the historicity of his characters and events.[55] His attitude, as expressed in his choice of a historical setting, has attracted less attention.[56] The first sentences of the novel are of crucial import-

194

[52] E.g., those of Scobie (supra n. 44) and Loicq-Berger (supra n. 45).

[53] See the introduction to Chion of Heraclea, *A Novel in Letters,* ed. I. Düring (Göteborg 1951; reprint New York 1979) for the documentary sources on which this novel is based and a discussion of its purpose.

[54] See, in particular, W. Bartsch, "Der Charitonroman und die Historiographie," diss. Leipzig 1934, 6–34, and cf. B. P. Reardon, "Theme, Structure and Narrative in Chariton," *YCS* 27 (1982) 15 n. 26.

[55] B. E. Perry, "Chariton and His Romance from a Literary-Historical Point of View," *AJP* 51 (1930) 100–104 with n. 11 (additions in Perry [supra n. 5] 353 n. 25); Bartsch (supra n. 54) 3–6; F. Zimmermann, "Chariton und die Geschichte," *Sozialökonomische Verhältnisse im alten Orient und im klassischen Altertum* (Berlin 1961) 329–45; Reardon, *Courants littéraires* (supra n. 5) 341 n. 67; Plepelits (supra n. 1) 15–20; Chariton, *Le roman de Chairéas et Callirhoé,* ed. G. Molinié (Paris 1979) 5–8; and Scarcella (supra n. 43) 344–52, 363–65.

[56] But cf. the important remarks of P. Grimal in *Latomus* 26 (1967) 842f. and of C. W. Müller, "Chariton von Aphrodisias und die Theorie des Romans in der Antike," *A&A* 22 (1976) 132f., and idem (supra n. 44) 379, 383, 387.

ance:[57] "I, Chariton of Aphrodisias, clerk to the rhetor Athenagoras, am going to tell you the story of a love affair which took place in Syracuse [πάθος ἐρωτικὸν ἐν Συρακούσαις γενόμενον διηγήσομαι]. Hermocrates, the Syracusan general, the man who defeated the Athenians, had a daughter by the name of Callirhoe ... " (1.1.1). The author firmly places himself in contemporary society and the plot of the novel in a distant heroic past. By modeling his introductory sentence on those of the classical historians he is not trying to pass as a historian[58] — contemporary historiography did not use this formula — but to communicate, right from the start, the spirit of the very age in which the plot is set. And that plot, he hastens to say, is a love story: again not the posture of a historian, but that of a deliberate and unconcealed novelist. He plays on the same contrast between fact and fiction when he ends his novel with the words τοσάδε περὶ Καλλιρόης συνέγραψα, "This is my account of Callirhoe" (8.8.16), συγγράφειν being the word used by authors of factual accounts in prose, notably by the historians,[59] while the reference to the heroine's name suggests, rather, love elegy.[60]

195

Our first criterion, "Time," is satisfied: writing in late Hellenistic or early imperial times, Chariton sets his action in the classical period, more precisely some time after 413 B.C., the date of the defeat of the Athenian naval expedition to Sicily. Next comes the criterion of "Characters." Hermocrates, the father of the heroine, is a historical figure known from Thucydides and Xenophon. His great historical achievement, the victory over the Athenians, already lies in the past — the allusion to it is kind

---

[57] For an excellent detailed analysis, see Müller (supra n. 56) 123–25.

[58] Such a view has often been expressed, e.g., by Plepelits (supra n. 1) 11: "Das Werk soll den Eindruck erwecken, als sei es im 5. oder 4. Jh. v. Chr. verfasst worden" — a view hardly reconcilable with the acceptance (also by Plepelits) of Chariton's self-introduction as to be taken at face value.

[59] On συγγράφω (Char. 8.8.16) and σύγγραμμα (Char. 8.1.4), see Bartsch (supra n. 54) 3, Zimmermann (supra n. 55) 330, Plepelits (supra n. 1) 10 and Müller (supra n. 56) 120 n. 29. All except Müller, however, seem to overstate the case: συγγράφω is in no way exclusively used for "Geschichte schreiben"; cf. Xen. Eq. 1.1, Pl. Min. 316D (on medical writers) etc. (LSJ s.v. II.1). The same of course goes for διηγέομαι (Char. 1.1.1), to which Bartsch and Plepelits refer, and for συντάσσω, σύνταγμα (Hld. 10.41.4) referred to by Weinreich (infra n. 91) 28.

[60] Cf. the titles of Parthenius's Ἐρωτικὰ παθήματα, many of which (e.g., 10, 11) mention the girl's name only. Cf. supra n.1.

of a leitmotif in the novel[61] — but as an individual he takes some direct part in the action in connection with his daughter's wedding, burial, disappearance, and homecoming. The Persian king Artaxerxes is the second unequivocally historical figure; he is involved with Callirhoe both in his public capacity of supreme judge and privately, falling in love with her. While Hermocrates may best be described as a background figure, Artaxerxes is one of the main agents of the story, and fully characterized. His queen, Stateira, takes part personally in the action as well, though less prominently. Some other figures, notably the Ionian nobleman Dionysius, may have received their names and some traits from historical persons,[62] but in any case they are not put on stage in their known historical roles. Of overall importance, from our point of view, are the facts that the hero and heroine are purely fictitious characters (even if a daughter of Hermocrates is known to have existed),[63] whose private experiences are at the center of the story, and that they are brought into direct relationship to historical figures. The criterion by which the *Alexander Romance* and its cognates failed to be typically historical novels is here almost programmatically fulfilled.

As regards "Setting," geographical and historical, the whole plot is enacted in a concretely depicted Mediterranean and Near Eastern world. There is elaborate description of traveling on land and sea, from Syracuse in the west via Miletus in Ionia to Babylon in the east, with mention of well-known cities, islands, rivers, etc., on the way. The administrative structure of the Achaemenid empire is there, with three satrapies specified and a couple of (probably imaginary) satraps taking part in the action. The consequences of Dionysius, the Ionian nobleman, being a Persian subject are well set out: he is summoned to trial before the Great King at Babylon and later has to take an active part in the war on the Persian

196

---

[61] Hermocrates' name appears more than fifty times in the text of the novel: see the Thesaurus Linguae Graecae, *Alphabetical Keyword-in-Context Concordance to the Greek Novelists* (Irvine, Calif. 1979, microfiche) s.v. and cf. Molinié's useful analytical index (supra n. 55) 223; Zimmermann (supra n. 55) 336f.; and Scarcella (supra n. 43) 344.

[62] See Perry (supra n. 55) 100f. n.11; Zimmermann (supra n. 55) 337f.; and Scarcella (supra n. 43) 345f.

[63] See Perry (supra n. 55) 101 n. 11, and idem (supra n. 5) 137–39; Zimmermann (supra n. 55) 337; and Scarcella (supra n. 43) 346f. Perry's thesis that the whole plot is based on legend or "a pre-existing popular or historiographical tradition" (138) can hardly be upheld; cf. Reardon, *Courants littéraires* (supra n. 5) 351f. n. 97; Müller (supra n. 56) 133 n.87; and Plepelits (supra n. 1) 30–32.

side. The war itself, caused by a rebellion in Egypt and described with a fair amount of specific detail from the mobilization of the Persian army onward, deeply affects the fortunes of the hero and heroine, at the end bringing about their reunion. The mainly private first part of the novel is thus (6.8) followed by a shorter part — about one-fourth of the whole — in which public affairs come to the fore.

Some obvious anachronisms appear in the historical framework. The most blatant one is letting the lifetime of Hermocrates (died 407) co-incide with the reign of Artaxerxes II Mnemon (404–363/57). Further-more, Miletus in fact was not again under Persian dominion until after 387,[64] and the Egyptian rebellion, the leader of which is cautiously kept anonymous, appears to be still more violently backdated, insofar as it is at all meant to describe an actual historical event.[65] But all this is hardly more than Scott allowed himself in *Redgauntlet*, taking similar temporal liberties and staging a purely fictitious rebellion. No doubt the general reader's demand for historical probability was more than satisfied by Chariton's drawing of the contours of a classical milieu, in combination with his occasional pastiche on the manner of the classical historians (culminating in a number of hidden quotations from Xenophon and others).[66] Accuracy and authenticity in historical fiction is of course to be seen in relation not to historical reality, but to the picture of an age which writer and reader share from reading the same history books. For instance, Chariton's image of the Great King and his court, colored as it is by his Greek spectacles, will have impressed his contemporary read-ers as authentic as long as it did not manifestly depart from the image given by Herodotus, Xenophon, and Ctesias. It is completely irrelevant that *we* happen to know better.

197   Admitting the general probability of the historical background for the

---

[64] See Scarcella (supra n.43) 349.

[65] There are different options regarding which rebellion or capture of Tyre was Chariton's model: P. Salmon, "Chariton d'Aphrodisias et la révolte égyptienne de 360 avant J.-C.," *Cd'E* 36 (1961) 365–76; Zimmermann (supra n. 55) 342f. (Alexanders' capture of Tyre in 332; the Alexander historians); Molinié (supra n. 55) 7f. (amalgam of actual events of 405, 389–387, 360, and 332); Scarcella (supra n. 43) 349. P. Grimal, trans., *Romans grecs et latins* (Paris [1958] 1980) 382 instead points at a fifth-century event, the Egyptian re-bellion in ca. 460–454 under Artaxerxes I.

[66] For an annotated list of Chariton's "Entlehnungen aus klassischen Autoren" see A. D. Papanikolaou, *Chariton-Studien,* Hypomnemata 37 (Göttingen 1973) 13–24; see also Perry (supra n. 55) 104–8 and Zimmermann (supra n. 55) 330f.

love story, different readers will have judged differently where the line is drawn between fact and fiction, exactly as is the case with modern historical novels and modern readers.[67] No doubt some believed the whole story to be authentic.[68] That, however, was not the fault of the author, who certainly knew he was not writing history and never pretended he was.[69] In this as in other important respects, he appears to differ from the author of the *Alexander Romance,* but to side with most modern writers of historical fiction. It is commonly maintained that Chariton chose the historiographical form in order to make the novel seem less "novel" to his readership, or that (in John Morgan's words) "he saw his fiction as still sheltering under the wing of historiography."[70] Viewing him against the background of modern practitioners of the same trade, I am more inclined to think that his aim was precisely to create that titillating sensation peculiar to historical fiction, which is the effect of openly mixing fictitious characters and events with historical ones.[71] This is not to try to pass the novel off as something else, but, rather, to make the most of the contrast; in his first and last sentences, Chariton shows that he is well aware of the possibilities.

If Chariton meets the general reader's demand for "truth," he certainly fails according to the severer norms of such critics as Lukács and Fleishman. His historical milieu is, precisely, contours, costumes, masks: historical persons and places named, historical events alluded to and customs described, and in addition the classical atmosphere created through stylistic means. But the characters themselves, who act against this back-

---

[67] Cf. Fleishman's discussion (supra n. 29) 4–7, starting from Sigrid Undset's *Kristin Lavransdatter.*

[68] Cf. Müller (supra n. 56) 126.

[69] E. L. Bowie, "The Novels and the Real World," in Reardon (supra n.4) 91–96, tries to distinguish between intention and effect: "the author *can,* even if he clearly does not expect to, be taken to be treating the real world of γενόμενα" (92); "the reader can treat the story as one which *might* have happened but eluded the classical historians" (93). Cf. also Bowie (supra n. 44) 685.

[70] Morgan (infra n. 90) 225. Cf., with different emphasis, Perry (supra n. 5) 139, 168; G. Schmeling, *Chariton* (New York 1974) 55f.; and Hägg (supra n. 3) 16f. More to the point, I. Stark, *Philologus* 128 (1984) 258.

[71] Treu (supra n. 5) 458 makes much the same observation but still seems to think that the purpose is to make the (naive) reader believe that if the secondary characters are historical, the protagonists are so too. Maehler in Reardon (supra n. 4) 50f. misses the point in a similar way, saying that "*all* [the] main characters are historical persons" (my italics).

ground, are hardly conceived of as individuals of an age different from that of the author, let alone as typical representatives of that past age. Instead, as has been stressed by Bryan Reardon in particular,[72] it is late Hellenistic man who speaks and acts, late Hellenistic life that is really depicted, against the classical decor.[73] Chaereas's apolitical behavior, says Reardon, is the greatest among Chariton's anachronisms. We cannot claim that all this is deliberate strategy on the part of the author, that, like some modern writers, he chose a historical milieu in order to make his contemporary topic and characters stand out all the more effectively against that background. The kind of historical consciousness needed to recreate a historical past, or to realize the problem at all, simply was not at his disposal.

198

For *Parthenope* the picture is much the same, as far as it is possible to judge from the fragments, but with some interesting new nuances. Our main source for the Greek text is a comparatively extensive papyrus fragment (some seventy lines in all);[74] in addition, there are some Greek literary testimonia[75] and the fragments of an eleventh-century Persian verse-romance, *Vāmiq and 'Adhrā*, ultimately based on the Greek novel.[76] Just as Chariton relies mainly on Thucydides for the historical connections of his main characters, the unknown author of *Parthenope* relies on Herodotus. Parthenope herself is the daughter of Polycrates, the tyrant of Samos; she appears, though anonymously, in Herodotus (3.124). Her lover Metiochus (Hdt. 6.39–41) is the son of Miltiades, the victor at Marathon. By bringing these two together as young lovers at the court of Polycrates, the author backdates Metiochus by some twenty or thirty years, and he creates an imaginary blood-relationship between

---

[72] See Reardon, *Courants littéraires* (supra n. 5) 341, and cf. Plepelits (supra n.1) 14f; Bowie (supra n. 69) 93f.; and Reardon (supra n. 54) 19–26.

[73] Cf. J. Bompaire, "Le décor sicilien dans le roman grec et dans la littérature contemporaine," *REG* 90 (1977) 55–68, displaying the use in Chariton and Aelius Aristides of a kind of "Syracusan myth." Bompaire uses *décor* in a more positive way — as part of the novelist's legitimate means of creating a historical atmosphere — than do modern literary critics of the historical novel.

[74] See Maehler in *ZPE* (supra n. 4) and cf. Scarcella (supra n. 43) 363 n.97.

[75] See Maehler in *ZPE* (supra n. 4) and T. Hägg, "The *Parthenope Romance* Decapitated?" *SymbOslo* 59 (1984) 76f. [No. **8** in this volume].

[76] See T. Hägg, "Metiochus at Polycrates' Court," *Eranos* 83 (1985) 92–102 [no. **9** in this volume], and B. Utas, "Did 'Adhrā Remain a Virgin?" *OrSuec* 33–35 (1984–1986) 429–41.

Polycrates and Miltiades, making them both descend from Aeacus, the son of Zeus; in Herodotus, only Miltiades claims such a descent, whereas Polycrates' father is an ordinary mortal with a very similar name, Aeaces. Furthermore, on the basis of the historical fact that, during his rule of the Chersonese, Miltiades remarried (with a Thracian princess, Hegesipyle), the author invents an unhistorical, typically novelistic motive for young Metiochus to leave the Chersonese: he flees from his stepmother's machinations.[77]

These are indeed the kind of manipulations we may expect from any author of a historical novel, modern or ancient, and there can be no doubt that the love story itself and the further adventures of the young couple are purely fictitious. The author of *Parthenope,* however, seems to have put rather more effort than Chariton did into the creation of a coherent historical background to his fiction. His Polycrates seems to have come more to the fore than Chariton's Hermocrates: together with his wife — who is possibly a daughter of King Croesus of Lydia (!) — he welcomes his fugitive relative Metiochus to his Samian court, entertains him in the evening, and shows an active interest in the young man. To create an authentic-looking environment the author introduces other historical figures as well and lets them mingle with the fictitious ones: Anaximenes of Miletus, the philosopher, serves as kind of toastmaster at the symposium on the first night, Eros being the topic of discussion, and a well-known poet, who is probably none other than Ibycus of Rhegium, sings of the beauty of the young couple, both these prominent figures illustrating the cultural activities traditionally associated with Polycrates' court.

199

While Chariton is content to let Hermocrates' historical achievement belong to the prehistory of the plot, making his public activities in the novel itself depend on the fictitious intrigue rather than the reverse, *Parthenope* appears to have had a less static historical setting: it also included the death of Polycrates, the ascension to power of his former secretary Maeandrius, and finally at least the beginning of the reign of Polycrates' brother Syloson. Maeandrius apparently tries to win Parthenope for himself, is rebuffed, and takes his revenge by selling her as a slave. Syloson, on the other hand, is referred to in positive terms in one of the frag-

---

[77] For detailed documentation of the historicity of this novel, see Hägg (supra n. 76) 92–98.

ments and may well have had a hand in the final reunion of the lovers. Incidentally, the characterization of Maeandrius as bad and Syloson as good conforms to the picture of the two rulers given by Herodotus. To all appearances, then, the fictitious love-story is enacted — as envisaged by our criterion "Setting" — against the background of a succession of historical events, each of which affects the fortunes of the lovers.

If *Callirhoe,* and even more so *Parthenope,* thus fulfill several of the basic criteria for the typical historical novel, the same does not apply, as far as I can see, to the other surviving "ideal" novels,[78] even when set in the past. Achilles Tatius makes a point of having himself met the protagonist and heard the story from his lips. The only reference to a potentially verifiable public event, a war between Byzantium and the Thracians, is probably just part of the fiction.[79] The mention of a "satrap" of Egypt (4.11.1; cf. 4.13.4) does not, as some have believed, refer to the Persian dominion,[80] but is an Atticist way of saying "prefect";[81] and the Egyptian robbers operating in the Delta, the *boukoloi,* who in the novel capture the lovers, are a phenomenon recorded by the historian Dio Cassius as late as A.D. 172[82] — i.e., not long before Achilles Tatius must have written his novel. His is consequently a contemporary novel.

Xenophon of Ephesus begins his story in a way reminiscent of the folktale's "once upon a time": ἦν ἐν Ἐφέσῳ ἀνήρ …, "There was a man

---

[78] Reservation must be made for the *Ninus* and *Sesonchosis* novels; the fragmentary state of preservation does not allow an assessment of what part history (or myth) may have played in their structure. On *Ninus,* see Perry (supra n. 5) 153ff.; on *Sesonchosis* as close in type to the *Alexander Romance,* see J. N. O'Sullivan, *ZPE* 56 (1984) 44. Anyway, as Dihle (supra n. 4) 55 points out, "Erzählungen aus grauer Vorzeit in exotischem Milieu" like these two cannot have had the same kind of appeal to a Greek reader as *Callirhoe* and *Parthenope.* For the view that they too are the products of a romantic nationalism, but in this case in Hellenistic Syria and Egypt, respectively, see M. Braun, *History and Romance in Graeco-Oriental Literature* (Oxford 1938) 6–18 and cf. Grimal (supra n. 56) 842f.

[79] Ach. Tat. 1.3.6, 7.12.4, 8.18.1; cf. Bowie (supra n. 44) 694f.

[80] Thus S. Gaselee, ed., *Achilles Tatius* (London 1917) 378 n. 2; *contra* E. Vilborg, *Achilles Tatius: Leucippe and Clitophon — A Commentary* (Göteborg 1962) 11, 85.

[81] Cf. Philostr. *VS* 1.22.3 (p. 31.1 Kayser), on which see W. Schmid, *Der Atticismus,* vol. 4 (Stuttgart 1896) 423, and G. W. Bowersock, *Greek Sophists in the Roman Empire* (Oxford 1969) 52.

[82] Ach. Tat. 3.9.2ff., 4.12; Dio Cass. 71.4.1–2. See F. Altheim, *Literatur und Gesellschaft im ausgehenden Altertum,* vol. 1 (Halle 1948) 121–24, and, on the role of the *boukoloi* in the novels generally, Scarcella (supra n. 3) 352–64; cf. also J. Schwartz, *AC* 45 (1976) 618–26.

in Ephesus …" (1. 1.1); and he ends in a similar vein, but is content with leaving it at that vaguely preterite impression. He never specifies the period by referring to any identifiable public event or naming any historical person. There is some quite specific geographical information, especially regarding the route of the brigands in Egypt (4.1.1–4), but it is probably more or less contemporary,[83] as is the author's dose of "social realism."[84] Nothing else in the décor invokes the classical period; on the contrary, the mention of Alexandria and Antioch sets the action in postclassical times, that of the Prefect of Egypt (a public figure, but anonymous)[85] makes it post-Hellenistic, and that of the Eirenarch of Cilicia in fact probably even post-Trajan.[86] These might conceivably all be anachronisms on the part of this not very sophisticated author, but the absence of any deliberate counterstroke must decide the question: this is no historical novel according to our definition, either in intent or in effect. The same is true for Longus, who likewise begins in a past tense — the author interprets a painting describing a love story that took place in the past *(praef.;* cf. 1.1.2 ἦν and 4.39) — but never makes any attempt to anchor his story in any particular period[87] or puts on stage any historical figure.

Heliodorus's novel has greater claims to being counted as historical; in fact, it has often been put on an equal footing with Chariton's for setting its action in a historical past.[88] There are, however, important differences between the two. It is true that Heliodorus deliberately sketches a pre-Hellenistic background for his story: his Egypt is under Persian dominion (which means ca. 525–330 B.C.), and Alexandria does not occur. It does not matter much, from our point of view, how consistently this Persian

---

[83] See H. Henne, "La géographie de l'Egypte dans Xénophon d'Ephèse," *RevHistPhilos* n.s. 4 (1936) 97–106, who corrects E. Rohde's and G. Dalmeyda's judgment of Xenophon's Egypt as pure fantasy.

[84] See Morgan (infra n. 90) 235 (with further refs.).

[85] Cf. T. Hägg, "The Naming of the Characters in the Romance of Xenophon Ephesius," *Eranos* 69 (1971) 30f. [No. 7 in this volume].

[86] Cf. H. Gärtner, "Xenophon von Ephesos," *RE* 2. Reihe 9 (1967) 2055–89, cols. 2086f.

[87] Geographical realism in Longus is discussed by H. J. Mason, *TAPA* 109 (1979) 149–63; P.M. Green, *JHS* 102 (1982) 210–14; and E. L. Bowie, *CQ* n.s. 35 (1985) 86–91.

[88] Even Müller (supra n. 44) 391 speaks of "allenfalls Gradunterschiede," while Dihle (supra n. 4) 54 acutely points to the differences.

Egypt is described or how historically accurate are his classical Delphi[89] and early-Meroitic Meroë;[90] all these are certainly amalgams of facts from different historical periods with a strong admixture of pure invention,[91] creating the general atmosphere of a distant historical past.[92] What does matter, however, is the total absence of identifiable historical figures or events. The Persian satrap Oroondates and his wife Arsace, the sister of the Great King, have simply been given typical names[93] (as have the satraps Mithridates and Pharnaces in Chariton); the Great King of the period is not specified, and King Hydaspes and Queen Persinna of Aethiopia, the parents of the heroine, are invented characters. No authentic figure like Hermocrates or Polycrates mingles with the fictitious characters at Delphi; the flying visit in the tale (2.25.1) of the Greek courtesan Rhodopis, known from Herodotus (2.134; cf. Strabo 17.1.33), is a poor substitute. Any dependence on factual happenings, like the description of the siege of Syene (Book 9), which may have been inspired by the siege of Nisibis in A.D. 350,[94] is concealed rather than utilized to create an impression of authenticity. It goes without saying that nothing in the fortunes of the protagonists is imagined as affected by events outside the universe created by the novelist for the occasion.

The kind of historical probability the *Ethiopica* still undoubtedly achieves relies on other means: as John Morgan has shown, it is by dress-

---

[89] J. Pouilloux, "Delphes dans les *Ethiopiques* d'Héliodore: la réalité dans la fiction," *JSav* (1983) 259–86 (shorter version in *REG* 97 [1984] xxivf.) finds a surprising amount of authenticity in this description; but the realism concerns Delphi of the imperial period, not the classical in which the action is set.

[90] Cf. J. R. Morgan, "History, Romance, and Realism in the *Aithiopika* of Heliodoros," *ClAnt* 1 (1982) 237–50, who finds more of the Meroë of Herodotus than that of later periods in Heliodorus's description. [See further No. **12** in this volume.]

[91] Cf. J. Maillon in R. M. Rattenbury and T. W. Lumb, eds., *Héliodore: Les Ethiopiques*, vol. 1 (Paris 1935) lxxxviiif., and O. Weinreich, *Der griechische Liebesroman* (Zurich 1962) 41. Iamblichus's *Babyloniaca* probably presents a similar amalgam: cf. U. Schneider-Menzel in Altheim (supra n. 82) 77–84 (on the personal names) and 89–92 (finding traces from the pre-Persian to the Parthian period); similarly Weinreich, p. 15.

[92] Morgan (supra n. 90) 236 n. 46 lists some of the obvious anachronisms.

[93] Cf. the notes on Hld. 2.24.2, 7.1.4, and 7.14.3 in Rattenbury and Lumb (supra n. 91) and see Morgan (supra n. 90) 247.

[94] See, most recently, Morgan (supra n. 90) 226 n.15, and G. N. Sandy, *Heliodorus* (Boston 1982) 4f. (with further refs.), who are both inclined to accept a late-fourth-century date for the novel. New arguments for Heliodorus's priority, however, have been advanced by M. Maróth, *Acta Ant. Acad. Scient. Hung.* 27 (1981) 239–43.

ing the story in narrative devices typical of historiography — expressing uncertainty, offering alternative explanations for events, providing authentic geographical and ethnographical information, etc. — that Heliodorus lends plausibility and an air of realism to his account.[95] By writing like a historian, or assuming "the historiographical pose," he wants his love-and-adventure story to appear as "history" (which, as Morgan explains, is not quite the same as "fact").[96] We may thus well choose to call the *Ethiopica* a historical novel, but bearing in mind that it has far less in common with the typical modern works of that designation than have *Callirhoe* and *Parthenope*. Of our criteria, it satisfies that of "Time" and, to a reasonable extent, that of "Truth,"[97] while essential traits are missing as regards "Characters" and "Setting."

Discussing the modern historical novel, Harry Shaw asks why, in this very extensive genre, there have been so comparatively few acknowledged masterpieces; even great writers have failed when venturing on a historical novel.[98] He finds what looks like an insoluble dilemma inherent in the genre: novels are built up around protagonists who are private individuals, and "milieu, minor characters, and plotted action are there to illuminate them." In historical novels, by contrast, the characters are ideally expected to represent, at the same time, "salient aspects of a historical milieu," and even to "elucidate historical process."[99] Succeeding in conveying the spirit of the age, the author is apt to fail in individual characterization, and vice versa. Returning from ideals to everyday practice, from the missing masterpieces to the flourishing popular genre of the historical novel, we may ask the analogous question: why is the genre so popular? — and seek the answer in roughly the same direction. It is precisely at the point of intersection between the historical and the private sphere, I believe, that the particular attraction of the typical historical novel lies. Or, at least, one of its attractions, for plain interest in history is of course a major part of the explanation too. Once we have relaxed from the demand for historical "truth" in the more profound sense, the

202

---

[95] Morgan (supra n. 90). For a different approach, see J. J. Winkler, *YCS* 27 (1982) 93–158.

[96] Morgan (supra n. 90) 223–26, 261f.

[97] Cf. ibid. 248.

[98] Shaw (supra n. 11) 30 (top) and 30–50, "The Problem with Historical Novels." Cf. Henderson (supra n.12) xvf.

[99] Shaw (supra n.11) 49.

"dilemma" can be turned into a strength. The author introduces private individuals with whom the reader can identify (they are "timeless" human beings rather than "representative" for a different age) and makes them personally witness and experience great historical events and figures. This is why the best-known periods and figures — a Napoleon, a Polycrates — are the favorites with writers of popular historical fiction: the more familiar the historical décor, the more titillating the reader's sense of taking part in the events through the medium of the fictitious characters, breaking time barriers as well as the barrier between the public and the private.

This is what Chariton and the author of *Parthenope* had discovered. They did not, like the writers of romanticized biographies, put a historical figure at the center of their fantasies, nor did they as conscientiously as Heliodorus pose as historians, giving to their love stories a feeling of being historical accounts. Rather, they were deliberately playing on the reader's naive delight in recognizing the great figures of history and at the same time viewing them from a new perspective.[100] But a touch was enough, a sketched background to what was after all the main thing, the love story itself. Again, it was not just any period and place that they chose for its setting; it was the Golden Age of Greece, and the climate of incipient classicism in which they lived[101] gave them a convenient opportunity of appealing to a sense of nostalgia for that heroic past — incidentally, another point of contact with Scott and the Romantic period in which the modern historical novel arose.[102] To all appearances writing

203

---

[100] Cf. Bowie (supra n. 44) 685: "The reader can fancy that he is enjoying a sentimental sidelight on conventional political history."

[101] See the illuminating remarks of Dihle (supra n. 4) 54f., who argues for a mid-first-century B.C. date. For a useful review of earlier attempts to date Chariton and the interesting (though not compelling) suggestion that Chariton's Athenagoras is identical with the rhetor Athenagoras (*Ant. Pal.* 11.150), active in the first decades of the second century A.D., see C. Ruiz Montero, "Una observación para la cronología de Caritón de Afrodisias," *Estudios Clásicos* 85 (1980) 63–69. The present argument is of course not dependent on as early a date as suggested above.

[102] See Fleishman (supra n. 6) 16f. and Sanders (supra n. 12) 1f. Other incentives for historical fiction than nostalgia are of course possible, e.g., a moralistic interest; that goes some way toward explaining why comparatively few modern authors have chosen the classical periods of antiquity as setting and so many the late antique period of decline. Cf. H. Riikonen, *Die Antike im historischen Roman des 19. Jahrhunderts: Eine literatur- und kulturgeschichtliche Untersuchung,* Commentationes Humanarum Litterarum 59 (Helsinki 1978) 34–39, 203–5, and the comments of E. J. Kenney in *CR* n.s. 31 (1981)

→

before classicism had yet become a commonplace, our two authors will have had a chance to convey, with the fresh charm of novelty, the "classical feel"[103] to their late Hellenistic readers.

Finally, to return to the generic considerations discussed at the beginning of this paper: can we legitimately speak of a subgenre, the "historical novel," of which *Callirhoe* and *Parthenope* represent an early form, *Waverley* and *Ivanhoe* a modern?[104] The best way to address the problem is probably to follow Lukács and Shaw in regarding the historical novel as just a temporary tributary of the great stream of the novel: it branches off for a while, then rejoins the main stream. The first novel we possess happens to be historical, the next three are not, and then, with the *Ethiopica,* history (of a kind) is there again; but Heliodorus has less in common with Chariton than with his immediate predecessors. The historical novel has no history of its own, but all the way it "depends on the formal techniques and cultural assumptions of the main tradition."[105] Setting the novel in a historical milieu, the writer achieves different results, depending both on the stage of development the novel as

282f. Needless to say, our two ancient novels have a deeper spiritual kinship with the Waverley novels of Scott (or, for that matter, with the *Iliad*) than with most modern historical novels set in antiquity. The parallel between the Homeric epic and "le roman historique à la Walter Scott" was drawn in an interesting article by P. Van Tieghem, "La question des genres littéraires," *Helicon* 1 (1938) 95–101, as an example of "ces genres non formels, mais psychologiques, qui mettent en jeu les mêmes facultés des auteurs, les mêmes goûts du public" (99).

[103] The expression is borrowed from Reardon (supra n. 54) 19 (in a slightly different context).

[104] I am of course not suggesting any influence from Chariton on Scott; but it is interesting to note that Scott apparently was influenced by Heliodorus, probably indirectly through Sidney's *Arcadia:* "Banquet turns to Battle" Hld. 1.1, *[New] Arcadia* II.27.5 (*Old Arcadia* p. 128.7 Robertson), *Ivanhoe,* chapter 41. See S. L. Wolff, *The Greek Romances in Elizabethan Prose Fiction* (New York 1912) 366, 463, and R. T. Kerlin, "Scott's *Ivanhoe* and Sydney's *Arcadia,*" *Modern Language Notes* 22 (1907) 144–46. Cf. Scott himself on his early reading, which at least included Madeleine de Scudery's *Cyrus: Waverley* pp. 13f. Lamont ("Waverley's" reading) and 350 (General Preface, 1829). Whether the *Ethiopica* in Underdowne's or any later translation ever came in his hands is impossible to say, but the early unpublished "fragment of a romance" (p. 361 Lamont, Appendix I) begins in a way strikingly similar to Heliodorus's novel: "The sun was nearly set behind the distant mountains of Liddesdale, when a few of the scattered and terrified inhabitants of the village of Hersildoun …"

[105] Shaw (supra n. 11) 23; cf. 30. Cf., for a similar viewpoint, Van Tieghem as quoted supra n. 102.

genre has reached and on the level of sophistication of the writer and his intended audience.

The stage that contemporary historiography has reached is an essential factor too. Historiography and historical novel can be shown often to go hand in hand; Scott's novels, for example, are unthinkable without the developments in historiography of the preceding decades.[106] It would be as absurd to demand from an ancient historical novelist like Chariton a sense of "history as a shaping force,"[107] which we do not find in the historians or biographers of his age — in fact, perhaps not until after the French Revolution[108] — as it would be to demand of him any other special quality of the advanced modern novel, for instance the psychological insights of a Dostoevski. It is all the more remarkable that still, as we have seen, a number of basic characteristics of the typical historical novel of our time are already to be distinguished in the first Greek novels of antiquity.

---

[106] See Fleishman (supra n. 6) 16–36, and, from a different viewpoint, L. Braudy, *Narrative Form in History and Fiction: Hume, Fielding and Gibbon* (Princeton 1970).

[107] Fleishman (supra n. 6) 15.

[108] Cf. Lukács (supra n. 9) 23.

Some Technical Aspects of the Characterization
in Chariton's Romance

[originally published in *Studi classici in onore di Q. Cataudella*, Vol. 2, Catania 1972 (pr. 1975), 545-556.]

In an article entitled *Chariton and his Romance from a Literary-Historical Point of View* (*AJP* 51, [1930], 93–134), B. E. Perry has called attention to Chariton's special gift for character drawing (esp. pp. 115–123). The subject has recently been treated on a full scale by J. Helms in his monograph *Character Portrayal in the Romance of Chariton* (Diss., Univ. of Michigan 1963, publ. The Hague & Paris 1966). It emerges very clearly from Helms's study — more clearly, perhaps, from his copious presentation of the material than from his own conclusions — that Chariton's real forte is "character revelation" in quoted *speech* (monologues and dialogues) and in *action,* whereas the narrator's own third-person statements[1] on traits of character are comparatively rare and, as a rule, lack the subtle nuances that are appreciable in the other means of characterization. It is also obvious that Chariton's method of character drawing is intuitive, at its best, resulting from a genuine talent for psychological observation rather than being influenced by theoretical considerations or following rhetorical rules.[2] In Perry's words, "the style of presentation is mimetic on the whole rather than sophistic" (p. 115). However, in this short article I shall not dwell on these undoubtedly most important aspects of Chariton's characterization but concentrate on a few minor points of narrative technique, supplementing in some respects the picture given by Perry and Helms. The technical points chosen will be Chariton's way of introducing his characters into the action, his means of identifying them

546

---

[1] Helms unfortunately fails to make a clear distinction between these statements and the integrated ones, i. e. the comments expressed *through other characters* (see, for instance, pp. 32 f., 45, and 54 f.).

[2] Helms's classification according to Aristotelian categories of characterization should, I believe (the author himself does not take up the issue), be taken only as a model for description and not as an argument for Chariton's actual and deliberate observance of the rules implied.

at later appearances, and the effect of the omniscient narrative perspective[3] on the appellations thus applied to the characters. As a background, I shall first briefly survey the *dramatis personae*.[4]

About 70 individuals are mentioned by Chariton as taking part in the action of his romance; about one-fifth of them are women. This figure does not include the deities who intrude into the action (Aphrodite, Eros, Pronoia, Tyche), persons who are mentioned only in the speeches of the characters (Adrastos II, 1, 6 etc.) or as relatives of the participants (Megabyzos V, 3, 4 etc.) or in similes (Alcibiades I, 1, 3 etc.), and the groups of people whose actions or feelings are recorded (the people of Syracuse I, 1, 11–12, the suitors I, 2, etc.) About half of the 70 participators occur only once, in a special function: an individual τις voicing the feelings of a group (V, 3, 1 etc.), a messenger (I, 3, 1 etc.), or the like. Of the remaining half, 19 persons are given proper names; the most important of these are Callirhoe and Chaireas, the hero and heroine of the romance, Dionysios, a Ionian nobleman, Artaxerxes, the Great King, and Theron the pirate. The rebel leader, who plays an important part in the second half of the romance, is left anonymous (he is called simply ὁ Αἰγύπτιος or (ὁ) βασιλεύς), and so are the mother and the son of Callirhoe (I, 1, 5 etc.; III, 7, 7 etc.), and a number of characters who play an important part in one scene but then disappear, more or less, from the action (the Italian suitor in I, 2, 2–4, the temple attendant in III, 6, 4–6 and 9, 1–4, the Egyptian soldier in VII, 6, 6–12 and VIII, 1, 6 and a few more). About 20 characters in all may be regarded as being of more than passing importance to the action, and on these the emphasis will be placed in the present study; as for the rest, the method of introduction is purely functional (for instance, III, 4, 11 καθεζόμενος οὖν ἐν τῷ πλήθει τις ἁλιεὺς ἐγνώρισεν αὐτὸν καὶ... εἶπε...), and the identification at the renewed appearance, if any, does not involve any problems, as following closely on the introduction (4, 12 τὸν πρῶτον εἰπόντα..., ὁ ἁλιεύς). The problems for the author do not arise, until the interval between the appearances is greater and the reader's memory and the author's consistency in character drawing thus are put to the test.

547

[3] Cfr. Chap. 3, "Points of View", of my *Narrative Technique in Ancient Greek Romances: Studies of Chariton, Xenophon Ephesius, and Achilles Tatius,* Stockholm 1971 (*Acta Instituti Atheniensis Regni Sueciae, 8°*, VIII).

[4] For the details, I refer to the "Index Analyticus Nominum Propriorum" in W. E. Blake's critical edition of Chariton's romance (Oxford 1938). My quotations of the Greek text are taken from that edition.

* * *

The most common *way of introducing* also the more important characters into the action is the *functional*. The person in question appears as the subject or object in a clause which forms part of the current narrative: V, 2, 2 ... ἠσπάσατο μὲν (sc. ὁ Μιθριδάτης) Περσῶν τοὺς ὁμοτίμους, Ἀρταξάτην δὲ τὸν εὐνοῦχον ὃς μέγιστος ἦν παρὰ βασιλεῖ καὶ δυνατώτατος πρῶτον μὲν δώροις ἐτίμησεν, εἶτα ... [5]. In nearly all the cases, the name is the main word, to which the occupation and other characteristics are added as appositions or subordinate clauses; only Pharnaces, the satrap, is mentioned the first time in the opposite manner, with the title as the main word (IV, 1, 7)[6]. It may be of interest to note that what is an exception in Chariton turns out to be the rule in another romancer, Xenophon Ephesius: he regularly mentions the designation for occupation, age or the like first and the proper name as an apposition. To Xenophon Ephesius the type is the main thing, to Chariton the individual. It should be added, however, that two of the official persons in Chariton's romance are introduced functionally by their *titles only,* namely, the Great King (I, 12, 6 etc.) and a general (IV, 5, 5–6); later on, in official contexts, their respective names (Artaxerxes and Bias) appear (IV, 6, 3; IV, 5, 8)[7].

548

Non-functional introductions are reserved for the hero and heroine and a few others. One way is through expressions for relationships: I, 1, 1 Ἑρμοκράτης εἶχε θυγατέρα Καλλιρόην τοὔνομα ... (cfr. I, 1, 3 Ariston). Another way gives the introduction a still more independent position: I, 1, 3 Χαιρέας γάρ τις ἦν μειράκιον εὔμορφον ... and I, 7, 1 Θήρων γάρ τις ἦν πανοῦργος ἄνθρωπος ... (cfr. VIII, 3, 10 Demetrios). In his most artful introduction, however, Chariton proceeds in the very opposite way. Instead of drawing a small portrait on his own authority, as he does of Callirhoe, Chaireas, and Theron, he makes Dionysios and his steward

[5] Also Plangon II, 2, 1; Polycharmos I, 5, 2; Rhodogoune V, 3, 4; Stateira V, 3, 1; Hyginos IV, 5, 1; Pharnaces IV, 1, 7; Phocas II, 1, 1. Mithridates, who is coupled with Pharnaces in IV, 1, 7, was first mentioned in III, 7, 3, without any explanatory adjuncts, as being as self-evident a figure as the Great King in I, 12, 6; 13, 1; II, 4, 7; etc.

[6] Mithridates, who is coupled with Pharnaces in IV, 1, 7, was first mentioned in III, 7, 3, without any explanatory adjuncts, as being as self-evident a figure as the Great King in I, 12, 6; 13, 1; II, 4, 7; etc.

[7] Instances of delayed naming occur also in the other romances: Ach. Tat. I, 7, 3; IV, 2, 1; VI, 2, 5; Hld. I, 18, 2; Xen. Eph. V, 5, 2. Cfr. also Lucian *Ver. Hist.* I, 36.

Leonas come to life through a dramatic dialogue,[8] preceded by the reproduction of Theron's visual impressions (I, 12, 6 ἐν δὲ τῷ μεταξὺ παρήει πλῆθος ἀνθρώπων ἐλευθέρων τε καὶ δούλων, ἐν μέσοις δὲ αὐτοῖς ἀνὴρ ἡλικίᾳ καθεστώς, μελανειμονῶν καὶ σκυθρωπός). The ensuing dialogue between Theron and a man in the suite, who turns out to be Leonas, gradually provides the usual introductory material for Dionysios and Leonas (name, social position, etc.), only in an unusual form.

Thus, we have seen that the proper name, insofar as the person is named at all in the romance, occurs already in the introductory phrase, except in four cases: Bias, Dionysios, Leonas, and Artaxerxes. Of these, only Artaxerxes is still anonymous, when the first episode in which he takes part is ended, but in his special case the title, βασιλεύς, may be regarded as equivalent to a name. What kind of additional information is given about the characters at the time of their introduction? As regards the men, all except Chaireas and his friend Polycharmos are conscientiously furnished with indications of social position or occupation, sometimes with a detailed description of their respective tasks (Theron, Leonas, Hyginos), sometimes with only a title. On the introduction of women, an indication of relationship is obligatory, as in V, 3, 4: ... προεκρίθη Ῥοδογούνη, θυγάτηρ μὲν Ζωπύρου, γυνὴ δὲ Μεγαβύζου, μέγα τι χρῆμα ⟨κάλλους⟩ καὶ περιβόητον ... The outward appearance, mentioned in the case of Rhodogoune, is also part of the introductions of Callirhoe and Chaireas; however, only *general* expressions for beauty occur, combined with comparisons, but no detailed description of individual traits. Intellectual or moral qualities are referred to in four cases: Demetrios (VIII, 3,10 παιδείᾳ καὶ ἀρετῇ τῶν ἄλλων Αἰγυπτίων διαφέρων), Theron (I, 7, 1 πανοῦργος ἄνθρωπος, ἐξ ἀδικίας πλέων τὴν θάλασσαν), Plangon (II, 2, 1 ζῷον οὐκ ἄπρακτον[9]), and Hyginos (IV, 5, 1 τῷ πιστοτάτῳ).[10] The only characteristic that Polycharmos is given is that he is φίλος ἐξαίρετος of Chaireas, as Patroclus of Achilles (I, 5, 2). The

549

---

[8] Cfr. Helms, p. 68.

[9] Perry paraphrases "Plango... is shrewd, practical" (p. 117), Blake translates "a shrewd sort of creature" (p. 22, cfr. Helms, p. 95). To my mind, "active" (or "practical") seems preferable to "shrewd". Cfr. the combination of ἄπρακτον and ζῷον in Epict. I, 10, 7: τί οὖν; ἐγὼ λέγω ὅτι ἄπρακτόν ἐστι τὸ ζῷον; Does Chariton allude to some popular philosophical expression of this kind?

[10] Cfr. also the description of the παράσιτος in I, 4, 1 and the ὑποκριτής in I, 4, 2, and Theron's own characterization of some intended accomplices in I, 7, 2.

age is mentioned in the case of Demetrios (VIII, 3, 10 ἡλικίᾳ προήκων), Dionysios (I, 12, 6 ἡλικίᾳ καθεστώς), and Callirhoe and Chaireas (I, 1, 1 παρθένου, 1, 3 μειράκιον), while the nationality is explicitly stated on the introduction of Dionysios and the Egyptian Demetrios.[11] For most of the other characters, the nationality may easily be inferred from the circumstances and setting of the introduction, but it may be noted that the pirate chief, Theron, is introduced without any ethnic label[12] (and remains without one for the whole action), in contrast to the Tyrian and Egyptian pirates in the other romances.[13]

550

In summary, the meagrest introductions are devoted to the official or even historical persons of the romance (Hermocrates, Artaxerxes, "The Egyptian", etc.). The hero and heroine are introduced with more details, but with the entire emphasis on their outward appearances. Most comprehensive are the pictures given of Dionysios — who, through the reflection in the mind of another character, is the only one to have his *momentary* appearance recorded (I, 12, 6 μελανειμονῶν καὶ σκυθρωπός) — and of Theron. A comparatively insignificant figure, Demetrios, is also honoured by the narrator with an unusually complete characterization: VIII, 3, 10 φιλόσοφος, βασιλεῖ γνώριμος, ἡλικίᾳ προήκων, παιδείᾳ καὶ ἀρετῇ τῶν ἄλλων Αἰγυπτίων διαφέρων. Never, however, not even in the last-mentioned instances, is there any question of character drawing on such a scale as to bring the action to a real standstill; mostly, the narrator is content with giving just one or two characteristics which are of importance for fitting the person into the current situation.

* * *

[11] The age immediately emerges also at the introduction of an anonymous νεανίας in I, 2, 2, and, of course, also in the case of the participating children (I, 12, 8; III, 7, 7 etc.); Ariston, Chaireas' father, is not explicitly referred to as "very old" until a later appearance (III, 5, 4). The nationality is a chief characteristic also at the introductions of a number of anonymous characters of limited participation (I, 2, 2; VII, 2, 2; 6, 6; VIII, 2, 1; 2, 12; 6, 4).

[12] Unless Blake is right in suggesting ἐκ Κιλικίας, instead of ἐξ ἀδικίας in I, 7, 1 (cfr. his app. crit. to p. 10, 3).

[13] Chariton generally takes it for granted that all his characters understand and speak *Greek*, even at the Persian court (see, for instance, the trial and the private conversations between Artaxates and Callirhoe). Only on one occasion, when Chaireas and Polycharmos arrive as deserters at the Egyptian military camp, does the author call attention to language barriers (VII, 2, 2) — only to forget it in Chaireas' later dealings with the Egyptian rebel leader and his war council.

When a character who has on his first appearance been introduced in one of the ways just described reappears outside the unbroken context of the introduction, the chief *means of identifying* him, as might be expected, is his proper name or an equivalent designation (βασιλεύς, ἡ βασιλίς, ὁ Αἰγύπτιος). However, some modifications deserve notice. For some persons, an additional identificatory element occurs at later appearances. Thus, Mithridates, who was first mentioned in passing in III, 7, 4, is identified by having his official title (in various versions) added to his name on several occasions: IV, 1, 7 δύο σατράπαι..., Μιθριδάτης ὁ ἐν Καρίᾳ ..., 1, 9 Μιθριδάτης δέ, ὁ Καρίας ἔπαρχος,[14] 2, 4 ὁ δὲ Μιθριδάτης ὁ σατράπης. Later the title is dropped and the name alone is used in about 60 cases; exceptions are only some occurrences in direct or indirect speech, where the mention of the title is organically motivated by context (IV, 5, 5; 5, 8; 6, 4: ὁ Καρίας ὕπαρχος). The same thing, in principle, is valid for later mentions of Polycharmos, Pharnaces, Phocas, Ariston, Artaxates, and Rhodogoune. Other characters entirely lack such additional means of identification. In this category we find, apart from Callirhoe and Chaireas, also Dionysios, Theron, and a number of less prominent participants: Demetrios, Hermocrates, Leonas, Plangon, and Stateira (when not identified by title *only*). As regards Theron, he is sometimes given the apposition ὁ λῃστής or ὁ τυμβωρύχος, but then always in quoted speech and in order to emphasize his *role,* not in order to remind the reader of his identity (for instance, II, 6, 3 "ἐγὼ τυραννήσω σώματος ἐλευθέρου, καὶ Διονύσιος ὁ ἐπὶ σωφροσύνῃ περιβόητος ἄκουσαν ὑβριῶ, ἣν οὐκ ἂν ὕβρισεν οὐδὲ Θήρων ὁ λῃστής;"). The same is true of Hermocrates; it is when he is referred to in speech and not when he acts that the title ὁ στρατηγός is added. To sum up, the identificatory elements are added — in the narrative proper as distinct from the quoted speech — mostly in the cases of characters who were not given a distinct scenic description the first time they appeared in the romance, such as Phocas, who is introduced in II, 1, 1 but does not become a person of flesh and blood until III, 7, 1-3 and 9, 5-12 (and consequently is still identified as ὁ οἰκονόμος in II, 2, 1; 7, 2; and III, 7, 1). On the other hand, the name only is evidently enough for the characters who were emphatically introduced (cfr. the preceding section, on the principal characters, on

[14] This is the reading of the MS., vindicated by F. Zimmermann (in F. Altheim & R. Stiehl, *Die aramäische Sprache unter den Achaimeniden,* 2, Frankfurt am Main 1960, p. 156, n. 8c). Blake accepts at this place (in conformity with IV, 5, 5; 5, 8; 6, 4) Cobet's conjecture ὕπαρχος. Cfr. below, n. 21.

Demetrios, and on Leonas). This correlation shows the thorough and conscientious work of the author.   552

Sometimes, as a reminder to the reader, some specific facts from the past are summarily repeated at the moment of reappearance: IV, 2, 2 Πολύχαρμος οὖν, ὁ συναλοὺς αὐτῷ φίλος...[15]. More usual are the repetitions of traits of character or outward appearance which were originally mentioned at the introduction. To a certain extent, the narrator also supplements or varies his explicit characterization on these renewed introductions.[16] Thus, the youth and beauty of Callirhoe and Chaireas are often referred to again, but at the same time the picture is supplied with new traits, belonging to their intellectual or moral qualities: of Chaireas μεγαλόφρων (I, 1, 8), οἷα δὴ καὶ φύσεως ἀγαθῆς καὶ παιδείας οὐκ ἀπρονόητος (VII, 2, 5), of Callirhoe φρονήματος πλήρης (I, 3, 6), οἷα δὲ γυνὴ πεπαιδευμένη καὶ φρενήρης (VI, 5, 8; cfr. VII, 6, 5). For Theron, the keyword πανοῦργος ("clever, smart") in the introduction is repeated on three later occasions,[17] twice varied with δεινός (I, 9, 6; 13, 2), while the influential position and the loyalty are the qualities repeatedly referred to in the case of the eunuch, Artaxates (V, 2, 2; VI, 2, 2; 3, 1; cfr. VI, 4, 8), and so on.

The character who is most often subjected to repeated or supplementary judgements — and here I count also those in direct speech, partly self-appreciations — is Dionysios. The three main categories mentioned already on his introduction — παιδεία, πλοῦτος, and γένος — are referred to again eight times, three times, and once, respectively. Gradually, new   553
main characteristics are added, such as ἀρετή, φιλανθρωπία, and δόξα, and also more specific ones: φιλογύναιος, φρόνιμος, χρηστός καὶ δίκαιος, and several others. His social position (ὁ πρῶτος τῆς Ἰωνίας) is likewise

[15] Cfr. the still more articulated identification of Rhodogoune in VII, 5, 5, repeating facts from V, 3, 4–9.

[16] See Helms, pp. 46 and 68.

[17] I, 13, 2; III, 3, 12; 3,17. Helms, by basing his study on Blake's English translation of the romance (Ann Arbor 1939) and not directly on the Greek text, has been led to adduce the instances in I, 7,1; III, 3, 12, and 3, 17 as evidence under the heading "He (sc. Theron) is a rascal" (pp. 89 f.), but that in I, 13, 2 under "He is shrewd" (p. 90). Helms's approach to the text via a translation, though questionable on grounds of principle, is seldom any real disadvantage in the case of Chariton, thanks to this romance's emphasis on *indirect* character revelation (in speech and action); only the direct statements of character traits, like the present ones, are liable to occasional misrepresentation by not being classified according to their original Greek wording.

impressed upon the reader (cfr. the occasional modification in II, 5, 4: Μιλησίων πρῶτος, σχεδὸν δὲ καὶ τῆς ὅλης Ἰωνίας), whereas his outward appearance is described only once (II, 5, 2) after the snapshot provided when he first appears in the action (quoted in the preceding section). It is important to note that also the characteristics supplied later on, like those given at the first introductions of the various characters, are *functionally* motivated; there is always an organic reason for mentioning a certain characteristic in a certain situation. The epithets are thus not mechanically attached once and for all to the persons, but the repetition or supplementation of the explicit characterization is closely dependent on the consistency and variation in the skilled indirect character portrayal.

* * *

I mentioned above that the identification of the characters showed differences as between the direct (or indirect) speech and the narrative proper: also when the reader's need of additional identificatory elements was reasonably satisfied and the character well established, such elements would occur as organically motivated by the fictitious situation in which the person was mentioned. We have also seen that some of the characters are sometimes identified in the narrative by name only, sometimes by title only. The most important cases are the Great King, who is called βασιλεύς much more often than by his name Artaxerxes,[18] the queen, who is called Stateira about as often as by the title, and Artaxates, who is more often referred to as ὁ εὐνοῦχος than by name. Furthermore, ὁ Αἰγύπτιος is mentioned a few times as (ὁ) βασιλεύς. I proceed to the direct speech and the more varied appellations used there, both when the person in question is addressed and when he is just mentioned. The Great King is thus some times called δεσπότης, the queen δέσποινα, and words for different kinds of relationship — γυνή, ἀνήρ, πατήρ, μήτηρ, etc. — are naturally used with reference to these two, to Chaireas and Callirhoe, and so on. Also more temporary roles give occasion to special appellations, as when the Great King is called ὁ δικαστής (V, 5, 3 etc.) or ὁ ἐχθρός (VII, 2, 4). The question to be discussed here is whether this use is transferred from its natural occurrence in the direct speech to apply also to the third-person narrative; in other words, whether a restricted *narrative perspective* (point of view) is observable to any extent outside the direct speech.

---

[18] See my *Narrative Technique* (above, n. 3), p. 145, n. 1.

As usual, Dionysios provides the most complete illustrative material. By his subordinates (Leonas, Phocas, Plangon, and, at the beginning, Callirhoe), he is regularly addressed as "δέσποτα" or "κύριε" ("Διονύσιε" only by Callirhoe in II, 5, 11, by Mithridates, by Artaxerxes, and in addressing himself); the same words are used mostly also for *mentions* in direct speech (exceptions: I, 13, 4; II, 2, 5; and others). Dionysios himself refers to the psychological implications of these appellations in ordering his servant to bring some food to Callirhoe from his table, on the day when he has met with his new slave and fallen in love with her: "μὴ εἴπῃ δὲ 'παρὰ τοῦ κυρίου' ἀλλὰ 'παρὰ Διονυσίου'" (II, 4, 2; cfr. 6, 5 "βλέπε μὴ δεσπότην εἴπῃς"). In the indirect reproduction of speech and thoughts, δεσπότης is likewise more common than the name: I, 13, 1 Λεωνᾶς δὲ ἐκέλευσε περιμένειν αὐτὸν περὶ τὴν θεραπείαν τοῦ δεσπότου πρῶτον ⟨γενόμενον⟩.[19] Outside of this immediate dependency, the picture is different. The viewpoint shifts quite freely between the participants, and no one is viewed through the eyes of another more than very occasionally.[20] Thus, when Dionysios is in close contact with some of his subordinates (in I, 12–III), the term δεσπότης is never used as the subject of a clause (except in a passive construction in III, 1, 3); when he acts himself, he is consequently seen directly, without intermediaries, and identified as the reader knows him, that is, as (ὁ) Διονύσιος simply. An intermediary position is taken by the clauses in which he is the object of some action performed by a subordinate: II, 1, 1 εὗρε δὲ (sc. ὁ Λεωνᾶς) ἔτι κατακείμενον τὸν Διονύσιον and II, 1, 7 ἀπῆλθε πρὸς τὸν δεσπότην. In such cases, there seems to be a free choice between the two principal possibilities; the subordination of the whole clause under the intention (thought etc.) of the subject is accordingly more or less pronounced. A mere striving for stylistic variation often seems to account for the change between the possible wordings (see, for instance, in III, 9, 10–11, immediately before and after the quotation of Phocas's utterance.)[21]

555

---

[19] Thus also in II, 1,1; 1, 6; 1, 9; 4, 9; 7, 4. The name in III, 7, 1; 7, 2; 9, 6.

[20] See the reference above, n. 3.

[21] The striving for variation occasionally leads to some confusion, esp. in the case of anonymous secondary characters, as when ἡ ζάκορος (III, 6, 4 and 6, 6) re-appears as ἡ ἱέρεια, ἡ πρεσβῦτις, ἡ γραῦς, and again ἡ ἱέρεια (III, 9, 1–4). Further instances in I, 4, 1–8; IV 2, 2–8; VIII, 8, 2. F. Zimmermann (loc. cit. above, n. 14) calls attention to the various titles applied to Mithridates (σατράπης, ὕπαρχος, ἔπαρχος, στρατηγός) and comments: "Die Variation des Ausdrucks ist eines der Stilprinzipien unseres Autors, die er offenbar Thukydides abgelauscht hat".

Similarly, the name Callirhoe is used in the narrative in the scene of the first meeting with Dionysios (II, 3, 5–8); when she is no longer physically present but is only lingering in the minds of Dionysios and Leonas, and in their speech (II, 4), there is a quite consistent use of other appellations, such as ἡ γυνή, ἡ ξένη, or ἡ δούλη. Not until after the occasion when Callirhoe is formally introduced to Dionysios does the *name* begin to occur in the corresponding positions (II, 5, 8 etc.). This subtly modulated choice of appellations gives to Chariton's narrative a dimension which is missing in the "flat" narrative style of, for instance, Xenophon Ephesius. In addition, it is possible, as Zimmermann has shown,[22] to trace the development of Dionysios' attitude towards Callirhoe precisely through the scale of the appellations which the author makes him apply to her in his direct speech, from νεώνητος and δούλη through ἡ ἄνθρωπος to γυνή.

556   To sum up, the direct speech shows a quite consistent change in the appellations applied to the characters according to the person speaking, the situation in which the utterance occurs, and, to a certain extent, the stage of development in the psychological relations between speaker and character mentioned or addressed. Chariton's own observation of these matters emerges clearly from the passages quoted above (II, 4, 2 and 6, 5). The indirect speech shows about the same scale of variations (though the material is less rich and thus only some of the variants occur there), and this use may be transferred also to cases in which a person is mentioned as the object of another person's doings — he is, so to say, seen for a moment through this other person's eyes. This is quite exceptional, however, and is restricted to the position of grammatical object; as the subject of the clause, a character is always mentioned with a neutral appellation which identifies him to the reader without expressing any nuance specific to the temporary surroundings. This is, in a small but significant detail, the consequence of the application of the "author's point of view",[23] which establishes a direct contact between narrator and audience. It provides the basis for a functional system of identification in the narrative frame, whereas the subtler nuances are saved for mentions within the direct or indirect reproduction of the characters' thoughts and speeches.

---

[22] "Kallirhoes Verkauf durch Theron: Eine juristisch-philologische Betrachtung zu Chariton" (*Aus der Byzantinistischen Arbeit der Deutschen Demokratischen Republik* 1, Berlin 1957, pp. 72–81), p. 81.

[23] See my *Narrative Technique* (above, n. 3), pp. 112–116.

4

Orality, Literacy, and the "Readership"
of the Early Greek Novel

[originally published in Roy Eriksen (ed.), *Contexts of Pre-Novel Narrative. The European Tradition*, Berlin, Mouton de Gruyter, 1994 (Approaches to Semiotics 114), 47–81.]

The texts I propose to discuss are the ancient Greek novels of love, travel and adventure — also labelled "the ideal Greek novel". This is a genre which presumably originated in the late hellenistic period and flourished in the first two or three centuries of the Roman empire.[1] I will concentrate on the early, "non-sophistic" type of novel and, most of the time, leave out of account the later, more well-known "sophistic" specimens, Longus' *Daphnis and Chloe*, Achilles Tatius' *Leucippe and Clitophon*, and Heliodorus' *Aethiopica*.

The earliest extant Greek novel is Chariton's *Callirhoe*, dated some time around the beginning of our era, which stands out as the first novel in the western tradition. It is a sentimental love story, set within a historical frame (Hägg 1987) and exhibiting the elements that were to become stock motifs of the genre: youth and beauty, love and jealousy, separation, search and reunion, apparent death, pirates, slavery, erotic rivalry. But this is a more serious and subtle work of literature than the enumeration of motifs might indicate. The author is more concerned with the psychology of the characters than with the external events; and the ideals propagated are chastity, courage, and humanity. The stylistic level is above what might perhaps be expected with a knowledge of modern "trivial" literature.

The second work to be included in my discussion, the *Ephesiaca* by Xenophon of Ephesus, belongs to the second century AD. It comes closer to common expectations of the genre, with its simple style and

---

[1] For general introductions to the genre, see Hägg (1983) and Holzberg (1986). All the principal texts, as well as most of the fragments, are now available in authoritative and readable English translations, in B.P. Reardon (ed., 1989). — My quotations of the Greek text of Chariton and Xenophon of Ephesus are (with a few minor divergences) from the editions of Blake (1938) and Papanikolaou (1973b), respectively; my translations quote, or are based on, those contained in Reardon's collection. [Manuscript completed in February, 1991.]

breathless succession of violent events set on various locations around the Mediterranean. Many scholars regard the transmitted version as an abbreviation of an originally larger and more elaborated work;[2] I doubt that this is the case and will treat the novel, with its obvious short-comings as a literary work, as a genuine (though late)[3] example of the early type of Greek novel.

Around the two surviving "non-sophistic" novels of Chariton and Xenophon there exist a small number of papyrus fragments of other, presumably early novels. They will also be brought into the discussion, but mostly as a group, since they are too short to provide individual answers to the kind of questions put in the present paper. The lost Greek original of the Latin *Historia Apollonii regis Tyri* would also rank among the "non-sophistic" novels, of the less accomplished, Xenophon-of-Ephesus type, though its exact nature can of course only be divined.

The questions to be asked concern orality and literacy, from a particular point of view. These are concepts which have been much discussed in classical studies of the last decades, starting with Eric Havelock's *Preface to Plato* (1963).[4] But that discussion — as distinct from the discussion of literacy versus illiteracy, recently magisterially resumed by William V. Harris (1989) — concentrates mostly on the archaic and (early) classical periods, whereas the texts to be discussed here belong to the late hellenistic and early imperial periods, half a millennium later. Still, the

---

[2] The case for abbreviation was made by Bürger (1892); my own doubts are explained in detail in Hägg (1966) [published here as no. **6**], with additional reasons given in Hägg (1983: 21). Further arguments against the abbreviation theory have been adduced by Ruiz Montero (1982; 1988: 156–160); cf. also Anderson (1984: 148, 150; 1989: 126 f.) and Treu (1989: 193).

[3] Specimens of the non-sophistic and the sophistic type of novel may thus overlap in time; that is why I prefer the term "non-sophistic" to "presophistic". But Xenophon, with his Atticizing linguistic veneer, is anyway no pure representative of the non-sophistic type.

[4] Most of Havelock's subsequent works are now conveniently collected in *The literate revolution in Greece and its cultural consequences* (1982), and his achievement summed up by himself in *The muse learns to write* (1986). For an informed and balanced discussion of the problems involved, see Andersen (1987; 1989); cf. also the pertinent remarks in Thomas (1990: 15–34). There is a good bibliography in Detienne (ed., 1988: 525–538). My (necessarily incomplete) probings into the abundant literature on literacy and orality from a comparative, anthropological viewpoint have revealed little of direct relevance to the type of problem I discuss here. As Finnegan (1988: 160) puts it, "Amidst all the speculation about consequences of literacy, why are there so few studies which investigate the consequences of orality, or of the loss of literacy, *or of a choice to use one rather than another?*" (my italics).

concepts are useful for the present purpose, and some of the insights reached in that discussion are important, I think, for the understanding of the later cultural situation, as well.

This does not mean that I intend to revive, or support with new arguments, the theories put forward by some earlier scholars that the ideal Greek novel — as a genre — had an oral origin. Reinhold Merkelbach, in an appendix to his famous study *Roman und Mysterium* (1962: 333–340 = [1984]), suggested that the surviving ancient novels — which he regarded as covertly religious texts — were the direct successors of oral miracle stories, so-called "aretalogies", used in the Graeco-Oriental mystery cults.[5] He called attention to a number of stereotyped phrases frequently repeated in some of the novels, especially in the *Ephesiaca*, which he viewed as the equivalents of epic formulas. While these recurring phrases may indeed indicate some connection with orality — and there will be occasion to return to them below — Merkelbach's specific explanation is hardly convincing; on any account, it presupposes that one also accepts his general theory that the genre has its roots in religion, the extant novels (except that of Chariton) being actual *Mysterientexte*.

I am also rather hesitant about the conclusions reached by Alex Scobie in an otherwise important study, "Oral literature, storytelling, and the novel in the Graeco-Roman world" (Scobie 1983: 1–73). He suggested that professional, itinerant story-tellers, *fabulatores* or profane *aretalogoi*, played a role in the early stages of the novelistic genre. But the evidence for their activities is scarce, and there is nothing to indicate that long and complex structures such as the novels were at any time on their repertoire. It is quite another matter that stories, story patterns, and modes of narration may have been taken over by the novelists from such performances.

Rather than having any kind of oral origin as a genre, the ideal Greek novel in my opinion is the typical product of a literate society. The long coexistence and reciprocity of orality and literacy in the archaic and classical periods had in the hellenistic age yielded to a more "bookish" culture[6] — at least as far as the *production* of literature is concerned. Cal-

49

---

[5] "[W]ie im Epos, Lyrik und Drama müssen mündliche Ursprünge angenommen werden, die sich erst später zur 'Literatur' entwickelten" (Merkelbach 1962: 333). Merkelbach has recently returned to the issue in a conference paper, which I know only through the published abstract (Merkelbach 1990).

[6] The importance of books as carriers of uniform Greek *paideia* to all parts of the hellenistic world is well described by Easterling (1985: 23–25).

limachus and the other poets figuring round the Alexandrian *Mouseion* are the early-hellenistic signs of this attitude: they are librarians writing books. The novel signifies much the same, though on another level, in the late hellenistic period. The author of *Callirhoe* is the secretary of a rhetorician. And the novels are, so to speak, second-generation *books*: books which primarily relate to earlier books, besides presumably allowing influx from contemporary oral sources.

In the first place, this intertextuality[7] is evident within the genre: Xenophon of Ephesus — with limited success, it is true — reuses elements of Chariton's novel in his own; and the sophistic novels without restraint borrow building-blocks from their simpler predecessors, although sometimes embellishing them almost beyond recognition. As regards the classicism which the novels exhibit to varying degrees, it is mostly directed towards literary texts: Homer, Herodotus, Thucydides, Xenophon. Thus, Chariton does not enter his classical historical setting by way of local tradition or his own imagination, but primarily through Thucydides and Xenophon, imitating also the historiographical style of his models.

Chariton's art of quotation is indicative of his attitude.[8] By a kind of collage technique, he frequently incorporates verses from Homer into his narrative. He reuses a famous line from Demosthenes' speech *On the crown* (1.3.1 = *De Cor.* 169), and he tacitly borrows a short passage from Xenophon's *Cyropaedia* (6.4.3):

> Char. 5.2.4: ... λανθάνειν μὲν ἐπειρᾶτο, ἐλείβετο δὲ αὐτοῦ τὰ δάκρυα κατὰ τῶν παρειῶν.
>
> "For all his efforts to avoid notice, tears ran down his cheeks."

While the Homeric quotations might be recollections from school, items like the verbatim quotation (only with change of gender) from the *Cyropaedia* (and there are more examples)[9] show the author writing with another book in front of him — physically or mentally.

Thus, even the earliest extant Greek novel is a pure desk product, the produce of a typically literate environment. But does that necessarily mean that the readership of the novels was restricted to that same cultural

---

[7] The various functions of intertextuality in the ancient novels are distinguished by Fusillo (1990).

[8] For his quotations and allusions, see Papanikolaou (1973a: 13–24) and Bowie (in press [1994]).

[9] See Papanikolaou (1973a: 20).

context? For whom was the novel created? These questions lead us on to   50
Ben Edwin Perry's theory that the emergence of the ideal Greek novel
should be seen in connection with the spreading of literacy in the hellenistic age. Perry (1967: 84, 174 f. *et passim*) draws the parallel with the
rise of the modern novel in eighteenth-century England, which satisfied
the needs of new groups of readers. "It is only in response to a continuing popular demand, or to one that is fostered by a numerous group or
class of persons with common interests, that the more important and
enduring literary forms, such as romance and tragedy, have been created"
(Perry 1967: 12). They do not come into existence by a combination of
existing genres, and they do certainly not start as exercises of the school
room: these had been the two explanations developed in Erwin Rohde's
famous *Der griechische Roman und seine Vorläufer* of 1876. Nor do they develop gradually and automatically from another genre: Eduard Schwartz
(1896) saw the novel as the continuation of hellenistic historiography,
and had many followers. No, says Perry (1967: 387), "new literary forms
are willfully created by individual writers in accordance with a positive
artistic purpose or ideal"; they are prompted by an actual demand which,
in turn, is the result of a new sociocultural situation.

In the hellenistic world, that new situation was the breakdown of
the classical *polis* society and the emergence of a cosmopolitan, big-city
culture. The old community of values, of which epic and drama were
the exponents and propagators, had been replaced by a multitude of
conflicting desires and centrifugal tendencies. The individual felt isolated and at a loss. The ideal novel, Bryan Reardon (1971) explains, is
the *myth* of late Hellenism: the lonely traveller in search for his beloved,
in search for a meaning in his life. What the mystery cults provided for
the masses and moral philosophy for the elite, the novel took care of
within the literary system.

This Perry-Reardon view of the general sociocultural and psychological background for the emergence of the new genre has been widely
accepted, while the more limited and precise question of identifying the
early novel's actual readership has remained an object of debate. Notably,
Perry's equation with the rise of the modern novel has been rejected: there
existed no literate middle class, or no middle class at all, in hellenistic
society, it is correctly pointed out; so we have to define more carefully
who these new readers "demanding" the new genre really were. Rather
than searching in the middle strata of society we should probably, it has
been suggested, look for the new readers close to the top: among people

in the professions, administration, and trade; among the *nouveaux riches*; and, in particular, among the women at the same next-to-the-elite level of society, who also drew the benefits of the spread of literacy in the hellenistic age.[10] And we should not, misled by modern analogies, look for tens of thousands of new readers; a substantial new group of readers, sufficient for the creation of a new genre, is necessarily something much more modest in scale in late-hellenistic Asia Minor or Egypt than in eighteenth-century England.

The last few years, however, have witnessed a massive frontal attack on the very corner-stone of the Perry-Reardon construction, the alleged "popularity" of the genre, the idea of new readers "demanding" a new genre. Berber Wesseling (1988: 76) concludes: "The intended audience … is probably the intellectuals in the first place but not exclusively." Kurt Treu (1989: 197) speaks of the novel as "insgesamt eine voraussetzungsreiche und anspruchsvolle Lektüre, die sich an entsprechend vorgebildete und interessierte Leser wandte." Susan Stephens (1990 and in press [1994]), scrutinizing the papyrological remains of novels, finds that "the novels were not 'popular' with the denizens of Greco-Roman Egypt" and is not willing to "construct another set of readers for the ancient novels" than the same "high culture" reading public which also read (and owned) Thucydides. Ewen Bowie (1990: 151, and in press [1994]), basing his argument primarily on the learned apparatus of allusions and the rhetorical style already to be found in Chariton, reaches the conclusion that the novelists "expected their readers to be of the same sort as those of other serious literature." William Harris's (1989: 227 f.) brief verdict well summarizes the new orthodoxy: "… the notion that [the Greek romance] was truly popular collides with two clear facts: the refined sophistication of the authors' Greek, and the relatively small number of papyrus fragments that survive. We should rather see the romance as the light reading of a limited public possessing a real degree of education."

Thus, the novel again stands as an accidental (or at least unexplained) creation, just an extra offer to those few who already enjoyed reading Thucydides, Poseidonius, Plutarch or Aristeides. It does not seem, how-

---

[10] On women and literacy in the hellenistic period, see the studies of Pomeroy (1977; 1984: xii, 59–72, 117–121), who, however, does not take the novel into consideration (except for mentioning it in passing, 1984: 80). Cole's study (1981) provides a good overview of female literacy and its limitations, also in the hellenistic period. Harris (1989), too, pays ample attention to "women's literacy", see Index s.v. and, in addition, p. 141.

ever, that those who have recently denied the "popularity" (in this sense) of the genre have seriously considered this consequence.[11] Bowie (1990: 150, and in press [1994]), for instance, searching for possible reasons why scholars have imagined the readers of the novels as "different" from those who read Plutarch and the historians or attended lectures of philosophers and sophists, finds the following four: the genre's sentimental treatment of love, the novels' (alleged) low quality, the lack of an ancient name for the genre, and the silence of other ancient authors with regard to novels. The crucial reason — that the new potential readership explains the very emergence of the genre — is not on the list. The earlier theories about the genre's origins, it is true, demanded no new readers: if the ideal novel was a combination of erotic poetry and travel romance (Rohde) or the continuation of historiography (Schwartz), it was of course meant for the same kind of readers as those earlier genres; if it was created in a rhetorical school context, it was primarily intended for people having that kind of higher education, the connoisseurs of sophistic elegance. But the sociocultural explanation is a different case: if the arguments put forward by Wesseling, Treu, Stephens and Bowie should be valid for the early novel — and not only for the three "sophistic" specimens, whose sophistic readership can never have been in serious doubt — we are back to square one, as far as the question of "origins" of the Greek novel is concerned.

52

The following discussion will start as a scrutiny of the principal arguments of Bowie and Stephens[12] and, to a lesser extent, those of Wesseling and Treu (who are, on the whole, more cautious in their conclusions). Yet its scope and application will be wider than this outer form may

---

[11] Stephens (in press [1994]) is an exception; her introductory discussion (ms., pp. 15) shows that she is clearly aware of the problem, although she is unable to produce a convincing alternative to the Perry-Reardon construction (which she chooses to attack only indirectly, by way of some quotations from the present writer's introduction to the genre, Hägg: 1983).

[12] I am greatly indebted to Ewen Bowie (Oxford) and Susan Stephens (Stanford) for letting me read and quote from their Dartmouth papers in advance of publication. (I refer to them as "in press", often without page numbers, whereas quotations from the abstracts are identified by year (1990) and page number.) Since my criticism below of these papers might lead readers to think otherwise, I wish to state at the outset that I regard both papers as important contributions to the topic under discussion, with justified criticism of some of the dimmer arguments sometimes used to support the "popularity" of the Greek novel and with interesting new material. My chief quarrel is with their conclusions (which are largely *ex silentio*).

signal: it is meant to be a critical examination of the various criteria one can — or cannot — use in the search for the readership of early fiction generally, in periods for which most of the "normal" sources for literary sociological studies, such as sales figures, library statistics and readers polls, are missing.[13]

Bowie (in press [1994]) begins by making the important distinction between intended and actual readership and by admitting that ideally each of the surviving novels should be treated independently, before any general theory concerning the "overall readership" can be reached. But he immediately gives in on both these points and does not systematically sustain even the distinction between "non-sophistic" and "sophistic" novels (though he seems to acknowledge that it is possible to discern two such groups).[14] Most of his general conclusions are, in fact, based on evidence concerning the three sophistic novels — with the predictable result that the readers of "the novel" turn out to have been identical with those who read other kinds of classical or classicizing literature. Bowie thus fails to address, in a consistent way, the only question really subjected to diverging opinions: Who read the *early* novels (surviving or lost), or for what kind of readers was the genre *originally created*?[15] It is true that due to the scarcity of evidence for the genre's formative period, such a discussion necessarily involves more speculation than Bowie is generally prepared to allow. But what little there is, should be given its proper weight (rather than be allowed to be neutralized by evidence relating to the sophistic specimens) and be tested against various hypothetical frameworks. For the only certain thing is that our knowledge of this genre's first stage is

53

---

[13] Treu (1989: 178 f.) provides a good overview of the "Quellenlage" for the ancient novel in this respect.

[14] The difference in language between Chariton and Xenophon of Ephesus, on the one hand, and Achilles Tatius and Heliodorus, on the other, is emphasized by Zanetto (1990), who concludes that difference in the intended audience (the "realtà del mercato") — rather than the individual writer's cultural context — is the real explanation.

[15] Stephens (in press [1994]) similarly confuses the issue. E.g., she declares that scholars who assume a qualitatively different reading public for the novel than for history or philosophy are creating an ideal ancient reader "whom we would be hard-pressed to find today — someone who happily reads Gibbon or Nietzsche, but eschews *Lolita* or *Tristam Shandy*" (ms., p. 2) [p. 406]. Still allowing for considerable rhetorical exaggeration, it must be authors like Longus and Achilles Tatius she puts on a level with Nabokov and Sterne, and not a Xenophon of Ephesus (we can easily find readers who happily read Foucault but eschew *Angélique et le pirate*). Her remark is thus peculiarly irrelevant for the real issue. On the readership of the sophistic novel, cf. Hägg (1983: 107 f.).

utterly fragmentary, and that there *was* more than we *have*. Our gravest mistake would be to construct a building using only the few scattered remains — and believe the result to be historically true.[16]

For the present purpose, it will suffice to discuss those points in Bowie's argument where he relies, to any significant extent, on evidence relating to the early novels. The most important one, already mentioned above, concerns the amount and range of classical quotations and allusions in Chariton's *Callirhoe*. Chariton, says Bowie, therefore "required a well-read reader to appreciate [their] force".[17] Now, Chariton seems to stand more or less alone in this respect among the early novels, save for the fragmentarily preserved *Parthenope*. This fact is admitted, but not exploited, by Bowie. If the existence of a learned apparatus in Chariton is an argument in favour of learned readers, may not its absence in Xenophon of Ephesus — and, presumably, in *Ninus*, *Chione* and Iamblichus' *Babyloniaca* (and the Greek model for *Historia Apollonii*?) — indicate that those novels were intended for less educated readers[18] and, consequently, that the early novel at large was not primarily directed at the elite?

Yet, whether we consider Chariton an exception or not, the point about his allusions is an important one, as is also the point that his characters "deploy rhetoric in a way he surely expected his [well-educated] readers to admire". I have myself earlier concluded that Chariton "aimed at the educated classes of the hellenistic cities of Asia Minor" (Hägg 1983: 98), and Bowie agrees. But does that really exclude a wider circulation, either intended or actual? I would like to suggest that a novelist like Chariton may have had several different audiences in mind. One of them would obviously be his own equals, socially and culturally (cf. Treu 1989: 180 f.). These will have been able to respond to the novelist's quotations

---

[16] Bowie's (in press [1994]) tentative limitation of the genre to AD 60–230 is such a building. It already starts collapsing when he reaches Petronius who, already in the 60s, "at least knew some form of the Greek novel" — and found the genre well-known and important enough to be worthy of a parody. Papyrus dates should not be allowed to function as *termini ante quos non*: it is true that there is no papyrus of Chariton antedating the second century A.D. — but the same applies to Aeschines, Aristophanes, Herodas, Sappho, and many other classical and hellenistic authors (according to Table vii in Willis 1968: 223–235, based on Pack's second edition; reserve must consequently be made for any papyri published after April 1964).

[17] Treu (1989: 185 f.) makes the same point.

[18] Similarly Wesseling (1988: 76).

and allusions in an appropriate way, and so will of course also his superiors in education and sophistication (though they might have found his art and ethos too naive, as Petronius presumably did). Simultaneously, however, he may have envisaged as a potential — and larger — audience people a step or two further down the sociocultural ladder.[19]

Would these less educated readers then not be more or less excluded by the many quotations and allusions, allegedly "requiring" a certain degree of education? To my mind, this is a modern misconception: that one should be expected, and oneself expect, to understand all — or else abstain.[20] Some parallels from antiquity and the middle ages may be helpful. In the middle ages, Christian pictorial art sometimes operated on two levels: there was a simple story or message, for all to understand; and there was a secret code for the few, details in the picture which were truly meaningful only to the initiated, and textual quotations for the literate. In classical Athens, tragic drama was watched by the whole citizenship, though the surviving texts present us with many subtleties which only the intellectual elite will have fully appreciated. The suspense and the emotional impact were there for all to experience, the sophisticated thought and form for the delight of the few.[21] Icelandic family sagas likewise, it has been plausibly argued, directed themselves to at least two different audiences, a reading public and an oral public, distinguished also by their degree of education: the former a small literate subgroup, including clerics, some wealthier people, and other saga writers (of which there were quite a few), the latter a large and socially mixed body of listeners to recitals, at farms and elsewhere.[22] In none of these cases are there good reasons to maintain that the intended audience was only, or even foremost, the few who were able to grasp the more sophisticated message. On the contrary, in terms of social function it

[19] Wesseling (1988: 75 f.) touches on this possibility, but does not develop the thought; remarkably enough, she seems more positive to allowing a "multilevel" audience in the case of the sophistic novels.

[20] Stephens (in press [1994]) also falls into this pit (ms., p. 4), though castigating others for not recognizing "the cultural biases and the *a priori* assumptions that we automatically bring to our project" (ms., p. 1). Besides, her reference, in n. 11, to Bartsch (1989) shows that again the issue is blurred by adducing evidence from the sophistic novels to support an allegedly general conclusion ("the novelists themselves" — who, precisely?).

[21] Cf. Stanford (1983), Heath (1987), and, in particular, des Bouvrie (1990).

[22] See Clover (1982: 188–204: "The Two Audiences", esp. 199–202) and (1985: 271, 282 f., with further refs.). Cf. also Foote (1974: 17 f.).

was the larger audience that mattered most; while, on the other hand, each individual artist will have been especially sensitive to the reception among his intellectual peers and fellow craftsmen. The former consideration guarantees a certain standard of general communicability, the latter encourages artistic subtlety.

These parallels suggest that it may not have been a *condition* for a reader of *Callirhoe* to be well-educated — though it would of course have constituted a definite advantage, because it would give fuller satisfaction (and, in the case of the highly educated, an alibi for reading light literature?). The narrative suspense, the emotional impact, the escapist function were there for all, the rhetorical and classicizing embellishment for some. Missing a subtle allusion hurts nobody; how many actual readers of Longus, for instance, through the centuries have noticed the numerous hidden references to earlier poetry which learned modern scholars have hunted down?[23] The really important thing, if exclusiveness should be avoided, is that the narrative structure and the phraseology do not pose too heavy demands. In the sophistic novels these are likely to be a substantial hindrance for the less literate, in Chariton presumably not (though these things are of course extremely difficult for us to assess).

Naturally, there is no way of actually proving that Chariton did address himself to others than his equals, and that his comparatively simple style was a conscious choice for this purpose. But we may at least be permitted to doubt that readers who did not recognize passages from Demosthenes and Menander, or were unable to appreciate certain rhetorical niceties, are a priori to be excluded from either the intended or the actual readership of his novel.

Remaining for a while with the intended, rather than actual, readership, we should briefly consider the possibility that the "new" readers are not only — or not primarily — readers of other classes than the elite, but of the other sex: women. At least since Erwin Rohde (1876: 356), a female audience for the ideal novel has been a favoured hypothesis, of course originating in easy (and perhaps dangerous) parallels with the rise of the modern novel.[24] I agree with Bowie and Stephens that there is

55

---

[23] Cf. Hunter (1983: 59–83).

[24] On women's role not only as prospective readers, but also as writers of novels in the formative phase of the genre, see now the impressive study of Spencer (1986); cf. also her contribution below [Eriksen, *Contexts of Pre-Novel Narrative*, 1994], pp. 285–302.

little hard evidence for women as an actual reading public; but the same is true for male readers of the early novel, and still there must have been an audience. There *was* a spread of literacy in the hellenistic age, though the extent might easily be exaggerated (cf. Wesseling 1988, 69–71); and there *were* highly educated women, as Bowie's (in press [1994]) own meticulous inventory shows. Consequently, there were also others in between: women not out-standing in learning so as to receive notice, but sufficiently educated to read a novel. It is all a matter of probabilities, and how one assesses them. To me, the early novels' preoccupation with women — particularly evident in *Callirhoe* and *Parthenope* — and with psychology, sentiments and private life, remains the best indication that the genre had women as an important target group right from the start.[25] Bowie is of course right in pointing to New Comedy as a genre with similar characteristics in this respect; but what do we know about its original audience and its hellenistic or Roman reading public, that excludes the possibility that comedy too had a large female constituency? It might be more to the point to compare the novel with an earlier imaginative prose work, Xenophon's *Cyropaedia*. With its emphasis on politics and strategy and hunting, and with romanticism relegated to a subplot, it appears to me to cater for a male readership. It did not beget a "popular" genre; when such a thing arose some two or three hundred years later, the proportions of love and public affairs were radically different.[26]

I shall not dwell on the roles played by women in the novels; here is a recent careful study by Brigitte Egger (1988), who concludes that the heroines of the novels are described in a way which would make them suitable objects of identification for contemporary emancipated women:[27] "Es werden die realen Beschränkungen des weiblichen Lebens

[25] That there are sexual descriptions in Longus and Achilles Tatius which (presumably) were not aimed at women and which (presumably) their male guardians would not allow them to read (Bowie, in press [1994]), is irrelevant here. That the three sophistic novels were intended for a (primarily) male audiencc, has not (to my knowledge) been contested.

[26] Comparison with the rise of the English novel is illuminating: the prospect of female readers with their particular spheres of interest (home, family, emotions, "love and morality") had its influence on male and female writers alike and thus, in important respects, determined the shape of the new genre (cf. Spencer 1986: 6, 20 f., 32 f., 77 f.). Pomeroy (1984: 81) similarly states: "The preferences of women readers certainly influenced the literary form of the modern novel."

[27] Johne (1989: 155–159), in a similar review "zur Rolle der Frau in der Gesellschaft und im Roman", also stresses the identification aspect.

literarisch bestätigt, sogar noch stärker gefasst als in der zeitgenössigen
Wirklichkeit …; gleichzeitig wird durch die Illusion unbezwinglicher
emotionaler und sexueller Wirkung der Frau der Wunsch nach Einfluss
und Bestimmung umgelenkt und beschwichtigt." Just one aspect should
be briefly mentioned here: their literacy (cf. Egger 1988: 42 f.). They do
read and write, and if not novels (as some of their sisters in early modern
novels), at least letters.[28] And one of the heroines, Parthenope, is even
a highly educated woman,[29] if we are to believe the Persian eleventh-
century verse romance which is an important source for our knowledge
of this lost Greek novel: at the age of two, she started studying, at seven
"she became an astronomer and a dexterous scribe" (verses 28–30); and
education obviously continued through her teens (verses 34–35):

56

> When her father [Polycrates of Samos] examined her in arts,
> he found a key to eloquence and a treasure of virtue.
> In deliberation the cultured child
> became without need of the instruction of the learned.[30]

This piece of evidence now comes in addition to the well-known fact
that Antonius Diogenes seems to have dedicated his novel to a woman
"fond of learning", his sister Isidora.[31]

So much, at this stage, for the intended readers. What means do
we have to identify the *actual* readers of the early novels? One source,
which is important for other ancient genres, is conspicuously missing:
the testimonia in other literature. There is no mention at all of the ideal
Greek novel, either in works of literary criticism or, even in passing, in

---

[28] In Chariton, the heroine both reads and — *sua manu* — writes letters (8.4.4–7 "she
took a writing tablet and wrote the following: …", 8.5.13 "When [Dionysius] recognized
Callirhoe's handwriting …"; cf. also 4.4.6–5.1). In Xenophon of Ephesus, private notes
exchanged between Habrocomes and Anthia's rival, Manto, play an important part
(2.5.1–5, 2.10.1; cf. also 1.12.2, 2.12.1 and 5.11.6–12.1). For the rich papyrus documentation
of women as letter writers in the hellenistic period, see Cole (1981: 234–236).

[29] It is of less consequence that Callirhoe in Chariton's novel (6.5.8) is described as πεπαιδευμένη; in the context, it means no more than "well-brought-up", as Reardon (in
Reardon, ed. 1989: 95) translates it.

[30] I quote this novel, Vēmiq and 'Adhrā by Abu'l-Qa-sim 'Unsurī, in the (so far unpublished) English translation of Bo Utas [now published as T. Hägg & B. Utas, *The Virgin
and her Lover: Fragments of an Ancient Greek Novel and a Persian Epic Poem*, Leiden 2003];
see further Utas (1984–86) and Hägg (1985) [published here as no. 9].

[31] Photius, *Bibl.* 111a. Cf. Bowie (in press [1994], ms., pp. 4 f.).

other writings, before AD 200 — i.e., in the first two or three hundred years of the genre's existence. Some remarks in Philostratus and Julian only tell us that novels were known to, and sometimes read by, intellectuals in the last centuries of the empire. *Pace* Bowie (in press [1994]), the fact that such references are missing in the earlier period — in Dio Chrysostomus, Plutarch and Lucian, for instance — remains a strong indication that the non-sophistic novel belonged to a different literary sphere from "serious" literature: they were certainly known to other writers, but not acknowledged.

The physical remains of novels, the papyrus fragments, are another potential way of getting information about their readership, at least as far as Egypt is concerned.[32] This is a material which, according to Stephens (in press, ms., p. 6), "in its chance selection and survival comes very close to a random sample, allowing us to examine the types and quantities, relatively speaking, of ancient reading matter before the winnowing effect of time, taste and classical scholarship".[*] If this holds true, comparison between the novel fragments and those of other types of Greek literature might be illuminating.[33] In Stephens' count, there are now 45 fragments of novels, dating from the first to the sixth centuries AD. Of these, four are of Chariton, six of Achilles Tatius, one of Heliodorus. The large majority belongs to novels which have not survived in a complete form. This is little in comparison not only with Homer (who, as the school author *par préférence*, is represented by well over 500 fragments), but also with lyric (161), tragedy (131) and New Comedy (63). Among

57

---

[32] We should remember that Egypt is probably periphery rather than centre, as far as the early novel is concerned; there is nothing to connect either *Callirhoe, Parthenope* or *Ninus* with that country — Asia Minor is the natural guess (at least for the first two).

[*] Quoted here according to Stephens' ms. (cf. n. 12); in her printed version of 1994, the whole passage is reformulated (p. 410): "Though they are now only a tiny sample of what the whole must have been, these papyrus fragments of abandoned or worn-out books, thus preserved, may in their sheer numbers serve as a kind of laboratory to study ancient literary tastes before the winnowing effects of time, taste, and classical scholarship."

[33] An important factor to take into account, however, when judging Stephens' statistical approach, is that papyri become numerous only one or two centuries after the putative emergence of the Greek novel; for the first century B.C., there are registered only 80 literary papyri in all, in the first century A.D. the number is 304, in the second century 956! (figures according to Willis 1968: 210, Table iii). What we assess, when counting papyri of *Callirhoe, Parthenope* and others, are *literate readers* in *Roman Egypt* (with emphasis on each word!) of early novels probably produced for a late hellenistic/early Roman audience in Asia Minor (cf. the preceding note).

classical prose authors, Demosthenes is to date represented by over 120 fragments, Thucydides by 75. The number of Old and New Testament texts between the second and the fourth century is 172.

On the basis of these and other figures, Stephens (in press [1994]) tries to prove two things at the same time: firstly, that the novels were not "popular", since the papyrus fragments of that genre are so comparatively few, and, secondly, that popularity cannot be measured by means of papyrus statistics. The latter demonstration is wholly convincing, which means that the former one necessarily fails.[34]

There is more of value and interest in Stephens' next effort to extract information from the novel papyri, namely, by examining their physical appearance: roll or codex, handwriting etc., again comparing with other kinds of literature. A few of the fragments have the look of expensive "coffee-table" books, others have belonged to simpler codexes. None — according to Stephens — betrays a really "popular" audience, as do contemporary fragments of the New Testament; on the contrary, they are "indistinguishable" from fragments of Sappho, Thucydides, Demosthenes and Plato. Nor is the proportion of codexes (instead of rolls, presumably the more prestigious form) in her opinion so great as to warrant the conclusion that the novel is less "serious" than other kinds of profane Greek literature.

This all means an important corrective from the side of a papyrologist to what earlier scholars, including the present writer, have thought possible to infer from the novel papyri.[35] But the significance for our main issue is perhaps not so great as Stephens seems to believe. The expensive

---

[34] E.g., she remarks (ms., p. 7) [p. 411]: "With [Thucydides] the fiction of popularity is difficult to maintain — Thucydides' Greek can never have been easy to read, nor was he, as Homer was, studied and copied in the grammar schools … yet on a statistical basis, Thucydides seems to have been among the most widely read prose writers in the ancient world."

[35] Treu, also a papyrus expert, conducts a similar investigation (1989: 189–192) and reaches similar conclusions. He sees no reason, however, even on the basis of the papyrus evidence, to restrict novel reading to the cultural elite: "Zu betonen ist, daß die Papyri die Lektüre der Romane für die mittlere Städte bezeugen und damit — so muß man annehmen — in Kreisen einer mittleren Bildungshöhe" (190). Treu (190 f.) also differs somewhat from Stephens in his assessment of the relative quality of the novel papyri: on a scale from luxurious to simple manuscripts, they belong in the middle and bottom part. The ostracon (Bodl. 2175) with a passage of *Parthenope* (which Stephens does not mention) is interpreted as "eines der seltenen direkten Zeugnisse für Wirkungen des Romans auf soziale Unterschichten" (192).

rolls no doubt indicate, as do also a couple of mosaics with novel motifs in a Syrian summer villa, that some of the well-to-do took a fancy to the novels, and paraded that fancy. But wealth and intellectuality do not necessarily go together. Rather than belonging to the intellectual elite, the owners of the summer villa and the buyers of the coffee-table editions of novels may have been members of the growing stratum of people working in the administration, in the professions, and in commerce. The less wealthy, or less ostentatious, among them may have been the owners or users of the more normal-looking papyrus material. With money and leisure literacy — as distinct from learning — entered this stratum of society, and it is probably here we find some of the first novel *readers* proper. Stephens' investigation does nothing to change this view.

On the other hand, it is hardly admissible to draw — as Stephens does — any firm conclusions from the absence in her material of such novel papyri as would betray a truly "popular" audience.[36] As I have suggested elsewhere (Hägg 1983: 93), it is probable that the further dissemination of the novels down the social scale, as far as it did take place, was primarily by means of recitals, within the household, among friends, or even publicly — i.e., the novel in such circumstances had an "audience" proper rather than a "readership".[37] I further suggested that scribes and secretaries — the colleagues of Chariton, the rhetorician's secretary — may have played a crucial role in this process. At any rate, literacy will have been very rare in the lower strata of society, and such literacy as is necessary to start reading for one's pleasure will have been almost non-existent. Hellenistic society, as we know it from Egypt, was primarily a "craft-literate" society:[38] writing was necessary for legal and commercial purposes and for communication, but — beyond writing one's name

[36] It is not only research on the novel that suffers from such philological one-eyedness, cf. Thomas (1990: 17); as she remarks, "illiterates tend lo leave no record".

[37] The ancient habit of reading books aloud, even in one's privacy, will no doubt have contributed to making the difference between private reading and recital less sharp than it is with silent private reading. Reading for oneself and for one's family/household will often have been more or less the same thing, or at least the one will easily have led to the other. For a critical review of the evidence for reading habits in antiquity, see Knox 1968; he states (p. 421) that "the normal way to read a literary text … was out loud, whether before an audience, in the company of friends or alone"; as regards letters and other documents, however, silent reading was nothing unusual.

[38] For the term, cf. Havelock (1986: 41, 65); in Harris's (1989: 7f.) terminology, it would correspond to "scribal literacy". Harris's "craftsman's literacy" (8, 146) is something different.

— it was mostly entrusted to professionals, to scribes; even those who did take care of the task themselves, were probably in most cases only little more than "semi-literate".[39] The intellectual elite, and the growing stratum of well-to-do who could afford a more advanced school education, still constituted a very small proportion of the population.[40] If the novel did spread below the top strata, it was consequently primarily by means which could leave no physical remains.[41]

External evidence, then, documents a reading public for the novel only among the comparatively well-to-do and comparatively well-educated. But this circumstance clearly does not allow us to *exclude* as a potential or actual audience either the intellectual elite (who may simply not have cared or wanted to mention their light reading) or a broader, more "popular" public, i.e., people who were less than fully literate, who would hardly read for their pleasure, and who could anyway not afford to buy books. It goes without saying that we are still moving, quantitatively speaking, in the upper strata of society.

Internal evidence makes the picture a good deal more detailed and colourful. Both form and substance of the novels themselves allow conclusions about the kind of readers the novelists expected or hoped for. I will concentrate mostly on form here,[42] with orality and literacy as

---

[39] "Semi-literates", in Harris's (1989: 5) definition, are "persons who can write slowly or not at all, and who can read without being able to read complex or very lengthy texts".

[40] Both Bowie (in press [1994]) and Stephens (in press [1994]) give more detailed resumés of what we know about literacy in hellenistic and Roman times; for a full-scale discussion of the matter, see now Harris (1989: esp. 139–146, 273–282). Stephens (in press [1994]) quotes Harris, p. 267: "the overall level of literacy is likely to have been below 15%", but that estimate in fact refers to Rome and Italy; for the Greek-speaking parts of the empire, no corresponding figure is ventured.

[41] Stephens (in press, ms., p. 9) [p. 413], mentions the possibility that the "slightly larger" lettering in some Old and New Testament papyri, as compared to non-Christian books, may have been intended to facilitate public reading. This is hardly anything that we should expect to find in novel papyri, even on my hypothesis. There is, after all, a difference between a holy text, meant to be recited at divine services, and a novel accidentally read aloud to, say, a household. It would have been interesting if Stephens had included in her investigation the papyri of the apocryphal apostle acts and similar "popular" Christian literature; they are potentially a more adequate object of comparison for the novels than the New Testament.

[42] Here I will have to reuse material already presented (in much greater detail) in my study of narrative technique in the novels (Hägg 1971); my excuses are that the debate has so far largely neglected that material and its potential importance for the question of readership, and that I now look upon it specifically from the orality/literacy viewpoint.

59

catchwords. But I begin by recapitulating some possible conclusions from contents and attitudes (leaving some of the more fanciful suggestions aside).

First we return to the women, from the present point of view. Women are the real heroes of the early novels: Callirhoe, Parthenope, Anthia. They are sympathetically drawn and altogether more alive than their pale husbands and lovers. A partly, some would say predominantly, female audience thus remains a fair assumption. It is also worth recalling that we have reasons to believe that two of the first novels known to us carried as their title only the name of the heroine: *Callirhoe, Parthenope*.[43]

Continuing with the internal criteria, some novels play mostly on sentimental strains, while others rely more on violence and adventure to capture their readers. This tells us something of the supposed taste of the prospective readers, but less about their sex or social position; that already some of the early novelists addressed a male rather than female audience, is however likely. One or two of the early novels want to share with their readers a nostalgic feeling for the classical period and its achievements in art and literature. As we have noted above, a certain amount of classical education is thus obviously taken for granted if the reader is fully to enjoy what is offered in these specimens of the genre.

To try to define, on the basis of contents and attitude, one particular group as the target for "the early novel", is thus impossible. The genre is not homogeneous from the start, nor will its public have been so.[44] The formal characteristics offer a similarly diversified picture of the expected audience. The historiographical style which Chariton adopts might give the impression that he directs himself to the same readership as the classical historians. But that style is more a coating than a mimesis in depth; one may compare the Doric-dialect flavouring of the choral odes of Attic drama. Anyone who reads a passage of Chariton after a passage of Thucydides will notice the fundamental difference.[45] The colouring is there for those who may relish it, but the intellectual effort needed for

---

[43] The fragments of *Ninus* do not support similar conclusions about Semiramis's role in that novel.

[44] Similarly Müller (1981: 394) and Reardon (ed., 1989: 10 f.).

[45] On Thucydides' key position in the progress from orality to literacy — as the first author clearly demanding a "Lesepublikum" 'reading audience' — see Andersen (1987: 43 f.). But of course this does not mean that all post-Thucydidean literature is of that kind.

the one is not needed for the other. The author wants to be inclusive, not exclusive.

Again, there are in the style and narrative technique of the early novels certain elements that seem to be typical of oral literature. To some extent, they may be explained by the mimetic attitude of the novelists: they imitate the style of classical authors like Herodotus and Xenophon, and these, in turn, preserved oral elements in their style. But this may not be the whole truth; we shall look closer at the evidence.

A typical feature is the frequent use of stereotyped linking phrases between the episodes: the preceding action is summarized in a clause with the particle μέν, the new action starts with a δέ clause:

> Char. 4.2.1 Καλλιρόη μὲν οὖν ἐν Μιλήτῳ Χαιρέαν ἔθαπτε, Χαιρέας δὲ   60
> ἐν Καρίᾳ δεδεμένος εἰργάζετο.
>
> So Callirhoe was burying Chaereas in Miletus while Chaereas was working in Caria in chains.

> Xen. Eph. 2.14.1 καὶ ἡ μὲν ἐν Ταρσῷ ἦν μετὰ Περιλάου, τὸν χρόνον ἀναμένουσα τοῦ γάμου· ὁ δὲ Ἁβροκόμης ᾔει τὴν ἐπὶ Κιλικίας ὁδόν· …
>
> So she found herself in Tarsus with Perilaus, awaiting the time for her marriage. Meanwhile Habrocomes was making for Cilicia …

Such phrases were in use already in the Homeric epics, and we also find them in Greek prose, from Herodotus on. Their function is to mark a caesura in the narrative flow, as does the beginning of a new section or chapter in modern printed texts, but still without really breaking the flow.[46] In addition, the retrospective summary in the μέν part is in itself important in oral communication, since the listener lacks the reader's opportunity to stop and look back himself if needed. In the δέ part of the linking phrase, which serves as a kind of heading for the following section, there are usually also identificatory and resumptive elements which remind the reader of the situation when he last left that thread of action, again without having to look back.[47] Maybe, the frequent use of this and other formulas of short-range repetition in a novel like that of Xenophon of Ephesus is not just a sign of the author's stereotyped

---

[46] The best treatment of the phenomenon is in Fränkel (1968: 83–85). Cf. also Immerwahr (1966: 58, 61), on Herodotus, and Hägg (1971: 314–316).

[47] For a detailed analysis of such linking phrases in Xenophon of Ephesus, in particular, see Hägg (1971), Ch. 4.

mind, as has been commonly taken for granted, but an indication that he addresses himself, in the first place, to an audience proper rather than a readership.[48]

The frequent use of detailed recapitulations of larger parts of the narrative is another characteristic of the early novels.[49] In Xenophon of Ephesus, they are mostly given in indirect speech, such as the following:

> Xen. Eph. 3.3.1 λέγει δὲ ὁ Ἀβροκόμης ὅτι Ἐφέσιος καὶ ὅτι ἠράσθη κόρης καὶ ὅτι ἔγημεν αὐτὴν καὶ τὰ μαντεύματα καὶ τὴν ἀποδημίαν καὶ τοὺς πειρατὰς καὶ τὸν Ἄψυρτον καὶ τὴν Μαντὼ καὶ τὰ δεσμὰ καὶ τὴν φυγὴν καὶ τὸν αἰπόλον καὶ τὴν μέχρι Κιλικίας ὁδόν.

> Habrocomes told him that he was an Ephesian and that he had fallen in love with a girl and married her; he mentioned the prophecies, the voyage, the pirates, Apsyrtus, Manto, his imprisonment, his flight, the goatherd, and the journey to Cilicia.

All these things have already been part of the narrative, but instead of writing simply: "Habrocomes told him of his background and adventures", the author obviously feels a need to remind his reader of each of the main points of the action. And this happens not just once or twice, but regularly — in various forms — through the text of this rather short novel.

Chariton's novel is also filled with retrospects and recapitulations of different kinds, with different kinds of surface motivation. A character may recapitulate in his mind all his former sufferings, or he may tell another character of his experiences:

> Char. 2.5.10 μόλις οὖν ἐκείνη τὰ καθ᾽ ἑαυτὴν ἤρξατο λέγειν· Ἑρμοκράτους εἰμὶ θυγάτηρ, τοῦ Συρακοσίων στρατηγοῦ. γενονένην δέ με ἄφωνον ἐξ αἰφνιδίου πτώματος ἔθαψαν οἱ γονεῖς πολυτελῶς. ἤνοιξαν τυμβωρύχοι τὸν τάφον· εὗρον κἀμὲ πάλιν ἐμπνέουσαν· ἤνεγκαν ἐνθάδε καὶ Λεωνᾷ με τούτῳ παρέδωκε Θήρων ἐπ᾽ ἐρημίας. πάντα εἰποῦσα μόνον Χαιρέαν ἐσίγησεν.

> So, reluctantly, Callirhoe began to tell her story. "I am the daughter of Hermocrates, the Syracusan general. I had a sudden fall, and lost

---

[48] For a similar interpretation of transitional phrases in medieval romances, see Crosby (1936: 106 f.).

[49] See Hägg (1971), Ch. 7, for a documentation of the abundance and variety of this kind of material in the early novels; I formulated my "oral hypothesis" for the first time on p. 332.

consciousness; and my parents gave me a costly funeral. Tomb robbers opened my tomb; they found me conscious again and brought me to this place, and Theron gave me to Leonas here in a deserted spot." She told them everything else but said nothing about Chaereas.

Or the author himself steps forward and summarizes what has happened earlier, in a way reminiscent of serial stories in our weeklies:

Char. 5.1.1–2 ὡς μὲν ἐγαμήθη Καλλιρόη Χαιρέᾳ, καλλίστη γυναικῶν ἀνδρὶ καλλίστῳ, πολιτευσαμένης Ἀφροδίτης τὸν γάμον, καὶ ὡς δι᾽ ἐρωτικὴν
ζηλοτυπίαν Χαιρέου πλήξαντος αὐτὴν ἔδοξε τεθνάναι, ταφεῖσαν δὲ πο-
λυτελῶς εἶτα ἀνανήψασαν ἐν τῷ τάφῳ τυμβωρύχοι νυκτὸς ἐξήγαγον ἐκ
Σικελίας, πλεύσαντες δὲ εἰς Ἰωνίαν ἐπώλησαν Διονυσίῳ, καὶ τὸν ἔρωτα
τὸν Διονυσίου καὶ τὴν Καλλιρρόης πρὸς Χαιρέαν πίστιν καὶ τὴν ἀνάγκην
τοῦ γάμου διὰ τὴν γαστέρα καὶ τὴν Θήρωνος ὁμολογίαν καὶ Χαιρέου πλοῦν
ἐπὶ ζήτησιν τῆς γυναικὸς ἅλωσίν τε αὐτοῦ καὶ πρᾶσιν εἰς Καρίαν μετὰ
Πολυχάρμου τοῦ φίλου, καὶ ὡς Μιθριδάτης ἐγνώρισε Χαιρέαν μέλλοντα
ἀποθνήσκειν καὶ ὡς ἔσπευδεν ἀλλήλοις ἀποδοῦναι τοὺς ἐρῶντας, φωράσας
δὲ τοῦτο Διονύσιος ἐξ ἐπιστολῶν διέβαλεν αὐτὸν πρὸς Φαρνάκην, ἐκεῖνος
δὲ πρὸς βασιλέα, βασιλεὺς δὲ ἀμφοτέρους ἐκάλεσεν ἐπὶ τὴν κρίσιν –
ταῦτα ἐν τῷ πρόσθεν λόγῳ δεδήλωται· τὰ δὲ ἑξῆς νῦν διηγήσομαι.

62

How Callirhoe, the most beautiful of women, married Chaereas, the handsomest of men, by Aphrodite's management; how in a fit of lover's jealousy Chaereas struck her, and to all appearances she died; how she had a costly funeral and then, just as she came out of her coma in the funeral vault, tomb robbers carried her away from Sicily by night, sailed to Ionia, and sold her to Dionysius; Dionysius's love for her, her fidelity to Chaereas, the need to marry caused by her pregnancy; Theron's confession, Chaereas's journey across the sea in search of his wife; how he was captured, sold, and taken to Caria with his friend Polycharmus; how Mithridates discovered his identity as he was on the point of death and tried to restore the lovers to each other; how Dionysius found this out through a letter and complained to Pharnaces, who reported it to the King, and the King summoned both of them to judgement — this has all been set out in the story so far. Now I shall describe what happened next.

This whole apparatus of repetitive material must have some kind of a functional explanation. No earlier Greek prose exhibits such a spectrum and such a frequency, even if each separate form is not unique (e.g., Chariton's authorial recapitulations in 5.1 and 8.1 imitate book openings in our manuscripts of Xenophon's *Anabasis*, and the final summing-ups, notably Char. 8.7–8, have an epic precedent in Odysseus's detailed report to Penelope in *Od.* 23.310–341). Nor do the later, sophistic novels excel in such material. If they use retrospects, it is mostly to supplement the primary narrative, not to repeat it. Heliodorus, whose complicated structure would need clarification, gives none; Chariton, whose narrative a normal (modern) reader would find extremely straightforward and clear, abounds with reminders and summaries, including a detailed recapitulation (in direct speech) of the whole story at the end.

It seems to be a reasonable hypothesis, at least, that the explanation has to do with the expected readership — that the early novelists directed themselves to people who had not yet moved definitely from orality to literacy, i.e., to inexperienced readers, or to listeners.[50] The author, the producer, was of course fully literate, but he expected the consumers to be less so. Not necessarily all the consumers, but the larger part — and, notably, those for whose spiritual needs the genre was created, if we keep to Perry's explanation.

63   One may speculate whether other characteristics of the early novel as well may betray such a cultural context. For instance, that may be the explanation for the dense net of anticipatory material: foreshadowings of various degrees of explicitness and various range.[51] As a counterpart to the recapitulatory material, the foreshadowings sometimes contribute to clarifying the main lines and stressing the main points of the action (cf. the combined recapitulation and foreshadowing in Char. 8.1.4–5). But mostly they are of a less specific nature than the recapitulations: oracles, omens and dreams, or just vague forebodings of coming events, either "authorized" by the narrator himself or uttered by one of the characters. Such items tend to create suspense and expectation and would thus no doubt stimulate inexperienced readers to keep on reading, listeners to stay listening — or to return for the recital of the next instalment. It is

---

[50] Wesseling (1988: 71–73) has the merit of taking seriously earlier suggestions that novels may have been recited rather than read. But her discussion, as far as it goes, suffers from not distinguishing between the early type of novel and the three sophistic specimens. There is indeed a world of difference between the kind of oral elements in Chariton and Xenophon which may have facilitated "popular" consumption and the stylistic brilliance in parts of Heliodorus destined to elicit applause from a sophistic audience (already Rohde [1876: 353 n. 1; cf. also pp. 304 f.] referred to the reported recitation of Heliodorus in a group of Byzantine φιλόλογοι: "Philip the Philosopher" [12th cent.?], *Commentatio in Charicleam*, p. 366.11 Colonna [in his ed. of Heliodorus]).

[51] See Hägg (1971), Ch. 6.

true that the sophistic novels, too, employ this technique (Achilles Tatius, in particular), and of course with much greater sophistication.[52] Yet, the explanation of the frequent foreshadowings need not be the same in both cases. The greater complexity of the sophistic novels well motivates the use of such devices, e.g., to bridge a long digression. In the case of the more straightforward early novels, on the other hand, a fully literate reading public would hardly have felt the need for as many anticipations as we find there. It would be different with an oral audience, or new readers in an orally dominated cultural context; after all, foreshadowings are an old epic phenomenon (cf. Duckworth 1933). Thus, while the form has obviously been transmitted from the non-sophistic to the sophistic novels, the function may have changed.

The many short-range "headings" in the δέ-part of the linking phrases (treated above) are of course an important part of the anticipatory arsenal. Furthermore, particularly in Chariton, the transition to a new episode — whether belonging to the same line of action or not — is the place where the narrator likes to step forward in person and speak directly to his audience. The informal, oral style he assumes on such occasions is well brought out in Bryan Reardon's (1989) translation:

> This, then, was what the robbers did. As for Callirhoe — she came back to life! (1.8.1).

> Fortune outwitted her, though; ... So now she brought about an unexpected, indeed incredible, state of things. How she did it is worth hearing (ἄξιον ... ἀκοῦσαι) (2.8.3).

> But once more, even on that day, the evil spirit vented his spite. How he did so I shall tell you (ἐρῶ) shortly; first, I want to relate (βούλομαι ... εἰπεῖν) what happened in Syracuse during the same time. That was as follows. The tomb robbers... (3.2.17/3.1).

64

Another potential indication of orality is the kind of stereotyped phraseology which we find in Xenophon of Ephesus, in particular. In addition to his linking phrases, with the line back to Homer and Herodotus, there are in Xenophon also other instances of stereotyped formulation in recurring narrative situations. According to Dalmeyda (ed., 1926: xxvii–xxxi), they contribute to this particular novel's "physionomie de

---

[52] Cf. Bartsch (1989), who may sometimes, however, overstate the sophistication.

conte populaire".[53] Merkelbach (1962: 333 [1984: 153]), as we have seen, takes them as an indication of an oral origin for the whole genre. Some examples:[54] powerful men are introduced with the stock phrase (ἀνὴρ) τῶν τὰ πρῶτα (ἐκεῖ) δυναμένων, 'one of the foremost men in the land';[55] a journey by sea is often indicated by the words διανύσας τὸν πλοῦν, 'having completed his voyage' (supplemented with the appropriate temporal or local specification);[56] lovesickness is habitually described with the words διέκειτο πονήρως, '[he, she] was in a bad way',[57] and the customary capitulation to its attacks is worded οὐκέτι καρτερῶν, οὐκέτι φέρειν δυνάμενος (or similarly), 'when he could hold out no longer'.[58] Like the epic formulas, they of course facilitate the author's task; but, more importantly in our context, they also make less demands on the listener or reader than a more elaborate literary style with variegated expressions even for standard situations. The message comes through, undisturbed by unnecessary literary "noise". It would also be unwise to condemn such a style from an aesthetic point of view, for, as George Saintsbury once stated, "it is certain as a matter of fact … that repetitions, stock phrases, identity of scheme and form, which are apt to be felt disagreeable in reading, are far less irksome, and even have a certain attraction, in matter orally delivered."[59]

From the stereotyped phraseology one may venture the step to the stereotyped scenes, motifs and plots of the genre. They too may — and,

---

[53] For a thorough structural analysis of Xenophon's novel, with particular attention paid to the folktale traits, see Ruiz Montero (1988: 97–164). Traits of oral narrative in both Xenophon and Chariton are discussed by Scobie (1983: 32–35). Zanetto (1990), too, interprets the use of formulas in these two novels as an indication of their readership, but the abstract is not specific on this point and orality is not explicitly mentioned.

[54] More examples can easily be collected through Papanikolaou's (1973b) Index verborum.

[55] Xen. Eph. 1.1.1, 2.13.3, 3.2.1, 3.2.5, 3.9.5, 5.1.4. Translations tend to disguise this kind of stereotyped expression: "among the most influential citizens of Ephesus", "one of the foremost men in the land", "I belong … to one of the leading families of Perinthus", "one of the leading men in Byzantium", "one of the most prominent men in the city", "from one of its [Lacedaemon's] leading families" — these are Anderson's (1989) English variations for Xenophon's stock phrase (in spite of this translator's proclaimed aim "to retain the characteristic monotony … of Xenophon's style and narrative manner" [p. 127]).

[56] Xen. Eph. 1.11.2, 1.11.5, 1.14.6, 3.1.3, 5.1.1, 5.6.1, 5.6.4, 5.10.3, 5.11.1, 5.15.1.

[57] Xen.Eph. 1.3.2, 1.4.6, 1.15.1, 1.15.4, 2.3.3, 2.4.2, 5.8.3; cf. also 1.5.9, 5.2.3, 5.12.3.

[58] Xen. Eph. 1.4.4, 1.5.5, 1.15.2, 2.3.3, 2.5.1, 2.12.2, 3.2.2, 3.2.10, 3.10.4 and 1.4.6, 3.2.12, 3.7.4, 4.5.4, 5.10.1; cf. also 3.2.7, 3.12.3.

[59] Quoted after Crosby (1936: 104).

in my opinion, should — be looked upon from the point of view of orality. This has not been done, in the way it has for the epic, presumably because the novel was "born" within a literate culture. But if we place the emphasis on the receivers, the audience, instead of the producers, true literacy cannot be taken for granted any more in the hellenistic than in the classical period.[60] No doubt, the typical scenes in epic, the stock characters in comedy, the well-known mythological stories used in tragedy, the standard disposition and *loci communes* of forensic rhetoric were all partly motivated by the way these genres were communicated to their public, and by the nature of their respective audiences. In an oral — or should we rather say "aural"?[61] — situation, not only redundance but also a certain amount of predictability is necessary for satisfactory reception; much depends on previous acquaintance, on recognition of at least part of the message.[62]

65

A parallel from a modern trivial genre, the TV soap opera, may help to illuminate one particular aspect of the early novel's stereotypy. Series of the *Dallas-Dynasty* type, while of course ending each episode in a way which makes the viewer eager to watch the next one as well, at the same time are so constructed that a viewer who has missed one or several episodes still has no serious difficulties; after a minute or two, he is à jour. This is less a result of the initial summary of the preceding episode than of a skilled use of types and stereotypes. It is also possible to start watching a particular series at any point, if one is only somewhat familiar with the conventions of the genre. In the same way, a listener who has missed one or several episodes of Xenophon's novel, through

---

[60] The problems of defining and identifying "literacy" in ancient society are well discussed by Thomas (1989: 18–20). However inadequate, I use in the present article the terms "true (or genuine) literacy", "quasi-literacy" (below, n. 65), "semi-literacy" (above, n. 39), "illiteracy" to cover the whole range.

[61] The word is used in a corresponding context by Russo (1978: 41f.); Andersen (1987: 44) similarly speaks of "auraler Aufnahme".

[62] Cf. Russo's (1978) interesting observations about the function of "regularity" or "recurrence" in the Homeric epic, distinguishing "five levels of regularity" from the hexameter verse and the formulas proper to thematic composition and "the epic outlook" or "world-view". *Mutatis mutandis*, most of the levels seem to have counterparts in the early Greek novel (including "the novelistic outlook" which would roughly correspond to Reardon's "late-hellenistic myth"). I do not agree, however, with Russo's (47) generalisations about the differences between epic and (modern) novel and between ancient and modern "spirit", unless popular literature, ancient and modern, and its readers be excluded.

absence or inattention, will hardly experience any loss, and also new listeners will soon feel at home and be able to appreciate whatever there is to appreciate. What is a vice in artistic epic, according to Aristotle, is a virtue in these trivial genres: remove one or several parts of the whole, and the novel (soap opera etc.) will still function. The episodic structure of a Xenophon of Ephesus and the stereotypy of plot, scenes and characters go hand in hand.

The stereotypes of the early Greek novel may thus reflect the orally dominated world in which the genre started, being part of its adaptation to the "oral consciousness"[63] of its readership (listeners and new readers alike). It is true that many of the stereotypes also meet us in the sophistic specimens which were directed at truly literate readers; but each writer then plays with them according to his own talent and taste and the preferences of his expected audience. They are part of the genre, but no longer functionally necessary: by them, the novel betrays its "popular" origin.

What I have attempted in this paper, is to explore another way of coming to grips with the early Greek novel's readership than those starting either from external data (testimonia, papyri) or from one type of internal evidence (contents, attitude), both ending, at best, with a *non liquet*. The other type of internal evidence, the narrative form, appears more promising; and I do not doubt that further investigation from the point of view of orality/literacy would reinforce the impression that the early novel — as a genre — belongs to another, more "popular" cultural context than contemporary "serious" literature. The features I have called attention to are only the most overt signs: recurrence, repetition, stereotyped phraseology etc.; if my hypothesis is correct, there should be other, less conspicuous traces of an oral context as well.

The important thing is that we free ourselves from the literacy/illiteracy dichotomy, as far as the novel is concerned. For an investigation of the "readership" of the early Greek novel, it is immaterial whether in late-hellenistic society five or 15 or 25% of the inhabitants were literate, in the sense that they had learnt to read and write: firstly, many, probably the majority, of these "literate" people were notwithstanding unqualified for sustained reading of a lengthy text; secondly, also "illiter-

66

---

[63] For the term, cf. Havelock (1986: 41). On the "co-existence of oral and written modes … as a normal and frequently occurring aspect of human cultures", see Finnegan (1988: 142; cf. 167f.).

ate" people could be part of the audience of the novel, namely, as listeners. The borderline, if we look for readers proper, goes rather between the intellectual elite, whose members were truly literate and capable of reading also for their pleasure,[64] and the "quasi-literates",[65] semi-literates and illiterates who all remained part of a predominantly oral culture — i.e., the borderline goes between literacy and orality.[66] But it is along this borderline that the novel *as reading-matter* may have been able to penetrate into the vast quasi- and semi-literate territory: listeners may have turned into readers because these texts were in some ways adapted for what might most properly be called "the aural mind". To what extent this really happened, we cannot know.

More comparative material must of course be brought in to prove the point about the early novel's "aurality", both from contemporary Greek literature, serious and more popular, and from other periods and literatures. In the present context, it may be permitted to end by emphasizing again the latter aspect. Ben Edwin Perry's (1967) comparison with the spread of literacy and the rise of the modern novel in mid-eighteenth century England, although no doubt pointing in the right direction, has been shown to be misleading in important respects. Maybe the middle ages could provide better illumination for part of our problem (to find one parallel to cover the whole complex is of course not possible).[67]

---

[64] Andersen (1987: 44), apparently referring to fourth-century Athens, speaks of "eine weitgehend isolierte literarische Schicht", created "durch die Wissenschaft, aber auch durch die Dichtung". The situation, as far as "serious" literature and "true" literacy are concerned, will hardly have been much different in the post-classical periods. With Atticism, the isolation even increases.

[65] I use this term to denote those who were formally able both to read and write but had not developed this ability into true literacy, from lack of training and/or inclination. They would normally use their ability only when forced by circumstances (to write a letter, receipt or contract, to read a decree, a technical manual etc.).

[66] This is not to deny that "the culture of the elite continued [in the hellenistic period] to have a strong oral component, with oratory and performance retaining their important roles" (Harris 1989: 125); but the borderline then goes, to be precise, between "bi-culturality" (those partaking of both cultures) and orality (including the quasi-literates and semi-literates).

[67] On medieval popular literature (romances, saints' lives etc.) as largely orally delivered (either recited by a professional story-teller or read aloud by a member of a family group), see Crosby (1936). The late middle ages probably provide the best parallel to our novels in this respect: "As manuscripts became more numerous and more of the laity learned to read, it is natural that the vogue for public recitation by the minstrel should give way somewhat before the private reading by one member of a family to others" (97).

I have already pointed to Icelandic family sagas and their "two audiences" (Clover 1982: 188–204) or "audiences of mixed origins" (Foote 1974: 17). Carol Clover, in a later study (1985: 270–283), discusses recurrent features and transitional narrator-formulas in the sagas from the viewpoint that "saga authors were presumably aware that their work would be both read (by a few) and heard (by many)".[68] But thirteenth-century Iceland is of course a very special cultural milieu;[69] and the family sagas, though sometimes labelled "historical novels", are very different from the Greek novels. In some respects, the *fornaldarsögur*, treated at another place in this book*, provide closer parallels in narrative technique to the type of early Greek novel extant in Xenophon of Ephesus and the *Historia Apollonii regis Tyri* — or, to put it in another way, with the Greek novel in so far as it incorporates traits of the folktale. A closer typological comparison between the two might well prove fruitful. For the present, however, these suggestions will have to suffice.

67

[68] Clover, in her critical *Forschungsbericht* (1985: 281), also writes: "the sagas are full of recurrent features (motifs, themes, 'rhetorical' devices, and plot structures, large and small); recurrence of this sort and to this extent is characteristic of oral narrative, not of literary narrative…". But there is no agreement among scholars about the reasons for these typically oral traits in the sagas: are they an organic part of the saga tradition, i.e., taken over from the oral predecessors of the written sagas, are they deliberate adaptations in order to meet the needs of the large mixed audiences (as Clover herself seems to believe), or do they not prove orality at all? "The problem is that although formulaic repetition is a defining characteristic of oral literature, it is by no means exclusive to oral literature, as one can readily see at a glance at such genres as detective novel or romance (medieval as well as modern) or the western or pornography" (Clover 1985: 282). On formulaic language and other "oral" traits in oral and written literature, see also Finnegan (1977: 69–72, 126–133; 1988: 78, 157–159, with further refs.). On "excessive repetition" in Old French and Middle English romances indicating that they were primarily intended for oral delivery, see Crosby (1936: 102–108).

[69] E.g., the potential occasions for recital of family sagas discussed by Foote (1974) will only to a limited degree have had counterparts in the late-hellenistic world.

* [Eriksen, *Contexts of Pre-Novel Narrative*, 1994.]

References

Andersen, Øivind 1987: "Mündlichkeit und Schriftlichkeit im frühen Griechentum", *Antike und Abendland* 33: 29-44.

— 1989: "The significance of writing in early Greece: A critical appraisal", in: Karen Schousboe–Mogens Trolle Larsen (eds.), 73-90.

Anderson, Graham 1984: *Ancient fiction: The novel in the Graeco-Roman world.* London & Sydney: Croom Helm.

— 1989: "Xenophon of Ephesus: An Ephesian tale", in: B.P. Reardon (ed.), 125-169.

Bartsch, Shadi 1989: *Decoding the ancient novel: The reader and the role of description in Heliodorus and Achilles Tatius.* Princeton, N.J.: Princeton University Press.

Blake, William C. (ed.) 1938: Charitonis Aphrodisiensis *De Chaerea et Callirhoe amatoriarum narrationum libri octo.* Oxford: Clarendon Press.

des Bouvrie, Synnøve 1990: *Women in Greek tragedy: An anthropological approach.* (Symbolae Osloenses fasc. suppl. 27.) Oslo: Norwegian University Press.

Bowie, Ewen L. 1985: "The Greek Novel", in: P.E. Easterling & B.M.W. Knox (eds.), 683-699.

— 1990: "Who Read the Ancient Greek Novels?", in: James Tatum & Gail M. Vernazza (eds.), 150-151.

— in press [1994]: "The readership of Greek novels in the ancient world." [Paper read at the Second international conference on the ancient novel, Dartmouth College, 1989.] [Subsequently published as: "The readership of Greek novels", in J. Tatum (ed.), *The search for the ancient novel*, Baltimore and London 1994, 435-459.]

Bürger, Karl 1892: "Zu Xenophon von Ephesos", *Hermes* 27: 36-67.

Clover, Carol J. 1982: *The medieval saga.* Ithaca & London: Cornell University Press.

— 1985: "Icelandic family sagas (Íslendingasögur)", in: Carol J. Clover & John Lindow (eds.), 239-315.

Clover, Carol J.–John Lindow (eds.) 1985: *Old Norse-Icelandic literature: A critical guide.* (Islandica 45.) Ithaca & London: Cornell University Press.

Cole, Susan Guettel 1981: "Could Greek women read and write?", in: Helene P. Foley (ed.), 219-245.

Crosby, Ruth 1936: "Oral delivery in the middle ages", *Speculum* 11, 88-110.

Dalmeyda, Georges (ed.) 1926: Xénophon d'Éphèse, *Les Éphésiaques ou Le roman d'Habrocomès et d'Anthia.* Paris: Les Belles Lettres.

Detienne, Marcel (ed.) 1988: *Les savoirs de l'écriture. En Grèce ancienne.* (Cahiers de philologie 14.) Lille: Presses Universitaires.

Duckworth, George Eckel 1933: *Foreshadowing and suspense in the epics of Homer, Apollonius, and Vergil.* Diss. Princeton.

Easterling, P.E. 1985: "Books and readers in the Greek world. 2. The hellenistic and imperial periods", in: P.E. Easterling & B.M.W. Knox (eds.), 16-41.

Easterling, P.E.–Bernard M.W. Knox (eds.) 1985: *The Cambridge history of classical literature*. Vol. 1. *Greek literature*. Cambridge: Cambridge University Press.

Egger, Brigitte 1988: "Zu den Frauenrollen im griechischen Roman. Die Frau als Heldin und Leserin", in: H. Hofmann (ed.), 33–66.

Finnegan, Ruth 1977: *Oral poetry: Its nature, significance and social context*. Cambridge: Cambridge University Press.

— 1988: *Literacy and orality: Studies in the technology of communication*. Oxford: Basil Blackwell.

Foley, Helene P. (ed.) 1981: *Reflections of women in antiquity*. New York, London & Paris: Gordon and Breach Science Publishers.

Foote, Peter 1974: "The audience and vogue of the sagas of Icelanders: Some talking points", in: Gabriel Turville-Petre & John Stanley Martin (eds.), 17–25.

Fränkel, Hermann 1968: *Wege und Formen frühgriechischen Denkens*. 3. Aufl., München: C.H. Beck.

Fusillo, Massimo 1990: "The text in the text: Quotations in the Greek novel", in: James Tatum & Gail M. Vernazza (eds.), 131–132.

Gärtner, Hans (ed.) 1984: *Beiträge zum griechischen Liebesroman*. Hildesheim: Georg Olms Verlag.

Goody, Jack 1987: *The interface between the written and the oral*. Cambridge: Cambridge University Press.

Hägg, Tomas 1966: "Die Ephesiaka des Xenophon Ephesios — Original oder Epitome?", *Classica et Mediaevalia* 27: 118–161 [No. **6** in this volume].

— 1971: *Narrative technique in ancient Greek romances: Studies of Chariton, Xenophon Ephesius, and Achilles Tatius*. (Acta Instituti Atheniensis Regni Sueciae, Series in 8o, 8.) Stockholm: Svenska institutet i Athen.

— 1983: *The novel in antiquity*. Oxford: Basil Blackwell/Berkeley & Los Angeles: University of California Press.

— 1985: "Metiochus at Polycrates' court", *Eranos* 83: 92–102 [No. **9** in this volume].

— 1987: "Callirhoe and Parthenope: The beginnings of the historical novel", *Classical Antiquity* 6: 184–204 [No. **2** in this volume].

Harris, William V. 1989: *Ancient literacy*. Cambridge, Mass. & London: Harvard University Press.

Havelock, Eric A. 1963: *Preface to Plato*. Cambridge, Mass.: Harvard University Press/ Oxford: Basil Blackwell.

— 1982: *The literate revolution in Greece and its cultural consequences*. Princeton, N.J.: Princeton University Press.

— 1986: *The muse learns to write: Reflections on orality and literacy from antiquity to the present*. New Haven & London: Yale University Press.

Havelock, Eric A.–Jackson P. Hershbell (eds.) 1978: *Communication arts in the ancient world*. New York: Hastings House.

Heath, Malcolm 1987: *The poetics of Greek tragedy*. London: Duckworth.

Hofmann, Heinz (ed.) 1988: *Groningen colloquia on the novel*. Vol. 1. Groningen: Egbert Forsten.

Holzberg, Niklas 1986: *Der antike Roman. Eine Einführung.* München & Zürich: Artemis Verlag.

Hunter, Richard L. 1983: *A study of Daphnis & Chloe.* Cambridge: Cambridge University Press.

Immerwahr, Henry R. 1966: *Form and thought in Herodotus.* (Monographs published by the American Philological Association 23.) Cleveland, Ohio: Press of Western Reserve University.

Johne, Renate 1989: "Zur Figurencharakteristik im antiken Roman", in: Heinrich Kuch (ed.), 150–177.

Knox, Bernard M.W. 1968: "Silent reading in antiquity", *Greek, Roman and Byzantine Studies* 9: 421–435.

Kuch, Heinrich (ed.) 1989: *Der antike Roman. Untersuchungen zur literarischen Kommunikation und Gattungsgeschichte.* Berlin: Akademie-Verlag.

Merkelbach, Reinhold 1962: *Roman und Mysterium in der Antike.* München & Berlin: C.H. Beck.

— [1984]: "Über die Geschichte des Romans im Altertum", in: Hans Gärtner (ed.), 153–160. [Reprint of Merkelbach 1962, 333–340.]

— 1990 "Novel and aretalogy", in: James Tatum & Gail M. Vernazza (eds.), 108.

Müller, Carl Werner 1981: "Der griechische Roman", in: Ernst Vogt (ed.), 377–412.

Ong, Walter J. 1988: *Orality and literacy: The technologizing of the word.* London & New York: Routledge. [First publ. London: Methuen 1982.]

Papanikolaou, Antonios Dem. 1973a: *Chariton-Studien. Untersuchungen zur Sprache und Chronologie der griechischen Romane.* (Hypomnemata 37.) Göttingen: Vandenhoeck & Ruprecht.

— (ed.) 1973b: Xenophon Ephesius, *Ephesiacorum libri V.* Leipzig: B.G. Teubner.

Perry, Ben Edwin 1967: *The ancient romances: A literary-historical account of their origins.* Berkeley & Los Angeles: University of California Press.

Pomeroy, Sarah B. 1977: "*Technikai kai mousikai*: The education of women in the fourth century and in the hellenistic period", *American Journal of Ancient History* 2: 51–68.

— 1984: *Women in hellenistic Egypt. From Alexander to Cleopatra.* New York: Schocken Books.

Reardon, Bryan P. 1969: "The Greek Novel", *Phoenix* 23: 291–309.

— 1971: *Courants littéraires grecs des IIe et IIIe siècles après J.-C.* (Annales littéraires de l'Université de Nantes 3.) Paris: Les Belles Lettres.

— (ed.) 1989: *Collected ancient Greek novels.* Berkeley, Los Angeles & London: University of California Press.

Rohde, Erwin 1876: *Der griechische Roman und seine Vorläufer.* Leipzig. [Reprint 5th ed., Darmstadt: Wissenschaftliche Buchgesellschaft 1974.]

Ruiz Montero, Consuelo 1982: "Una interpretación del 'estilo KAI' de Jenofonte de Efeso", *Emerita* 50: 305–323.

— 1988: *La estructura de la novela griega.* (Acta Salmanticensia. Estudios filologicos 196.) Salamanca: Ediciones Universidad de Salamanca.

Russo, Joseph 1978: "How, and what, does Homer communicate? The medium and message of Homeric verse", in: Eric A. Havelock & Jackson P. Hershbell (eds.), 39–52.

Schousboe, Karen–Mogens Trolle Larsen (eds.) 1989: *Literacy and society*. Copenhagen: Akademisk Forlag.

Schwartz, Eduard 1896: *Fünf Vorträge über den griechischen Roman*. Berlin. [2nd ed., Berlin: De Gruyter 1943.]

Scobie, Alex 1983: *Apuleius and folklore*. London: The Folklore Society.

Spencer, Jane 1986: *The rise of the woman novelist. From Aphra Behn to Jane Austen*. Oxford: Basil Blackwell.

Stanford, William Bedell 1983: *Greek tragedy and the emotions. An introductory study*. London: Routledge & Kegan Paul.

Stephens, Susan A. 1990: "'Popularity' of the ancient novel", in: James Tatum & Gail M. Vernazza (eds.), 148–149.

— in press [1994]: "The popularity of the ancient novel: Fiction or fact?" [Paper read at the Second international conference on the ancient novel, Dartmouth College, 1989.] [Subsequently published as: "Who read ancient novels?", in J. Tatum (ed.), *The search for the ancient novel*, Baltimore and London 1994, 405–418.]

Tatum, James–Gail M. Vernazza (eds.) 1990: *The ancient novel: Classical paradigms and modern perspectives*. Hanover, N.H.: Dartmouth College.

Thomas, Rosalind 1990: *Oral tradition and written record in classical Athens*. Cambridge: Cambridge University Press.

Treu, Kurt 1989: "Der antike Roman und sein Publikum", in: Heinrich Kuch (ed.), 178–197.

Turville-Petre, Gabriel–John Stanley Martin (eds.) 1974: *Iceland and the mediaeval world: Studies in honour of Ian Maxwell*. Victoria: University of Melbourne.

Utas, Bo 1984–86: "Did 'Adhra remain a virgin?", *Orientalia Suecana* 33–35: 429–441.

Vogt, Ernst (ed.) 1981: *Griechische Literatur*. (Neues Handbuch der Literaturwissenschaft 2.) Wiesbaden: Akademische Verlagsgesellschaft Athenaion.

Wesseling, Berber 1988: "The audience of the ancient novel", in: H. Hofmann (ed.), 67–79.

Willis, William H. 1968: "A census of the literary papyri from Egypt", *Greek, Roman and Byzantine Studies* 9: 205–241.

Zanetto, Giuseppe 1990: "Il romanzo greco: Lingua e pubblico", in: James Tatum & Gail M. Vernazza (eds.), 147–148.

5

Epiphany in the Greek Novels:
The Emplotment of a Metaphor[1]

[originally published in *Eranos* 100, 2002, 51–61]

Gods appearing in anthropomorphic form to human beings, or, at least, fictitious characters believing they are seeing gods on earth, is a fairly common motif in the Greek novels.[2] By Greek novels, in this context, is meant the five extant so-called "ideal" Greek novels, dating between about the birth of Christ and the late fourth century AD. The motif of epiphany is most conspicuous in the narrative of the oldest among the five, Khariton's *Kallirhoe*, probably written between 50 BC and AD 50. Thus, much of the paper will deal with Khariton, analysing in some detail his clever handling of the motif and calling attention to the interesting insights he gives into ancient beliefs concerning epiphany. Some typical, shorter appearances of the motif in the later novels[3] will also be reviewed, before attention is finally turned more closely to one episode in Longus' *Daphnis and Khloe* (AD 150–250?) where a sophistic variation on the theme is introduced.

In defining what role the epiphanies play in the narrative pattern of each novelist, the following specific questions will underlie the discussion. To what extent are these "true" epiphanies, in the sense that

---

[1] This is an annotated and augmented version of a communication presented to "Epiphanies: A conference and a workshop on the methods and study of ancient religions", Rhethymno, 1–4 July 2001, organised in honour of Professor Robin Hägg by the University of Göteborg, the University of Bergen, and the University of Crete.

[2] For a recent short discussion of ancient epiphanies, with an extensive bibliographical note, see H.S. Versnel, "What did Ancient Man See when he Saw a God? Some Reflections on Greco-Roman Epiphany", in: D. van der Plas (ed.), *Effigies Dei*, Leiden 1987, pp. 42–55.

[3] These are Xenophon of Ephesus, *Ephesiaka* (AD 50–150?), Akhilleus Tatios, *Leukippe and Kleitophon* (AD 150–200?), and Heliodoros, *Aithiopika* (AD 350–375?). All dates are approximate and open for discussion. See further articles by various hands in G. Schmeling (ed.), *The Novel in the Ancient World*, Leiden 1996, and, for Xenophon, J.N. O'Sullivan, *Xenophon of Ephesus: His Compositional Technique and the Birth of the Novel*, Berlin & New York 1995. All the novels are available in new English translations in B.P. Reardon (ed.), *Collected Ancient Greek Novels*, Berkeley 1989.

the characters witnessing them really believe that they are seeing gods, and to what extent should we rather speak of metaphors? What kind of people — socially, intellectually — are witness to this phenomenon, and in what contexts? What is the author's own attitude to the epiphanies that his characters experience: is this to him just part of a literary mythology, ultimately going back to Homer, or does he believe himself in gods appearing on earth in crucial situations to help or harm human beings?

To what extent such epiphanies, as they are described in the Greek novels of the Imperial period, also tell us something about actual beliefs among the Greek population of the Roman Empire, and thus have an historical as well as a literary interest, is a question better left to specialists in the history of ancient religions. The fact that Khariton's *Kallirhoe* is an historical novel, set in the Classical period of Greek history, is a complicating factor in that connection: the author may reflect contemporary belief or construct a distant past or present an amalgam of both.

Moreover, how to interpret the epiphanies is, of course, part of the larger problem what religious intent and, possibly, message these novels may have had on diffent levels. Does the conspicuous role religion plays in them, on the surface, simply mirror the actual role of religious customs and beliefs in Graeco-Roman society, or should at least part of it be ascribed to literary convention? Did some of the novels, as Reinhold Merkelbach and others have argued,[4] address themselves to special religious groups and contain religious messages hidden from those not initiated, and what role may the epiphanies play in such a scenario? While emphasis in the present short paper will be on epiphany as a literary motif, some of the wider issues will be touched upon as well.

Our first instance of epiphany is a key scene in Khariton's novel. We are at the beginning of Book II, of eight books in all, and the heroine, Kallirhoe, finds herself a slave on a country estate outside Miletus in Ionia. This needs some explanation. At the beginning of the novel, she is married, in her home-town Syracuse, to her young lover, Khaireas.

---

[4] R. Merkelbach, *Roman und Mysterium in der Antike*, Munich 1962; idem, *Die Hirten des Dionysos: Die Dionysos-Mysterien in der römischen Kaiserzeit und der bukolische Roman des Longus*, Stuttgart 1988. Cf. also K. Kerényi, *Die griechisch-orientalische Romanliteratur in religionsgeschichtlicher Beleuchtung*, Tübingen 1927 (reprint Darmstadt 1962), and the discussion of R. Beck, "Mystery Religions, Aretalogy and the Ancient Novel", in Schmeling (ed., above, n. 3), 131–50.

When she is just a couple of months pregnant, their marriage is tragically interrupted: in a fit of jealousy and rage, Khaireas kicks his wife in the stomach, she appears to be dead and is entombed. But inside the sepulchre she wakes up, only to be captured by grave-robbers and brought by ship to Ionia. Here, Theron the pirate sells her to Leonas, the steward (διοικητής) of Dionysios, the richest man in Miletus.

This Dionysios has recently become a widower, he is in deep mourning, and now his steward Leonas wants to console him by presenting to him the newly acquired slave girl, Kallirhoe. Dionysios refuses to hear anything about the beautiful girl, but Leonas cleverly persuades him to leave Miletus to visit his country estate where Kallirhoe is kept. This is where we enter the narrative. Plangon, the estate-manager's wife who takes care of Kallirhoe, says to her (2.2.5–6):[5]

> "Come to Aphrodite's shrine and offer up a prayer for yourself. The goddess makes her appearance here (ἐπιφανὴς δέ ἐστιν ἐνθάδε ἡ θεός); and, besides our neighbours, people from the city come here to sacrifice to her. She listens especially to Dionysios, and he has never failed to stop at her shrine." They then told her of the appearances of the goddess (τῆς θεοῦ τὰς ἐπιφανείας), and one of the peasant women said, "Lady, when you see Aphrodite you will think you are looking at a picture of yourself."

So this is a country shrine where Aphrodite regularly appears to her worshippers; people even come all the way from the metropolis to sacrifice. The rural, traditional character of the cult is emphasized. But the motif is not introduced just for its picturesque qualities, it prepares the ground for a narrative device that Khariton is going to use. As he reminds us, Kallirhoe herself is Aphrodite's double, a leifmotif of the novel, which will now become productive in the immediate development of the plot.

Kallirhoe, following Plangon's advice, visits the shrine, but prays — contrary to all normal behaviour in front of this goddess — that she shall never attract any man again. Aphrodite, however, has the opposite intent. She restores Kallirhoe's beauty after the hardships she has gone through, so that the country folk marvel at her (2.2.8, ὥστε θυμάζειν τοὺς ἀγροίκους καθ᾽ ἡμέραν εὐμορφοτέρας αὐτῆς βλεπομένης). And now Dionysios himself is on his way to his country estate (2.3.5–6):

53

---

[5] Khariton is quoted according to the text and translation of G.P. Goold (Loeb Classical Library, Cambridge, MA 1995).

While Dionysios was riding out to the country, Kallirhoe, having seen a vision of Aphrodite during the night (τῆς νυκτὸς ἐκείνης θεασαμένη τὴν Ἀφροδίτην), wanted to pay homage to her once more. She was standing there in prayer when Dionysios jumped down from his horse and entered the shrine ahead of the others. Hearing the sound of footsteps, Kallirhoe turned round to face him. At the sight of her Dionysios cried, "Aphrodite, be gracious to me, and may your presence bless me (καὶ ἐπ᾽ ἀγαθῷ μοι φανείης)!" As he was in the act of kneeling, Leonas caught him and said, "Sir, this is the slave just bought. Do not be disturbed. And you, woman, come to meet your master." And so Kallirhoe bowed her head at the name of 'master' and shed a flood of tears, learning at last what it means to lose one's freedom. But Dionysios struck Leonas and said, "You blasphemer, do you talk to gods as you would to men (ὡς ἀνθρώποις διαλέγῃ τοῖς θεοῖς;)? Have you the nerve to call her a bought slave? No wonder that you were unable to find the man who sold her. Have you not even heard what Homer teaches us? 'Oft in the guise of strangers from distant lands / the gods watch human insolence and righteousness.'" Then Kallirhoe spoke. "Stop mocking me," she said, "and calling me a goddess, when I am not even a happy mortal (θεὰν ὀνομάζων τὴν οὐδὲ ἄνθρωπον εὐτυχῆ)." As she spoke, her voice sounded to Dionysios like that of a goddess (ἡ φωνὴ τῷ Διονυσίῳ θεία τις ἐφάνη), for it had a musical tone and produced a sound like that of a lyre. In great confusion, therefore, and too embarrassed to say more, he went off to the house, already aflame with love.

Not only country folk, it now appears, but the well-educated nobleman Dionysios himself believes in epiphany — at least for the moment. He rebukes his steward, referring to Homer's dictum about gods often visiting human beings "in the guise of strangers from distant lands" (Od. 17.485: θεοὶ ξείνοισιν ἐοικότες ἀλλοδαποῖσιν) — not a very good parallel, in fact, the point being that Aphrodite has just appeared to him resembling nobody but herself. Even Kallirhoe's voice seems divine to Dionysios. Yet, his belief in epiphany is not strong enough to prevent him from falling in love with the godlike slave girl; and he will soon be trying to make her his new wife. Kallirhoe will finally agree, persuaded that Khaireas is dead and intent on having her child by Khaireas born and raised in lawful wedlock.

Uniquely for the Greek novels, the heroine thus marries twice; likewise uniquely, Khariton thus needs two representations of the motif "love at first sight". The epiphany scene is his ingenious way of meeting the challenge. The normal setting for "love at first sight" in this group of novels is a religious festival where the young hero and heroine see each other for the first time and immediately fall in love. Accompanying this event there is regularly the crowd's acclamation of the couple's divine beauty. In Kallirhoe's case, even the authorial voice itself has proclaimed her divine, Aphrodite-like beauty right at the start (1.1.2: ἦν γὰρ τὸ κάλλος οὐκ ἀνθρώπινον ἀλλὰ θεῖον, οὐδὲ Νηρηΐδος ἢ Νύμφης τῶν ὀρειῶν ἀλλ᾽ αὐτῆς Ἀφροδίτης). The spectators readily believe that hero and heroine are gods appearing on earth; there is a constant oscillation in the novels between metaphor — "divine beauty" — and religious awe (e.g., Khar. 1.1.16 θάμβος ὅλον τὸ πλῆθος κατέλαβεν, ὥσπερ Ἀρτέμιδος ἐν ἐρημίᾳ κυνηγέταις ἐπιστάσης). Typically, at the beginning of Xenophon's novel (1.2.7), some of the onlooking Ephesians worship the heroine Antheia as the goddess Artemis herself as she advances in the procession towards the temple, others think she is a double created by the goddess:[6] ... καὶ ἦσαν ποικίλαι παρὰ τῶν θεωμένων φωναί, τῶν μὲν ὑπ᾽ ἐκπλήξεως τὴν θεὸν εἶναι λεγόντων, τῶν δὲ ἄλλην τινὰ ὑπὸ τῆς θεοῦ πεποιημένην· προσηύχοντο δὲ πάντες καὶ προσεκύνουν... Next the hero, Habrokomes, comes along amid the ephebes and all eyes are turned on him instead of Antheia (1.2.8). The crowd hails him as καλός and an "incomparable image of a handsome god (οἷος οὐδὲ εἷς καλοῦ μίμημα θεοῦ)". So, unlike the heroine, he is unhesitantly defined a μίμημα, not the real thing. The godlike youngsters meet, see each other, and fall in love (1.3.1).

Taking these stereotyped and symmetrical scenes of mutual love at first sight as his point of departure,[7] Khariton has created his asymmetrical epiphany scene at a crucial point of his narrative. The importance he attributes to it in his plot may be seen from an anticipation in Book I as well as several retrospects after the event. In 1.14.1, Theron the pirate has contrived a spectacular entry for his slave girl on sale:

> Unveiling Kallirhoe and loosening her hair, he opened the door and told her to go in first. Leonas and all in the room were struck with amazement at the sudden apparition (ἐπιστάσης αἰφνίδιον κατεπλάγησαν), as if they had set eyes on a goddess, for rumour had it that Aphrodite could be seen in the fields (ἐπιφαίνεσθαι, 'manifested herself').

---

[6] Xenophon of Ephesus is quoted according to the Teubner edition of A.D. Papanikolaou, Leipzig 1973.

[7] On the "symmetrical" love in the novels, see D. Konstan, *Sexual Symmetry: Love in the Ancient Novel and Related Genres*, Princeton 1994.

This prepares the reader for the scene in the shrine that we have just witnessed. Later in the narrative, the description of the magnificent wedding between Dionysios and Kallirhoe is again replete with references to the bride as the goddess Aphrodite in person. The boatmen who are going to transport her from the country estate to Miletus are "overwhelmed with awe (δείματι) on seeing her, as though Aphrodite herself were coming to embark", and kneel in homage (3.2.14). In Miletus, there is speculation about the bride's identity (3.2.15): "the humbler folk (τὸ ... δημωδέστερον πλῆθος) were persuaded that she was a Nereid who had risen from the sea or a goddess who had come from Dionysios' estate: this was the gossip of the boatmen." By implication, the more sophisticated city-dwellers were less credulous.[8] When Kallirhoe appears in bridal attire, the whole crowd shouts (3.2.17): "Aphrodite is the bride (ἡ Ἀφροδίτη γαμεῖ)!" This is the very climax before the narrative shifts back to Syracuse to recount what happened to Khaireas after Kallirhoe was killed and buried.

There are more specific retrospects to come. Long after the epiphany scene, Khaireas — who is not dead, of course, as Kallirhoe believed — in his search for his kidnapped wife arrives at the shrine of Aphrodite and discovers the golden statue of Kallirhoe that Dionysios has put up beside the cult statue as a votive offering. Khaireas faints when he recognizes her traits in the statue, but the shrine attendant (ἡ ζάκορος) misunderstands his reaction (3.6.4):

> "Be not alarmed, my son; the goddess has frightened many besides you: for she appears in person and lets herself be clearly seen (ἐπιφανὴς γάρ ἐστι καὶ δείκνυσιν ἑαυτὴν ἐναργῶς). However, this is a sign of good luck. Do you see this golden statue? This girl was once a slave, and Aphrodite has made her the mistress of us all." "Who is she?" said Khaireas. "She is the lady of this whole estate, my son, and the wife of Dionysios, the first man in Ionia."

In this manner, as an aftermath of the supposed epiphany, Khaireas gets the bad news that his wife is now married to another man; and the plot takes another important turn.

[8] Xen. Eph. similarly at one place ascribes such credulity to barbarians (2.2.4):... καὶ ἄνθρωποι βάρβαροι μήπω πρότερον τοσαύτην ἰδόντες εὐμορφίαν θεοὺς ἐνόμιζον εἶναι τοὺς βλεπομένους. Heliodoros 1.7.2 combines the social and ethnic inferiority of such believers: his barbarian bandits believe ὑπ᾽ ἀγροικίας that Kharikleia might be a living cult image.

In 3.8–9, we return again to the shrine for a last retrospect.[9] Kallirhoe has given birth to her child and Dionysios arranges a magnificent sacrifice to thank Lady Aphrodite "at whose shrine we first saw each other" (3.8.2, παρ᾽ ἧ πρῶτον ἀλλήλους εἴδομεν) — to Dionysios' mind, it was the usual matter of mutual love at first sight. He weeps at the sight of Kallirhoe with "their" son in her arms, "a beautiful sight," says Khariton, "the like of which no painter has ever yet portrayed, nor sculptor fashioned, nor poet described before now; for none of them has represented Artemis or Athena with a baby in her arms" (3.8.6) — so Kallirhoe is still a goddess, but now a virgin one for the sake of the paradox. Kallirhoe then sends the others away to be alone with the goddess, to pray and to cry over her misfortunes. She calls the priestess (τὴν ἱέρειαν) who comes and tries to comfort her (3.9.1):

> "My child, why are you crying amid such blessings? Why, even strangers are paying you homage now as a goddess (ὡς θεὰν … προσκυνοῦσι). The other day two fine young men sailed by here, and one of them nearly expired at the sight of your statue, οὕτως ἐπιφανῆ σε ἡ Ἀφροδίτη πεποίηκεν."

This final twist on the epiphany topic is in the form of a play on words. The two most recent translations of Khariton's novel into English neatly display the latitude of meaning. Bryan Reardon translates:[10] " — that is how famous Aphrodite has made you", while George Goold chooses the other alternative: "so like a goddess on earth has Aphrodite made you." The pun is perhaps a sign that we should not take the talk about epiphany too seriously. Khariton, as we remember, let Dionysios recover quickly from his instantaneous belief that Kallirhoe really was Aphrodite, while the other people believing in epiphany are all simple minds, servants, peasants, boatmen, "humbler" city-dwellers, or the temple staff *ex officio*, whom author and reader may join in regarding with a touch of good-humoured irony.

As we have seen, the post-classical technical terms for epiphany (ἐπιφαίνεσθαι, ἐπιφανής, ἐπιφάνεια) are repeatedly used in relation to this particular scene at the country shrine of Aphrodite.[11] This usage is quite

---

[9] Cf. also the more general reminder in 5.9.1: … ἡ Στάτειρα τῆς κλίνης ἀνέθορε δόξασα Ἀφροδίτην ἐφεστάναι.

[10] In Reardon (ed., above, n. 3), pp. 17–124.

[11] In this sense, only ἐπιφανής seems to occur before the Hellenistic period (Hdt. 3.27.3), the others first epigraphically from the 3rd century BC onwards, and then often in the literature of the Imperial period.

exceptional, in fact the word-group reappears just on one occasion in these novels, in Akhilleus Tatius' *Leukippe and Kleitophon* 7.12.4 (and retrospectively in 8.18.1). We are in Ephesus, and Sostratos, the heroine's father, arrives from Byzantion as the head of a religious embassy to Artemis of Ephesus. The explanation is:[12]

> The Byzantines, you see, had experienced an apparition from Artemis (τῆς Ἀρτέμιδος ἐπιφανείσης) during their war against the Thracians, and after their victory they reckoned that they should send her a sacrifice to acknowledge her help in their military triumph. The goddess had also appeared to (ἐπιστᾶσα) Sostratos personally one night: the dream indicated that he would find his daughter in Ephesus and his brother's son as well.

In contrast to Khariton, Akhilleus Tatius does not weave the motif of epiphany into the plot or develop its potentials. The epiphany of Artemis is just reported, as in an historiographical account, and its reality is not questioned: it is real enough through the effect the epiphany had on the outcome of the war.

The fact that the technical terms for epiphany appear nowhere else in these novels, does not mean that no more epiphanies, or pseudo-epiphanies, are reported. Quite the opposite. We have already, in passing, seen several examples of how the novelists tend to emphasize the beauty of their protagonists by letting people around them mistake them for gods, or liken them to gods. In Heliodoros' *Aithiopika*, the heroine Kharikleia is repeatedly described in this author's detailed ekphrastic manner so as to evoke in every ancient reader the mental picture of Artemis, laurel crown, bow, quiver and all (1.2.2; cf. 3.4.5–6) — she was "a creature of such beauty that one might have taken her for a goddess (θεὸς εἶναι ἀναπείθουσα)", says Heliodoros (1.2.1),[13] and does not have to tell us what goddess he is referring to. The less sophisticated Xenophon, as we have seen, in the corresponding scene (1.2.7) lets the spectators identify the divine model for us. Heliodoros, to be true, also does so afterwards, but then in his more

---

[12] Akhilleus Tatios is quoted according to the edition of E. Vilborg, Göteborg 1955, and the translation of J.J. Winkler in Reardon (ed., above, n. 3), pp. 170–284.

[13] Heliodoros is quoted according to the Budé text of R.M. Rattenbury and T.W. Lumb, Paris 1960, and the translation of J. Morgan in Reardon (ed., above, n. 3), pp. 349–588.

learned manner (1.2.6): "Some [among the watching brigands] said she must be a god — the goddess Artemis, or the Isis they worship in those parts (τὴν ἐγχώριον Ἶσιν) …". We are in Egypt, and in fact the description of Kharikleia-Artemis at this point also has some traits that a well-informed Greek reader will have been able to associate with Isis: Kharikleia, while equipped as Artemis, bends over the injured Theagenes in the pose of Isis tending the dead body of Osiris. The epiphany takes the form of a typically Heliodoran riddle. The author delivers another variation on the "godlike" motif in 1.7.2 when the barbarians who had stayed at home inspect the booty and look upon the girl, "whose beauty seemed to exceed that of humankind (θεσπέσιόν τι χρῆμα)" — "had they carried off the priestess too, they wondered, or was this girl the statue of the goddess, a living statue (ἢ καὶ αὐτὸ ἔμπνουν μετῆχθαι τὸ ἄγαλμα) …?" Even if the lifelike/living cult image must have been a commonplace, in literature and life, there is a fair chance that Khariton's country-shrine Aphrodite is in the back of Heliodoros' head.

Another form of epiphany, expressed without recourse to the specific terminology, takes place when a god appears to one of the characters in his or her sleep. The typical terms for expressing this are ἐφίστασθαι for the god appearing, θεᾶσθαι (or similarly) for the person experiencing the vision. We have already seen Khariton stating summarily that Aphrodite appeared to Kallirhoe in the night between her two visits to the country shrine (2.3.5), and that Sostratos in Akhilleus Tatios was visited by Artemis who told him that he would find his daughter at Ephesus (7.12.4). There are more detailed descriptions of such nocturnal visions at other places, and of gods less propitious. In Xenophon's *Ephesiaka*, Habrokomes has a terrifying vision on board the ship from Rhodes (1.12.4):[14]

> A woman appeared to (ἐφίσταται) Habrokomes, fearful in appearance and superhuman in size, and dressed in a bloodred robe; having appeared (ἐπιστᾶσα) she seemed to set the ship alight; the rest perished, but he swam to safety with Antheia. As soon as he had seen this, he was in a panic (ταῦτα ὡς εὐθὺς εἶδεν ἐταράχθη) and expected something dreadful from the dream (ἐκ τοῦ ὀνείρατος); and the dreadful happened.

Soon afterwards, their ship is attacked by Phoenician pirates, many are killed in fight, the rest burnt with the ship, but Habrokomes and Antheia

[14] Translation adapted from that of G. Anderson in Reardon (ed., above, n. 3), pp. 125–169.

are captured alive and brought as slaves to Tyre. The dream is thus one of those woven into the plot as anticipations or forebodings of events to come, for the reader as well as the dreaming character. But who is the awesome woman of the vision? That she is larger than life would indicate that she is a goddess, and guesses have included Hekate, Isis and Tykhe.[15] A similarly frightening and equally unidentifiable goddess appears to Kleitophon in Akhilleus Tatios (1.3.4), foreboding, among other things, the violent separation of the couple; while Artemis, on a later occasion (4.1.4), appears to his beloved Leukippe to assure her that all will end well, and that she will remain a virgin until she is eventually married to Kleitophon.

In Longus' novel, Daphnis is on two occasions (2.23; 3.27) visited in his sleep by three eloquent Nymphs, appearing "as tall, beautiful women, half-naked and barefooted, their hair flowing free — just like their images", as Longus playfully adds (2.23.1, τοῖς ἀγάλμασιν ὅμοιαι). This is, of course, how gods and goddesses are recognized when appearing in this kind of epiphany;[16] there is in the novels, as far as I am aware, no instance of a god appearing incognito, in the guise of an ordinary mortal, as in Homer. The three Nymphs appear both times in response to prayer (or other verbal communication) and in order to ensure their continued worship by granting Daphnis relief from his troubles.

The nightly visions that we have encountered so far in several of the novels are rather stereotyped in form and function, no doubt reflecting a general belief in gods communicating with human beings through dreams.[17] Our last example of epiphany in the novels will be of a more sophisticated, literary kind. Not surprisingly, it occurs in Longus, and the god making his apparition, in full daylight, in the garden of old Philetas, is of course Eros. It is Philetas himself who tells Daphnis and Khloe in ecphrastic graphicness about his unique experience (2.4–6):[18]

[15] Cf. the discussion of this dream by M. Plastira-Valkanou, "Dreams in Xenophon Ephesius", *Symbolae Osloenses* 76, 2001, pp. 137–49, at p. 139f., with further refs. For Hekate, cf. Lucian, *Philops.* 22.

[16] Cf. Versnel (above, n. 2), p. 46.

[17] On this topic generally, see S. MacAlister, *Dreams and Suicides: The Greek Novel from Antiquity to the Byzantine Empire*, London & New York 1996.

[18] Longus is quoted according to the Teubner edition of M.D. Reeve, 3rd ed. Leipzig 1994, and the translation of C. Gill in Reardon (ed., above, n. 3), 285–348.

"As I went [into my garden] today around midday I saw, under the pomegranates and myrtles, a boy (βλέπεται παῖς), with myrtle berries and pomegranates in his hands. His skin was white like milk, and his hair was reddish-gold like fire, and his body glistened as though he'd just bathed (λευκὸς ὥσπερ γάλα καὶ ξανθὸς ὡς πῦρ, στιλπνὸς ὡς ἄρτι λελουμένος). He was naked and alone, and he was enjoying himself fruit picking, as though it was his own garden. I pounced on him to try and catch him, frightened that he'd break down the myrtles and pomegranates in his naughtiness. But he escaped from me easily, with quick, light movements, sometimes running under the rosebushes and sometimes hiding under the poppies like a young partridge. ..."

So the nameless intruder easily escapes — different from kids and calves that Philetas has chased, "this was something tricky (ποικίλον τι χρῆμα) and impossible to catch" (2.4.3). But Philetas is soon charmed (ἔθελγε) out of his anger and begs the boy for a kiss, in return for fruit and flowers unlimited (2.4.4). The boy begins gradually to disclose who he is (2.5.2): "I am not really a boy (παῖς), even though I look like one, but I'm even older than Kronos and the whole of time itself." He gives a long description of his activities, still without mentioning his name, and says that he is now looking after Daphnis and Khloe. He ends (2.5.5): "and be happy that you're the only man who's seen this boy (παιδίον) in your old age." Then he hops away through the leaves, like a young nightingale (2.6.1): "I saw wings growing from his shoulders and a little bow between his wings, and then I saw neither them nor him."

"You are consecrated to Eros, my children, and Eros is looking after you", Philetas concludes his long narrative (2.6.2), identifying at last by name his self-invited guest; and, says Longus (2.7.1), "Daphnis and Khloe enjoyed this very much, treating it as a story rather than as fact (ὥσπερ μῦθον οὐ λόγον ἀκούοντες)." Not even the naive children of Longus' creation believe in epiphany![19] The narrative goes on with Philetas' well-known hymnic praise of Eros (2.7.1–7), and with the children's fruitless attempts to follow his Theocritan cure for love, "a kiss and an embrace and lying down together with naked bodies".

---

[19] Others interpret the words μῦθον οὐ λόγον differently, cf. W.E. McCulloh, *Longus*, New York 1970, p. 98 ("a story, not just a report", paraphrased as "the pleasure of story as against mere information", or "myth [in the strong sense] over against abstract philosophizing or theologizing", or "myth as religiously edifying, as against a mere story"), and B.P. Reardon, "Μῦθος οὐ λόγος: Longus's Lesbian Pastorals", in: J. Tatum (ed.), *The Search for the Ancient Novel*, Baltimore & London 1994, pp. 135–147, at p. 146 ("a fable, not a rational account").

The element of religious awe that characterizes the other novelistic epiphanies is conspicuously absent from this one. The childish intruder is strange and "tricky", but does not inspire fear; Philetas is first angry, then charmed, but never frightened. In the following hymn, Philetas describes Eros as a relentless natural force; but in the epiphany he is reduced to an idyllic figure who plays a harmless game of identification, supplying a number of verbal clues, until finally the wings grow out and the bow appears to prove that he is really the god. No portentous presence, no *proskynesis*. We have indeed moved a long way from Khariton's evocation of popular belief in epiphany, and his repeated use of the motif for the development of his plot, to Longus' largely ornamental play with the concept, with little relevance to the role the god plays in the action of the novel. For even if Longus' Eros is gentler and more caring than the vain and contentious god who directs the events of the other novels,[20] he is nevertheless far from the innocuous creature of the epiphany.[21]

Fundamentally different as they are, these are the two most accomplished uses of the epiphany motif in the Greek novels. Yet, as we have seen, all the novelists include epiphanies in their narratives, be it in the form of gods appearing to mortals in dreams, or — most typically — as a means of emphasizing the hero's and (in particular) the heroine's "godlike" beauty, the one quality that separates them from ordinary people and marks them as exceptional human beings. Or is there more to it than that? *Are* they in fact gods, or at least reflections of the gods of a divine myth that underlies the fiction, as Karl Kerényi proposed?[22] It is

[20] Cf. A. Billault, "Characterization in the Ancient Novel", in: Schmeling (ed., above, n. 3), pp. 115–129, at p. 129, and M.C. Mittelstadt, "Love, Eros, and Poetic Art in Longus", in: *Fons Perennis* (Festschrift V. D'Agostino), Torino 1971, 305–332.

[21] It is probably significant that advocates of the religious interpretation of the novel have so little to say about the epiphany (but all the more about the "hymn" and the god's role generally in the novel), cf. Merkelbach (above, n. 4) 1962, p. 205, and 1988, p. 164, and H.H.O. Chalk, "Eros and the Lesbian Pastorals of Longos", *Journal of Hellenic Studies* 80, 1960, pp. 32–51, at pp. 33–35, 41. Kerényi (above, n. 4) does not even mention this epiphany. R.L. Hunter, *A Study of Daphnis & Chloe*, Cambridge 1983, p. 32, just notes that "Eros here is the mischievous child with whom we are all only too well acquainted". Only O. Schönberger (ed.), Longos, *Hirtengeschichten von Daphnis und Chloe*, 3rd ed., Berlin 1980, p. 185, tries to vindicate the epiphany quality of the ekphrasis by pointing out the boy's beauty and "Glanz" (στιλπνός) as traits typical of epiphanies.

[22] Kerényi (above, n. 4), pp. 95–122 (Ch. 5, "Göttlichkeit und Leiden"). The key phrase is (p. 102): "… daß wir derartige göttliche Erscheinungen im griechischen Roman überhaupt als einen Widerschein der plasmatisch umgebildeten *Göttersage* zu betrachten haben."

proper to end with a brief discussion of Kerényi's argumentation, to my knowledge the only sustained interpretation of the epiphany motif in the novels that has been presented, and to confront it with the alternative, secular-literary interpretation.

While Reinhold Merkelbach reads the novels as mystery texts, with hero and heroine as gods appearing under aliases, Kerényi insists that the religious structures he believes to have detected in the novels are to be regarded as "literarisch vermittlete Mysterienmotive, säkularisiertes religiöses Gut, verbürgerlichter Mythos".[23] And while Merkelbach does not discuss Khariton's novel, which he considers as the exception to the rule that the ancient novels are *Mysterientexte*,[24] Kerényi (pp. 98f.) takes Khariton as his prime example and as the very gateway to his interpretation of the epiphany motif. His key scene is not the epiphany in the country shrine, but Kallirhoe on board the vessel that takes her from the country estate to her wedding in Miletus (3.2.14, partly quoted above). Kallirhoe comes directly from the shrine, he notes, when the boatmen take her for Aphrodite and kneel in homage; and the most important element, to Kerényi, is what happens when she is sitting in the boat: προθυμίᾳ δὲ τῶν ἐρεσσόντων λόγου θᾶττον ἡ ναῦς κατέπλευσεν εἰς τὸν λιμένα, "So ardently did they row that in less time than it takes to tell the ship sailed into the harbour." The swiftness of the voyage is expressed, in this literary version of the motif, by the common idiom λόγου θᾶττον and caused by the boatmen's προθυμία, 'eagerness'. It would thus pass as an unobtrusive part of any narrative. Yet, according to Kerényi, it receives its full significance only if we view it as part of an aretalogical context: the goddess emerges from her shrine, is greeted with *proskynesis*, and demonstrates her divine status by a miracle, the instantaneous transfer to Miletus — this is one of her typical ἀρεταί. Kerényi produces a number of parallels for wondrously swift (or just smooth) sea crossings in various Greek and Latin texts, arguing that they all have their archetype in Isis sailing to find Osiris' body.

Several other instances of epiphany in the novels are likewise shown to contain details in description or vocabulary that seem to link them with similar scenes in overtly religious texts. For instance, ἐναργῶς in Khar. 3.6.4 (quoted above) is "[e]in Fachausdruck der aretalogischen ἐπιφάνεια-Literatur".[25] The problem, as always in these matters, is whether

60

---

[23] Kerényi (above, n. 4), p. 201 n. 3 ("Nachbetrachtungen" in the 2nd ed.).

[24] Merkelbach, *Roman und Mysterium* (above, n. 4), pp. 339f.

[25] Kerényi (above, n. 4), p. 96 n. 16; cf. Versnel (above, n. 2), p. 48.

the accumulation of many potential links amounts to proof, in the absence of any quite convincing case. Merkelbach's conviction that precisely Khariton, whom Kerényi adduces as his crown witness, wrote a purely literary novel without a religious substructure, does not strengthen the argument. We had better turn to the alternative, the literary tradition going back to Homer, which Kerényi too concedes as a partial explanation of the novelists' obsession with godlike characters.

In fact, Khariton himself gives clear support to that line of thought. For him, it is not just a matter of a tradition ultimately going back to Homer, but a direct link to the epic model established through numerous quotations embedded in the narrative. A couple of these are significant in our case. When Kallirhoe, through Eros' machinations, is on her way eastwards, heading for the Persian court and another unwanted suitor, the Great King himself (4.7.5),[26] Fame runs on before her, "announcing to everybody the arrival of Kallirhoe, the renowned Kallirhoe, the masterpiece of Nature, 'like unto Artemis or to Aphrodite the golden' (Ἀρτέμιδι ἰκέλη ἢ χρυσείη Ἀφροδίτη)." This line occurs twice in the *Odyssey* (17.37 and 19.54), both times with reference to Penelope. In 6.4.6, in turn, it is the Great King who, during his spectacular hunting party, imagines Kallirhoe as truly like (ἀληθῶς οἵη …) Artemis the archer roving over the mountains, with a three-line quotation from the description of Nausikaa in *Odyssey* 6.102–4.[27]

In Homer, of course, it is in these cases not a matter of people believing that they see Artemis or Aphrodite when they see Nausikaa or Penelope. It is the poet who makes the comparison, and the notion of an epiphany is not spelled out. On other occasions, however, it is — exactly as in the novels — a question of a figure being at a loss as to what to believe, as when Odysseus first addresses Nausikaa, eloquently speculating as to whether she is Artemis herself or a mortal (*Od.* 6.149ff.). The Homeric epics also bestow epithets of the kind θεοειδής, θεοείκελος etc. on their heroes. It is obvious that these similes, scenes of awe and bewilderment, and epithets together form the background to the "godlike", "divinely beautiful" cliché of later erotic poetry and romantic prose, as well as to

[26] There is another possible play on the word ἐπιφανής in that context: her travelling party is said to be more celebrated than the simultaneous one of Khaireas, ἐπιφανέστερον γὰρ καὶ βασιλικώτερον ἦν τὸ κάλλος.

[27] Longus 4.14.2 has a similar epic-inspired simile: Εἴ ποτε Ἀπόλλων Λαομέδοντι θητεύων ἐβουκόλησε, τοιόσδε ἦν οἷος τότε ὤφθη Δάφνις. Cf. also Akh. Tat. 1.4.2.

the various ways of making it functional in a narrative context. Erwin Rohde suggested that the novelists had simply taken over this usage from Hellenistic poetry as part of the erotic narrative technique,[28] but is dismissed by Kerényi with the rather facile argument that Akhilleus Tatios, otherwise the chief successor to earlier Greek eroticism, exhibits the fewest examples of this topos.[29]

No attempt will be made here to trace, in more detail, the ways of influence. To judge from the extant texts, however, it appears that Khariton is the one who takes the further step of developing the "godlike" commonplace into epiphany proper, as a religious experience among common people, and making this an organic part of his plot. In contrast to the other novelists, he clearly alludes to the contemporary concept of ἐπιφάνεια by applying the post-classical technical terminology to the ancient phenomenon. Whether there are also reflections of aretalogical structures in his narrative pattern, is more difficult to tell; there is always the possibility that the similarities are due to the common background in actual cult practice.

---

61

[28] E. Rohde, *Der griechische Roman und seine Vorläufer* (1876), 3rd ed. Leipzig 1914, repr. Darmstadt 1974, pp. 152 n. 1, 154–56.

[29] Kerényi (above, n. 4), pp. 95f.

Xenophon's *Ephesian Story*

The *Ephesiaca* of Xenophon Ephesius
— Original or Epitome?

[originally published as 'Die Ephesiaka des Xenophon Ephesios — Original oder Epitome?', *Classica et Mediaevalia* 27, 1966 (pr. 1969), 118–161. Translated and bibliographically updated by the author for this volume.]

I

With the article "Xenophon von Ephesos" by H. Gärtner in the most recent volume of the *RE*[1] (IX A 2, 1967, 2055-2089), we have a reliable and well documented survey of modern research on this seemingly simple but still problematic novelist. Gärtner, however, goes far beyond the format of a pure survey, particularly in his discussion of the theory of a "Helius interpolation" in Xenophon's novel recently put forward by R. Merkelbach. According to Merkelbach, *Roman und Mysterium* (pp. 91-113), in the 3rd century AD a "Helius redactor" reworked the original "Isis novel" and thus created a propaganda instrument in the cult of *Sol invictus*. Gärtner (coll. 2074-2080) carefully examines this thesis

119

---

[1] The following abbreviations are used in the article: Bürger = K. Bürger, "Zu Xenophon von Ephesus", *Hermes* 27, 1892, 36-67. — Dalmeyda = Xénophon d'Éphèse, *Les Éphésiaques ou le roman d'Habrocomès et d'Anthia.* Texte ét. et trad. par G. Dalmeyda, Paris 1926. — Gärtner = H. Gärtner, "Xenophon von Ephesos", *RE* 2. Reihe, IX A 2, 1967, 2055-2089. — Kerényi = K. Kerényi, *Die griechisch-orientalische Romanliteratur in religionsgeschichtlicher Beleuchtung,* 2., erg. Aufl., Darmstadt 1962. — Mazal 1962/63, 1964 and 1965 = O. Mazal, "Der griechische und byzantinische Roman in der Forschung von 1945 bis 1960", *Jahrb. der Österr. Byz. Ges.* 11/12 (1962/63), 9-55; 13 (1964), 29-86; 14 (1965), 83-124. — Merkelbach = R. Merkelbach, *Roman und Mysterium in der Antike,* München & Berlin 1962. — Pack[2] = R.A. Pack, *The Greek and Latin literary texts from Greco-Roman Egypt,* 2nd ed., Ann Arbor 1965. — Perry = B.E. Perry, *The ancient romances. A literary-historical account of their origins,* Berkeley & Los Angeles 1967. — *RAC* = *Reallexikon für Antike und Christentum.* — *RE* = *Realencyclopädie der classischen Altertumswissenschaft.* — Rohde = E. Rohde, *Der griechische Roman und seine Vorläufer,* 4. Aufl., Darmstadt 1960 (is cited according to the page numbers of the 1st edition, Leipzig 1876, which are marked in the margins of later editions). — Zimmermann = F. Zimmermann, "Die Ἐφεσιακά des sog. Xenophon von Ephesos. Untersuchungen zur Technik und Komposition", *Würzburger Jahrbücher für die Altertumswissenschaft* 4, 1949/50, 252-286.

and convincingly demonstrates its weak basis in the text of the novel. It
is to be regretted that he has not, with the same thoroughness, tackled
another, older theory which also concerns the original form of this novel.
For it is maintained that the version of the *Ephesiaca* that has come down
to us is not the original one but only a later abbreviation, an epitome of
the original work. Concerning this question, Gärtner (coll. 2072–2074)
has confined himself to a short summary of previous research. Though
he mentions one voice negative to the abridgement hypothesis (Rattenbury),[2] in his presentation of the "evidence" he is entirely on the side of
those who regard the novel as an epitome. Thus, there is the risk that the
abridgement hypothesis which was already well established, will now be
considered as fully proven. I shall therefore make an attempt to demonstrate what is, to my mind, the weak basis of the theory and open the
question anew for discussion.

E. Rohde, *Der griechische Roman* (p. 401), was the first to point out the
possibility that the *Ephesiaca* is an epitome: "In places, this story almost
reads as no more than a summary (*Inhaltsangabe*) of a story; one might
almost get the idea of not having a fully developed novel before one's
eyes, but just the *skeleton* of a novel, an *extract* (*Auszug*) from an originally much more substantial book." This hypothesis was taken up by K.
Bürger in *Hermes* 27, 1892, 36–67, and further developed. Bürger tracks
down a number of inconsistencies and gaps in the story and maintains
that he has found the concrete traces of an excerptor and thus proven the
theory. Of scholars who have subsequently occupied themselves with this
novel, the majority has by and large accepted Bürger's conclusions;[3] some

---

[2] See below, n. 4.

[3] E. Mann, *Über den Sprachgebrauch des Xenophon Ephesius.* Progr. Kaiserslautern 1896, 4
and 41. — Wilamowitz, *Gött. Gel. Anz.* 163, 1901, 34. — F. Garin, *Studi ital. di filol. class.*
17, 1909, 442 and 459 n. 2. — O. Schissel von Fleschenberg, *Die Rahmenerzählung in den
ephesischen Geschichten des Xenophon von Ephesus*, Innsbruck 1909, 5. — A. Calderini in
Caritone di Afrodisia, Le avventure di Cherea e Calliroe, Torino 1913, 36. — Dalmeyda
pp. XXVI f. *et passim.* — Kerényi pp. 105, 232 and 236. — A. Wifstrand, *Εἰκότα* V, Lund
1945, 15 and 17 (= K. Hum. Vetenskapssamf. i Lund, årsber. 1944–45, 83 and 85). — Zimmermann pp. 253 and 286. — O. Weinreich in the postscript to Heliodor, *Aethiopica.
Die Abenteuer der schönen Chariklea*, Zürich 1950, 331. — R. Helm, *Der antike Roman*, 2.,
durchges. Aufl., Göttingen 1956 (= Studienhefte zur Altertumswiss., 4), 43. — P. Grimal
in the introd. to *Romans grecs et latins*, Paris 1958, XX. — R. Nuti in *Il romanzo classico.*
A cura di Q. Cataudella, Roma 1958, 183. — Merkelbach p. 91. — A. Papanikolaou,
"Chariton und Xenophon von Ephesos. Zur Frage der Abhängigkeit", in Χάρις Κ. Ἰ.
Βουρβέρη, Athens 1964, 305 n. 6 and 320. — Perry p. 346. — It has no doubt contributed

→

have expressed a certain scepticism about them,[4] but to my knowledge   120
no one has presented a critical examination of Bürger's arguments. With
this general acceptance it has followed, on the one hand, that scholars
have avoided dealing with those parts of the novel that Bürger singled
out as abbreviated (thus, e.g., Schissel and Zimmermann),[5] on the other,
that difficult problems of textual criticism and peculiar linguistic phenomena could with some relief be blamed on the excerptor. It may be
looked upon as symptomatic for the treatment of this problem today that
Merkelbach (p. 91 n. 1) remarks in passing: "A new editor of Xenophon
should in the critical apparatus mark the places where the epitomizer
has abbreviated the text."[*] A further consequence is that in discussions
about potentially abbreviated editions of other ancient novels, the *Ephesiaca* is often referred to as a certain case of epitomizing.

  In this situation, the first requirement must be a careful examination
of the evidence that Bürger brought forward; what has later been added
by other scholars concerning small details will be included just in a few
cases, since it is without exception a matter of further construction on
the basis of Bürger (this is also true for Dalmeyda in the introduction
and footnotes to his edition and for Gärtner in the *RE*). After examining
Bürger's results (II) I shall briefly touch on other possible explanations   121
for peculiarities in the narrative style of the *Ephesiaca* (III) and deal with
the problem of the number and length of its various "books" (IV); finally, there will follow a survey of other abridgement hypotheses in the
field of ancient popular fiction (V).

to the general acceptance of the abridgement hypothesis that Dalmeyda in his edition,
which is the only modern one of the novel, gives his full support to Bürger's exposition:
"Cette impression, fort juste, a été confirmée de façon décisive par l'excellente étude de
K. Bürger, et la lecture attentive des *Éphésiaques* ne fait que suggérer de nouveaux arguments à l'appui de ses judicieuses observations."

[4] E.H. Haight, *Essays on the Greek romances,* New York 1943, 41. — Th. Sinko, *Eos* 41,
1940–46, 34. — R.M. Rattenbury, *Gnomon* 22, 1950, 75. — Q. Cataudella in *Il romanzo
classico*, Rome 1958, XI n. 2. — A. Lesky, *Gesch. der griech. Lit.,* 632, 920.

[5] In the works referred to in nn. 1 and 3 above.

[*] [This advice was followed by A.D. Papanikolaou in his Teubner edition of the *Ephesiaca*
(Leipzig 1973), cf. *Praefatio* pp. xi–xii; in an additional apparatus, between the *apparatus
fontium* and the *apparatus criticus*, Bürger's conjectural demarcation of abbreviated sections is diligently registered and, as it were, codified. Cf. further my review of the edition
in *Gnomon* 49, 1977, 457–462, reprinted in the present volume as No. **17.**]

II

Bürger first states that in comparison with the other "sophistic novels of love", Xenophon's novel exhibits "a quite remarkable brevity and dryness in its narrative style (*Darstellung*)" (p. 36); further, that this characterization is not valid for the *whole* novel — for in this novel too, there are sections that are provided with full rhetorical ornamentation (e.g., I 2; 10; 13; 14; II 6); the merely narrative parts differ strongly from those "rhetorical digressions (*Abschweifungen*)" (p. 37). In particular, he points at two episodes with similar contents, namely, the failed attempts of Manto (II 3–5) and Cyno (III 12,4) to win the favour of the hero, Habrocomes, by cunning and violence (pp. 38–40). In the first case, full use is made of the motif through artful speeches, monologues and letters (altogether ca. 3 pages in the Teubner edition);[6] in the latter, the episode is brought to a conclusion in one single sentence. That far, one may agree with Bürger in his description of the "double face" of the novel. But it must be stressed immediately that there are no clear borderlines between the two kinds of narrative style — they run into each other, and all intermediate stages occur. Bürger's conclusion, however, is dubious: "Since it is not easy to imagine for what reasons an author might be induced to produce a composition of such a contradictory nature (*Zwiespältigkeit*), already what has been demonstrated so far seems to be enough to justify the conclusion that we are dealing with the excerption of a narrative that was originally uniformly structured with regard to rhetoric" (p. 41). Still, Bürger goes on to show the "traces of the excerption" in the text. We shall come back to these traces later, but pause at this point to examine the validity of the conclusion just quoted and to consider its consequences.

Are we really entitled to assume that every author must form his work quite homogeneously? Is he not free, on one occasion to work out a certain theme with the greatest care, using all rhetorical means, but on another to deal with the same theme using only few words — especially, if his imagination and range of variation with regard to style are not exactly great? In Xenophon's case, attention has often been called to

122

---

[6] *Erotici Scriptores Graeci*. Rec. R. Hercher, T. I, Leipzig 1858. In the following, all *quantitative* data (pages and lines) are counted according to the Teubner edition, whereas the text is always (if nothing else is stated) *quoted* according to Dalmeyda's Budé edition (see above, n. 1).

the monotony of his language ("the utterly simplified syntax", Gärtner col. 2071), the stereotyped character of his phraseology (Rohde p. 407 nn. 1 and 2, Bürger p. 44 n. 1, Dalmeyda pp. XXVII ff.), and so on, all characteristic of the whole novel, not only of the parts that have been described as "abbreviated".* Consequently, he may not even have had the ability to clothe the whole "skeleton" of the novel uniformly with rhetorical flesh. Or he may not have felt any obligation whatsoever to do so. The Greek novels do not belong to a genre with as strictly fixed rules as the officially acknowledged kinds of literature of the classical period. They are, as B.E. Perry, *The ancient romances* (pp. 99 f., 118, 175 ff.), has recently emphasized, to a high degree dependent on the initiative and ability of every single author. Moreover, the absence of formal fetters seems to apply to the "presophistic"[7] novels (Chariton, Xenophon). Others (Longus, Achilles Tatius, Heliodorus), it is true, who belonged to the stylistic movement of the Second Sophistic, reached a higher literary level (and were thus probably not suited or meant for the same wide audience as the former). Even so, the existence of these sophistically shaped works of art does not allow us to read the same ideal into an earlier period or another writer, if the material at hand does not give us sufficient support to do so. Thus, Bürger's reference to Achilles Tatius and Heliodorus when restoring the original shape of the *Ephesiaca* has no value as evidence. Rather, we have to inspect the text itself to see whether it is likely or not that the detailed descriptions that Bürger supplements, have ever been there.

We may be able to get closer to an answer to this question by investigating a narrative device that occurs very often in this novel, the retro-

---

* [For a full-scale investigation of Xenophon's style and its oral character, see now J.N. O'Sullivan, *Xenophon of Ephesus: His compositional technique and the birth of the novel*, Berlin & New York 1995.]

[7] Cf. W. Schmid, *Neue Jahrb. für das klass. Altert.* 13, 1904, 485 (also in the appendix to Rohde, 1914³, 610). The term "presophistic" is not necessarily to be understood as a *chronological* indication. Perry, p. 109: The two phases in the development of the novel "may be called the presophistic and the sophistic respectively, in order to indicate their historical sequence; but since the difference between the two kinds is due less to the age in which they appear than to the mentality and educational background of the authors themselves, and the class of readers for whom they wrote, it follows that romances of the presophistic type (or the non-sophistic), may be produced in the same age as that in which the sophistic type is coming to the fore, as they were in the second century after Christ." — The same principal attitude is to be found also in O. Schissel von Fleschenberg, *Entwicklungsgeschichte des griechischen Romanes im Altertum*, Halle 1913, VIII f.

spective recapitulation.[8] The linear narrative of the novel is now and then interrupted by the insertion of a short summary of events that have been narrated earlier in the novel. Formally, such a summary is put into the mouth of one of the acting characters, as direct or indirect speech. We take as an example the point where two servants, Leucon and Rhode, relate their adventures from the day they were separated from Habrocomes:

V 10, 1 καὶ πίπτουσι πρὸ τῶν ποδῶν αὐτοῦ καὶ τὰ καθ᾽ αὑτοὺς διηγοῦνται, τὴν ὁδὸν τὴν εἰς Συρίαν ἀπὸ Τύρου, τὴν Μαντοῦς ὀργήν, τὴν ἔκδοσιν, τὴν πρᾶσιν τὴν εἰς Λυκίαν, τὴν τοῦ δεσπότου τελευτήν, τὴν περι-ουσίαν, τὴν εἰς Ῥόδον ἄφιξιν.

The line of action summarized here is to be found piecemeal at different places earlier in the novel: II 9,1-2; II 10,4; V 6,3-4. The main points of what they have experienced are carefully listed in the nominal recapitulation. Now, a recapitulation of this completeness is, of course, rare in the novel. The lines of action devoted to the main characters, Anthia and Habrocomes, are much more detailed when they are first narrated than those of the secondary characters, and consequently the recapitulations have to be more selective. Yet, through the pure number of single recapitulation elements (altogether ca. 120 in retrospective recapitulations of this kind), a large proportion of the main action is covered. In this way, we have in the novel itself a kind of key (*Fazit*) to its contents, even if it is incomplete and sometimes ambiguous.

What results can we obtain from this "key" for the abridgement hypothesis? Firstly, an investigation of the separate elements of the formally fixed recapitulations shows that in practically all cases a clear correlate is to be found in the preceding narrative.[9] This confirms what is already

124

[8] Cf. O. Schissel von Fleschenberg, *Wiener Studien* 30, 1908, 241; A. Calderini in the introd. to his trans. of Chariton (see above, n. 3), p. 148 f.; R.M. Rattenbury in Héliodore, *Les Éthiopiques*, T. II, 2. éd., Paris 1960, 87 n. 1; Zimmermann, p. 265. — I shall present an investigation of this narrative device in another context; here I restrict myself to summarizing the results relevant for the present limited question. [The investigation was published in T. Hägg, *Narrative technique in ancient Greek romances: Studies of Chariton, Xenophon Ephesius, and Achilles Tatius* (Acta Instituti Atheniensis Regni Sueciae, Series in 8o, VIII), Stockholm 1971, Ch. 7.]

[9] The reference seems to be unclear in four cases only, but without giving any grounds for the abridgement hypothesis: III 3,1 τὴν φυγήν must refer to the happenings in II 10,1 or II 12,2, but does not fit either very well; V 9,9 τὴν φυγήν probably refers to V 3,3, but the chronology of the recapitulation makes the reference unclear (cf. Dalmeyda p. 69 n. 1, und F.W. Schmidt, *Jahrb. für class. Phil.* ed. A. Fleckeisen 52, 1882, 199); V 10,11 τὴν ἔκδοσιν is ambiguous (cf. Xenophontis Ephesii *de Anthia et Habrocome Ephesiacorum libri V.* Rec. P.H. Peerlkamp, Haarlem 1818, 58 and 373; Dalmeyda p. 72; M. Hadas, *Three Greek romances*, New York 1953, 165); V 14,1, cf. below, n. 10.

obvious when reading the novel and has not been denied by Bürger, namely, that no substantial gaps are to be found in the course of the main action. It is difficult to imagine how such exact summaries of the contents as, for instance, Anthia's "catalogue" in V 14,1–2[10] could be correct otherwise (unless a very thorough and talented epitomizer had occupied himself with the work, which does not seem to conform with the picture generally drawn). Another result of the investigation is of greater importance for the present question, while at the same time, it is by nature not as unambiguous. As far as one can rely on it, however, it seems emphatically to contradict the abridgement hypothesis. It appears that the retrospects stress the *same* episodes as the primary narrative. The love between Habrocomes and Anthia, the oracle (I 6,2), the oaths (II 1,4–6), the episode with Manto (II 3 ff.) and that with Perilaus (II 13, III 4–8) are the most common elements of the recapitulations; and, at the same time, they are the junctures in the plot of the novel, in the form it is transmitted, that exhibit the most meticulous rhetorical outfit. Let us look at the examples Bürger refers to! The Manto episode, as we have seen, is frequently mentioned in the retrospects. The Cyno episode, on the other hand, which was accorded a summary piece of narrative in III 12,3–6, without direct speech or any other rhetorical embellishment, is neglected in the retrospects as well: the name Cyno is not mentioned in the regular recapitulations,[11] while the name Manto occurs three times in such positions (III 3,1; 8,7; V 10,11), and is thus regarded as a familiar concept by the author. We may notice the same relation concerning the Perilaus episode compared to the Psammis and Polyidus episodes.[12] Now, if one states, as Bürger (pp. 36 ff.) does, that the original version contained Cyno, Psammis and Polyidus episodes with the same rhetorical apparatus as the Manto and Perilaus episodes, then it will be necessary to find an explanation also for the fact that the relative importance of these episodes in the primary narrative corresponds so well with their roles in the recapitulations. Another example: the impressive shipwreck

125

---

[10] Analysed by O. Schissel von Fleschenberg, "Technik der Romanschlüsse im griechischen Liebesroman", *Wiener Studien* 30, 1908, 234 ff. — Schissel interprets V 14,1 ξύλα as "Scheiterhaufen" ("pile of wood, stake"), which cannot be correct; one should rather think of the "wooden beams" in IV 6,4–5.

[11] The mention in IV 4,2 is not retrospective. The whole episode is recapitulated in IV 2,1, it is true, but only to reestablish the connection with III 12,6.

[12] The name Perilaus: III 8,7; V 14,2. The whole episode: III 10,4; V 5,5; V 14,1; cf. also III 9,5–8. — Psammis and Polyidus: only V 14,2.

scene which Bürger depicts following models in the other novels and inserts in II 11,10, instead of the meagre description transmitted: Why is there not a single reference to it later in the novel? A conscientious epitomizer may have omitted allusions to events that do not occur in his epitomized version of the novel; but no doubt it must be looked upon as highly improbable that he should also, with almost scrupulous care, have deleted from the stereotyped retrospects even references to episodes which, though abbreviated, are still left in the epitome, just in order to keep a subtle inner balance. Obviously, the results of this investigation cannot be regarded as final proof against the abridgement hypothesis; for the material is fragile and we cannot, of course, demand absolute consistency or mathematical precision from the original author either, with regard to his shaping of the retrospects. Still, it would be odd if the epitomizer had not, even once, been caught up in the tight net of recapitulations; at some place at least he should have betrayed himself by letting a retrospect say too much or something different from the primary narrative! Instead, we now see in the recapitulations, even if in an inexact and fragmentary way, a kind of reflection of the action of the novel, precisely in its "uneven" form.

We now return to Bürger's exposition. After his description of the "double face" of the novel summarized above, he procedes, "in order to complete the evidence", to show "in detail the traces of the excerption, as they may be detected in the form of unclear points and contradictions in every excerpted work" (p. 41). He thus employs the same method as he had used with success in his dissertation on the Lucianic tale of the ass.[13] He places the main emphasis on Xenophon's description of a shipwreck and robber attack in II 11,10-11; this is, in his view, the first clearly abbreviated passage in the novel, but at the same time the *only* one where he can make the assumption of excerption not only "probable, but necessary" (p. 48). Therefore, we too have to examine this passage thoroughly; it is quoted according to the text of Dalmeyda:[14]

II 11,10-11 οἱ δὲ ἔμποροι λαβόντες τὴν Ἀνθίαν εἰς τὸ πλοῖον ἦγον καὶ νυκτὸς ἐπελθούσης ᾖεσαν τὴν ἐπὶ Κιλικίας· ἐναντίῳ δὲ πνεύματι κατεχόμενοι καὶ τῆς νεὼς διαρραγείσης μόλις ἐν σανίσι τινὲς σωθέντες ἐπ᾽ αἰγιαλοῦ τινος ἦλθον· εἶχον δὲ καὶ τὴν Ἀνθίαν. (11) ἦν δὲ ἐν τῷ τόπῳ

[13] C. Bürger, *De Lucio Patrensi*. Diss. Berlin 1887. See below, section V.

[14] On the text in II 11,11, cf. A. Wifstrand, *Εἰκότα* V, Lund 1945, 17, and *Εἰκότα* VI, Lund 1957, 13 (= K. Hum. Vetenskapssamf. i Lund, årsber. 1944-45, 85 and 1956-57, 29).

ἐκείνῳ ὕλη δασεῖα. τὴν οὖν νύκτα ἐκείνην πλανώμενοι ἐν αὐτῇ [τῇ ὕλῃ] ὑπὸ τῶν περὶ τὸν Ἱππόθοον τὸν λῃστὴν συνελήφθησαν. (The narrative then shifts to a section of the parallel line of action centred on Habrocomes, II 12; after 23 lines it returns to Anthia:) II 13,1–2 οἱ δὲ περὶ τὸν Ἱππόθοον τὸν λῃστὴν ἐκείνης μὲν τῆς νυκτὸς ἔμειναν εὐωχούμενοι, τῇ δὲ ἐξῆς περὶ τὴν θυσίαν ἐγίνοντο. παρεσκευάζετο δὲ πάντα καὶ ἀγάλματα τοῦ Ἄρεος καὶ ξύλα καὶ στεφανώματα· (2) ἔδει δὲ τὴν θυσίαν γενέσθαι τρόπῳ τῷ συνήθει. (The sacrificial ritual is described in 4 lines; after this short digression, the narrative returns to the present situation:) ἔδει δὲ τὴν Ἀνθίαν οὕτως ἱερουργηθῆναι.

We may summarize Bürger's arguments (pp. 41–48) as follows: (1) Shipwrecks are usually exploited by the novelists for long-winded rhetorical ornamentation (cf. Ach. Tat. III 1–5; Hld. V 27; Petron. 114; *Hist. Apoll.* 11–12); here, however, the motif is disposed of in a single sentence. (2) In addition, this sentence is unclear and incoherent: between the contrary winds and the rescuing, the action is too rapid and abrupt; "the excerptor has left out the main part ... and superficially conjoined the poor remnants from beginning and end by καί" (p. 43). (3) The description of the robber attack is also scanty; cf. the narrative with a similar motif in Ach. Tat. III. (4) The robber chief Hippothous is introduced in a way "only conceivable, according to all rules of grammar and logic, if he had been mentioned previously" (pp. 43 f.); the lack of any introduction of this important character is especially striking because Xenophon has worked out a stereotyped way of introducing his characters. (5) When, after the interruption, the narrative returns to the robbers and Anthia, "the sacrifice" is mentioned in the definite form; yet it has not been spoken of previously. (6) The clause ἔδει δὲ τὴν Ἀνθίαν οὕτως ἱερουργηθῆναι is incomprehensible (unless a motivation is added, as in Ach. Tat. III 19,3) — why *must precisely Anthia* be sacrificed? (7) Later (II 14,1), Habrocomes accidentally meets with Hippothous οὐ πρὸ πολλοῦ τοῦ ἄντρου τοῦ λῃστρικοῦ; but a "robber's cave" has not been mentioned earlier in our story. — So far the circumstantial evidence; Bürger believes he has found the final proof in the retelling of the same episode in III 3,3. Before proceeding to that piece of evidence, however, we shall examine the former ones.

Concerning the first and third arguments, I refer to the objections already raised above: the novelists, it is true, draw from the same sources and often shape their motifs in similar ways, but surely that does not mean that one is entitled to *demand* from a certain author at a certain place a specific realization of a motif. Furthermore, Xenophon has already in I 13-14 dragged out the motif "distress at sea", and that was perhaps enough for him. The second argument in fact only says that one or two elements in the description have perhaps dropped out; it is arbitrary to assume a fully developed scene with pathos and direct speech. The fourth point is the strongest one: Hippothous should really, at least according to the rules that prevail in this novel and are well analysed by Bürger (pp. 44 f.), have been properly introduced before his name could be used as a means of identification for the band of robbers. The fifth and seventh arguments are worth considering, but not really conclusive; such small slips may easily be blamed on the author, especially here where the train of thought has been interrupted by the insertion of a section from the Habrocomes action (II 12) and by the first part of the Perilaus episode (II 13, 3-8), respectively. The sixth argument, finally, is due to a misunderstanding. It belongs to the author's stereotyped way of expressing himself after a digression that he resumes the main narrative again by repeating some words that occurred before the digression (cf. I 8,1-3; V 4,8-10). It follows that ἔδει after the digression is not at all meant to denote any compulsion to sacrifice precisely Anthia, but only refers to the observation of the usual ritual, exactly as the same phrase was used before the digression. The word should thus neither be replaced with ἐδόκει (as Bürger p. 45 suggests in passing, referring to the parallel in III 3,4 ταύτην ἔδοξε τῷ Ἄρει θῦσαι), nor be interpreted as a sign of epitomizing. If there is something we miss in this context, it is only the same as what seemed offensive with regard to τὴν θυσίαν, the omission of any mention of the *decision* to sacrifice Anthia.

Later in the narrative Bürger finds the final confirmation of his impression that the passage discussed has been distorted precisely through the activity of an epitomizer. Hippothous, the robber chief, and Habrocomes have met accidentally. Hippothous tells his companion the story of his life and is then informed about Habrocomes' misfortune (III 2-3,1). It occurs to him that Anthia, Habrocomes' wife, may be identical with the girl he captured but lost again. He supplements his story in the following way: III 3,3-4 "ἄλλο" ἔφη "σοὶ [ὀλίγου] διήγημα παρῆλθον οὐκ εἰπών· (4) πρὸ ὀλίγου τοῦ τὸ λῃστήριον ἁλῶναι ἐπέστη τῷ ἄντρῳ κόρη καλὴ πλανωμένη, τὴν ἡλικίαν ἔχουσα τὴν αὐτὴν σοί, καὶ πατρίδα ἔλεγε τὴν σήν· πλέον γὰρ οὐδὲν ἔμαθον· ταύτην ἔδοξε τῷ Ἄρει θῦσαι." This report thus concerns the same events as those narrated in II 11,11 and 13,1-2. According to Bürger (p. 46), "it is a matter of course that such secondary narratives as just tell the reader what he already knows are kept as concise as possible." (There is a parallel instance in Xen. Eph. III 9,4–7.) "Now", Bürger continues, "the narrative is short enough in our passage too, but still almost more detailed, remarkably enough, than the primary description earlier in the novel; and, the most striking thing about it: however short it is, it still brings something that is quite new and something that is rather different from what was narrated previously." What is quite new is to be found in the words from καὶ πατρίδα to ἔμαθον, what is different is that Anthia has now arrived in the neighbourhood of the cave quite alone, not accompanied by the merchants. In Bürger's view, these things must originally have been told in the first narrative, in II 11,11, as well, namely, how Anthia was separated from the merchants, etc. He is well aware of the hypothetical nature of any attempt to supplement what has been lost, but ventures to outline the contents of the original version in the following way: "she (that is, Anthia) has in her confusion approached the robbers of her own accord, without suspecting their true character, and trustingly begged them for help, thus providing an opportunity for her fatherland too to be mentioned in a lament on her sad fate" (p. 47).

Now, is it really "irrefutably established that what is alluded to here in the short recapitulation, cannot possibly have been missing in the first description of these events" (Bürger p. 48)? And "that the descripton of the adventure with the robbers must have been infinitely more extensive in the original text" (p. 46)? Firstly, it seems dubious to establish as a fact that a recapitulation must in every respect be more summary than the first description. Rather, it depends on the *function* of the secondary narrative whether it should be detailed or not. In the present description (III 3,3–4), it is not only the "new" details which Bürger mentions that appear; in the passage quoted above, reference is made as well to the girl's beauty and age, and later in the same speech Hippothous returns to Anthia's appearance and dress: III 3,5 ἦν δὲ καλὴ πάνυ, Ἀβροκόμη, καὶ ἐσταλμένη λιτῶς· κόμη ξανθή, χαρίεντες ὀφθαλμοί. All this is, of course, not mentioned in the primary description in II 11,11 since it has no function there (the *reader* is aware of Anthia's beauty from the very beginning, cf., in particular, I 2,5–7); but here the motivation is obvious: Habrocomes needs exactly this information to be able to recognize the girl as Anthia. In *this* context, the mention of her *patris* too makes sense, and not as the reflection of a lament mentioning her home in the primary description of the scene, as Bürger would explain it.[15] Consequently, what is "new" in the secondary

130

description is neither striking nor offensive, only what is "different" may motivate suspicions about the first passage. The whole matter is reduced to the difference between the following two clauses: II 11, 11 πλανώμενοι ἐν αὐτῇ [τῇ ὕλῃ] ὑπὸ τῶν περὶ τὸν Ἱππόθοον τὸν λῃστὴν συνελήφθησαν, III 3,4 ἐπέστη τῷ ἄντρῳ κόρη καλὴ πλανωμένη — thus in fact only the question of number: if we make Anthia the subject in II 11,11 and change the verbal forms accordingly, the two statements are no longer incompatible.[16] But if we also take into consideration Bürger's other evidence examined above, especially the missing introduction of Hippothous, we may be justified in postulating a real lacuna in II 11,11.[17] What is lost may have been a couple of clauses in the same simple narrative style as the surrounding clauses exhibit. In any case, neither the parallel scenes in other novelists nor, as we have seen, the secondary narrative in III 3,4 allow us to conclude that originally there was at this place an extensive rhetorical showpiece. A small lacuna, originating by chance and inadequately supplemented by someone who had neither the ambitions nor the overwiew of an epitomizer, seems to me the simplest solution of the problem.

Bürger then continues (pp. 48–59) with a list of other places where he also believes there are traces of the epitomizer, even if "in fact, such a conclusive case cannot be made at any other place" (p. 48). We shall make as representative a selection as possible and add some comments.

[15] Bürger (p. 47) suggests as an alternative solution that in the complete version Anthia was asked for her name and descent, as in IV 3,6 and V 4,4; as a comparison he also adduces Heliodorus I 21 f. But these passages cannot in any way be regarded as good parallels; in all three cases, Anthia's or Chariclea's answers are interesting for the reader *only because they are false*, and that is why they are quoted by the author; a *truthful* answer on Anthia's part would have had no corresponding value as a motif.

[16] Or is Hippothous' report perhaps deliberately tendentious (as Manto's letter in II 12,1; cf. also Rhenaea's lie in V 5,7)? However, the continuation agrees badly with that interpretation; there Hippothous tells straight out about his decision to sacrifice Anthia.

[17] If we regard a lacuna here as probable, what does this mean for the abridgement hypothesis in general? Let us look at the similar discussion about Λούκιος ἢ Ὄνος! A. Mazzarino, *La Milesia e Apuleio*, Torino 1950, 91, writes about the "esempi tipici" that together constitute the chain of evidence for the epitomizing of *Onos*: "comunque, dal punto di vista metodico, è da rilevare che *basterebbe uno solo* di essi per riconoscere la verità della tesi generale, essere l'"Ὄνος un epitome" etc. But this cannot possibly be true; one lone "mistake" with regard to the content may always be explained differently (lacuna in the transmission, contamination etc.). The compelling proof (to the extent such a thing is possible in this kind of question) can be achieved only through a *chain* of such circumstantial evidence, all reducible to the same causal explanation, the deliberate abbreviation.

II 12,1. Manto's letter to Apsyrtus is, according to Bürger (pp. 48–50), so mutilated as to make it faulty and incomprehensible. "The goatherd" appears with the definite article in spite of the fact that Apsyrtus cannot have heard about him earlier, the first clause (ἔδωκάς με ἀνδρὶ ἐν ξένῃ) is "completely incomprehensible". — From a rigidly logical point of view, these remarks are justified — but not if the case is seen in its context and with the eyes of an ordinary reader. The *reader* already knows the goatherd and takes no offence at the definite form; it is certainly a "mistake" on the part of the author, but an easily understandable one: as he writes in II 11,3 μεταπέμπεται τὸν αἰπόλον, so he does here in the secondary narrative: II 12,1 μετεπεμψάμην τὸν αἰπόλον, without putting himself in the situation of the recipient of the letter. The first clause of the letter is a very brief summary of what has been narrated in detail earlier (II 5–7), but it is comprehensible to the fictitious receiver of the letter as well as the reader. The letter is conceived in a wholly functional manner; what has been told earlier is mentioned only in passing, what is new (partly also to the reader, namely, the tendentious altering of the events to Manto's advantage) is told in more detail. The author may, of course, just as well as an epitomizer, be credited with a purely functional point of view.

III 7,3 and 9,2. After a long section with Anthia as the central character, the action switches to Habrocomes in III 9,2; this is done without any indication of his place of residence: III 9,2 ὁ δὲ Ἀβροκόμης ἐζήτει καὶ ἐπολυπραγμόνει εἴ τις ἐπίσταιτο κόρην ποθὲν ξένην αἰχμάλωτον μετὰ λῃστῶν ἀχθεῖσαν· ὡς δὲ οὐδὲν εὗρεν, ἀποκαμὼν ἦλθεν οὗ καθήγοντο. It appears only gradually, even indirectly, that Habrocomes and Hippothous now happen to be in Tarsus in Cilicia, whereas the author had last left them in Cappadocia (III 3,7). Otherwise, the author always handles changes of the place of action with pedantic care.[18] Bürger is therefore of the opinion that a whole independent section describing the journey from Mazacus in Cappadocia to Tarsus in Cilicia has been omitted through the activity of the excerptor. He finds the confirmation of this assumption in "half" a transitional phrase in III 7,3: ὁ μὲν ⟨οὖν⟩ τοιαῦτα ἐθρήνει, περιβεβλήκει δὲ ἅπασαν καὶ ἠσπάζετο χεῖράς τε καὶ πόδας "νύμφη" λέγων "ἀθλία, γύναι δυστυχεστέρα". (4) ἐκόσμει δὲ αὐτὴν ... According to Bürger, the missing section must have been situated exactly at this place; the clause has the characteristics of the Xenophontic transitional phrase,[19] but "this clause cannot belong to the following, since nowhere is there the required opposite to the ὁ

132

[18] At one more place, the mention of a journey is missing: in V 9,5, Hippothous suddenly appears in Taras, although there was earlier (V 9,3) only the general indication "Italy"; but the case is not equivalent to III 9,2, since here the name Taras itself does occur.

[19] The stereotyped form and use of these transitional phrases in Xen. Eph. are analysed in detail by Bürger, pp. 51–53. — Bürger, pp. 54 ff., notices that the particle μέν is missing in two transitional phrases (III 12,1 and IV 1,5) and finds in this further traces of the excerptor; but the general stereotypy in style certainly does not need to be combined with an absolute consistency of use.

μὲν οὖν" (p. 53). — Some objections may be raised. This clause is made particularly similar to the other transitional clauses only by accepting Hercher's supplement οὖν, which is not necessary and has not been adopted by Dalmeyda;* the μέν alone hardly needs an "opposite" but may correspond with the following δέ, whereby two elements in the same chain of action are connected. The pluperfect περιβεβλήκει, it is true, is summarizing, as is often the case in the concluding clauses before the transitions, but this is not true for the following verb or for the clause as a whole; no other section in the parallel action of the novel is interrupted in the middle of events that are described in detail or immediately after a passage of direct speech. And even if we should imagine a Habrocomes section at this place, III 9,2 will remain partly unsatisfactory: the introductory clause does not have the resumptive elements (geographical names and suchlike) that generally mark the beginning of a new section.[20] Thus, it is simpler (if we are to suppose a lacuna at all;[21] even Bürger finds no "conclusive evidence" here) to assume an eventual omission to have occurred immediately before III 9,2, and not an omission of an independent section but of a short clause informing about the journey, perhaps also mentioning the quartering and the enrollment of a new band of robbers (we find similar brief information, e.g., in V 1,1–2 and V 8,1, and in IV 1,3, respectively).

III 11–12. These two chapters are, according to Bürger (p. 54), "particularly severely abbreviated"; still, he says, the epitomizer has succeeded in shaping the section almost without causing offence. A "betraying" νυκτὸς γενομένης (III 12,5), however, has been left from the more detailed narrative (which had been equipped "with exact indication of the whole course of time"). — But this particular indication of time, "when night came", has been introduced just in order to point to the particular circumstances surrounding the cruel murder, and should not be understood as the accidental remainder of a pedantically communicated time schedule. There are, on the whole, few indications of time in the novel; what happens in daytime needs no particular specification of time, only when exceptionally we hear about nocturnal happenings, is the time indicated (thus also, with the same expression and isolated, in III 2,12).

V 5,1–2. The "confusion" in the first clause, we are told, is due to the redactor; in the first part of the clause, the arrival of Polyidus is only expected, in the second it is already taken for granted; the parentheses in 5,2 became necessary owing to the abbreviation (pp. 57 f.). — Again, the impression of a lack of continuity in the clause goes back to Bürger's hypercritical attitude; the pluperfect form ἐπέπυστο expresses quite logically the condition prevailing when

---

* [nor by Papanikolaou in his Teubner edition of 1973.]

[20] Cf., e.g., II 14,1 and IV 5,1, looking back at II 12,3 and IV 4,1, respectively.

[21] Perhaps only a slip on the part of the author? It would not be surprising if, after having mentioned Perilaus' doings in Tarsus (III 9,1), he passed without further ado over to Habrocomes' experiences in the same city (9,2), forgetting in the process that his hero's last place of residence was Mazacus.

Polyidus arrives: "she *knew* (that is, already in advance) that he was bringing the girl with him, but from fear … she said nothing to him (that is, at his arrival) but made plans", and so on. With regard to the parentheses, they are of a kind that occurs often in Xenophon: they provide a piece of information exactly at the point where it is necessary for understanding the context or useful in making the narrative as simple as possible (cf. I 8,2; 13,4; II 9,1; III 2,5; 5,9; 10,4; V 4,5). Such a method should not be ascribed to lack of skill on the part of an epitomizer but to the economy of the author.

V 5,7–6,2. Here, the redactor has acted "in his most radical manner", says Bürger (p. 58); still, there are no particular stumbling-blocks to discover, a fact that does not prevent the following conclusion: the original 8–12 pages (that is, four sections that would "otherwise" occupy 2–3 pages each) have been abbreviated into 19 lines. The arbitrary character of all such arguments and calculations has already been sufficiently emphasized above.

V 6,2–3. Here too, as in V 5,1, Bürger (pp. 58 f.) finds two different points in time abruptly juxtaposed; namely, the parents' searching activities and their death; in addition, the subject οἱ γονεῖς is "quite unnecessarily" repeated in both clauses; and that a transitional clause occurs with Habrocomes instead of the parents as its main focus, makes the proof complete. — The first argument can only be described as a subjective feeling. The second one is not valid either because, on the one hand, Xenophon often repeats a noun instead of using a pronoun (cf. Dalmeyda, p. xxviii) and, on the other, in this special case he wants to avoid ambiguity by repeating the noun (between the two times the parents are mentioned, there are two additional concepts in the plural, οἱ Ἐφέσιοι and τοὺς ἀναζητήσοντας). Finally, Habrocomes as the subject in the transitional clause just indicates that the short mention of the fate of the parents is to be regarded as a digression in the Habrocomes action (connected by association with Habrocomes' intention to return home); the material at hand gives no reason for assuming that there was originally an independent line of action focussed on the parents.[22]

---

[22] Bürger p. 59 and Dalmeyda p. 64 n. 1 also find the information about the death of the parents in V 6,3 and V 15,3 incompatible, a fact they would likewise ascribe to the epitomizer. — The same fact is mentioned *three* times: V 6,3 ὑπὸ ἀθυμίας δὲ καὶ γήρως οὐ δυνηθέντες ἀντισχεῖν οἱ γονεῖς ἑκατέρων ἑαυτοὺς ἐξήγαγον τοῦ βίου. — V 6,4 τεθνήκασι δὲ αὐτῶν οἱ πατέρες, — V 15,3 ἔτυχον γὰρ ὑπὸ γήρως καὶ ἀθυμίας προτεθνηκότες. The epitomizer lets "the miserable parents at one time take their own lives and at another die from old age", says Bürger. But if we adduce V 6,4 as well and take into account the author's usual technique of recapitulation, the consistency seems flawless; in the second mention of their death only the *fact* is interesting, in the third one the temporal relationship as well (προ-, that is, *before* their children's arrival in Ephesus) but not the way they died (-τεθνηκότες is neutral as in V 6,4 τεθνήκασι). ὑπὸ γήρως καὶ ἀθυμίας is a literal (but incomplete) repetition of the accompanying circumstances, but *not* (as Bürger and Dalmeyda interpret the clause) a new, positive statement about the direct causes of death.

By studying these and some additional passages in the *Ephesiaca* we have, according to Bürger (p. 59), "got to know in detail the redactor's (*Bearbeiter*) method …, how he has taken over some sections fairly unaltered, compressed others drastically and completely left out still others." A rough calculation on the basis of Bürger's investigation gives the result that he considers about two thirds of the transmitted text to be unabbreviated (I; II 1-11,10; III 2-11; IV 2 and 6; V 1-2 and 10,6-15).[23] But here too, spread over the whole story, he finds "as in every excerpted work" (p. 61) a great number of smaller and larger lacunas. Exception is of course made for places "where the manuscript itself has lacunas which naturally do not concern us here." He then lists (pp. 61-64) several lacunas where only a single word is to be supplemented and also some where he finds more extensive elements of a clause missing. Not infrequently, these remarks appear to hit on genuine corruptions (and many textual critics[24] since Bürger have laboured with these), but often the reason for suspicion is weak or quite arbitrary: Bürger has suggested a number of supplements only in order to achieve a more beautiful parallelism, inviolable logic or an even better (that is, pure Attic) language. But even if, for the moment, we leave out of account this ambition to bring Xenophon's novel closer to the model provided by the sophistic novels proper, his method remains questionable. The lacunas present in the only extant manuscript[25] are naturally not considered as the traces of an epitomizer. But what happens in the discussion with the intermediate stages that must have existed between the original version — or the original epitomized version — and our *codex unicus*? In these too, lacunas will very probably have occurred which have nothing to do with the "abbreviated character of the work". Rather, particularly in the case of the novels we have to allow for a not very careful transmission (Wilamowitz[26] speaks of the "barbarization of unprotected texts" [*Verwilderung*

---

[23] Yet, the epitomizer's hand is sometimes noticeable in the "unabbreviated" sections as well, says Bürger (pp. 64 f.); this is the case, e.g., in I 8,2 (the description of the canopy, cf. J. Palm, "Bemerkungen zur Ekphrase in der griechischen Literatur", *K. Hum. Vetenskaps-Samf. i Uppsala, Årsbok 1965-66*, Uppsala 1967, 193 f.; see also above on V 5,1-2) and in III 10,1-3 (the transition from indirect to direct speech, cf. e.g. H. Fränkel, *Wege und Formen frühgriechischen Denkens*, 2nd ed., München 1960, 80 ff.).

[24] Listed by Gärtner col. 2089. See, in addition, G. Giangrande, "Konjekturen zu Longos, Xenophon Ephesios und Achilleus Tatios", *Miscellanea critica* I, Leipzig 1964, 97-118.

[25] *Cod. Laurentianus conv. soppr. 627* (13th century), cf. Dalmeyda pp. xxxiii f., Perry pp. 344 f. (with lit.) and Gärtner coll. 2087 f.

[26] *Gött. Gel. Anz.* 163, 1901, 34. Cf. Zimmermann, p. 286.

ungeschützter Texte] with reference to Chariton, see below, V), and small
lacunas of precisely the kind discussed here seem to be better explained   136
as the result of neglect on the part of copyists than of any ambition to
abbreviate. It is not easy to understand why an epitomizer should have
deliberately left out single words that were necessary for the context,[27]
nor, on the other hand, why a text that was once epitomized, should
have been treated worse by copyists than an original text.

If one attempts to combine Bürger's various results and put them in
relation to the actual state of affairs in the text of the novel, there emerges
a rather contradictory picture of the epitomizer and his activities. He has,
on the one hand, spared no effort to preserve the whole series of episodes
and the whole route. He allows no unmediated transitions, he carefully
controls the recapitulations, he inserts small informative parentheses in
order to make the narrative flow easily. He has at some places radically
compressed the account (at a rate of about 1:15), yet without leaving behind any traces for the sharp-sighted critic. On the other hand, he has
once (II 11,11) broken the logical coherence in a clumsy way, omitted the
introduction of one of the most important figures in the novel, Hippothous (but kept the phrases of introduction for the most insignificant
secondary characters), and also, at several places, omitted a word or half
a clause without thinking of the coherence of the clause or the content.
This care in larger matters and incomprehensible negligence in smaller
simply cannot be reduced to a common denominator.[28] It seems to me
to be the basic error of Bürger's investigation that he tries to solve the   137
real problem, the rhetorical unevenness, by adducing material of a totally different character. Firstly, he points at inconsistencies and alleged
gaps in the action. Though this may in principle be justified, it is car-

---

[27] The absurdity of such an assumption may, for instance, be illustrated by a "discovery"
made by Dalmeyda, p. 38 n. 1: III 3,3 τὴν κόμην must refer to the hair of the dead Hyperanthes; but in III 2,13 it was not mentioned that Hippothoos cut off any lock of his
beloved's hair and brought it with him, something Dalmeyda blames on the epitomizer.
Examination of the text in III 2,13 shows, however, that the words in question, ἀφελὼν
λείψανα, are strange in themselves and may thus arouse the suspicion that we have to
do with an unintended, accidental lacuna, not a deliberate abbreviation. An epitomizer
would rather have used an altogether understandable phrase to summarize the course
of action, for instance: "I buried him" — he would certainly not have kept the whole
detailed description and only cancelled a couple of words, such as "the hair"!

[28] Thus in principle the same objections that Gärtner (coll. 2076 f.) raises against Merkelbach's hypothesis of a "Helius redactor" (see above, I): this "would thus force us to
think of the redactor, on the one hand, as a fairly sensitive writer and, on the other, as
a highly unskilled propagandist for his god."

ried much too far, without taking account of what is generally to be expected from a simple novel of entertainment with regard to smaller mistakes and logical defects.[29] Secondly, as we have seen, Bürger has also tried to attribute the linguistic irregularities and the omission of single words to the same general cause. On the other hand, he has made no attempt to find out the motives or principles of a potential epitomizer from the shape of the transmitted text. What purpose will this form of novel have served? It is not a matter of eliminating all rhetoric in favour of pure adventure (we find rhetoric in large quantities in the first and last books and elsewhere too, in the monologues and dialogues),[30] nor

---

[29] I also include in this category the mistake that Dalmeyda p. 43 n. 1 and Gärtner col. 2074 find in Xen. Eph. III 7,3: in II 13,8, Anthia has totally concealed her marriage to Habrocomes; in spite of this, in III 7,3 Perilaus even knows the name of her husband. — Let us look at the scene in III 7,3! Perilaus bewails his loss of Anthia; the author lets him as a striking contrast mention Habrocomes, the happy man for whom Anthia has chosen death out of love; it is in this context natural for the author not to take into consideration that Perilaus "in reality" knows nothing at all about Habrocomes. It is a common mistake among advocates of the abridgement hypothesis that they do not look at each motif or each scene of the novel as a closed unit from which the author tries to achieve the maximal effect on each occasion; instead, they demand a long-range consistency that obviously exceeds the level of ambition of a writer of entertainment. — On some mistakes in Ach. Tat. (V 11,6 and VII 14,2), cf. Achilles Tatius, *Leucippe and Clitophon*. A comm. by E. Vilborg, Gothenburg 1962 (= Studia Graeca et Latina Gothoburgiensia, 15), 98 and 123.

[30] Therefore, the *Ephesiaca* provides no good support for Kerényi's hypothesis of the abridgement as a natural, late development of the form of the novel: "it belongs to a time in which the showpieces of rhetorically schooled writers were already hard reading, or served the needs of a social class that had not even previously been educated enough to enjoy such things" (p. 236). — O. Weinreich tries another hypothesis in his afterword to Heliodor, *Aethiopica*, Zürich 1950, 331: "The epitomizing proves the popularity of the novel: whoever found the original edition too voluminous, bought the cheaper one." Against this hypothesis one may point out, as Gärtner (col. 2073) does, "the sparse attestation (*Bezeugung*)" (no papyrus fragments, see below, III; one sole manuscript, see above, n. 25; only occasional traces in later literature, see Gärtner, col. 2087). This *argumentum e silentio* must not be overestimated, however, since our prospects of assessing the popularity or distribution of an ancient novel are limited by geographical as well as social factors. On the one hand, we have the papyri, which are representative for Egypt alone; on the other, the literary allusions and the Byzantine selection of works for copying, none of which is apt to reflect the taste of the average ancient reader of novels. — However, Gärtner's (col. 2073) own theory of some kind of private abridgement enterprise, is no more plausible; in that case, a pure anthology form (without the scrupulous preservation of the skeleton) would have been more appropriate — but, of course, the theoretical *possibility* of such a one-time event cannot be excluded. See below, V.

of selecting the showpieces, since the whole course of events has been brought along. Surely, one cannot demand more consistency from an epitomizer than from an author, but an epitome must necessarily be produced for a certain purpose, to satisfy a concrete need. Furthermore, one misses in Bürger an analysis of the concrete method by which the abridgement was produced. Is he of the opinion that the skeleton sections retain the author's words after deleting the superfluous, or that the epitomizer has himself retold the plot in his own words? In the first case, one would expect deficient connections between the clauses, false references etc. as traces of the abbreviation. In the second case, a detailed analysis of lexicon, style, prose rhythm etc. might perhaps work out the differences between original and abbreviated sections, of course on the condition that the author and the epitomizer are not identical, as Rohde (p. 401 n. 1) suggests, and that a longer period of time has to be postulated between the two, as most scholars think.[31] No such data have yet been presented to support the abridgement hypothesis, either by Bürger or by later advocates of this hypothesis.[32]

138

III

139

We may thus regard the assumption that the *Ephesiaca* is an epitome of a more extensive novel as not proven by Bürger's argumentation. Unfortunately, so far no papyrus fragment with the text of this novel has appeared, as has happened in the case of Chariton and Achilles Tatius; such fragments might perhaps have solved the question definitely. A fragment (2nd/3rd century AD) of an "Antheia novel" has been found,[33] it is true, but there seems to be no connection, as regards contents, with

---

[31] Gärtner (col. 2073) is inclined to date the epitomizing to the Byzantine period.

[32] E.Mann, *Über den Sprachgebrauch des Xenophon Ephesius.* Progr. Kaiserslautern 1896, 41, would attribute the "inconsistency in the use the most common Atticistic traits" to the "less knowledgeable later excerptor". In contrast, W. Schmid, *Bursians Jahresbericht* 108, 1901, 227, states: "if one takes into consideration that, beginning with the 2nd century, the novelists' hunt for Attic elegance in-, not decreases, one would rather prefer to attribute the incorrect forms to X. himself, not to his epitomizer, and regard the former, for the time being, roughly as Chariton's (older?) contemporary." In fact, all five "incorrect forms" that Mann p. 41 uses to illustrate his thesis are to be found in the "unabbreviated" sections of the novel!

[33] F. Zimmermann, *Griechische Roman-Papyri und verwandte Texte,* Heidelberg 1936, 78–84. Pack[2] 2627.

the *Ephesiaca*. It is worth noting that two of the proper names in the fragment (Antheia and Euxeinos) occur in the *Ephesiaca* as well, but the other names (Lysippos, Thraseas, Kleandros, Lysandros) appear only in the fragment, and the situation described in it does not fit the framework of the *Ephesiaca*. Of course, the story preserved in the fragment may still have played a role in the prehistory of our novel. One need not assume that Xenophon created his story from his own imagination, but he has, of course, like the other representatives of this genre, drawn his material from the large common stream of narrative transmitted orally or in writing.[34] Only the final composition, the fitting of the various episodes into precisely this narrative frame, and the uniform stylization must be attributed to the author of the novel. It follows that the author, in the stage when he conceived his story, may have "abbreviated" some material that he had taken over from a more detailed description. In *that* sense the Cyno episode, for instance (see above, II), is a brief version of the widespread motif of Potiphar's wife, which is commonly (also in our novel, in the Manto episode) told in more detail.[35] It is also conceivable that Xenophon's description of the robber expedition in Egypt (Book IV), which Gärtner (col. 2073) notes as abbreviated, builds on a detailed geographical description that has been abbreviated, partly even abruptly, to fit this place in the novel.[36] This kind of short version or

140

---

[34] Cf. F. Wehrli, "Einheit und Vorgeschichte der griechisch-römischen Romanliteratur", *Mus. Helv.* 22, 1965, 133–154.

[35] The story of Joseph and Potiphar's wife: M. Braun, *Griechischer Roman und hellenistische Geschichtsschreibung*, Frankfurt am Main 1934 (= Frankfurter Studien zur Religion und Kultur der Antike, 6), 23–117; idem, *History and romance in Graeco-Oriental literature*, Oxford 1938, 46–95 (the Cyno episode p. 55); S.Trenkner, *The Greek novella in the classical period*, Cambridge 1958, 64–66. — Cf. also Perry pp. 82 f., about short versions in New Comedy, in which the narrative material often (in prologues etc.) "had to be shortened and reduced to summary outlines". — In the epic too, of course, such skeleton narratives are common (e.g., *Il.* 6, 160 ff. about Bellerophon and Anteia; the tempo is even higher than that of Xenophon!).

[36] H. Henne, "La géographie de l'Égypte dans Xénophon d'Éphèse, *Rev. d'hist. de la philos. et d'hist. gén. de la civil.* 4, 1936, 97–106, concludes that Xenophon himself probably never visited Egypt; his description of the country is, however, not to be regarded as pure phantasy but as "reminiscences scolaires ou littéraires" (a combination of knowledge taken from books, the use of a map of the Nile Delta, and oral information?). — It may be noted in this context that Gärtner, col. 2084, in his discussion of the relationship between Xen. Eph. and Chariton, readily takes over the strange argument of F. Garin *(Studi ital. di filol. class.* 17, 1909, 426 f.), according to whom Xenophon's geographical framework

→

178

abbreviation has, of course, in principle nothing to do with the assumption of an abridgment of the finished novel, but the possibility cannot be ruled out that under certain circumstances the two kinds may leave behind similar "traces" in the text.

In this context, we may also take into consideration the inadequate motivation that occurs at various places in the novel, for instance, when Habrocomes departs for Egypt in III 10,4 or for Italy in IV 4,2. To my mind, the simplest explanation is to regard these deficiences as the traces of a kind of contamination of motifs, although not noticeable to such a high degree as Perry demonstrates in the Latin novels (Apuleius and *Historia Apollonii*).[37] The author draws his motifs from different sources and tells them for the qualities each possesses in itself, without attaching much importance to fitting them in a natural way into the larger framework of the action. Thus, the motivation at the transition from one episode to another, if it occurs at all, becomes artificial or even absurd. It is perhaps possible to explain another peculiarity of the *Ephesiaca* in the same way as well, namely, the "loose ends" in the story. Some details appear to be brought in for a definite purpose, but then come to nothing (e.g., Anthia's false information in IV 3,6 and V 4,4 or the tamed dogs in IV 6,6–7 and V 2,5–6).[38] The author has brought them

141

is dependent on that of Chariton, e.g.: "Habrocomes arrives in Alexandria (III 10,4) because Chaereas too wants to search for his missing Callirhoe in Africa (III 3,7 f.)." We are supposed to believe that Xenophon, who obviously had at his disposal a detailed material about Egypt (in addition to the geographical facts and names in IV 1 and V 2–2, also knowledge of the Isis and Apis cults in I 6,2, III 11,4, IV 3,3, V 4,8–11 etc.), would have situated a fifth of his plot in this country only because Chaereas *once* in Chariton's novel (III 3,8) is given Africa (Λιβύην) as his particular area in the search for Callirhoe; this plan, however, is never carried out, none of the main characters in Chariton's novel ever sets foot on Africa's soil!

[37] Pp. 254–282 and 294–324. — Perry, however, writes (p. 300): "*Contaminatio* is a peculiarly Latin literary phenomenon. Its presence in Greek literature after Homer, including the Greek romances, can be only rarely if ever detected" (further developed p. 321 n. 3). Now, Perry gives no definition of his own of the concept (cf. Schanz-Hosius, *Gesch. der röm. Lit.* I, 1927⁴, 129) and does not make clear where he draws the line between *contaminatio* and the kind of combination of disparate motifs that he too assumes for the Greek novels (cf., e.g., p. 320). — Cf. also A. Lesky, "Motivkontamination", *Wiener Studien* 55, 1937, 21–31 (= A.L., *Gesammelte Schriften,* Bern & München 1966, 327–334) with important considerations of matters of principle and examples from Hesiod, Apollodorus and Petronius.

[38] On the dogs, cf. Bürger p. 57 and Gärtner col. 2074. — One further example: I 14,4, cf. F. Garin, *Studi ital. di filol. class.* 17, 1909, 424 f., Dalmeyda p. xxx, and A. Papanikolaou in *Χάρις Κ. Ἰ. Βουρβέρῃ*, Athens 1964, 315 f.

along together with motifs that he has taken over, but has then forgotten them again (and we need not think of a "later" abbreviation). A careful author with specific literary ambitions, as for instance Heliodorus, may hide the joints and delete the traces of contamination; a less ambitious or skilful author, in contrast, does not care about the inconsistencies. That absurd motivations and logical gaps do not diminish a novel's popularity, if only the separate composite parts are attractive, is shown by widely circulated 'popular books' (*Volksbücher*) of the type of the *Historia Apollonii regis Tyri*.

IV

In brief statements about the state of our novel, one further argument is often adduced as an important support for the validity of Bürger's abridgement hypothesis.[39] Bürger himself, in contrast, deliberately refrained from using that argument, and it is in fact incompatible with his results. The *Suda* (s.v. Ξενοφῶν Ἐφέσιος) attributes *ten* books to the novel, while the transmitted version is divided into *five* books. If the information in the *Suda* is to be trusted, a length of about 140 pages must be assumed for the original version if the book length of the transmitted version is taken as the norm, or of about 200 pages according to the average length of the books of the other novels, or even about 300 pages, the size of Heliodorus' ten books.[40] Now, as we have seen, Bürger in his analysis took precisely the unevenness of the text as his point of departure and arrived at the conclusion that only about a third of the transmitted whole (that is, about 25 pages) is to be regarded as more or less abbreviated. Is it really possible to imagine that the narrative material in these 25 pages was originally related five, six or ever ten times more

---

[39] E.g., by Weinreich, Grimal, Merkelbach and Perry at the places referred to above, n. 3. Now also by Gärtner, see below, n. 42. — Rohde p. 401 n. 1 called attention to the information provided by the *Suda* and proposed "an *epitome* of the original story which reduced it to half its size"; in the 2nd ed., however, a reservation was inserted pointing at the possibility of "a different book division".

[40] The length of the books in the Greek novels, counted according to the Teubner editions (for Heliodorus, ed. I. Bekker, Leipzig 1855, for the others ed. R. Hercher, Leipzig 1858–59): Char.: 8 books., 154 pp., 24-19-23-16-20-17-14-21, average 19 pp. — X.E.: 5 books, 71 pp., 17-14-14-6-20, average 14 pp. — A.T.: 8 books, 176 pp., 21-30-22-19-26-17-16-25, average 22 pp. — Long.: 4 books, 86 pp., 21-22-21-22, average 22 pp. — Hld.: 10 books, 309 pp., 36-38-19-25-36-21-39-27-29-39, average 31 pp.

fully and still, in spite of the extraordinarily high degree of abbreviation, no essential gaps in the coherence or greater differences in style have occurred? Xenophon's style is *invariably* simple, additive, paratactic etc. (cf. Gärtner col. 2070–2072). Yet, K. Kerényi (*Die griechisch-orientalische Romanliteratur*, p. 236), evidently has no such reservations when he calls the *Ephesiaca* "probably the most extensive novel of the period in question." He thinks, of course, of the indisputable richness of narrative material in the novel — but is it really possible to decide the actual extent of a literary work only by mechanically adding up the concrete elements of the plot? To my mind, the striving for simplicity and a high tempo in the narrative, which can be noted also in parts of the novel that nobody has marked as abbreviated (in contrast to the retardatory style of Achilles Tatius and Heliodorus), excludes such an assumption. Theoretically, it might also be suggested that the abbreviation had been achieved mainly through the suppression of a series of inserted stories without organic links to the main action. Yet, to my knowledge, nobody has found any obvious points in the *Ephesiaca* where such insertions might have been made, as is the case with the Ὄνος (see below, V). Finally, a later, expanded edition of the novel in ten books would also be conceivable (as, for instance, Apuleius expanded the original story of the ass into eleven books, see below, V), or one might simply assume a different book division. However, all speculations on the basis of the information given in the *Suda* are futile if one considers the "uncertainty of all numbers occurring in our manuscript tradition".[41]

As was mentioned in passing above, Bürger (p. 41 n. 1) does not believe that the number stated in the *Suda* is reliable. Instead,[42] he regards

143

---

[41] Thus A. Lesky, *Gesch. der griech. Lit.,* 1963², 921, on account of different numbers referring to the *Babyloniaca* of Iamblichus, see below, V. — On the change to έ instead of ί, already suggested long ago, see Gärtner, col. 2072.

[42] It is incomprehensible how Gärtner col. 2072 thinks he can *combine* the evidence of the *Suda* number with that of the different book lengths and even, in addition, make it compatible with the thesis championed by O. Schissel von Fleschenberg, *Die Rahmenerzählung in den ephesischen Geschichten des Xenophon von Ephesus*, Innsbruck 1909, namely, that "Ch. II 1 of the epitome belongs to Book I of the original" (p. 48). Are we to imagine an original novel of 10 books, with logical book divisions and uniform book length, which an epitomizer has abbreviated unevenly? If he had *kept* the book divisions, that might possibly have explained the different lengths of the books; but if he also reduced the number of books from ten to five and introduced new book divisions, we are as far from explaining the unevenness of the book lengths as before. See below, n. 44.

the transmitted book division as the original one and sticks to the remarkable difference in length between the Xenophontic books, which
is most striking between the fourth (6 pages) and the fifth (20 pages).[43]
But does this difference really reflect the abbreviation, as Bürger himself has seen it? It is true that he regards the particularly short fourth
book as abbreviated for the most part; but more than half of the fifth
book too should consist of excerpted sections (and among them is the
"most radically" abbreviated section, V 5,7–6,2, see above, II) and still,
the book is now, with its 20 pages, longer than the unabbreviated first
book (17 pages) and the two books that are only abbreviated in smaller
parts (Book II and III of 14 pages each). Considerations of this kind
cannot get us anywhere, as long as we do not know when or according to what principles the book division was done.[44] The other novels

[43] See above, n. 40.

[44] Literature on ancient book division: Th. Birt, *Das antike Buchwesen in seinem Verhältnis zur Litteratur,* Berlin 1882, 286–341 (the basic investigation); idem, *Kritik und
Hermeneutik nebst Abriss des antiken Buchwesens,* München 1913 (Handb. der klass. Alter-
tumswiss. I:33), 292–295; K. Dziatzko, *RE* III, 1899, 940 f., 951 f.; idem, *Untersuchungen
über ausgewählte Kapitel des antiken Buchwesens,* Leipzig 1900, 141 f., 156 f.; W. Schubart,
Das Buch bei den Griechen und Römern, 2nd ed., Berlin & Leipzig 1921, 43, 51–55; P.
Junghanns see below n. 55; C. Høeg in *Studi e testi* 124, Città del Vaticano 1946, 1–5; C.
Wendel, *Die griechisch-römische Buchbeschreibung verglichen mit der des Vorderen Orients,*
Halle (Saale) 1949 (= Hallische Monographien, 3), 44–59; F.G. Kenyon, *Books and readers
in ancient Greece and Rome,* 2nd ed., Oxford 1951, 16 f., 52, 64 f.; E. Arns, *La technique
du livre d'après Saint Jérôme,* Paris 1953, 103–118; *Geschichte der Textüberlieferung,* Vol. I,
Zürich 1961, 44 f.; F. Wieacker, *Textstufen klassischer Juristen,* Göttingen 1960 (= Abh.
der Akad. der Wiss. in Göttingen, Phil.-hist. Kl., 3. Folge, Nr. 45), 67 f., 120–122. — At
this place, it is only possible to indicate briefly a few of the as yet unsolved problems that
obstruct the fruitful use of the book division for the abridgement hypothesis: (1) *Book
length*. According to Birt (*Ant. Buchw.,* 295, 302, 324; *Abriss,* 293), the novelists (as also
the epistolographers) use the format of the 'book of poetry' (*Gedichtbuch*), that is, the
single books are considerably smaller than those of most prose authors (poetry: 700–1100
lines, prose: 1500–2500 lines); he mentions as an example only Longus: 529 (?), 716 1/2,
684, 735 lines (cf. Longos, ed. O. Schönberger, Berlin 1960, 26 f.). Have considerations
of genre or practical purposes decided this small format? What is the lowest admissible
number of lines? — (2) *Unevenness*. Birt (*Ant. Buchw.,* 287 f., *Abriss,* 294) finds a striving
for "uniformity of book length" (due to library practice?, Schubart, 51), but he also gives
examples of the opposite: Aelian, *de nat. anim.* Book 6: 1103 1/2 lines, Book 8: 600 lines,
Euclides, *Elem.* Book 4: 584 lines, Book 11: 2018 1/2 lines (*Ant. Buchw.,* 323, 328). Later
on, after the introduction of the codex, "the maximum falls … to a degree that the good
period does not experience" (*Ant. Buchw.,* 300–302): Nonnus, *Dion.* Book 31: 282 lines,
Book 48: 978 lines. — (3) In *private copies*, the logical book divisions are often replaced

→

too exhibit considerable, if not as striking, differences of book length (Chariton between 14 and 24 pages, Achilles Tatius 16–30, Heliodorus 19–39), and yet (to my knowledge) nobody has for that reason thought of a later abridgement.

by accidental ones which depend wholly on the length of the rolls available (Dziatzko *Unters.,* 156 f., Wendel, 47 f.). Thus, one may either consider a private and accidental new division of the *Ephesiaca* or even ask whether this novel has ever had logical book divisions. Perhaps it was divided from the start according to the writing material at disposal; at any rate, *none* of the transmitted book divisions is self-evident (not even the one in the "unabbreviated" first section, between Books I and II, see above, n. 42). Can we really take library copies for granted in the case of the non-sophistic novels? — (4) *The transition from roll to codex*: "it begins — not later than the mid-2nd century — with Christian literature; beginning in the 3rd century, there follows the transcription of legal texts from rolls to codices, and with regard to classical literature, the transcription process takes place mainly in the 4th century." (H. Widmann, *Archiv für Gesch. des Buchw.* 8, 1967, 598; cf. C.H. Roberts, "The Codex", *Proc. of the Brit. Acad.* 1954, 169–204; Wieacker 120 ff.; T. Kleberg, *Buchhandel und Verlagswesen in der Antike,* Darmstadt 1967, 69–86). What is the position of the novels in this development? Chariton: 3 papyrus fragments from rolls (Pack[2] 241–243, 2–3. Jh.) and a late parchment codex (Pack[2] 244, 6th/7th century). Ach. Tat.: 2 fragments from papyrus *codices* (Pack[2] 1 und 3; 3rd and 2nd(?) century), 1 from a roll (Pack[2] 2, 3rd/4th century). Of the remaining almost 30 novel(?) fragments (many are very small, often written on the verso of various documents) at least 2 derive from codices (Pack[2] 2619, pap., 3rd/4th century, and 2638, parchm., 6th century). Unfortunately, conditions in other parts of the Greek world cannot be checked. If we assume, for the earlier novels, a readership of little literary education, the parallel with the Early Christian use of the codex form lies close at hand (cf. C.C. McCown, "Codex and roll in the New Testament", *Harvard Theol. Rev.* 34, 1941, 219–250, and Roberts 185 ff.; his characterization, p. 187, "literate but not literary", will be applicable to the readers of novels as well). Even if the categorical view of Birt, "the codex the book of the poorer" *(Abriss,* 351) has to be modified (Roberts 179, 186 f.), the fact is that the roll remained the only acknowledged form of book in literary circles even at a time when in practice the codex was widely spread (Roberts 176: "in the first two centuries of the Empire polite society acknowledged one form and one form only for the book — the roll"); silence reigns regarding the codex exactly in the same way as no notice is taken of the existence of the novel! Did Xenophon perhaps from the start publish his novel in codex form and keep the division into books just as a convention? In that case, it was of no importance if he went below the "normal size" of a book or cared less for the rules of "uniformity". — (5) In conclusion: If the novel was written on rolls, the cause of the unevenness may be the writing material that happened to be at hand (for the original edition or for a private copy *before* the transcription into a codex); if it was written directly in a codex, the rules of uniformity have no meaning any longer.

V

Is it then conceivable at all, in principle, that our novel could be an epitome? To shed light on this question we shall now give a brief survey of the surviving novelistic literature of antiquity[45] from the particular point of view of whether or under what circumstances epitomized versions of works of fiction existed, or at least have been assumed by scholars to have existed. It goes without saying that such an examination of parallel cases cannot provide the solution of our problem, but it seems important that our case is not viewed in isolation. On the other hand, it is not enough just to refer to other "abbreviations", for behind this term, as will be clear, there hide quite different phenomena, with regard to motivation as well as procedure. In each case, therefore, at least the main characteristics have to be indicated. It must be stressed that the following survey cannot be complete[46] nor offer personal opinions concerning the various problems. I shall only attempt to let the material relevant to our question come forth from the often extensive discussions of the single novels or novelistic works, and to summarize it briefly.

As is well known, epitomes of technical treatises of all kinds, historiographical works etc. occur in great number, sometimes produced by the authors themselves, but more often appearing in later periods.[47] The causes for such enterprises are easy to understand; it is the facts that are

---

[45] The information on later research in this area provided in the report of O. Mazal (see above, n. 1) has been indispensable to me.

[46] For instance, I have deliberately refrained from attempting a summary of the textual tradition of the *Alexander Romance*; it offers a rich sample of different redactions, interpolations, epitomes and collections of excerpts, for which I refer to R. Merkelbach, *Die Quellen des griechischen Alexanderromans*, München 1954, 61–74, 118–120. More recent literature in Mazal 1962/63, pp. 30–50, and J. Trumpf, "Eine unbekannte Sammlung von Auszügen aus dem griechischen Alexanderroman", *Class. et Mediaev.* 26, 1965, 83–100.

[47] I. Opelt, "Epitome", *RAC* 5, 1962, 944–973. This article contains, besides a fundamental discussion of the genre "epitome", a list of 160 epitomes of Greek and Roman works. The epitomes of the *Clementine Romance* (see below) are listed under "theological epitomes" (Nos. 125-128), otherwise no epitomes of literature of entertainment are mentioned, cf. col. 945: "The e(pitome) is created and above all used by historiography and non-literary writing (*Fachschriftstellerei*). The three characteristics most essential to the e(pitome): briefness; emphasis on the contents, not the form of the original work; and restriction to narrative and descriptive prose, show clearly that the e(pitome) is meant to serve the purpose of brief instruction." [The entry s.v. "Epitome" in *Der neue Pauly*, Vol. 3, Stuttgart & Weimar 1997, 1175-77, likewise excludes the category fiction.]

interesting and important, also in abbreviation and often regardless of
the literary form. It must be different with fiction written to entertain.
What purpose do novels stripped of their rhetorical ornamentation serve
and who would take the trouble to produce such epitomes?[48] We may
in this context leave aside the summaries of novels that a scholar like
the Patriarch Photius (9th century) inserted in his *Bibliotheca*; they were
part of a larger context and never meant for a life of their own as independent literary works. Yet, we have precisely in Photius an indication
of the existence of two versions in different detail of a work that must
be said to belong to the literature of entertainment. Photius also gives
some interesting, though not unambiguous, information about the differences between the two versions.

Photius (*Bibl.* cod. 129)[49] reports that he has read the *Metamorphoses*
of a certain Lucius of Patrae; furthermore, that the two first books[50] of
this work "are virtually a transcript" (μόνον οὐ μετεγράφησαν) of the story
Λοῦκις ἢ Ὄνος of Lucian — or may perhaps, Photius asks himself, the
relationship between the two works be the opposite? He then decides on
Lucian as the imitator: καὶ γὰρ ὥσπερ ἀπὸ πλάτους τῶν Λουκίου λόγων ὁ
Λουκιανὸς ἀπολεπτύνας καὶ περιελὼν ὅσα μὴ ἐδόκει αὐτῷ πρὸς οἰκεῖον
χρήσιμα σκοπόν, αὐταῖς τε λέξεσι καὶ συντάξεσιν εἰς ἕνα τὰ λοιπὰ συνα-
ρμόσας λόγον, "Λοῦκις ἢ Ὄνος" ἐπέγραψε τὸ ἐκεῖθεν ὑποσυληθέν. Both
works are full of πλασμάτων μὲν μυθικῶν, ἀρρητοποιΐας δὲ αἰσχρᾶς — but
still the tendency of the Lucianic story, he says, is satirical, while Lucius
has taken the metamorphoses and other nonsense quite seriously.

Of the two works Photius read, the longer one is lost, but the shorter
one, the *Onos*, has been transmitted among Lucian's works; in addition,
the *Metamorphoses* of Apuleius builds on the same story about the ass.
The relationship between these three works has been much discussed;[51] in

---

[48] Similar doubts (and comparisons with modern practice) in Th. Sinko, *Eos* 41, 1940–46,
34, who stresses the stylistic *uniformity* of the *Ephesiaca* ("tota enim epitome eodem
stilo scripta est"), apparently without knowledge of the point of departure of Bürger's
investigation.

[49] Photius, *Bibliothèque*, T. 2, texte ét. et trad. par R. Henry, Paris 1960, 103 f.

[50] Has Lucius only copied the first two books of a longer work, *or* has Photius only checked
the relationship between model and copy in the first two books, *or* did the model too
have only two books? On this much-discussed question, which prevents us from using
the information in deciding the extensiveness of the model, cf. Perry pp. 216 and 368 f.
— In addition, the relationship "*two* books in the original — *one* book in the epitome"
tells us nothing after the introduction of the codex, cf. I. Opelt, *RAC* 5, 1962, 959.

this context, we can only refer to a few points of special importance for our question. Modern research has confirmed Photius' impression that the *Onos* is an epitome. Thus, we need not take into account the other hypothesis, that the lost *Metamorphoses* was an expansion of the *Onos*. These results have been reached partly through an internal analysis of the *Onos* (which exhibits mistakes with regard to contents or logic), partly through detailed comparison with Apuleius' novel, which independently of the *Onos* derives from the lost *Metamorphoses* of Lucius (and in which the explanation for some of the mistakes in the abbreviated work is to be found).[52] Furthermore, the investigations have established as likely that the epitomizing was accomplished both by eliminating smaller parts of the main action (ἀπολεπτύνας in Photius) and by leaving out some inserted stories (περιελὼν etc.).[53] Yet, opinions differ widely about how long the original was, from equating it with Apuleius' novel (ca. 290 pages)[54] to a length of only 3–5 pages[55] more than the 35 that the *Onos* covers. A majority of scholars now takes a middle course, believing that the original was not much longer than the *Onos* (Perry p. 216 suggests 50 Teubner pages altogether), but still contained some inserted stories.[56] Apuleius has considerably increased the number of such insertions (probably drawing his material from other Greek sources) and also quite freely paraphrased what he took over directly,[57] whereas the *Onos* epitomizer for his part has eliminated the few inserted stories and perhaps some additional "super-

149

---

[51] Literature and summary of the discussion in A. Lesky, "Apuleius von Madaura und Lukios von Patrai", *Hermes* 76, 1941, 43–74 (= A.L., *Gesammelte Schriften,* Bern & München 1966, 549–578). See also Mazal 1964, pp. 67–69. [Of later discussions, H. van Thiel, *Der Eselsroman,* Vol. I–II, München 1971–72, is fundamental.]

[52] Cf. Bürger's dissertation (above, n. 13).

[53] Against Lesky, E. Paratore, *La novella in Apuleio,* 2nd ed., Messina 1942, 115, denies the existence of inserted stories in the model; he is of the opinion that the *Onos* is still to be considered an "excerptum", partly in that it contains only *two* of the originally several books, partly in that it eliminates the "abbondanza descrittiva". Cf. also Paratore in *Studi in onore di G. Funaioli,* Roma 1955, 351–353, where he defends the same view against A. Mazzarino, *La Milesia e Apuleio,* Torino 1950.

[54] Kerényi pp. 151–205.

[55] P. Junghanns, *Die Erzählungstechnik von Apuleius' Metamorphosen und ihrer Vorlage,* Leipzig 1932 (= *Philologus,* Suppl. 24,1), 118–120, cf. Lesky (see above, n. 51), p. 48.

[56] Yet, the consensus, in principle, regarding this question between, e.g., Lesky, Perry and Mazzarino at the places referred to above, in no way means that they also attribute the *same* inserted stories to the model!

[57] Cf. Perry pp. 281 f., 376–378.

fluous" material as well, but otherwise kept the words and syntax of the original — all this in accordance with Photius' information. On the other hand, Photius' impression that only the shorter work had a satirical tendency does not seem compatible with this picture of the epitomizing procedure nor probable in itself.[58] Maybe we should assume with Perry (pp. 216 f.) that Photius has misunderstood some naive utterances of Lucius, the "hero" of the ego narrative, which occurred only in the longer work, as the author's actual opinions; but, as Lesky (p. 49) stresses, Photius could of course have no doubt that the shorter work was satirical since it circulated under Lucian's name. Thus, we cannot state anything with certainty about the true reasons for the epitomizing.

In connection with Apuleius, we shall also have a brief look at Petronius' *Satyrica*.[59] According to K. Müller,[60] there was "at the head of our medieval transmission of the text … a single, incomplete copy" which contained only a smaller part (Books 14-16) of the extensive original work. From this derive both the whole of the *Cena Trimalchionis* (= Book 15?) and an extract produced in the 9th century, which is in its turn transmitted in two versions, the "long excerpts" (identical with the model except for a few lacunas) and the "short excerpts" which have taken over about two fifths of the model. The fact that only a few books of the novel have survived into the Middle Ages, is probably to be attributed to external, accidental circumstances; but how and why did the first extract, the model for the extant excerpts, come into existence? Müller[61] assumes that in the 9th century a scholar worked

150

---

[58] E. Rohde and others, however, have defended the information given by Photius, see Lesky (above, n. 51), p. 49 n. 26.

[59] On the title, cf. Perry pp. 191 f.

[60] Petronius, *Satyrica — Schelmengeschichten*. Lat.-deutsch von K. Müller und W. Ehlers, München 1965, 414-417. — For earlier theories, mainly based on F. Bücheler's fundamental investigations, see Schanz-Hosius, *Gesch. der röm. Lit.* II, 1935[4], 509 f., 518 f., and W. Kroll, *RE* XIX:1, 1938, 1203, 1212.

[61] Petronii Arbitri *Satyricon*. Cum app. crit. ed. K. Müller, München 1961, XXXVI ff. (cf. J. Delz, *Gnomon* 34, 1962, 678 f.). — Perry p. 191, too, sees in the remains of the novel not "excerpts" in the strict sense, but "pieces of salvage from a badly damaged manuscript, representing everything intelligible that some copyist in the ninth century, or earlier, was able to make out from the torn or blotted pages before him". Cf. also Pétrone, *Le satiricon,* texte ét. et trad. par A. Ernout, 3rd ed., Paris 1950, XIII n. 3 (and p. XX on the lacunas in the "long excerpts": "parfois elles semblent se réduire à un mot ou à une phrase, parfois c'est toute une suite d'événements qui a été supprimée").

from a severely damaged manuscript, partly copying in complete form
what was still readable, partly making excerpts, and also supplementing the text with his own explanatory additions. Since the *Cena* was
placed in the middle of the codex and was therefore better preserved,
he copied it separately *in extenso* as well. The "short excerpts", finally,
are in Müller's view an expurgated edition for use in schools. Probably,
then, we cannot in the case of the *Satyrica* assume a primary intent to
epitomize, but only a redaction of what had survived by accident.

The *Ephemeris belli Troiani* of Dictys of Crete is transmitted in a Latin
version by a certain Septimius (4th century).[62] Septimius says himself
in an introductory letter that he has translated the first five books of the
work in their complete form from the Greek, but has summarized in
one book the remaining five (or four)[63] which dealt with the return of
the heroes from Troy. The condensed narrative style in Septimius' sixth
book appears to confirm fully this information, and we need not search
far for the reasons for this case of epitomizing. The translator and his
audience were mainly interested in the actual war description of the first
five books, though the main points of the description of the homecoming
too, in abbreviated form, could maintain their position as "historical"
facts. — A papyrus fragment of the *Greek* Dictys, published in 1907,[64]
brought further confirmation of Septimius' declaration; he had in fact
translated, or rather paraphrased, the Greek text, but not really — in
the first half of the work — abbreviated it, as some scholars had believed
earlier because of the simple or even meagre narrative style. It caused

151

---

[62] Dictyis Cretensis *Ephemeridos belli Troiani libri a Lucio Septimio ex Graeco in Latinum
sermonem translati.* Accedit papyrus Dictyis Graeci ad Tebtunim inventa. Ed. W. Eisenhut, Leipzig 1958. — Cf. also Schanz, *Gesch. der röm. Lit.* IV:1, 1914[2], 85–90, and the
introduction to *The Trojan war: The chronicles of Dictys of Crete and Dares the Phrygian.*
Transl. with an introd. and notes by R.M. Frazer, Bloomington & London 1966.

[63] Epistula, 1,17 ff. Eisenhut: "itaque priorum quinque voluminum, quae bello contracta
gestaque sunt, eundem numerum servavimus, residua de reditu Graecorum quidem in
unum redegimus" (quidem *edd. vett.,* quinque *lbb.,* quatuor *De., Mei.*). Prologus, 2,12
f. Eisenhut: "igitur de toto bello novem volumina in tilias digessit Phoeniceis litteris"
(novem *De., Mei.,* sex *lbb.,* ἐννέα *Eudokia,* θ' *Suda*).

[64] *The Tebtunis Papyri* 2, ed. Grenfell-Hunt-Goodspeed, London 1907, No. 268. — On the
relationship between original and translation: E. Patzig, *Byz. Zeitschr.* 17, 1908, 382–388;
N.E. Griffin, *Amer. Journ. of Philol.* 29, 1908, 329–335; M. Ihm, *Hermes* 44, 1909, 1–22;
R.M. Rattenbury in J.U. Powell, *New chapters in the history of Greek literature,* 3rd ser.,
Oxford 1933, 224 f.; Eisenhut, pp. VII f.

surprise that the Greek narrative was "not more detailed and better, but shorter and inferior" in comparison to the Latin one (Patzig p. 386).[65] With regard to content, the two versions largely coincide; in style, the Latin version is "a rather free redaction (*Bearbeitung*) with all sorts of additions, mostly of a rhetorical nature" (Ihm p. 1). The extant fragment is too short and partly lacunose, however, to allow a general judgement on the method of the translator.[65a]

The Troy Romance of Dares of Phrygia too has survived in a Latin version, *De excidio Troiae historia* (6th century), which professes to be a true translation from the Greek.[66] Yet no Greek fragment has so far confirmed that assertion. In this case as well, some have regarded the book as an epitome because of its short form, either abbreviated when translated or epitomized later from a full translation (or from a more detailed Latin original).[67] O. Schissel von Fleschenberg[68] rejects these theories. In his opinion, they are based on false analogies with the later embellished versions of the Troy Romance[69] and have no support in the Latin text; he would himself regard the greater part of the novel as a fairly true rendering of a Greek original.

In the anonymous *Historia Apollonii regis Tyri* we possess in Latin a story that with regard to both content and form has many points of

[65] The earlier expectations about the character of the original were influenced by the fuller descriptions of the topic in Byzantine authors, in particular, in Malalas (*Chron.* V), cf. Griffin pp. 329 f. — Some even believed that the discovered Greek text was only an *abridgement* of a more detailed original, cf. Christ-Schmid, *Gesch. der griech. Lit.* II: 2, 1924[6], 811; against this thesis: Patzig p. 387, Ihm p. 2, Eisenhut pp. VII f.

[65a] [A new fragment, Pap. Oxy. 2539 (2nd/3rd century), was published by J.W.B. Barns in *The Oxyrhynchus Papyri* 31, London 1966; cf. M. Treu in *Gnomon* 40, 1968, 354.]

[66] "quam (i.e. historiam Daretis Phrygii) ego summo amore conplexus continuo transtuli. cui nihil adiciendum vel diminuendum rei reformandae causa putavi, alioquin mea posset videri. optimum ergo duxi ita ut fuit vere et simpliciter perscripta, sic eam ad verbum in latinitatem transvertere" (from the Prologus, text according to Daretis Phrygii *de excidio Troiae historia*. Rec. F. Meister, Leipzig 1873, 1).

[67] Schanz-Hosius, *Gesch. der röm. Lit.* IV:2, 1920, 84–87. Cf. also the introduction to Frazer's translation (above, n. 62), pp. 11–15.

[68] *Dares-Studien*, Halle a. S. 1908, p. 6: "… the original Greek Dares, which in the extant Latin version underwent a free redaction which is no epitome, as has been the opinion till now, but a redaction that besides single smaller changes, has been expanded in its total extension by about 11 chapters."

[69] In particular, *Le Roman de Troie* of Benoît de Sainte-More, see Schissel p. 160.

contact with the *Ephesiaca*. It is an old matter of controversy[70] whether the Latin version is the original one or just a Greek work in translation; further, in the latter case, whether the translator brought with him the Christian interpolations (and would thus be placed in the 5th/6th century) or we should assume a translation already in the 3rd century and a later Christian redaction. We cannot pursue the various theories here, but merely state that in spite of the important arguments of E. Klebs,[71] most scholars today assume a Greek model; in the translation process, it was "reworked quite freely and, considering the shortness of the 'History', probably abbreviated" (K. Svoboda p. 220). The idea that there has been an abridgement is recurrent, and since we lack any external evidence (no fragment of a Greek text has been found, the author/translator mentions no model), it is motivated through the "popular character" (or similarly), which one would not be happy to find in the Greek original. To my knowledge, no detailed argument for the abridgement hypothesis has been presented anywhere,[72] but behind the suspicions voiced it is possible to discern the same criteria as in the case of the *Ephesiaca*: the shortness, the popular character, further the disproportion between the different narrative modes: dramatic scenes "are scattered plentifully throughout the otherwise meagre, at times actually summary, narrative, producing a halting, uneven effect, an alternate speeding up and slowing down of the action" (Ph.H. Goepp p. 169).[73] In addition, we have a number of careless motivations, inconsistencies and loose connections; Schanz-Hosius (p. 90), however, who exemplify these deficiencies, do not regard them as signs

[70] A good survey of the *status quaestionis* is to be found in K. Svoboda, "Über die Geschichte des Apollonius von Tyrus", *Charisteria F. Novotny octogen. oblata,* Prague 1962, 213–224 (= Opera Univ. Purkynianae Brunensis, Fac. Philos., Vol. 90). Cf. also Schanz-Hosius, *Gesch. der röm. Lit.* IV:2, 1920, 87–92; P.J. Enk, *Mnemosyne,* Ser. 4, 1, 1948, 222–237; *The Old English Apollonius of Tyre,* ed. P. Goolden, Oxford 1958, ix–xii; Mazal 1964, pp. 48–50.

[71] E. Klebs, *Die Erzählung von Apollonius aus Tyrus. Eine geschichtliche Untersuchung über ihre lateinische Urform und ihre späteren Bearbeitungen,* Berlin 1899. — Also Schanz-Hosius ibid. and Perry pp. 304 f., 320 ff., argue for a Latin original.

[72] The most detailed motivations in Rohde pp. 416 ff., and U. Wilcken, *Archiv für Papyrus-Forsch.* 1, 1901, 258 n. 2. — Cf. W. Schmid, *RE* II, 1896, 144; Kerényi p. 235 f.; Merkelbach p. 161. [Cf. now G. Schmeling in Schmeling (ed.), *The novel in the ancient world,* Leiden 1996, 534.]

[73] Ph.H. Goepp, "The narrative material of Apollonius of Tyre", *ELH* 5, 1938, 150–172.

of an abridgement: "In our little piece we have a fairy tale (*Märchen*), and many peculiarities may be explained and excused by its fairy-tale character."[74] — The first reasonably secure point in the transmission of the *Historia* is the Christian version of the 5th/6th century (*R*). From this derive the two different redactions (*RA* and *RB*) that may be reconstructed from the extant manuscripts.[75] Literal agreements prove that they originate from the same Latin model, but many differences in content have resulted from interpolations and/or abbreviations; "sometimes the one, sometimes the other version is more detailed" (Svoboda p. 223). Finally, it should at least be mentioned that there are further Latin redactions from the Middle Ages that are characterized partly by abbreviation, partly also by expansion and additions.[76]

The so-called *Pseudo-Clementines*[77] are often characterized as a Christian novel; novelistic narrative material which probably derives from a pagan novel, intermingles with theological discussions and homilies. From a common original which has not survived,[78] there descend two different works, both composed in the 4th century: the *Homilies*, transmitted in their Greek version, and the *Recognitions* which we only possess in the Latin translation of Rufinus.[79] These two versions have been composed through the "revision, transposition and cancellation" of elements

154

---

[74] Perry pp. 294–324, explains many inconsistencies etc. as the result of a *contaminatio*, see above, III.

[75] Printed in parallel in *Historia Apollonii regis Tyri*. Rec. A. Riese, Leipzig 1893². [In its Teubner successor, ed. G. Schmeling, Leipzig 1988, three different redactions, A, B, and C, are printed separately.]

[76] Klebs pp. 334–361.

[77] Cf. B. Rehm, *RAC* 3, 1957, 197–206; Mazal 1964, pp. 80–86; F. Paschke, *Die beiden griechischen Klementinen-Epitomen und ihre Anhänge. Überlieferungsgeschichtliche Vorarbeiten zu einer Neuausgabe der Texte*, Berlin 1966. I mainly follow Paschke's *Forschungsbericht* (pp. 1–78), from which the literal quotations are taken. — Cf. also Perry pp. 285–293.

[78] According to Kerényi (pp. 67–94), Merkelbach (p. 177) and others, a pagan novel lies behind the original. *Contra* Rehm *RAC* 3, 1957, 200 f., cf. Paschke p. 17. — In Kerényi, the theory was not expressly connected with the idea of an abridgement; but cf. S. Trenkner, *The Greek novella in the classical period*, Cambridge 1958, 101 f.: many, insufficiently motivated points in the narrative "must be survivals of a longer version of the story, carelessly adapted by pseudo-Clement to the biography of St. Clement of Rome"; likewise Perry p. 291.

[79] *Die Pseudoklementinen*. I. *Homilien*, ed. B. Rehm, prepared for print by J. Irmscher, Berlin & Leipzig 1953 [2nd ed. prepared by F. Paschke, Berlin 1969]; II. *Rekognitionen*, ed. B. Rehm, prepared for print by F. Paschke, Berlin 1965.

in the model, furthermore through the redactors' own additions.[80] The *Homilies* are described as more "heretic" in the selection of material, the *Recognitions* as more "orthodox"; further, the novelistic material is more fully preserved in the *Recognitions*, the theological sections in the *Homilies*. — An actual abridgement of the *Homilies* is first to be found in the epitome which expurgates the "dogmatically offensive content" and is thus "composed, in the first place, of excerpts from the travel accounts and from the novelistic material." Still further off from the original version we find the "metaphrastic epitome" of Symeon Metaphrastes (10th century). Yet, the frame story remains "practically intact" throughout the whole series of redactions.[81] The complicated transmission history of the *Pseudo-Clementines* which in this context could just be outlined in its reasonably secured main lines, is in each phase determined, as we have seen, by the theological content of the work and the current attitude to it.

We now arrive at the novels proper, more exactly, those composed and transmitted in Greek. Chariton's *Chaereas and Callirhoe* is written in a plain narrative style, without inserted stories or chronological transpositions. The narrative is of uniform fullness the whole novel through and could not in itself arouse any suspicion of epitomizing. The situation changed, however, with the discovery of a parchment manuscript (6th/7th century) with a section from Chariton's novel (VIII 5,9–6,1 and 6,8–7,3).[82] This so-called *Codex Thebanus* (*Theb.*) exhibited a great number of smaller deviations from the earlier *codex unicus*, the Florentine manuscript *Laurentianus* 627 (13th century, *F*): transposition of single words, different forms of the same word, omission or addition of details in the narrative which on the whole conveyed the same course of action. U. Wilcken, the discoverer of the new manuscript, came to the

155

---

[80] Rehm, *RAC* 3, 1957, 198: "H and R at some places agree almost word for word, at others again they diverge strongly, in such a way that sometimes H, sometimes R gives the impression of being closer to the original." [For a new assessment of the relationship, see M. Vielberg, *Klemens in den Pseudoklementinischen Rekognitionen. Studien zur literarischen Form des spätantiken Romans* (Texte und Untersuchungen, 145), Berlin 2000, 171–194.]

[81] Likewise in the older Arabic epitome of the *Pseudo-Clementine Hom.* and *Rec.* that I. Opelt, *RAC* 5, 1962, 967 ff., uses to exemplify in detail the general principles of epitomizing.

[82] U. Wilcken, "Eine neue Roman-Handschrift", *Archiv für Papyrus-Forsch.* 1, 1901, 227–272.

conclusion that the two texts were "two redactions of Chariton's original text, undertaken independently of each other", and that these redactions were "abridgements of the original" (p. 251). The fuller forms are always, in his opinion, logical, often necessary, and would thus belong to the original; the abbreviated ones are awkward. *F* is more abbreviated than *Theb.* Wilcken adduces Bürger's results concerning the *Ephesiaca*; though he is not prepared to exclude the possibility of a similar unevenness in the abbreviation of the two redactions of Chariton, he finds great differences in the working methods: "in the Florentine manuscript, Chariton's work is in the main preserved, whereas in the *Ephesiaca* whole sections have been omitted" (p. 252).[83] Wilcken's theory was first rejected by Wilamowitz,[84] who characterized the deviations as "stylistic variants" which are particularly common in the transmission of light literature. He was also of the opinion that at least *F* was protected against the assumption of an abridgement by the discovery of an earlier papyrus (Pap. Fayum 1, 2rd/3th century); for the text in this papyrus which is much closer to the date of the composition of the novel, agrees to a large extent with that of *F*.[85] Later on, after a careful examination, F. Zimmermann too rejected the idea of two abbreviated redactions.[86] He showed that at the most diverging points, *F* has the best readings, that is, those most in accordance with Chariton's linguistic usage, whereas *Theb.* exhibits an inferior and "barbarized" (*verwildert*) text. W.E. Blake endorsed Zimmermann's results and mainly followed *F* in his critical edition of 1938.[87] Since then, nobody seems to have revived the theory that the transmitted text was an abbreviated version of the novel.

---

[83] Wilcken p. 252, also compares his result with that of Klebs on the two extant Christian versions of the *Historia Apollonii*, *RA* and *RB* (see above), and finds great similarities; still, in the case of the two redactions of Chariton, he is inclined to assume only abbreviation, no interpolations.

[84] *Gött. Gel. Anz.* 163, 1901, 32–34. Cf. also W. Schmid, *Bursians Jahresbericht* 108, 1901, 275 f., A. Calderini in Caritone di Afrodisia, *Le avventure di Cherea e Calliroe,* Torino 1913, 221 f., and Christ-Schmid, *Gesch. der griech. Lit.* II:2, 1924⁶, 809.

[85] The reliability of *F* was confirmed through the discovery of two more papyrus fragments, see F. Zimmermann, *Hermes* 63, 1928, 193–224 (discusses Pap. Fay. 1 und Pap. Oxy. 1019), and *Papyri Michaelidae,* ed. with transl. and notes by D.S. Crawford, Aberdeen 1955, No. 1 (p. 1: "The text shows about the same frequency of variation from the Florentine Codex … as do the Fayum and Oxyrhynchus papyri").

[86] "De Charitonis codice Thebano", *Philologus* 78 (N.F. 32), 1923, 330–381.

[87] Charitonis Aphrodisiensis *De Chaerea et Callirhoe amatoriarum narrationum libri octo.* Rec. W.E. Blake, Oxford 1938, xi.

With regard to Achilles Tatius' *Leucippe and Clitophon*, the story begins already in the 17th century with C. Salmasius. On the basis of the many variants in the two most important groups of manuscripts, he assumed two editions of the novel, both prepared by the author himself.[88] This hypothesis has never gained acceptance, but the discovery of papyri with fragments of the novel has caused new hypotheses of a similar kind. These are based on those smaller deviations from the medieval manuscripts, in wording as well as word forms, that are observable in the papyri. The last editor of the text, E. Vilborg (pp. XLIV and LXXIII), however, finds these variants too insignificant to support a theory of different redactions;[89] they just show "that none of the papyri hitherto found represents the same branch of tradition as the archetype of our medieval MSS" (p. XXXV). On the other hand, and more importantly, one of the three[89a] papyri (Pap. Oxy. 1250, beginning of 4th century?)[90] also deviates from the manuscripts with regard to the sequence of the narrated elements. In the fragment which — expressed in the terms of the traditional sequence — begins in II 7,7 and ends in II 9,3, Chs. 2 and 3,1–2 of the same book have been inserted between Chs. 8 and 9; the transitional phrases have been modified accordingly. Many scholars are of the opinion that the sequence of the papyrus is superior with regard to content and thus constitutes the original one. Two possible explanations have been advanced. Either all that has been transmitted through both channels derives from Achilles Tatius' original version and

[88] Ἐρωτικῶν Ἀχιλλέως Τατίου *sive de Clitophontis et Leucippes amoribus libri VIII.* Opera et studio C. Salmasii, Lugduni Batavorum 1640, "ad lectorem" (ad fin.).

[89] Achilles Tatius, *Leucippe and Clitophon,* ed. E. Vilborg, Stockholm 1955 (= Studia Graeca et Latina Gothoburgensia, 1). — The variants in Pap. Mediolanensis (Vilborg, pp. XVI f.) and its early date (2nd century AD) made the editor, A. Vogliano, *Studi ital. di filol. class.*, N.S. 15, 1938, 121–130, think of a precursor to the transmitted novel: "la tela, su cui Achille Tazio ritessè poi il suo romanzo" (others, starting from various considerations of content, arrive at a similar result: Q. Cataudella, *La parola del passato* 9, 1954, 38–40, and P. Grimal in *Romans grecs et latins,* Paris 1958, 871–873). A. Colonna, however, the most recent editor of this papyrus (*Papiri della Università degli Studi di Milano*, Vol. III, Milano 1965, 50–54), shares Vilborg's opinion of the question.

[89a] [One further papyrus, P. Colon. inv. 901 (end of 3rd century), has been published by A. Henrichs in *Zeitschr. für Papyr. und Epigr.* 2, 1968, 211–226; this too "follows on the whole the vulgate text of the MSS."] [See now also W.H. Willis, "The Robinson-Cologne papyrus of Achilles Tatius", *Greek, Roman and Byzantine Studies* 31, 1990, 73–102.]

[90] *The Oxyrhynchus Papyri* 10, ed. Grenfell-Hunt, London 1914, 135–142.

the incorrect sequence in the archetype was caused by a leaf that fell out
of a codex and was then copied at the wrong place.[91] Or there were two
different redactions, in the opinion of A. Calderini, one shorter which
is the original one, and one expanded in which Chs. 1 and 3,3 of the
second book are added and the sequence is deliberately changed.[92] But
the opposite opinion too is represented, most recently and in greatest
detail by C.F. Russo.[93] He finds the version of the medieval manuscripts
superior, it is coherent and efficient, whereas that of the papyrus has instances of "incoerenza temporale e stilistica" (p. 401): "π ha manipulato
il testo originario del romanzo", namely, "con lo scopo di abbreviarlo"
(p. 402). Yet, this has been achieved only by transposing and cancelling
certain sections, not by stylistic abbreviation, for the remaining parts are
"testualmente piene, non sono condensate, riassunte." The motives for
the abbreviation, according to Russo, were commercial: an anthology
of the extensive novel, intended for a wide audience.

158

Two more novels should be briefly mentioned in this context. The
Babyloniaca of Iamblichus is known both through a significant number
of fragments and through a summary in Photius *(Bibl.* cod. 94). The
summary ends with Book 16, but Photius does not expressly state that
this is really the last book of the novel; and the *Suda* (s.v. Ἰάμβλιχος) at-

---

[91] F. Garin, *Riv. di filol. e di istruz. class.* 47, 1919, 351–357; Vilborg p. XLII, who, however, considers it impossible to take the consequences of this view in his arrangement
of the text.

[92] *Studi della scuola papirologica* I, Milano 1915 (R. Accad. scient.-lett. in Milano), 82–84.
— A. Colonna, *Boll. del Com. per la prep. dell'Ediz. Naz. dei Class. Greci e Lat.,* fasc. I (=
Atti della R. Accad. d'Italia, rendic. della cl. di scienze mor. e stor., ser. VII, suppl. al vol.
I), Roma 1940, 61–83, speaks of two parallel redactions already in the 3rd century (none
of them "better" or "more original"), "in cui interi episodi erano situati diversamente, e
diverse erano alcune frasi, alcune parole nel testo" (pp. 82 f.); in the 9th or 10th century,
the redactions were contaminated and in the process the archetype of our manuscripts
(with its inconsistencies and its redundancy) created.

[93] "Pap. Ox. 1250 e il romanzo di Achille Tazio", *Atti della Accad. Naz. dei Lincei, 1955,*
ser. VIII, rendic., cl. di scienze mor., stor. e filol., Vol. X, 397–403. — H. Dörrie, *De Longi*
Achillis Tatii Heliodori memoria, diss. Göttingen 1935, 86–88, also defends the traditional
sequence against that of the papyrus; but he evidently assumes no kind of abbreviation
in the papyrus edition. — R.M. Rattenbury, *Class. Rev.* N.S. 6, 1956, 230 f., likewise
supports the sequence of the medieval manuscripts, but finds Russo's abridgement hypothesis not quite satisfactory: "it is perhaps more likely that the papyrus never contained more than excerpts and that the rearrangement of this passage was designed by
the excerptor to consolidate and simplify the material that he used". Cf. also Russo in
Gnomon 30, 1958, 585–590.

tributes no less than 39 (variant reading: 35) books to the *Babyloniaca*. If the book number of the *Suda* has not been totally corrupted in the transmission of the text,[94] we may put forward three alternative suggestions for a solution: (1) different editions of the novel with different divisions into books,[95] (2) two editions with the same frame story, one shorter (which Photius read) and one longer, equipped with more inserted stories (that of the *Suda*),[96] or (3) only *one* edition which was summarized by Photius up to and including Book 16, but which then continued with new adventures in 23 (or 19) further books.[97] As has been pointed out,[98] however, it is not easy to imagine what might have been narrated after the happy reunion in Book 16. An important argument *for* a continuation are two fragments of Iamblichus in the *Suda* that according to U. Schneider-Menzel (p. 77), "cannot be accommodated anywhere in the preserved sixteen books". But other scholars are of a different opinion[99] and the question remains undecided.

For Heliodorus, finally, Gärtner (col. 2073) has postulated an intermediate stage between the transmitted version of the *Aethiopica* with its complicated structure and the summary of Photius (*Bibl.* cod. 73) with its chronological sequence of events. The Patriarch's procedure in this case differs "completely from his common practice of retelling" and therefore, in Gärtner's opinion, he must have followed a reworked edition or a hypothesis of the novel. This theory, however, has not yet been substantiated.*

Our survey of abridgements, certain or hypothetical, has shown that we cannot *a priori* exclude the possibility that the *Ephesiaca* was epitomized. At the same time, however, it must be emphasized that none of

---

[94] Thus Th. Sinko, *Eos* 41, 1940–46, 36. Cf. also Lesky (see above, n. 41).

[95] Thus, e.g., Rohde p. 364 n. 2, and R. Henry in Photius, *Bibliothèque*, T. II, Paris 1960, 207.

[96] *Iamblichi Babyloniacorum reliquiae.* Ed. E. Habrich, Leipzig 1960, 70.

[97] U. Schneider-Menzel in F. Altheim, *Literatur und Gesellschaft im ausgehenden Altertum*, Vol. I, Halle/Saale 1948, 57 nn. 4 and 77.

[98] Rohde p. 364 n. 2; Habrich ibid.; Lesky ibid. Cf. W. Kroll, *RE* IX, 1916, 641.

[99] Hercher in *Erotici Scriptores Graeci*, Vol. I, Leipzig 1858, 217; Rohde p. 366 n. 1; Habrich ibid. [Now also S.A. Stephens & J.J. Winkler, *Ancient Greek novels: The fragments*, Princeton, NJ 1995, 180 f., 202 f.]

* [Gärtner himself retracted his theory in "Charikleia in Byzanz", *Antike und Abendland* 15, 1968, 47–69, at 53 n. 20.]

the verified abridgements or redactions constitutes a really good parallel to Xenophon; none exhibits the symptoms that first led Rohde and Bürger to the assumption of epitomizing, in particular, the unevenness, the alternation of meagre and rhetorically full narrative. The frequent but always summary cross references between Xenophon and "other epitomized novels" that occur in the debate as a support for this or that abridgement hypothesis, appear not to be founded on the actual state of affairs. In the case of the Latin Dictys, it is true, we may speak of an "unevenness", but the circumstance that only the five (or four) last books have been abbreviated is due to consistent consideration of the special contents of these books. The same may be said, *mutatis mutandis*, of the later epitomes of the *Pseudo-Clementine Homilies*.[100] The *Historia Apollonii* is described as uneven in about the same sense as the *Ephesiaca*, but in that case too the assumption of an abridgement seems to be based on the subjective view that a Greek original must be homogeneous and well-formed. For Dares and the first five books of Dictys as well, a more detailed and "superior" Greek model has been assumed, but the discovery of a fragment of the Greek Dictys gave no support for that assumption. Instead, the only thing that we may state with certainty is that the Latin redactions often brought *new* material: the Latin Dictys is stylistically fuller than the Greek one, the *Historia Apollonii* contains a large amount of purely Latin material, pagan as well as Christian, and Apuleius' novel is an extreme example of an expansion and "elevation" (*Aufhöhung*, Lesky) of the slimmer and plainer model.[101] That redactors sometimes also select from the model and make omissions, goes without saying, but should not be mistaken for a primary intention to abbreviate.

Certain tendencies towards an arbitrary selection are perhaps traceable within the Greek tradition as well, namely, in "barbarized" texts such as the *Codex Thebanus* of Chariton's novel. "Redactions" of novelistic works that differ with regard to *contents* are well testified, such as the *Homilies* and *Recognitions* of the *Pseudo-Clementines* and the versions *RA* and *RB* of the *Historia Apollonii*; but the result of the selection is neither with regard to narrative technique nor stylistically to be looked upon as a real

160

---

[100] Therefore the statement of Christ-Schmid, *Gesch. der griech. Lit.* II: 2, 1924[6], 810 n. 9, referring to Xen. Eph., is not correct: "of the Pseudo-Clementine Recognitions as well we have two epitomes that eliminate the dogmatic content". Precisely this motive *as regards content* is missing in Xenophon!

[101] Cf. Perry pp. 253 f., 373 f.

161 contraction or condensation. Such a characterization is still less applicable to two other cases: the Petronius "excerpts" are a string of pearls with clear borderlines between the literal extracts from the original (even if some interpolations may be recognized), and the alleged "papyrus edition" of Achilles Tatius largely agrees in wording with the transmitted version (even if the transitions are somewhat changed). It is true that Photius speaks of a *stylistic* abbreviation in the case of the *Onos*, but the extant text is not strikingly condensed or uneven; the traces of epitomizing are remaining references to omitted episodes and some places where stories might have been inserted — the kind of traces that have *not* been demonstrated in the *Ephesiaca*. What we have been looking for in vain is a well testified parallel case in ancient fiction in which the whole course of action has been preserved, though partly reduced to a bare skeleton — and in which this state of affairs is actually the result of a later deliberate epitomizing.

Conclusion

As we have seen, the hypothesis that the *Ephesiaca* is an epitome can be proved neither with the book number given in the *Suda* nor with the uneven length of the books. It is of course equally impossible just to rely on the subjective impression of a "too strong" contrast between skeleton-like and rhetorically full sections, because we do not know the author's personal qualifications or other works of his pen. Many peculiarities may be explained by a less skilful composition of the story from the start, others are very probably to be interpreted as signs of troubles during the transmission of the text. The burden of truth no doubt rests with anyone who prefers the more complicated solution of the problem, the later deliberate abbreviation of the novel. Bürger's discussion, his numerous arguments notwithstanding, has in my view failed to prove the abridgement hypothesis. His arguments are based partly on misleading comparisons with the "sophistic" novels, partly on too high demands on the logic etc. of a simple work of entertainment. In that capacity, Xenophon's novel, in its transmitted form, will readily have served its purpose.

7

The Naming of the Characters in the Romance
of Xenophon Ephesius

[originally published in *Eranos* 69, 1971, 25–59]

The naming of the characters in Xenophon's *Ephesiaca* (2nd cent. A.D.?)[1] deserves attention in at least two different respects. The first is the unusually high frequency of named characters in the romance. In the introduction to his edition of the text G. Dalmeyda pointed out this fact, regarding it as one of the features which give to this romance a "physionomie de conte populaire": "l'auteur ne met jamais en scène un personnage, même s'il ne paraît qu'une fois et dans un très court épisode, sans lui donner un nom: on dirait d'un conte fait à un auditoire d'enfants."[2] In the first part of this article I shall investigate more in detail the author's practice in these matters and discuss the possible explanations for his giving — or not giving, since Dalmeyda overstates his case — a proper name to a character.

The second aspect of the naming which I shall deal with is directly interrelated with the first: what *kind* of names does the author give to his characters? "Dass unsere griechischen Romanschriftsteller gern *sprechende Namen* wählten und bei der Namenwahl überhaupt sorgfältig verfuhren…ist bekannt." How far does this general statement of K. Kerényi's hold good for Xenophon?[3] It is an obvious fact that the

[1] This date seems to be the most probable, though there are no quite unequivocal dating criteria. On this question and on the romance of Xenophon in general, I refer to the recent artiele by H. Gärtner in *RE*, 2. Reihe, IX, 1967, 2055–89.

[2] Xénophon d'Éphèse, *Les Éphésiaques ou le roman d'Habrocomès et d'Anthia*, Texte établi et traduit par G. Dalmeyda, Paris 1926, pp. XXVII f. In quoting the Greek text of the romance, I use this edition.

[3] K. Kerényi, *Die griechisch-orientalische Romanliteratur in religionsgeschichtlicher Beleuchtung*, 2. ergänzte Aufl., Darmstadt 1962, p. 170. Kerényi treats of some of the names in Xenophon on pp. 170–2 (n. 72). Earlier, some notes on the subject were offered by Locella (cited in P. H. Peerlkamp's edition of Xenophon Ephesius, Harlem 1818, p. 304) and by E. Rohde, *Der griechische Roman und seine Vorläufer*, 4. Aufl., Darmstadt 1960, p. 402, n. 2 (the page numbers are those of the first edition of 1876). Gärtner, op. cit. (see n. 1), col. 2069, briefly discusses the matter.

26

two principal characters, Habrokomes and Antheia,[4] have been given genuinely "significant" names, but things are less clear as regards many of the other characters. Thus, I shall examine here to what extent one may suppose an intentional choice of etymologically significant names or of names which were possibly meant to provoke special associations through their earlier use (in myth, history or literature). By adducing epigraphical material, I shall also attempt to trace the relative frequency of each name in the contemporary Greek world and possible geographical or social limitations in their use. Finally, some tentative conclusions will be given regarding the principles that may have guided Xenophon in choosing the names and, as far as possible, regarding the impression that the names chosen may have made on a contemporary reader.

Named and nameless characters

There are in Xenophon's romance 33 characters (23 men, 10 women) who are given individual names,[5] whereas 11 persons take part in the action without being named. The frequency of named characters in itself, though certainly high in a romance of only 71 pages (in the Teubner edition), has a natural explanation in the narrative structure. The romance consists of a chain of short episodes, enacted at different places and with Habrokomes and Antheia (and, to a certain degree, the robber Hippothoos) as the only common characters. Thus, many different persons are introduced; each of them plays an important part in one or two episodes and then leaves the action completely. The remarkable thing is, however, the *proportion* between the named and the nameless characters. In the two romances which are most comparable with Xenophon's, those of Chariton and Achilles Tatius, about a third of the individuals mentioned receive proper names; in Xenophon, as many as three characters out of

---

[4] For obvious reasons, I transliterate the personal names as closely to the Greek spelling as possible in this article, instead of using Latinized forms. For the form Antheia, see n. 22.

[5] Two more personal names occur, namely, Μεμφῖτις, which is the name falsely given by Antheia in IV, 3,6, and Μενέλαος, who is said to have built a canal in Egypt (IV, 1,3); probably, the brother of Ptolemy I is intended (*RE* XV: 1, 1931, 830-1, "Menelaos 6"), though Xenophon seems to be the only informant of this special fact (see H. Henne, "La géographie de l'Égypte dans Xénophon d'Éphèse", *Revue d'histoire de la philosophie et d'histoire générale de la civilisation* 4, 1936, 99).

four are named. I shall examine the individual cases and seek to deduce the immediate reasons for naming or not naming a character.

Table 1 shows the named characters, Table 2 the nameless. For each individual are given first the place(s) in which he or she appears in the romance (with the place of introduction in italics)[6] and then a figure for the frequency of the name or its substitute, respectively. These figures show roughly the relative importance of each character in the plot; only in one case, that of Lampon the goatherd, is the figure misleading in this respect, because the man is called simply ὁ αἴπολος twelve times in addition to the five mentions by name. In stating that these figures generally give a satisfactory idea of the importance of the characters, I have already hinted at the principal — and self-evident — function of the name-giving. In any narrative, the name is a natural means of identifying a person who recurs frequently in the course of narration in cases in which the use of a pronoun alone is not clear enough. In a simple and straightforward narrative like Xenophon's, it is indispensable, functioning as a substitute for characterization (regardless of the question whether it is "significant" in itself) and being in some cases the only really individual trait which the author bestows upon a character.[7] Now, 15 names in Xenophon recur ten times or more, 11 names between five and nine times, and only 7 names less than five times. Only in this last group may the practical function be seriously disputed, and I shall now examine each of these cases separately.

In V, 11,2 we are told that Hippothoos and Antheia find a lodging in the house of an old woman "named Althaia"; in that connection she is also referred to as τὴν ξένην, but the name is never repeated and she is never mentioned at all in the rest of the romance. Another old woman, Chrysion, is introduced by name before she starts her narration in III, 9,4 and is then mentioned once as τῆς πρεσβύτιδος τῆς Χρυσίου (*both* characterization *and* name) after the narration (9,8), but never again. Also the young man Androkles is mentioned twice only, and that in the same paragraph (V, 1,6). In these three cases we may indeed question the practical function of the naming. The situation is somewhat different in two more cases

29

---

[6] The places where a name occurs in the text, though the individual is not physically present in the action, are placed within brackets.

[7] On the general characteristics of Xenophon's narrative, see further my *Narrative Technique in Ancient Greek Romances: Studies of Chariton, Xenophon Ephesius, and Achilles Tatius*, Stockholm 1971 (Acta Instituti Atheniensis Regni Sueciae, 8°, VIII).

Table 1. Named characters in the *Ephesiaca*.

Name	Place(s) of occurrence	Frequency
Ἀβροκόμης	*I 1,1 et passim*	218
Ἀγχίαλος	*IV 5,1–6*; IV 6; (V 9)	11
Αἰγιαλεύς	*V 1,2–12*; V 2; (V 10)	9
Ἀλθαία	*V 11,2*	1
Ἀμφίνομος	*IV 6,4–7*; V 2; V 4; (V 9)	10
Ἀνδροκλῆς	*V 1,6*	2
Ἀνθία, Ἄνθεια	*I 2,5 et passim*	188
Ἄραξος	*III 12,2–5*; (IV 2); (IV 4)	8
Ἀριστόμαχος	*III 2,5–10*	3
Ἄψυρτος	*I 14,7*; I 15; II 2–7; 10; 12; (III 3*)*	23
Εὔδοξος	*III 4, 1–3*; III 5	7
Εὐίππη	*I 2,5*; I 5; 10; (III 5)	4
Εὔξεινος	*I 15,3–4*; I 16; II 1–2	10
Θελξινόη	*V 1,5–12*	7
Θεμιστώ	*I 1,1*; I 5; 10; (II 8)	4
Ἱππόθοος	*II 11,11*; II 13–14; III 1–3; 9–10; IV 1; 3–6; V 2–4; 6; 9; 11–13; 15	64
Κλεισθένης	*V 9,3*; V 13; 15	4
Κλυτός	*V 5,4–8*	6
Κόρυμβος	*I 13,3–6*; I 14–16; II 1–2	22
Κυνώ	*III 12, 3–4*; IV 4	5
Λάμπων	*II 9,3–4*; II 11–12	5
Λεύκων	*II 2,3*; II 3–4; 7; 9–10; V 6; 10–13; 15	27
Λυκομήδης	*I 1,1*; I 5; 10; (II 8)	6
Μαντώ	*II 3,1–6*; II 4–5; 7; 9–12; (III 3, 8; V 10)	23
Μεγαμήδης	*I 2,5*; I 5; 10; (III 5)	5
Μοῖρις	*II 5,6*; II 9; 11–12; (III 8; V 14)	11
Περίλαος	*II 13,3–8*; II 14; III 3–9; (V 14)	24
Πολύιδος	*V 3–1–2*; V 4–5; (V 14)	15
Ῥηναία	*V 5,2–8*	6
Ῥόδη	*II 2,3*; II 3; 5; 7; 9–10; V 6; 10–13; 15	23
Ὑπεράνθης	*III 2,2–13*; (III 3; V 15)	13
Χρυσίον	*III 9,4–8*	2
Ψάμμις	*III 11,2–5*; III 12; IV 3; (V 14)	8

Table 2. Nameless characters in the *Ephesiaca*.

Designations	Place(s) of occurrence	Frequency
ὁ ἄρχων τῆς Αἰγύπτου	*III 12,6*; *IV 2*; *V 3*; *5*	8
θεράπαινά τις	*II 5,3–4*	2
οἰκέτης πιστός	*II 2,5*	1
τις οἰκέτης	*II 12,1*	1
τις τῶν οἰκετῶν	*III 6,4*	1
ὁ πατήρ [*sc.* τοῦ Ὑπεράνθου]	*III 2,7*	1
πορνοβοσκός	*V 5,7*; *V 7,9*	9
πρεσβύτης τις (ὁ δεσπότης)	*II 10,4*; *V 6,3*; (*V 10,11*)	3
πρεσβῦτις	*V 9,1*	2
τις τῶν Ῥοδίων	*V 13,2*	1
ὁ τροφεύς (ὁ πρεσβύτης)	*I 14,4*; *14,6*	2

of low frequency, Aristomachos and Kleisthenes, because the distribution of the occurrences over the text is greater (see Table 1) and thus the identifying function is more relevant (though, in fact, at least Kleisthenes is circumstantially identified by other means, too, on his re-introduction in V, 13,6). In the cases of Euippe and Themisto, the mothers of Antheia (I, 2,5) and Habrokomes (I, 1,1), respectively, one more motive may be adduced: the proper names have a natural function when the author gives the pedigrees for the two principal characters of the romance.

The cases in which the naming of a character seems to serve no practical purpose are thus reduced to three — Althaia, Chrysion and Androkles. These three belong to the same category as most of the nameless characters, that is, the nine persons in Table 2 who recur three times or less in the romance. If we try to find some difference between named and nameless characters with the same low frequency, the social position obviously comes to the fore. None of the three named characters is indicated as unfree, whereas four of the anonymous ones are definitely servants or slaves (one θεράπαινα, three οἰκέται) and one more, ὁ τροφεύς, probably

30

belongs to the same category. Now, it is evident that the low social status is in these cases combined with a very subordinate role in the action — the slave may serve as an agent in the delivery of a letter, and so on — and as soon as the part to be played is more important, even slaves are given their individual names, as is shown in the cases of Leukon and Rhode. As for the rest of the anonymous characters with a low frequency, there is nothing either in their social position or in their roles in the action[8] that differs from the same qualities in the three named ones; for instance, the old man in II, 10,4 and the old woman in V, 9,1 might well have received proper names with the same right as Althaia and Chrysion — as long as we are judging the whole thing as a matter of function or else of intention. Before returning to this discussion, I shall look at the two nameless characters who differ from the rest in having important parts to play in the romance, the prefect of Egypt and the brothel-keeper.

The *praefectus Aegypti* is introduced into the action in III, 12,6 by the words: οἱ δὲ εὐθὺς συνέλαβον τὸν Ἁβροκόμην καὶ δήσαντες ἀνέπεμπον τῷ τῆς Αἰγύπτου ἄρχοντι. He then recurs six times, designated as ὁ ἄρχων τῆς Αἰγύπτου and once with the variant wording τὸν διοικοῦντα τὴν Αἴγυπτον (IV, 2,7). The absence of a proper name is not to be explained as due to his being only an abstract authority who does not make a personal appearance in the romance; it *is* the man himself who takes part in the action, and he is furnished with thoughts, feelings and speech to the same extent as other comparable characters in the romance. The reason for not giving the prefect a name is probably to be found in other circumstances. The *praefectus Aegypti* is an official of such importance that his naming would meet with difficulties of a special kind; a fictitious name would immediately give itself away as such and thus spoil the impression of authenticity at which the romance as a whole seems to aim (it keeps far from the recounting of ἄπιστα, in spite of the miraculous ingredients in IV, 2), while an authentic (Roman) name would definitely fix the time of the action.[9] Chariton introduces historical persons like Hermokrates and

[8] The slightest role is played by the Rhodian, male or female, who is for once distinguished from the mass in V, 13,2.

[9] Striking parallels to the anonymity of the prefect are afforded by the early Christian panegyrists, who developed, as H. Delehaye puts it, a veritable "horreur des noms propres": "Dans les panégyriques des martyrs on chercherait en vain, je ne dis pas le nom du magistrat qui a prononcé la condamnation–on pouvait l'ignorer–, mais celui de l'empereur, responsable des édits de proscription. Il est vaguement désigné comme ὁ κρατῶν τότε, ὁ τότε κρατῶν..." (*Les passions des martyrs et les genres littéraires*, 2ᵉ éd., Brussels 1966, pp. 150–2). (I owe this reference to Docent L. Rydén.)

Artaxerxes into the action, and Iamblichus mentions Berenike by name,[10] but Xenophon, on the other hand, seems to avoid all that might give a historical setting to his romance. He never even mentions the Romans — though the mere existence of the prefect presupposes, of course, that the action takes place on and around a Mediterranean dominated by the Romans — and he generally keeps the events on a private level. There are no specific details that limit the universal application of the action; similar incidents might be happening "now", in the eyes of the contemporary audience, as well as "once upon a time". As far as I can see, the presence in the romance of one more official, the eirenarch of Cilicia, who *has* an individual name (Perilaos), does not weaken the argument; in that case, the office is much less important, and a fictitious name would in all likelihood pass without comment from most readers.

A few words may be added here about the actual wording of the title *praefectus Aegypti* in the romance. It does not seem to be identical with the official Greek title, either generally or at any special period. The proper Greek counterpart to the Latin title was ἔπαρχος Αἰγύπτου, which is used in the edicts from 89 A.D. and onwards.[11] In less official connections other expressions are used: ἡγεμών is the usual term in the papyri,[12] ἐπίτροπος occurs in early literary sources, notably in Philo,[13] and ἄρχων seems to be exclusively literary (all the instances that are generally referred to come from Cassius Dio[14].) Josephus uses for the prefect's official activities the verbs διοικεῖν (BJ VII, 420) and διέπειν (IV, 616 and V, 45).[15] Obviously, Xenophon uses neither the official title nor that of daily life but has recourse to the literary one. Furthermore, he does not treat it as a fixed

32

[10] Char. I, 1,1 ff. and IV, 6,3 ff.; Iambl. Babyl. 17 and 20 (in Photius Bibl. cod. 94).

[11] *RE* XXII: 2, 1954, 2353.

[12] O. W. Reinmuth, *The Prefect of Egypt from Augustus to Diocletian* (Klio, Beiheft 34, Leipzig 1935), p. 9. According to H. Hübner, *Der Praefectus Aegypti von Diokletian bis zum Ende der römischen Herrschaft* (Erlanger Beiträge zur Rechtsgeschichte, Reihe A, Heft 1, Munich 1952), p. 16, the same distinction is valid later too: ἔπαρχος Αἰγύπτου (or ἐπ. Αὐγουστάλιος) as "Amtsbezeichnung", ἡγεμών "vornehmlich als Anrede".

[13] For example, Philo XIX, 163 (p. 150, Cohn & Wendland). According to A. Stein, *Die Präfekten von Ägypten in der römischen Kaiserzeit* (Dissertationes Bernenses, Ser. I, Fasc. 1, Bern 1950), p. 179, the use of this term is due to a misconception, ἐπίτροπος being the equivalent of *procurator* and the special status of Egypt thus being disregarded.

[14] Cassius Dio 53,29,3; 54,5,4; 58,19,6; 63,18,1; 71,28,3. The statement in *RE* XXII: 2, 1954, 2353, that Dio also uses ἐπίτροπος ("Dio LIII 29 und passim"), must be wrong (cf. W. Nawijn's *Index Graecitatis* to Dio in vol. 5 of Boissevin's ed., Berlin 1931, p. 337).

[15] Stein, op. cit. (see n. 13), p. 180.

title to the same extent as Cassius Dio, who always places τῆς Αἰγύπτου between article and participle and in all cases, except one (63,18,1), uses the whole expression as an apposition to the Roman name (for instance, 53,29,3 Αἴλιος Γάλλος ὁ τῆς Αἰγύπτου ἄρχων). Xenophon is freer, changes the word order, inserts τότε once (III, 12,6) and even chooses another verb, διοικεῖν, in one case (IV, 2,7). The same tendency is still more marked in his treatment of the title of the eirenarch; in II, 13,3 he paraphrases it in the following way: ὁ τῆς εἰρήνης τῆς ἐν Κιλικίᾳ προεστώς, in III, 9,5 we read that Περίλαός τις...ἄρχειν μὲν ἐχειροτονήθη τῆς εἰρήνης τῆς ἐν Κιλικίᾳ..., but nowhere is the official title ὁ εἰρηνάρχης or εἰρήναρχος to be found.

In the case of the brothel-keeper, ὁ πορνοβοσκός another explanation of the anonymity seems reasonable. His *occupation* is directly responsible for his function in the romance — whereas many of the other characters act entirely as private persons — and he is the only one of his kind to take part in the action, in contrast to the many robbers who need individual names to be distinguished from each other. Furthermore, it is particularly easy to use the occupation instead of a proper name in this case, as πορνοβοσκός was a well-known stock character in comedy.[16] A literary influence of the same kind may be traceable also in the case of the nameless τροφεύς.[17] One more parallel is afforded by the fact, mentioned above, that Lampon the goatherd is more often designated by his occupation (ὁ αἰπόλος) than by his name. In all three cases, there is only one representative of each occupation taking part in the action, and thus the title serves just as well as or perhaps even better than a proper name — the title is by nature "significant", not only through literary tradition but also through the associations of daily life.

It is time to return to the point of departure, the general statement by Dalmeyda. As we have seen, not all but as many as three-quarters

---

[16] Ὁ πορνοβοσκός occurs in both the Middle and the New Comedy, even as the titles of plays by Euboulos (fragments 88 and 89 in J. M. Edmonds, *The Fragments of Attic Comedy*, vol. II, Leiden 1959, pp. 120 ff.) and Poseidippos (fragment 22 in Edmonds, vol. III A, Leiden 1961, p. 236).

[17] Thus O. Schissel von Fleschenberg, *Die Rahmenerzählung in den ephesischen Geschichten des Xenophon von Ephesus*, Innsbruck 1909, p. 17. On the nurse (τροφός) and the παιδαγωγός as nameless types in Sophocles and Euripides (but *not* in Homer: Eurykleia, Phoinix), see R. Hirzel, *Der Name: Ein Beitrag zu seiner Geschichte im Altertum und besonders bei den Griechen*, Leipzig 1918 (Sächs. Akad. d. Wiss., Philol.Hist. Kl., Abh. 36: 2), pp. 64 f.

of the characters in the *Ephesiaca* receive individual names. Generally, it is possible to show that there were practical reasons for the naming of a character. Most of the *named* characters recur several times in the romance, though often within one restricted part of the plot, and then the name is used as the only or the chief means of identification. On the other hand, most of the *nameless* characters play extremely subordinate parts in the action, being mentioned just a few times within the compass of one or two paragraphs. To the latter rule there are two notable exceptions, the prefect of Egypt, whose anonymity is probably due to a general desire to avoid mentioning facts that would fix the action in a definite historical situation, and the brothel-keeper, a type character and also the single representative of the trade in this romance.

34

The exceptions to the former rule, or rather tendency, deserve more discussion, because they illustrate the author's narrative style in general. In each single episode, the hero or heroine meets with one or two other characters, who are, in fact, "primary characters" as long as their participation lasts. All these, except the prefect and the brothel-keeper, naturally have proper names (but not many other characteristics), and the author uses a stereotyped formula with few variations for their introduction and naming. It is quite natural that this formula should persist also in some cases in which its practical function is small or even non-existent; as in many other respects, the author sticks to a technique which he has once adopted without much thought of its suitability in the individual case. Here, in the simplified and clear-cut manner of narration, in the repetition of stiff formulas, etc., rather than in the naming of the characters as such, we find the resemblances to the folk-tale[18] and possibly traces of an oral technique.[19] From this angle it is also possible to throw light on the really remarkable feature, the *few nameless* characters in this romance. The author simply reduces his narration to the "primary characters" in each episode, only seldom mentioning individually an unimportant agent; usually, he either leaves out completely the small

[18] There are many striking similarities between the narrative technique of Xenophon and that of the "Volksmärchen", as described by, for instance, M. Lüthi, *Es war einmal: Vom Wesen des Volksmärchen*, Göttingen 1962, pp. 33–35.

[19] Cf. R. Merkelbach, *Roman und Mysterium in der Antike*, Munich & Berlin 1962, pp. 113, n. 4, and 333.

concrete details in the action, which would involve other persons than the protagonists, or he introduces a collective group (the inhabitants of a certain town, etc.) to take part in the action. Thus, his general tendency to summarize means also the exclusion — with only a few exceptions — of the swarming crowd of unimportant, nameless individuals which we find in the other romances.

The choice of names

To judge an author's intentions in giving the characters individual names, it is of primary importance to know what *kind* of names he chooses. The names in Xenophon's romance will be investigated here along three different lines. (1) Is the name etymologically *significant*,[20] that is, does it have a significance which is easily discernible and which has an obvious bearing on the character's moral qualities, outward appearance or role in the action? It is in this connection unimportant, of course, whether the etymology is historically correct or not, as long as the name is likely to provoke definite associations, in the mind of a Greek reader, with a certain sphere. (2) Is the name definitely connected by its earlier use in myth, history or literature with one person or type to which the author may be thought to allude by choosing the name for one of his fictional characters? Such names may also be called "significant", but, in order to distinguish this category from the former, I shall here use the term *literary*. (3) Was the name used for persons living in the author's own day? In that case, was it a common or an uncommon name, and is it possible to trace any limits in its application, as regards geographical regions, ethnic origins or social status? If there is a positive correlation in these respects between the use in daily life and that in the romance, the name may possibly be regarded as *realistic*.

It goes without saying that these three categories do not exclude each other: a name may have an obvious meaning and at the same time be commonly used in daily life, and so on. The investigation will be carried out, however, along the separate lines, in order to show the possibilities

---

[20] For a general discussion of the notion of significant names (including those which I here call "literary" for short), I refer to J. C. Austin, *The Significant Name in Terence* (Univ. of Illinois Studies in Language and Literature, 7: 4, 1921), Urbana 1923, pp. 9–23. "Redende Namen" in Greek literature are dealt with in outline by F. Dornseiff in *Zeitschrift für Namenforschung* 16, 1940, 24–38 and 215–8.

in each case; afterwards, the different principles will be weighed against each other and the motive for the actual choice of a certain name discussed. I should also make it clear from the start that the material that will be used in the investigation, especially in the second and third parts, is of such a kind — as regards both quantity and state of preservation and accessibility — that it has not been possible for me, with this limited aim, to make more than a preliminary and cursory inventory of it from the standard works and the available indices. What I shall present here are, therefore, mere soundings, for which I make no claims to completeness, but, even so, I hope that the conclusions which they will yield will at least indicate, with a tolerable degree of probability, the direction in which the answers to the questions are to be looked for.

1. *Significant names*

The names of the hero and the heroine of the romance, Ἀβροκόμης[21] (LSJ s.v. "with delicate hair") and Ἀνθία or Ἄνθεια[22] (from ἄνθος, "flower") were without any doubt chosen in order to stress their youth and beauty. In the case of Antheia this is confirmed by the description in I, 2,5: ἤνθει δὲ αὐτῆς τὸ σῶμα ἐπ᾽ εὐμορφίᾳ. Significant in the same direction are also Ὑπεράνθης, the beautiful young boy whom Hippothoos loves (III, 2,2), and Θελξινόη (θέλγω, "charm", and νόος, "mind"), who plays the corresponding part in the first-person story of Aigialeus (V, 1,5). Yet another name is in accordance with the part which the person plays in the romance: Κυνώ, "bitch", which in its transferred sense is markedly pejorative (Hesychius: Κυνώ· ἡ ἀναιδεστάτη. Cf. also LSJ s.v. κύων II). Both her function in the story and the characterization on her introduction are exclusively negative: III, 12,3 … γυναῖκα ὀφθῆναι μιαράν, ἀκουσθῆναι πολὺ χείρω, ἅπασαν ἀκρασίαν ὑπερβεβλημένην, Κυνὼ τὸ ὄνομα. A positive correlation may also be traced between name and person in the cases of Περίλαος, the eirenarch, whose office gives him a

37

---

[21] Ἀβροκόμης, with the *spiritus lenis* (as in Herodotus and in Xenophon's Anabasis, see below), is the usual spelling in the MS., see Dalmeyda, op. cit. (see n. 2), p. 3, n. 1.

[22] The MS. vacillates between the two forms. F. Zimmermann, "Die Ἐφεσιακά des sog. Xenophon von Ephesos: Untersuchungen zur Technik und Komposition", *Würzburger Jahrbücher für die Altertumswissenschaft* 4, 1949/50, 252–86, prefers the form Ἄνθεια (which is found in a papyrus fragment of a romance, see below n. 34) and adduces the support of an epigraphical expert, G. Klaffenbach (p. 265, n. 3).

prominent position among the people (II, 13,3), and Εὔδοξος "of good repute", who is a physician (III, 4,1); in these cases, however, the names have no great bearing on the actual function of the characters in the plot. The young girl, who is Antheia's personal servant and Leukon's companion, has the name Ῥόδη (ῥόδον, "rose"), which may also be meant to be significant, but this assumption cannot be proved by anything in the meagre characterization which the author bestows upon her (II, 2,3; 3,3). It is equally impossible to judge whether the name Μεγαμήδης of Antheia's father (I, 2,5) is meant to be characterizing (μήδεα, "counsels, plans, prudence"), or whether the name Λεύκων of the young slave (II, 2,3; 3,6) gives any hint of his outward appearance (λευκός, LSJ s.v. II b: "of the human skin, *white*, *fair*, sts. as a sign of youth and beauty"); none of these persons is described explicitly by the author. The case of Amphinomos, which may also belong here, will be discussed in the section on literary names.

In a few more cases there seems to be a slight connection between the significance of the name and the context in which it appears; the name does not add to the characterization of the individual, but the author apparently had its etymology in mind. In Syracuse Habrokomes stays πλησίον τῆς θαλάσσης παρὰ ἀνδρὶ Αἰγιαλεῖ πρεσβύτῃ, ἁλιεῖ τὴν τέχνην (V, 1,2); the name, "inhabitant of the coast", is accommodated to his present dwelling-place and his occupation — it is quite another matter that it does not correspond to his origin (he was born and grew up in Sparta, as he tells himself in V, 1,4).[23] In II, 14,5 we are told that Habrokomes and Hippothoos rest themselves and their horses: ἦν γὰρ <καὶ> τῷ Ἱπποθόῳ ἵππος ἐν τῇ ὕλῃ κρυπτόμενος. This name is regarded by Kerényi[24] as a genuinely significant name with a symbolic meaning, but I regard this as highly speculative; be that as it may, in this connection at least the name and the realistic detail are simply combined to make a play on words, and the horses are never alluded to again in the story. A third instance of the same kind is, I believe, the chief pirate, called

38

---

[23] Rohde, loc. cit. (see n. 3), calls this "eine sonderbare Gedankenlosigkeit des Xenophon" – "man müsste in diesem Namen geradezu eine *Prophezeiung* seiner Schicksale suchen". This is obviously to deny the author the straightforward play on words but to call for a symbolism in name-giving which would escape the ordinary reader; who noted, by the way, an allusion in the choice of Ἀγχίαλος for the robber from Laodicea in Syria, a town which often (though not in Xenophon) has the by-name ἡ ἐπὶ (or πρὸς) θαλάσσῃ?

[24] Op. cit. (see n. 3), pp. 170-2.

Κόρυμβος, who is introduced in I, 13,3 with an unusually full description: ... νεανίας ὀφθῆναι μέγας, φοβερὸς τὸ βλέμμα· κόμη ἦν αὐτῷ αὐχμηρὰ καθειμένη. Probably, it is more than a mere coincidence that his *hair* is given special attention and that the word κόρυμβος, "top", may be used in a transferred sense for a certain kind of hair-dressing.[25] Thus, the names in these cases are apparently not chosen in order to characterize their bearers in any deeper sense but are exploited for the sake of puns which originate from their meanings, just as the author does with the truly significant name Antheia in the passage cited above (I, 2,5).

There are, of course, more personal names in Xenophon with quite lucid meanings, such as Εὐίππη, Λάμπων, Λυκομήδης and Πολύιδος, but, as far as I can see, it is not possible to find any correspondence between name and character in these cases. Sometimes, the moral qualities and the behaviour of the person in question even seem to be contrary to the etymology of the name. Thus, Ἀνδροκλῆς (V, 1,6) and Ἀριστόμαχος (III, 2,5) do not at all play the parts of renowned heroes in the romance; as the rivals of Aigialeus and Hippothoos, respectively, they are rather negatively depicted. The pirate who cunningly tries to win the favour of Antheia during her forced stay at the pirates' headquarters at Tyre (I, 15,3–II, 2,2) is called Εὔξεινος, "hospitable"! Κλυτός, "renowned", is a timorous slave (V, 5,4–8), and Χρύσιον, "my little treasure", is the name given to the talkative old woman in III, 9,4. If the author had the etymologies in mind at all in such cases, he must have meant the names to be *ironically* significant. It may be suspected, however, that such an intention was beyond what we may justly expect from this author,[26] especially since there is no explicit stressing of the moral characteristics of these individuals — the characterizations given above are read out of

39

[25] Exactly what kind of hair-dressing the term κόρυμβος (or κρωβύλος) referred to is uncertain; it may have been different kinds at different times (see *RE* VII, 1912, 2120–4). LSJ s.v. κρωβύλος: "roll or knot of hair on the crown of the head". The sense of κόρυμβος, which occurs in Antipater of Sidon (*Anth. Pal.* 6,219,3), is discussed by A. S. F. Gow & D. L. Page, *The Greek Anthology: Hellenistic Epigrams*, Cambridge 1965, vol. 2, p. 85. Cf. also F. Bechtel, *Die historischen Personennamen des griechischen bis zur Kaiserzeit*, Halle 1917, p. 601 (under the heading "Personennamen aus Bezeichnungen von ... Haartrachten"), and L. Robert, *Noms indigènes dans l'Asie Mineure gréco-romaine*, I, Paris 1963, p. 268, n. 1.

[26] It is more natural to look for such names in an author like Apuleius; W. Ehlers, in the Tusculum edition of the *Metamorphoses* (Munich 1958, pp. 521–3), lists the following: Arete (IX, 17,2), Aristomenes (I, 6,4), Pythias (I, 24,5) and Socrates (I, 6,1).

their behaviour — and since there are other characters in the romance (Euippe, etc.) for which neither a positive nor a negative correlation between name and role is to be found. This question will be taken up again when the names have been investigated from the other points of view as well.

2. *Literary names*

Most of the personal names in Xenophon are to be found earlier in Greek literature as the names of mythical, historical or fictional characters.[27] Six of them occur already in Homer, six more are met with for the first time in Herodotus, and, to take a late example, no less than fourteen are mentioned in the mythological handbook which is traditionally called the Bibliotheke of Apollodoros (1st or 2nd cent. AD). Mostly, the names are given to different persons in the different works in which they occur; only a few names seem to be more or less definitely connected with *one* mythical or historical person each. In order to find out if Xenophon picked the name of any of his characters from a special context, possibly with the intention that the reader should also associate the figure in the romance with the model, I have made comparisons between some of Xenophon's characters (as regards outer and inner qualities, as well as function in the plot) with their namesakes in earlier literature. As a selection has to be made, I have chosen to deal with the works of Homer and Herodotus, in the first place, because they are at the beginning of the tradition and because the agreements in names with Xenophon are comparatively frequent. Then I shall examine separately two names by which most authors before Xenophon refer to the same two persons, one mythical (Apsyrtos) and one historical (Eudoxos), and finally discuss the occurrences in other ancient romances of names identical with or similar to those of Xenophon.

---

[27] The main source for this part of the investigation has been W. Pape & G. E. Benseler, *Wörterbuch der griechischen Eigennamen*, 3. Aufl., Brunswick 1863–70. Supplementary collections from special indices have been made in the cases in which completeness seemed especially desirable: comedy (including recent papyrus finds and the Romans, Plautus and Terence), Herondas, *Anthologia Palatina*, Alciphron and, of course, the romances, both Greek (for Heliodorus the index of I. Becker's Teubner edition, Leipzig 1855, for the rest that of R. Hercher, Leipzig 1858–59, and for the fragments that of F. Zimmermann, *Griechische Roman-Papyri und verwandte Texte*, Heidelberg 1936) and Latin (Petronius, Apuleius and Historia Apollonii regis Tyri).

Ἀγχίαλος occurs in Homer as the name of three different persons, all with very peripheral roles: a Greek warrior who is killed by Hector (Il. 5,609), the ruler of the Taphians with the epithet δαΐφρων (Od. 1,180 and 418) and a Phaeacian (Od. 8,112). There is no agreement with Xenophon's picture of the Syrian robber who tries to outrage Antheia but is stabbed to death by her (IV, 5). — In the Iliad (9,555) as well as in all later works in which the name appears, except for Xenophon, Ἀλθαία is the mother of Meleager, who curses her own son and (according to one version of the myth) is even responsible for his death. In Xenophon, she is an old women on Rhodes, in whose house Hippothoos and Antheia find a lodging, and she lacks all individual traits (V, 11,2). — In the Odyssey (16–22, see esp. 16,394) Ἀμφίνομος is the foremost but also the noblest among the suitors; he has the rightous mind, but hardly anything more definite, in common with the compassionate robber who saves Antheia from the hungry dogs in IV, 6 and V, 2. — The name Ἱππόθοος is borne by two persons in the Iliad, by the leader of the Pelasgians who is killed by Ajax (2,840–3 and 17,288–318) and by one of Priam's sons who is mentioned only in an enumeration (24,251). In Xenophon, Hippothoos is the third character in importance, but his characteristics change from episode to episode: sometimes he is the ruthless robber who even tries to kill Antheia on two different occasions (II, 13 and IV, 6) and sometimes Habrokomes' best friend and helper (II, 14–III, 3; III, 9–10; V, 8–14); in his own story he is the ill-fated lover of a young boy (III, 2). In none of these functions does he show any distinct similarities with his namesakes in the epos. — Λυκομήδης is a Homeric warrior who is characterized as κρατερός and ἀρηΐφιλος, who slays an enemy but who is not individualized beyond this (Il. 9,84; 12,366; 17,345–6; 19,240). In the *Ephesiaca* the name is applied to Habrokomes' father, an important man in Ephesus, who is characterized only by his behaviour: he is worried about his son (I, 5,5) and irresolute (I, 7,1), he feels sorrow (I, 10,7) and regret (V, 6,3) — in short, there are no resemblances. — Πολύιδος occurs twice in Homer, first as the name of a Trojan, who is a son of an interpreter of dreams and is killed by Diomedes (Il. 5,148), and then as the name of a seer from Corinth with the epithets γέρων ἀγαθός, whose son is killed at Troy (Il. 13,663 and 666). The Polyidos who in Xenophon leads the fight against the robbers in Egypt is described as νεανίσκον ὀφθῆναι χαρίεντα, δρᾶσαι γεννικόν (V, 3,1) and has nothing in common with the epic figures.

41

It seems quite clear that Xenophon has in no case chosen a certain name in order to allude directly to a character in Homer. Only once, in the case of Amphinomos, is there a vague correspondence in the moral qualities of the two characters, the noble suitor and the noble robber, but it is by no means sufficiently marked to be called an allusion; it may be a sheer coincidence or perhaps the name is meant in both cases, independently, to be significant (νόμος, "law", etc.), though also in a very vague sense.

In Herodotus[28] Ἀβροκόμης is a son of Darius, killed at Thermopylae (Hdt. 7,224; also mentioned in Isocrates 4.140). In Xenophon's Anabasis (I, 3,20; 4,3–5; 7,12) another Ἀβροκόμας is the satrap of the Great King in Phoenicia at the time of Cyrus' expedition. Thus, both are Persians who fight against the Greeks; they do not play heroic parts in these sources, and there are no comments on their outward appearances or inner qualities. In the romance, Ἀβροκόμης is a Greek (from Ephesus), and he is described as beautiful, proud and persevering; it seems to be out of the question that Xenophon should have intended the name of his hero to allude directly to these colourless Persians, as they are depicted in Herodotus and Xenophon the historian. — There is the same lack of resemblances between, on the one hand, the two beautiful young boys Ὑπεράνθης and Κλεισθένης in the romance (III, 2 and V, 9–15, respectively) and, on the other, their namesakes in Herodotus; there, the former is another son of Darius who is killed at Thermopylae (Hdt. 7,224), whereas the latter is the great Attic reformer of the late sixth century (Hdt. 5,66–73; 6,131) or his grandfather, the tyrant of Sicyon (Hdt. 5,67–69; 6,126 and 128–31). Κυνώ, who is evil personified in Xenophon (III, 12), has nothing more than the name in common with the Persian woman in Herodotus (1,110 and 122) who saves the little boy Cyrus from death and brings him up as her own son.[29] — Furthermore, two characters in Xenophon bear names which belong to Egyptian pharaohs in Herodotus; Μοῖρις (Hdt. 2,13 and 101) and Ψάμμις (Hdt. 2,159–161);[30] Herodotus does not comment upon their personal qualities but only describes their achievements — in the case of Moiris, different constructions, notably the lake of Moiris west of the Nile, and in the case of Psammis a military expedition to Aethiopia, among other things. The Syrian Moiris of the romance, who marries Manto and falls in love with Antheia (II, 5,6; 9; 11–12), is thus without resemblances to the Pharaoh, whereas Psammis is a βασιλεύς also in the romance (though "Indian")[31] and actually travels in Egypt towards Aethiopia (III, 11 and IV, 3).

[28] On the names which are common to Herodotus and Xenophon Ephesius, see B. Lavagnini, "La patria di Senofonte Efesio" (1926), reprinted in *Studi sul romanzo greco*, Messina & Florence 1950, p. 156.

[29] Besides these two women with the name Κυνώ, I have only found one Κυννώ, namely, in Herondas' fourth mime; she does not, however, show any resemblance to any of the former.

[30] Cf. Lavagnini, loc. cit. (see n. 28): Moiris is a misunderstanding on the part of Herodotus, who took the Egyptian word for the construction (the lake) to be the name of the constructor (the Pharaoh); Psammis is the short for Psammetichos II. Psammis also occurs as the name of a Persian in Aeschylus' Persae, 959.

[31] "Indian" is not necessarily to be taken literally: "Im allgemeinen Sprachgebrauch heissen die Aksumiten nicht Aethiopen, sondern Inder, einfach weil sie in der für die hohe Kaiserzeit wichtigsten (vgl. Xen. Eph. 4,1,5 u.ö) Kontaktregion des ägyptisch-indischen Handels leben" (A. Dihle, *Umstrittene Daten: Untersuchungen zum Auftreten der Griechen am Roten Meer*, Cologne & Opladen 1965, p. 75).

This last-mentioned case, Psammis the Pharaoh and Psammis the "Indian king" visiting Egypt for commercial reasons, is thus the only one in which a similarity can be traced, though it is a slight one. If Xenophon was really influenced directly by Herodotus in his naming of the characters — what makes this somewhat more probable[32] than in the case of Homer is that the names which Herodotus and Xenophon have in common are comparatively *rare* in other literary sources — this influence was evidently of a very superficial kind. Xenophon took the names but he never cared to choose them in such a way that the correspondences would apply also to the characters themselves and their functions.

Apart from Althaia (mentioned above in the section on Homer), there seems to be one more name which was definitely connected with one mythical character in all Greek literature before Xenophon, namely, Ἄψυρτος, Medea's brother, who was murdered during her and Jason's flight from Colchis. With this child or youth (according to different versions of the myth) the chief pirate in the romance has obviously no point of contact (I, 14–II, 12). — On the other hand, a certain connection is traceable between the name of the old Ephesian physician in the romance, Εὔδοξος (III, 4–5), and the fact that one or two historical physicians are mentioned in literary sources with precisely this name, notably the famous astronomer and physician from Cnidus, ὁ μαθηματικός, of the 4th cent. B.C.[33]

Thus, the associations which the names of mythical characters like Althaia and Apsyrtos were likely to provoke did not apparently bother Xenophon, nor, to any appreciable degree, the contexts in which the names appeared in classical writers. Only in the case of one historical person, the physician Eudoxos, is there an obvious correspondence, but the importance of this is somewhat weakened by the possibility, mentioned earlier, that this name may he interpreted as significant through its etymology as well. I shall now turn to the literature which is nearer to Xenophon, both in time and in kind, and see if the points of contact are more frequent there than earlier.

---

[32] Lavagnini, loc. cit. (see n. 28) regards the Herodotean influence on Xenophon "non dubbia e non discutibile", but this is, in my opinion, a definite overstatement. Cf. also n. 49.

[33] Diogenes Laertius, VIII, 86–91; in ch. 90, more persons with this name are mentioned, possibly one more physician.

In what remains of ancient romantic literature, only four of Xenophon's personal names recur in the same forms, applied to fictitious characters. Ἄνθεια and Εὔξεινος appear in a small fragment of a romance, which has been hypothetically connected with the *Ephesiaca* as representing an earlier stage than the version which has been transmitted.[34] Nothing in the characterization points to an identity, however, between the bearers of the same names in the fragment and the romance. — The name Μεγαμήδης, which in Pape & Benseler is recorded only for Xenophon,[35] is now also to be found in a fragment, the so-called Chione romance,[36] in which a man called Megamedes seems to be one of the principal characters. This has led to the interesting theory that Xenophon intentionally connected his romance with an earlier popular one by making his heroine, Antheia, the daughter of one of its characters with this unusual name.[37] There are only late parallels to this, however — thus, Kleitophon and Leukippe from the romance of Achilles Tatius are the parents of the hero in a Christian legend[38] — and Xenophon himself does not explicitly allude to any such relationship. — In Longus, Ῥόδη is the wife of Megakles, Chloe's father (IV, 36,3); she is not characterized, however, and bears no resemblence in her function to the young slave girl in Xenophon. — Three other names in Xenophon recur in related literature but then only as the traditional names of mythical characters: Althaea in Apuleius (VII, 28,4), the Lapith woman Θεμιστώ as an object of comparison in a fragment,[39] and Εὐίππη as a woman loved by Odysseus in one of Parthenius' stories (3).

I have noted also the following *similar* names: Xenophon's Χρύσιον (an old woman) — Petronius' Chrysis (a young girl, Petr. 128); Λάμπων (αἰπόλος) — Λάμπις (βουκόλος, Longus IV, 7,1); Κλυτός (slave) — Clytius (teacher, Apuleius I, 24,6); Αἰγιαλεύς (fisherman)[40] — Αἰγιαλός (king, Parthenius 1,1); Λεύκων (loyal slave) — Λευκώνη (young, unhappy wife, Parthenius 10,1). The only notable connection besides the name is the one between the goatherd in Xenophon and the cowherd in Longus.

---

[34] Zimmermann, op. cit. (see n. 27), p. 78.

[35] As a patronymic, Μεγαμηδείδαο is found in the Homeric Hymn to Hermes, 100.

[36] Zimmermann, op. cit. (see n. 27), p. 44.

[37] B. Lavagnini, "Le origini del romanzo greco" (1921), reprinted in Studi sul romanzo greco, Messina & Florence 1950, pp. 95 f., and Kerényi, op. cit. (see n. 3), p. 171 (n. 72).

[38] Migne, *PG* 116,93 ff. (*Passio SS. Galactionis et Epistemes*). See H. Dörrie, "Die griechischen Romane und das Christentum", *Philologus* 93, 1938, 273–6.

[39] Zimmermann, op. cit. (see n. 27), pp. 46 ff.

[40] Also in Alciphron (I, 9 Schepers) there is a fisherman by the name of Aigialeus.

As we have seen, the points of agreement between the naming of Xeno-phon's characters and that of the characters in other romances are not frequent. There are some distinct ones, however, even though the extant facts do not permit any wider conclusions about possible allusions or dependencies. It should be borne in mind that there is extremely little left of the romantic literature which apparently flourished already in late Hellenistic times and that we cannot consequently estimate with any certainty how much Xenophon had in common with or even directly took over from his predecessors in the genre; the few scraps preserved hint that it *may* have been quite a lot.

45

Finally it may be mentioned that Xenophon seems to have been the first author in the Greek literature — as far as it has been preserved and as far as it is covered by the indices consulted[41] — to have used the names Ἄραξος and Ῥηναία for persons (they occur earlier in the liter-ary sources only as geographical names). Κόρυμβος occurs only later in Greek literature, in Nonnus 13,141, but is to be found also in Cicero (Att. 14,3), as the name of an emancipated slave (Corumbus). Of very low frequency are also Megamedes (see above), Moiris (most occurrences late) and Chrysion;[42] above are listed the few places where Habrokomes, Hyperanthes and Psammis occur in the literature.

3. *Realistic names*

In order to get an idea of the position of Xenophon's names in the daily life of his times — whether they were in use at all for living persons and, if so, how common they were — I have searched for the names in epi-graphical and non-literary papyrological material from Greek-speaking regions through Classical, Hellenistic and Roman times.[43] The result is

---

[41] See n. 27.

[42] In addition to the instances mentioned by Pape & Benseler (see n. 27), a Chrysion occurs in Alciphron (IV, 14,2 Schepers) in an enumeration of *meretrices*. According to F. Bechtel, *Die attischen Frauennamen*, Göttingen 1902, p. 111, this name is "aus der schmei-chelnden Anrede hervorgegangen" (as, for instance, in Aristophanes, *Acharn.* 1200). Cf. also Robert, op. cit. (see n. 25), p. 19, n. 2.

[43] The limits of the investigation were fixed by the lack of comprehensive collections of inscriptions from some regions and the lack of indices to certain existing corpora or to parts of them. The main source has been the volumes of *Inscriptiones Graecae* (*IG*), which include indices of proper names; of vols. I and IX:1 the *editio minor* has been used. Sup-plementary collections have been made in *Supplementum Epigraphicum Graecum* (*SEG*)

→

46   reported in Table 3.[44] The occurrences are grouped in large geographical units according to where the inscriptions[45] were found; a general classification according to the ethnic origin of each bearer of a name was impossible, because only a minority of the persons is designated in this respect in the inscriptions. Nor has it, in view of the limited scope of this investigation, been possible to group the inscriptions according to their dates (dates are often not provided by the editors). As far as I can see, this is not, however, of any vital importance for the present study, since even a simple spot test confirms that the Greeks were very conservative in their naming customs; if a certain name occurs (and is not too uncommon) in Classical times, one may take it as certain that it recurs in the

47   material from both Hellenistic and Roman times.[46] Now, in dealing with Xenophon, who certainly belongs to Roman times, the main question must be which names were possible for practical use at such a late stage,

---

1–21 (1923–65), *Tituli Asiae Minoris* (*TAM*) I, II and III: 1, *Inscriptions grecques et latines de la Syrie* I–V (ed. L. Jalabert & R. Mouterde), *Monumenta Asiae Minoris* (*MAMA*) I–VIII, *Forschungen in Ephesos* II, III and IV: 3, *La Carie* II (ed. L. & J. Robert), *Inscriptiones Creticae* I–IV, *Inscriptiones antiquae orae septentrionalis Ponti Euxini* I, II and IV, and *Inscriptiones in Bulgaria repertae* I–II (ed. G. Mihailov). The Egyptian material (papyri, inscriptions, etc.) comes from F. Preisigke, *Namenbuch*, Heidelberg 1922. I have not been able to include systematically the vast amount of documentary papyri published since the compilation of the Namenbuch, the supplement of D. Foraboschi being only in its initial stage (Fasc. 1, *A–Βίλος*, Milan & Varese s.a.).

[44] Naturally, I have tried to avoid double recordings of the same person, which may have been caused either by actual repeated mentions of one person in the same or in different inscriptions or by the same inscription recurring in several of the corpora used. All the same, lapses in this respect may occur, especially in the case of high-frequency names which are more difficult to check, but the general tendencies should hardly be disturbed by minor inexactitudes of this kind.

[45] From this point onwards, "the inscriptions" or "the epigraphical material" (without further specifications) means the *whole* material used, that is, including the small proportion provided by the papyri.

[46] I have tested this on the Attic material, which is published according to periods: *IG* vol. I up to 403/02 B.C., vol. II up to Augustus, vol. III Roman times. For instance, the name Aristomachos occurs four times in the first, 26 times in the second and six times in the third volume; this distribution is closely related to the bulk of the inscriptions published for each of the periods and is consequently not an indication of differences in the popularity of the name. Unfortunately, the handbooks do not give much help in these matters, there is much discussion about the formation of names and about the earliest instances and their localization but very little about the relative frequency, the survival and distribution during later periods, social differences, etc. (some exceptions are referred to in n. 65).

and in that case the total number of occurrences is more important than an exact dating of each inscription in which a name is found.

Some distortions which are unavoidable on account of the nature of the material should also he noted. Naturally, the proportions between the occurrences of a certain name in different regions must not at once be taken as indicating actual differences in the popularity of the name; they may simply reflect the different numbers of inscriptions available from each region. Furthermore, there is no proportional distribution of the inscriptions over the different periods of time; thus, most of the epigraphical material from mainland Greece belongs to the 5th and 4th centuries B.C., as other regions had different periods of political and economical prosperity, which are reflected in the relative number of inscriptions. Finally, this type of material cannot be expected to give a true cross-section through the social classes or the sexes. A concentration on the upper classes and the men is natural, since much of the material is made up of more or less official documents; grave inscriptions, manumission documents and certain kinds of papyrological material only partly make up for this distortion.

These reservations having been made, some more positive statements may also be ventured. If a name is very rare or is not found at all in this material, this fact strongly indicates that the name was at least uncommon in daily life, with reservations for the lower classes and for possible local fluctuations. If, on the other hand, the name is frequent in these sources and seems to be spread all over the Greek world, this cannot be regarded as mere chance; the name must have been "common", though its position in this respect, in comparison with Greek personal names in general, does not emerge from this investigation.

In the figures of the table (Table 3) a distinct group of frequent names may be discerned. Ἀριστόμαχος, with its 170 occurrences, is the most common name beyond all comparison. Then come, with decreasing frequency, Εὔξεινος (69 occurrences; always in the form Εὔξενος in the inscriptions), Ἀνδροκλῆς (55), Εὔδοξος (37), Λάμπων (30), Λυκομήδης (28; sometimes in the form Λυκομείδης) and Λεύκων (25). All these names seem to have had a wide distribution geographically. Possibly, it may be thought peculiar that Androkles is absent in the material from Asia Minor, but it is quite possible that this is accidental, since the material from this region is not particularly large. Next come the two most common female names, Ῥόδη (18) and Χρυσίον (14), and then Κλεισθένης (11), Περίλαος (11), Ὑπεράνθης (9), Κόρυμβος (7), Θεμιστώ (4), Πολύιδος (3),

48
50

Table 3. Occurrences of Xenophon's personal names in epigraphical and papyrological material from different parts of the world.

	Attica	Peloponnesus	Central & Northern Greece	Moesia & Thracia	Pontus Euxinus	Islands of the Aegean	Crete	Cyprus	Asia Minor	Syria	Egypt	Cyrene	Italy & Sicily	Total
Ἀβροκόμης													1	1
Ἀγχίαλος					2									2
Αἰγιαλεύς		1												1
Ἀλθαία														0
Ἀμφίνομος	1								1					2
Ἀνδροκλῆς	21	7	4		1	11	4			1		6		55
Ἀνθία			1											1
Ἄραξος														0
Ἀριστόμαχος	41	17	24	5	1	42	1	1	16		9	4	9	170
Ἄγυρτος														0
Εὔδοξος	16	3	7			4			4		2	1	1	37
Εὔιππη		1												1
Εὔξε(ι)νος	17	4	14		4	15			5		3	2	5	69
Θελξινόη														0
Θεμιστώ	2						1		1					4
Ἱππόθοος														0
Κλεισθένης	3	1			1	6								11
Κλυτός														0
Κόρυμβος	3	1				1			2					7
Κυνώ														0
Λάμπων	3		9			8			1		8		1	30
Λεύκων	8	1	3		3	4	2				2		2	25
Λυκομήδης	11	4	2			5	1		1		4			28
Μαντώ						1								1
Μεγαμήδης														0
Μοῖρις											1			1
Περίλαος	3	1	2			1			1		3			11
Πολλίδος						2								3
Ῥηναία														0
Ῥόδη	8	1	3			2	1		1		1		1	18
Ὑπεράνθης	3	1					4					1		9
Χρύστον	4				6	2			2					14
Ψαμμ											1			1

Ἀγχίαλος (2) and Ἀμφίνομος (2). Some of these names show a remarkably uneven geographical distribution. Of 11 inscriptions with the name Kleisthenes, four come from Euboea, of nine men with the name Hyperanthes, at least five are Cretans,[47] and of 14 women called Chrysion, no less than six apparently lived near Panticapaeum on the Black Sea.[48] It may also be mentioned that, among the 30 occurrences of the name Lampon, four come from Boeotia and five from the island of Thasos. It is quite possible that these names were bound by special ties to certain regions or places, but the evidence of the inscriptions may also be due to mere coincidences. What is important for this study is that there is no unanimous tendency towards one special region for several or all of the names; it is not possible to bind the author geographically by means of the personal names. In the case of Ephesus[49] the material is even quite negative; in the inscriptions from that town which I have gone through I have only found one of the names in the romance, Aristomachos, that is, the generally most common name among those investigated here.

In the whole material, the following names have been found only once each: Ἀβροκόμης, Αἰγιαλεύς, Ἀνθία, Εὐίππη, Μαντώ, Μοῖρις and Ψάμμις. Nine names do not occur at all: Ἀλθαία, Ἄραξος, Ἄψυρτος,

51

---

[47] In addition to four instances in *Inscriptiones Creticae* III, there is also one Cretan mentioned by this name in an inscription from Attica (*SEG* 19, 105).

[48] Cf. also Robert, op. cit. (see n. 25), p. 19, n. 2, on Χρυσίον: "il n'est pas rare à Héraclée du Pont".

[49] As Lavagnini, op. cit. (see n. 28), has demonstrated, the by-name "Ephesius" need not mean that Xenophon really was an Ephesian by birth; it may simply be a label which announces that he is, among many Xenophontes, the one who wrote the *Ephesiaca*. On the other hand, Lavagnini's efforts to show that Xenophon definitely did not know anything of Ephesus but took his information from Herodotus are not quite convincing. The crucial point, on which the whole proof is based, is the distance between the city of Ephesus and the Artemision, which Herodotus (I, 26,2) and Xenophon Ephesius (I, 2,2) both state as being "seven stades". This is not the place to discuss Lavagnini's arguments in detail, but a few statements may be made. (1) The situation of the town was, in principle, the same in the archaic period (to which Herodotus is referring), before Croesus forced the inhabitants to move nearer to the Artemision, and after the Lysimachean re-foundation of the town about 290 B.C. (2) Processions to the sanctuary did not only pass through the Magnesian Gate but also through the "Coressian" Gate (cf. J. Keil, *Ephesos*, 5. Aufl., Vienna 1964, p. 54, n. 9). (3) Whichever way the procession usually took, it must have been the most natural thing to measure the distance between the town and the Artemision where it was shortest, namely, starting from the "Coressian" Gate, and in that case "seven stades" is valid for Xenophon's time as well as for the period before the middle of the 6th cent. B.C.

Θελξινόη, Ἱππόθοος, Κλυτός, Κυνώ, Μεγαμήδης and Ῥηναία. Of course, this does not entitle us to conclude that they were not in use at all in daily life — the many names with one single occurrence each are warnings enough of the frailty of the material — but certainly they cannot have been common within the regions and the classes of people which the inscriptions cover. A good illustration of one of the deficiencies of the material alluded to above is the fact that, of the ten names of women which occur in the romance, no less than seven belong to this category, with one occurrence or none at all in the epigraphical material, whereas the majority of the male names belong to the more frequently recorded ones. There is no reason to believe that Xenophon actually chose realistic names for one sex but not for the other.

52

I shall now examine more closely these low-frequency names and, where feasible, also adduce epigraphical or papyrological material from other sources.[50] The instance of Habrocomes which is included in the statistics is to be found in an inscription from Italy (possibly from Rome; *IG* XIV, 1318);[51] the name occurs at least once more, namely, as the name of an Athenian in an inscription from Samos (date: 346/45 B.C.).[52] — Aigialeus, an ethnicum as regards the type of formation (τὸ Αἰγιαλός), occurs in an inscription from Epidaurus (*IG* IV, 926₁) and outside this material also in an inscription from Smyrna;[53] the name Αἰγιαλός is more common (five occurrences). — Anthia occurs in a Boeotian inscription (*IG* VII, 1973), and besides this also in the form Ἄνθεια in Messene (*IG* V:1, 1482);[54] the shorter form, Ἀνθία, is furthermore attested as the name of an Egyptian woman mentioned in the "Tax rolls from Karanis" (171–174 A.D.).[55] — Euippe (in the form Εὐίππα) is met with once in an

---

[50] In order to allow comparison between the figures of the table, this additional material has not been introduced into the statistics.

[51] The abbreviations for the epigraphical corpora are given above in n. 43.

[52] J. Kirchner, *Prosopographia Attica*, vol. 1, Berlin 1901, s.v. Furthermore, the name Habrokomes has been conjectured in *IG* XII:8, Samothrace 201, and also in the metrical inscription from Ostia, which has been published under the title "Carmen sepulchrale Abrocomae (?)" (*SEG* 16,614). The celebrated person seems to have been a beautiful youth of Oriental origin, but only the two first letters of his name, AB (in a long syllable) remain, and other names are possible. Date: 1st half of the 2nd cent. A.D.

[53] A. Fick & F. Bechtel, *Die griechischen Personennamen*, 2. Aufl., Göttingen 1894, p. 333: "nicht bloss mythisch"; p. 307: "Smyrna, Ion. Inschr. no. 153".

[54] See Klaffenbach, cited in Zimmermann, loc. cit. (see n. 22).

[55] *Michigan Papyri*, vol. IV, parts I–II, Ann Arbor 1936–39, Nos. 223–225. In nearly 30 occurrences of the same women's name, the variant spelling Ἄνθεια is attested only once (224,6).

inscription from Mantinea (*IG* V:2, Ma 335; 1st cent. B.C.?), while the male counterpart Εὔιππος occurs more often (six times). — Manto is found in an inscription from Tenos (*IG* XII:5, 872; 4th or 3rd cent. B.C.).[56] — For Moiris and Psammis the instances in the table come from Egyptian sources,[57] but at least the former name was in use in other regions too[58].

Among the names which are non-existent in the primary material for this investigation, some are represented at least by related names. Male counterparts of Althaia and Thelxinoe are mentioned, Ἀλθαῖος (Eretria, *IG* XII: 9 index, two occurrences) and Θελξίνοος (Sparta, *IG* V:1, 124). For Hippothoos we find the female counterpart Ἱπποθόη in a grave inscription from Rome (*IG* XIV, 1720). — Klytos is not recorded in the material but has been in use as the name of historical persons;[59] the variant Κλύτιος is recorded in an inscription from Ephesus (Forschungen in Ephesos II, 57; 3rd cent. B.C.). — For Hippothoos and Megamedes there are indications of epigraphical evidence in the secondary literature, which mentions instances from Miletus[60] and Teos,[61] respectively. — As has been mentioned in the section on literary names, two of the names occur as geographical appellations: Cape Araxos, the northern point of Elis, and Rhenaia, variant of the more common name Rheneia for the island next to Delos. Kyno also exists as a geographical name, sometimes used as a shorter form for Κυνῶν πόλις and Κυνὸς πόλις in Egypt.[62] It is an established fact that geographical names could be used for persons in the unchanged form[63] and not only transformed into ethnica like Αἰγιαλεύς

53

---

[56] L. Zgusta, *Kleinasiatische Personennamen*, Prague 1964, § 868-1, adduces a name Μαντουν (from Pisidia), which is either indigenous or to be associated with the Greek Μαντίας and Μαντώ.

[57] In addition to the instances recorded by Preisigke (see n. 43), one Ψάμις and one Ψάμμις are also mentioned in the "Tax rolls from Karanis" (see n. 55).

[58] See Preisigke. For Moiris, cf. also *Inscr. Cret.* II:XXIV on a certain Μοῖρις Τιμοπόλιος Ῥιθύμνιος, Bechtel, op. cit. (see n. 25), p. 323, who adduces an instance of the name from Miletus (*Milet*, H. III, Berlin 1914, 122 I_{89}, "um 500"), and Lavagnini, loc. cit. (see n. 28), who adduces one from Smyrna (*CIG* 3147,37).

[59] Κλύτος Ἀκαρνάν, στρατηγός (191 B.C.): Liv. 36,11–12 and *IG* IX. 1:2 (*ed. minor*), p. XXVII. See also Pape & Benseler s.v.

[60] Bechtel, op. cit. (see n. 25), p. 220. ἵππος is a common component in Greek names generally and enjoyed a special popularity in Eretria, but the combination Hippothoos seems to be absent in that material. See F. Bechtel, "Das Wort ἵππος in den eretrischen Personennamen", *Hermes* 35, 1900, 326–31.

[61] Lavagnini, op. cit. (see n. 37), p. 95, n. 4 (with a reference to *CIG* II, 3064_{29}).

[62] *RE* XII: 1, 1924, 26 f.

[63] Bechtel, op. cit. (see n. 25), pp. 550–62; E. Fraenkel, "Namenwesen", *RE* XVI: 2, 1935, 1643.

and Μεμφῖτις[64] in Xenophon. Thus, the three names mentioned may also, apart from other possible derivations, be regarded as transferred geographical names.

54   This inventory of the names that are absent from the primary material of the investigation shows that every one of them is nonetheless quite possible as a realistic name: some actually occur in other sources, some are represented by related names, and some were in use as geographical names. We may conclude that Xenophon obviously did not use imaginary names of his own invention, nor did he take over from literary sources any names that would be unthinkable in daily life.[64a]

An easily defined social group among the characters of the romance are the slaves, four of whom are given individual names: Klytos, Lampon (unfree goatherd), Leukon and Rhode. Were these names realistically chosen, so that they might be classed as typical slave names? To judge from the material available for comparison,[65] this does not seem to have been the case; only Ῥόδα occurs there as the name of a slave, and once only.[66] However, this state of things seems to have a historical explanation and must not be looked upon as an unrealistic trait in the romance. It is true that there was a definite distinction between the names of slaves and those of citizens in all Greek communities (except for Laconia, apparently) during the Classical period, but the differences were gradually obliterated, with the result that no separate categories of

---

[64] Antheia calls herself Memphitis when she wants to be considered as an Egyptian (IV, 3,6). The word does not occur as a proper name in Preisigke's *Namenbuch* but only as an adjective of nationality in his *Wörterbuch der griechischen Papyrusurkunden*, III, Berlin 1929-31, Abschn. 13, s.v. Bechtel, op. cit. (see n. 25), p. 541, gives an instance of the male name Μεμφίτης.

[64a] A supplementary search in later volumes of the *SEG* (22–24, 1967–69) — made possible through a delay in the publication of this article — supports this conclusion. Worth mentioning is esp. one instance of the name Klytos (*SEG* 24,1105 11, Moesia, 1st cent. B.C.), further two new instances of Moiris from regions other than Egypt (*SEG* 23,86, Attica, 304/3 B.C.; 24,649, Thracia, 2nd cent. B.C.) and one Manto (?, *SEG* 24,579, Macedonia, 2nd or 3rd cent. A.D.).

[65] H. Collitz & F. Bechtel, *Sammlung der griechischen Dialekt-Inschriften*, 4:2, Göttingen 1901, pp. 311–26; S. Copalle, *De servorum Graecorum nominibus capita duo*, Diss. Marburg 1908; M. Lambertz, *Die griechischen Sklavennamen*, I–II (Gymn. Progr. Wien 1906/07 and 1907/08).

[66] Lambertz, op. cit. (see n. 65), II, p. 15.

names are discernible in the Roman period.[67] The romance gives one more illustration of this, the names Antheia and Thelxinoe, earlier typical names of courtesans,[68] are used for two free-born women of the highest class, the wives of Habrokomes and Aigialeus respectively.

In contrast to the historical vagueness of the romance, referred to in the first part of this article, there is the desire of the author to place the action in a definite geographical setting. He mentions the names of many countries and towns, usually only the best-known ones but in the case of Egypt also names of smaller places, some of them otherwise unknown;[69] all this gives an air of authenticity. Therefore, it is legitimate to ask also if the names of the characters were chosen to give any local colour. As far as any conclusions can be drawn from the available material, however, there seems to be no tendency in that direction. The names of the Ephesians in the romance (Habrocomes, Antheia, their respective parents and Eudoxos) are not represented in the inscriptions from that town (Forschungen in Ephesos and *SEG*), and I have not been able to find anywhere else any indications that these names were taken from any prominent citizens of that town (in the same way as, for instance, Chariton uses the Syracusan Hermokrates as a link between history and fiction). Perilaos and Chrysion are absent in the Cilician material investigated (*MAMA* II–III and *SEG*), just as the persons who are involved in the Syrian and Phoenician adventures have no namesakes in the inscriptions from those territories (Jalabert & Mouterde and *SEG*). However, the epigraphical material available from these regions is not very large. The Egyptians in the romance, Polyidos, Rhenaia, Araxos and Kyno, are not recorded in the papyri and inscriptions from that country, and the characters of the story enacted at Sparta (V, 1) have no counterparts in the Laconian material (*IG* V: 1 and *SEG*); only the male counterpart to Thelxinoe is found in an inscription from Sparta, as was mentioned above.

To a great extent this lack of correspondence may be explained by the gradual internationalization of the Greek proper names, many of which were from the beginning limited to particular regions. As has

[67] Lambertz, op. cit. (see n. 65), II, pp. 31 and 42.

[68] Hirzel, op. cit. (see n. 17), pp. 74 f.

[69] Cf. Henne, op. cit. (see n. 5), who modifies the negative judgement of Dalmeyda, op. cit. (see n. 2), p. 49, n. 2.

been noted above, no distinct local borderlines are discernible, at least for the high-frequency names in this material. Of course, there may have been differences in popularity, and likewise the figures in the table for some of the low-frequency names may point to actual and not coincidental fluctuations in the use of names — but to prove this another type of investigation would be needed. For the present purpose it is enough to state that personal names in general tended to become, or were already, the common property of the whole Hellenic world in Xenophon's time; consequently, the possibilities of lending local colour to the action in this way were restricted, even for an author who really endeavoured to do so. In the case of Xenophon, one may doubt even this; no Latin names occur (the prefect is anonymous), nor any Oriental ones, at least not undisguised, in spite of the occurrence of Phoenicians, Syrians, Cilicians and Egyptians in the action. In this respect, a reservation is necessary, however. Just as the "Indian" Psammis has an originally non-Greek (though Hellenized) name,[70] it is not impossible that some of the more uncommon names which Xenophon uses were intended to give a foreign accent to the narration. Under the Greek forms, names like Araxos and Rhenaia may hide genuine Oriental names.[71]

If the results of the three separate lines of investigation are brought together, some distinct trends are observable. Among the names which seemed to have been chosen, more or less evidently, to describe the characters, most turn out to be uncommon or even non-existent in the epigraphical material (notably Habrokomes, Antheia, Thelxinoe and Kyno). This obviously lends support to the assumption that they were really meant to be significant, since the etymology of an uncommon name is naturally more apt to have an unweakened effect on the audience than that of a name frequently used in daily life. Aigialeus and Hippothoos also belong to this infrequent category, which makes their use for plays on words natural. A comparatively unweakened meaning may be assumed for some other names, Hyperanthes, Perilaos and Korymbos, though they are somewhat more common in the epigraphical

[70] See n. 30.

[71] On Hellenized names of Oriental origin in the romance of Iamblichus, see U. Schneider-Menzel in F. Altheim, *Literatur und Gesellschaft im ausgehenden Altertum*, I, Halle/ Saale 1948, pp. 77 ff.

and papyrological material.[72] Still more frequent are Eudoxus, Rhode and Leukon, and therefore no confirmation of their being significant is offered; on the other hand, the case of Amphinomos and Megamedes in this respect seems to be strengthened. To the category of names which may possibly be interpreted as ironically significant belong some of those which show the highest frequencies in daily life (Aristomachos, Euxeinos and Androkles), and this fact seems to settle the question. In all likelihood, they were chosen by the author simply because they were near at hand and not with any ironical purpose. In the case of such common names, the etymological meaning had certainly faded, and thus any special intention of this kind would have had to be indicated explicitly by the author if it were to he observed and enjoyed by the contemporary Greek audience.

The type of significant name which resides not in the etymologies but in the associations which the name is apt to provoke in an educated reader seems to be alien to Xenophon. If he took some names directly from Herodotus, his intention was obviously not to allude to the characters in question; he chose names such as Habrokomes and Hyperanthes only because they were etymologically significant. It must also be remembered that Xenophon's dependence upon Herodotus may be only indirect; he may be relying on an already established tradition of using these names as significant.[73] One thing that would support this hypothesis is the use of the name Kyno, which is applied to quite opposite characters in Herodotus and Xenophon; the rest of the characters are at least more colourless, as regards their moral qualities, in Herodotus and are thus less obtrusive when transferred. One further circumstance is worth noting. Psammis, Moiris and Kyno do not have only Herodotus as the common denominator but also a geographical region, Egypt, where they were used as personal or geographical names. Thus, Xenophon, with his predilection for geography, and especially Egyptian

58

---

[72] I think that it would definitely be going too far to deny the possibility that any names that may occur in daily life were significant (as, for instance, A. P. Smotrytsch, "Die Vorgänger des Herondas", *Acta Antiqua* 14, 1966, 63, does in sorting out all the names which have been found in inscriptions from Cos). In each case, we must weigh how natural the assumption of genuin significance is against the frequency in daily life (as far as we can trace the latter).

[73] Hirzel, op. cit. (see n. 17), p. 74, mentions the form Hyperanth*os* as a type name for beautiful boys.

topography, may well have received the stimulus directly, without Herodotus as an intermediary.

The names of well-known mythological or historical figures, like Althaia, Apsyrtos and Kleisthenes, are given, as we have seen, to the characters of the romance without any discernible symbolical meaning, and this is true also when the names in question were uncommon in daily life, as seems to be the case especially with the first two. Eudoxos remains a doubtful case; it is possible to explain it as significant — by etymology or by association with the historical physician of that name — whereas it was so common in daily life that it may also have been chosen without any special intention. However, there seems to be no instance of a symbolical name-giving of a more studied type — in the same way as, for instance, Longus introduces a Philetas in his romance and Apuleius a Socrates[74] — and this is in accordance with the general impression which Xenophon gives of telling a simple story to a large audience, without pretensions and subtleties. The reservation that must be made in this respect was hinted at above: too little is preserved of the earlier romantic literature to make it possible to judge the degree of Xenophon's dependence on this, and thus the possible allusions to characters in the works of his predecessors escape our notice.

The etymologically significant names should not be regarded as subtleties over the heads of an ordinary audience. In Greek literature this practice has a long tradition deriving from Homer and it was especially developed in the New Comedy;[75] it also seems to have been characteristic of early fiction in general.[76] Xenophon, however, uses such names with a certain moderation. He does not invent any quite unrealistic names;[77] the material adduced here shows that all his names were either demonstrably used for individuals in daily life or, in the very few remaining cases, theoretically could quite possibly be so used, occurring, for instance, as

[74] On Longus (II, 3) see O. Schönberger, in his edition of Daphnis and Chloe (Berlin 1960), p. 163. On Apuleius (I, 6), cf. above n. 26.

[75] See the works cited in n. 20 above.

[76] Cf., for instance, I. Watt, *The Rise of the Novel*, London 1957, p. 19. Some studies on the naming of characters in modern literature are listed in R. Wellek & A. Warren, *Theory of Literature*, London 1955, p. 336, n. 17.

[77] This is in accordance with the practice of Lucian but in opposition to that of Alciphron, as characterized by K. Mras, "Die Personennamen in Lucians Hetärengesprächen", *Wiener Studien* 38, 1916, 339.

geographical names. Further, he gives really significant names to only about a third of his named characters. For most of the unimportant characters, he seems to have chosen the names quite at random among those in use in daily life, utilizing them for individualization but not for characterization. Whether he had any additional intentions in his choice of everyday names, such as to give a more authentic character to the fictitious events of his story, must remain undecided. One may perhaps venture the suggestion, however, that the impression which Xenophon's personal names made upon a contemporary audience — and which we are unable to experience spontaneously — was an impression more of realism than of literary invention.

Parthenope
and the Oriental Reception
of the Ideal Novel

The *Parthenope Romance* Decapitated?*

[originally published in *Symbolae Osloenses* 59, 1984, 61–92]

"The tales of the Egyptian martyrs have the character of decapitated Greek romances, provided with a new Christian head and a new 'happy' ending", the late John Barns is reported to have said.[1] In his published work similar statements occur, though in a less pointed form, e.g.: "One of the permanent features of the Egyptian mind was its taste and talent for romantic story-telling. In one martyrdom at least, that of *Eustathius and Theopistē*…, the influence of the Greek romance, with many of its favourite motifs, situations and devices, is unmistakable."[2] This then is a counterpart to Barns's more famous claim that the Greek genre of the novel owes its origin, "at least in part", to popular romantic stories circulating in Ptolemaic Egypt, in Demotic as well as in Greek translation.[3] Thus, in a manner of speaking, the genre paid back to Christian Egypt its old pagan debt.

---

* The core of the present article was contained in a paper read at the symposium of Platonselskabet: Nordisk selskab for antikkens idétradition held in Gothenburg, 8–11 June 1983. — For the abbreviated references "Coquin" and "Maehler", see below, nn. 18 and 50.

[1] I owe this quotation from J. W. B. Barns's teaching at Oxford to Professor R. H. Pierce (University of Bergen), to whom I am indebted for the reference to Coquin's publication of the Parthenope martyrdom and other invaluable help as well.

[2] E. A. E. Reymond & J. W. B. Barns (eds.), *Four Martyrdoms from the Pierpont Morgan Coptic Codices*, Oxford 1973, 1.

[3] J. W. B. Barns, "Egypt and the Greek Romance", *Mitteil. aus der Papyrussamml. der Österr. Nationalbibl.* N.S. 5, 1956, 29–36, p. 35. Cf. B. P. Reardon, *Courants littéraires grecs des IIe et IIIe siècles après J.-C.,* Paris 1971, 328–32, and T. Hägg, *The Novel in Antiquity*, Oxford 1983, 96–101. When Barns himself, in his inaugural lecture of 1966, briefly returns to the question, his formulations are judiciously balanced ("Egyptians and Greeks", *Pap. Brux.* 14, 1978, 14): "That the two worlds [*sc.* the Egyptian and the Greek] could meet, however, is shown by the scanty remains of a hybrid literature in Greek — translations from Demotic, or Greek compositions expressing Egyptian ideas or designed to appeal to Egyptian taste. I believe that the Greek prose romance, a late phenomenon in which Oriental influence has long been suspected, for all its Greek presentation and classical borrowings owes an especial debt to Egypt. The debt was reciprocal; some late Demotic romances show unmistakable Greek influence."

Put in general terms, Barns's suggestion is hardly controversial; and we may at once extend it to apply to a certain class of Christian martyrdoms at large, not just those that happened also to circulate in Egypt in Coptic versions, like the Eustathius legend.[4] It is indeed as natural that motifs from the Greek novels should recur in martyrdoms of the "epic" or "adventure" type[5] as it is that they appear in other popular Christian literature, like the apocryphal Acts of the Apostles.[6] As regards the martyrdom specifically mentioned, the *Passio SS. Eustathii et soc.,*[7] it is easy enough to substantiate the claim.[8] The story falls into three distinct parts: conversion, adventures, and martyrium. The following summary emphasizes the novelistic traits, most of which naturally occur in the adventure part.

Placidas, a Roman general serving under Trajan, belongs to a noble family and is exceedingly rich (Greek version: 378C, Coptic version: fol. 2*a*); though a pagan, he is righteous (378D; the Coptic version develops at length this topic, including also his wife and two sons, 2*b*). During a hunt (a motif abruptly dropped, 380C, 4*a*), Christ appears to Placidas, who is converted together with his wife; in baptism they receive the names Eustathius and Theopiste.

62

---

[4] Both Budge (below, n. 7) p. vi and Barns (above, n. 2) p. 1 speak of the *Passio SS. Eustathii et soc.* as if it were assuredly Egyptian in origin. As long as this has not been demonstrated (cf. below, n. 9, on the absence of Egyptian colouring), it would perhaps be safer to regard its circulation in Coptic as showing the Egyptian taste, rather than talent, for romantic story-telling.

[5] H. Delehaye, *Les passions des martyrs et les genres littéraires* (Subs. Hag., 13 B), 2nd ed. Bruxelles 1966, divides the martyrdoms into "passions historiques", "panégyriques", and "passions épiques"; the Eustathius martyrdom is regarded as formally belonging to the last group, though Delehaye uses some other terms to characterize it as well: "passion romanesque", "roman hagiographique" (the martyrium is rather loosely appended), or simply "roman d'aventures" (pp. 227–9).

[6] See esp. R. Söder, *Die apokryphen Apostelgeschichten und die romanhafte Literatur der Antike*, Stuttgart 1932 (reprint Darmstadt 1969).

[7] *Bibl. Hag. Gr.* 641, *Bibl. Hag. Lat.* 2760, *Act. SS.* Sept. VI, 123–37. Greek text (with Latin trans.) also in Migne, *PG* 105, 376–417 (the "Acta Antiqua" at the bottom of the pages), Coptic version (with Engl. trans.) in E. A. W. Budge (ed.), *Coptic Martyrdoms etc. in the Dialect of Upper Egypt* (=*Coptic Texts*, 4), London 1914 (reprint New York 1977), 102–27 and 356–80.

[8] Cf. H. Delehaye's article of 1919, "La légende de Saint Eustache", reprinted in his *Mélanges d'hagiographie grecque et latine* (Subs. Hag., 42), Bruxelles 1966, 212–39, p. 221, where some of the similarities with the Greek novel are briefly indicated.

Tribulations come, as Christ has warned them. Having lost all his possessions, Eustathius sets out with his family for Egypt (no motivation for this
destination is given, 392C, 9*a*).⁹ "When the skipper saw that Eustathius' wife
was very beautiful, he fell in love with her" (392C, 9*a*). So Eustathius is separated from his wife: the skipper, "a barbarian", keeps her as payment for the
passage (392D, 9*b*); and later from his sons as well: they are carried away by
wild animals (393C, 10*a*). He nearly commits suicide (393C, 10*a*), but instead
bursts out into a recapitulatory monologue of lament (393D–396C, 10*b*–11*b*).
Having worked in a village for several years, he then serves as a watchman in
an orchard for fifteen years (396D, "ten years" 11*b*). Meanwhile his wife, though
living with the skipper in his country, with God's help manages to preserve her
chastity (396D, 16*a*); and his sons, who were saved from the animals by shep-
herds and farmers, are reared by them as their own (393C–D, 10*a*–*b*), without
knowing that they are brothers (396D, 11*b*).

The rest of the adventure part of the story is largely taken up by complex
recognition scenes with ample portions of recapitulatory speech. Two of the
emperor's soldiers on search (ἀναζήτησις) for Eustathius finally find and succeed
in identifying him (397D–401D, 13*b*–14*a*), and he is reinstalled as a general. His
two sons, recruited as soldiers in his army, recognize each other (405D–408C,
17*a*) and are recognized by their mother (408C–D, 17*a*–*b*); and Eustathius is
recognized by his wife (408D, 17*b*), who proudly declares: "The Lord Christ is
my witness, that neither that man (sc. the skipper) has defiled me nor anyone
else, but I have guarded my chastity (σωφροσύνη) until this day" (409C, 18*a*).
Eustathius tearfully embraces and kisses his beautiful wife (409C, 18*b*). The
rumour of the happy reunion is spread, and all the soldiers gather and rejoice
with the family (412C, 19*a*; cf. 401D–404C, 14*b*).

In Rome to celebrate his victory over the barbarians, Eustathius is asked by
the emperor — now Hadrian — to sacrifice to Apollo as a thanksgiving for
both victory and reunion; but he refuses, and the martyrium is enacted.

Most of the motifs emphasized in my summary are commonplace in
the Greek novels: beauty, nobility, wealth; travelling, separation, search-

---

⁹ Similarly unmotivated departures for Egypt occur in the novels (Xen. Eph. 1.10.5 and
3.10.4, Ach.Tat. 2.31.6; cf. T. Hägg, *Narrative Technique in Ancient Greek Romances,*
Stockholm 1971, 174 and 185 n. 1, with further references), but there they are obvious
pretexts for moving the action to Egyptian soil. In our martyrdom, on the other hand,
this destination amounts to a "loose end": no Egyptian local colouring is given, it is not
even clear whether the ship really lands in Egypt (the river which Eustathius and his
sons cross with such a fatal result, is anonymous: τινα ποταμόν 392D, 9*b*). On the geographical anonymity which (with two or three exceptions) characterizes the whole story
(distinguishing it from the Greek novels with their concrete geographical background),
cf. Delehaye (above, n. 8) p. 217.

ing; monologues of lament, recapitulations; chastity preserved against all odds; and so on. The strong bent toward sentimentality is perhaps particularly revealing: the heroes burst into tears, for sorrow or joy, on at least half a dozen different occasions. Among the complete novels proper, Chariton and Xenophon Ephesius most readily come to mind; the *Pseudo-Clementines* and the *Historia Apollonii regis Tyri* are still closer, if we pay special attention to the particular variant of the separation/ recognition motif which our story exhibits. This motif alone may not be sufficient to prove dependence on the Greek novel — such *Wieder-erkennungsmärchen* are widely spread[10] — but the accumulated mass of indications in vocabulary, motifs, and narrative devices should make the balance incline decisively in that direction: this martyrdom, like others of the adventure type, is no doubt heavily indebted to the popular, or non-sophistic, Greek novel.

However, it is difficult to be more specific than that. Even if we feel confident that a certain motif ultimately derives from a pagan novel, how do we know whether it has reached the martyrdom directly or by way of, for instance, some other Christian tale? Some may be typical folk-tale motifs, some typical aretalogical features,[11] and how in this case can one prove that they are borrowed instead from a novel? Or, to arrive at a question of special importance to the student of the Greek novel: does the accumulation of evidence allow us to assume that the author of the martyrdom had one particular novel as his model for the adventure part of his story, a model from which he borrowed the basic structure and a reasonable part of the padding, a model which we could venture to reconstruct? Or is the influence of a much more general nature: a new story built up of borrowed elements? In short, we face the same kind of problem as in the case of the *Pseudo-Clementines* or the *Historia Apollonii*, and the fragmentary state of our knowledge of the non-sophistic novel of late Hellenistic and early imperial times makes any attempt at

---

[10] See Delehaye (above, n. 8), with the older bibliography listed.

[11] At the end of the martyrdom, when the bodies of Eustathius and his family are found inside the brazen bull undamaged by the fire, the multitude cries out: ἀληθῶς μέγας ἐστὶν ὁ Θεὸς τῶν Χριστιανῶν (417C) as does the crowd when Charicleia steps down unharmed from the stake (Hld. 8.9.16) and when Habrocomes and Antheia have been reunited on Rhodes (Xen. Eph. 5.13.3); on this "aretalogical ending", see K. Kerényi, *Die griechisch-orientalische Romanliteratur in religionsgeschichtlicher Beleuchtung* Tübingen 1927 (2nd ed. Darmstadt 1962), 61 (with further references) and 136; cf. also Söder (above, n. 6) pp. 101–2 and Delehaye (above, n. 5) p. 181.

an answer hazardous. The general influence we have, but do we anywhere have a decapitated Greek novel?

II

By coincidence, it may be that we now in fact possess such a specimen; or, at least, a suitable test case: the Coptic martyrdom of S. Parthenope, earlier known only in Arabic under the name Bartānūbā, to be tried against the Greek *Parthenope Romance*, newly tentatively reconstructed on the basis of papyrus fragments and various testimonia. The obvious connecting link, fragile as it may be, is the name of the heroine.

The martyrdom of "Bartānūbā" is contained in the Saidic recension of the Coptic *Synaxarium* for 21 Tybi (16 January).[12] The Arabic text was edited (from a 17th cent. MS) by J. Forget in 1909[13] and again by R. Basset in 1915.[14] W. E. Crum, commenting on these editions, equated "Bartānūbā" with the Greek Πρωτονίκη.[15] Quite recently another Greek counterpart, Παρθενεία, was suggested by S. Khalil,[16] who regards it as an "eloquent" name: the heroine's struggle to preserve her virginity is the central theme of this martyrdom. However, it is now clear that neither of these suggestions is correct; the underlying Greek name is Παρθενόπη. This was indeed suggested already in 1914 by E. Amélineau, but only en passant and in such an unexpected place,[17] from the point of view of scholars interested in either the Greek novel or Coptic martyrdoms, that it seems to have escaped notice. The definite proof was provided only in 1981 through R.-G. Coquin's publication of a *Coptic* fragment of the martyrdom,[18] in which the heroine's name is written Παρθενόπη.

64

---

[12] De L. O'Leary, *The Saints of Egypt*, London & New York 1937 (reprint Amsterdam 1974), 100. Not mentioned in H. Delehaye, "Les martyrs d'Égypte", *AB* 40, 1922, 5–154 and 299–364, nor in Baumeister (below, n. 44).

[13] *Corp. Script. Christ. Or.* 49, 1909, 399–403 (Arabic text) and 78, 1922, 382–7 (Latin trans.).

[14] *Patr. Or.* 11, 1915, 653–61 (Arabic text with French trans.).

[15] Egypt Expl. Fund, *Archaeological Report* 1908–1909, 63; *JEA* 4, 1917, 51–2.

[16] "Sainte Bartānūbā ou Sainte Partheneia?", *AB* 97, 1979, 381–5. Khalil emends the Arabic form of the name into Bartānūyā.

[17] "Les Coptes et la conversion des Ibères au Christianisme", *RHR* 69, 1914, 143–82 and 289–322, pp. 302–3.

[18] "Le roman de Παρθενόπη/ Bartānūbā (ms. *IFAO*, Copte 22, ff⁰ 1ʳ⁻ᵛ 2ʳ)", *Bulletin de Centenaire*, Suppl. au *BIFAO* 81, 1981, 343–58 + Pl. XLII.

This Coptic fragment, from a 9th or 10th century codex of mixed contents, contains about one fifth of the martyrdom (§§ 2.6–5.4 and 11.16–19). Besides giving us the correct name of the heroine, it shows, according to Coquin, that the Arabic version in the *Synaxarium* is a fairly true translation of the Coptic text[19] (which may in turn be a translation from a lost Greek original).[20] Coquin now provides a complete French translation of the martyrdom, based on the Coptic fragment, as far as it goes, and on four different Arabic manuscripts; more important variant readings are given in footnotes.[21] This translation is the basis of my following summary and discussion of the story.

In the days of Emperor Constantine — we are told — a beautiful young girl, twelve years of age, baptized Parthenope, was received in a monastery near Byzantium. Her beauty and virtue, education and modesty awoke everybody's admiration and made the Mother and Sisters love her (§ 1). But the Devil got jealous and arranged that the emperor, who was looking for a young bride, should hear about this unique and perfect maiden. He consulted his magnates and on their advice sent people to fetch her (§ 2). On seeing her, they wondered at her beauty and at once abducted her from the monastery, in spite of the Mother's and Sisters' tears and her own despair, and brought her into the emperor's presence (§ 3). Seeing that the rumour was true, the emperor rejoiced and had her brought alone into his bed-chamber, where he invited her to become his lawfully wedded wife, enjoy riches, and be the mother of future emperors (§ 4). She, however, managed to decline in a cunning way, appealing to his Christian faith and his sense of righteousness: she is already *God's* servant and bride, the emperor has no right to claim her for himself (§ 5). The godfear-

---

[19] Coquin p. 346: "l'arabe est, dans l'ensemble, fidèle au copte et le résume à peine".

[20] Coquin (p. 346) leaves the question open. Delehaye (above, n. 12) pp. 149–52 and Reymond & Barns (above, n. 2) pp. 18–9 seem to agree that Coptic martyrologies are as a rule translations from the Greek, though there are also original compositions in Coptic; Baumeister (below, n. 44) p. 149 would regard most of the later legends (time of Shenute, 5th cent.) as composed in Coptic. As regards our text this is of course a problem only if we consider it as Egyptian at all in origin, cf. below, n. 67.

[21] The sole basis of Forget's and Basset's editions (above, nn. 13–14) was a Paris 17th cent. MS., *B.N. ar. 4869* (= *P¹*). Practically the same text, according to Coquin (pp. 345–6), is contained in the unedited *B.N. ar. 4881* (= *P²*), whereas a text of better quality is provided by a Louxor MS. (= *L*) recently discovered and presented by Coquin (*AB 96*, 1978, 351–65). A fourth text containing the martyrdom, Beirut, *Bibl. Or.* 614 (= *B*), is reported to give "un texte très remanié": "la suite des événements et l'issue finale sont les mêmes, mais le style est corrigé et n'a plus la sobriété du récit du *Synaxaire*"; cf. below, nn. 27 and 69. Coquin knows of three further MSS. (containing lives of saints) in the "Couvent de S. Antoine, près de la Mer Rouge …, les mss *Hist.* 92, 98 et 114", but he has not been able to consult them.

ing emperor admired her intelligence and had her sent back to the monastery, where Mother and Sisters rejoiced at her deliverance and preserved virtue and had her tell them everything (§ 6).

But the Devil did not give up: he hurried to Persia to proclaim the maiden's fame among the heathens. The Persian king himself received the rumour and sent his soldiers, carrying fraudulent letters to Constantine, to search for the Greek monastery, abduct Parthenope and bring her to him at once (§ 7). They found her, identifying her by her astounding beauty, and brought her lamenting her fate but hoping to become a martyr — into the presence of the king, who was filled by desire and admiration for her beauty. He had her brought into his bed-chamber, where he offered her riches and power and invited her to become his lawfully wedded wife and the mistress of his eunuchs and concubines (§ 8). Feigning consent she asked for a respite to rest, wash and dress appropriately and for a fire so as to sacrifice, alone, to her God. She was promised this, and also, in case she died before the king, that her body should be brought back to the monastery to be buried in her ancestors' tomb (§ 9). The king swore by his gods to do all this, gave a feast for his men, and had all Parthenope's wishes carried out. She prepared herself in various ways, prayed and offered incense, approached the fire and prayed to Christ to receive her soul, emphasizing her virginity (§ 10). She then threw herself into the fire and gave up the breath of life; but the fire did not touch her body or clothes. The eunuchs and concubines found her dead; their wailing called the king to the room. Though deceived he kept his oath: dressed in royal cerements, looking as if asleep, Parthenope was brought to the monastery, where everyone, after being told what had happened, rejoiced at her virginity, wisdom, and martyrium (§ 11).

III

There are, both in these general outlines of the story and in several details of motifs, narrative technique, and even phraseology, clear points of resemblance with the ideal Greek novels. We shall consider them in turn.

The heroine is a young girl, only twelve years old. Similarly, Antheia in Xenophon Ephesius is fourteen, Chloe in Longus thirteen when the story proper begins. Among many qualities enumerated, such as modesty, intelligence, and education,[22] Parthenope's physical beauty is particularly emphasized: "douce de visage, parfaite et jolie de taille, très belle à entendre et à voir, accomplie en tout sens" (§ 1.8–9). This initial

66

[22] Cf. the παιδεία ideal particularly fostered by Chariton: of Callirhoe (6.5.8; 7.6.5; cf. 1.12.9), of Chaereas (7.2.5), of Dionysius (1.12.6 *et passim*), and of Demetrius (8.3.10).

→

"authorial" description is repeated and varied,[23] whenever the girl is viewed by anybody: "quiconque le voyait, s'émerveillait de la beauté de son aspect et de sa taille ... (§ 1.12–13); the soldiers sent out to fetch her marvel at her beauty (§ 3.1; § 8.3); the emperor and the king are further witnesses to her beauty (§ 4.2–3; § 8.8–9). The Devil is of course particularly eloquent in this matter: "... une jeune fille vierge, à qui ne ressemblait aucune femme parmi toutes les femmes du monde, parfaite en toute forme, beauté, intelligence, continence, sagesse, maintien et foi" (§ 2.4–6). This repeated mention of the heroine's beauty and of the immediate effect her physical appearance has on people is in exact accordance with practice in the novels.[24]

Again, the insistence on the *fame* of Parthenope's beauty preparing the way (§2.2–7; § 7.2–3; § 8. 13), as opposed to her physical presence accomplishing the whole task, is particularly reminiscent of Chariton: the rumour of the beautiful virgin Parthenope first reaches the imperial palace at Constantinople, then even Persia and its royal court, just as Callirhoe's fame is first spread on Sicily and in Italy and further still (1.1.2) and finally reaches the Great King (4.7.5–6; 5.2.6; cf. 2.7.1).[25] Although the circumstances leading to the Great King's decision to have Callirhoe brought to Babylon are indeed much more complex than the crude motivation given in the martyrdom for Parthenope's abduction ("ce roi ... aimait les plaisirs impurs" or "aimait les femmes", § 7.3–4), Callirhoe's reputation for excep-

---

(Cf. παιδεία in a different context in the Parthenope fragment, lines 40 and 70 Maehler). Xenophon's Habrocomes too is once said to receive education (1.1.2), but otherwise this is not part of the characterization of the heroes and heroines of the novels.

[23] For the similar repetition and variation of characterization in Chariton, see T. Hägg, "Some Technical Aspects of the Characterization in Chariton's Romance", *Studi classici in onore di Q. Cataudella*, Vol. 2. Catania 1972, 545–56, p. 552. [No. 3 in this volume.]

[24] Compare § 3.1 "ils furent émerveillés de sa beauté", § 8.3 "ils furent stupéfaits de sa beauté", § 8.9 "il ... s'émerveilla de sa beauté" with Xen. Eph. 1.12.1 τὸ κάλλος τῶν παίδων καταπεπληγότες, 2.2.1 κατεπλάγη τὴν εὐμορφίαν, 2.2.4 ἐτεθαυμάκεσαν τὸ κάλλος, 5.7.3 τῶν τεθαυμακότων τὸ κάλλος, or (less stereotyped) Char. 1.1.16; 1.14.1.; 2.2.2; 5.3.9 *et passim*.

[25] Φήμη is more often alluded to in Chariton than in the other novelists: it is described as "running about" (διέτρεχε 1.1.2; 1.5.1; 8.1.11; διέδραμε 2.3.8; τρέχει 3.2.7) or "running in advance" (προέτρεχε 4.7.5; προεπεδήμησε 3.4.1; προκατελάμβανε 5.2.6; cf. also 2.7.1; 3.3.2; 4.6.8; 5.3.2; 6.8.3). Similarly, in the *Chione Romance* (cf. below, n. 65): ταχέως δὲ διεφοίτησε ἀνὰ τὴν πόλιν ἄπασαν ... φήμη (Col. II.3–7). In the martyrdom the Devil "partit en hâte au pays des Perses" (§ 7.2), and, the MS. *B* adds, "se mit à faire le tour des rues et à crier disant que" etc. (p. 353 n. 5). Chariton's Fame is almost as concretely

→

tional beauty still plays a decisive role (4.6.4; 7), and the Great King does fall in love with the girl, like his colleague in the martyrdom.

The agent behind the rumour of Parthenope's beauty is the Devil, who cannot stand her excellence: "Mais le diable, l'ennemi de toute justice, en devint jaloux" (§ 2.1). He is thus similarly characterized, and plays the same role for the commencement of the action proper, as Eros in Chariton and Xenophon Ephesius: μηνιᾷ πρὸς ταῦτα (sc. Habrocomes' beauty and chastity) ὁ Ἔρως· φιλόνεικος γὰρ ὁ θεὸς καὶ ὑπερηφάνοις ἀπαραίτητος (Xen. Eph. 1.2.1; cf. 1.2.9 and 1.4.5, and Char. 1.1.3–4; 6; 12). His first intrigue having failed through Constantine's Christian faith, the Devil, "l'ennemi, l'adversaire détestable, … ne cessa pas de combattre cette bienheureuse Parthénopée …" (§ 7.1–2), but tried the Persian king next. Something of the same fighting spirit is shown by Chariton's Eros: Callirhoe's rejected suitors mobilize him as the companion of Jealousy in their plot against Chaereas (1.2.5), and all through the novel he keeps endangering the heroine's chastity by inflaming other men with love for her (cf., e.g., 2.4.5, quoted below), until at last his principal, Aphrodite, thinks that Chaereas has suffered enough under his torments (8.1.3) and effects a recognition and reunion.[26]

Moreover, there is in one of the Arabic manuscripts an addition, which Coquin obviously regards as a piece of free embroidery on the theme: "le diable alluma le feu de l'amour pour elle dans son (sc. the emperor's)

---

described,running through the whole town, οἰμωγὴν ἐγείρουσα διὰ τῶν στενωπῶν (1.5.1; cf. 5.2.6). Compare also § 7.3 "Sa renommée parvint au roi" with Char. 5.2.6 διέβαινε δὲ ἡ φήμη μέχρις αὐτοῦ τοῦ βασιλέως (cf. 2.7.1 and 4.1.8). Xenophon Ephesius and Heliodorus never allude to Φήμη (though in Xen. Eph. 1.12.1 the "name" of Habrocomes and Antheia runs [διεπεφοιτήκει] through the town), Longus only once or twice (4.25.3, cf. *pr.* 1), and Achilles Tatius in a few places in ways rather less reminiscent of the martyr-dom: 6.9.3; 6.10.3–5 (about Φήμη as the daughter of Διαβολή — cf. our "renom" proclaimed by "le Diable"!); 7.16.3. (My investigation has on this point, as on several others, been greatly facilitated through the use of the Thesaurus Linguae Graecae *Alphabetical Keyword-in-Context Concordance to the Greek Novelists* (Irvine, Cal. 1979, available on microfiche), which covers the five complete novels.)

[26] Another possibility would be that the author of the martyrdom has found in his pagan model a βάσκανος δαίμων, like the one that intrudes three times in Chariton's action (1.1.16; 3.2.17; 6.2.11; cf. Xen. Eph. 3.2.4); as a mover of the action it alternates with Eros and Tyche. Christian vocabulary when referring to the devil would make the association immediately suggest itself (cf. Lampe, *PGL* s. vv. βάσκανος and δαίμων), e.g. *Passio S. Polycarpi* 17.1 (p. 14.21–2 Musurillo): ὁ δὲ ἀντίζηλος καὶ βάσκανος καὶ πονηρός, ὁ ἀντικεί-μενος τῷ γένει τῶν δικαίων (compare our martyrdom's "l'ennemi, l'adversaire détestable", § 7.1). Achilles Tatius once uses βάσκανος as the epithet of ἔρως (2.34.1).

cœur, au point qu'il allait mourir par la force de sa passion pour elle" (§ 2.8, MS.*B*, p. 351 n. 8). This whole addition — if an addition it is[27] — easily allows itself to be rendered into the Greek idiom of the novels. Xenophon's Antheia remembers the πῦρ ἐρωτικόν that accompanied her and Habrocomes at their wedding (3.6.2; cf. Ach. Tat. 1.17.2), and Achilles Tatius repeatedly and at length wallows in the metaphor "fire of love" (esp. 5.15.5–6).[28] Metiochus, discussing Love in the Parthenope fragment (lines 56–8), tries to refute this very image of Eros the fire-making child.[29] Also the idea that love threatens to kill the afflicted is a commonplace of the novels; for instance, Chariton's Chaereas after his first meeting with Callirhoe goes home "deadly wounded" (1.1.7), and the following night is frightful for them both, the fire burning (1.1.8 τὸ γὰρ πῦρ ἐξεκαίετο), the healthy Chaereas pining away and approaching death (1.1.8–10). The same illness threatens the life of Xenophon's loving couple (1.5.8–9 ἀλλὰ καὶ ἔτι μᾶλλον ὁ ἔρως ἀνεκαίετο. ; ὅσον οὐδέπω τεθνήξεσθαι προσδοκώμενοι). However, the most complete and structurally relevant parallel to our martyrdom passage is again provided by Chariton, this time describing Eros' attack on one of Chaereas' rivals, the Ionian nobleman Dionysius (2.4.5–7): the trouble-loving Eros (again the typical ἐφιλονείκει) cannot stand the man's chastity, he makes the fire in his heart burn more violently (ἐπυρπόλει σφοδρότερον ψυχήν), and Dionysius cries out to his loyal steward Leonas "I am lost" (ἀπόλωλά σοι), accusing him of having brought the "fire" — the beautiful Callirhoe — into his house and heart (πῦρ ἐκόμισας εἰς τὴν οἰκίαν, μᾶλλον δὲ εἰς τὴν ἐμὴν ψυχήν). Characteristically Chariton himself provides a variation on the theme later on, when it is the Great King's turn to fall in love with Callirhoe (6.3.2 on Eros having entered his heart) and his loyal eunuch's turn to try to find a remedy for his master's burning illness (6.3.3 ἠσθάνετο μὲν τυφομένου τοῦ πυρός). We may note that in both these cases, as in our martyrdom passage, the one that suffers this particular attack of Eros is not the hero, but one of his powerful rivals,

68

---

[27] Coquin's characterization of this (unedited) manuscript is quoted above, n. 21. The fact that in at least three places (§ 2.8; § 7.2, above, n. 25; §7.4, below, VII) its variants show striking similarities with the idiom of the Greek novels makes a reconsideration of the relationship between the manuscripts desirable; perhaps *B* translates another Coptic version that more closely approaches the original. The reconsideration would of course have to include the three unexamined Arabic manuscripts.

[28] Cf. also Ach.Tat. 1.6.6; 1.11.3; 6.19. For many more places, see J. N. O'Sullivan, *A Lexicon to Achilles Tatius*, Berlin & New York 1980, s.v. πῦρ 2b.

[29] On this topos, see Maehler pp. 16–7 with n. 35.

at a moment when the heroine is (or, in the martyrdom, soon enough will be) completely at his mercy. And in all three instances the dynast in the event shows unexpected constraint and magnanimity.

We return to the unanimously transmitted version of the story. Hearing the rumour the emperor consults "ses grands" before deciding to send for Parthenope. In the queer embryo, or fragment, of a consultation scene given (§ 2.6–8), the advisers' main function is to confirm that they too have heard the rumour. Full exploitation of this motif, with pros and cons and typically enacted (in Herodotean tradition) in Oriental court milieu, is met with in the novels (e.g., Char. 4.6.5 and 5.8.6–7: the Great King consulting with his friends).

In order to escape the marriage offered her by Constantine, Parthenope delivers a well-invented and embellished speech (§ 5, "Plaidoyer de Parthénopée"). She emphasizes that she, his slave, does not deserve the honours he has promised her (as Callirhoe does when confronted with similar offers, Char. 6.5.9). After some further flattering and ingratiating turns comes her trick: what would the emperor, as a rightful judge, think of a man who carried away another man's bride? The emperor willingly falls into the trap, condemning such a man, whereupon the girl reminds him that she is in fact God's servant and betrothed, and so makes him release her. Among the many episodes in the Greek novels in which, temporarily separated from her husband or fiancé, the heroine tries to evade an unwanted new marriage there is, I think, no exact parallel to this particular trick. But it is obvious that it would function well in such a context, if only we substitute "already married (or betrothed) to X" for "God's betrothed". For various reasons, the fact that the heroine is already married or betrothed is generally concealed in the novels, so the proposing magnates there could easily be induced to give the same answer as the emperor. As regards the remaining prerequisite, that even tyrants are basically honest and pious men who keep their word, this at least fits in with Chariton's idealistic view of the world, though hardly with the novels at large. Neither Chariton's Great King (6.3.7–8), nor of course his noble Dionysius (2.4.5; 10; 2.5.3; 2.6.2–3), would touch another man's wife (or slave).[30]

When Parthenope is brought back to the monastery, we are told that everyone goes out to meet her, rejoicing and thanking Christ, and that she tells them all that has happened (§6.4–6). The emotional participa-

[30] Iamblichus' tyrant Garmus is completely different (2; 16), and so are the various masters and mistresses in Xenophon Ephesius (1.16.5; 2.5.2 etc.; religious awe, not respect for her civil status, saves Antheia in 3.11.4 5 and 5.4.6–7).

69

tion of a crowd (in particular, of the citizens of the hometown) in the hero-and-heroine's vicissitudes and the report given to the people (or the gods) after the happy homecoming are typical features of the novels.[31]

The "fraudulent letters" to Constantine, carried by the Persian king's soldiers (§7.4–6), are a further motif which is dropped without being exploited. The exchange of letters is common in the novels; for instance, more or less deceitful letters to and from the Great King, two of his satraps, and other people involved play a part in Chariton's intrigue (4.4–7). Whether the martyrdom's letters had any similar function to these we cannot say.

Abducted a second time, Parthenope says to herself (§8.5–7): "Que faire en ce mauvais combat, pire que le premier? J'ai été emmenée chez un roi craignant Dieu et il ne m'a pas fait de mal. Cette fois-ci, c'est un homme idolâtre, ne connaissant pas Dieu. Peut-être, trouverai-je l'occasion d'être martyre vraiment?" Rhetorical outbursts of lament like this one, spoken by the hero or heroine in the form of a monologue, prayer, or (less often) part of a dialogue, are regular features of the novels, sometimes almost ritually repeated to accompany every new turn of the action. The two ideas that we see combined in Parthenope's monologue are stock ingredients in the novelistic counterparts as well: the impending evil is compared to the earlier one(s) and found worse, and suicide is considered the best or only way out of it. I quote one example each from Xenophon Ephesius and Chariton. Antheia, again in the hands of pirates, bewails her fate (Xen. Eph. 3.8.6): "πάλιν" ἔφησε "λησταὶ καὶ θάλασσα, πάλιν αἰχμάλωτος ἐγώ· ἀλλὰ νῦν δυστυχέστερον, ὅτι μὴ μετὰ Ἀβροκόμου …". In Babylon, Callirhoe has just been told that the Great King is in love with her; left to herself, she curses her beauty (Char. 6.6.4–5): "ὦ κάλλος ἐπίβουλον, σύ μοι πάντων κακῶν αἴτιον. διὰ σὲ ἀνηρέθην, διὰ σὲ ἐπράθην…. πάντων δέ μοι βαρύτατος ὁ ἔρως ὁ βασιλέως…". The poor girl can think of only one noble remedy: "ἀπόσφαξον σεαυτήν".[32]

The Persian king begins his speech to Parthenope by declaring that he has not been able to sleep because of her reported beauty (§ 8.13–14). The Great King's sleeplessness caused by his incipient love to Callirho

---

[31] See, in particular, Char. 8.6–8. The role played by the crowd in the novels is surveyed by A. Calderini, *Caritone di Afrodisia*, Torino 1913, 94–5.

[32] Other examples: Char. 1.11.2–3; 1.14.6–10; 3.8.9; 3.10.4–8; 5.1.4–7; 5.5.2–4; 5.10.6–9; 6.2.8–11; 7.5.2–5. Xen. Eph. 5.5.5; 5.7.2; 5.8.7–9. Cf. Hägg (above, n. 9) pp. 262–4 (with further lit.). [No. 3 in this volume.]

is a motif which Chariton develops at some length (6.1.6–12); earlier, Dionysius' insomnia in the corresponding situation has been described (2.4.2–10).[33]

The whole final complex, in which Parthenope manages to delay the marriage with the Persian king, arrange a ceremonial suicide, and have her body transported home (§§ 9–11), has several traits that smack of the novel. Parthenope simulates acceptance of the king's offer of marriage, as Xenophon's Antheia does before Perilaus the Eirenarch, agreeing to marry him (because she sees no alternative), asking for a respite of thirty days, and finally trying to kill herself by poison in the very bridal chamber, while Perilaus is feasting with his friends (2.13.6–8; 3.3.7–6.5).[34] We find this last detail as well in the martyrdom, where the king feasts with his men, while his bride *in spe* prepares for her suicide (§ 10.2). The descriptions of how Perilaus-and-friends and king-and-servants, respectively, find the dead girl also have some points in common (3.7; § 11.4–10).

On the other hand, there is of course a fundamental difference between the Antheias of the novels and our Parthenope. Antheia's death is only an apparent death: what she thought was deadly poison is just a sleeping-draught, and she wakes up in the burial-chamber (3.8.1); and Heliodorus' Charicleia escapes from the pyre not only with her body unharmed by the flames, but alive (8.9.14–16). In contrast, Parthenope's death is real and irrevocable. What Mother and Sisters rejoice at, when her body is brought home, is her preserved virginity, her wisdom (σοφία in the Coptic fragment), and her martyrium (μαρτυρία) — the new kind of "happy" ending Barns referred to.

[33] The sleepless lover is of course a well–known literary topos (and hardly a sign of "realism", as Coquin p. 356 would have it); cf., in the novels, Char. 1.1.8; Xen. Eph. 1.4–5.1; Ach. Tat. 1.6.2 4; Long. 2.9.2; 3.4.2; *Hist. Ap.* 18. References to other literature in E. Rohde, *Der griechische Roman*, 4th ed. Darmstadt 1960, 157 nn. 3–4.

[34] Among many scenes of deception in the novels (see Calderini, [above, n. 31] pp. 106–10 with references to the relevant passages), there is another one which shows specific points of similarity with ours: Heliodorus' Charicleia before the pirate Trachinus (5.26 29). Charicleia is invited to share in all the riches (26.1, cf. § 8.15–6), she forces herself to take on a charming look and praise the pirate's humanity (26.2, cf. § 9.2), and to gain time her protector Calasiris uses a ruse similar to Parthenope's: he asks the pirate to allow the bride to be left alone and undisturbed in the bridal-chamber to make her toilet so as to be presentable to such a bridegroom (29.1, cf. § 9.3–8). However, even if Charicleia is prepared to die rather than accept Trachinus' love (29.4), the rest of the action takes another course than in the martyrdom.

71

Keeping this basic difference in mind, we shall look at some other peculiar, and possibly significant, traits in the description of Parthenope's martyrium. Parthenope not only asks for a respite to refresh herself after the tiresome journey,[35] she has one further demand, more important for what she is planning (§ 9.5–7): "Il me faut du combustible et un endroit écarté et isolé, dans un lieu retiré, où il n'y a personne, pour que je présente mon offrande à mon Dieu, avant d'entrer chez toi, et sans que personne voie mon offrande." Having arranged all this, the king "ordonna d'y allumer le feu" (§ 10.4). Parthenope prays, offers her incense, "et sortit là où était le feu; elle ferma la porte jusqu'à ce que le feu soit allumé" (§ 10.6–7). Then she prays again,[36] asking Christ to receive her sacrifice (her soul and her virginity),[37] and throws herself into the fire (§ 11.1). This description seems rather peculiar and circumstantial for the situation. There is really no motivation for the fire: she can pray to her God without a fire.[38] In fact, her prayers are duplicated: the first prayer is followed by the offering of the incense, the second one by her "real" sacrifice. And the insistance on complete privacy seems strange for the enactment of a *martyrium*: a suicide, and that in secret, is not what you would expect from a Christian martyr, even if you might find some distant parallels.[39] It all makes sense, I think, only if we consider the whole description as being adapted from a pagan novel. Then, the fire for sacrificing is natural (while the first prayer and the incense of course belong to the Christian adaption), and the privacy is necessary,

[35] § 9.2–3: "mais je suis très fatiguée par la route, en ce pénible voyage"; cf. Chariton's concern for his heroine's well-being after tiresome travelling (1.11.5; 1.14.3; 2.2.2–3; 8.7.3).

[36] Cf. the prayers of Habrocomes before the cross (Xen. Eph. 4.2.4) and the pyre (4.2.8) and of Charicleia before the pyre (Hld. 8.9.12).

[37] In her prayer, Parthenope says: "ton sceau est aussi sur mon visage, apposé dans mon aspect" (§ 10.9). This is certainly not, as Coquin (p. 355 n. 2) suggests, "une allusion à une croix tatouée sur le corps", but a way to say that she crosses herself before entering the fire, like other martyrs before her: *Passio S. Dasii* 11 (p. 278.17–8 Musurillo) ὥπλισέν τε τὸ μέτωπον αὐτοῦ τῇ σφραγῖδι τοῦ τιμίου σταυροῦ τοῦ Χριστοῦ, cf. *Passio S. Cononis* 6.5 (p. 192.6) and *Passio S. Crispinae* 4 (p. 308.1). Our martyrdom's "sceau" thus mirrors the Greek of σφραγίς, σφραγίζω (cf. Lampe, *PGL* s. vv., B).

[38] Coquin's explanation (p. 357), with reference to Persian religious practice, seems too sophisticated for this simple tale.

[39] Coquin (p. 358), polemizing against Khalil's (above, n. 16) views of the martyrdom's Christian inspiration, calls attention to the suicide: to him, suicide to preserve virginity is rather "une survivance socio-culturelle" from Graeco-Roman antiquity than "une manifestation de la mentalité chrétienne, même si une justification religieuse est donnée

→

because what we witness is not a true suicide (which could be enacted in public), but a *trick*. Exactly how it was performed in the model we cannot know, but we may recall the magic stone which saved Charicleia from the flames (Hld. 8.10.1 1) or Leucippe's false belly in Achilles Tatius' sacrificial scene (3.15; 21). What we are able to divine, however, is the continuation: the heroine, who has cleverly made the king swear to bring her "dead" body home the very same day (§§ 9.11–10.1), is accordingly lifted up and carried away "elle était semblable à une dormeuse" (§ 11.12)![40] — and, once safely home, she of course wakes up from her sleep.[41] It is she herself (or her accomplices?) that tells her story, not the king's agents (§ 11.15), and the rejoicing concerns preserved chastity, cleverness, and — saved life.

72

IV

The present analysis has quite deliberately focussed on novelistic motifs and techniques in the martyrdom. There are of course other features which do not at all, or not as clearly, fit into the novelistic pattern, as we know it, and there are also other ways to interpret and classify some of the features here described as typical of the ideal Greek novel. For instance, some of the motifs remind one of the folk-tale, such as the various tricks tried by the girl to evade or postpone the threatening outrage/marriage at the hands of the tyrant/ruler.[42] But the non-sophistic novels too employ

---

de ce geste: la sauvegarde de la virginité, le sacrifice de la vie à Dieu". It may be added that suicide does exceptionally occur in historical martyrdoms: in Pergamum, during the reign of Marcus Aurelius (?), Agathonice throws herself into the fire (without expecting a sentence, unless there is a lacuna in the Greek text, as has been suspected) so as to share the fate of Carpus and Papylus, who have been properly condemned and executed (*Passio SS. Carpi et soc.* 46, p. 28.8 Musurillo; cf. the Latin version p. 34.26-7, where execution takes the place of the suicide); cf. further W. H. C. Frend, *Martyrdom and Persecution in the Early Church*, Oxford 1965, 197–8, 272, and Index s. vv. "Suicide" and "Martyrdom, voluntary". However, Parthenope's secret suicide is very different from an act of open demonstration like Agathonice's.

[40] Similarly Callirhoe, lying (apparently) dead on the bier, looks like "the sleeping Ariadne" (Char. 1.6.2).

[41] Apparent death, with "resurrection" following, belongs to the stock motifs of the novel; cf., for instance, Char. 1.8.1; Xen. Eph. 3.8.1; Iambl. 3 4; 6; *Hist. Ap.* 25-27.

[42] Coquin (p. 357 with n. 1) briefly discusses the use of this "thème folklorique", with further references. Cf. also S. Thompson, *Motif-Index of Folk-Literature*, Vol. 4, Helsinki 1934, K500–699, "Escape by deception" (esp. 522.0.1 "Death feigned to escape unwelcome

→

folk-tale motifs, so such an observation does not disprove the hypothesis of a novelistic origin, it just points to another possibility. Further, some motifs may be described as typical of a certain time or milieu rather than exclusively "novelistic". The preservation of the martyr's body intact is one example: this motif occurs in embryonic form in some of the old historical acts and then becomes a favoured topos in many legends,[43] especially in Egypt, where it takes on particular forms agreeing with old native beliefs of the restoration of the body. What we then have to consider is the particular form the motif exhibits in our text, and this is indeed far from the Egyptian "Legenden vom unzerstörbaren Leben",[44] but close to the apparent-death scenes of the novels. But the appeal this motif has had for the author of the martyrdom may of course in turn be due to that wider popularity. Other motifs, such as the young Christian girl who fights for her faith and chastity against superior force, may have had a backing in real life and in authentic reports of martyrdoms.[45] A double or triple inspiration for the inclusion of a certain motif is quite conceivable. The important thing here is that we have been able to isolate, spread throughout the martyrdom, a number of elements which all — even if alternative explanations are possible in one case or other — seem to have one common denominator, the ideal Greek novel.

We may proceed one step further. Not only do these elements fit into the picture of the ideal Greek novel in general, but several of them seem to belong to one particular branch: the early, non-sophistic novel, as represented to us by Chariton — the simpleminded, truly *ideal* type, with an emphasis on human relations and sentiment. We find no traces of the more violent and sensational type, as represented by Iamblichus

73

marriage"); further, Vol. 5, 1935, R10 "Abduction", R175 "Rescue at the stake", T320 "Escape from undesired lover", T326 "Suicide to save virginity". For the general problem, see A. J. Festugière, "Lieux communs littéraires et thèmes de folk-lore dans l'Hagiographie primitive", *WS* 73, 1960, 123–52.

[43] As early as the *Passio S. Polycarpi* 15–16 (p. 14.6–14 Musurillo) the flames are said to leave the body unharmed. Among many later examples we may note the *Passio SS. Eustathii et soc.* (416D–417C, 21*b*–22*a*), cf. above n. 11.

[44] See T. Baumeister, *Martyr Invictus*, Münster 1972 (ref. owed to R. Bjerre Finnestad).

[45] Cf., for instance, Eusebius' report (*Hist. eccl.* 6.5.1–5) on the "famous" (περιβόητον) Potamiaena of Alexandria, young (τῆς ἀοιδίμου κόρης) and beautiful (καὶ γὰρ οὖν αὐτῇ ἀκμαῖον πρὸς τῇ ψυχῇ καὶ τὸ τοῦ σώματος ὡραῖον ἐπήνθει), whose "crime" was chastity (μυρία μὲν ὑπὲρ τῆς τοῦ σώματος ἁγνείας τε καὶ παρθενίας, ἐν ᾗ διέπρεψεν, πρὸς ἐραστὰς ἀγωνισαμένης) and punishment the fire. See also *Hist.eccl.* 8.14 (esp. §§ 2, 12, 14–17) on Maxentius and Maximinus (ref. owed to T. Christensen).

and Xenophon Ephesius (who would surely have been able to supply material for legends of martyrs of the common blood-stained kind). Nor is there in the Parthenope martyrdom, as far as I can see, anything exclusively typical of the sophistic novels of Longus, Achilles Tatius, and Heliodorus. Many motifs, it is true, are typical of the genre as a whole, but it is the execution and the placing of emphases that count.

The next step is of a still more tentative nature. If it is true that a number of features in the Parthenope martyrdom derive from the non-sophistic, ideal Greek novel, would it be possible to decide whether they have been taken over from one particular model or have been chosen freely from a whole tradition, perhaps even by way of other Christian works (apocryphal Acts of the Apostles, other lives of martyrs or saints)? A comparison with the Eustathius martyrdom is instructive. Reading that martyrdom, and others of the "epic" kind, one is reminded of Barns's remark that the producers of Egyptian martyrdoms seem to have been paid "by the yard": the martyrologies "were padded out with stock passages to the requisite size".[46] In fact, this martyrdom is complete, as *martyrdom*, without most of the novelistic stuff: Eustathius, from the start a successful general in the emperor's service, could after his conversion at the hunt have refused obedience at once and been executed with his family, the rest is padding. The Parthenope martyrdom is different. Here the plot itself is "novelistic": the girl's renowned beauty, the forced abductions from the monastery, her feats of intelligent negotiation with emperor and king, all these constituents organically lead up to the martyrium. And there are no "authentic" details at beginning and end, except for the location of the monastery on a "mountain"[47] outside Constantinople and the no less superficial linking of the story with a particular Roman emperor, Constantine (who with his mother Helen receives some lines of eulogy at the beginning, § 1.1–5). So, there is no trace of any "basic" story to be padded out; this is obviously one of those martyrdoms which, at the most, start from the authentic name of a martyr, but are otherwise entirely fictitious.[48]

74

---

[46] Reymond & Barns (above, n. 2) p. 3.

[47] Cf. Amélineau (above, n. 17) p. 303 n. 4 and Coquin p. 351 n. 7. This may be an *interpretatio Coptica* without foundation in any putative Greek original version of the martyrdom.

[48] Its entirely fictitious character is stressed by Amélineau (above, n. 17) p. 307, Khalil (above, n. 16) p. 385, and Coquin p. 356.

In such a case, the easiest thing for the author no doubt would be to adapt to his own purposes an existing story. A couple of motifs left unexploited — the council called in (§ 2.6–8) and the fraudulent letters (§ 7.4–6) — may perhaps be interpreted as the remnants of a model. And, more important: as we have seen, the Parthenope martyrdom exhibits a number of features, in motifs as well as narrative structure, which seem to point to one particular kind of Greek novel. Considering all this, I think it is legitimate to suggest that there was one sole, or one main, literary model for the whole martyrdom. Thus we have arrived at the point where the name of the heroine becomes important.

V

Coquin (pp. 357–8) actually points to the possibility that there is some kind of connection between the Parthenope martyrdom and the Greek novel of *Metiochus and Parthenope*. He does not develop the idea,[49] however, and does not seem to be aware of the considerable advance in our knowledge about this novel owing to H. Maehler's brilliant reconstruction work, based on three Berlin papyrus fragments (one of them not previously identified or published) and the scraps of secondary tradition.[50]

As Coquin remarks, the name Parthenope is attested in both pagan and Christian Egypt, in Greek as well as Coptic sources,[51] though it does not seem to have been very common in any period. We may note, just as an odd piece of coincidence, that one of the instances, a small and unornamented tombstone now in the Cairo Museum,[52] refers to a young Christian girl by the name of Parthenope, who died on Choiak 20 (of an unknown year), at the age of twelve, like our heroine (from such materials martyrdoms may be written …). The name, which in

---

[49] He drops the question with the words (p. 358): "On peut se poser la question, bien que la trame générale et plusieurs épisodes ne paraissent pas avoir été empruntés".

[50] "Der Metiochos-Parthenope-Roman", *ZPE* 23, 1976, 1–20 + Pl. I-II. Supplemented by M. Gronewald, "Ein neues Fragment aus dem Metiochos-Parthenope-Roman (Ostrakon Bodl. 2175 = Pack² 2782)", *ZPE* 24, 1977, 21–2.

[51] Coquin (p. 345 nn. 4–9) cites the relevant sources.

[52] W. E. Crum, *Coptic Monuments*, Le Caire 1902 (reprint Osnabrück 1975), No. 8334; G. Lefebvre, *Recueil des inscriptions grecques-chrétiennes d'Égypte*, Le Caire 1907 (reprint Chicago 1978), No. 300. Perhaps from Akhmim. No date proposed in either publication.

Greek mythology was carried by a Siren, is well attested outside Egypt 75
too in Roman imperial times; for instance, in the vast epigraphical material from Rome collected by H. Solin it occurs 33 times.[53] The conclusion is that there may very well have existed — in Egypt or elsewhere in
the Roman Empire — a Christian martyr by the name of Parthenope;
although there seems to be no evidence for her existence beyond our
martyrdom, the name itself is "realistic" enough.

At the same time, Parthenope is obviously an "eloquent" name, fitting for the story of virginity unto death. So we have the following
three possibilities: (1) the name is authentic (there was a martyr called
Parthenope), or (2) it was chosen because of its etymological meaning
(to tell a fictitious story of a virgin martyr), or (3) it was simply taken
over from the pagan *Parthenope Romance* (which because of its popularity was chosen as a model for a fictitious martyrdom). Whichever of
these explanations for the naming we prefer, there is a fair chance that
the *Parthenope Romance* was the model for the core of the martyrdom;
for even if the name should happen to be authentic, the story is certainly not, and the identity of name have made the choice of model
obvious.

We shall now turn to the novel itself to see whether the known facts
about it, and the tolerably certain assumptions, admit of a combination
with the novelistic elements of the martyrdom.

VI

Our knowledge of the *Parthenope Romance* relies on the following
sources: [54]

Fragments

(a) P. Berol. 7927 + 9588 (= Pack² 2622) + 21179 (Maehler, above, n. 50).
These three fragments are part of the same roll (71 lines in all; 2nd cent. AD)

[53] *Die griechischen Personennamen in Rom. Ein Namenbuch*, Vol. I, Berlin & New York 1982,
pp. 399–400; the social distribution: "27 incerti, 2 wahrscheinlich Freigelassene, 4 Sklaven
und Freigelassene" (1st/5th cent. AD). The Siren's special connection with Naples may
mean that the name was more frequent in the West than in the Eastern provinces.

[54] Earlier literature is listed in F. Zimmermann, *Griechische Roman-Papyri und verwandte
Texte,* Heidelberg 1936, 52–63, the few later contributions in Maehler. Cf. esp. R. M. Rattenbury, "Romance: Traces of Lost Greek Novels", in J. U. Powell (ed.), *New Chapters in
the History of Greek Literature*, 3rd Series, Oxford 1933, 211–57, pp. 237–40.

and give us one scene of dialogue. Maehler concludes that it is a symposium scene taking place in Polycrates' palace on Samos; the participators are Polycrates, Parthenope (his daughter, anonymous in other sources), Metiochus (the son of Miltiades), and Anaximenes (the philosopher), who has proposed the theme of discussion, Eros. Metiochus has just arrived (?);[55] he and Parthenope have met before (?),[56] but are not yet married, nor even (openly) lovers: Metiochus in his speech repudiates love, which upsets Parthenope. The scene would thus belong to the earlier part of the novel: not at the very beginning, but before separation.

(*b*) *O. Bodl.* 2175 (= Pack[2] 2782; Gronewald, above, n. 50). Gronewald concludes that this small fragment (8 lines; "Roman period") contains part of a letter from Metiochus to Parthenope, when they are separated: Metiochus says he cannot sleep from the day she [went away (?)].

(*c*)? *P. Oxy.* 435 (=Pack[2] 2623). Beginnings of two columns (20 lines in all; 2nd/3rd cent. AD), containing the names Κερκυραῖοι and Παρθε[νόπ]ης (?). Attributed to this novel by Zimmermann (above, n. 54) p. 62: Parthenope "befindet sich in der Gewalt irgendwelcher Machthaber", she is offered freedom in return for payment, the people of Corcyra rejoice. The scene, if correctly interpreted, should thus belong to the time of separation. Maehler (p. 4 n. 13), however, does not regard the reasons for the attribution sufficient,[57] and leaves this piece out of account.

Testimonia

The following scattered references to Parthenope and/or Metiochus are, in the first place, to various scenic performances. However, I follow Maehler (pp. 3–4) in using them for the reconstruction as well, on the assumption that they are likely somehow to mirror the basic plot of the novel. The same uncertainty applies to the illustrations in pictorial art (below, *k–l*).

---

[55] Thus Maehler p. 15, interpreting lines 31–32 σήμερον ... τοῦ παιδὸς ἥκοντος. Or does "the boy" refer to Eros?

[56] Thus Maehler p. 16, interpreting lines 35–36 λαβ[όντες ...]ου πάθους ἀνάμνησιν. It is true that πάθος in the novels often means "die Erfahrung der Liebe", but it may also refer to other kinds of "experiences", such as Callirhoe's (apparent) death by maltreatment in Char. 1.5.1; here reference may, for instance, be to the violent happenings in the Chersonese alluded to in lines 17–19 (Maehler p. 14). Anyway, it seems awkward not to assume that this is Parthenope's first meeting with Metiochus, who (initially) plays the arrogant renouncer of Eros (Rattenbury [above, n. 54] p. 239 well compares his attitude to that of Habrocomes in Xen. Eph. 1.1.5).

[57] Sceptical also K. Ziegler, *RE* XVIII (1949) 1935-6.

(*d*) Scholion on Dionysius Periegetes, 358 (*Geogr. Gr. Min.* II p. 445 Müller), and Eustathius' commentary on the same line (*ibid.*, p. 280). Greek text of both quoted by Maehler (p. 3 n. 9). The line commented on calls Naples μέλαθρον ἁγνῆς Παρθενόπης, which causes the scholiast to stress that this P. is one of the Sirens and not — as spectators of some ὀρχηστιχῇ ἱστορίᾳ might believe — the P. of Samos, ἡ τὸν ἄνδρα ζητοῦσα Ἀναξίλαον περιήει ("die auf der Suche nach ihrem Mann zu Anaxilaos gelangte", Maehler).[58] The scholiast later on returns to this Samian P., and what he then says is — apart from some misunderstandings — rather faithfully echoed by Eustathius; the following four elements are common to both: (1) Parthenope preserved her virginity (παρθενίαν) in spite of the advances of (ὑποπεσοῦσα schol., ἐπιβουλευθεῖσα Eust.) many men, (2) she fell in love with Metiochus, [who came there] from Phrygia (ἀπὸ ... Φρυγίας schol., but Φρυγὸς Eust.; cf. Maehler p. 19), (3) she cut off her hair (ἀκοσμίαν ἑαυτῆς καταψηφιζομένη, Eust. adds), and (4) went to live in Campania (a specification directly referring to the line commented on). Eustathius does not keep the two Parthenopes apart, but adds that it was perhaps διὰ τὴν τοιαύτην σωφροσύνην that Dion. Per. called P. ἁγνήν. The scholiast, for his part, had already in (1) explained the name Παρθενόπη with reference to the girl's preserved παρθενία.

(*e*) Lucian, *Salt.* 2 (quoted in Maehler, p. 2 n. 7). Phaedra, Parthenope, and Rhodope are mentioned as ἐρωτικὰ γύναια, τῶν πάλαι τὰς μαχλοτάτας who are typical objects for mimetic dance.

(*f*) Lucian, *Pseudol.* 25 (quoted in Maehler, p. 3 n. 8). Ninus, Metiochus, and Achilles are mentioned as characters impersonated by a rhetor in the theatre.

(*g*) Lucian, *Salt.* 54 (quoted in Maehler, p. 12 n. 21). Among subjects suitable for dance are mentioned Polycrates' πάθος and his (unnamed) daughter's μέχρι Περσῶν πλάνη.

The following two testimonia refer to the assumed historical setting of the novel, as represented by Herodotus. How much of it the novelist

77

---

[58] See Maehler p. 3 n. 10, citing classical parallels (Hdt. 4.71.3, Lys. 8.8. Dem. 18.44 and 150–1) for περιιέναι and περιέρχεσθαι + acc. meaning "aufsuchen, gelangen zu", none of which, however, carries conviction; the object is always either a country or persons in the plural (πάντας etc.; cf. also Xen. Eph. 3.4.2 περιήει μὲν καὶ τοὺς ἄλλους ἄνδρας which means that περι- makes sense. It should be noted that περιιέναι, sometimes (as here) combined with a participle like ζητῶν, is typically used in the novels to describe the hero or heroine "roaming, going round" (a town etc.) searching for the beloved (e.g., Char. 7.1.2; Xen. Eph. 5.8.1); perhaps there is some corruption hiding in our scholion text? A third possibility, which is perhaps less likely, is that the verb here (as sometimes περιέρχεσθαι, LSJ s.v. I 3) means "cheat". This would indeed suit the new context suggested below (Parthenope cheating Anaxilas, as in the martyrdom she cheats Constantine), but in that case we miss an added σοφίᾳ (cf. Hdt. 3.4.2), δι' ἀπάτης (Plut. Nic. 10.4) or ἀπάτη (Hld. 5.10.2).

really assimilated into his plot, we do not know – probably very little, like Chariton.

(*h*) Herodotus 3.124 (cf. Maehler pp. 11–2), on the (unnamed) daughter of Polycrates, who tried in vain to prevent her father from going on his fatal visit to the Satrap Oroetes. Polycrates threatens that if he returns alive she will for a long time remain a virgin (παρθενεύεσθαι), which she says she would prefer to being deprived of her father.

(*i*) Herodotus 6.39–41 (cf. Maehler p. 14), on Miltiades' dealings on the Chersonese, his Thracian wife Hegesipyle, and his son (by his first wife) Metiochus. When Miltiades has been forced to leave the Chersonese, Metiochus' ship is captured by Phoenicians, who bring him to Darius; there he is treated well and given a Persian wife.

Finally, there are two representations of Parthenope and Metiochus in pictorial art:

(*k*) Floor mosaic (c. AD 200) from a Roman villa near Antioch-on-the-Orontes (cf. Maehler pp. 1–2 and Pl. I), showing Parthenope and Metiochus (names inscribed over their heads) standing in a somewhat theatrical pose: P., her left hand raised, addresses M., who is dressed as a Roman officer.

(*l*) Another mosaic (in two parts), probably from the same place (cf. Maehler p. 2 and Pl. II), showing the two sitting back to back, but turning their heads to look at each other. M. is dressed as before; P.'s dress has slipped down from her shoulder, which would indicate an erotic situation.[59]

These then are the sources for the reconstruction of the *Parthenope Romance* that have been available up to the present. Can we now add the Parthenope martyrdom as well? To try to answer that we have to look first at what specific points of resemblance there are between novel and martyrdom, besides the name of the heroine. In so doing we had better accommodate our expectations to the nature of the evidence: on the one hand, only one random scene preserved, one piece of a letter, and some hints of the basic separation-and-search theme; on the other, a martyrdom of some ten normal-size pages, for which the author may have selected material from a novel of perhaps 150 pages. The chances of finding conclusive proof are evidently rather small.

---

[59] Maehler (p. 2) interprets their expression as "erregt, vielleicht verwirrt oder erschrocken", and builds on this interpretation in his later attempt (p. 19) to relate the illustration to a particular episode of the novel (see below, n. 70); he seems to have overlooked the erotic implication of the deranged dress.

VII

The heroine's virginity, which is basic to the martyrdom, is stressed also in the novel testimonia (*d*) and (*h*), while (*e*) seems oddly inconsistent with the general picture. However, chastity (if not necessarily virginity) is a basic feature of the ideal novel in general, and the "eloquent" name Parthenope may account for the special emphasis and form this feature has acquired in the sources. So, while undoubtedly an important point of resemblance, the virginity motif alone proves nothing.

The martyrdom shows Parthenope being offered marriage by two rulers, Constantine and the Persian king. The novel's Parthenope suffers the attempts of "many men" (*d*). One of them may be Anaxilas, probably the tyrant of Rhegium, whom she "visits"[60] (*d*); another may well be the Persian king, if we are allowed to bring in testimonium (*g*). Maehler writes (p. 12): "dann (*viz.*, if the theatrical performance mentioned by Lucian is based on the novel) wäre Parthenope nicht nur nach Westen (Rhegion und Campanien), sondern auch nach Osten bis nach Persien verschlagen worden, ähnlich wie Kallirhoe bei Chariton, und auch Polykrates' Ende hätte darin wohl eine Rolle gespielt — nachweisen freilich lässt sich das einstweilen nicht". This ingenious suggestion has perhaps received its confirmation in our martyrdom; at least, the coincidence is striking. That, for the beautiful heroine of a Greek novel, a πλάνη to Persia necessarily leads to erotic complications involving the ruler of the country need hardly be added.

A small detail, for what it may be worth: in the novel, Parthenope cuts off her hair, presumably to be able to steer clear of new lovers and suitors (*d*); in the martyrdom, an apparently difficult passage of the Arabic text (§ 1.10) may be interpreted to mean that after her arrival in the monastery this Parthenope too had to cut off her hair.[61] If so, the situation is of course different, but a reminiscence from the novel is possible.[62]

The thought of the beautiful Parthenope has kept the Persian king from sleeping (§ 8.13–14), as the longing for her keeps Metiochus sleepless in (*b*). The motif is commonplace enough, but it may be remarked

79

---

[60] Cf. above, n. 58.

[61] Coquin (p. 351 with n. 4) translates (§ 1.10): "Elles apprêtèrent ses cheveux", but informs us that the Arabic verb used is unexpected, that the earlier editors translate "couper", and that the MS. *B* has a "correction".

[62] The motif as such is common; Maehler (p. 3 n. 12) gives some parallels, to which should be added Iambl. 4 (+ fr. 17 Habrich), 13, and fr. 61 p. 47.4–7 Habrich.

that Chariton similarly echoes himself in describing the insomnia of Dionysius and of the Great King.

We pass from these, rather few, direct points of contact to a circumstantial type of evidence. Maehler's and Gronewald's comments on the Parthenope fragments (*a*) and (*b*) clearly bring out how close this novel is to that of Chariton. Besides the similar attachment to classical history and historiography — Chariton to Thucydides, the *Parthenope Romance* to Herodotus — there are several remarkable parallels in motifs and phraseology. A. Dihle's linguistic analysis, which places the *Parthenope Romance* in the same pre-Atticist context as Chariton, closes the net further.[63] There is indeed a fair chance that the same man has written both *Callirhoe*[64] and *Parthenope* — and perhaps *Chione* as well, whether including or not the new fragment reminiscent of Chariton recently published by M. Gronewald.[65] Only, our imperfect knowledge of the novel's early history prevents us from wholly excluding the possibility of a close imitator of Chariton (or vice versa) — much closer then, in spirit and language, than ever Xenophon Ephesius. However that may be, the intimate connection between Chariton and the *Parthenope Romance* is a fact, and this permits us to link the Parthenope martyrdom yet more closely to the *Parthenope Romance*; because, as already noted above (IV), the martyrdom's novelistic traits agree best with Chariton.

Enough concrete examples of the agreement have been given in my analysis of the martyrdom (III): the rumour of the heroine's beauty spreading, the role played by Eros (and/or the βάσκανος δαίμων), the noble magnate/ruler, the Persian king (sleepless for love; a barbarian, but not barbarous), and so on. As in Chariton, the emphasis is on speech, thought, and sentiment, whereas the external events (abductions and other adventure elements) are dismissed in a few sentences. The extension of the action from West (Sicily/South Italy) to East (Persia), but — untypically for the novels, at least in the imperial period — excluding

---

80

[63] "Zur Datierung des Metiochos-Romans", *WJA* N.F. 4, 1978, 47–55.

[64] This may be the original title (cf. Char. 8.8.16 and *P. Michael.* 1), the type *Chaereas and Callirhoe* representing a later fashion; see K. Plepelits (trans.), Chariton von Aphrodisias, *Kallirhoe* (Bibl. d. griech. Lit., 6), Stuttgart 1976, 28–9.

[65] "Ein neues Fragment zu einem Roman", *ZPE* 35, 1979, 15–20. Cf. esp. the important considerations pp. 19–20. The *Chione Romance* in Zimmermann (above, n. 54) pp. 40–6.

Egypt, is also common to both. A detail of vocabulary may be added, to be found only in the Arabic MS. *B* (in which we also found the Chariton-like kindling-of-love passage): the Persian king is described as one who "aimait les femmes" (§7.4). This corresponds exactly to the Greek φιλογύναιος or φιλογύνης, which occurs three times in Chariton (1.12.7 and 2.1.5 of Dionysius, 7.6.7 of Chaereas), but in no other Greek novel. Maehler (pp. 19–20) mentions φιλότεκνος in the Parthenope fragment (line 12) as a possible indication of close relationship to Chariton, because this author is particularly fond of compounds with φιλο-;[66] the present instance is more telling still, exhibiting the very word exclusively used by Chariton.

Looking at the problem from the point of view of the martyrdom, we may note that the imitation of a Chariton-structured *Parthenope Romance* would account for the choice of a Persian king as one of the suitors. To Coquin (pp. 356–7), the marked contrast in the characterization of the Christian Emperor Constantine and the pagan King of Persia is an indication that the martyrdom was composed in Egypt, "pour tourner en dérision les occupants perses (619–629 A.D.)". This seems rather far-fetched (even if a criterion for date and provenance[67] alike would indeed be welcome); the contrast is exactly that between Greek and barbarian in a novel of Chariton's type, only "translated" into Christian terms.

---

[66] Maehler (pp. 19–20) refers to A. D. Papanikolaou, *Chariton-Studien* (Hypomnemata, 37), Göttingen 1973, who p. 158 lists all "Adjektivbildungen mit φιλο-" in Chariton: 13 in all, occurring at 30 places, whereas Xenophon Ephesius exhibits only three such compounds. It should be added, however, that φιλότεκνος actually is to be found in Iamblichus (together with φίλανδρος, fr. 35 p. 31.11-12 Habrich), and — more important, as a qualification of Maehler's and Papanikolaou's statements — that Chariton is really special in this respect only in comparison with Xenophon (and Longus: only φιλόκαλος); these compounds become popular again in Achilles Tatius (φιλάνθρωπος, φιλόθηρος, φιλόμυθος, φιλόξενος, φιλοπάρθενος) and Heliodorus (φίλαβρος, φιλάνθρωπος, φιλέλλην, φιλέμπορος, φιλήκοος, φιλόνεικος, φιλόνεος, φιλοπλούσιος, φιλόστοργος, φιλότιμος, φιλοχρήματος), most of them with only one occurrence each. As a matter of curiosity it may be noted that the common word φιλάνθρωπος (with derivatives) shows a distribution which is revealing for each novelist's character: it is found 20 times (i.e., once every 8 pages) in Char. and 25 times (once every 12 pages) in Hld., the two "ideal" novels *par préférence*, while it occurs only twice in Xen. Eph., five times in Ach. Tat., and once in Longus!

[67] The fact that the Parthenope martyrdom seems to be transmitted only in Coptic and Arabic and has a place in the Coptic synaxary, makes it a plausible supposition that it does originate in Egypt, but I can find no confirmation in the text itself: the "mountain" detail (§ 2.3) may be due to the Coptic translator (see above, n. 47), and the "coloration

→

VIII

All the above considerations taken together strongly indicate, to my mind, that the author of the Parthenope martyrdom was not just generally influenced, directly or through Christian intermediaries, by the non-sophistic Greek novel, but that he had one particular model before his eyes, the *Parthenope Romance*. Chronologically, there are no difficulties: from papyri and mosaics we know that this novel was still popular around AD 200, and Chariton and the *Chione Romance* were read and copied in Egypt as late as the 7th century.[68] That the author had this novel before his eyes does not, of course, mean that he took over the whole plot — the model was indeed both decapitated and subjected to further amputation — nor that he cannot have borrowed some of the narrative material from other sources as well. But it does mean that we have an explanation for the untypical overall structure of this martyrdom, with a suicide in privacy as its climax instead of a public declaration of the heroine's Christian faith followed by her execution — and also that we have an additional factor to take into account when trying to reconstruct the *Parthenope Romance*.

That any reconstruction from the scanty remains we possess is an extremely hazardous business, goes without saying.[69] However, this demonstration would hardly be complete without at least an attempt to show how (or if) the new potential source can be combined with the earlier known evidence. Paragraph numbers refer to the martyrdom, italicized letters to the fragments and testimonia listed above (VI).

Parthenope is the daughter of Polycrates, the tyrant of Samos (*a*). She is young (only twelve?, § 1.7), virtuous, intelligent, well educated, and extremely beautiful, admired by all (§ 1.8–9, 12–14). Eros, jealous of her chastity, intrudes and spreads the rumour that there lives on Samos a young maiden, who is perfect

nationale" which Coquin (pp. 356–7) discovers obviously resides in the depiction of the Persian king alone. The typically Egyptian martyrdoms are indeed very different in character, cf. Delehaye (above, n. 12) pp. 149–50 and his *Passions* (above, n. 5) pp. 225–6. Yet the Greek novels, including the more truly "ideal" type, were obviously popular in Egypt in the imperial period, so martyrdoms stamped on them may well have been produced alongside the more sensational, bloodstained, and miraculous kind.

[68] Witness the *Codex Thebanus deperditus*, U. Wilcken, *APF* I, 1901, 227–72.

[69] Reservation must be made for the additional uncertainty caused by the different Arabic versions; Coquin's translation gives only partial information on the MS *B*, which may well prove to provide a better basis for reconstruction (cf. above, n. 27).

in all respects; there is no woman in the world like her (§2.1–6). [Suitors assemble, but are] all turned down by Parthenope, true to her name (*d*). Then Metiochus arrives, the son of Miltiades, driven away from the Chersonese (*a, i*), perhaps on his way back (unmarried!?, cf. *i*) from Darius and having passed Phrygia (*d*). He takes part in a symposium arranged by Polycrates (back, alive, from Oroetes!?, cf. *h*); Parthenope is also allowed to be present, and Eros is the subject for discussion set up by Anaximenes the philosopher (*a*). They fall in love (*d*) and are betrothed (or married); Metiochus, however, has to leave; and his bride is to join him later in his town (§ 5.9–11).

Eros intrudes again, or a *baskanos daimon* (the rejected suitors?): the rumour reaches some magnate or ruler (Anaxilas?, *d*), who falls in love with Parthenope on sight/unseen, without knowing that she is already betrothed/married, and arranges her abduction (§§ 2–3). Brought into his presence Parthenope receives a promise that she will become his lawfully wedded wife, share his riches, bear his sons (§ 4). She answers that she is his slave and not worthy of this honour; appealing to his righteousness, she asks him to state his opinion of a case in which a girl, who is already betrothed/married to one man, is carried away by another (§ 5.1–12) She gets the expected answer, reveals that she is already betrothed/married to Metiochus (§ 5.13–19), and is released and brought back home, where she is greeted with joy, tells her story, and thanks the gods (§ 6). 82

[Leaving home again for some reason (abducted again? or to join Metiochus?),] Parthenope wanders around searching for Metiochus, having cut off her hair [to escape attention]; [but in spite of this] many men try to win her (*d*). The wanderings include a stay in Campania (*d*), perhaps a visit to Anaxilas, the tyrant of Rhegium (*d*, in case he is not identical with the first magnate/ruler), [who is one of her suitors], and perhaps also the detention by a powerful man on Corcyra (*c*). During the wanderings (or perhaps already before leaving Samos?), she receives a letter from Metiochus, who complains that he has been sleepless since the day they parted (*b*).

Eros does not give up: he lets the rumour of Parthenope reach as far as Persia, where the king, "a lover of women" (φιλογύναιος), arranges to have her brought to him by force; deceptive letters (to Polycrates?) play some role in that connection (§ 7). The soldiers sent out recognize Parthenope by her astounding beauty; on her way to the king the girl laments in a monologue this new abduction, worse than the former one, and opts for suicide (§ 8.1–7). The king, filled with desire by her beauty, orders her to be brought into his bed-chamber, where he tells her he has not been able to sleep because of her and then proceeds to offer her marriage, riches, and dominance over all his eunuchs and concubines (§ 8.8–18). She feigns compliance, asking only for a respite in order to rest, wash herself, and dress; she also asks to be left alone and to have a fire lit so as to sacrifice to her gods; and the king grants her all this (§ 9.1–10). She adds that she has a presentiment that she will die before him, and makes him swear by his gods that on the day she dies he will have her body carried to her home town to be buried in her ancestors' grave (§ 9.11–15; § 10.1–2). The king feasts with his men and has everything arranged according to the girl's wishes (§ 10.2–4). Parthenope, left alone, prepares herself in various ways, prays and sacrifices, and then throws herself into the fire, which does not harm her (§ 10.4–12; 11.1–3). When she does not appear, the eunuchs and concubines open the door and find her lifeless; they are shocked and bewail her youth and exile (§ 11.4–6). The king, brought to the place by their moaning, is likewise shocked, but remembers his oath and has her on the very same day carried, "looking as if asleep", to her home (§ 11.6–13). [Safely there she wakes up from her apparent death and] tells her story; everyone rejoices at her chastity and cleverness, [which has saved her life].

This may have been the happy ending, or part of it: the reunion with Metiochus remains to be told. But an alternative would be instead to cut off head and tail of the two episodes selected for the martyrdom, i.e., to suppress their abduction-from-home and happy-homecoming parts and simply range the two episodes among others of a similar kind which happen to Parthenope during her wanderings (*d,g* πλάνη). This would leave room for a recognition-and-homecoming end à la Chariton instead, which may — just possibly — be what the two mosaics illustrate: Metiochus would then, like Chaereas (and like Rhodanes in Iambl. 22), play the victorious general (he wears his uniform in both mosaics), and the mosaics would depict the pathetic recognition itself (*k*) and the ensuing reunion of the two lovers (*l*).[70]

It must be kept in mind that the above is purely an *exempli gratia* reconstruction, which probably relies rather too heavily on the new potential witness to the novel's plot and which necessarily distorts the proportions (what is Metiochus doing all the time?). But like *exempli gratia* supplements in papyrology and epigraphy, it is meant to bring out the inherent possibilities, or some of them, in as concrete a form as possible — and, it is hoped, to provoke a fruitful discussion.

Postscript. When this article was already in press, further search and inquiry led to the surprising discovery that Metiochus and Parthenope did in fact enjoy a prosperous *Nachleben* in the east right through the middle ages. Dr. Bo Utas (Uppsala) called my attention to an edition of a Persian eleventh-century verse novel preserved in fragments, the *Wāmiq-o-Adhrā* of 'Unṣurī, edited by Maulavi Mohammed Shafi (The

[70] Maehler (pp. 18–9) suggests that (*l*) refers to a certain incident in the symposium scene (*a*); the overlooked erotic implications apart (cf. above, n. 59), it seems to me less likely that such a quickly passing incident should be chosen for illustration, than a crucial standard scene like the recognition. But, of course, at the present state of our knowledge this is all what Gronewald (above, n. 65) p. 20 would call "ein müssiges Spiel".

Panjab University Press: Lahore, 1967), the existence of which seems to have escaped the notice of students of the Greek novel. The editor is aware of the fact that the Persian novel "is based on the material of some Hellenistic romance" (p. 3), but he makes no attempt to identify this model. However, from the information and the translated extracts he gives in his English introduction, there can be no doubt that we are concerned with the *Parthenope Romance*: the action starts on Samos, the heroine is the daughter of Polycrates, and her Arabic name ʿAḏhrā means "virgin". At this island the young hero arrives, "fleeing from his home due to tyranny"; they meet at the temple of Hera, fall in love, and exhibit all the usual symptoms of love sickness.

How far the preserved fragments (some 372 verses in all) carry us, is not stated in the introduction. In collaboration with Dr. Utas, I hope to be able to present, in due course, a translation of the fragments (and various other testimonia) and a commentary which discusses the consequences of this new find for the reconstruction of the novel. For the present it can be noted that the popularity of precisely this novel in late antiquity has been confirmed. Through what intermediaries it reached eleventh-century Khurāsān and ʿUnṣurī (ob. prob. 1049/50) is not clear, but there seems to have been an Arabic version, as well as a Persian prose novel by Al-Berūni, which may have been the immediate source for our verse novel. And the story does not end with ʿUnṣurī: "the names of Wāmiq and ʿAḏhrā began to be used by poets as of typical lovers", and even when ʿUnṣurī's novel was eventually lost, there appeared from the 15th century onwards numerous more or less freely invented stories about the same couple.

84

9

Metiochus at Polycrates' Court

[originally published in *Eranos* 83, 1985, 92–102]

The discovery that the Persian poet 'Unṣurī's (d. *c.* 1040 AD) verse-romance *Vāmiq and 'Adhrā* (*V&A*), a substantial fragment of which was published in 1967, is based on the Greek novel of *Metiochus and Parthenope* (*M&P*) gives us an unexpected opportunity to shed some further light on the Greek fragments of that novel which were (re)published and exhaustively discussed by H. Maehler in 1976.[1] A detailed comparative treatment of the Greek and Persian fragments and a reconstruction of the whole will have to wait till later; it has to take into account not only the new major Persian fragment (some 372 double verses in all) but also a number of 'Unṣurī verses quoted in various lexical works, the summary of part of the plot found in the 12th-century compilation *Dārāb-nāmah* of Abū Ṭāhir Ṭarsūsī, and other testimonia scattered in Oriental sources.[2] The chief object of the present brief note is to see to what extent the Persian version may help us to restore the principal Greek fragment in the part where the two overlap, namely, the description of Metiochus' participation in a symposium at Polycrates' court. But first, as a background, some observations on the historicity of the novel in the light of the new evidence.[3]

---

[1] The Persian fragment vas published by M. Shafi, *Wāmiq-o-'Adhrā* of 'Unṣurī, Lahore 1967, and is now also available (with Russian trans.) in I. Kaladze, *Epičeskoe nasledie Unsuri* ("The Epic Heritage of Unsuri"), Tbilisi 1983. For the identification of *V&A* as based on *M&P*, see the postscript to T. Hägg, "The *Parthenope Romance* Decapitated?", *SO* 59, 1984, 61–92, pp. 83f. [No. **8** in this volume]. The principal Greek fragment (*P. Berol.* 9588+21179+7927) was (re)published by H. Maehler, "Der Metiochos-Parthenope-Roman", *ZPE* 23, 1976, 1–20.

[2] For a survey of the various Oriental sources, see B. Utas, "Did 'Adhrā Remain a Virgin?", *Or. Suec.* 33–34, 1984–85 (forthcoming); [in fact published in vol. 33–35, 1984–86, 429–441] cf. also Kaladze's monograph (above, n. 1) and, for the lexical quotations, H. Ritter in *Oriens* 1, 1948, 134–139. The *Dārāb-nāmah* passage is summarized by Shafi (above, n. 1), pp. 2f.

[3] I am indebted to B. Utas for translation of the Persian material and for discussion of many of the problems involved.

1. Historicity

The combination of two names in the Berlin fragment, (l. 3) Χερρο-
[νησίτης?] and (l. 15) Ἡγησι[πύ]λη, led Maehler to the conclusion that
the hero of the novel, Metiochus, must be identical with Miltiades'
son of that name mentioned by Herodotus (6.41). He was also able
to show that the heroine, Parthenope, is the daughter of Polycrates,
anonymously mentioned in Herodotus (3.124), and that the symposium described takes place on Samos in Polycrates' lifetime. Since Polycrates was trapped and executed by the Persian satrap Oroetes in 522/1,
whereas Metiochus must have been born some time between 528 and
516/5,[4] the novelist is obviously guilty of an anachronism similar to that
of Chariton, who puts on stage simultaneously Hermocrates of Syracuse (killed in 407) and King Artaxerxes II (reigned 404-359). But in
the present case, it should be observed, the mistake is particularly easy
to account for, since there are two persons named Miltiades in Herodotus, both connected with the Thracian Chersonese: besides the great
Miltiades (before 550-*c.* 489), the father of Metiochus and later victor
at Marathon, there is also his paternal uncle and namesake (c. 590–after
528); M. senior was the *oikistēs* of the Chersonese and its ruler till his
death (Hdt. 6.34-38), while M. junior ruled there *c.* 516/5-493/2 (Hdt.
6.34, 39-41). Herodotus' own account is not unambiguous, as modern
debate has shown,[5] and sometimes in later tradition, e.g., in Cornelius

---

[4] For the notoriously vexed Miltiades chronology, see H. T. Wade-Gery, *JHS* 71, 1951,
212-221; N. G. L. Hammond, *CQ* 50, 1956, 113-129; H. Berve, *Die Tyrannis bei den
Griechen*, Vol. 1-2, München 1967, pp. 79-85, 564-569; K. Kinzl, *Miltiades-Forschungen*,
Diss. Wien 1968, *passim;* and J. K. Davies, *Athenian Propertied Families 600-300 B.C.*,
Oxford 1971, pp. 299-304. Miltiades' first marriage, in which Metiochus was born, falls
somewhere within the period 528-516/5 BC (cf. Wade-Gery, p. 212). Hammond's (p. 118)
more precise dates — marriage c. 522, birth of Metiochus c. 520 — build on a series of
unverifiable assumptions.

[5] Cf. Hammond (above, n. 4), pp. 113-117, who distinguishes no less than three men of
the name Miltiades in Herodotus (and in some other sources probably dependent on
him); *contra* Berve (above, n. 4), p. 566 and Kinzl (above, n. 4), pp. 13-15. Another debated question, whether Miltiades was in fact (enforcedly) absent from the Chersonese
between 514 and 496/5 (cf. F. Prontera, *PP* 27, 1972, 111-123, pp. 122f.; *contra* E. Lanzil-
lotta, *MGR* 5, 1977, 65-94), need not concern us here; the close reading of Hdt. 6.40
needed for that interpretation cannot anyway be expected from our novelist.

Nepos' biography *(Milt.* 1–3),[6] the two are simply amalgamated into one. This "combined Miltiades" suited our novelist excellently: one of his constituent parts ruled the Chersonese in the same period as Polycrates ruled Samos (c. 538–522/1), the other provided the author with the irresistible motif of the persecuted stepson.

Regarding Miltiades' family affairs, our historical sources (Hdt. 6.39.2, 41.2; Marcell. *Vita Thuc.* 2, 10–12; Plut. *Cim.* 4) give just the bare facts: he first married an Athenian lady, who bore him Metiochus (and probably his daughter Elpinice as well);[7] having arrived in the Chersonese, he married the Thracian princess Hegesipyle, who became the mother of Cimon.[8] As was already partly discernible from the Greek fragments, the novelist put into this framework the story of the stepmother, Hegesipyle, who to promote the interests of her own children *(M&P* ll. 15f.) slanders and persecutes her stepson *(M&P* ll. 13, 21; *V&A* vv. 42ff.). To judge from the Persian version, the end of this family drama was not, as Maehler (p. 14, commenting on ll. 17–22) suggests, formed on Herodotus' report (6.40–41) of the expulsion (in 493) of Miltiades and Metiochus from the Chersonese. Instead, the novelist seems at this point

94

---

[6] See Kinzl (above, n. 4), pp. 109–120, who concludes that the confusion goes back to Nepos' immediate source (Ephorus?, Kinzl p. 151). Similar confusion can be discerned in Paus. 6.19.6, cf. Berve (above, n. 4), p. 566. Hammond (above, n. 4), p. 123 n. 4 unconvincingly tries to explain away the contradiction in the Pausanias passage, disregarding the emphatically placed πρῶτος τῆς οἰκίας ταύτης, which must imply that there were later members of the family who *did the same,* namely, ⟨τὴν⟩ ἀρχὴν ἔσχεν ἐν Χερρονήσῳ τῇ Θρακίᾳ.

[7] Hammond (above, n. 4), p. 121 and Davies (above, n. 4), pp. 302f., contrary to most other authorities, prefer to regard Elpinice a daugther of Hegesipyle; that, however, would mean that she lived "in matrimonio" (Nep. *Cim.* 1.2) with her (full) brother, not just her half-brother, Cimon (Nep. *loc. cit.* explicitly speaks of wives "eodem *patre* natas"), which seems less likely (in spite of Plut. *Cim.* 4.3 κόρης). Cf. n. 8.

[8] The number of children, or sons, in each marriage is a matter of ambiguity. Hdt. 6.41.2 only states that Metiochus was the oldest of Miltiades' children (παίδων), not distinguishing in that connection between the two marriages. Marcell. § 11 speaks of "children" (παίδων) in the first marriage, "a child" (παιδίον) in the second; § 12, however, if correctly transmitted (ὁ for [the second] οἱ would be an easy correction), seems to imply that there was more than one child in the second marriage as well (thus, hesitantly, H. Berve, *Miltiades,* Berlin 1937 [= Hermes, Einzelschr., 2], p. 6 n. 2). *M&P* ll. 15 f. τῶν ἑαυτῆς [---π]αίδων with reference to Hegesipyle would side with § 12 against § 11; cf. also Davies (above, n. 4), p. 304 on some indirect (and inconclusive) evidence for one or two further daughters of Miltiades and Hegesipyle. Hammond (above, n. 4), p. 118 mistakenly supposes that Marcell. 11 παίδων, 12 οἱ παῖδες must refer to *sons.*

to have left history for romance: Vāmiq /Metiochus discovers that his stepmother plans to take his life by poison and sees no other way out than to flee from the country *(V&A* vv. 53–55).

Together with his true companion Ṭūfān/Theophanes (?)[9] Metiochus secretly leaves for Samos. The Persian fragment makes it perfectly clear that he arrived in Samos directly from the Chersonese, which means that we get no support for the mysterious ἀπὸ Φρυγίας in one of the late Greek testimonia for the novel *(Geogr. Gr. Min.* II p. 445 a 8 Müller);[10] perhaps it is just a slip for ἀπὸ Θρᾴκης. But why precisely Samos as the destination? The reason stated in *V&A* (v. 69) is that Metiochus is a blood-relation to Polycrates. Greek tradition, however, does not seem to record any such relationship between Miltiades' family, the Philaids,[11] and the tyrant of Samos. One may be tempted to speculate, whether the novelist perhaps made Metiochus' Athenian mother, about whose family nothing seems to be known for certain,[12] in some way related to Polycrates; but the solution is probably simpler than that, and at once more astonishing. According to our historical sources, Miltiades senior traced his descent back to Aeacus, the son of Zeus (Hdt. 6.35.1 ἀπ᾽ Αἰακοῦ, Marcell. 2 πρὸς Αἰακὸν τὸν Διός). Polycrates, on the other hand, is introduced by Herodotus as "the son of Aeac*es*" (3.39.1 Π. τὸν Αἰάκεος).[13] Once more, by mistake or for the sake of the intrigue, our novelist has mixed things up. We find the confirmation in one of the lexical quotations from ῾Unṣurī, perhaps the very first verse of the romance: "A fine

95

---

[9] "Theophanes" was suggested by C. Bosch in Ritter (above, n. 2), p. 139.

[10] See Maehler (above, n. 1), p. 3 n. 11 and Hägg (above, n. 1), p. 76.

[11] Cf. F. Schachermeyr, *RE* XIX: 2, 1938, 2113–2121 s.u. "Philaidai"; Wade-Gery (above, n. 4), p. 218 n. 29; Hammond (above, n. 4), p. 121; Berve (above, n. 4), p. 759; Davies (above, n. 4) No. 8429 (with Table I).

[12] See *RE* XV: 2, 1932, 1681 *s.v.* "Miltiades 2"; Wade-Gery (above, n. 4), p. 219 (with n. 43); Berve (above, n. 4), p. 569; Kinzl (above, n. 4), p. 50; Davies (above, n. 4), p. 302 (daughter of Hippias?). Nor is it known what happened to her when Miltiades left for the Chersonese and remarried: was she dead, had he divorced her (thus Davies, *loc. cit.,* and others), or did he marry the Thracian princess without a formal divorce from his Athenian wife? Berve's statement in his monograph of 1937 (above, n. 8), p. 6 that she "anscheinend in jungen Jahren starb" seems to be a mere conjecture without any basis in the ancient historical sources and does not reappear in his synthesis of 1967 (above, n. 4), p. 567; it now happens, however, that it receives support, for what it is worth, from *V&A* v. 42: "(Vāmiq was) a clever young man whose mother was dead."

[13] No variant reading Αἰακοῦ is recorded in the critical editions at this or other places in Herodotus where the name Αἰάκης occurs in the genitive.

city, named Samos, where happily ruled a king, / Called Polycrates, worthy of greatness, an offspring of *Aeacus son of Zeus*".[14] The confusion of the two names, organically embedded as it is in the intrigue, must go back to the original Greek author.

Through these innocent manipulations the novelist has managed to bring together in his story two of the great names in Herodotus, Polycrates and Miltiades. Miltiades is only a background figure, the father who fails to protect his son against his new wife's machinations *(V&A* vv. 42 ff., *M&P* 1.6?), while Polycrates takes a more active part in the plot. The picture given of the Samian tyrant, at least as glimpsed through in the fragments, is most positive; it is no doubt generally inspired by Polycrates' proverbial good fortune (εὐτυχίη, Hdt. 3.40.1, cf. Strabo 14.1.16)[15] and riches rather than by any specific historic account. His magnificence (μεγαλοπρεπείη, Hdt. 3.125.2) and the display of wealth at his court are a recurrent motif in the novel from the description of Polycrates' own wedding *(V&A* vv. 4–14, cf. v.12 "all this wealth, the greatness and fame of King Polycrates") through the symposium scene. He is depicted as a noble man (v. 124 "that good-natured ruler"), he receives Metiochus with respect and warmth (vv. 132–135), and — to judge from the summary in the *Dārāb-nāmah* — he had, before the inopportune death of his wife, even agreed to let Metiochus marry his daughter. What later made him change his mind is not clear; there is of course the possibility that following Herodotus (3.124) the novelist let Parthenope provoke her father's anger by opposing his intention to visit Oroetes.

Polycrates' attracting intellectuals and poets to his court is also illustrated in the novel: Anaximenes the philosopher is present at the symposium and is the one who formulates the questions put to Metiochus in order to test him *(M&P* ll. 30ff., *V&A* vv. 143ff., probably v. 178 too), and on another occasion a well-known minstrel, behind whose corrupted name probably hides Ibycus,[16] is featured celebrating in song the beauty of the young couple *(V&A* vv. 261ff.). Incidentally, neither Anaximenes nor Ibycus is mentioned by Herodotus, and Ibycus' presence at Poly- 96

---

[14] Trans. Shafi (above, n. 1), p. 4. Cf. Ritter (above, n. 2), p. 135 No. 3, with Bosch's comment.

[15] Cf. V. La Bua, "Il papiro Heidelberg 1740 e altre tradizioni su Policrate", *MGR* 4, 1975, 1–40, p. 9.

[16] This identification was suggested, with much hesitation, in Ritter (above, n. 2), p. 135 No. 4, and now seems to be confirmed by Utas' findings (above, n. 2).

crates' court, though a commonplace in modern handbooks, is curiously weakly attested in ancient sources; the much-debated "Ibycean" poem addressed to (young) Polycrates apart,[17] our novel would seem to be the only pre-Byzantine testimony to that presence.

There is in the novel fragments no trace of the tradition adverse to Polycrates which, while scarcely visible in Herodotus' account (but cf. 3.142.3), comes out unmasked in some of the later sources,[18] as when Clearchus moralizes over the tyrant's licentious way of life (fr. 44 Wehrli, Ath. 12.540e-541a) or Diodorus Siculus reports about his ruthless piracy and greed (10.16) and about the outrages committed against citizens and foreigners alike in Samos (1.95.3). Our author is a classicist at heart, if not necessarily in his language.[19]

The Herodotean influence is noticeable in the further development of the action as well. After Polycrates' death the young couple, still unmarried, passes into the hands of another ruler, identified by B. Utas as Maeandrius, Polycrates' former secretary, whom the tyrant had left in charge when setting out on his fatal journey to the Persian satrap (Hdt. 3.123; 142.1, 3). The novelist obviously has him play the role of an evil despot: he throws the lovers into prison, demands Parthenope for himself, and on her refusal sells her as a slave (*Dārāb-nāmah*). Herodotus too, in the greater part of his account, presents Maeandrius in a rather unfavourable light (3.143-146; contrast 142), as do some late writers (cf. Luc. *Cont.* 14). On the other hand, the tyrant's brother Syloson, who was installed by the Persians after they had driven Maeandrius away,

97

---

[17] *P.Oxy.* 1790 = fr. 282 Page. Cf. C. M. Bowra, *Greek Lyric Poetry,* Oxford 1936, pp. 258 ff.; D. L. Page, *Aegyptus* 31, 1951, 158-172, pp. 168ff.; J. Labarbe *AC* 31, 1962, 153-188, pp. 181 f., 186f.; J. P. Barron, *CQ* 14, 1964, 210-229, pp. 217-227; M. L. West, *CQ* 20, 1970, 205-215, pp. 206-209; J. Peron, *RPh* 56, 1982, 33-56, pp. 36-40. West's solution seems preferable: there was only *one* tyrant called Polycrates, his father Aeaces was a tyrant as well, and Ibycus came to Samos during Aeaces' rule, which is compatible with *Suda's* (s. v. Ἴβυκος) statement that it happened "in the time of Croesus, the 54th Olympiad" (=564-60 *BC);* this means that the poem, whether by Ibycus or not (cf. Page's doubts), does not anyway show that Ibycus was active on Samos during Polycrates' own reign.

[18] For a detailed analysis of the various Polycrates traditions, see La Bua (above, n. 15); on Herodotus' picture of P., see H. J. Diesner, *A. Ant. Hung.* 7, 1959, 211-219, esp. pp. 217f.; K. H. Waters, *Herodotos on Tyrants and Despots,* Wiesbaden 1971 (= Historia, Einzelschr., 15), pp. 25-30; and La Bua, p. 18 n. 1 (with further refs.). A useful survey of the ancient sources on Polycrates is provided by Berve (above, n. 4), pp. 582-587.

[19] Cf. A. Dihle, *WJA* N.F. 4, 1978, 47-55, who finds that both linguistic evidence and the kind of "Historismus" displayed in the novel point to a date in the 1st cent. BC.

seems to have had a positive role to play in the plot, to judge from the one verse mentioning his name which happens to have survived ("King Syloson had an auspicious star …").[20] This again conforms with Herodotus' picture (3.140–141, 144, 149), as opposed to that of several later sources, according to which Syloson's "harsh rule" led to the depopulation of the island (Arist. fr. 574 Rose, cf. Strabo 14.1.17). If there were, as V. La Bua maintains,[21] from an early date and originating in Samos two distinct traditions, one consistently in favour of the Polycratean family and one against it, being pro-Maeandrian and anti-Persian, then our author sides with the former. It may even be, though this is at the present stage a mere suggestion, that the happy ending of the novel was staged on a Samos ruled by Syloson (*c.* 521–*c.* 515). If so, the story is more consistently and diligently put into a coherent historical framework — Polycrates, Maeandrius, Syloson — than is any of the ideal Greek novels we previously knew.

The heroine's wanderings, "in search of her husband", somehow take her to another Herodotean tyrant, Anaxilas of Rhegium (Hdt. 6.23; 7.165); this is stated in one of the Greek testimonia (scholion on Dion. Per., 358 = *Geogr. Gr. Min.* II, p. 445a3–4 Müller) and now, thanks to Utas' identification of the corrupted name forms, receives confirmation in a couple of lexical quotations from ʿUnṣurī.[22] Anaxilas ruled 494–476, so we find ourselves again in the time of Miltiades junior and Metiochus. One further identification is tempting, though less certain than the others: the name of Polycrates' wife, who plays an important role in the first part of the novel, may be read as Nanis,[23] the name which in later tradition (Parth. 22 = Hermesianax fr. 6 Powell) is given to King Croesus' daughter, who is said to have betrayed Sardes to Cyrus in 547/6 (a variant of the Tarpeia motif).[24] If the identification is correct — the difficulties lie in the spelling of Croesus' name and the circumstance that

---

[20] Trans. Shafi (above, n. 1), p. 4.

[21] V. La Bua, "Sulla conquista persiana di Samo", *MGR* 4, 1975, 41–102, pp. 44f., 52–55, 89–91.

[22] Utas (above, n. 2); cf. the different interpretations in Ritter (above, n. 2), pp. 136f. Nos. 7 and 13, and Kaladze (above, n. 1), pp. 87f. Nos. 6 and 17.

[23] The transmitted form is Yānī; the change to Nani(s) is minimal, the difference between the Arabic letters for initial y and n being just the placement of dots (which are often omitted in the manuscripts).

[24] Anonymous daughters of Croesus appear in Xen. *Cyr.* 7.2.26.

he seems to be called King of Phrygia instead of Lydia[25] — the novelist
has managed to enlist among his background personages another one of
Herodotus' great figures, and a friend of Miltiades senior at that (Hdt.
6.37–38.1), and made him become posthumously (and with chronological, if no other,[26] plausibility) the father-in-law of Polycrates!

2. *The Overlapping Part*

The Greek papyrus fragment consists of two columns. Of Col. I (*P. Berol.* 9588+21179) the last 33 lines are preserved, but in a fairly mutilated state: the first third, or more, is missing of each line. Though it is
possible to guess rather much of the contents, no single whole sentence
can be restored with confidence. Col. II (*P. Berol.* 7927+21179) is in a
better state of preservation: in most of its 38 lines only the first four
or five and (in the upper part) the last two or three letters are missing.
Consequently, as regards Col. II, only little improvement on what is in
reality a fairly complete Greek text can *a priori* be hoped for from our
Persian version, which is not only a thousand years younger, but may
have passed through one or several intermediaries,[27] and is versified at
that. On the other hand, it provides a good test-case for what help can
be expected in other, less well preserved parts, if only there is a reasonable overlap in contents.

The first part of Col. I (ll. 1–24) seems to record a conversation between Polycrates and Metiochus. What the tyrant is referring to in his
speech is not immediately evident (cf. below), but Metiochus in his answer obviously dwells on his stepmother's machinations against him. The
conversation is followed by a short transitional passage, in which Polycrates announces the beginning of the drinking (l. 27 πότου καιρός) and
briefly refers to Anaximenes and the subject of discussion apparently suggested by him. In the Persian version, there seems to have been no direct
counterpart to the dialogue: there, the symposium proper, with flutes and

---

[25] See Shafi (above, n. 1), p. 38 of the Persian text, v. 77; cf. Kaladze (above, n. 1), pp. 134,
196, and Utas (above, n. 2).

[26] Cf., however, the alleged historical connection between Polycratean and Lydian τρυφή
(Clearchus fr. 43–44 Wehrli).

[27] For preliminary discussion of the potential intermediary stages between the Greek
original and 'Unṣurī's romance, see T. Hägg, "The Oriental Reception of Greek Novels",
SO 61, 1986 (forthcoming) [No. 10 in this volume], and Utas' forthcoming article (above,
n. 2).

all (v. 137), starts immediately after Vāmiq has arrived in the palace and been greeted, for the first time, by Polycrates (vv. 131-135). Then it is the Persian version's turn to be the more detailed. We are told that it is Polycrates' intention to test the young stranger's ability in speech, and "the outstanding sage" Anaximenes is introduced. He is said to be watching the young couple's behaviour and to observe their "furtive glances", which makes him formulate a question about love to Vāmiq in order to be able to look into his heart (vv. 139-151). Whatever restorations we attempt in the Greek transitional passage, it cannot have contained this much.

The easiest solution of the problem is to suppose that the conversation between Polycrates and Metiochus has simply been left out in the Persian version and that the contents of *V&A* vv. 139-151 *preceded* that conversation in *M&P*. We may reconstruct the following sequence of events: Metiochus arrives in the palace and is greeted by Polycrates (*V&A* vv. 131-135). He is invited into the dining-hall; Polycrates' wife Nanis (?) is present as well (apparent from v. 219), and Parthenope is brought there (v. 136). Polycrates wants to test Metiochus, and Anaximenes is introduced, makes his observations and puts his question (vv. 139-151). During the dinner, Metiochus is made to tell about the reasons for his flight from the Chersonese *(M&P* ll. 1-24). Then it is time for the symposium proper, and for Metiochus' speech on Eros. The suppression of the dinner conversation in the Persian version is probably due to the fact that the circumstances around Vāmiq's flight had already been narrated at its proper place in the chronological sequence (*V&A* vv. 40ff.). Whether that was the case in the Greek novel as well, and the dinner conversation thus only a kind of recapitulation, must remain an open question; it is of course possible that 'Unṣurī, or some predecessor of his, preferred to straighten out a story which was originally told with more of a retrospective technique.

Metiochus' speech on Eros takes up the largest part of Col. II (ll. 37-62). After a short disclaimer of his competence for the task, reported in indirect speech, Metiochus eloquently and at length ridicules the conventional picture of Eros as a small child who travels round the world shooting his arrows at people. Why should precisely Eros, primeval and divine, never grow up, as human children do? How could a child travel like that and have such power? Metiochus himself regards love, of which he professes to have no personal experience, as "a movement of the intellect (κίνημα διανοίας), provoked by beauty and increased through habit" (ll. 60–62).

To these 26 short lines of Greek prose correspond 14 preserved double-verses in the Persian version (vv. 152–165), to which should probably be added some eight verses missing after v. 152.[28] Vāmiq also begins by disclaiming, in view of his youth and inexperience, any competence to deal with the subject proposed, but he does so in direct speech and in some detail (vv. 153f., plus the missing verses?). Although this necessarily means that there cannot be any close resemblance in wording with the brief indirect statement in *M&P,* we can at least see that Maehler and Merkelbach are on the right track in their restorations in lines 38 and 39, respectively (Maehler pp. 9, 16): Μητίοχος ὑποτιμησάμεν[ος | μὴ ἔχειν λόγον εἰ]κότα ἢ μάθησιν πρέπουσ[αν | τῇ τοιαύτῃ διαλ]έξει… We find a faint echo at the end of v. 153: "An old heart is more experienced in the world; it is more approved as regards culture and *knowledge*", cf. μάθησιν.

Arriving at the exposition of the topic itself, Vāmiq starts where Metiochus ended (v. 155): "Although I do not know the character of it *(scil.* love) …", cf. *M&P* ll. 59f. ἐγὼ [δὲ γ᾽ οὔ]πω (*scil.* τοῦ πάθους εἴληφα πεῖραν). He then proceeds to a short description of the young Eros (vv. 156–161), who is not, however, a small child as in the Greek (ll. 48, 54 βρέφος). The closest parallel is in v. 158: "Keeping a flaming fire in one hand, a bow and an arrow in the other", cf. ll. 4244 ἔχω[ν | πτερ]ᾲ καὶ τῷ [ν]ώτῳ παρηρ{κ}τημένον ⟨τ⟩όξον κα[ὶ τῇ | χειρὶ] κρατῶν λαμπάδα. The fire and the arrow piercing people's hearts are in the following verses embroidered on in a way which has few points of contact with the Greek text.[29] Most important of all, the ridiculing and repudiation of the Eros of mythology and the rationalistic explanation of love, which are the most conspicuous features of Metiochus' speech, are totally absent in that of Vāmiq, who is content to *describe* young Eros without rejecting the idea. He then switches over to a curious description of an alternative, *old* Eros (vv. 162–165), feeble-looking but dangerous, who has no counterpart whatsoever in the Greek text.[30]

[28] The existence and length of this lacuna follow from Utas' calculations, based on the facsimile reproduction of the manuscript in Shafi's edition (above, n. 1).

[29] *V&A* v. 157 "in action *quarrelsome* like a warrior" sounds like a translation of φιλόνεικος, the characterization of Eros in Char. (1.1.4, 6.4.5) and Xen. Eph. (1.2.1), but there seems to be no room for that adjective in Metiochus' description.

[30] This lack of agreement made Kaladze (above, n. 1), pp. 37–39 (too hastily) reject the idea that *V&A* could have anything to do with *M&P.*

After this different speech on Eros, 'Adhrā's reaction cannot very well be the same as Parthenope's. Angry at Metiochus' rejection of love (ll. 65–68), Parthenope embarked on what seems to have been a defence of the traditional Eros we meet in art and literature (ll. 68–71, end of fragment). 'Adhrā, on the other hand, reacts with a renewed feeling of love towards Vāmiq (vv. 166ff.), and her answer to him begins (v. 169): "O, man of good counsel, eloquent, clear-sighted [---] guide", contrast Parthenope l. 69 κενὸ[ς] ὁ τοῦ ξένου λῆρος...! Still, what follows apparently bears a greater resemblance to the original speech than could be expected. 'Adhrā rejects the notion that Eros could be old (as Parthenope probably rejected the rationalistic view of love) and vigorously defends young Eros: lovers are young, consequently Love too (vv. 170–176). This defence is obviously directed more against Metiochus' arguments than against Vāmiq's descriptions, especially so in the last two verses (175f.): "Know that everything grows old except love which stays [young]. If love were anything but young, it means that it would be harmed by old age." As we remember, Metiochus on the contrary thought it absurd that Eros should *not* grow up as everybody else.

If the hero's speech on love should be typical for the relationship between the Greek original and the Persian version, it is obvious that we can expect very little of word-to-word correspondence, even at places where the two actually overlap. Some of the original content is left out completely (rationalistic view of love), some of it is taken over but put into a context which fundamentally changes its meaning (young Eros not ridiculed but sympathetically described), and there are in *V&A* also completely new items inserted into the common framework (old Eros). On the other hand, the common framework is there (successive speeches on love by the two secret lovers), and a grave remodelling of one item (the hero's speech) is not permitted to have its full consequences on the following (the heroine's answer). The last circumstance cannot have been advantageous for the logical coherence of the Persian romance, but is clearly a positive factor in our reconstruction work.

The preliminary conclusion is that *V&A*, once as many as possible of its scattered members are collected and systematized, will be able to advance considerably our general knowledge of *M&P*, its setting, plot and characters, but only to a lesser extent contribute to the actual restoration of the preserved Greek text. I end by offering a sample of observations of the latter kind; Maehler's text, commentary (with restorations by various hands), and translations[31] provide the starting-point throughout.

ll. 3 f. πῶς Χερρο[νησίτης ---| --- ἐπά]γαγκες εἰς γάμον; "Warum sollte ein Chersonesier notwendigerweise zur Heirat ungeeignet sein?" (Maehler 1976), "Wieso sollte ein Chersonesier als Schwiegersohn nicht in Frage kommen?" (Maehler 1983). To judge from *V&A*, the γάμος referred to at this early stage can hardly be Parthenope's, as hitherto taken for granted. There is no competition of suitors, as F. Zimmermann had in mind,[32] nor does Polycrates plan any marriage for his daughter or even yet know that she and the young stranger have fallen in love on their first meeting at the shrine of Hera (*V&A* vv. 84–89, 102–116). Presumably the marriage is instead that of Miltiades to Hegesipyle, who might conceivably have been called a "Chersonesian": "Why [did he] necessarily have to marry [a woman from] the Chersonese?", or similarly.[33]

l. 6 τοῦ πατρὸς ὀλ{ε}ιγωρία, "die seinem Vater widerfahrene Gering-schätzung" (Maehler 1983).[34] Probably a subjective rather than an objective genitive (cf. Maehler 1976, p. 13): Metiochus' father, Miltiades, obvi-ously allowed himself to be duped by Hegesipyle's slander of her stepson (cf. *V&A* vv. 45–49, 93 etc.), and (the result of) "his father's negligence" is what Polycrates now promises to make good (l. 7 διορθώσομαι).

ll. 8f. κ]αταστήσας εἰς ὑψηλό[[ν]]τερον | [ἀξίωμα ---] "ihn in einen höheren (Stand?) erheben" (Maehler 1983). Instead, Merkelbach's sug-gestion τόπον, relating to Metiochus' place at Polycrates' table (Maehler 1976, pp. 8, 13), seems to be confirmed by *V&A* v. 133: "(and) had him sit in a more honoured seat", a piece of information which is pointless

102

---

[31] Besides the scraps of translations given in Maehler's commentary of 1976 (above, n. 1), there is also a continuous translation by his hand in B. Kytzler (ed.), *Im Reiche des Eros,* Vol. 2, München 1983, pp. 730f.

[32] F. Zimmermann, *Griechische Roman-Papyri und verwandte Texte,* Heidelberg 1936, p. 59; cf. his trans. in *Antike* 11, 1935, 292–316, p. 298 ("Wie könnte ein Mann aus der Chersonesos für die Ehe in Betracht kommen?").

[33] It is difficult to guess the actual wording, εἰς being the crux. One would have expected some phrase with πρός, such as λαμβάνειν (Marcell. 11, Hld. 7.28.2 etc.) or ἄγεσθαι (Jos. *Vita* 4 etc.) πρὸς γάμον (for a sample of other phrases with πρὸς γάμον, see Hld. 2.31.4, 4.6.6, 4.14.2, 7.24.4, 8.2.2). However, εἰς instead of πρός in various functions is a phe-nomenon observed in post-classical Greek (cf. Schmid, *Att.* IV 614, 627), and we find a rather close parallel in Diod. Sic. 2.5.1, where διδόναι εἰς γάμον occurs instead of the usual δ. πρὸς γ. (Chio 10, Xen. Eph. 2.12.2 etc.).

[34] Similarly already in F. Zimmermann, *Aegyptus* 13, 1933, 53–61, p. 58, and 15, 1935, 277–281, p. 279.

as it stands isolated in the Persian version, without the dinner conversation and without any previous mention of his being offered or taking any seat at all.

If the suggested new interpretation of ll. 3 f., 6 and 8f. is correct, we no longer find Polycrates discussing Metiochus' suitability as a husband to Parthenope (which is far too early) but simply engaged in a dialogue with the young man about his reasons for leaving home, and seemingly taking his side against his father. This may in turn have induced Metiochus to defend his father (ll. 10–13, esp. 12 φ[ι]λότεκνος, cf. Maehler 1976, p. 13), putting the whole blame on Hegesipyle and her concern for her own young children (ll. 15f.; cf. above, n. 8).

ll. 23 f. [κατέφυγον ἐπὶ] τὸν σὸν οἶκον καὶ τὴν [σωτηρίαν ἕξειν ὑ]πέ[λ]αβον. These restorations, by Merkelbach and Maehler, respectively (Maehler 1976, p. 8), seem to suit the context better than Maehler's translation of 1983: "doch dass (das Weib sogar) dein Haus und (deinen Herd damit) vergiften würde, das hätte ich nicht vermutet" (nothing in *V&A* indicates that Hegesipyle should have had any contact with Samos). Cf. *V&A* v. 121: "He (*scil.* Vāmiq) has come to Samos for the protection of the king, he has come to this illustrious court" (similarly, vv. 68–70, 93–95). Yet there is another attractive possibility. Welcoming Vāmiq, Polycrates says, among other things (v. 135): "You have come to your own home and city", which matches our Greek line remarkably well, if differently restored: ἥκεις εἰς] τὸν σὸν οἶκον καὶ τὴν [σὴν | πόλιν ---], only the speaker appears to be the wrong one. Maybe there was another change of speakers some lines earlier, Polycrates taking over from Metiochus (but cf. ll. 24f.), or Metiochus here quotes Polycrates' words of welcome. What makes it particularly tempting to equate l. 23 with v. 135 is the possible doublemeaning of οἶκος: while it has reached *V&A* simply as "house" or "home" (Persian *khānah*), in the Greek Polycrates surely meant "your own *family*", alluding to their alleged common descent from Aeacus (cf. above).

The Oriental Reception of Greek Novels:
A Survey with some Preliminary Considerations

*For Frithiof Rundgren**

[originally published in *Symbolae Osloenses* 61, 1986, 99–131]

The Greek novels of love, travel, and adventure — a genre which emerged in late Hellenistic times and flourished in the first centuries AD — experienced a rich *Nachleben* in Byzantium and the West. The "sophistic" specimens of the genre were read and discussed by distinguished scholars like Photius (9th cent.) and Psellus (11th cent.), they were imitated by a number of Byzantine novelists in the 12th century, and again in the 13/14th centuries they had their share in the emergence of the Byzantine courtly romance. Two of them, Heliodorus and Achilles Tatius, are extant (in full or part) in about two dozen MSS each, which attests to a considerable diffusion (even if their 12th-century imitator Eustathius Makrembolites with 43 MSS beats them in this particular popularity test).[1] The story of their reception then continues in the Renaissance and Baroque epochs, when they are translated, imitated, and sometimes creatively assimilated into the national literatures of Western Europe.

    This part of the Greek novel's afterlife is fairly well known in its general outlines,[2] though much remains to be done by way of filling in the

* The present article was conceived as a contribution to a *Festschrift* in honour of Professor Frithiof Rundgren, holder of the Chair of Semitic Languages at Uppsala University, to be presented to him on his 65th birthday. When the topic proved more fruitful than expected and the article came to exceed the fixed limits, it was decided, in understanding with the editors of the *Festschrift*, to publish it separately; but it remains dedicated to the great scholar and esteemed friend for whom it was originally written. — I am grateful to S. Gero, T. Kronholm, R. H. Pierce, and B. Utas for reading and commenting on various earlier drafts. The responsibility for any errors or omissions and for the views put forward is solely mine.

[1] See A. Cataldi Palau in *RHT* 10, 1980, 75–113. To be sure, most of the MSS (of Eust. Makr. as well as of Ach. Tat. and Hld.) are of a very late date (15th/16th cent.).

[2] For a general survey, with further refs., see Hägg 1983, pp. 73–80, 192–213, 240 f., 249 f.

details.[3] The novel's reception in the East is less well catered for: in fact, it is seldom even realized that there was such a thing,[4] and the subject has (to my knowledge) never been studied in any detail. The main reason for this neglect, as far as classical scholars are concerned, is obvious: the language barrier. It is not given to everyone to move — like the distinguished dedicatee of this article — with equal ease within the domains of Classical and Oriental studies; and if there is anything a classicist gets to learn in the course of his professional training, it is never to venture outside the boundaries set by his linguistic competence. This is no doubt a sound rule, in principle, but one all too easily misused as an excuse for neglect and ignorance. The late and reluctant use of extant Arabic translations in the constitution of Greek texts is only the most blatant manifestation of a persistent tendency.[5] The wider perspective, the study of the classical legacy in the Islamic world, still remains "a neglected outpost of classical scholarship", as R. Walzer stated thirty years ago.[6] As for our topic, there are in fact certain scattered hints and data available even to the outsider in Oriental studies, and the aim of the present article is to collect some of them and see what pattern they form. Working my way through translations and secondary sources of various kinds, I have, however, grown increasingly convinced that this is a topic that would richly repay a closer study; if somebody equipped with the necessary languages is moved to take it up, the article will have served more than its merely clarifying purpose.

We shall in turn consider three ways in which the Greek novels may have lived on in the various Oriental literatures: (1) translated in their full original form, (2) translated in adapted form, or (3) used as sources for "creative borrowing".[7] The emphasis will be on Arabic literature, Muslim or Christian, but some attention will also be paid to Syriac, Persian, and

---

[3] Cf., e.g., G. N. Sandy's recent careful mapping of the Greek novel's influence on "minor" English and French novelists in *A & A* 25, 1979, 41–55, and 28, 1982, 169–191.

[4] It is indicative that von Grunebaum's important study (1946, 1963) is missing in the two detailed bibliographies of the relevant period, O. Mazal's in *JÖBG* 11–12, 1962–63, 9–55; 13, 1964, 29–86; 14, 1965, 83–124, and G. N. Sandy's in *CW* 67, 1974, 321–359.

[5] Cf. Klein-Franke 1980, pp. 6–8, 15 f. (with a quotation of E. R. Curtius' incisive remarks in his *Büchertagebuch,* Bern & München 1960, p. 7); Walzer 1962a, pp. 33–35; Grunebaum 1963, p. 376.

[6] Walzer 1962a, p. 29 (in a reprinted essay of 1956).

[7] The expression borrowed from Grunebaum 1946, p. 294; cf. Walzer's similar concept "productive assimilation" (1962a, p. 11).

Coptic literature, in their own right or as intermediaries between Greek and Arabic. For the sake of the argument some of the general cultural background will have to be indicated, but it goes without saying that no complete picture can be attempted: all along, the selection of facts and viewpoints has been made with our special topic in mind.

1. Translations

Do we possess any Arabic translation of a Greek novel, or any medieval Latin version made by way of Arabic? This seems a reasonable question, considering the Arabic transmission of other classical or post-classical prose works. The value such a translation would represent is self-evident: although not providing the original wording, it could still help us to arrive at a better text of any of the five extant novels (a couple of them are poorly transmitted) or, better still, present us with the full version of some lost or only fragmentarily preserved novel. Unfortunately, however, no translation of the kind seems to be recorded, if we may rely on the unanimous silence on this topic in modern critical editions and collections of fragments. Our next question then will be: is there any chance at all that Greek novels ever passed into Arabic (or any other Oriental language), so that future discoveries are possible, or was our first question naive and uninformed — do the historical conditions and the known mechanisms of selection plainly exclude the translation of this kind of Greek literature? This is clearly where we have to start.[8]

How early, where, and under what precise circumstances the translation of Greek literature into Arabic started is still a matter of scholarly dispute,[9] but it seems fairly safe to state that organized translation activity on a larger scale began only some time after the ʿAbbāsid dynasty had come to power around AD 750 and that it continued for about 300 years, the period AD 800–950 being its heyday. The medical centre at Jundīshāpūr (Gundēshāpūr), founded in the Sassanian period, played a key role at the start, but the newly-founded capital, Baghdad, soon took over the lead. While translation, mostly from Persian or Greek into Syriac, had been carried out by the scholars themselves at Jundīshāpūr,   102
it became an art or science of its own in Baghdad, where expert schools

---

[8] For the following discussion the works mentioned in the list of references by Gottschalk, Grunebaum, Kunitzsch, Peters, Rosenthal, Rundgren, and Walzer have been particularly helpful. Klein-Franke 1980 contains an extensive bibliography on the subject.

[9] Cf. Kunitzsch 1975, pp. 271 ff.

of translators worked in the service of scholars who often themselves could read only Arabic. The result of this great "translation movement"[10] is imposing, not least in terms of quantity: the list of works translated — of which only a small part has survived — comprises some of the major Platonic dialogues, almost the whole Corpus Aristotelicum, various Hermetic and Neoplatonic treatises, well over hundred medical and philosophical works of Galen alone (and, mainly through him, parts of the Corpus Hippocraticum), books of "Artemidorus", Dioscorides, Ptolemy, Euclid and other scientific writers, not to mention a host of late antique commentaries on Aristotle and others.[11]

This standard list shows that utility, for practical or theoretical purposes,[12] was the prime criterion for a work to be selected for translation, the favoured subjects being medicine and pharmacology, alchemy, astrology, and the exact sciences; furthermore logic and linguistics (for the interpretation of the Qur'ān), and of course philosophy and theology. This "utilitarianism" alone might seem to rule out the novels; and R. Walzer even emphatically states: "neither Greek poetry nor artistic prose was ever translated into Classical Arabic".[13] As we shall see, this is probably an exaggeration,[14] but it may well hold true for the (more or less) "official" activity just described. However, before looking closer at that question, we have to consider another factor which, besides utilitarianism, limited the scope of this Arabic translation movement, namely, the use of intermediary languages between Greek and Arabic.

It would seem — though here again scholars differ in their estimate[15] — that most of the Greek literature that passed into Arabic did so by

[10] See, in particular, Peters 1968, pp. 57–67, with further refs.

[11] For a useful review of current work on these translations, see Paret 1959–60 and, for later developments, Kunitzsch 1975. The complete picture is given by the massive volumes of Sezgin I-VIII and Ullmann 1970–72.

[12] Cf. Rosenthal 1965, p. 18.

[13] Walzer 1945–46, p. 162 (and, similarly, 1962b, p. 180). Equally sweeping statements are easy to find elsewhere, e.g., Peters 1968, p. 26, and Kunitzsch 1975, pp. 269 f. Cf. the more balanced account in Rosenthal 1965, pp. 24 f., 344.

[14] To some extent, it is of course a question of how to define "artistic prose" (or "Prosakunst"); and as for poetry, of whether one demands the translation of whole works (epics, dramas), or is content to find smaller items; on Homeric verses (and other Greek poetry in Arabic tradition), see Kraemer 1956 and 1957 (and cf. Grunebaum 1963, p. 387 with n. 30), on the pseudo-Menandrean sententiae, see Ullmann 1961.

[15] Most of the scholars cited in n. 8 above agree that the use of a Syriac intermediary is the normal procedure, the direct translation more of an exception, even in the "best" period (9th cent.); but for the opposite view, see, e.g., Paret 1959–60, p. 393.

way of a Syriac version, either one existing already or one made specially for the purpose.[16] This is due to the fact that the translators were generally recruited among one or other of the Christian minorities which the Caliphate had inherited from its Byzantine and Sassanian predecessors. Most of them were Syrian Nestorians, intellectuals (priests, physicians) who still spoke their native Syriac but had to use Arabic in their professional work. Their native culture was hellenized, but many of them were no doubt as ignorant of the Greek language as were their Muslim employers. Their practical bilingualism made them the ideal translators into Arabic, if only the work they were set to translate, be it originally Greek, Persian, or Indian, existed in a Syriac version.

103

Thus the selection process actually starts some centuries earlier in early Byzantine Syria and in Sassanian Iran (where Nestorianism, having in the latter half of the 5th century been banned from Syria, was allowed to coexist with Zoroastrianism). Greek was of old well established in Syria and kept its position within the various Christian Syrian milieux for at least some generations after the Arabic conquest. But there were other, non-linguistic limitations upon the translation activities carried out here: besides the Christian texts, the Syrians chose for translation mostly such pagan literature as was neutral from a religious point of view (medicine, philosophy, science) whereas "from their Christian point of departure they were apt to reject, as incompatible with Christianity, the large mass of Greek belles lettres with its basis in pagan mythology".[17] This would certainly exclude the novels: not only does the action take place in the ancient Greek world with gods, religious feasts, and oracles playing a prominent part, but one or two of the novels even overtly propagate pagan cults. Nor could the novels plead exceptional educational value to excuse their paganism: they had no place in the late antique school curriculum[18] and did not belong to those works that a St. Basil would recommend for reading as part of the Greek cultural heritage. Allowing for the possibility of exceptions from the general rule — it is likely that

---

[16] See Peters 1968, p. 63.

[17] Rundgren 1964–65, p. 53 (my trans.).

[18] It is often assumed that the Greek literature which eventually passed into Arabic is more or less identical with that fostered in the late Greek schools of philosophy at Alexandria, Antioch and other places in the East, which survived under Christian rule (and even, in some cases, under Arabic rule). See, in particular, Meyerhof 1930 (and in *Islamic Culture* 11, 1937, 17–29), and cf. Grunebaum 1942, p. 291 n. 133; Walzer 1962a, pp. 2 f.; Peters 1968, pp. 15–17; Kunitzsch 1975, pp. 270–273.

unlikely things should happen, as Aristotle observes — the Christian Syrian milieu will have constituted a needle's eye through which the pagan novel is not likely to have passed.

By contrast, Christian novels and related literature of Greek origin understandably enjoyed much popularity in that environment. The *Pseudo-Clementines*, probably originally written (and rewritten) in Syria, were translated into Syriac as early as the fourth century,[19] and an epitomized version of the *Recognitions* later passed into Christian Arabic literature.[20] Various apocryphal Acts of the Apostles, like the *Acts of Thecla* likewise appear in Syriac,[21] and so do of course Acts of Martyrs in great numbers.[22] The pagan *Alexander Romance* of Pseudo-Callisthenes may seem a more astonishing choice; but Alexander is of course no ordinary hero of a love story, but an historical and legendary figure of great attraction, and the romanticized account of his achievement was welcomed almost everywhere — not least in the Orient, for natural reasons.[23] By way of a (lost) early 7th-century Pahlavī version it took its place in Syriac literature, probably already in that same century and in an Eastern Syrian (Nestorian) environment.[24] In the extant MSS the Syriac translation is constantly accompanied by a short compilation referred to as "The Christian Legend Concerning Alexander", which is a curious mixture of elements of the romance with Biblical and other materials. In the 9th century the Syriac version, with the Christian legend incorporated, was translated into Arabic, whence it passed on into other Islamic literatures;

[19] Baumstark 1922, p. 68; Rehm 1969, pp. VII-IX (with refs. to the various editions).

[20] Graf I, p. 303; Rehm 1969, p. VIII.

[21] Baumstark 1922, pp. 68 f.

[22] Baumstark 1922, pp. 93–95.

[23] E.g., there is an early (5th-century) Armenian translation, now available in English trans.: A. M. Wolohojian, *The Romance of Alexander the Great by Pseudo-Callisthenes*, New York & London 1969.

[24] Cf. Nöldeke 1890, pp. 11–17; Baumstark 1922, p. 125; Cary 1956, p. 11; Boyle 1977. The Syriac version, inclusive of the Christian legend, is available in the English trans. of E. A. W. Budge (Cambridge 1889). On the 8th-century Arabic version (preserved in two 14th-century MSS) of what seems to be a Greek epistolary novel of Alexander, "rattaché de quelque manière au Roman du ps.-Callisthène" (p. 213), see M. Grignaschi in *Muséon* 80, 1967, 211–264. Yet another aspect of the Oriental Alexander tradition is treated in T. Nagel, *Alexander der Grosse in der frühislamischen Volksliteratur*, Walldorf-Hessen 1978.

half a millennium later this Arabic version was the model for an (extant) Ethiopic translation.[25] There was also another "pseudo-documentary" work, the romantic *Life of Secundus the Silent Philosopher*, which made its appearance in various Christian literatures, including the Syriac.[26] According to B. E. Perry, it was accepted there neither strictly as a biography nor as a novel, but as "being conceived in broad perspective as martyrology and wisdom literature of an edifying kind, comparable and spiritually akin, in spite of its non-Christian origin and character, to the lives of saints and martyrs and the oracles of the prophets and patriarchs of old".[27] To answer such a description, the standard pagan novel of love clearly needed much more drastic an adaptation or amputation than did the books of Alexander and Secundus; to a possible case of such amputation we shall return below (2).

If the pagan novels were not able to pass the Christian Syrian needle's eye, there were other ways that led to Baghdad. If only they were available in the 9th century in Greek manuscripts, they might — though the chances are perhaps not too great — have belonged to those works which were translated directly from Greek into Arabic (whether by means of a Syriac "working version" or not). There is evidence of translators in the 9th century who did learn to master Greek and actively sought for Greek manuscripts of rare works in the ex-Byzantine countries — the Nestorian Ḥunayn ibn Isḥāq being the most famous among them — and there were contacts and exchange between the Arabic and Byzantine learned

105

---

[25] Graf I, pp. 545 f. The Ethiopic version is translated by E. A. W. Budge (London 1896, revised ed. 1933). Cary 1956, p. 12 n. 19, reports of a recent discovery of "an Arabic Pseudo-Callisthenes in Constantinople which may prove to be the lost intermediary", namely, between the extant Syriac and Ethiopic versions (MS Aya Sofya 3003–4, dated AD 1466); I have found no further ref. to this MS (not mentioned in *EI*² iv, 127b). (Ten MSS are known of the much later Arabic translation made in 1769–71 by the Orthodox priest Yuwāṣif ibn Suwaidān from a Middle Greek vernacular version; see J. Trumpf in *ByzZ* 60, 1967, 3–40, pp. 22–27, and A. Ch. Lolos in *Graeco-Arabica* 3, 1984, 191–202.) On the afterlife of the *Alex. Rom.* in the East generally, see Boyle 1977.

[26] Baumstark 1922, p. 169; Perry 1964, pp. 53–55. Perry proposes no date for the Syriac version (which is extant in a 9th-century manuscript), but he regards the Syriac and the Armenian translations as the two oldest Oriental versions of this text and places (pp. 57 f.) the Armenian one round the 6th century.

[27] Perry 1964, p. 63.

milieux (even if it is no more than a myth that the Patriarch Photius actually visited Baghdad as an ambassador).[28] The Bayt al-Ḥikma, "House of Wisdom", at Baghdad is said to have accommodated a large collection of Greek manuscripts.[29] As for the general availability of manuscripts of the novels in the 9th century, we may recall that in Constantinople Photius had access to at least four novels: Achilles Tatius, Heliodorus, Iamblichus and Antonius Diogenes — the latter two being lost to us, except for some fragments and Photius' detailed descriptions in the *Bibliotheca*. It is probable that libraries at Alexandria and Antioch and elsewhere in the Eastern provinces had contained copies of the novels as well — indeed, the genre was most at home in those parts and thus it is at least conceivable that such manuscripts should have ended up at Baghdad.

So, if utility could sometimes perhaps give way to interest simply, it will hardly have been impossible to procure a copy of a pagan Greek novel for translation. We may imagine, for instance, that Iamblichus' *Babyloniaca*, with its action played exclusively in ancient Mesopotamia and with its admixture of magic and ethnographical curiosa, might have awakened the interest of some of the latter-day inhabitants of that same country; or that Achilles Tatius' scientific digressions and Antonius Diogenes' geographic fantasies should have attracted others. Again, the *Aethiopica*, written in the 3rd or 4th century by Heliodorus of Emesa in Syria, who places the Sun-god in the centre of his pantheon: did it never attract, for instance, members of that alternative translators' milieu, the Syriac-speaking "Sabians" (Ṣābi'a) of Ḥarrān (Carrhae) with their syncretistic religion, including Neoplatonic features and the cult of stars and planets?[30] No positive answer to these questions seems to be available at present; but it is, from this point of view, reassuring to know that as yet only a minor part of the extant Arabic manuscripts has been edited or else subject to scholarly examination. Collections were earlier

---

[28] Cf. Peters 1968, pp. 22–27, 61 f. The notion that Photius visited Baghdad (thus, e.g., Walzer 1945–46, p. 167) or Samarra (Peters 1968, p. 23) and found there the Greek books he describes in the *Bibliotheca* (Hemmerdinger 1956) is based on a misinterpretation of Photius' words in his preface to the *Bibl.* His embassy, if it was ever realized, may indeed have led him to Samarra; but of that we know nothing, and anyway the *Bibl.* was composed before the departure; see Treadgold 1980, pp. 16–36.

[29] *EI*² i, 1141a; *CHIslam* II, p. 582; Hemmerdinger 1956.

[30] *EI* IV 22b–23b; *EI*² iii, 228a; cf. Meyerhof 1930, pp. 410–412, and Gottschalk 1965, p. 118.

systematically searched mainly for great names like Aristotle and Galen, and though much progress in cataloguing has been achieved lately,[31] new discoveries still belong to the order of the day. That a manuscript containing the Arabic version of a Greek novel, in full or abbreviated form, should come to light one day, is thus not merely wishful thinking, as the corresponding expectation would be with regard to Greek manuscripts in European libraries.[32] "So wie ein Archäologe nur dort den Spaten in die Erde sticht, wo er erwartet, auf einen Fund zu stossen, so haben auch die Generationen von Gelehrten die arabische Literatur auf das hin untersucht, was sie darin zu finden hofften."[33] Let us hope that someone soon expects to find a novel.

106

Up to now, our considerations have admittedly been of a largely hypothetical nature. To find a confirmation that we may be on the right track, we have to make an excursion to Persian literature of the early 11th century and, more exactly, to the verse romance of *Vāmiq and 'Adhrā* (hereafter: *V & A*) composed by 'Unṣurī (d. *c.* AD 1040), poet laureate to Sultan Maḥmūd of Ghazna. It has long been recognized by specialists in Persian literature that this story goes back, in the last instance, to some ancient Greek novel.[34] It is true that B. E. Perry — to my knowledge the only classical scholar to have discussed this possibility — was rather reserved towards the idea of direct dependence;[35] but at that time, apart from a fair number of disconnected verses quoted in lexical works etc., our knowledge of 'Unṣurī's work mainly depended on a 16th-century Turkish version of the story.[36] Only since the recent publication of substantial new fragments, both Persian and Greek, is it possible to state with confidence that *V & A* betrays a Greek origin not just generally, but is in fact based — through whatever intermediaries — on the Greek

---

[31] See, in particular, Sezgin I-VIII.

[32] Compare the vain hope, nourished through the centuries, of finding the complete Iamblichus MS mysteriously alluded to in various sources (see Rohde 1960, p. 392 n. 2, and L. di Gregorio in *Aevum* 38, 1964, 1-13).

[33] Klein-Franke 1980, p. 154.

[34] Cf. V. F. Büchner in *EI* IV, 1108a ("freie Nachdichtung" [of a Hellenistic novel]?); Ritter 1948 (p. 139: "keinen Zweifel, dass [*V & A*] auf einen hellenistischen Abenteuer- und Liebesroman zurückgeht"); Grunebaum 1963, p. 585; Rypka 1968, p. 175 (with further refs. to contributions of Russian and Persian scholars).

[35] Perry 1959, p. 14 n. 29.

[36] *EI* IV, 1107b, 1210b–11a.

novel of *Metiochus and Parthenope* (hereafter: *M & P*, a work considered to be close in date and style to Chariton's extant novel *Chaereas and Callirhoe* (1st cent. BC or AD).[37]

The new Persian material referred to — substantial manuscript fragments (372 verses in all) from the beginning of the novel, describing *inter alia* the hero and heroine's first meeting — was discovered and published, in 1967, by M. M. Shafi.[38] The new Greek papyrus fragments were published and studied, in 1976, by H. Maehler (to whom, however, the Persian fragments were unknown); the preserved part is a symposium scene enacted on Samos, and Maehler was able to show that the heroine, Parthenope, is the daughter of Polycrates the tyrant, and the hero the son of Miltiades.[39] Since 'Adhrā means "virgin" and the names Samos, Polycrates, Syloson (the latter's brother), Miltiades, and others recur in more or less easily recognizable form in the Persian text, there can be no doubt about the basic identity of the two novels, though separated in time by a thousand years.[40]

For further information about 'Unṣurī's novel, the precise contents of the fragments, and Vāmiq and 'Adhrā's later vicissitudes in Persian literature as a typical loving couple (the names meaning simply "The Lover and the Virgin"),[41] I refer to a forthcoming article by B. Utas.[42] Here I shall just briefly and tentatively discuss by what intermediaries the Greek novel may have reached 11th-century Iran, since this directly bears on our previous, Arabic-centred considerations. It is possible to present a fairly strong case for the existence of an Arabic intermediary. Not only do hero and heroine carry purely Arabic names, but we also

[107]

[37] Cf. Hägg 1984, p. 79.

[38] Shafi 1967. Dr. B. Utas kindly called my attention to this edition, and we have now (1984) embarked on a joint study of the text, which will, I hope, result in the publication of an English translation of the Persian fragments, a tentative reconstruction of the original Greek novel, and the tracing of its Oriental tradition. What is said in the present article on this tradition is consequently of a very preliminary nature. The Persian fragments are now also available in a Russian translation in Kaladze 1983.

[39] See Maehler 1976 and Hägg 1984, pp. 75–77, for the papyrus fragments and further testimonia.

[40] On the names, see Ritter 1948; for the identification, the postscript to Hägg 1984, pp. 83 f.

[41] See H. Ethé in Geiger & Kuhn II, p. 240, and Shafi 1967, pp. 2, 7 f.

[42] "Did 'Adhrā Remain a Virgin?", *Or. Suec.* 33–34, 1984–85 (forthcoming) [in fact published in vol. 33–35, 1984–86, 429–441].

find in a late 10th-century source, Ibn an-Nadīm,[43] the information that a book by this very title was composed by Sahl b. Hārūn (d. AD 830), who was secretary to the Caliph al-Ma'mūn and head of the "Library of Wisdom" at Baghdad.[44] When, some 200 years later, the great Islamic scholar al-Bīrūnī (d. *c.* AD 1051) says that he translated the story of *V & A*[45] — from Arabic into New Persian, we may presume[46] — it is at least possible that Sahl's Arabic version was his model; and al-Bīrūnī's prose version in turn may, as Shafi suggests,[47] have been his contemporary 'Unṣurī's immediate source for his verse romance.

If the existence of an Arabic intermediary seems likely — though not beyond doubt (cf. below) — and, if so, the later passage into New Persian presents no great problems, the earlier stages of the transmission are all the more obscure. What was Sahl's model for his Arabic version? It is not quite out of the question that he translated directly from the Greek, for this is the period when Greek was known by some of the professional, scientific translators; but Sahl, in spite of his association with the "Library of Wisdom", is not known to have belonged to those. Or was his model in Pahlavī? He was himself a Persian by birth, and he belonged to "der bedeutenden Gruppe von Schriftstellern, die im Arabischen alte persische litterarische Tradition fortgesetzt haben".[48] It is indeed tempting to combine these facts with a piece of information contained in an admittedly late and perhaps not very reliable source, the literary biographer Daulatshāh (15th cent.). He tells us that one day the governor of

108

---

[43] *Fihrist*, p. 120 (ed. Flügel), trans. Dodge 1970, pp. 262 f.

[44] On Sahl, see *EI* IV, 67; Brockelmann I, 516, and S I, 213; Gottschalk 1965, p. 123; Sezgin I, 272 f. Sahl was a Shu'ūbī, i.e., he opposed the Arabic dominance within Islam and, a Persian by birth, worked for the revitalization of Persian culture. His literary activities seem to have been mostly within the belles-lettres sphere; he was famous for a book of fables, in which he imitated *Kalīla wa-Dimna*, and for a treatise in praise of greediness (which has survived).

[45] Al-Bīrūnī's *Fihrist*, printed by C. E. Sachau in his ed. of *Chronologie orientalischer Völker*, Leipzig 1878 (reprint 1923), p. XXXXIV.

[46] It is doubtful whether al-Bīrūnī knew any Greek at all (see Shafi 1967, p. 1, with further refs.), and (according to G. A. Saliba in *Al-Bīrūnī Commemorative Volume*, Karachi 1979, pp. 255 f.) "his knowledge of Syriac was rather superficial". F. Rosenthal's contribution to the *Biruni Symposium* (ed. E. Yarshater & D. Bishop, Leiden 1976), "al-Bīrūnī between Greece and India", was not available to me.

[47] Shafi 1967, pp. 1 f.

[48] J. H. Kramers in *EI* IV, 67a.

Khorāsān, the Amīr 'Abdu'llāh b. Ṭāhir (AD 828–844), was approached by a man who offered him a book as a present, namely, "the Romance of Wāmiq and 'Adhrā, a pleasant tale which wise men had compiled for King Nūshirwān". The Amīr, however, immediately ordered the book and other similar "compositions of the Magians" to be destroyed.[49] The veracity of this story has been doubted on the grounds that it is strange for an old Pahlavī book from the days of Khusrau Anūshīrvān (Chosroes I, reigned 531–578) to carry an Arabic title;[50] but certainly Daulatshāh's account permits of the interpretation that it was in Arabic translation that the old romance was presented to the Amīr, and the coincidence in time with Sahl's translation is striking. However, there are other reasons to treat Daulatshāh's information with the utmost caution: at this late date "Vāmiq and 'Adhrā" had become a type-name for a romantic couple, which might have been given more or less at random to the old Pahlavī verse romance of the anecdote, and the placing of that alleged piece of Pahlavī poetry precisely in the reign of Khusrau can be purely conventional, reflecting the nationalistic myth of a great literary past.[51]

So, if we clearly cannot accept Daulatshā's information as evidence *tout court*, there are, on the other hand, good reasons to pursue this line a little further: the anecdote may after all contain at least a kernel of truth; the coincidence with Sahl's date as well as with his Persian origin is certainly worth attention; and there is nothing improbable in itself that a Greek novel should have passed Sassanian Iran on its way to 'Abbāsid Iraq (we saw, for instance, the *Alexander Romance* take that way, although it passed Syriac as well). Hellenism and philhellenism have of course a long tradition in Iran, from Alexander through the Seleucid and Parthian periods up to Shapur I (*c.* AD 240–270) and Khusrau I.[52] Antagonism towards Rome does not necessarily exclude openness to Greek influence, for which through the centuries there were numerous occasions, normal

---

[49] E. G. Browne's trans. of Daulatshāh's *Lives of the Poets*, p. 30, as quoted by himself in Browne II, pp. 275 f. Cf. also Browne I, pp. 12 f., 346 f.

[50] Horn 1901, p. 178.

[51] The "doubtful authority" of Daulatshāh is stressed by both V. F. Büchner in *EI* IV, 1107b, and Shafi 1967, p. 1, but neither of them articulates his doubts, as regards this specific piece of information; I owe to B. Utas the two reasons for caution specified here. Cf. further his own contribution (above, n. 42).

[52] Cf. Peters 1968, pp. 41–54; O. Klíma in Rypka 1968, pp. 53–58; Rundgren 1976, pp. 140 f.; *CHIran* III, Index, *s.vv.* "Hellenism", "Greeks in the Iranian Empire", and "Byzantine Empire" (see esp. pp. 568–592); and R. N. Frye, *The History of Ancient Iran* (München 1984), pp. 172–175.

interchange between neighbouring countries quite apart. To mention just a few concrete examples: inhabitants of captured Byzantine territories and prisoners of war were resettled in Sassanian Iran;[53] in peace-time Greek artists and workmen were borrowed for building activities;[54] and, as is well known, King Khusrau welcomed at his court of Ctesiphon Greek intellectuals no longer wanted in Justinian's Christian empire.[55] Furthermore, he founded the medical school of Jundīshāpūr, which was to play such an important, literally international role for learning well into the Islamic period. Greek residents, and knowledge of the Greek language, are therefore to be reckoned with at various dates and at various places in Sassanian Iran, not only among the Nestorians. Thus it is at least conceivable for a Greek novel to have been translated directly from Greek into Pahlavī, Sassanian Iran providing the means for it to get round the Christian Syrian needle's eye.

Our hypothetical chain of translations is already long enough — from Greek into Pahlavī into Arabic into New Persian prose and verse — and further links would of course be possible (in particular, Syriac before or after Pahlavī).[56] But the fact that the story in ʿUnṣurī's version is still recognizable as a Greek novel should perhaps warn us not to increase unnecessarily the number of intermediaries. Rather, what has been presented above may be described as a maximum view. In fact, the other extreme has recently been argued by I. Kaladze, who advances the bold hypothesis that ʿUnṣurī himself knew Greek (allegedly from his stay in "Byzantine" Nisibis) and translated the story directly from Greek prose into Persian verse.[57] B. Utas, in his forthcoming study, is also prepared, on linguistic grounds, to dismiss the idea of a Pahlavī or Syriac intermediary and, in addition, suggests that Sahl's *V & A* was perhaps another story altogether, unconnected with *M & P* as well as with ʿUnṣurī's *V & A*.[58] It is to be hoped that further scrutiny of ʿUnṣurī's version, especially

---

[53] Peters 1968, pp. 44 f. (with further refs.); *CHIran* III, pp. 570 f.

[54] *CHIran* III, pp. 570, 591 f.

[55] See Agathias 2.28–32 and cf. Peters 1968, p. 47 (on "the philosophical and philhellenic interests of Khusraw"), and *CHIran* III, pp. 161, 571, 591 f.

[56] V. F. Büchner, *EI* IV, 1108a, speaks of the possibility of a "syrische Vermittlung" between Greek and Pahlavī; Syriac between Pahlavī and Arabic, on the other hand, would conform to the way of transmission of the *Alexander Romance*, cf. above, p. 104.

[57] Kaladze 1983, p. 52; cf. Utas (above, n. 42).

[58] Utas (above, n. 42).

of the forms of the Greek proper names,[59] and a close comparison of the overlapping parts of the Greek and Persian fragments[60] will bring us nearer to a solution of this problem.

110   It is perhaps significant that *M & P* — the only novel, so far, which demonstrably had an Oriental *Nachleben* in translation — belongs to the early, "non-sophistic" type and did not, as far as we know, survive the "dark centuries" in its original language to be received by the Byzantine humanists. Its popularity in the Roman imperial period, on the other hand, is proved by the papyrus fragments, some literary testimonia, and a couple of mosaics from Syrian Antioch (dated round AD 200).[61] It may then be unwise to concentrate our attention, as we did earlier, on 9th-century Byzantium and the novels that were read and copied by the humanists there and which were later favourably received in Western Europe. It may well be that the novels of the more popular kind, which circulated in the hellenized parts of the Orient in late antiquity, had at least as great a chance of an Eastern *Nachleben*, only through different channels. This idea receives some indirect support from B. L. Perry's investigation of the origin of the well-known 13th-century Florentine manuscript (*Cod. Laur. Conv. Soppr.* 627), which is, among other things, the *codex unicus* for the two non-sophistic novels of Chariton and Xenophon Ephesius.[62] He finds that it was written, near the middle of the 13th century, somewhere "on the western borders of Syria and Armenia" and that it attests to an "isolated Asiatic tradition of a whole series of rare Greek texts, and recensions of ancient texts, which were not propagated in Byzantium or in the West".[63] In other words, viewed from our perspective: the sophistic novels travel the main road via humanistic Constantinople, whereas the non-sophistic ones[64] survive in

---

[59] On the use of linguistic evidence to prove the existence of Pahlavī intermediaries between Greek and Arabic, cf. Kunitzsch 1975, esp. pp. 277–281. Utas (above, n. 42) bases his exclusion of a Pahlavī intermediary on a preliminary study of the proper names in *V & A*.

[60] For a beginning, see T. Hägg, "Metiochus at Polycrates' Court", *Eranos* 83, 1985, 92–102 [No. **9** in this volume].

[61] See Maehler 1976.

[62] Perry 1966; cf. Perry 1967, p. 344 n. 2.

[63] Perry 1966, pp. 424–430; quotations pp. 425, 424. Cf. Perry 1967, pp. 347 f. n. 9.

[64] Not exclusively the non-sophistic ones, however: the *Cod. Laur.* contains Longus (the only complete MS of this novel) and Achilles Tatius as well; cf. Perry 1966, pp. 418, 425.

more hidden circumstances in the East and come to our knowledge only by accident, so to speak: through a sole manuscript, copied in the 13th century on the eastern borders of the Byzantine empire; through the find, in Egypt, of a 7th-century parchment containing fragments of Chariton and the *Chione Romance*;[65] through the fragments of a Persian translation of an Arabic translation …

We may surmise that any non-sophistic novel which survived in the East in translation owed its survival to a process which had little in common with the organized translation activities devoted to philosophy, medicine, and the like. We are concerned with several centuries of practical bilingualism among educated people in the hellenized East, especially among those employed in trade and administration. Greek kept its position as an administrative language in eastern provinces like Egypt and Syria even after the Arabic conquest: it was only gradually ousted by Arabic from about AD 700.[66] This bilingualism will have offered rich — though naturally unrecorded — opportunities for the passage of such light literature as these novels from one language into the other. As regards the further passages during the Islamic period conditions appear to have been different. At least, the scraps of information we possess about *V & A* point at the court milieux (of caliphs, governors, sultans) as providing particularly fertile soil for the survival and renewal of the genre.[67] The competence to translate was at that time maybe to be found exclusively in the neighbourhood of the professional translation centres — witness Sahl — but the customers, or audience, were no doubt others than those who ordered Aristotle.

We can now see why the Arabic *M & P* — if that is a correct description of Sahl's *V & A* — escaped the net cast for Greek novels in Arabic translation: not only is it apparently lost (or, at least, not yet discovered), but it circulated under an impenetrable Arabic title, and *anonymously* (or under the translator's name). It is therefore tempting to speculate about the origin of other stories which likewise have titles made up of the names of two lovers and occur in the same contexts as *V & A*. One

III

[65] The *Cod. Thebanus deperditus*, publ. by U. Wilcken in *APF* I, 1901, 227–272.

[66] Cf. Rosenthal 1965, pp. 14–16; Gottschalk 1965, pp. 116 f.; Kunitzsch 1975, pp. 271–273.

[67] These court milieux are where Arabic and Persian *adab* literature, or belles-lettres, was generally cultivated; see Lichtenstadter 1974, pp. 106 f.

example is the "romantic epic" *Shād-bahr u 'Aynu'l-ḥayāt*, a title which like *V & A* occurs in lists of both al Bīrūnī's and 'Unṣurī's writings and means "Happy of Fate and Life Source";[68] could it have something to do with Chariton's *Chaereas and Callirhoe*? Again in Ibn an-Nadīm's famous catalogue, *Kitāb al-Fihrist* (composed *c.* AD 988), no less than 136 stories about lovers are listed:[69] it is obvious that, alongside Indian and genuinely Persian romantic stories, Greek novels as well may be at the bottom of some of them. In addition, the *Fihrist* gives a mysterious list of eleven titles under the heading "Names of the Books of the Greeks in the field of Night-Stories and Histories", to which B. E. Perry and F. Rosenthal have already called attention.[70] These few hints will have to suffice. As R. Walzer stated on several occasions: besides the papyri, the Arabic versions (and, we may add, translations of lost such versions) are our best hope for increased knowledge of ancient Greek literature.[71] This obviously applies to the novels as well.

2. Adaptations

Early translations of popular works of fiction, in the West as well as in the East, were often, at the same time, adaptations: and so 'Unṣurī's *V & A*, having perhaps passed a couple of intermediaries, is in many ways another novel than the original *M & P*. But in the present context I reserve the term "adaptations" for such more drastic, deliberate changes of a story's nature which allow it — or rather: parts of it — to function in a totally new context. As an example, it happens that we are again

---

[68] See Shafi 1967, pp. 1 f., and Rypka 1968, p. 175, for this and other titles. For two further 11th-century Persian romantic epics, *Varqa u Gul-shāh* and *Vīs u Rāmīn*, and on the supposed Pahlavī source of the latter, see Rypka 1968, pp. 132, 177. Cf. also the material collected by Grunebaum 1963, p. 585 n. 88. That the Greek *Ninus Romance* should have had some influence on the later metamorphoses of Semiramis in Oriental tradition, ending up in the romantic heroine Shīrīn in a Persian epic and a romance, is another possibility which might repay a closer look; cf. Eilers 1971, pp. 47–59, and the review by F. Rundgren in *Or. Suec.* 23–24, 1974–1975, 225 f.

[69] *Fihrist* (ed. Flügel), pp. 304 ff., trans. Dodge 1970, pp. 719–724. For a survey of Arabic book titles within the "amusement" sector, see Dodge 1954, pp. 537–539.

[70] *Fihrist* (ed. Flügel), pp. 305 f., trans. Dodge 1970, p. 718; cf. Perry 1961, pp. 12 f.; Rosenthal 1962, p. 37, and 1968, p. 186 n. 2.

[71] Cf. Walzer 1945–46, p. 171, and 1962a, pp. 180 f.

able to use *M & P*. As I have tried to demonstrate elsewhere,[72] there is a fair chance that precisely this novel was utilized for the composition of a Christian martyrdom; namely, for the story of the young Christian girl Parthenope, who had to fight against a Roman emperor, Constantine, and a Persian king for her virginity and faith, and who chose suicide rather than surrender. This martyrdom was presumably composed in Greek, but it has survived in full only in Arabic; it was translated into Arabic by way of Coptic, and parts of the Coptic version have recently been discovered and published.[73]

If it is correct that the Parthenope martyrdom builds on *M & P* — besides the name of the heroine, a number of motifs and elements of narrative technique point in that direction[74] — we are in a position to study the Christian adaptor at work. The motif "virginity", which was in all likelihood strongly underlined already in the pagan novel (cf. the heroine's "eloquent" name), has been taken over and further elaborated. The two rulers who threaten the girl's virginity also look like figures from a novel. But the second-most important limb of the story has been amputated, the hero Metiochus; and the girl's fiancé, to whom she refuses to be unfaithful in spite of temptations and threats, is Christ. There can be no ordinary happy ending with recognition and reunion; instead, the girl throws herself into the fire and expires (no trick, no apparent death, as presumably in the model), and so becomes a celebrated martyr. It goes without saying that the story has been stripped of all references to pagan gods and cults; the role played in the novels by Fate (Tyche) or personifications like Fame has been taken over by the Devil, and only in the final scene of prayer and sacrifice are there some details which betray the pagan origin. More important, the suicide itself is a motif which hardly suits a martyrdom, but which the adaptor had to swallow, if he wanted to use the novel's plot.

Unfortunately, neither date nor provenance of the Parthenope martyrdom can be determined. The Coptic fragment belongs to a 9th/10th-century codex, and the extant Arabic manuscripts are later still. The bare existence of a Coptic version of course means that the story circulated

113

---

[72] Hägg 1984.

[73] Coquin 1981.

[74] For details, see Hägg 1984.

in Egypt, but as far as I can see there is nothing in the story itself which necessarily links it to that country;[75] the Greek original, if any, may have been written anywhere in the eastern parts of the Christian Roman empire, and the only certain *terminus post quem* is Constantine's reign. Anyway, as regards our supposed model, *M & P*, its popularity in the East not only far into the imperial period, but into the early Byzantine period, seems to be confirmed; the way is paved for its other Oriental reappearance as *V & A* as well.

What guaranteed the Parthenope martyrdom a large readership and survival to our days is the fact that it became part of the Sahidic recension of the Coptic *Synaxarium* for 21 Tybi (16 January), on which day the commemoration of the girl's death was celebrated.[76] This *Synaxarium* is extant in Arabic in several manuscripts. In addition, the Arabic version of the story has been transmitted in other manuscripts, separately from the *Synaxarium*.[77] Thus, through its metamorphosis into a martyrdom, the pagan novel was able to live on for more than a millennium in Christian Arabic literature. In a similar manner, many elements of the ancient Greek novels (motifs, narrative technicalities) were assured a *Nachleben* in the various literatures of Oriental Christianity: they were first absorbed by popular Christian literature in Greek, such as the apocryphal Acts of the Apostles, martyrdoms, and lives of saints, then translated or imitated in similar products in Coptic, Syriac, Armenian, Arabic, Ethiopic etc. Whereas it may be considered as an established fact that separate elements of the novels were utilized in this way by Christian writers, it still remains to be investigated whether the Parthenope martyrdom is unique in being (in my opinion) built almost entirely on the plot of one particular pagan novel. It is to be expected, however, that a thorough and systematic search of the great

[75] Coquin 1981, pp. 356–357, finds some Egyptian "coloration nationale"; *contra*: Hägg 1984, p. 80 (with n. 67).

[76] *Corp. Script. Christ. Or.* 49, 1909, 399–403 (Arabic text), and 78, 1922, 382–387 (Latin trans.); *Patr. Or.* 11, 1915, 653–661 (Arabic text with French trans.); the text of both is based on a 17th-century MS. However, these two editions are now superseded by Coquin 1981, who for his French translation has collated three more Arabic MSS, besides the Coptic fragment.

[77] One of the MSS that Coquin 1981 has collated (Beirut, *Bibl. Or.* 614) belongs to such a separate tradition and gives "un texte très remanié"; in addition, Coquin knows of three further MSS which contain the Parthenope martyrdom alongside other lives of saints.

treasures of ancient story-telling that lie hidden in the various synax-aria in Oriental languages[78] would yield more instances of this particu-lar kind of afterlife.[79]

3. Creative borrowing

The third kind of reception of the Greek novel in the East, the "pro-ductive assimilation"[80] of this particular Classical inheritance into the various branches of Oriental narrative literature, is probably the most important, and at the same time the most elusive and difficult one to study. It demands from its investigator an intimate knowledge of both the Classical and the Oriental material as well as awareness of the compli-cated network of influence between the cultures and between the literary genres within each culture. In comparison, translations are a simple and straightforward object of study; the influence of one specific Greek work on (say) a specific Arabic work may also sometimes be open to demon-stration; but when it comes to the identification of motifs or narrative elements from the novels, which — to use Prof. Rundgren's words in a similar context — may occur as "erratische Blöcke" in Oriental litera-ture,[81] the difficulties tend to be formidable. The novels lack the kind of distinctive terminology or original ideas which make the correspond-ing search in the fields of philosophy, grammar,[82] or the exact sciences more immediately promising; the novels, in contrast, consist of strings of rather commonplace motifs (some originating from the folk-tales) and mostly use a narrative technique resembling that of popular story-telling in general. Their sheer triviality thus tends to obscure the ways of borrowing and process of assimilation.

There is also a more specific reason: many scholars, from P.-D. Huet

---

[78] The Ethiopic Synaxarium, *Maṣḥafa Sĕnkĕsār*, is available in the English trans. of Budge 1928, who calls it "a vast storehouse of Christian legends and traditions and popular folk-lore" (I, p. XI). The Coptic-Arabic Jacobite Synaxarium is published, with French trans., in various volumes of *Patr. Or.*: 1:3, 1907; 3:3, 1909; 11:5, 1915; 16:2, 1922.

[79] R.-G. Coquin has in a letter kindly drawn my attention to the "romantic" character of the story of Θαλάσσιον/Bāḥrān; cf. Graf I, p. 542, and add the Ethiopic version in *Patr. Or.* 1, 1907, 589–597, and Budge 1928, IV, pp. 987–991.

[80] See above, n. 7.

[81] Rundgren 1970–71, p. 83.

[82] Cf. Rundgren 1976.

to G. Anderson,[83] have claimed — and there is nothing improbable about the claim, only the same difficulties when it comes to proof — that the emergence of the Greek novel in Hellenistic times is due to influence from the old Oriental narrative literature.[84] We thus run the risk of arguing in a circle: what we are apt to identify as a "Greek-novel element" in an Arabic piece of narrative may be a motif or a narrative device which the Greek novelists originally borrowed from the East — and which has perhaps arrived in Arabic literature through other channels, without making the Hellenistic detour. Finally, the fact that comparatively little remains of precisely the early and popular ("non-sophistic") Greek novel, which may be particularly relevant in this Eastern context,[85] still more reduces the chances of finding unambiguous cases of influence and borrowing.

The Oriental literary material which potentially has, directly or indirectly, assimilated elements of the Greek novel is very large, even if we exclude, in this context, the Christian literature. Besides the mass of pure fiction, of which the *Arabian Nights* (hereafter: *AN*) is only the most obvious example, a search of this kind would have to include the narrative parts of other productive genres as well, such as historical and biographical works (of a more or less romanticized character).[86] However, for the present purpose I shall restrict my comments to a small corpus of texts from the *AN*, namely, the eight or nine stories or parts of stories which the Arabist G. E. von Grunebaum has singled out as being clearly

[83] Huet's *Traité de l'Origine des romans* of 1670 is best consulted in the critical, annotated ed. by A. Kok (Amsterdam 1942); cf. esp. pp. 120 ff., 148 ff. Anderson's recent book (1984), while not solving, as it claims, the problem of the origins of the novel, has the great merit of assembling a rich material from Oriental sources (from Sumerian myths to Arabic and Persian narrative literature and modern folk-tales) which shows more or less close resemblance to the story-patterns and motifs of the ancient Greek and Roman novels. The handling of this material, however, leaves much to be desired: many of the parallels adduced are less than convincing, the author completely fails in making a distinction between phenomenologically explicable similarities and really significant ones, and he makes no real effort to sift his material chronologically or trace the actual ways of influence. Cf. further below, n. 87.

[84] For the various theories of an Oriental (Egyptian etc.) origin, see Reardon 1971, pp. 318 ff. Lacôte 1911, in a largely neglected study, advocated an *Indian* origin, pointing at the story-within-a-story structure exhibited by Antonius Diogenes, in particular; *contra*: Keith 1928, pp. 365–370 ("The Romance in Greece and India").

[85] Cf. above, (1), and Perry 1959, pp. 13 f.

[86] Cf. Rosenthal 1965, pp. 345 ff., and 1968, pp. 186 ff. ("The Historical Novel"). Lichtenstadter 1974, pp. 106–111, gives a useful survey of Arabic *adab* or belles-lettres.

dependent on Greek novels,[87] most of them exhibiting the typical "combination of travel adventures with a love action".[88] I shall briefly indicate on what more specific traits of the stories von Grunebaum bases his conclusion — his detailed and circumspect analysis deserves to be read in full by everyone interested in the Greek novel — before adding some comments of my own bearing on our previous discussion.

First, it is important to note that these stories, or parts of stories, according to von Grunebaum differ *in their general pattern* from the rest of the *AN*, a pattern in which he recognizes the Greek novel. Furthermore, common *motifs* are not so conspicuous a part of the Greek heritage in the *AN* as are common "patterns of style, patterns of presentation, and emotional conventions".[89] The reason why the Greek influence has passed relatively unnoticed is that the elements do not occur in isolation but are mixed with elements of different provenance: Indian, Persian, Arabic, Jewish etc. They tend to occur as "floating details" in new narrative contexts: "the organic system in which, and for which, they were developed [*sc.*, in the Greek novel] is torn asunder, some impressive details are preserved and applied where they are considered fitting but with no view to their real function".[90] The whole Greek environment — personal and geographical names, historical and mythological allusions, gods and cults — is replaced by a genuinely Islamic milieu. When such items are sometimes actually taken over, their origin is effectively concealed, as when "resignation to the whims of Fate" appears as "resignation to the will of Allāh",[91] rather like the kind of Christian substitution which we observed in the Parthenope martyrdom.

116

---

[87] Grunebaum 1942; the stories in question are listed on pp. 282 f., with page references to E. Littmann's German trans. of *AN*, 1921–28. (This edition was unavailable to me, so my own references to the *AN* are to a later edition of the same translation, with a different pagination: Littmann 1953, I-VI.) Cf. also Grunebaum 1946, pp. 305–310; 1963, pp. 389–395 (with important additions in the notes, pp. 577 ff.). Many other points of contact between the *AN* and the Greek (and Roman) novels are discussed by Anderson 1984; cf., in particular, pp. 152–156 on Lollianus' *Phoenician Tales* (carried away, however, by his own overall thesis of Oriental models for the novels, Anderson does not even consider the possibility that the influence may have gone *from* Lollianus *to* the *AN*). On Petronius and the *AN*, see also Dornseiff 1938.

[88] Grunebaum 1946, p. 305.

[89] Grunebaum 1942, p. 278.

[90] Grunebaum 1942, p. 281.

[91] Grunebaum 1942, p. 282.

The narrative pattern most commonly overtaken is at once the basic one of the novel: love (at first sight) — separation — travel adventures (*inter alia*: shipwreck; attack by pirates; attempt to seduce the chaste hero; new marriage of the heroine, who however preserves her chastity) — reunion.[92] The happy ending, no constant feature in other parts of the *AN*, is obligatory.[93] The glorification of chastity is paramount, and the beauty of both protagonists is stressed. Otherwise there is a certain vagueness in the characterization of the heroes, and some of them show a passivity resembling that of the heroes of the novels; furthermore, they are generally not endowed with supernatural powers, in contrast to the heroes of other Arabic tales.[94] The attitude to love and some of the terminology used for its description are similar,[95] e.g., love as suffering or disease, "the close connection in the lovers' mind of love and death",[96] the extreme sentimentality (tears, fainting-fits) — being a lover almost becomes a "profession".[97] The Islamic condemnation of self-destruction makes the motif "(attempted) suicide" rare, but it is probably significant that it does occur a couple of times in these tales.[98] Further shared motifs are "apparent death" (through drugging), letters, dreams, the participation of the people in the fate of the lovers, and the amazement (*ekplēxis*) reaction.[99] There is an "oracle", in the guise of a horoscope, forecasting the dangers as well as the happy ending;[100] we meet the familiar figure of the accompanying friend,[101] witness the "funeral of, and erection of a mausoleum for, the hero, who, however, is still alive",[102] and experience various recognition scenes.[103] The Greek influence is also apparent, ac-

117

---

[92] For all the references, with Greek parallels, see Grunebaum 1942, esp. pp. 282 f.

[93] Grunebaum 1942, p. 289.

[94] Grunebaum 1942, p. 283. Characterization in general, however, and especially that of the women, is a field in which von Grunebaum finds these *AN* tales to be comparatively independent (cf. Grunebaum 1942, p. 285).

[95] Grunebaum 1942, pp. 283–285.

[96] Grunebaum 1946, p. 308; 1963, p. 392.

[97] Grunebaum 1946, p. 308; 1963, p. 393.

[98] Grunebaum 1942, p. 283 (with n. 68); 1946, pp. 307 f.; 1963, p. 392.

[99] Grunebaum 1942, p. 289.

[100] Grunebaum 1942, p. 282 n. 58; 1946, p. 307; 1963, pp. 391 f.

[101] Grunebaum 1942, pp. 282 n. 58, 289.

[102] Grunebaum 1942, p. 283; 1946, p. 307; 1963, p. 392.

[103] Grunebaum 1942, p. 282 (with the warning that the "recognition" motif occurs in "non-Greek" *AN* stories as well).

cording to von Grunebaum, in some patterns of style (antithesis, parallelism of clauses)[104] and in the use of such rhetorical devices as the detailed description (*ekphrasis*) of gardens, palaces etc. and the theoretical discussion (*zētēma*) of topics like "the nature of love".[105]

All these are indeed essential elements of the Greek novel; but, it needs to be stressed once more, in the *AN* they do not all occur in one single story, and they are mostly contaminated with motifs of other extraction. Reading the stories singled out by von Grunebaum, one never gets the feeling that this "is" a Greek novel, just barely camouflaged to fit the Islamic surroundings; so great is the difference in both substance and spirit. Yet attentive examination reveals still more details, notably in phraseology and narrative technique, which escaped von Grunebaum but seem to confirm his thesis; there will be occasion below to specify some of them.[106] First, however, we shall take a look at the possible ways of influence.

Von Grunebaum emphatically excluded the possibility that the resemblances could be due to a common, independent inflow, into both novel and *AN*, from older Near Eastern sources: "The style and form patterns which from the novel have found their way into the *AN* are Greek; and even if they were not originally Greek, they did not pass into the *AN* directly from a hypothetical oriental source, but unmistakably came through the medium of later Greek literature".[107] He had to leave open,

---

[104] Grunebaum 1942, p. 286.

[105] Grunebaum 1942, pp. 286 f. For the interest in this Platonic topic at the court of the Caliph al-Ma'mūn in 9th-century Baghdad, see F. Rosenthal in *Islamic Culture* 14, 1940, 387–422, p. 421. Did Sahl b. Hārūn (cf. above, pp. 107 f.) perhaps take part in such discussions — and quote from *M & P*?!

[106] Some further similarities in motifs: Littmann 1953, V, p. 314/Char. 8.8.12–14 (the faithful friend rewarded by marriage to sister of heroine/hero); V, p. 378/Char. 2.2.2–3 (heroine's beauty in bath admired by women); V, p. 393/Char. 3.7.4 (hero/heroine sees in dream the beloved suffering, wakes up with a cry); V, pp. 653–655/Ach. Tat. 5.1 (enchanted tourist in Alexandria); V, p. 658/*Hist. Ap.* 33 (heroine offered for sale at slave auction); V, pp. 690–694 (much in Maryam the Belt-Maker's "prehistory" reminiscent of Chariton's Callirhoe); V, p. 701/Char. 1.1.14 ("ward das helle Tageslicht finster vor ihrem Angesicht"). The way the hero's love for the heroine is awakened in the story of Saif al-Mulūk and Badī'at al-Jamāl, through a *picture* (Littmann 1953, V, pp. 247 ff.; on this motif, see Rohde 1960, p. 53 [50] n. 4), provides us with an alternative explanation of the motif appearing in two Syrian mosaics illustrating the *Ninus Romance* (cf. Maehler 1976, p. 1 [with further refs.]; Hägg 1983, Fig. 4): Ninus lying on his bed with a picture of a girl in his hand — this may be the very beginning of the love story.

[107] Grunebaum 1942, p. 281.

however, the question of when and through what channels this influence was exercised, admitting that "there exists no documentary evidence to prove the actual transmission of the classical elements".[108] Tentatively, and comparing with other Greek influence on Arabic literature, he pointed at 7th-century Syria, where "the vitality of the classical forms of life up to the very eve of the Muslim conquest is attested", noting as well (as we did above, pp. 110 f.) "the close administrative cooperation between the Arabs and the conquered Greeks".[109] Briefly returning to the question in 1963, von Grunebaum seems rather to embrace F. Rosenthal's view that the Arabic acquaintance with the Greek novels is no earlier than the 9th century.[110] Neither of the two scholars, however, substantiates this assertion or tries to give a concrete form to the idea of the "appearance" of the Greek novel in Arabic in the 9th century — are we to envisage translations (by whom, and of what novels?) or more indirect ways of influence?

As is well known, the compilation of the *AN* was a long and complex process, which continued from (at least) the 9th through the 12th century; the Arabic work was inspired by, and partly built on, a similar Persian collection, which in turn drew on Indian sources, in particular.[111] Consequently, both possibilities are theoretically open: the Greek influence may not have been exercised until the Arabic formative process in the 9th century (or even later), but may as well, wholly or in part, belong to the prehistory of the *AN*, working on its (Persian? Syriac? Arabic?) sources. This is not the place, and I certainly do not have the competence, to enter into a full discussion of these intricate problems. Yet it seems to me that any attempt at a solution must start from two ends: not only by further analysis of the *AN* tales themselves, but also by tak-

118

---

[108] Grunebaum 1942, p. 290, with n. 124 on "the methodology of establishing literary or cultural dependence whenever full documentation of the actual borrowing cannot be obtained"; cf., in a similar vein, Rundgren 1976, p. 138.

[109] Grunebaum 1942, p. 291.

[110] Rosenthal 1968, p. 186 n. 2 (commenting on the titles of Greek novels (?) listed in the *Fihrist*, cf. above, n. 70); Grunebaum 1963, p. 581 n. 56: "Bekanntschaft mit der griechisch-byzantinischen Romanliteratur beginnt wohl nicht vor dem neunten Jahrhundert, also wenigstens hundert Jahre nach dem Eindringen persischer Belletristik" (with a ref. to the 1st ed. of Rosenthal's work, 1952, p. 164 n. 2).

[111] Cf. Horovitz 1927; Grunebaum 1963, pp. 376 f.; Lichtenstadter 1974, pp. 112–114.

ing into account the kind of data assembled and discussed in the first section of the present article. The two approaches meet in the crucial issue: what kind of Greek novel, the popular or the sophistic (or both), is it that found its way into the *AN*?

This is a distinction that von Grunebaum fails to make himself;[112] but if we examine his evidence closely it becomes clear that most of the motifs, patterns, and expressions referred to (cf. the exemplification above) either characterize the genre as a whole or are most typical of the non-sophistic novels. Only some of the special rhetorical devices noted are more familiar from the sophistic specimens, but their appearance in the *AN* may be explained in another way: since they are not exclusively typical of the novels, they may alternatively be looked upon as part of a more general influence of Greek rhetoric on Arabic literature.[113] Comparing the "Greek" features in the *AN* tales with novels like that of Achilles Tatius, von Grunebaum speaks of "a loss of refinement", a lowering of the artistic level, or "the inevitable recrudescence of the popular character".[114] If instead we assume that most of the influence derived from novels like Xenophon's *Ephesiaca* or still less "sophisticated" specimens, lost to us except for a few fragments but mirrored in some early Christian literature,[115] then there is no need for the popular character to "recrudesce" — it was there all the time. This, in turn, would mean that we should rather ascribe these common features to an early influence from Greek popular novels on the sources of the *AN* than to the existence, in 9th-century Baghdad, of actual translations of the sophistic novels.

Some additional observations on the narrative structure and phraseology of our "Greek" *AN* tales in fact confirm their typological closeness to the kind of novel represented by Xenophon. There is the same naive and stereotyped handling of the parallel action, with fixed linking phrases

119

---

[112] von Grunebaum's general description of the Greek novel (see esp. Grunebaum 1942, pp. 280, 283, 286) reveals that he is chiefly acquainted with the three sophistic specimens.

[113] Cf. Grunebaum 1942, pp. 286 f.

[114] Grunebaum 1946, p. 306 (1963, p. 390). He furthermore speaks of the Greek novel in general as being on a much higher artistic level than the apocryphal Acts of the Apostles (1942, p. 280), without considering what was probably the general standard of the early, popular novels. Perry 1959, pp. 13 f., while referring to von Grunebaum, tacitly corrects these misconceptions.

[115] Cf. Hägg 1983, p. 161.

of the type "Also stand es um Saif el-Mulūk und den Wesir Sāʾid. Sehen wir aber nunmehr, was die Prinzessin Badīʿat el-Dschamāl tat!"[116] The ever recurring fainting-fits — for sorrow or joy, horror or love — are likewise described in a stereotyped phraseology close to Xenophon's: "… dann sank er ohnmächtig nieder. … Als er wieder zu sich kam …".[117] We recognize the outbursts of lament, with more or less detailed retrospective contents, which regularly interfoliate the action in the periods when hero and heroine are separated; only in the *AN* they burst out in verses, in the novels in rhetorical prose.[118] One of the tales exhibits a long final recapitulation in indirect speech, in which the hero tells his sister of what he has experienced.[119] And so on: it would be possible to prolong this list of similarities, and to set up similar lists for Chariton and the *Historia Apollonii regis Tyri*. But this is no doubt a highly dangerous kind of material, if you are out for historical connections, as dangerous as common motifs. It needs a careful investigation of the narrative conventions generally in the *AN*, before any conclusions about a Greek influence on our selected tales can be drawn. And the possibility of an influx in the reverse direction, from older Oriental narratives into the Greek popular novel, must be constantly kept in mind.

To end on a somewhat less austere note, I would like to call attention to the frame-story into which one of von Grunebaum's selected *AN* tales is inserted. It is the story of the Prince Saif al-Mulūk and the Princess Badīʿat al-Jamāl,[120] which is preceded by a long introductory tale[121] building up the listeners' expectations as to the unique qualities of the story itself. We are told that once upon a time the Persian King

---

[116] Littmann 1953, V, p. 293 (cf. pp. 299, 308, 310; 377, 387, 456, 465 etc.). For the corresponding linking phrases in Xen. Eph., see Hägg 1971, pp. 158 ff. (on Char., pp. 141 ff.).

[117] Littmann 1953, V, p. 395 (cf. pp. 407, 421, 432, 433, 443, 453, 454 etc.). Corresponding phrases in Xen. Eph. 1.9.2–3; 2.4.5; 3.9.7 etc.; cf. Char. 8.1.8–10 (very similar to Littmann 1953, I, p. 497).

[118] Littmann 1953, V, pp. 297–303; 460, 474, 475, 480; 694 f. etc. For the corresponding monologues in the novels, see Hägg 1971, pp. 262 f., 273 f., 283.

[119] Littmann 1953, V, pp. 499 f. (cf. pp. 409, 423; 473 f.); on the novels, see Hägg 1971, pp. 253–255, 257–261, 267–273, 278–280, 328 f. — Compare the end of another *AN* story, where all the adventures are recorded and laid in an archive as a reminder of "des Schicksals Wechselfällen" (Littmann 1953, I, p. 500), with the end of Xen. Eph.

[120] Littmann 1953, V, pp. 228–315.

[121] *Ibid.*, pp. 219–227.

of Khorāsān, a true connaisseur of old tales, ordered the wise merchant Hasan to tell him a story, more wonderful than any he had yet heard; if he succeeded, he would become the king's grand vizier, if not, he would lose all his possessions and be forced to go into exile. Hasan asks for one year's respite and sends five highly educated mamlūks, with five thousand dinars each, to five different countries to search for the most wonderful story ever heard. The one who finally succeeds is the fifth of them, who was sent to Syria and Egypt. In Damascus he is brought to a learned old man, who is a celebrated story-teller, and asks him if he happens to know the story of Saif and Badīʿat. Astonished at the specific question the old man admits that he knows that story, but adds that it is not the sort of story told at street corners. He invites the mamlūk to his house, produces a book containing the story, and allows the mamlūk to copy it, on the condition that he shall not tell the story in the streets; "und weiter nicht vor Frauen noch vor Sklavinnen, weder vor Sklaven, noch vor dummen Menschen, noch auch vor Kindern; vielmehr sollst du sie nur Königen und Emiren, Wesiren und Männern der Wissenschaft, Schriftgelehrten und ähnlichen Leuten vorlesen".[122] Full of joy the mamlūk returns to Hasan, the merchant, who rewards him richly, himself copies the manuscript anew, and goes to read it to the king, who for the occasion summons "jeden Emir von hoher Verstandeskraft, jeden trefflichen Mann der Wissenschaft, jeden Feingebildeten und Dichter und klugen Richter".[123] The story proves a complete success, Hasan receives his reward, and the king has the story copied in golden letters and laid in his own treasury.

Besides the insistence on the special status of this story — expectations which the story actually told hardly meets — we may note some specific details: the story is discovered in *Syria*, and it is about a prince of *Egypt*;[124] while certainly not amounting to a Greek novel, it still exhibits a fair number of elements typical of that genre; and it is described as no ordinary oral tale, but is found in an old *book* and is *copied* and *read*. The story's title is known in advance, the manuscript is discovered after long and purposive searching, and a copy of a copy of the manuscript finally

---

[122] *Ibid.*, p. 226.

[123] *Ibid.*, p. 227.

[124] The story itself has little to do with Egypt, but the writer shows some acquaintance with Egyptian localities; see Littmann 1953, VI, p. 690.

ends up in a Persian archive. Nothing is said, of course, about languages and translations. It seems to me that this could perhaps be some kind of reflection, in the form of a tale, of how a famous Greek novel like *M & P* might have found its way, via Syria, to the various Muslim courts of the East. If the story that happens to have been put into the frame may show traces of an early Greek influence on the sources of the *AN*, the frame-story itself would rather reflect the later, deliberate acquisition and translation of Greek novels and, at the same time, tell us something about the prestige these may have enjoyed. It may be added, for what it is worth, that the Persian king of the frame-story, who was the ultimate cause of the quest for the Story of Stories and has the fictitious name Muḥammad ibn Sabāïk, has been identified as no other than the great Sultan of Ghazna, Maḥmūd ibn Sebüktigin (reigned AD 998–1030),[125] to whose court were attached, among other notabilities, our old acquaintances al-Bīrūnī and 'Unṣurī.[126]

References

Anderson, G. 1984. *Ancient Fiction: The Novel in the Graeco-Roman World*. London, Sydney & Totowa, N.J. 1984.

Baumstark, A. 1922. *Geschichte der syrischen Literatur*. Bonn 1922.

Boyle, J. A. 1977. "The Alexander Romance in the East and West", *BRL* 60, 1977, 13–27.

Brockelmann, C. I-II, S I-III. *Geschichte der arabischen Litteratur*. I-II. Weimar, Berlin 1898–1902. Supplementband I-III. Leiden 1937–42.

Browne, E. G. I-II. *A Literary History of Persia*. [I-II.] London 1902–06.

Cary, G. 1956. *The Medieval Alexander*. Cambridge 1956.

CHIran = *The Cambridge History of Iran*. I-V. Cambridge 1968–83.

CHIslam = *The Cambridge History of Islam*. I-II. Cambridge 1970.

Coquin, R.–G. 1981. "Le roman de Παρθενόπη/Bartānūbā (ms. *IFAO, Copte* 22, ff° I^{r-v}2^r)", *Bulletin de Centenaire*, Suppl. au *BIFAO* 81, 1981, 343–358.

---

[125] Thus Horovitz 1927, pp. 104 f.; cf. Littmann 1953, VI, pp. 691 f.; on Maḥmūd, *CHIslam* I, pp. 147–149; II, pp. 3 f.

[126] In fact, 'Unṣurī himself figures in the Persian version of this frame-story: the quest for the story is there arranged specifically in order to excel another story, procured by 'Unṣurī, in which the Sultan has taken particular pleasure; see Horovitz 1927, pp. 104 f.

Dodge, B. 1954. "The Subjects and Titles of Books Written during the First Four Centuries of Islam", *Islamic Culture* 28, 1954, 525–540.

— 1970. (trans.) *The Fihrist of al-Nadīm: A Tenth-Century Survey of Muslim Culture.* I-II. New York & London 1970.

Dornseiff, F. 1938. "Petron und 1001 Nacht", *SO* 18, 1938, 50–55.

EI = Enzyklopaedie des Islām. I-[V]. Leiden & Leipzig 1913–38.

EI²= The Encyclopaedia of Islam. New Edition. 1-. Leiden 1960–.

Eilers, W. 1971. *Semiramis: Entstehung und Nachhall einer altorientalischen Sage.* Wien 1971. (Österr. Akad. d. Wiss., Phil.-hist. Kl., Sitzungsber. 274:2.)

Geiger, W. & Kuhn, E. I-II. *Grundriss der iranischen Philologie.* I-II. Strassburg 1895–1904.

Gottschalk, H. L. 1965. "Die Rezeption der antiken Wissenschaften durch den Islam", *AAWW*, Phil.-hist. Kl. 102:7, 1965, 111–134.

Graf, G. I-V. *Geschichte der christlichen arabischen Literatur.* I-V. Città del Vaticano 1944–53. (Studi e testi, 118. 133. 146. 147. 172.)

Grunebaum, G. E. von 1942. "Greek Form Elements in the Arabian Nights", *JAOS* 62, 1942, 277–292. [Reprinted in Grunebaum 1976.]

— 1946. *Medieval Islam. A Study in Cultural Orientation.* Chicago 1946.

— 1963. *Der Islam im Mittelalter.* Zürich & Stuttgart 1963. [3rd revised and enlarged ed. of Grunebaum 1946.]

— 1976. *Islam and Medieval Hellenism. Social and Cultural Perspectives.* London 1976.

Hägg, T. 1971. *Narrative Technique in Ancient Greek Romances.* Stockholm 1971.

— 1983. *The Novel in Antiquity.* Oxford 1983.

— 1984. "The *Parthenope Romance* Decapitated?", *SO* 59, 1984, 61–92 [No. 8 in this volume].

Hemmerdinger, B. 1956. "Les 'Notices et extraits' des bibliothèques grecques de Bagdad par Photius", *REG* 69, 1956, 100–103.

Horn, P. 1901. *Geschichte der persischen Litteratur.* Leipzig 1901.

Horovitz, J. 1927. "Die Entstehung von Tausendundeine Nacht", *Review of Nations* 4, 1927, 85–111.

Kaladze, I. 1983. *Epičeskoe nasledie Unsuri* ("The Epic Heritage of Unsuri"). Tbilisi 1983.

Keith, A. B. 1928. *A History of Sanskrit Literature.* Oxford 1928.

Klein-Franke, F. 1980. *Die klassische Antike in der Tradition des Islam.* Darmstadt 1980.

Kraemer, J. 1956–57. "Arabische Homerverse", *ZDMG* 106, 1956, 259–316; 107, 1957, 511–518.

Kunitzsch, P. 1975. "Über das Frühstadium der arabischen Aneignung antiken Gutes", *Saeculum* 26, 1975, 268–282.

Lacôte, F. 1911. "Sur l'origine indienne du roman grec", in *Mélanges d'Indianisme offerts ... à S. Lévi.* Paris 1911, pp. 249–304.

Lichtenstadter, I. 1974. *Introduction to Classical Arabic Literature.* New York 1974.

Littmann, E. 1953. (trans.) *Die Erzählungen aus den Tausendundein Nächten.* Wiesbaden [1953] (repr. Darmstadt [1984]).

Maehler, H. 1976. "Der Metiochos-Parthenope-Roman", *ZPE* 23, 1976, 1–20.

Meyerhof, M. 1930. "Von Alexandrien nach Bagdad", *SPAW*, Phil.-hist. Kl., 1930, 389–429.

Nöldeke, Th. 1890. "Beiträge zur Geschichte des Alexanderromans", *Denkschriften der K. Akad. d. Wiss., [Wien]*, Phil.-hist. Cl. 38:5, 1890.

Paret, R. 1959–60. "Notes bibliographiques sur quelques travaux récents consacrés aux premières traductions arabes d'oeuvres grecques", *Byzantion* 29–30, 1959–60, 387–446.

Perry, B. E. 1959. "The Origin of the Book of Sindbad", *Fabula* 3, 1959, 1–94.

— 1961. "Two Fables Recovered", *ByzZ* 54, 1961, 4–14.

— 1964. *Secundus the Silent Philosopher.* Ithaca, N.Y. 1964. (Philological Monographs publ. by the American Philological Association, 22.)

— 1966. "The Greek Source of Some Armenian Fables and Certain CloselyRelated Matters of Tradition", in *Polychronion.* Festschrift F. Dölger. Hrsg. v. P. Wirth. Heidelberg 1966, pp. 418–430.

— 1967. *The Ancient Romances: A Literary-Historical Account of their Origins.* Berkeley & Los Angeles 1967.

Peters, F. E. 1968. *Aristotle and the Arabs. The Aristotelian Tradition in Islam.* New York & London 1968.

Reardon, B. P. 1971. *Courants littéraires grecs des IIe et IIIe siècles après J.-C.* Paris 1971.

Rehm, B. 1969. *Die Pseudoklementinen.* I. *Homilien.* Hrsg. v. B.R. 2. Aufl. Berlin 1969. (GCS, 42².)

Ritter, H. 1948. [Review of] *Dīwān-i* Abū l-Qāsim Ḥasan b. Aḥmad ʿUnṣurī (Tahrān 1323/1945), in *Oriens* 1, 1948, 134–139.

Rohde, E. 1960. *Der griechische Roman und seine Vorläufer.* 4. Aufl. Darmstadt 1960.

Rosenthal, F. 1962. "The Tale of Anthony", *Oriens* 15, 1962, 35–60.

— 1965. *Das Fortleben der Antike im Islam.* Zürich & Stuttgart 1965.

— 1968. *A History of Muslim Historiography.* 2nd rev. ed. Leiden 1968.

Rundgren, F. 1964–65. "Aristoteles hos araberna", *Religion och Bibel* 23–24, 1964–65, 50–58.

— 1970–71. "Arabische Literatur und orientalische Antike", *Or. Suec.* 19–20, 1970–71, 81–124.

— 1976. "Über den griechischen Einfluss auf die arabische Nationalgrammatik", *Acta Societatis Linguisticae Upsaliensis,* N.S. 2:5, 1976, 119–144.

Rypka, J. 1968. *History of Iranian Literature.* Dordrecht 1968.

Sezgin, F. I-VIII. *Geschichte des arabischen Schrifttums.* I-VIII. Leiden 1967–82.

Shafi, M. 1967. (ed.) *Wāmiq-o-Adhrā* of ʿUnṣurī. Lahore 1967.

Treadgold, W. B. 1980. *The Nature of the Bibliotheca of Photius.* Washington, D.C. 1980.

Ullmann, M. 1961. *Die arabische Überlieferung der sog. Menandersentenzen.* Wiesbaden 1961. (Abh. für die Kunde des Morgenlandes, 34:1.)

— 1970–72. *Die Medizin im Islam.* Leiden & Köln 1970. *Die Natur- und Geheimwissenschaften im Islam.* Leiden 1972. (Handbuch der Orientalistik. 1. Abt., Erg. bd. VI: 1–2.)

Walzer, R. 1945–46. "Arabic Transmission of Greek Thought to Medieval Europe", *BRL* 29, 1945–46, 160–183.

— 1962a. *Greek into Arabic. Essays on Islamic Philosophy.* Oxford 1962. (Oriental Studies, 1.)

— 1962b. "Arabische Übersetzungen aus dem Griechischen", *Miscellanea Mediaevalia* 1, 1962, 179–195.

Hermes and the Invention of the Lyre.
An Unorthodox Version*

[originally published in *Symbolae Osloenses* 64, 1989, 36–73]

The Greeks generally ascribed the invention of the lyre to Hermes. We find the earliest, and also the most detailed, surviving version in the Homeric *Hymn to Hermes* (24–61), presumably composed in the late sixth or early fifth century B.C.[1] The story briefly goes like this.[2] On the very day of his birth, Hermes was leaving the Cyllenian cave in search for Apollo's cattle, when he found a tortoise (24 χέλυς) browsing outside the dwelling. At once realizing its musical potentialities, he brought his new "toy" (32 ἄθυρμα) back into the cave and killed it (41–42): 37

> ἔνθ᾽ ἀναπηλήσας γλυφάνῳ πολιοῖο σιδήρου
> αἰῶν᾽ ἐξετόρησεν ὀρεσκῴοιο χελώνης.
>
> There he tossed it upside down and with a chisel of gray iron he scooped out the life of the mountain-turtle.[3]

---

* Research for the present article was principally conducted during a two-month stay in 1987 at the Dept. of Classics, Memorial University of Newfoundland, made possible through an exchange agreement between MUN and the University of Bergen. I wish to thank the Head of Department, Dr. John Whittaker, and his colleagues for providing a stimulating scholarly milieu and excellent working conditions.

[1] On the date, see H. Görgemanns, "Rhetorik und Poetik im homerischen Hermeshymnus", in H. Görgemanns & E. A. Schmid (eds.), *Studien zum antiken Epos*, Meisenheim am Glan 1976, 113–128 (early fifth century) R. Janko, *Homer, Hesiod and the Hymns*, Cambridge 1982, 133, 140–143 ("close of the sixth century"), 149 f.; and G. S. Kirk in *Cambr. Hist. Class. Lit.* I, 1985, 115 ("between the late sixth and early fourth century").

[2] Besides the standard texts and commentaries by L. Radermacher (Sitzungsber. Akad. Wiss. Wien Phil.-hist. Kl. 213:I, 1931), Allen-Halliday-Sikes (Oxford 1936), J. Humbert (Paris 1936) and F. Càssola (Milano 1975), my discussion also profited from the annotated translation by A. Barker in his *Greek Musical Writings* I, Cambridge 1984, 42–46 and from the illuminating analysis of S. C. Shelmerdine, "Hermes and the Tortoise: A Prelude to Cult", *GRBS* 25, 1984, 201–208. W. Hübner, "Hermes als musischer Gott", *Philologus* 130, 1986, 153–174 discusses important aspects of the Hymn, with extensive and up-to-date bibliographical documentation.

[3] Text Humbert (above, n. 2), trans. A. N. Athanassakis, *The Homeric Hymns*, Baltimore 1976. On ἀναπηλήσας, cf. Shelmerdine (above, n. 2) 205 f.

He then fixed stalks of reed into holes made through the shell, stretched oxhide over it, and added two arms, a crossbar, and seven strings of sheep-gut.[4] He began to play on it with a plectrum, improvising a song about the love of Zeus and Maia, his parents. But soon his attention turned in another direction, so he hid the lyre in his cradle and set out again for Apollo's cattle. Later in the hymn (419–510), the theme of the lyre is resumed: Hermes appeases Apollo by playing and singing, and he finally surrenders the instrument itself to his brother as a recompense for the stolen cows.

38

The other full-scale treatment of the topic that we know of was by Sophocles in his satyr play *Ichneutae*, only extant in fragmentary form (fr. 314 Radt, esp. lines 284–376).[5] In its search for Apollo's stolen cows, the chorus of satyrs arrives at the Cyllenian birth cave, led there by a curious sound. In the course of a dialogue between the satyrs and Cyllene, the nurse of "less-than-six-days-old" (279) Hermes, the circumstances surrounding the invention of the lyre gradually and partly emerge: a speechless animal has got a voice after its death (300, 328);[6] the animal was pot-shaped, had a spotted skin, was similar to a horned beetle, etc. (302, 307); the boy, turning it upside down (?, cf. 287 ἐξ ὑπτίας κ[...]),[7] [killing it], and gluing an oxhide over the shell (310, 314, 374–376), has produced what he calls a "lyre" (312) and is now happily playing on it

---

[4] On the *realia* behind the poetic description, see, most recently, P. Phaklares, "Χέλυς", *AD* 32, 1977, 218–233; P. Courbin, "Les lyres d'Argos", *BCH* Suppl. 6, 1980, 93–114; H. Roberts, "Reconstructing the Greek Tortoise-Shell Lyre", *World Archaeology* 12:3, 1981, 303–312; D. Paquette, *L'instrument de musique dans la céramique de la Grèce antique*, Paris 1984, 145–171; and A. Bélis, "À propos de la construction de la lyre", *BCH* 109, 1985, 201–220. The exact function of Hermes' "stalks of reed (47 δόνακας καλάμοιο)" is unclear, cf. Courbin 102–107 (to fasten the arms to the shell), Roberts 308 f. (to prevent the shell from being deformed under the strain of the tightened strings), Barker (above, n. 2) 43 n. 17 ("to fix and support the oxhide membrane"), and Shelmerdine (above, n. 2) 206 f. with n. 20 ("to form a bridge" and "fasten the bridge to the shell").

[5] Text in *TGF* IV ed. S. Radt, Göttingen 1974; comm. A. C. Pearson, *The Fragments of Sophocles* I, Cambridge 1917, 224–270; trans. D. L. Page, *Select Papyri* III (LCL, 1962) 26–53. I follow Radt's text and line numbering.

[6] 300 θανὼν γὰρ ἔσχε φωνήν, ζῶν δ᾽ ἄναυδος ἦν ὁ θήρ (cf. 328), cf. *H. Herm.* 38 ... ζώουσ᾽. ἢν δὲ θάνῃς, τότε κεν μάλα καλὸν ἀείδοις. On the subsequent history of this paradox, see E. K. Borthwick, "The Riddle of the Tortoise and the Lyre", *Music and Letters* 51, 1970, 373–387, and cf. Allen-Halliday-Sikes on *H. Herm.* 25.

[7] Cf. *H. Herm.* 41 (quoted above). For parallels of ὕπτιος in tortoise contexts, see Allen-Halliday-Sikes ad loc.

(326 f.). This was the sound that brought the searching satyrs to the cave, and they now suspect the oxhide to have come from one of Apollo's cows (374–376).

This description, as far as it goes (and is discernible in the fragment), is reasonably compatible with the version in the Hymn, except for one significant difference: here, the theft of the cattle *precedes* the construction of the lyre. Besides its dramatic function, this order neatly explains how little Hermes could have access to oxhide for his sound-box. The dramatist, whether following some lost predecessor or not, thus improved on the logic of the story.[8] Yet he seems basically to have exhibited the same version of the invention of the lyre as the Hymn,[9] and I shall in the following refer to it as the "orthodox version": the infant Hermes kills a tortoise and constructs the lyre from its shell.

In later Greek and Roman literature, there are a number of references to Hermes and the lyre,[10] but no further full treatment of the topic survives. It is the purpose of the present paper, however, to demonstrate that at least one such treatment has existed and, furthermore, that it is partly retrievable by means of a major new fragment (in Persian, as it happens) and some other scattered evidence of ancient origin, which has hitherto been overlooked. But we shall first review the shorter references of the Hellenistic and Roman periods to see how far they conform to the orthodox version, as known to us from the Hymn and the Satyr Play.

Apart from the strictly mythological contexts, such as handbooks and explanatory scholia, it is in musicological and, in particular, astronomical treatises that we find most such references, the Lyre being a constellation and Hermes its originator. It starts, in the third century B.C., with

39

---

[8] W. Burkert, "Sacrificio-sacrilegio: il 'trickster' fondatore", *Studi storici* (Roma) 25, 1984, 835–845, p. 841, suggests that this order might be the original one, linking sacrifice (of cows and tortoise alike) with the creation of music. It remains to explain why the author of the Homeric Hymn should have changed this logical order.

[9] Commentators tend to stress the differences rather than the similarities, cf. Pearson (above, n. 5) 226 f. and Allen-Halliday-Sikes (above, n. 2) 270 f., 277, but then often with the whole story rather than the lyre-invention part specifically in mind. Verbal coincidences, showing that "Sophocles was well acquainted with the Homeric text", are listed by Pearson (228).

[10] The references may be less numerous than one would expect, but (as we shall see) Allen-Halliday-Sikes (above, n. 2) 277 definitely overstate the case in speaking of "little or no impression", "silence" and neglect.

Aratus and Eratosthenes. The former, in his *Phaenomena* (268 f.),[11] only briefly alludes to the invention:

καὶ Χέλυς ἥδ᾽ ὀλίγη. τὴν ἄρ᾽ ἔτι καὶ παρὰ λίκνῳ
Ἑρμείης ἐτόρησε, Λύρην δέ μιν εἶπε λέγεσθαι ...

And here is the tiny Tortoise. Hermes, when still beside his cradle, pierced it and called it a Lyre.

40   Aratus here verbally echoes the Hymn (21 ἐνὶ λίκνῳ, 42 ἐξετόρησεν)[12] as well as the Satyr Play (312 ...]υν δ᾽ αὖ λύραν ὁ παῖς καλεῖ).

Both the relevant works of Eratosthenes, the epic poem *Hermes* and the prose collection of constellation myths called *Catasterismi*, are lost, but the epitome (first or second century A.D.) transmitted under the latter name[13] has an entry on the Lyre (ch. 24) probably derived from Eratosthenes:

κατεσκευάσθη δὲ τὸ μὲν πρῶτον ὑπὸ Ἑρμοῦ ἐκ τῆς χελώνης καὶ τῶν Ἀπόλ-
λωνος βοῶν, ἔσχε δὲ χορδὰς ἑπτὰ ἀπὸ τῶν Ἀτλαντίδων.

It (sc. the lyre) was first constructed by Hermes from the tortoise and Apollo's cows, and it got seven strings after the (seven) daughters of Atlas.

This epitomized version permits us to discern two things only: the lyre is constructed from the tortoise itself (an important point, as will be clear later on), and material from Apollo's cows is used in the construction. On the latter point it agrees with Sophocles against the Hymn,[14] on the former with both.

[11] Text J. Martin, Firenze 1956.

[12] Neither G. A. Mair's explanatory translation (LCL, 1955) "pierced for strings" nor the entry in LSJ s.v. τορέω II "work, shape" take account of Aratus' obvious allusion to *H. Herm.* 42 (quoted above); he boldly says "pierce" for "kill". The confusion already starts with the *scholia vetera* on Aratus (p. 211.5 Martin): χέλυν ἐκδείρας ὁ Ἑρμῆς κατετόρευσε λύραν, where other scholiasts use κατασκευάζω (p. 210.17, 212.10).

[13] Text quoted from Eratosthenes, *Catasterismorum reliquiae* ed. C. Robert, Berlin 1878, 138. On Eratosthenes, including his *Hermes*, see G. A. Keller, *Eratosthenes und die alex-andrinische Sterndichtung*, Diss. Zürich 1946. The dissertation (Univ. of Southern California, 1970) by T. Condos, "The *Katasterismoi* of the Pseudo-Eratosthenes: A Mythological Commentary and English Translation", was available to me only through the abstract in *DA* 31, 1971, 6029A.

[14] Robert *ad loc.* suspects that the words about Apollo's cows are an interpolation, perhaps from Apollodorus (cf. below); but he could not know the *Ichneutae*. Whether the cows provided the cover of the sound-box (as in Sophocles), strings (as in Apollodorus) or arms (from the horns), is suppressed in the epitome.

As regards Eratosthenes' *Hermes*, the few remnants (fr. 1-16 Powell) only tell us that his hero was "still young" (ἔτι νέος) when he constructed the lyre,[15] and that it had eight (!) strings. Other fragments confirm that the epyllion devoted much attention to the god's early childhood.[16] We have no reason to doubt, in spite of the slight variation in the number of strings, that Eratosthenes chose basically the same version of the invention for his poetic treatment as for his prose work, and that both were ultimately inspired by the Hymn.

In the prolific and entangled Aratus tradition, which absorbs a variety of items from Eratosthenes as well,[17] Hermes and the lyre naturally appear now and then. The Greek *scholia vetera* on Aratus[18] on the whole keep well within the orthodox version of the invention, only in one instance harmonizing the baby's age into "on his third day" (p. 211.15 Martin τριταῖος ὢν ἀπὸ τοῦ τόκου) for the Hymn's "on the first day" and Sophocles' "less than six"; whether this implies that the theft precedes the invention, is not stated. No new details are added, as regards the invention, in the free Latin adaptations of the *Phaenomena* by Cicero (42-44) and Germanicus (270 *lyra Mercurio dilecta* simply),[19] whereas, in the fourth century A.D., Avienus (618-621)[20] is somewhat more explicit than his Greek model by stating that "sinews" were used for strings (619 *curva religans testudine chordas*, 621 *formaret nervis*), a slight deviation from the orthodox version with its sheep-guts.

Two further astronomical treatises, probably both belonging to the Augustan age, refer to the invention in similarly general terms: Hyginus (*Poet. Astr.* 2.7.1),[21] referring to Eratosthenes, only parenthetically

---

[15] Fr. 13 Powell, from Theon of Smyrna p. 142 Hiller (with an obvious emendation of the transmitted ἐστι).

[16] Thus Keller (above, n. 13) 121; on the lyre, pp. 104 f., 123-125.

[17] For the texts, see E. Maass, *Commentariorum in Aratum reliquiae*, Berlin 1898. The most recent comprehensive investigation is by J. Martin, *Histoire du texte des Phénomènes d'Aratos*, Paris 1956; cf. the elucidatory review of R. Keydell, *Gnomon* 30, 1958, 575-584.

[18] Ed. J. Martin, Stuttgart 1974, 210-212.

[19] Cicero's *Aratea* ed. J. Soubiran, Paris 1972, 168 f.; *The Aratus ascribed to Germanicus Caesar* ed. D. B. Gain, London 1976, 29, 60, 94.

[20] Ed. J. Soubiran, Paris 1981, 181, 210 f. Cf. further the commentary in D. Weber, *Aviens Phaenomena, eine Arat-Bearbeitung aus der lateinischen Spätantike*, Wien 1986, 159-161.

[21] Ed. A. Le Bœuffle, Paris 1983; on the probably Augustan date, see p. XLIII.

states that Hermes made the lyre from a tortoise, while Manilius (5.324 f.)²² speaks of "the shape of the tortoise-shell (*testudinis forma*), which under the fingers of its heir (i.e., Hermes) gave forth sound only after death (*tantum post fata sonantis*)", translating into his convoluted style the paradox we already know from Hymn and Play.²³ Apparently, our ancient astronomical references all keep well within the orthodox version; there will, however, be occasion to return to the medieval continuation below.

Among the other, miscellaneous references, the earliest is in Nicander's *Alexipharmaca* (559–562)²⁴ of the second century B.C.: the limbs of the mountain tortoise, we are told, are one of the possible ingredients of a drug against salamander poison — the tortoise whom Hermes "endowed with a voice though voiceless, for he separated the chequered shell from the flesh (561 σαρκὸς γὰρ ἀπ᾽ οὖν νόσφισσε χέλειον | αἰόλον) and extended two arms from its edges." Eutecnius' prose paraphrase (ch. 20, p. 54.24–28 Geymonat),²⁵ while deliberately restructuring and expanding, nonetheless adds no extraneous elements to this description (e.g., τῶν γὰρ δὴ σαρκῶν τὴν χέλυν αὐτῆς ἀποφαίνει γυμνήν). The scholia on Nicander²⁶ likewise stay loyal to the text they explain.

In the *Bibliotheca* of Apollodorus (3.2),²⁷ compiled in the first or second century A.D., Hermes' first days are described in rather close adherence to the Homeric Hymn. As in Sophocles' play, however, the theft of the cows precedes the invention of the lyre. Accordingly, the short account of the construction of the instrument appears to be indebted to both these sources:

43   καὶ εὑρίσκει πρὸ τοῦ ἄντρου νεμομένην χελώνην. ταύτην ἐκκαθάρας, εἰς τὸ κύτος χορδὰς ἐντείνας ἐξ ὧν ἔθυσε βοῶν καὶ ἐργασάμενος λύραν εὗρε καὶ πλῆκτρον.

---

²² Text and trans. quoted from Manilius, *Astronomica* ed. G. P. Goold (LCL), 1977, 326 f.

²³ Above, n. 6.

²⁴ Text and trans. quoted from Nicander, *The Poems and Poetical Fragments* ed. A. S. F. Gow & A. F. Scholfield, Cambridge 1953, 130 f.

²⁵ Eutecnii *Paraphrasis in Nicandri Alexipharmaca* ed. M. Geymonat, Milano 1976, 54. See p. 18 f. on Eutecnius' habit, testified elsewhere, of adding new elements to Nicander's mythological descriptions.

²⁶ *Scholia in Nicandri Alexipharmaca cum glossis* ed. M. Geymonat, Milano 1974, 192 f.

²⁷ Text and trans. quoted from Apollodorus, *The Library* ed. J. G. Frazer (LCL), Vol. 2, 1946, 4–9.

And before the cave he found a tortoise browsing. He cleaned it out,
strung the shell with chords made from the kine he had sacrificed, and
having thus produced a lyre he invented also a plectrum.

We note one deviation: here the slaughtered cows do not, as in Sophocles,
provide material for the sound-box, but for the strings; whether guts or
sinews (as in Avienus), we are not told.

Nicomachus, the first/second-century mathematician and musicolo-
gist,[28] is as austere as the astronomical writers, referring only to the fact
that Hermes invented the lyre from the tortoise and provided it with
seven strings (p. 266.2–3 Jan).

Pausanias (8.17.5)[29] is geographically precise (ὄρος Κυλλήνης Χελυδό-
ρεα), but otherwise content with a general report. The only conspicuous detail is the term ἐκδέρω for "removing the shell from the body",
a word obviously chosen to provide an etymology for the name of the
mountain (-δέρω | Χελυ-δόρεα).[30]

Philostratus (ca. 200 A.D.), depicting in his *Imagines* (1.10.1)[31] Amphion playing the lyre before Thebes, is similarly sparse in describing
the invention itself; he specifies, however, that Hermes used two horns
for arms, a crossbar and a tortoise shell. Later (1.10.2) it emerges that
the horn is goat-horn and that boxwood was used in the construction as
well. There is also a fairly detailed description of the shell and the seven
strings (νευραί). In the Homeric Hymn, the material used for the arms
is not specified, but goathorn would no doubt be a reasonable guess. Archaeology and early art seem exclusively to attest *wooden* arms,[32] whereas
poetry and myth may still have favoured an animal material. One may
compare Polyphemus' imaginary lyre in Lucian (*Dialogi Marini* 1.4),
made of a stag's skull, with horns and all.

44

[28] *Musici Scriptores Graeci* ed. C. Jan, Lipsiae 1895, 266.

[29] Ed. M. H. Rocha-Pereira, Vol. 2, Leipzig 1977.

[30] Cf. Radermacher (above, n. 2) 74, 189 f.; the same verb then occurs in the scholium
quoted above, n. 12.

[31] Ed. O. Schönberger, München 1968.

[32] See Bélis (above, n. 4) 203 f. For the view that goat-horn was the original material for
arms, see Th. Reinach, "Lyra", in Daremberg-Saglio-Pottier, *Dict. Ant.* III, Paris 1904,
1437–1451, p. 1439 f., with documentation from literature and later art (coins, Pompeian
paintings, Roman sarcophagi); and cf. the discussion in J. Duchemin, *La houlette et la
lyre*, Paris 1960, 118 f.

We have reviewed most ancient literary references of any substance and have found nothing that conflicts with the core of the orthodox version (though bare references like that of Germanicus or Nicomachus, of which there are more, of course say little or nothing in this respect). Only Lucian, in his dialogue between Hephaestus and Apollo (*Dialogi Deorum* 7.4),[33] gives us a glimpse of something different:

> χελώνην που νεκρὰν εὑρὼν (sc. ὁ παῖς) ὄργανον ἀπ᾽ αὐτῆς συνεπήξα-
> το ...
>
> He picked up a dead tortoise somewhere, and made himself a musical instrument out of it ...

The beginning of the dialogue makes it clear that here Hermes is still the new-born baby we know from the orthodox version, and the continuation on the construction of the lyre specifies, among other things, arms, crossbar and seven strings in terms recalling the Hymn. But Hermes finds the tortoise dead — that is the truly unorthodox detail in this account. A thorough search of scholia of presumably ancient origin will, as we shall see below, provide further occasional glimpses of something contrary to the literary mainstream. Yet these scattered pieces fall into place only when we take account of a major new testimony: the anonymous Greek novel of *Metiochus and Parthenope* (=*M&P*), as partly recoverable by means of a fragmentarily preserved eleventh-century Persian verse-romance, ʿUnṣurī's *Vāmiq and ʿAdhrā* (= *V&A*).

For the Greek original, our main source is a major papyrus fragment,[34] describing a symposium at Polycrates' court on Samos and staging Polycrates himself, his wife, his young daughter Parthenope, her lover Metiochus (the son of Miltiades!), and the philosopher Anaximenes; they discuss Eros. The Persian romance, which can be shown to be based (through whatever intermediary/ies) on *M&P* and of which considerably more is preserved (a fragment of some 380 double-verses and a great number of lexical quotations),[35] happens to overlap with the Greek

45

---

[33] Text and trans. M. D. Macleod (LCL), Vol. 7, 1961, 296 f.

[34] Published by H. Maehler, "Der Metiochos-Parthenope-Roman", *ZPE* 23, 1976, 1–20.

[35] Published by M. Shafi, *Wāmiq-o-Adhrā* of ʿUnṣurī, Lahore 1967, and again, with Russian trans. and comm., by I. Kaladze, *Epič eskoe nasledie Unsuri*, Tbilisi 1983. For the present paper, I am indebted to Bo Utas (Uppsala) for translation and discussion of the

→

papyrus, and continues where the latter breaks off. A poet is introduced, by name of Īfuqūs apparently none other than Ibycus![36] He plays the *barbaṭ* and celebrates in his song the beauty of ʿAdhrā /Parthenope and Vāmiq/Metiochus. Then the question is asked: Who was the inventor of the *barbaṭ*? Fuluqrāṭ/Polycrates expresses bewilderment at the different versions he has heard, but Vāmiq volunteers to tell what he regards as the old and authoritative story.

The following 37 double-verses (199–235) are taken up by this story; it will be summarized below. It should be noted, however, that — as a comparison of the overlapping parts shows[37] — the Persian romance cannot be expected to reproduce the Greek original faithfully throughout; sometimes it is very close, sometimes it distorts, omits, or adds material of its own. Thus, before any detail of this invention story is accepted as in substance original, it will have to be carefully weighed, with regard to its internal logic, general probability in an ancient Greek context, and compatability with the other invention evidence, orthodox or diverging.

(1) The wise man Hurmuz — So Vāmiq relates — once passed over a mountain to worship the Omnipotent. There he came across the carcass of a tortoise from which all the flesh had rotted away; but the sinews were still in place, dried and stretched, and when the wind passed through, a sound came from inside. [*Short lacuna.*] (2) The tone from the shell refreshed Hurmuz' heart, he felt joy and knew it was caused by the sound. So he picked up the shell, brought it with him and hung it in the wind to issue the joyous sound. 46

(3) After much brooding, he himself built an instrument similar to the tortoise, twisting and drying a gut to stretch over it. And again, the tone brought forth by the wind softened his heart, and he thought: How could this sound be made permanent? My instrument is no good, unless it functions without the wind blowing. [*Interpretation uncertain; possibly long lacuna within the speech.*] So he started rebuilding it, moving the frets (?) from inside to outside (?), and pondered for a long time how to make a peg to attach the string(s); but all in vain.

Persian material. We are currently working on a joint edition of the entire Greek and Persian material pertaining to this novel [published in 2003 as *The Virgin and her Lover: Fragments of an Ancient Greek Novel and a Persian Epic Poem*, Leiden]. Cf. B. Utas, "Did ʿAdhrā Remain a Virgin?", *Orientalia Suecana* 33–35, 1984–86, 429–441.

[36] For this identification, see Utas (above, n. 35) 434.

[37] See T. Hägg, "Metiochus at Polycrates' Court", *Eranos* 83, 1985, 92–102 [No. **9** in this volume].

(4) At last, one day when he went for a walk, he saw an old man at the road-side, bent by his years and in deep thoughts. Hurmuz asked him: Why are you depressed? You surely cannot have as good a reason as me. [*Short lacuna?*] For I am not able to finish my instrument properly, I do not know how to make it function. (5) The old man, looking up, explained to him how it might be done. Hurmuz was pleased to have it built by a human hand, and quickly at that. According to Vāmiq's wise teacher, this old man was called Hažrah-man. He attached many strings, ordering them according to their likeness to different human characters. [*Exact interpretation uncertain; the next two double-verses still more obscure and omitted here.*] (6) A stroke on the strings, [Hažrah-man explained,] is like a movement in our body, grasping and letting them go is like breathing. [*Lacuna of unknown length.*] Our nature is built into it, and so its essence has been elevated (?). Now the *barbaṭ* was finished [and he started playing on it].

Vāmiq's elaborate story — here presented in brief paraphrase — was enthusiastically received by his Samian audience, and ʿAdhrā's love was kindled. What are we then to make of it? First, it is obvious that "Hurmuz" must be Hermes (even if the correct Persian form would be *Hurmus*).[38] But is *barbaṭ* — one of the Persian words for "lyre" or "harp" — simply to be equated with "lyre", or is it conceivable that this is instead specifically the story of "the invention of the *barbitos*"?

At first sight the latter possibility looks attractive. The βάρβιτος (or βάρβιτον) was a distinct type of stringed instrument, like the lyre built from a tortoise shell, but with longer arms and strings, and accordingly deeper pitch.[39] It was used in Dionysian revelries and at symposia, being especially suited for accompanying the human voice. Its invention is ascribed to Terpander, the seventh-century Lesbian poet and musician (Pindar fr. 125 Snell, *apud* Athen. 14.635d–e), or to Anacreon (Neanthes fr. 5 Müller, third century B.C., *apud* Athen. 4.175d–e), but no particular story seems to have been connected with either invention.[40] In literature, the *barbitos* is mostly associated with the eastern Greek poets: the Lesbians and Anacreon. J. M. Snyder concludes that it "came from Asia Minor to

[38] A lexical quotation from *V&A* (Kaladze A: 33–34) gives the correct form *Hurmus*. *Hurmuz* generally stands for Ormus (Ahura Mazda).

[39] Cf. S. Michaelides, *The Music of Ancient Greece: An Encyclopaedia*, London 1978, 48 f.; Baker (above, n. 2) 14; Paquette (above, n. 4) 173–185; and, in particular, J. M. Snyder, "The *Barbitos* in the Classical Period", *CJ* 67, 1972, 331–340.

[40] As for Terpander, Pindar (according to Athenaeus) only says that he "invented the *barbitos* in antiphonal answer (ἀντίφθογγον) to the Lydian *pectis*" (trans. Snyder [above, n. 39] 335); the report of Anacreon's supposed invention completely lacks embedding.

the eastern Greek colonies sometime in the seventh or early sixth century B.C."[41] It then moved further westward; in Attic vase-painting, it surfaces round 520.[42] It continues to be referred to in ancient literature as a typically archaic Greek instrument (e.g., Dion.Hal. 7.72.5). Each of these historical facts would agree with the supposition that our novelist had this particular type of lyre in mind as Ibycus' instrument at the fictitious Samian symposium; and since there was no invention myth for the *barbitos*, he might well have been tempted to fill the gap.

Yet the story itself lends no support to this idea: it is introduced as being the authoritative version among several contenders; the invention is described as something brand new and revolutionary, not just as a modification of an instrument Hermes himself had invented as a baby; and, unless hidden in a *lacuna*, no particular attention is paid to the construction of the arms, the most conspicuous feature of the *barbitos*. We must conclude that this is really about the invention of the lyre, in general. Our author (presumably)[43] used βάρβιτος (-ον) simply as a synonym for λύρα, as often happens in Greek literature (e.g., *Anacreontea* 2 and 23 West); similarly, in the *Hymn to Hermes*, the same instrument is indiscriminately referred to as φόρμιγξ (64), χέλυς (153), λύρη (423) and κίθαρις; (499).[44] Yet, if among the synonyms he chose precisely *barbitos* (-on), a term otherwise unattested in the Greek novels and fragments,[45] he no doubt did so to contribute to the local colour of Polycrates' court, associating the word with archaic lyric, perhaps even directly with Ibycus.[46]

48

[41] Snyder (above, n. 39) 334.

[42] Paquette (above, n. 4) 175.

[43] The use of the Persian *barbaṭ* does of course not necessarily mean that the novelist used *barbitos*, but it appears to be the most natural inference.

[44] Cf. Barker (above, n. 2) 25 n. 19, who after discussing the earlier indiscriminate use adds: "In the fourth century a clear classification with appropriate terminology was developed …, but literature commonly neglects these technicalities even after that date."

[45] Cf. F. Conca, E. De Carli & G. Zanetto, *Lessico dei romanzieri greci* I, Milano 1983.

[46] Although the word is not attested among our Ibycus fragments, the novelist may well have read it in that poet. If not, the distinct association of the *barbitos* with Anacreon (Critias fr. 1.4 D–K *apud* Athen. 13.600e), and of Anacreon with Polycrates, was surely enough. (It was rather the *sambyke* that was Ibycus' invention, according to Neanthes fr. 5 Müller *apud* Athen. 4.175d–e). Cf. further Theocritus' reference to Simonides' *barbitos* (16.45), possibly another piece of "local colour" (though Gow *ad loc.* rather judges it as just "a poetical synonym for κιθάρα"), and Bacchylides' invocation of his *barbitos* (*Enc.* fr. 20B.1, 20C.2 Snell-Maehler).

We shall now analyze the Persian story, section by section, trying to distil the Greek essence and define its relationship to the orthodox version.

(1) Hermes is here a (wise) man, not an (infant) god. There can hardly be any doubt that he was a god in the Greek novel, but lost that dignity in the Islamic context. He was perhaps described as being on his way to his father Zeus on Olympus, though of course not to "worship" in the sense of the Persian version. It may be noticed, for what it is worth, that Mount Olympus instead of Cyllene is given as Hermes' birthplace in Philostratus (*Imag.* 1.26.1; *Vita Apoll.* 5.15), but without mention of the tortoise episode, while, on the other hand, Mount Olympus is still today a habitat for the lyre-producing tortoise par excellence, the *Testudo marginata*.[47] A trace of Hermes' divinity is in fact left in section (5), where he is content with the help of "a human hand" to build his instrument, probably implying that, as a god, he might be thought to have resented a man being cleverer than he. That kind of incongruity — a deliberate change of the original story at one place not having been consistently followed up in the sequel — is manifestly also present in the part of the Persian version which overlaps with the Greek fragment.[48]

If Hermes as a mortal is a secondary trait, his grown-up status, on the other hand, seems to be a logical, even necessary part of our version, and thus likely to be original. In fact, we find support elsewhere in Greek tradition.[49] If we first look at the story of Hermes stealing Apollo's cattle, with which the orthodox version of the invention story is linked, it sometimes occurs independently of the latter and with Hermes as an adult. It is true that already Alcaeus, in his *Hymn to Hermes* (fr. 308 LP), alludes to the child Hermes stealing the cows, with a well-known echo in Horace (*Carm.* 1.10.9–12); but there has obviously also been a strong parallel tradition, in both literature and art, with the god fully grown.

49

---

[47] See R. C. H. Pritchard, *Encyclopedia of Turtles*, Neptune, N. J., 1979, 349 (colour plate), 407: "restricted to southern Greece, from the Taygetos Mountains to Mount Olympus." Cf. further below, p. 54 f.

[48] See Hägg (above, n. 37) 100 f.

[49] See H. Herter, "Hermes: Ursprung und Wesen eines griechischen Gottes," *RhM* 119, 1976, 193–241, pp. 230–233 (with further refs).

The Battus incident, as told in the second century A.D. by Antoninus Liberalis (23) with Hesiod (fr. 256 Merkelbach-West *ed. maior*),[50] Nicander (fr. 40 Schneider and Gow-Schofield) and Apollonius Rhodius ("in his epigrams") among the alleged sources, is a case in point: Hermes, driving the stolen cattle, is observed by Battus, who swears not to denounce him, if only he receives a recompense; but when Hermes later returns in disguise to test Battus, he finds him easily bribed into breaking his oath and so transforms him into a stone. No trace here of an infant driving the cattle, as in the corresponding incident with the old man in the Hymn (210). And when Ovid, in the *Metamorphoses* (2.676–707), tells the same story, he next has Hermes fly to Athens to fall in love with the beautiful Herse (724 ff.).[51] His Hermes, then, is probably a youth, but no baby.

50

In Corinthian and Attic vase-painting of the late seventh and the sixth centuries, there are a number of representations of Hermes driving the stolen cattle; he is always depicted as a mature man with a beard.[52] There is, however, a handful of late-archaic or classical vases which do show Hermes as a child, three of them with clear reference to the birth story and cattle theft: a Caeretan hydria (Louvre E 702, ca. 530 B.C.), a cup of the Brygos Painter (Vatican, Helbig 639, ca. 490 B.C., ARV 369,6), and the fragments of a red-figure crater of ca. 450 B.C. (Bern, private owner).[53] There is no question here of the child actually driving the cattle; in all three cases, he is represented lying or sitting in bed inside the cave. In the two complete vases, we see Apollo coming to reclaim his cows, who are also, and most prominently, in the picture. The Brygos cup and the

[50] It is uncertain how much of the story really goes back to the Hesiodic Μεγάλαι Ἠοῖαι: Allen-Halliday-Sikes (above, n. 2) 270–272 and others seem to refer the whole lot to Hesiod, whereas Merkelbach-West say "perpauca hic Hesiodea esse vix monendum est" and, in their *ed. minor* (OCT, 1983), break off long before the cattle episode. Most of the other sources indicated by Ant.Lib. are metamorphoses collections. Cf. also R. Holland, "Battos", *RhM* 75, 1926, 156–183.

[51] F. Bömer *ad Met.* 2.679, who notes this, takes it as an example of Ovid sacrificing tradition and logic for the instant needs of his story, but Ovid may as well follow a tradition which does not couple cattle theft with birthstory.

[52] The material is collected in N. Ph. Yalouris, "Ἑρμῆς Βούκλεψ", *AE* 2, 1953/54, 162–184, pp. 171–179, and discussed by P. Zanker, *Wandel der Hermesgestalt in der attischen Vasenmalerei*, Bonn 1965, 60 f., and E. Simon, *Die Götter der Griechen*, München 1969, 296–298.

[53] See Zanker (above, n. 52) 61–63, and, for the new fragments, R. Blatter, "Hermes, der Rinddieb", *AK* 14, 1971, 128 f.

crater are of course late enough to have been inspired by the Homeric Hymn. As regards the Caeretan hydria, the presently adopted low date of the Hymn would preclude such a dependence. But since we already have the child as cattle thief in Alcaeus, that is no problem; it was not the author of the Hymn who invented the motif. In fact, an iconographical difference between the older vase-painting and the two later ones may be significant: only in the latter does the child recline in something that could be identified as the *liknon*, "winnowing-fan", of the Hymn; in the Caeretan representation, he lies stiffly on a small bed.

If the literary evidence shows us that there were two parallel traditions — the mature and the infant Hermes, respectively, as cattle thief — early art thus both confirms this and demonstrates that the former one was dominant throughout the archaic period, and consequently no doubt original. It may be added that the Indo-European cattle-raiding myth, of which this appears to be a variety, is of course alien to the burlesque created by a baby taking the leading part.[54] That feature, as we meet it in the Homeric Hymn and its followers, seems purely incidental to the myth.

The same is probably true for the Hymn's story of the baby inventing the lyre.[55] In Attic vase-painting, Hermes with the lyre is generally a bearded man.[56] While it is true that such representations do not intend to illustrate the invention episode itself, but just present the god with one of his attributes, the absence of any allusion on Attic vases to the baby-and-tortoise incident is at least worth noting. Not even the Caere-

[54] Cf., e.g., B. Lincoln, *Priests, Warriors, and Cattle* (Berkeley 1981), who emphasizes the cattle raid as a proof of manhood, demonstrating physical prowess and true warriorship. Our literary instance (on which Lincoln does not comment) is obviously an inversion of the norm. In case one prefers to describe Hermes' deed as theft (*H. Herm.* 18 βοῦς κλέψεν) rather than heroic raiding (*ibid.* 14 ἐλατῆρα βοῶν), even the "trickster" god (cf. Burkert, above, n. 8) is basically no comic figure. On Hermes vacillating between cattleraider and thief, see N. O. Brown, *Hermes the Thief: The Evolution of a Myth*, Madison 1947, 3–7, 81 f.

[55] Cf. C. Robert, "Zum Homerischen Hermeshymnus", *Hermes* 41, 1906, 389–425, p. 417 (whose excessive cutting up into pieces of the actual Hymn should not be allowed to discredit his often pertinent observations), and, in particular, the discussion in Radermacher (above, n. 2) 201–203, arguing *inter alia* that Hermes as a child and Apollo as a grown-up is an inversion of the normal relationship between the two brothers.

[56] Zanker (above, n. 52) 83 mentions only one Attic vase, a red-figure crater of the Dinos Painter (Gotha 73, ARV 1154,33), on which Hermes with the lyre appears as a young boy.

tan hydria and the Brygos cup, with their representation of the infant thief in his cradle, exhibit any traces of the lyre[57] (nor, incidentally, do the fragments of Alcaeus' *Hymn to Hermes*). In later Greek and Roman art, it does happen that Hermes is represented together with a tortoise,[58] as he often is with other animals as well (cock, scorpion etc.), but this again is probably just one of his attributes.[59] Consequently, it has no great bearing on our argument that this Hermes too, like Hermes with the lyre, is (in most cases) fully grown.[60] In the surviving objects of art, one looks in vain for a quite clear case of Hermes (whether a baby or not) and the tortoise being depicted with reference specifically to the lyre production.[61] An intriguing piece of information, however, is given by Pausanias (2.19.7), who reports that, in the sanctuary of Apollo Lycius at Argos, there is a statue of "Hermes having caught a tortoise to make a lyre" (Ἑρμῆς ἐς λύρας ποίησιν χελώνην ᾑρηκώς).[62] We should have liked to know the date of the statue, whether Hermes was a baby, and how his intention to make a lyre of the tortoise was represented (unless it is just Pausanias himself who associates tortoise with lyre).

52

---

[57] *Pace* Settis (below, n. 58) 85 n. 349, who suggests that "perhaps" the tortoise shell is represented on the Brygos cup, hanging on the left side of the *liknon*. But the detail referred to (cf. the clear ill. in Yalouris [above, n. 52] 177, Pl. 7*a*) is very different from the lyres of Attic vase-painting; and a reference here to the lyre episode would no doubt have been quite explicit.

[58] The most complete survey is in S. Settis' learned monograph, ΧΕΛΩΝΗ. *Saggio sull' Afrodite Urania di Fidia*, Pisa 1966, 84–94.

[59] See S. Eitrem, "Hermes 1", *RE* VIII:I (1912) 738–792, cols. 757–759.

[60] Settis (above, n. 58) 86; exceptions p. 84 f.

[61] Settis (above, n. 58) 85 mentions some instances in which such an interpretation has been advanced. In itself, it would be no surprise if the Hymn had inspired artists, especially in the Hellenistic period, to represent the baby Hermes with his "toy". Yet it is difficult to prove that a certain representation of a boy with a tortoise (such as the fountain statue in the Palazzo dei Conservatori, Cat. Stuart Jones No. 32) is really meant as Hermes (or derives from such a representation), or even that the killing of a tortoise (as on a couple of gems, A. Furtwängler, *Die antiken Gemmen* I, Leipzig & Berlin 1900, Pl. 15:59–60; cf. M. Bieber in *MDAI(A)* 37, 1912, 175 n. 3) really refers to Hermes' lyre construction rather than depicting a sacrifice. (I thank Espen B. Andersson for assistance on these matters.)

[62] Discussed in L. R. Farnell, *The Cults of the Greek States* V, Oxford 1909, 27, 42 f. Incidentally, the "Marathon Boy" (ca. 340 B.C.) has been interpreted as representing "young" Hermes rejoicing over finding the tortoise, which he carried in his left hand, see F. Chamoux, "Hermès Parammon", *Études d'archéologie classique M. Launey* II, Paris 1959, 29–40, p. 38.

53   To find literary evidence for a fully-grown Hermes inventing the lyre, we have to turn to the scholiasts. A scholium on Dionysius Thrax (§2),[63] explaining the connection between the words λύρα and λύτρα — the "lyre" was the "ransom" given by Hermes to Apollo for the cattle — says that Hermes came across the tortoise when he "once found himself in Arcadia": φασὶ γὰρ ὅτι ποτὲ Ἑρμῆς ἐν Ἀρκαδίᾳ ἀναστρεφόμενος εὗρε χελώνην … Neither this wording nor the continuation about the cattle and the "ransom" reveal any connection with the god's birth. There is, however, one still clearer piece of evidence, which we shall study more closely, since it becomes a corner-stone in the following deliberations.

    The Greek scholia on Aratus, as we saw above, contained nothing remarkable about the invention of the lyre. But in some Latin scholia on Germanicus' translation of the *Phaenomena* (the "Scholia Strozziana" p. 150.10–151.4 Breysig),[64] there is a curious piece which localizes the invention in Egypt and deviates from the orthodox version in other significant ways too. It is, however, no genuine part of the Germanicus tradition; it intruded into it from the so-called *Aratus latinus* (p. 150.19–151.15 Breysig, p. 230 f. Maass), which is a seventh-century Latin translation of a Greek compilation based on Aratus and Eratosthenes.[65] But this particular piece does not belong there either: far from being part of the Aratus-Eratosthenes tradition, as it is sometimes presented,[66] it was interpolated into some *Aratus latinus* manuscript from the discussion of musical terminology in the *Etymologiae* (3.22.8) of Isidorus (Bishop of 54 Seville ca. 601–636).[67] Isidorus, in turn, had copied the information from Servius' commentary on Virgil's *Georgica* (4.463).[68] Since the four

---

[63] *Scholia in Dionysii Thracis Artem Grammaticam* ed. A. Hilgard, Lipsiae 1901, 173.32–174.4 (cf. 308.15–17). In the principal, thirteenth-century ms., the scholia in question are attributed to Stephanus, a Byzantine grammarian of unknown date.

[64] *Germanici Caesaris Aratea cum scholiis* ed. A. Breysig, Berlin 1867.

[65] See Martin (above, n. 17) 37 ff.

[66] E.g., in Cicéron, *Les Aratea* ed. V. Buescu, Bucharest 1941, 198 n. 1, and Weber (above, n. 20) 160. The root of the evil is Robert's edition (above, n. 13) 138 f., though Robert corrects himself on p. 202, n. 2.

[67] See A. von Fragstein, *Isidor von Sevilla und die sogenannten Germanicusscholien*, Diss. Breslau 1931, 20, who, however, mistakenly makes Isidorus himself the interpolator (p. 72); cf. P. Wessner in *Gnomon* 10, 1934, 151–154. I quote Isidorus from the ed. of W.M. Lindsay, Oxonii 1911.

[68] Thus Fragstein (above, n. 68) 20, 72, 77, and J. Fontaine, *Isidore de Seville et la culture classique dans l'Espagne wisigothique*, 2nd ed. Paris 1983, 435.

sources convey the same message, with only stylistic variations, and the line of descent can be demonstrated beyond reasonable doubt, it will do to quote Servius (ca. 400 A.D.):[69]

> CAVA TESTUDINE periphrasis citharae, cuius usus repertus est hoc modo: cum regrediens Nilus in suos meatus varia in terris reliquisset animalia, relicta etiam testudo est. quae cum putrefacta esset et nervi eius remansissent extenti intra corium, percussa a Mercurio sonitum dedit. ex cuius imitatione cithara est composita.[70]

> "Hollow tortoise": a periphrasis for "lyre", the use of which was invented in the following way. When the Nile had returned to its course, leaving behind on land various animals, a tortoise too was left. After it had rotted, while its sinews remained stretched inside the shell, it issued a sound when hit by Mercurius. From its likeness the lyre was constructed.

This remarkable version unmistakably detaches the invention of the lyre from the Cyllenian birth-story context; there is nothing to indicate that Hermes is other than an adult. But the new location is strange. In our Persian text, Hermes finds the tortoise on a mountain, in Servius near the Nile, after the flood-water has receded. The former appears more genuine. Firstly, it agrees with the orthodox version, in which the birth-cave is situated on the slopes of Mount Cyllene in Arcadia, and the reptile is explicitly described as a "mountain tortoise" both in the Hymn (33, 42) and later (e.g., Nicander, *Alex.* 559). Secondly, ancient tradition, as represented by Pausanias (8.17.5; 23.9; 54.7), places the lyre-producing variety in the mountains of Arcadia, and archaeological finds and modern reconstructions seem to confirm the literary evidence on this point. The species referred to is obviously the *Testudo marginata*,[71] whose large shell, measuring 22–30 cm in length, was ideal for producing a sizeable soundbox for a lyre.[72] The *Testudo graeca* is reported to be

55

---

[69] Vol. 3, ed. G. Thilo, Leipzig 1887, 355.

[70] Isidorus (3.22.8) only changes the frame (*Lyram primum a Mercurio inventam fuisse dicunt, hoc modo: --- ad cuius speciem Mercurius lyram fecit ...*), whereas the interpolated *Aratus latinus* and the Germanicus scholia dependent on it restyle both the frame, once more, and some of the core; cf. the display in Fragstein (above, n. 67) 20.

[71] See above, n. 47.

[72] See Roberts (above, n. 4) 303 f. The two shells described by Courbin (above, n. 4) are smaller (ca. 16 cm.); Paquette (above, n. 4) 247, however, on the basis of vase paintings, regards 25–30 cm. as normal.

too small for that purpose, and so, presumably, is its Egyptian relation, the *Testudo kleinmanni*.[73]

Now, in fact, the carapace of the latter *was* utilized in Egypt, at least in the New Kingdom, as a sound-box, although not for lyres; the instrument produced in this way was a small lute, mostly played by female dancers.[74] On the other hand, the logic of Servius' story would seem to require not a land-tortoise, like the *kleinmanni*, but an aquatic turtle left on land by accident, in which case something like the huge Nile soft-shell, the *Trionyx triunguis*,[75] might be implied. There is no report, however, that its large flat shell was ever used, or indeed would be usable at all, as a sound-box. So, though there is an air of verisimilitude about Servius' version, with turtles left on land to rot and shells functioning as natural sound-boxes, on closer inspection the actual combination (turtle for tortoise, lyre for lute) appears to be unrealistic. The location implied in the novel's version presents no such inconsistencies, and is apt to be the primary one. It is likely that Servius' source relocated the invention story to Egypt as a consequence of Hermes' later special association with that country, as Hermes Trismegistos. It may be relevant that Diodorus Siculus (I. 16.1) mentions the Egyptian Hermes as the inventor of, among many other things, a lyre with three strings;[76] this might have prompted the relocation.

56   Next, the fact that our Persian Hermes found the tortoise dead. This agrees both with Lucian, as we saw above, and with Servius. It is also conceivable that any one of the bare references to Hermes and the lyre, in which no special point is made of "killing" or "flaying", might belong here. But the prime witnesses to the orthodox version are quite clear on this point. There is emphasis on the contrast between the living mute animal and the dead sounding instrument, and the Hymn even endows the killing itself with sacrificial connotations.[77] Our version, on the other hand, with support in the concrete details from Servius' description, is clearly rationalizing. The flesh has rotted away; Hermes is

---

[73] Pritchard (above, n. 47) 414 f.: 4–5 inches.

[74] See H. G. Fischer in *Lexikon der Ägyptologie* V (1983) 627 f. ("Schildkröte") and E. Hickmann, *ibid.* III (1979) 942–944 ("Laute") and 996–999 ("Leier").

[75] Pritchard (above, n. 47) 599 (colour plate), 640 f: up to 3 feet. On its role in Ancient Egypt, see Fischer (above, n. 74).

[76] Cf. Keller (above, n. 13) 99 f., 127–129.

[77] See Burkert (above, n. 8) 841 and Shelmerdine (above, n. 2).

not only released from killing, he no more has to remove the body from the shell. That process, which seems to cost the baby Hermes with his iron tool no effort at all, is in reality complicated enough; in the recent British reconstruction experiment, the carcass first had to be boiled for several hours.[78] Where the orthodox version is burlesque myth with ritual overtones, ours is down-to-earth and presumably based on practical experience.

Again in agreement with Servius, putrefaction has left the tortoise's sinews stretched over the shell: the lyre is already equipped with strings. The use of sinews for strings is not in accordance with the main witnesses to the orthodox version, but it does occur, as we shall see below on section (3). Now, the essential thing in our new version is not the material, but the fact that Hermes finds an instrument that is already sounding affected by the wind (according to the novel) or hit by Hermes' foot (Servius). He does not really *invent* the lyre, he *finds* it (and later tries to *imitate nature*). Readers and commentators of the *Hymn to Hermes* are sometimes troubled, not so much by the invention story's lack of realism — a baby as inventor etc. — as by its deficient internal logic: how is it possible, even on the story's own terms, that immediately on seeing the grazing tortoise Hermes bursts into happy laugh, thinking of the poor creature's future usefulness for producing music (29–37)?[79] Our unorthodox version, if not realistic either, is at least perfectly logical in this respect.

Between the two ways of making the "lyre" sound — naturally, as an effect of the wind blowing through the sinews, or fortuitously, by the shell being hit — priority should again be accorded to the novel as against the scholium. Both versions are no doubt accommodated to the respective physical setting, the Greek mountain and the Egyptian riverside. The former, however, also takes account of the widespread association of the sound effected by the wind blowing with the sound of

57

---

[78] See Roberts (above, n. 4) 304.

[79] One way to account for this is to make a virtue of necessity, stressing, like Görgemanns (above, n. 2) 123, Hermes' character of musical autodidact, who without help of god or men (v. 440–442) "selbst aus eigenem Einfall, vom Zufall (dem Fund der Schildkröte) begünstigt, die Lyra erfunden hat" — Hermes the εὑρετής par excellence. To K. Kerényi, *Hermes, Guide of Souls*, Zürich 1976, 26, this is an instance of divine "seeing through". Hübner (above, n. 2) 161, finds in v. 31 an instance of anticipatory "Metaphorik," ambiguously vacillating between lie and revelation.

musical instruments, mostly "wind instruments" proper but sometimes also string instruments, such as harp and lyre.[80] The closest the extant Greek novels come to this is probably Achilles Tatius' description (2.14.8) of a wonderful Spanish river, whose water "sounds like a *kithara*" (ὡς κιθάρα λαλεῖ) when struck by the wind; the water is the string, the wind the plectrum.

(2) The reason stated for Hermes bringing the shell home is more emotional in the novel than in the Hymn: the music refreshes his heart, it causes joy. The baby, on the other hand, was for the moment more intent on the instrument's practical utility, both for his own profit (30, 34 f.) and to create festivity and accompany dancers (31 f.). But the novel's insistence on the heart-refreshing effects of music agrees better with the sentiments expressed later in the Hymn, with Hermes playing and Apollo laughing when he hears the lovely sound of music (420–423)[81] — music which expels the desperate cares (447) and is associated with joy (449, 482), pleasure (484) and delight (506). And agreeing with these sentiments, it at once agrees with the commonplace Greek view of music, starting with Homer.[82] The *Ichneutae* (325–327 Radt) similarly has Hermes curing his sorrows with the lyre. The whole present section too, then, may well derive from the Greek novel; only, the fact that the cultural environment of the Persian verse-romance was also music-loving, should warn us not to take all details, or the placement of emphasis, as necessarily original.

(3) Most note-worthy in this section is the idea that Hermes, in order to perpetuate the sweet sound, should not simply try to attach arms, strings etc. to the shell itself, but sets out to build an instrument *similar to* the shell with its sinews. But for the exact parallel in Servius and his followers (*ex cuius imitatione, ad cuius speciem, in cuius similitudinem*),[83] one might have been inclined to regard this feature as an innovation of

---

[80] See the material from various cultures collected in W. H. Roscher, *Hermes der Windgott*, Leipzig 1878, 50–54. (Our instance would no doubt have been welcomed by Roscher, whose thesis about Hermes originating as a wind god has been generally rejected.)

[81] Caution should be taken, however, not to give the Hymn's words too modernly romantic an interpretation ("for the sweet throb of the marvellous music went to his heart, and a soft longing took hold on his soul", trans. H. G. Evelyn-White, LCL; similarly Athanassakis and Humbert); see M. Kaimio, "Music in the Homeric Hymn to Hermes", *Arctos* 8, 1974, 29–42, esp. p. 35.

[82] See Kaimio (above, n. 81) 34–38 and cf. Görgemanns (above, n. 2) 121 f.

[83] Cf. also Cassiodorus *Var.* 2.40.14 (ed. Å. J. Fridh, CCSL 96, Turnholti 1973): *Hanc (sc. citharam) igitur ad imitationem variae testudinis Mercurius dicitur invenisse,* perhaps taken over from Servius.

another cultural context, in which genuine tortoise-shell lyres were no longer on display. With Servius as support, however, we should probably accept this part of the story too as original. In fact, lyres made of wood did occur in Greece simultaneously with those of shell, and a couple of representations in fifth-century vase-painting, showing patterns which do not naturalistically reproduce that of a real tortoise shell, have been tentatively interpreted as depicting wooden sound-boxes.[84] In addition, the close relatives of the *lyra*, the *phorminx* and the *kithara*, were wooden instruments from the start.[85] Doubtless wood became increasingly common in later periods for the *lyra* too as a substitute for shell,[86] and so our novelist may be suspected of representing his own time rather than mentally entering that of Polycrates and Ibycus. If so, it is just one of his minor anachronisms.[87]

Among the construction details specified in the description, guts replace the tortoise's sinews as strings. This brings our version in accordance with the Hymn (which specifies: "sheepguts"), but at the same time with what was probably common practice in antiquity.[88] Otherwise, the various exponents for the orthodox version differ as regards the material used for strings. Apollodorus and others, apparently endeavouring to attach the lyre invention closer to its immediate mythical context, let the slaughtered cows produce the material (guts or sinews?). Avienus, in his Latin adaptation of Aratus (621, quoted above), speaks of "sinews", a material no doubt particularly close at hand for a writer, since the Greek and Latin words for "sinew" (νεῦρον, *nervus*) are often used for "string". At the other extreme, flax is substituted in a Pindar scholium with a rationalizing tendency, explaining that "the use of sinews had not yet been invented."[89] The drying

59

---

[84] Paquette (above, n. 4) 145, cf. Baker (above, n. 2) 14.

[85] The unstable terminology in antiquity for the string instruments may have caused confusion; cf. that Servius speaks of *cithara*, which Isidorus changes into *lyra*.

[86] Michaelides (above, n. 39) 190.

[87] On the historicity of the novel, see Hägg (above, n. 37) 92–98.

[88] Cf. the scholium on Ar. *Ranae* 231 (p. 282.21–22 Dübner) ὡς καὶ χορδὰς λέγομεν ἔτι νῦν τὰς ἐκ τῶν νεύρων, ὅτι παλαιὸν ἐντέριναι ἦσαν, and see Michaelides (above, n. 39) 190; Roberts (above, n. 4) 311; Barker (above, n. 2) 4; and Paquette (above, n. 4) 146 for somewhat differing opinions on this matter.

[89] *Hypothesis Pythiorum* a (p. 1.12–14 Drachmann II) Ἑρμῆς δὲ χέλυν εὑρὼν τετράχορδον λίνα ἀντὶ χορδῶν ἐνημμένην, ἐπειδὴ οὔπω τῶν νεύρων ἡ χρῆσις εὕρετο ... But later Apollo improved on the instrument (p. 2.2–3): δοκεῖ δὲ οὗτος τὰ λίνα ἐξελὼν τοῖς νεύροις ἐντεῖναι τὴν λύραν. Cf. Pollux *Onom.* 4.62 (p. 219.20 Bethe) μέρη δὲ τῶν ὀργάνων νευραί, χορδαί, λίνα, μίτοι ...

and twisting of the guts in our version is surely a detail from life, though already Homer (*Od.* 21.408) speaks of "well-twisted sheep-gut."[90]

60
The application of arms, otherwise an important topic in the orthodox version as well as in reports of modern attempts at reconstructing the ancient lyre,[91] is not even mentioned here — probably because the real crux, the fastening of animal horns or wooden arms to a real tortoise shell, does not come up, the whole thing being (presumably) made of wood. The hide covering the sound-box of the tortoise-shell lyre is for the same reason no topic here.

On the other hand, the construction of a peg to attach and tighten the string — Hermes seems to be content with one string so far — is realized as a problem; so it is in practice, but never in the orthodox invention story. Originally, the Greeks used strips of raw leather for this purpose, but these were later replaced by other contrivances, such as pegs of wood, metal or ivory,[92] and our author again appears to have the more modern device in mind.

The reference to frets (the Persian has *parda-hā*) being moved from inside to outside is more mysterious. Possibly, the Greek text here mentioned the μαγάς, "bridge",[93] whatever part of the carapace served that supporting function for the sinews/strings; and the Persian author (or some intermediary), unfamiliar with the lyre, interpreted it as something like the frets of a guitar or lute.[94]

(4) While the infant hero of the orthodox version was ready in almost no time with his construction — "born at dawn, by midday he played

---

[90] See Barker (above, n. 2) 30 with n. 34 (with further refs.).

[91] See Roberts (above, n. 4) 304 f. and Bélis (above, n. 4).

[92] Cf. W. D. Anderson, *Ethos and Education in Greek Music: The Evidence of Poetry and Philosophy*, Cambridge, Mass., 1966, 5 f., 211 f. (with further refs.); Michaelides (above, n. 39) 190; Roberts (above, n. 4) 305–308; and Barker (above, n. 2) 4. The term κόλλοψ, κόλλαβος applies to both strip of leather and peg. Paquette (above, n. 4) 147 f., analyzing vase-painting representations, distinguishes a greater variety of fastening devices.

[93] Lucian (*Dial.Deor.* 7.4) mentions "pegs" and "bridge" together in this context: ἔπειτα κολλάβους ἐμπήξας καὶ μαγάδιον (v.l. μαγάδα) ὑποθεὶς καὶ ἐντεινάμενος ἑπτὰ χόρδας … The use of ἐμπήγνυμι implies that Lucian too lets Hermes anachronistically employ pegs instead of strips of leather. The *Hymn to Hermes* and the other primary witnesses to the orthodox version omit any mention of pegs (strips) and bridge.

[94] An alternative, though less likely, explanation would be that the description was influenced by the old Egyptian lute, which sometimes had frets (and sometimes used a tortoise shell as sound-box), see Hickmann (above, n. 74) 942.

his lyre"[95] (*H. Herm.* 17) — ours, in spite of much brooding and trial, needs help from outside. His helper, the old man he meets on his walk, can of course have no real counterpart in the orthodox version. Here even Servius leaves us in the lurch, just stating without any details that Hermes constructed the lyre in the likeness of the tortoise. We are thus at a point where the Persian adaptator (or an intermediary) *may* have entered on an elaboration of his own, just as in the symposium speech he lets Vāmiq introduce an old Eros as an alternative to the conventional young one, without support, as far as we can see, in the parallel Greek text.

Yet there are clues to suggest that this part is original too. First, we in fact find an old man in the Hymn as well, though his role is different: Hermes, driving the stolen cattle, meets an old man working in his vineyard. He earnestly entreats the man not to tell anyone what he has just seen (87–93), but when Apollo comes along next day, the old man immediately informs against the baby thief (187–212). He is consistently referred to as "the old man" (ὁ γέρων) simply, as ours is, and it is only in the more pointed version of the same story, which we read in Antoninus Liberalis (summarized above), that he receives a name, Battus. Now, even if "the old man's" function in the Hymn differs from that in our Persian text, the two descriptions are similar. In our story, Hermes finds the man "bent double by the passing of year and month, his head bowing down in thoughts, his hand propping up his cheek" (trans. B. Utas), which sounds like an elaboration of the Hymn's (90) ἐπικαμπύλος ὤμους, "with bowed shoulders." By itself, this could be a mere coincidence, a stock description of old age, but viewed together with the other clue (cf. below), the introduction of the old man and his description are likely to be a reminiscence of, even an allusion to, the orthodox version's first and foremost representative, the Hymn.

(5) The second and decisive clue is the statement, in the present section, that Hermes is pleased with having a "human" helper in building the instrument. As was concluded above, in section (1), this must be interpreted as an unintentional remnant of an original version in which Hermes was a god; and so, the human helper motif must already have been present in the Greek novel.

What human helper, then, for Hermes would a Greek writer be inclined to introduce into the invention story, and why? It should be

61

62

---

[95] Trans. Athanassakis.

someone who is already associated in some special way with the early lyre. Since the helper is defined as a mortal, Apollo, who sometimes takes Hermes' place as the inventor,[96] is ruled out. Orpheus and Amphion are possible candidates, or Cerambus ("the first of men to use the lyre": Ant. Lib. 22.3); but Terpander seems to fit the circumstances best. To him, as we saw above, Pindar attributed the invention of the *barbitos*. If our author used the word *barbitos* more or less loosely as a synonym for *lyra*, he may have wished to accommodate this second "inventor of the lyre" together with Hermes in the same invention story.

But there is more to it: Terpander is also, in several sources,[97] given the credit for having introduced the *seven-string* lyre. This claim has often been accepted as an historical fact by modern scholars as well: the first part of the seventh century is considered a possible date for that innovation, which would have replaced the earlier lyre-type instruments with three or four strings.[98] In fact, as far as the Persian text, which is rather fragmentary and obscure at this point, allows us to follow the helper's construction activity, it is precisely the strings and their arrangement that are in focus. Even if the figure "seven" is not mentioned, the strings are said to be "many", whereas Hermes himself in his unsuccessful attempts seems to have operated with one string only. This, in a crude

63

[96] Apollo as inventor: Callim. *Del.* 253, see W. H. Mineur, Leiden 1984, *ad loc.* and K. J. McKay, *Erysichthon: A Callimachean Comedy*, Leiden 1962, 166 f. Cf. also Pl. *Resp.* 399d–e, Diod. Sic. 5.75.3, Paus. 9.30.1, [Plut.] *De mus.* 14 (1135f-36a). Brown (above, n. 54) 91 f., however, overstates the matter, saying that "both Hermes and Apollo were regarded as patrons of the tortoise-shell lyre; some preferred Hermes, and some Apollo …" In fact, Hermes is the rule, Apollo the exception, and those who mention Apollo as inventor never specify the tortoise-shell form; some confusion with the cithara (which was Apollo's instrument, cf. *Hymn. Hom. Ap.* 131, Pind. *Pyth.* 5.65, Bion 10(7).8) lies near at hand (*pace* Brown 93). If Brown is correct in regarding Hermes as a usurper of Apollo's musical hegemony in general, it still does not follow (nor does our literary and archaeological material warrant) that the tortoise-shell lyre specifically was originally regarded as Apollo's invention.

[97] E.g. Strabo 13.2.4 (cf. Page *PMG* p. 363), Plin. *HN* 7.204, [Plut.] *De mus.* 30 (1141c), Nicomachus *apud* Boeth. *De inst. mus.* 1.20.

[98] Among other considerations, the fact that the *Hymn to Hermes* regards the seven-string lyre as the very prototype has been taken to indicate that the change from fewer to seven strings must have taken place fairly early, or about Terpander's time. But the Hymn of course only provides a *terminus ante quem*, and, as we shall see below, the matter is in no way settled. Cf. Anderson (above, n. 92) 44 f.; Michaelides (above, n. 39) 190 f.; Baker (above, n. 2) 4, 208 n. 18 (and Index s.v. Strings of instruments, number); and Paquette (above, n. 4) 87, 90, 146 f.

way, epitomizes the development of the lyre as the Greeks traditionally viewed it.[99]

In reality, seven-string instruments are already attested in the Greek Bronze Age, notably the lyre-like instrument depicted on the Aghia Triada sarcophagus.[100] Regarding the tortoise-shell variety of lyre, on the other hand, the earliest unambiguous attestation, regardless of the number of strings, is provided by a hydria of ca. 700 B.C. from Analatos and a number of lead figurines from the sanctuary of Artemis Orthia at Sparta, dated 700–635 B.C. — i.e., belonging roughly to Terpander's period.[101] There is also the attractive hypothesis that a number of tortoiseshell fragments with drilled holes, which were recently found in the late-Bronze-Age sanctuary at Phylakopi, should have belonged to lyres. However, this is just a possibility, and the excavators' confident conclusion that "lyre music was a feature of ritual in the sanctuary throughout its life" seems unwarranted.[102]

We return to the text. Our novelist, in trying to harmonize two rivalling invention claims, if that is what he does, was not alone. Diodorus (5.75.3, cf. 3.59.5–6) seems to suggest that Hermes *re*invented the lyre after Apollo had destroyed his own similar invention,[103] and an excerpt from Nicomachus (1, p. 266 Jan) is closer still to the novelist, featuring precisely Terpander beside Hermes. Nicomachus first states, in full accordance with the Homeric Hymn, that Hermes is said to (φασι) have

64

---

[99] Cf. J. Chailley, *La musique grecque antique*, Paris 1979, 69 on the number of strings ("de la lyre archaïque à 3 cordes à la cithare tardive à 18 cordes") as a matter of concern not only for modern musicologists but for the Greeks themselves; so their historians, "pour chaque corde, ont cru devoir avancer un nom d'inventeur au reste variable d'un auteur à l'autre." The pseudo-Plutarchean compilation *De musica* (first/second century A.D.) 3–12 (1131f–1135d) is a good illustration of the frenetic hunt for inventors.

[100] Cf. B. Aign, *Die Geschichte der Musikinstrumente des ägäischen Raumes bis um 700 vor Christus*, Diss. Frankfurt am Main 1963, 44 f. For up-to-date information on the Bronze Age material, see C. Renfrew, *The Archaeology of Cult: The Sanctuary at Phylakopi*, London 1985, 325 (ref. by Robin Hägg).

[101] Aign (above, n. 100) 95 f., 204 f., 232–235.

[102] Renfrew (above, n. 100) 325 f., 384. The circumstance that most of the shells lack drilled holes is too easily dismissed. Nor is the potential use for other purposes seriously discussed; cf. that in Egypt tortoise shell was employed for combs, bracelets, knife hilts, bowls etc. (Fischer [above, n. 74] 627), and that the drilled shells found at Locri Epizephyrii have been interpreted as belonging to objects (bowls?) equipped with metal handles (Settis [above, n. 58] 90).

[103] Cf. Brown (above, n. 54) 93 f.

invented the lyre and equipped it with seven strings. He then, Nicomachus continues, handed over the skill to Orpheus — not to Apollo, as in the Hymn.[104] Orpheus, in turn, taught others, but after he had been killed, his lyre was thrown into the sea and carried to Lesbos, where it was found and brought to Terpander. He took it to Egypt and showed it to the priests, "as if he himself had been its first inventor (πρωθευρη-τής)." Τέρπανδρος μὲν οὕτω λέγεται τὴν λύραν εὑρηκέναι — this is the reason, Nicomachus suggests, why Terpander (too) is said to have invented the lyre. The same rival claim[105] may have prompted our author to introduce the old man as Hermes' mortal helper: the novelist's solution, as opposed to the scholar's.

For the name of the old man, Vāmiq adduces the authority of his own wise teacher. This may imply awareness that the innovation might be ascribed to others as well, as indeed it was; or it may simply serve to distinguish this old man from that of the Hymn, the "Battus" of the later tradition. The name itself, *Hažhrah-man*, is Iranian in form, in contrast to most other names in the novel, which are just more or less distorted transliterations of Greek names.[106] If the Greek original did call the man Τέρπανδρος, it is possible that the translator looked upon it as a "speaking name" and wanted to convey its meaning in Persian. According to this hypothesis, *Hažhrah* may be a contraction of *hažhīrah* meaning, among other things, "beautiful, good, agreeable", whereas the second part, *man*, appears to lack a satisfactory etymology.[107]

The helper episode as such is thus, with a reasonable degree of certainty, vindicated for the Greek original; but it does not follow that all its details are authentic. Rather, it is likely that the description of the construction technicalities was influenced by such string instruments as were actually known to the adaptator(s) (cf. above on the "frets"). On the other hand, it is probable that the original description should occasionally shine through the disguise. For instance, the idea that the strings

---

[104] Orpheus is the first recipient also in Isidorus *Etym.* 3.22.8 *ad cuius speciem Mercurius lyram fecit et Orpheo tradidit* and his *Chron.* 3955.77a (p. 437 ed. Th. Mommsen, MGHAA 11:2, Berolini 1961) *hac aetate alter Mercurius lyram repperit et Orfeo tradidit.*

[105] Nicomachus seems to be the only extant witness to the tradition that Terpander "invented the lyre" (without qualifications such as the "seven-string" or the "*barbitos*-type" lyre), but our novelist may of course have met it somewhere in this unqualified form.

[106] See Utas (above, n. 35) 435.

[107] I owe the elucidation of the Persian name to Bo Utas, who also tentatively suggests that *man* may be short for *mand* "furnished with".

were adapted to different characters faintly resembles the Greek view of various "harmonies" corresponding to special characters and emotions, as discussed by Plato in the *Republic* (398e ff.), with echoes in the pseudo-Plutarchean *De musica* (15–17, 1136b–37a).[108] But the notion of each separate string carrying such an association seems strange and may be due to some misunderstanding on the way.

(6) The equation of the musical instrument with a breathing human body may also have had some foundation in the original, though no quite accurate parallel from a Greek source readily presents itself. But in Isidorus' musicological section (*Etym.* 3.22.6) there is a curious Greek-Latin etymology for chorda "string":[109] *chordas autem dictas a corde, quia sicut pulsus est cordis in pectore, ita pulsus chordae in cithara* — the "beating of the string" compared to the "heart's beating in the breast". Rather than relying on one source, Isidorus in this section presents a "rhapsody" of loans,"[110] but it may still be significant that in the next sentence he mentions Hermes as the inventor of the strings and the one who "first confined sound to sinews (strings)."[111] There is at least some likelihood that a passage combining Hermes as inventor with lyre-and-strings likened to a living body[112] figures somewhere behind Isidorus' etymologically angled statement. Whether the ultimate source for that combination was our

66

---

[108] Cf. Barker (above, n. 2) 164 (with refs.), 169 (on the sophist Damon).

[109] There is a related etymological explanation in Cassiodorus *Var.* 2.40.12 (ed. Å. J. Fridh, CCSL 96, Turnholti 1973) … *nihil tamen efficacius inventum est ad permovendos animos quam concavae citharae blanda resultatio. Hinc etiam appellatam aestimamus chordam, quod facile corda moveat.* Contrast the Greek scholiast on Ar. *Ranae* 231 (quoted above, n. 88) with the correct explanation that "strings" are called χορδαί because they were (originally) made of guts, χορδαί.

[110] See Fontaine (above, n. 68) 434.

[111] *Etym.* 3.22.6 *Has primus Mercurius excogitavit, idemque prior in nervos sonum strinxit.* This piece of information stands isolated from the story of Hermes' invention of the lyre in 3.22.8, which Isidorus took over from Servius (cf. above). Fontaine (above, n. 68) 434 speaks of the clear "sédimentation des emprunts" in this section.

[112] The-body-a-lyre becomes a topos ("l'homme cithare de Dieu") in Patristic literature, cf. Ambrosius, *De interpellatione Job et David* 4(2).10.36 (ed. K. Schenkl, CSEL 32, Pragae 1897) *Confitebor tibi in cithara, deus meus. habet citharam suam anima nostra; … cithara est caro nostra, quando peccato moritur, ut deo vivat: cithara est, quando septiformem accipit spiritum in baptismatis sacramento. testudo enim dum vivit, luto mergitur; ubi mortua fuerit, tegmen eius aptatur in usum canendi et piae gratiam disciplinae, ut septem vocum discrimina numeris modulantibus obloquatur. similiter caro nostra …* For discussion and further refs., see J. Fontaine, "Les symbolismes de la cithare dans la poésie de Paulin de Nole," in W. den Boer (ed.), *Romanitas et Christianitas*, Amsterdam & London 1973, 123–143, esp. 126 f.

novel, is, of course, impossible to say; but it is fair to note that similar things are to be found in another novelist, Achilles Tatius, who likes to dissect human psychological and physiological functions, not seldom in close combination with mythographical expositions.

The examination in detail of the Persian text is thus completed. Before collecting the threads, we should look for other passages of the extant Greek novels in which special attention is paid to music and musical instruments. Generally, music plays only a minor role in the novels;[113] no author is obsessed with music in the way some of them are with art. As a natural part of Greek social and religious life, playing on the *aulos* and *syrinx* occurs in Chariton in connection with symposia and sacrifices (4.5.7, 6.2.4), but there is nowhere any detailed description of an instrument, and the sound of the kithara is mentioned only to illustrate the sweetness of Callirhoe's voice (2.3.8). Festivities of various kinds cause most of Heliodorus' references to song and music as well, again without any elaboration and with the *aulos* and *syrinx* as the favoured instruments (3.1.5, 4.17.1, 5.16.2), besides the human voice. The servant girl Thisbe is described as a skilled *kithara* player (1.11.3, 2.8.5), but only in passing. In Achilles Tatius, too, social playing on the *kithara* is mentioned a couple of times; the heroine regularly practices on the instrument (1.19.2, 2.7.1–2), and a slave gives a musical performance after dinner, singing of Apollo and Daphne to his own accompaniment on the *kithara* (1.5.4). The description of his instrumental prelude to this amorous song is the only time in the novels that the technicalities of playing a string instrument are dwelt on in any detail. As for the lyre, it occurs only once in the novels, and then in an enumeration of the various instruments that the nymph Echo learnt to play (Longus 3.23.2).

To find something closer in type to our story of the invention of the lyre, we have to turn to Longus and, in particular, Achilles Tatius and their treatment of the *syrinx*. The pan-pipes of course plays a prominent part in the description of the pastoral setting of *Daphnis and Chloe*, and at one point the entire myth of Pan and Syrinx is told (2.34). We hear of Pan's courtship and Syrinx' refusal, flight and transformation into reeds. Pan cuts the reeds in anger, then discovers what has happened and "invents the instrument" (τὸ ὄργανον νοεῖ), gluing together with wax reeds of unequal length.[114]

---

[113] For a survey, see P. Liviabella Furiani, "La musica nel romanzo 'erotico' greco tra natura e cultura", *QIFP* 1, 1984, 27–43.

[114] Text M. D. Reeve, Leipzig 1982.

Now the same aetiological myth is told by Achilles Tatius as well (8.6), though with important differences. He first describes, in his most circumstantial and mannered ecphrasis style, how a pan-pipes is constructed and played. Then follows the myth itself, with the story up to the metamorphosis reduced to the most essential facts, but with Pan's doings thereafter more elaborated. As in Longus, he cuts down the reeds in anger, discovers his fatal mistake, and regrets what he has done. The rest is totally different (8.6.10):[115]

> Συμφορήσας οὖν τὰ τετμημένα τῶν καλάμων ὡς μέλη τοῦ σώματος καὶ συνθεὶς εἰς ἓν σῶμα, εἶχε διὰ χειρῶν τὰς τομὰς τῶν καλάμων καταφιλῶν ὡς τῆς κόρης τραύματα· ἔστενε δὲ ἐρωτικὸν ἐπιθεὶς τὸ στόμα καὶ ἐνέπνει ἄνωθεν εἰς τοὺς αὐλοὺς ἅμα φιλῶν· τὸ δὲ πνεῦμα διὰ τῶν ἐν τοῖς καλάμοις στενωπῶν καταρρέον αὐλήματα ἐποίει, καὶ ἡ σῦριγξ εἶχε φωνήν.

68

> So he collected the fragments of reed as though they had been the maiden's limbs and put them together as though to form a single body; and then, holding the pieces in his hands, kissed them, as though they had been her wounds. As he put his lips to them he groaned from love, and breathed down upon the reeds while he kissed them; and his breath, pouring down through the holes in them, gave musical notes, and the pan-pipes found its voice.

What Longus expresses in the words, "he invents the instrument", is here described as the purely accidental result of Pan's desperate attempt to reconstruct his beloved. His breath just happens to pass through the joined reeds, which show themselves to function as a musical instrument. The similarity to our new version of Hermes and the lyre is evident. Pan is deprived of his inventive genius, as is Hermes, and a rational spirit has entered into the mythical context. The same spirit is evident also in Ovid's version of the myth (*Met.* 1.689–712): there, it is the wind that blows through the reeds and produces the sound, giving Pan the idea to construct a musical instrument — a still closer parallel to our Hermes and the sounding tortoise-shell.[116]

---

[115] Text E. Vilborg, Stockholm 1955, trans. S. Gaselee & E. H. Warmington (LCL), 1969.

[116] Longus chooses another expedient: the maiden Syrinx is described as not only beautiful, but also endowed with a good singing-voice (2.34.1 παρθένος καλὴ καὶ τὴν φωνὴν μουσικὴ), a trait missing in Ovid and Achilles Tatius. This makes the result of the transformation logical enough (2.34.3): καὶ ἡ τότε παρθένος καλὴ νῦν ἐστὶ σῦριγξ μουσική. Servius' version of the myth (*in* Verg. *Ecl.* 2.31) is too condensed to exhibit any of these distinctive features.

Conclusion

The results of the analysis may be summed up from three points of view: the faithfulness of the Persian translation of *Metiochus and Parthenope*, the character of this Greek novel in the light of the analysed section, and the consequences of the new version of the invention of the lyre for our understanding of the myth.

69   It appears, rather surprisingly, that the greater part of the invention story, as found in ʿUnṣurī's 11th-century verse-romance, is in fact likely to follow the Greek original rather closely. As shown by parallels in ancient literature, this is certainly the case with its first half, describing a fully-grown Hermes finding a dead tortoise, which emits music in the wind, and trying to construct a similar instrument himself to imitate nature. And there are good reasons to regard the other half too as genuine in substance: unsuccessful in his attempt, Hermes on a walk meets an old man, possibly Terpander, who helps him to produce a functioning many-stringed lyre. While the outline of the story thus seems to have been taken over rather faithfully, some of the concomitant circumstances (e.g., Hermes being a man, not a god) and much of the descriptive detail (partly omitted in my paraphrase above) should no doubt be ascribed to the Persian poet (or some non-Greek intermediary). The musicological matter is to be looked upon with particular caution in that respect.

With regard to *M&P*, we learn from this episode that the rationalizing attitude to traditional mythology, as displayed in Metiochus' speech on Eros preserved in the Greek papyrus fragment, was extant in other parts of the novel as well. No doubt, it was part of the novelist's characterization of his hero, who, consequently, was more distinctly characterized than his pale counterpart in Chariton's novel. The inclusion of an elaborate myth of this kind brings the author closer than previously suspected to Achilles Tatius, who among the extant novelists takes a special delight in such material. Achilles Tatius' treatment of the aetiological myth of the invention of the pan-pipes in fact shows some close points of resemblance with our invention myth. Yet our author's ambition, if correctly observed, to accommodate historical facts (Terpander and the seven-stringed lyre) in the framework of a more conventional mythical account, gives him a distinct profile. At the same time, we recognize again, as in the Greek fragments, the Chariton-like novelist who endeavours to create a historical atmosphere for his love-story, perhaps using the archaic-sounding term *barbitos* for "lyre",

though also, slightly anachronistically, making Ibycus appear with a $\quad$
wooden lyre (with pegs) in his hands.

The myth itself is a more complex issue. We have established the existence of an unorthodox version, part of which was already extant (but not noticed) in Servius and (perhaps) glimpsed in Lucian, but which only the novel enables us to study in a detailed and internally logical form. Hermes does not really *invent* the lyre, he finds an instrument produced by nature and, enchanted by its music, tries to imitate it. How far is this version the novelist's own creation, and what does he owe to sources lost to us? Lucian and Servius are of course late enough possibly to be dependent on the novelist, whose style and attitude place him fairly close to Chariton — i.e., he is probably not later than the first century A.D.

In at least one important feature, it appears that our version is more "original" than the orthodox one, namely, in staging a fully-grown Hermes. Various evidence suggests that both the cattle-theft and the invention of the lyre were originally told without any connection with the birth-story. But already in Alcaeus the *child* Hermes steals the cattle, and a vase-painting of ca. 530 B.C. shows Hermes lying on his cot with the stolen cows looking on. It is a significant fact, however, that the lyre is missing in both these pre-hymnal sources. This indicates that the author of the Homeric *Hymn to Hermes* may have been the first to connect all three stories: birth, invention and theft. Sophocles, for his satyr play, gladly appropriated the burlesque created by this combination — the baby as inventor and thief — only improving on the internal logic by placing the theft before the invention. The impact of the Hymn and Satyr Play made this the orthodox version, reflected in mythographical, astronomical and musicological literature and in later art. Yet, in its shadow the earlier version with a fully-grown Hermes inventing the lyre must have lived on, in sources lost to us, eventually to be received by our novelist.

If this is correct, there is a fair chance that the *killing* of the tortoise as well is an innovation of the author of the Hymn. The scene with Hermes meeting the grazing tortoise and addressing it has a real point only if he is a small child, who meets the animal on its own level.[117] The author $\quad$

---

71

[117] Hübner (above, n. 2) 160, speaking of "eine fiktive Übertragung der Menschenwelt auf das Tierreich" etc., misses both the humour and the child's perspective. The latter aspect is curiously absent in E. Szepes' analysis of the scene as well: "Humour of the Homeric Hermes Hymn", *Homonoia* 2, 1980, 5–56, pp. 34–37.

then imaginatively staged a sacrificial killing, deliberately anticipating that of the two cows later in the Hymn. The myth which he thus reshaped — and which our novelist much later utilized — had no doubt simply made Hermes, on his wanderings in Arcadia, come across a tortoise shell, from which he constructed the lyre, using parts of other dead animals as well: goat(?)-horns for arms, sheep-guts for strings, oxhide to cover the sound-box. There is no reason why precisely the tortoise should have been sacrificed for the purpose, while the other animal parts were just available. Hermes' creative genius was displayed by the combination of these dead parts into a sounding instrument.

If these two features — fully-grown Hermes and dead tortoise — are probably old, it is not unlikely that the rest of the story is the invention of the novelist, who deliberately lets his hero reject the orthodox version. This is not done explicitly, as the similar rejection of the conventional Eros earlier in the novel, but the readers, like the novel's Polycrates, are expected to know that version and recognize the novelties: the wind playing on the tortoise shell and thus giving the god the idea of music, the construction of a sham tortoise-lyre instead of using the shell itself, the necessity to find a human helper to make the instrument function.

Of course there is always the possibility that some of this is taken over from some Hellenistic source. There is nothing to indicate, however, that the known Hellenistic treatments of the subject, such as Eratosthenes' epyllion, displayed any of these features. It all rather bears the stamp of the rationalizing novelist, who takes a pride in doing away with the supernatural and tries to accommodate the different claims to the invention of the lyre he has met in literature. The fictional setting of the story, with Polycrates explicitly announcing that this is a controversial issue and Metiochus volunteering to sort things out, may even be interpreted as an internal indication of the novelist's claim to originality. However that may be, it is quite clear that this Hermes is too humanized and deprived of his divine faculties to derive from the old myth.

The faint afterlife of the unorthodox version may also be taken to indicate that it originated with our author. Lucian may well have read the novel and used part of it for his contaminated version (baby, but dead tortoise), but it is equally possible that he just knew the old pre-hymnal myth from the same source(s) as the novelist. Servius' version, on the other hand, shows enough specific agreements with the novel to warrant dependence, presumably with some Egyptian source as an intermediary. His condensed and egyptized account, taken over almost

72

literally by Isidorus and the Aratus tradition, happened to become the only witness to the unorthodox version to survive the Middle Ages until the Persian verse-romance now tells us the whole story.

And the moral? Simply a reminder of a generally recognized fact, to which, however, enough attention is not always paid in practice: that Greek "myths", in the shape we have received them, are mostly literary products, bearing the stamp of their time and of the individual author. The new unorthodox version helps us to see that the orthodox one as well is a piece of literature, not a traditional tale.[118] Behind these two, we may discern the more genuine myth. The impact which the Hymn exercised on later literature should not deceive us: such success gives it no retro-active authority, it remains a unique creation of its author, humorous, grim — and not too consistent. Serious interpreters have found in it the Divine Child, who legitimizes its status through wonderful exploits;[119] or Hermes' notorious Ambiguity expressing itself in his instantaneous transformation from a baby, who rejoices in its new toy, into an accomplished artisan;[120] or an instance of ritual killing out of which Music is born.[121] Certain mythical archetypes were no doubt used by the author in his composition, but the actual joining of the elements is his, and we have every chance of going seriously wrong if we attach too much importance to that accidental combination.

73

---

[118] Cf. the discussion in W. Burkert, *Structure and History in Greek Mythology and Ritual*, Berkeley 1979, 1–34.

[119] For refs., see Herter (above, n. 49) 232 f.

[120] L. Kahn, *Hermès passe ou les ambiguités de la communication*, Paris 1978, 124; and the lyre is the "produit ambigu de l'enfance d'un dieu qui se fait adulte" (*ibid.*).

[121] Cf. W. Burkert, *Homo Necans*, Berkeley 1983, 39, Shelmerdine (above, n. 2) 206, and, in particular, Burkert (above, n. 8) 841, 845.

Heliodorus and Nubia

The Black Land of the Sun
Meroe in Heliodoros' Romantic Fiction

[originally published in V. Christides & Th. Papadopoullos (eds.), *Proceedings of the Sixth International Congress of Graeco-Oriental and African Studies, Nicosia 30 April — 5 May 1996*, Nicosia 2000 (*Graeco-Arabica* 7–8, 2000), 195–220.]

One of the most intriguing descriptions of Nubia in ancient literature is to be found in a Greek novel of Late Antiquity, the *Αἰθιοπικά* or "Aithiopian Story".[1] Its title is derived from Αἰθιοπία, the Greek name for the Middle Nile region, that is Egypt south of Aswan and the northern part of the present Sudan (as far as the confluence of the White and Blue Nile) — or what we today commonly refer to as Nubia. The novel's author is a certain Heliodoros who presents himself in the last words of the novel as "a Phoenician from the city of Emesa [in Syria], one of the clan of Descendants of the Sun, Theodosios' son, Heliodoros" (10.41).[2] In fact, we know nothing else about this Heliodoros, not even for certain in what century he wrote. The novel has been dated by some in the second century AD, by many in the third, and by others still as late as the second part of the fourth century. At present, there seems to have emerged a consensus

---

[1] I prefer to use the spelling Aithiopia, Aithiopian etc. to avoid confusion with modern Ethiopia. — Thanks are due to Vassily Christides whose invitation to the delightful First International Colloquium on Graeco-Oriental and African Studies at Neapoli in Laconia in July, 1997, made me embark on this study; to the participants in the colloquium; and to László Török and Richard Holton Pierce who kindly read and commented on the penultimate version of the paper.

[2] I quote throughout from John Morgan's English translation (in B.P. Reardon [ed.], *Collected Ancient Greek Novels*, Berkeley 1989, 349–588), except at places where my argument needs a more literal rendering of the Greek. There are two critical editions of the Greek text: Héliodore, *Les Éthiopiques (Théagène et Chariclée)*, Vol. 1–3, ed. R.M. Rattenbury and T.W. Lumb, trans. J. Maillon (Collection des Universités de France), 2nd ed. Paris 1960; and Heliodori *Aethiopica*, ed. A. Colonna, Roma 1938 (this text is also available with facing Italian trans. in Eliodoro, *Le Etiopiche*, ed. A. Colonna [I Classici greci e latini TEA], Milano 1990). For a good introduction to this novel, see J.R. Morgan, "Heliodoros", in: G. Schmeling (ed.), *The Novel in the Ancient World*, Leiden 1996, 417–456; for its relation to history and historiography, the same author's "History, Romance, and Realism in the Aithiopika of Heliodoros", *ClAnt* 1, 1982, 221–265, is fundamental.

that it most probably belongs to the third quarter of the fourth century,[3] the main argument being Heliodoros' description in Book 9 of the technique the Aithiopians employ in besieging the city of Syene (Aswan). This description of what seems to be a purely fictitious event shows striking similarities with the account of the historical siege of Nisibis in Mesopotamia in AD 350 that the future Emperor Julian gives in two panegyric speeches to Constantius (*Or.* 1.22-23; 3.11-13). The Byzantine tradition that Heliodoros became a Christian later in life, even a bishop (at Trikka in Thessaly), would then not be chronologically impossible; but it cannot be supported by any external evidence and may simply be a convenient alibi for Christians who wanted to read a pagan love story.

196

The young heroine of the novel, Charikleia, turns out to be the daughter of the King and Queen of Aithiopia, Hydaspes and Persinna. She is white, while her parents are black; the explanation, we are told (4.8; 10.14-15), is that in the very moment of her conception the queen happened to look at a painting of the naked Andromeda who was released from the rocks by Perseus. And Andromeda, though an Aithiopian princess, was represented as white in the picture, as she in fact always is in Graeco-Roman art.[4] Now, the queen understandingly did not dare to present her white baby to the king; so Charikleia was exposed, and her adventures until she is finally recognized as the princess of Meroe fills the whole novel. In Delphi she meets a young Thessalian nobleman, Theagenes. They instantly fall in love; and together, or temporarily separated by external forces, the beautiful young couple make their winding way back to "the black land of the Sun" (ἠελίου πρὸς χθόνα κυανέην),

---

[3] Cf. Colonna (1990) 23-25; P. Chauvin, *Chronique des derniers païens*, Paris 1990, 321-325; G.W. Bowersock, *Fiction as History: Nero to Julian*, Berkeley 1994, 149-160; and Morgan (1996) 417-421.

[4] Thus K. Schauenberg, "Andromeda I", in: *LIMC* 1:1, Zürich and München 1981, 774-790, p. 788. Beazley's suggestion (in *CVA. Oxford* I III I on Pl. 4, 7-8) that an Attic 4th-century BC head vase in Oxford (Beazley, *ARV²* II 1550, no. 2) should be an exception to this general rule, is rejected by Schauenberg, "Achilleus als Barbar: ein antikes Mißverständnis", *A&A* 20, 1974, 88-96, p. 90 (and Pl. 3), who thinks this vase depicts "eine äthiopische Herrscherin von uns nicht bekanntem Namen", perhaps from a lost tragedy. (Cf. also Frank Snowden in J. Vercoutter, J. Leclant, F.M. Snowden, Jr., and J. Desanges, *The Image of the Black in Western Art*, Vol. 1, Cambridge, MA, and London 1976, 160, and Fig. 180.) Memnon, the Aithiopian king and hero at Troy, is also regularly represented as white, see Schauenberg, ibid. See further O.A.W. Dilke, "Heliodorus and the Colour Problem", *PP* 35, 1980, 264-271, and M.D. Reeve, "Coneceptions", *PCPhS* 215, 1989, 81-112.

as the Delphian oracle had promised (2.35.5; 10.41.2). Their wedding at
Meroe forms the happy ending of the novel.

It is in the last three books of the novel that most of the description
of Meroe, its history, geography, and ethnography, is to be found. The
concrete details of this romantic setting have now and then been used
by scholars, either to date the novel or to illuminate Meroitic history.[5]
No very convincing or conclusive results have been attained, which has
to do with the nature of the text. This is a novel, and an historical novel
at that: the action presupposes that Egypt is under Persian domination
and that Alexandria does not yet exist, which means that it takes place
some time after 525 and before 332 BC.[6] So the novelist wants to depict
Greece, Egypt, and Meroe as they were some seven or eight hundred
years before his own time. That his sources are mainly literary and that
they are mixed, ought not therefore to have come as a surprise to anybody, nor that his creative imagination decides how he is to select and
use his sources. Those who blame the author for having had recourse
to old literary sources like Herodotos instead of trying to gather such
factual information as may have been obtainable in his own time, seem
neither to be acquainted with historical fiction as a genre, nor even to
have considered the novel's dramatic date.[7]

Once we grant Heliodoros the privilege of using Greek literature on

197

---

[5] See, e.g., F.M. Snowden, *Blacks in Antiquity: Ethiopians in the Greco-Roman Experience*, Cambridge, MA 1970, 143; G. Vantini, "Greek and Arab Geographers on Nubia ca.
500 B.C.–1500 A.D.", *Graeco-Arabica* 3, 1984, 21–51, p. 25; and S.Ya. Bersina, "Milanese
Papyrus No. 40", *Meroitica* 10, 1989, 217–224, p. 222; other instances are referred to in
Morgan (1982) 249 n. 126. For more circumspect discussion, see C. Conti Rossini, "Meroe ed Aksum nel romanzo di Eliodoro", *RSO* 8, 1919–20, 233–239; E. Feuillatre, *Études
sur les* Éthiopiques *d'Héliodore. Contribution à la connaissance du roman grec*, Paris 1966,
33–44, with the review by J. Leclant in *REG* 81, 1968, 629–632; W. Vycichl, "Heliodors
Aithiopika und die Volksstämme des Reiches Meroë", in: E. Endesfelder et al. (eds.),
Ägypten und Kusch (Schriften zur Geschichte und Kultur des Alten Orients, 13), Berlin
1977, 447–458; Morgan (1982) 237–250; and R. Lonis, "Les Éthiopiens sous le regard
d'Héliodore", in: Baslez et al. (ed.), *Le Monde du roman grec* (Études de littérature ancienne, 4), Paris 1992, 233–241.

[6] On the *Aithiopika* as an "historical novel", see T. Hägg, "*Callirhoe* and *Parthenope*:
The Beginnings of the Historical Novel", *ClAnt* 6, 1987, 184–204, at p. 200f. [No. 2 in
this volume].

[7] Even John Morgan, despite his unrivalled understanding of Heliodoros' art, sometimes
lapses into this fallacy: "… Heliodoros' knowledge of Ethiopia was bookish; furthermore it was *out of date*" (Morgan 1982, 248), "There is little *awareness* of contemporary
events…" (Morgan 1996, 435) — my italics.

Aithiopia as his main inspiration for the setting of the last part of the novel's action, the problem of sources may be looked upon in a more relaxed manner. Herodotos would then rightly be his main Greek source for the depiction of pre-Hellenistic Meroe, in particular, Herodotos' so-called Aithiopian logos in 3.17–25 (*Fontes Historiae Nubiorum*[8] [in the following: *FHN*] I, 65; cf. also *FHN* I, 56–64 and 66). Agatharchides, Eratosthenes, Strabo, Diodorus Siculus and others might be expected to supply additional colourful material,[9] although the author would filter their accounts to prevent too obvious anachronisms: Alexandria and the Ptolemies, for instance, would not be allowed to figure in the novel, not to speak of the Romans. There is of course also the tantalizing possibility that in some cases he may have used contemporary sources, perhaps even of a documentary kind — only with the same caution. His range of sources would thus be much the same as the well-informed modern historian expects them to be, only that the author's priorities would be exactly the opposite of the historian's: if the historian hopes to find genuine third- or fourth-century-AD information about Meroe and deprecates its scarcity or absence, the author's intention was to construct an historical milieu without such lapses into too obvious a contemporaneity.

It is the historian's luck that an ancient novelist would not be so strict about anachronisms as his modern serious counterpart; nor, even if he so desired, have been in the position to check the details of his description against reliable historical accounts. It should also be taken into account that recent epigraphic and archaeological finds have shown Heliodoros' corresponding description of Delphi to be less fanciful than was earlier believed, and that it is imperial rather than classical Delphi that offers the parallels.[10] So, there is indeed a case to be made for an intensified study of Heliodoros' description of Meroe against the background of our present more detailed knowledge of Nubian culture — a knowledge accumulated through the successive rescue excavations and surveys of Lower Nubia earlier this century, and presently supplemented by the on-

---

[8] T. Eide, T. Hägg, R.H. Pierce and L. Török (eds.), *Fontes Historiae Nubiorum*, Vol. 1: *From the Eighth to the Fifth Century BC*, Bergen 1994; Vol. 2: *From the Fourth to the First Century BC*, Bergen 1996; Vol. 3: *From the First to the Sixth Century AD*, Bergen 1998.

[9] Cf. Feuillatre (1967) 136–142, who, however, finds less of Herodotos in Heliodoros than he would have found natural, and more of the later writers, and of Xenophon.

[10] See J. Pouilloux, "Delphes dans les *Ethiopiques* d'Héliodore: la réalité dans la fiction", *JS* 1983, 259–286, and G. Rougemont, "Delphes chez Héliodore", in: Baslez et al. (ed., 1992) 93–99; the latter sifts the evidence with greater attention to the literary aspects.

going archaeological activities in Upper Nubia, the actual centre of the Meroitic kingdom.[11] But it is important first to reconstruct the Meroe of Heliodoros' imagination: to see how consistent it is, how it functions and how it relates to the action of the novel. Like the Homeric world, it will basically be a fictional world, a composite world that never existed as a whole but shows traits of different ages, with poetic imagination gluing the constituent parts together, more or less successfully. Without trying to reconstruct the imaginary whole we risk misrepresenting the parts, those small concrete details usually selected for *Quellenforschung*.

Heliodoros' Aithiopia is imagined as a kingdom with the city of Meroe as its power centre and royal seat. During all the seventeen years that the action encompasses, Hydaspes is the βασιλεὺς Αἰθιόπων (10.34.2), Persinna the βασίλισσα Αἰθιόπων (4.8.1). The most elaborate title given to the king is "King of the Aithiopians who dwell to the East and to the West (ὁ τῶν πρὸς ἀνατολαῖς καὶ δυσμαῖς Αἰθιόπων ... βασιλεύς)" (9.6.2), obviously an allusion to the old idea of the *Aithiopes*, the "scorched-faced", as living closest to the rising and the setting sun (*Odyssey* 1.22f.).[12] This title does not fit the actual novelistic context in which Aithiopia figures not as a mythical place somewhere on the confines of the earth,

---

[11] Cf. the yearly reports by Jean Leclant in *Orientalia*. Another important addition to our knowledge is the recent publication of John Garstang's excavations of Meroe City in the beginning of the century: L. Török, *Meroe City: an Ancient African Capital*, Vol. 1-2, London 1997 (hereafter Török 1997a). For the sum of our present knowledge, see the new handbook by L. Török, *The Kingdom of Kush: Handbook of the Napatan-Meroitic Civilization* (Handbuch der Orientalistik, 1. Abt., 31), Leiden-New York-Köln 1997 (hereafter Török 1997b); for Nubia's relationship to the Greek and Roman world, S.M. Burstein, *Graeco-Africana: Studies in the History of Greek Relations with Egypt and Nubia*, New Rochelle, NY 1995.

[12] See Morgan's footnotes 113 and 200 to his translation. Herodotos too (7.69–70) refers to two Aithiopian peoples — who differ only in language and hair — the "eastern" ones (οἱ ... ἀπὸ ἡλίου ἀνατολέων Αἰθίοπες) living in Asia (apparently neighbours of the Indians), the others in (north) Africa (οἱ ... ἐκ τῆς Λιβύης), beyond (ὑπὲρ) Egypt. Cf. further A. Lesky, "Aithiopika", *Hermes* 87, 1959, 27–38, pp. 35f.; Morgan (1982) 237 (with n. 49); and Eide (1999).

[13] The Homeric concept of Aithiopia is, however, fittingly evoked both in the oracle which adumbrates the happy ending of the novel (2.35.5 ἴξοντ' ἡελίου πρὸς χθόνα κυανέην) and in Charikles' dream (4.14.2), prefiguring Charikleia's abduction from Delphi: γῆς ἐπ' ἐσχατόν τι πέρας οἴχεσθαι φέροντα, ζοφώδεσί τισιν εἰδώλοις καὶ σκιώδεσι πλῆθον, "[the eagle] flew off with her to one of the world's remotest extremities, a place teeming with dark and shadowy phantoms". Oracles, dreams, and other omens move in the mythical sphere, the action proper in the world.

as in Homer,[13] but firmly situated as the historical southern neighbour
of Egypt, what we now call Nubia. Royal titles, however, may preserve
archaic traits which no longer correspond to the actual facts, so we should
refrain from accusing the novelist of an anachronism at this place–within
his Greek romantic universe the title he created functions well enough.
It is another matter that this Greek concept of "East and West" has no
place in the historical Kushite or Meroitic royal titulary of the period:
from the earliest hieroglyphic documents on, the leitmotif is rather the
old Egyptian concept of "Two-lands", originally referring to Lower and
Upper Egypt.[14] The second time Heliodoros elaborates on Hydaspes' title,
in a letter from the Persian satrap, he chooses instead a honorific form
of address: "gracious (φιλανθρώπῳ) and blessed (εὐδαίμονι) king of the
Aithiopians" (10.34.2). It may be added that none of the expanded titles
or epithets has any similarity with the royal titles found in the surviving
Greek documents of late antique Nubia; the honorific epithets rather
have a Ptolemaic ring.

199

The kingdom is hereditary. Early in the narrative, in Book 4, it is
even intimated that a female succession to the throne would be possible:
Queen Persinna asks the Egyptian priest Kalasiris to help finding and
bringing back home her daughter Charikleia, hoping that the king's desire for "a child to succeed him" (τῆς ἐκ παίδων διαδοχῆς, 4.12.3) would
make him willing to accept the white girl as his legitimate daughter after all. This is echoed in clearer terms by Kalasiris when, after finding
Charikleia in Delphi, he awakes in her the expectation of exchanging
"the life of an outcast in a foreign land for the throne that is yours by
right, where you will reign (βασιλεύουσαν) with your beloved at your
side" (4.13.2). Finally back in her native city, Meroe, Charikleia raises
her claim to be the king's daughter, and the ensuing discussion repeatedly alludes to the "line of succession" (again διαδοχή, 10.13.5; 15.2; 16.4;
16.5) in which she stands if her claim should be legitimate. Yet, remarkably enough, this topic is not brought up again in the final chapters of
the novel when Charikleia's true identity has at last been emphatically
proven. She is wedded to Theagenes and they are each honoured with a
priesthood in the Meroitic cult, he as priest of the Sun, she as priestess
of the Moon, each accepting the insignia of priesthood, the white mitre,
from the king and queen (10.41). But it is not explicitly stated that they
will thereby also one day succeed Hydaspes and Persinna as rulers of the

[14] Numerous examples in the Egyptian texts in *FHN* I-II.

Aithiopians;[15] or, if so, whether Charikleia herself, as the one who by blood belongs to the royal house (γένους τοῦ βασιλείου, 10.12.1), will then be the supreme ruler, with Theagenes as her Prince Consort, as Kalasiris' prediction in 4.13.2 had led us to expect.

This is still more remarkable, for in other classical texts we find a tradition about the ruling queen of Meroe, the *Kandake*.[16] The common source for several of our Greek and Roman witnesses to this tradition and to Aithiopian kingship in general (cf. *FHN* II, 105–107) seems to be Bion of Soloi, an early Hellenistic writer who composed an historical work also called *Αἰθιοπικά*. According to Pliny (*Nat. Hist.* 6.183), Bion had himself visited Nubia; it is all the more deplorable that his book has not survived. The reference to the Aithiopian "eunuch and minister of the Kandake" (εὐνοῦχος δυνάστης Κανδάκης βασιλίσσης Αἰθιόπων) in the Acts of the Apostles (8.27, *FHN* III, 194) is well-known; and the author of the *Alexander Romance* gladly enlarged upon the topic, inventing a romantic meeting between Alexander and "Queen Kandake" (Ps. Call. 3.18–24, *FHN* II, 85). Not so our novelist, in spite of the opportunity it would have given him to bolster further the happy ending of the story. The fact that he leaves the earlier hints at a female succession as kind of a loose end in the story must lead us to conclude that the tradition of the Kandake was unknown to him.[17] Bion's *Aithiopika* apparently did not belong among his sources, nor the *Alexander Romance* among his reading matter — unless, of course, the Kandake's absence in Herodotos' Aithiopia made him resist the temptation.

The royal court (ἡ βασίλειος αὐλή, 4.12.1), we are told, is also the home of the Aithiopian wise men, the gymnosophists or "naked sages". They function as a high council, συνέδριον (10.2.1; 10.31.1), for the king, one of them taking on the function of president (πρόεδρος, 10.11.1) of the counsellors (σύνεδροι, 10.2.1; 10.10.1; 10.35.2). Their function is, precisely, to give the king counsel "about what to do" (σύμβουλοι τῶν πρακτέων,

200

---

[15] In contrast, their ascent to a ruling status was hinted at in 8.17.5 where Heliodoros, in his usual quest for paradoxes, states that Theagenes and Charikleia, now captured by the Aithiopians, were "guarded by those who were soon to be their subjects (ὑπηκόων)".

[16] This is not a personal name, as some classical writers assume, but a title, probably the designation for the king's wife and/or the Queen Mother (?). The historical background for the tradition of the ruling Kandake is discussed by László Török in the comments to *FHN* II, 85 (with further references); the first historically attested ruling queen of Kush is Queen Shanakdakheto in the late 2nd century BC (*FHN* II, (148), (149)).

[17] Morgan (1982) 249 seems to take for granted that Heliodoros knew the tradition.

10.2), especially, it seems, in religious matters; they are never mentioned in connection with the king's decisions in his war against the Persians in Egypt (which may simply mean that Heliodoros did not invent the *synedrion* until he reached Book 10). In one capacity only are the gymnosophists allowed to overrule the king (10.10.1): they have "judicial authority" (δίκη ... καὶ κρίσις) over the rulers (τοὺς βασιλεύοντας).[18] Yet, when Charikleia makes her πρόκλησις, "appeal to law" (10.10.2), in order to escape being sacrificed in the victory rites, the king protests, emphasizing that the sages are allowed "to judge cases only between the rulers and their native subjects (τοὺς ἐγχωρίους)", whereas Charikleia is a foreigner and a prisoner of war (10.10.4). The naked sages, it may be added, are also part of Philostratos' Aithiopia as described in his *Life of Apollonios of Tyana* (ca. AD 220);[19] but there they live in the borderland between Egypt and Aithiopia and are not endowed with any political functions.

Except for this high council, no political institutions or government officials are mentioned, only a ceremonial office holder, the chamberlain or court usher (εἰσαγγελεύς, 10.22.6; 10.34.1) whose duty is to introduce the various embassies arriving at court. This title was used by Herodotos in his description of the Persian court (3.84.2; cf. Diod. Sic. 16.47.3) and is also attested for the Ptolemaic court in Egypt (*PTebt* 179); but neither *eisangeleus* nor *synedrion / synedros / proedros* occur among the numerous Greek terms attested for late antique Nubian officials and institutions in our documentary material.[20] Again the historical setting takes precedence over any potential influence from contemporaneous institutions or terminology.

The priestly titles present a less clear case. The terms used for the Aithiopian office of priest and priestess in the novel are ἱεροσύνη, ἱεράομαι, whereas the typical designation for a priest in the late antique documents from Philai and Nubia as well as in some Greek literary sources

---

201

[18] Morgan (1982) 237 and (1996) 434 suggests that this is a reminiscence of the Meroitic priesthood's special power in relation to the kings prior to Ergamenes, as reported by Agatharchides in Diod. Sic. 3.6.3-4 (see *FHN* II, 142 with Comments); cf. Strabo 17.2.3 (*FHN* III, 187).

[19] For further literary references to gymnosophists and wise men in relation to Aithiopia, see Morgan (1982) 237 (with n. 50).

[20] Cf. T. Hägg, "Titles and Honorific Epithets in Nubian Greek Texts", *SO* 65, 1990, 147–177.

concerning Nubia is προφήτης. Now, ἱερεύς also occurs at some places in the documents, and it is possible that *prophetes* is used as the technical term for an Egyptian priest in Nubian — that is, in this period, Nobadian or Blemmyan — service, *hiereus* for a native priest. This, however, is debated;[21] and anyway no conclusions can be based on the fact that Heliodoros happens to use the most common and "unmarked" Greek word for his Aithiopian priesthood. But the topic of Greek titles in Nubia leads over to another interesting feature of Heliodoros' description of the Meroitic state, namely, its Hellenic inclinations.

Thus, the very first time Aithiopia is mentioned in the novel, we are told that somebody intends to bring a young Athenian slave girl, an excellent musician, as a gift to the Aithiopian king, to be the queen's "confidante and companion in things Greek" (συμπαιστρίαν καὶ συνόμιλον τὰ Ἑλλήνων, 2.24.3).[22] More importantly, it is repeatedly stated in the last books that the Aithiopian rulers as well as the gymnosophists cultivate the Greek language; and they speak it not only as a practical means of communication with foreigners (9.25.3; 10.31.1), but also as the esoteric language of the elite to which they take recourse when they do not wish to be overheard or understood by the common people (10.9.6; 10.39.1; cf. 10.35.2; 10.38.3; 10.40.1). Their correspondence with the Persian satrap is obviously also conducted in Greek (10.34). In war, the king has at his disposal a detachment of Greek-speaking soldiers to guard his foreign prisoners (9.1.5; cf. 9.24.2 where one the guards is referred to as "a half-caste Greek", μιξέλληνά τινα).

Now, all this has an intriguing historical counterpart in the widespread use of Greek in late antique Nubia for inscriptions (e.g., the triumphal inscription of the Nobadian king Silko in the fifth century, *FHN* III, 317) and for letters (e.g., that of the Blemmyan king Phonen to his Nobadian counterpart, *FHN* III, 319). Furthermore, as evidence for a more thorough-going Hellenic influence, we have the Greek titles for officials just mentioned, some used in the late antique successor states

---

[21] See Hägg, "Titles" (1990), 163–165 (with references to the texts and the scholarly discussion).

[22] G.N. Sandy, *Heliodorus*, Boston 1982, 15, takes for granted that it is the girl's "musical talent" that makes her attractive to the Aithiopian court; but the text emphasizes her "Greekness" in general. A passage in the *Periplus of the Erythraean Sea* (1st cent. AD), 49, confirms that slave musicians from the Mediterranean were exported as far as India as gifts to kings; cf. E.H. Warmington, *The Commerce between the Roman Empire and India*, 2nd ed. London 1974, 262.

to Meroe, some first attested in the Christian Nubian kingdoms of the medieval period. The titles are Greek, even if the texts in which they appear happen to be written in Coptic or Old Nubian. Greek seems to have been a court language, at least for some time. And as a church language, it is well known that Greek survived in Nubia well into the thirteenth century.[23]

But what about the ancient kingdom of Meroe itself? Among our Hellenistic literary sources, Agatharchides (in Diod. Sic. 3.6.3; *FHN* II, 142) offers the enigmatic information that King Ergamenes, the historical Arkamaniqo (cf. *FHN* II, 114), who reigned in the second quarter of the third century BC, had received a Greek philosophical education. Our material evidence is more manifold and eloquent. Influences from Hellenistic and Roman civilization are richly in evidence in architecture as well as in artefacts and sculpture, whether imported objects or indigenous products stylistically reminiscent of Mediterranean art. In the former category, the head of Augustus found at Meroe City is the best known single specimen.[24] In the latter, the so-called Royal Baths at Meroe are a case in point; the painted sandstone statues (third century BC to first century AD) found in a water sanctuary include reclining figures of royal ancestors and philosophers, and members of the Dionysiac cortège with their musical instruments, all in a local style heavily influenced by Alexandrian art[25] — congenial surroundings for the Athenian slave girl and musician who was meant to become the confidante of Queen Persinna! Even a number of Greek-Egyptian *auloi* have been excavated at Meroe. Local pottery of the so-called Roman-Nubian style was produced not only in the northern province, but in central Meroe as well. And so on.

Several channels of influence readily present themselves. The basic factor is, of course, that Egypt and Meroe were neighbours in the Nile Valley, the artery of communication between the Mediterranean, Eastern Africa and the Orient. More specifically, as early as the 270s BC Ptolemy

---

[23] Cf. T. Hägg, "Some Remarks on the Use of Greek in Nubia", in: J.M. Plumley (ed.), *Nubian Studies*, Warminster 1982, 103–107, and idem, "Greek Language in Christian Nubia", in: A.S. Atiya (ed.), *The Coptic Encyclopedia*, Vol. 4, New York 1991, 1170–1174.

[24] Cf. L. Török, "Augustus and Meroe", *Orientalia Suecana* 38–39, 1989–1990, 171–190.

[25] See Török (1997a) 66–90, figs. 75–81, Plates 35–52. Also illustrated in S. Wenig, *Africa in Antiquity: The Arts of Ancient Nubia and the Sudan*, Vol. 2: *The Catalogue*, New York 1978, figs. 61ff.

II's raid upstream into Nubia heralds the continuing Ptolemaic interest in controling part of the Middle Nile Valley.[26] The treaty of Samos in 20 BC, which followed C. Petronius' military campaign far south into Nubia (*FHN* II, 166; III, 190, 204-205), established Roman rule over the northernmost part of Lower Nubia, the so-called Dodekaschoinos, for centuries; according to Prokopios (1.19.28-35; *FHN* III, 328), it was only under Diocletian (in AD 298) that the Romans withdrew their troops and retired to the old frontier at Aswan. The great number of Greek inscriptions and graffiti found in the Dodekaschoinos is eloquent testimony of the imperial presence.[27] Since the Kingdom of Meroe apparently kept their representatives in the Dodekaschoinos through most of this period, there were in this buffer zone centuries of coexistence between Meroites and Greek-speaking Roman military and administrative personnel. Some Greek and Demotic inscriptions from Philai (*FHN* III, 265-266, cf. 260-261) provide us with glimpses of Meroitic ambassadors on special missions there in the mid third century AD (compare the gymnosophist's role as an ambassador to Egypt in the novel, 2.31-32). Even if the larger part of the actual population in the zone seems to have been newcomers and intruders, Nobadian and (later) Blemmyan tribes, the continuous Meroitic presence at the highest social level must have meant that Meroe itself received its constant influx of Egyptian Hellenism, with Lower Nubia as an intermediary.

Furthermore, our written sources, documentary as well as literary, attest already from Hellenistic times to the penetration of Greek travellers into the heart of Meroe and as far as the Red Sea coast, for commerce, elephant hunting, or exploration purposes (e.g., Pliny, *Nat. Hist.* 6.183, 191f., 194f.; *FHN* II, 100-104; papyrus letters on elephant hunting: *FHN* II, 120-121). Ptolemy listed the names and positions of many Nubian settlements from Hiera Sykaminos to Meroe and beyond (4.5-7; *FHN* III, 222). Cleopatra is said to have addressed Aithiopian visitors to the court in their own language (Plutarch, *Ant.* 27.4; *FHN* III, 218); Dio Chrysostom recognizes Aithiopians among his audience in Alexandria (32.36; *FHN* III, 221); and Ailios Aristeides, on his tourist trip to the Dodekaschoinos, interviews an Aithiopian official through interpreters

203

---

[26] Cf. Burstein (1995) 179f. with further refs.

[27] For a survey of this material, see S. Donadoni, "Les inscriptions grecques de Nubie", *Graeco-Arabica* 3, 1984, 9-19.

(36.55; *FHN* III, 230). These are but a few scattered details of the larger picture, a Meroitic kingdom apparently wide open to Graeco-Roman influence, chiefly along the Nile but, presumably, by way of its Red Sea ports as well.[28]

Yet, so far there is no material evidence that the Greek language was ever used in Meroe by its native population, as it was in Hellenistic and Roman Egypt; Meroe, after all, was an independent state, at no time a province under Macedonian or (except for the Dodekaschoinos) Roman rule. The inscribed monuments and objects that have survived are all in the Meroitic language and script, except for a few imported or closely imitated artefacts (glass vases, rings) with Greek inscriptions.[29] Still, the connections with Egypt must have meant that the Greek language was well known in Meroe in the late Hellenistic and imperial periods; and it is indeed possible that it was already at that time in use as a *lingua franca* for tradesmen along the Middle Nile and in diplomacy, as it manifestly was in late antiquity. Now that scholars have begun to reconsider the so-called "fall of Meroe" in the fourth century, finding cultural continuity between Meroe and the successor states of the area rather than a more definitive break, it may be legitimate to ask whether the seemingly unquestioned use of Greek even for internal communication between Blemmyes and Nobades is also a direct inheritance from the Kingdom of Meroe.

Then, Heliodoros would not be quite so fanciful or unreasonably chauvinistic after all in his picture of the role of the Greek language in Meroe — only that he of course places it in the wrong period! But read Rome for Persia, the Emperor for the Great King, the Prefect of Egypt for the Satrap — then Greek as the *lingua franca* of the region falls well into place. This may of course be a coincidence: what suited his romantic construction, happens to have had an historical analogy — but one never knows about novelists and their mixture of fiction and fact. As Stanley Burstein suggests,[30] Heliodoros' claim that the Meroitic kings studied

---

[28] Comprehensive account in J. Desanges, "L'Hellénisme dans le royaume de Méroë", *Graeco-Arabica* 2, 1983, 275-296. Among the latest contributions to the topic, D. Wildung, "Meroe and Hellenism", in: D. Wildung (ed.), *Sudan: Ancient Kingdoms of the Nile*, Paris-New York 1997, 370-380, is valuable for its superb illustrations, Burstein (1995) 105-123 for its critical discussion. See now also Török (1997b) 424ff., 516ff.

[29] See Desanges (1983) 282-285 (*SEG* XXXIII 1983, 1364 bis, cf. 1365).

[30] Personal communication, 16.04.97.

Greek may well be based on Ergamenes' Greek education, as described by Agatharchides and repeated by Diodoros; and information about the use of Greek in imperial diplomacy south of Egypt may well have reached the author through personal contacts with, say, Roman officials or soldiers transferred from Egypt to Syria. The notion that as ambitious and diligent an author as Heliodoros, just because he wrote an historical novel, should have been uninterested in the conditions presently prevailing in the country he had chosen as his scene, seems as absurd as its opposite. Information of this kind was floating around in the Eastern Mediterranean world, and he surely listened and absorbed.

We return to the fictitious world of the novel, with Greek as the language of the Meroitic elite. As will have become evident, there is no naive expectancy in Heliodoros' novel that everyone whom the Greek-speaking hero and heroine meet will be able to understand what they say, as we find it in the earlier novels of Chariton, Xenophon and Achilleus Tatios[31] — and also, more remarkably, in Philostratos' description of Apollonios of Tyana's experiences in northern Aithiopia (*Vita Apoll.* 6.1–27), contrary to his general habit of explicitly emphasizing Greek as the *lingua franca* of the wise.[32] The role of indigenous languages in the Roman empire and on its fringes was well appreciated by Heliodoros the Syrian, as it was perhaps not by authors from the old Hellenic regions; and not only appreciated, but creatively employed in the plot construction and for local colour. But it is mainly a matter of distinguishing between Greek and "the other", "une vision dichotomique de la réalité linguistique", as Suzanne Saïd puts it:[33] communication among Aithiopians, Egyptians, and Persians often takes place without reference to any language barriers (4.12; 9.6.1–2 etc.), in spite of the fact that author and reader are aware of their existence (8.17.2). Narrative economy takes precedence over realism.

Alongside the spoken language, the Meroitic script is used as an exotic ingredient as well as a secret code, and finally as an authenticating factor in the recognition process. For when the new-born Charikleia

---

205

[31] See S. Saïd, "Les langues du roman grec", in: Baslez et al. (ed., 1992) 169–186, pp. 169f., for the few exceptions to this rule.

[32] Cf. Saïd (1992) 170–174, with an explanation (173f.) which is not quite convincing. On Heliodoros, ibid. 174–178; cf. also Morgan (1982) 258–260.

[33] Saïd (1992) 175.

was exposed, her mother provided her with "a waistband of woven silk embroidered in native characters (γράμμασιν ἐγχωρίοις) with a narrative of the child's circumstances" (2.31.2). This narrative, the plot requires, should not be disclosed to the girl herself or to Charikles, the Delphic priest in whose custody she grows up. It may be read only by Meroites, such as the Gymnosophist Sisimithres who first found her (2.31.2) and was later instrumental in the recognition (10.14) — and by Egyptians! Charikles shows the band to his Egyptian guest Kalasiris, who finds that it is embroidered "in the Aithiopian script" (γράμμασιν Αἰθιοπικοῖς), yet "not the demotic variety but the royal kind (οὐ δημοτικοῖς ἀλλὰ βασιλικοῖς), which closely resembles the so-called hieratic (ἱερατικοῖς) script of Egypt" (4.8.1). Kalasiris is thus able to read the narrative, solve the riddle of the Delphic oracle's words about returning to "the black land of the Sun", and lay plans for the abduction of Charikleia from Delphi.[34]

This ingenuously contrived plot is built on some pieces of knowledge that the author obviously possessed about languages and writing systems employed in Meroe; but the actual historical situation was still more complex.[35] For monumental inscriptions, the Kushites from the eighth through the early third century BC used Egyptian hieroglyphs and an accompanying "traditional" Egyptian language; Kalasiris the Egyptian priest would presumably have had no difficulties in reading such inscriptions had he visited Gebel Barkal or Kawa. But for writing in ink on papyrus, ostraca, or textiles, as is the case here, Egyptians as well as Meroites of the period in which the action is supposed to take place would have used a simpler, cursive form of the hieroglyphs, a writing conventionally called "hieratic". Since the texts written in hieratic script would not necessarily be of a religious or otherwise formulaic character, this script "tended, although the medium of a learned elite, to embody more nearly current language".[36] It is futile to speculate what this might have meant for the language and script that Queen Persinna used on her baby's waistband;

---

[34] Cf. also the ring engraved with the royal crest (βασιλείῳ ... συμβόλῳ, 4.8.7) and inscribed with sacred characters (γράμμασι ... ἱεροῖς, 8.11.8), one of Charikleia's tokens of recognition. These signs, however, are never interpreted, but function only, together with the pantarbe jewel, as part of the ring's magic attributes.

[35] See R.H. Pierce in *FHN* I, pp. 13–16, and II, pp. 362–365; and L. Török in *FHN* II, pp. 359–361.

[36] R.H. Pierce in *FHN* II, 363.

but for the verisimilitude of the story it is certainly enough that her "royal" letters were (reasonably enough) similar to the Egyptian hieratic script, as Heliodoros notes, assuming his historiographical pose.[37] The simplification we have to buy is that all emphasis is on the script, whereas the language that necessarily goes with it, Egyptian, receives no comment. The queen thus writes, we have to assume, in Egyptian rather than in her native Meroitic (or her acquired Greek).

But there is more to this, since Heliodoros takes care also to specify what script was *not* used: the "demotic" variety, which the Egyptian priest obviously would not have been able to read. This would seem to rule out the possibility that the author is referring to what the Greeks styled the Demotic Egyptian script, which in the sixth century BC developed from the hieratic script and was still in use up to Heliodoros' day, until succeeded by what we call Coptic writing. Rather, he appears to be using this term for the indigenous Meroitic script, of which in reality both a hieroglyphic and a cursive variety were employed; the earliest surviving texts are from the second century BC. Though the signs are derived from Egyptian counterparts, the Meroitic language which they convey would have made such texts incomprehensible to Kalasiris (as indeed they still are to us).

206

By introducing Meroitic cursive alongside Egyptian hieratic in an Early Meroitic context, Heliodoros is of course guilty of an anachronism (though certainly one of the more pardonable). But it raises the question about where he got his partial knowledge of the writing systems of Meroe from. Herodotos has nothing to say about Aithiopian scripts, only at one point explains (2.36.4) that the Egyptians "use two kinds of writing, one called 'sacred' (ἱρά), the other 'common' (δημοτικά)". Agatharchides (in Diod. Sic. 3.3.5; *FHN* II, 142), in turn, reports that the Aithiopians think the Egyptians are Aithiopian settlers who have preserved Aithiopian customs, such as, apparently, their script: for they have two systems of writing, "one named 'common' (δημώδη), that everybody learns, another called 'sacred' (ἱερά), that only the priests among the Egyptians know, who learn it from their fathers as a secret tradition. Among the Aithiopians, however, everybody uses these signs." The point, then, is that all (literate) Aithiopians know this script because it is theirs from the start, while among Egyptians only those who preserve the secret tradition from

---

[37] For this characteristic of Heliodoros' style, see Morgan (1982) 227–234.

their Aithiopian founding fathers have the necessary knowledge. By way of comparison we may note that Heliodoros lets Hydaspes preach to the Egyptian priests at Syene that all things Egyptian, beginning with the Nile, derive from Aithiopia (9.22.7).

The passage from Agatharchides may well have been the inspiration for Heliodoros' description of Meroitic scripts,[38] although he twists the evidence somewhat to serve his own purpose. Kalasiris is an Egyptian priest: it is thus logical that he can read the hieratic signs (whereas an ordinary Egyptian would know only the demotic signs, according to Agatharchides). All Aithiopians use these signs: thus, Queen Persinna could have written them (Agatharchides, like Heliodoros in this context, does not bother to differentiate between the Meroitic and Egyptian *languages*). What Heliodoros adds on his own is only the remark that Kalasiris would not have been able to read the text on the waistband, had it been written in the 'common' script. The simplest explanation is that Heliodoros did know about contemporary (or, at least: post-third-century BC) conditions in Meroe, with a cursive script that Egyptians could not read. *His* 'demotic' script is thus Aithiopian, whereas the one to which Agatharchides refers is Egyptian. Heliodoros' source for contemporary writing systems in Aithiopia may have been some literary account lost to us, or oral informants.

If the role played in the novel by different languages and scripts, though simplified, appears to build on actual knowledge of Meroe and be intended to give a realistic touch to the story, the personal names bestowed on its Meroitic actors present a less consistent or persuasive picture. Charikleia, of course, got her Greek name far away from Meroe; but one would have expected her parents to bear, if not genuinely Meroitic names, at least such that gave the reader associations to the traditional Aithiopia (e.g., Memnon, cf. 4.8.3). Instead, the author has been content to give them names, Hydaspes and Persinna, that lead rather to India and Persia.[39] King Hydaspes' nephew, however, is named Meroebos, a

---

207

[38] The somewhat different terms used for the two varieties of script in Agatharchides and Heliodoros need not disturb us: first, Agatharchides' text has reached us only with Diodoros as an intermediary, and these are things he may have changed for stylistic reasons: second, if in fact Heliodoros too knew Agatharchides through Diodoros, he may himself have preferred to use the standard terms for Egyptian writing.

[39] Cf. Morgan (1982) 247.

"speaking" name (Μερό-ηβος, "youth of Meroe"), no doubt created for the occasion to adorn the seventeen-year-old son of Hydaspes' late brother, "a striking example of young manhood" (ἀξιοπρεπές τι νεανίου χρῆμα, 10.23.4), apparently now, with Hydaspes' help, the successor of his father on the throne of some neighbouring country. It is also possible that Sisi-mithres, the chief gymnosophist, is so called to give the impression of a Meroitic name (cf., e.g., the Meroitic priestly title *ssimete* or *sasimete*),[40] even if it is in reality a Hellenized Persian one.

No other place in the Kingdom of Meroe than the capital itself is named in the novel; Heliodoros has not helped himself from Ptolemy's list of toponyms. Theagenes and Charikleia get transferred from Syene to Meroe City as Hydaspes' prisoners; but the king's long march home with his victorious army is only described as far as Philai, then the narrative perspective shifts to Meroe, by way of letters that Hydaspes sends from Philai to the gymnosophists and the queen (10.2). The account of the expectations and preparations for the army's return home replaces any description of the route taken. It looks as if Heliodoros disposed of some specific information about the stretch between Syene and Philai — he lets the Aithiopian army turn away from the river and march inland until they reach Philai where Hydaspes installs a garrison (10.1.2)[41] — but none about communication further south in the Middle Nile region. Meroe City, however, and the Island of Meroe with its surrounding rivers — the Nile, the Astaborrhas, and the Asasobas — are described in some detail (10.5). The basic facts (names, measurements etc.) are obviously taken from an historical source (cf. Strabo 17.2.2; *FHN* III, 187), but the novelist has transformed the description of Meroe into one concordant with Aithiopia as an opulent fairyland, with giant animals and trees and marvellously rich crops.

208

---

[40] See, e.g., *FHN* II, 152.25, 183.4 and 184.3. For other examples of the use of this title and interpretations of its meaning, see L. Török in *FHN* II, p. 735 n. 361 (e.g., *ssimete ktke-s*, "*ssimete* of the Kandake").

[41] This is among Morgan's (1982) 249f. examples of Heliodoros' "distorted view of geography"; but Heliodoros is better informed than Morgan would allow. Philai is indeed an island, but its (Roman) garrison was placed on the East bank of the Nile, and it was reached from Syene by an inland road "skirting the river cataract for some three miles, according to the Antonine itinery"; thus M.P. Speidel, "Nubia's Roman Garrison", in: *ANRW* II.10.1 (1988), 773 (cf. the map p. 774). It is of course in Philai camp, not on the temple island, that Heliodoros lets Hydaspes rest his soldiers and install his garrison.

Besides this self-contained description, the topography and buildings of Meroe City peek through now and then in the account of the victory festivities which fills most of Book 10. In the royal palace (τὰ βασίλεια) inside the city, Persinna receives her husband's letter (10.3; 10.4.4; cf. 4.8.3 on its interior decorations); the messengers then ride through "the better quarters of the city" (10.3.2 τὰ ἐπισημότερα τῆς πόλεως) proclaiming the victory; the people rejoice and festoon their sanctuaries (τὰ τεμένη) with flowers. Persinna has herds of various sacrificial animals taken "across the river to the sacred glade" (εἰς τὴν περαίαν ὀργάδα) to await the victory ceremony (10.4.1). "Next she went to the gymnosophists, who had their abode in the temple of Pan (τὸ Πανεῖον)" in order to bring them the letter from Hydaspes; they withdraw into the *adyton* to read it.

This is about the level of concreteness all the way. The description could suit any ancient town, except for a few details. The cult of Pan is one such specific detail: "the people in Meroe worship Herakles, Pan, and Isis, in addition to some barbarian god", says Strabo (17.2.3; *FHN* III, 187).[42] The sacrificial glade on the other side of the river is another; it becomes the scene of the rest of the action. The sacrifice there will take place in honour of the Sun and the Moon; only men are allowed to participate (except for the queen who is Priestess of the Moon, 10.4.5), and the inhabitants of Meroe cross the Astaborrhas in small boats or by the bridge (τὸ ζεῦγμα, 10.4.6). Persinna welcomes her home-coming husband "at the temple gate, inside the sacred precinct" (τοῦ νεώ τε ἐν προπύλοις καὶ περιβόλων ἐντός, 10.6.1). Two square pavilions (σκῆναι) have been erected outside the precinct (10.6.2–3); under the domed roof of one of them the King and Queen have their thrones (cf. 10.16.1), while the other shelters statues of the national gods and the ancestors of the royal house, Memnon, Perseus and Andromeda; the gymnosophists sit at their feet. There are three altars (10.6.5): two close to each other to the Sun and the Moon, and one to Dionysos (i.e., Osiris). The sacrifice can begin.

The earliest Greek testimony for the topography and ritual of the Meroitic sun cult is in Herodotos' "Aithiopian logos" (3.17–25; *FHN* I,

---

[42] Similarly Diod. Sic. 3.9.1 (*FHN* II, 143). Cf. already Theokritos 7.113 (*FHN* II, 116) ἐν δὲ θέρει πυμάτοισι παρ᾽ Αἰθιόπεσσι νομεύοις, "and in summer may you (Pan) herd your flock among the most distant of the Aithiopians". Morgan's suggestion (1982, 238 n. 55; 1989, 559 n. 230) that *Pantheion* should perhaps be read instead of *Paneion* trivializes Heliodoros' account.

65).[43] Kambyses sends his spies to Aithiopia to find out about the famous "Table of the Sun" (3.18):

> On the outskirts of the city (ἐν τῷ προαστείῳ) there is a meadow (λει-μών) full of boiled meat from every kind of quadruped. During the night those of the citizens who at any moment are in office take care to place the meat there; during the day anybody who so wishes may go there and eat. The natives say that it is the earth that produces the meat each time.

The meadow outside the city roughly corresponds to Heliodoros' holy glade on the other side of the river (the words ὀργὰς πρὸ τοῦ ἄστεως in the king's letter 10.2.2 clearly echo Herodotos), and the meat from every kind of quadruped has a counterpart in Heliodoros' list of various animals, from oxen to zebras and griffins, that are transported to the scene of the sacrifice. Except for this, there seem to be no similarities. Again, we may note that the novelist does not avail himself of the most obvious material at his disposal in the Greek literary tradition about Aithiopia, but creates his own spectacle and his own wonders.

209

What, then, can be said about this novelistic setting and the historically and archaeologically ascertained facts about Meroe and its sun cult? The early epigraphical documents in Egyptian do state that the ruler of Kush was "the son of Amen-Rê", the Sun-god (cf. *FHN* I, 9, 21ff., 37; II, 71, 84), and the tradition was known to Greek writers, such as Bion of Soloi (*FHN* II, 105–106), as well. This comes in addition to the old Greek mythical concept of Aithiopia as the home of the sun. That Heliodoros lets Persinna call the Sun "the founder of our race" (ὁ γενεάρχης ἡμῶν, 4.8.2) is consistent with both. The excavations of Meroe City at the beginning of our century brought confirmation in the sense that there was indeed a temple of Amun in the city.[44] But the main ceremonies in the novel take place on the other side of the river, involving building structures of such a temporary nature that archaeology can hardly be expected to confirm (or disprove) their existence. One should take warning from

---

[43] Other early references to the Sun in connection with Meroe are in Mimnermos 12.9–11 and Aischylos fr. 323 M. See further Lesky (1959) 29–31, and Morgan (1982) 238 (with n. 54).

[44] For the early (seventh-third century BC) temple of Amun, see Török (1997a), 25ff., for the late (third century BC-third century AD) temple, ibid. 116ff.

the excavators' pathetic attempts to identify Temple M 250, a chapel on a double podium, with Herodotos' "Table of the Sun";[45] one thing is that the building proves to be as late as first century BC, another that the historian's description does not speak of a building at all.

Heliodoros' topographical description is vague, and vaguely verisimilar. This is also true for the description of the cult itself. Apart from the animals brought to the glade, the expectation of the spectators is that human beings as well — namely, the white prisoners, Theagenes and Charikleia — should be part of the thanksgiving offerings to the Sun for the victory, "the firstfruits of the war" (αἱ ἀπαρχαὶ τοῦ πολέμου, 10.7.1, cf. 9.1.4; 24.5; 26.1). This threat, and how it is finally averted, partly with the help of the gymnosophists who oppose human sacrifice on grounds of principle, dominates the action up to the end of the novel; and several specific details of the ceremonies are intertwined in the narrative. The different kinds of animals appropriate to each god, the Sun, the Moon, and Dionysos-Osiris, are specified, with explanations suggested in a manner to make it look an authentic historical account (10.6.5; cf. 10.28.1). The human victims to the Sun and the Moon must be chaste, and their chastity is tested (10.7–8); this is a titillating motif we know from other novels as well. Those who officiate at the sacrifice must be a married man and a married woman; that is why Charikleia the virgin cannot be allowed to slay Theagenes by her own hand as each of them romantically demands (10.21.2, 10.33.1), and why Theagenes and Charikleia may finally, after their marriage, themselves assume that particular priesthood (10.41.1).

Human sacrifice in itself was part of Meroitic martial practices; there is ample iconographical evidence for "the triumphal massacre of the enemy by the victorious king or warlord",[46] e.g., the lower podium reliefs in Temple M 250 at Meroe City (late first century BC, cf. *FHN* II, 179).[47] But to proceed from that fact — or, as Giovanni Vantini does, from the generally accurate geographical descriptions of the novel[48] —

[45] Cf. Török (1997a) 102ff.

[46] L. Török in *FHN* III, 274, Comments.

[47] See Török (1997a), 106ff., figs. 21–22, Plates 71–81.

[48] Vantini (1984) 25, summarizing an apparently unpublished paper of his, "Eléments de religion méroïtiques dans le roman 'Les Éthiopiennes' [sic] d'Héliodore" (1973). Vycichl (1977) 448f. gives a similar description, but finally (457f.) concludes that Heliodoros is no good source after all.

to the conclusion that Heliodoros gives us an authentic description of Meroitic cult, is unwise. The details he successively provides are, as we have seen, intimately connected with the progress of his plot, and no doubt the products of his creative imagination.

Seated on a high throne (ἐφ᾽ ὑψηλοῦ) beside the pavilion, the king receives embassies from various nations (ἔθνη)[49] who are bringing gifts to congratulate him on his victory (10.22.6; cf. 10.25.1). One is reminded of the victory thrones (δίφροι) erected in the fourth century AD at various places by Aksumite rulers, inscribed fragments of which have been found also in Meroe;[50] but this is likely to be sheer coincidence. Anyway, the reception of these embassies gives the novelist a natural opportunity to sketch the political landscape surrounding his Kingdom of Meroe.

The first to be received is no ambassador proper, but the king's young nephew Meroebos (10.23). As we have seen, he is a king himself, helped by Hydaspes to succeed his father on the throne; but Heliodoros never states over which country he reigns. The ordinary reader probably never notices; for this flourishing black (10.24.2) youth is introduced by the author to be a suitable husband for his white cousin Charikleia, once the royal couple have accepted her true identity. This unexpected turn of events plus the giant wrestler whom Meroebos brings as his gift (10.25) take all attention away from the identity of his kingdom; when the wrestler reenters the scene to fight against Theagenes, he is just referred to as "the Aithiopian" (10.30.7–8 etc.), contrary to the general rule that the gifts are chosen to represent the various nations bringing them. The whole Meroebos episode is clearly staged for special reasons of the plot and not in order to characterize Meroe's political and ethnographical environment.

The other gift bringers, however, serve precisely that purpose: ambassadors are received from the Seres (10.25.3), from Arabia Felix (10.26.1), from the Troglodytai (10.26.2), from the Blemmyes (10.26.2–3), and from the Aksumites (10.27), each with the ethnographically appropriate gifts. Except for the Aksumites, these peoples are defined as subject to tribute

211

---

[49] Morgan (1989) 575 translates ταῖς ἐκ τῶν ἐθνῶν ἡκούσαις πρεσβείαις (10.22.5) as "the embassies from the *provinces of our empire*" (my italics), implanting a definite political structure where Heliodoros is vague.

[50] Cf. T. Hägg, "A New Axumite Inscription in Greek from Meroe: A Preliminary Report", in: *Meroitistische Forschungen 1980* (Meroitica, 7), Berlin 1984, 436–441, and *FHN* III, 285–286.

to the Kingdom of Meroe (10.27.1); and they have already appeared as auxiliary forces in Meroe's war against the Persians in Upper Egypt, as narrated in Books 8–9.[51] This is perhaps where Heliodoros most obviously leaves his "classical" Meroe for later periods: only the Troglodytai have a Herodotean alibi (4.183.4; *FHN* I, 66), the Blemmyes (modern Beja) are first mentioned in Greek literature by Theokritos (7.114; *FHN* II, 116), and the Seres[52] and "Wealthy Arabs" later still.[53] But since all the names were familiar to readers of Greek literature at least from the time of Strabo and Diodorus Siculus on, there is no reason to think that Heliodoros' contemporary readers would have found them objectionably "modern".

The historically most interesting fact is that the Aksumites (Αὐξωμῖται) are described as "friends and allies" (φίλιοι … καὶ ὑπόσπονδοι, 10.27.1) rather than vassals as the rest. Since this distinction has no consequences for the plot of the novel — the Aksumites present their exotic gift, a *kamelopardalis* or giraffe, and then disappear from the action — it is legitimate to seek for an extra-textual explanation. In fact, as many have noted,[54] Aksum's prominence among Meroe's neighbours is likely to reflect its historical importance in the region in Heliodoros' own time. The Kingdom of Aksum was formed from tribal kingdoms only in the first century AD; in the next centuries Aksumite interventions into the affairs of neighbouring states are attested, and by the middle of the fourth its economic dominance and military force may have been decisive for the end of Meroe as a centralized kingdom (though the details in this process are far from clear).[55] The few words in the novel about friendship

---

[51] Morgan (1982) 240f. and (1989) 576 n. 244 reasonably suggests that Arabia Felix, bringing as their gifts cinnamon and other spices, corresponds to the auxiliaries from "near the Land of Cinnamon" (9.16.2). The Arabian Gulf and "the Cinnamon-producing country" are mentioned together in Strabo 17.1.5 (τοῖς πλέουσι τὸν Ἀράβιον κόλπον μέχρι τῆς κινναμωμοφόρου).

[52] The Seres, "Chinese", begin to appear frequently in Graeco-Roman literature in Augustan times (Verg. *Georg.* 2.121, Hor. *Carm.* 1.29.9, Char. 6.4.2 etc.). Cf. A.D. Papanikolaou, *Chariton-Studien. Untersuchungen zur Sprache und Chronologie der griechischen Romane* (Hypomnemata, 37), Göttingen 1973, 162f., Morgan (1982) 242 n. 79, and A. Dihle, "Serer und Chinesen", in: A. Dihle, *Antike und Orient*, Heidelberg 1984, 201–215.

[53] On the web of sources and traditions, cf. Morgan (1982) 236, 240–242, his footnotes (1989) 548 and 576, and the detailed discussion in Vycichl (1977) 451–457.

[54] E.g., Conti Rossini (1920–21) and Morgan (1982) 242 and (1989) 577 n. 247.

[55] See Burstein (1995) 207–213 and Török (1997b) 475f., 483–487.

and treaty between Meroe and Aksum can hardly be used as evidence in the reconstruction of the historical events of the fourth century, even if it is likely enough that there were such intermediate periods between the known armed conflicts between the two states (witnessed by the inscribed Aksumite victory thrones).[56] Nor can we date the composition of the novel on this basis; Heliodoros may well have described Meroe and Aksum as equals, even if the Kingdom of Meroe had already disintegrated and Aksum taken over the lead in the area — and he happened to know it. The only justifiable inference is that Heliodoros used sources about Meroe that reported a situation still prevailing at least in the first part of his own fourth century.

212

If friendship with Aksum appears in the novel without influencing its plot, the reverse is true for the war between Meroe and Persian Egypt. It is instrumental in finally bringing Charikleia and her lover home to Meroe City, while at the same time deferring and complicating that homecoming;[57] it allows the author to elaborate on warfare in great detail (as a second Homer) and present his ecphrastic description of the siege of Syene (in some particulars based on Julian or his source); and it serves to illustrate in action the concept of the noble and brave Aithiopians (King Hydaspes is supreme in both respects). All the more reason to doubt that there is any actual historical chain of events mirrored in the narrative. The general idea of rivalry and fighting between Egypt and its southern neighbour, with Syene, Elephantine, and Philai as strategically important places in the frontier zone, is of course historical enough; inscriptions confirm that there were in the Roman period cohorts garrisoned in all three.[58] This continuous situation is also exploited, though on a smaller scale, in the exchange of letters between Kandake and Alexander in the *Alexander Romance* (3.18; *FHN* II, 85). Further, Herodotos reports that the Aithiopians under King Sabakos invaded Egypt and stayed there for fifty years; it has been suggested that "Sabakos" here stands for the reigns of the Twenty-Fifth Dynasty rulers

[56] All these texts, in Ethiopian as well as Greek, are now available in É. Bernand, A.J. Drewes, and R. Schneider, *Recueil des inscriptions de l'Éthiopie des périodes pré-axoumite et axoumite*, Vol. 1–2, Paris 1991.

[57] The narrative strategy in the last books is analysed in detail by J.R. Morgan, "A Sense of the Ending: The Conclusion of Heliodoros' *Aithiopika*", TAPhA 119, 1989, 299–320; the siege on p. 308.

[58] Cf. *FHN* III, 220 and Speidel (1988).

Shabaqo, Shebitqo and Taharqo over Egypt ca. 716–664 BC (Hdt. 2.137; 2.152.1; *FHN* I, 60 and 63). And in his "Aithiopian logos" Herodotos relates how King Kambyses of Persia, after conquering Egypt in 525 BC, undertook an ill-planned and unsuccessful campaign against Aithiopia (3.25; *FHN* II, 65). These Herodotean narratives together may well have been Heliodoros' general inspiration, since one included Aithiopia in control, the other occurred in the right period; but there are no specific similarities between the descriptions. Nor are there, as far as I can see, any links between the surviving accounts of C. Petronius' campaign in the 20s BC (cf. above) and Heliodoros' Egyptian-Nubian war. So the idea itself and the setting are realistic, but the actual narrative above all a magnificent work of his imagination, though sometimes helped by extraneous material such as reports of the siege of Nisibis.

There is one detail, however, in the description of the war that merits further attention from the point of view of historicity. Heliodoros mentions a dispute over "the emerald mines" as one of the causes for the war. We are told that the gymnosophist Sisimithres had once acted as an Aithiopian ambassador to the Satrap of Egypt but been expelled from the country "[b]ecause he told the satrap to keep his hands off the emerald mines (τῶν σμαραγδείων μετάλλων), claiming that they belong to Aithiopia" (2.32.2; cf. 10.11.1). Later, the war starts because King Hydaspes wants to regain possession of these mines and "the city of Philai" which is held by a Persian-Egyptian garrison (8.1.3). Having defeated the Persians, he is officially recognized as the rightful master of both (9.6.5; 9.26.2). No more details about the mines, their situation etc., are ever given, and the mines themselves play no role in the action. But the author's insistence on this specific *casus belli* is a clear sign that he knows it to be historically verisimilar.

The emerald mines in question are in fact situated in the Red Sea Hills between Lower Nubia and the Red Sea. The first reference to emeralds in connection with Aithiopia in extant ancient literature appears to be in Pliny's book on minerals (*Naturalis Historia* 37.69; *FHN* III, 201).[59] The bright green emeralds from Aithiopia are found, he says, "at a distance of 25 days' journey from Koptos", citing as his source Juba, the king of Mauretania (d. ca. AD 23) who was also a learned writer in Greek. Strabo (17.1.45) locates emerald mines six or seven days from Kop-

213

[59]As pointed out by Morgan (1982) 246, already Theophrastos, *De lapid.* 34, associates precious-stones industry with Syene, but without specifying emeralds.

tos. The *Alexander Romance* (3.18.7; *FHN* II, 85) mentions "a crown of emeralds and unpierced pearls" among the Aithiopian gifts brought to Ammon, "protector of the Egyptian frontier". But the most interesting and specific information is found in the treatise "On the twelve stones on the breast-plate of Aaron" (*De XII gemmis* 19–21; *FHN* III, 305) by Bishop Epiphanios of Salamis on Cyprus (ca. AD 315–403). He speaks (in the 5th-century Latin rendering of his lost work) of a mountain called Smaragdinum, "which was once wet (with oil)[60] by Nero, as is commonly reported, or by Domitian" (19). This mountain, he alleges, is situated on an island outside Berenike on the Red Sea coast and has been under Roman control. He continues (21):

> Now, Beronice, as it is called, is contiguous with the district of Elephantine, and also with Telmis (= Kalabsha in Lower Nubia), which is now held by the Blemmyes. The mines of this mountain, however, have caved in. There are also other mines (*metalla*) established in the mountains in the barbarian district of the Blemmyes, near Telmis, where the barbarians now dig to extract emeralds.

What interests us is not Epiphanios' somewhat confused view of the geography of the region, but the information about contemporary historical events. "Now" (*nunc*, twice), he says, the Blemmyes hold Kalabsha and "the barbarians" (*barbari*, the Coptic version has "the Kushites") are extracting emerald from the mines in the vicinity. This was written about AD 394. Another contemporary source, the *Notitia Dignitatum* (*or.* XXXI.35, 65), edited between July 392 and May 394, implies, however, that the Romans still had strongholds in precisely this region.[61] The mines thus seem to have passed out of their hands and into those of the "barbarians" about AD 394. They obviously remained so for some time, for when in ca. AD 423 the diplomat and historian Olympiodoros "was staying around Thebes and Syene to do research, the tribal chiefs and priests of the barbarians around Talmis (Kalabsha), i.e., the Blemmyes, formed a desire to meet him" (fr. 37; *FHN* III, 309). He went, and *inter alia* reports the following, according to Photios (*Bibliotheca* cod. 80 p. 62a22–26):

---

[60] The rocks of the mountain were dyed with a green oil so as to enhance their colour and sparkle, Epiphanios explains at another place.

[61] For the details of this argument, see L. Török in the Comments on *FHN* III, 305.

214

He says he learned that in these regions there were also emerald mines (σμαράγδου μέταλλα) from which the kings of Egypt used to obtain emeralds in abundance. "These too," he says, "the priests of the barbarians urged me to visit, but this was not possible without a royal order (βασιλικῆς προστάξεως)."

The mines are obviously worked by the Blemmyes, although it is not clear from whom the "royal order" is to be issued. What is important in our context, is that a transfer of power in the Dodekaschoinos from Roman Egypt to its southern neighbour took place in ca. AD 394, and that the emerald mines as well changed hands. Could this possibly have been a direct inspiration for Heliodoros? Or perhaps some similar conflict earlier in the century, if it should be too late to place the composition of the novel in the mid 390s?[62] In the *Historia Monachorum* (1.2; *FHN* III, 307) we read — though without reference to the emerald mines — of an "Aithiopian" incursion in the direction of Syene, which took place roughly between AD 388 and 395; on this occasion, however, the conflict ended with Roman victory. Ca. AD 400, the Roman poet Claudian speaks of the Nile as flowing "through the thousand black kingdoms of Aithiopians" and winding "through Meroe and the fierce Blemmyes and black Syene" (*Carmina minora* 28.15–19; *FHN* III, 308). This confirms both that the Blemmyes were at the time in control somewhere in the Middle Nile Valley and that these names and places had a certain topicality in the Graeco-Roman culture of this period. Claudian left his native Alexandria for Rome in ca. 394!

What we may conclude from all this concurring literary evidence is, at the very least, that warfare in the frontier zone south of Syene was common — and commonly known — in the late fourth century, when Heliodoros probably wrote, and that he strikes a realistic *contemporary* note in making rivalry over the emerald mines a prominent *casus belli*.

---

[62] AD 350 (the third siege of Nisibis) is the *terminus post quem* (cf. above, n. 3), but we have no similarly definite *ante quem*. I cannot follow Morgan (1996) 419 when he states: "In either case [namely, whether Heliodoros had read Julian or they independently used a common source], Heliodoros' motive can only have been to exploit public awareness and interest, and he cannot, therefore, have been writing very long after the event: the novel was probably completed in the years between 350 and 375." And further (419): "We can thus reconstruct a speculative biography: Heliodoros wrote the *Aithiopika* around 360, and was holding high office in the Thessalian church around 400." The flaw in this argument is that nothing prevents us from assuming the opposite, namely, that Heliodoros did *not* intend his readers to recognize the siege of Nisibis in his siege of Syene. Why should he? The narrative is exciting as it is; and attention drawn away from his historical Egyptian milieu to contemporary Mesopotamia would hardly be in his interest.

It is time to round off this discussion of fact and fiction in the *Aithiopika* with a few words on the issue of blackness. It is true that the heroine is white, in spite of being the daughter of the black King and Queen of Meroe, which might lead one to believe that whiteness is represented in the novel as superior to blackness. This is not so. In the few places where the black skin of the Aithiopians is specifically noted, there is no negative implication. For instance, Charikles' first meeting with Sisimithres describes the Aithiopian as "a man of imposing (σεμνός) appearance, whose intelligence (ἀγχίνοιαν) in particular was plain to see in his expression; he had not long come of the age of manhood, and his skin was as black as it could be (τὴν χροιὰν δὲ ἀκριβῶς μέλας)" (2.30.1). Note how his blackness comes last in the description, as the climax. With regard to Charikleia's young Aithiopian cousin Meroebos it is not stated that he is black until he blushes: "even in his black skin (ἐν μελαίνη τῆ χροιᾷ) he could not conceal his blush" (10.24.2) — he had first been presented just as "a striking example of young manhood" (10.23.4) — and the reason why Charikleia and Meroebos are not united in marriage, as King Hydaspes wishes, is not the different colour of their skins, but simply that Charikleia loves Theagenes. Hydaspes himself is depicted as righteous, pious, and wise, not least in contrast to his Persian adversaries. Queen Persinna is virtuous and loyal, while Arsake, the wife of the Persian Satrap of Egypt, is evil and lustful. The Aithiopian gymnosophist Sisimithres is again intelligent, compassionate, and pious, with no flaws in his character such as the action reveals in both the Delphian priest Charikles and his Egyptian counterpart Kalasiris.[63] It is the old Greek ideal of the "blameless" Aithiopians, developed into a philosophical utopia, that takes precedence over any ethnographical description (such as is used for Meroe's allied tribes) or emphasis on Greek vs. "barbarian" nature (as the Persians and Egyptians are characterized).[64]

---

[63] The character traits given to the Aithiopians in the novel are summarized by Lonis (1992) 234. Cf. also T. Szepessy, "Die Aithiopika des Heliodoros und der griechische sophistische Liebesroman", *AAntHung* 5, 1957, 241–259, pp. 244–251, and H. Kuch, "A Study on the Margin of the Ancient Novel: 'Barbarians' and Others", in: Schmeling (1996) 209–220, pp. 218f.

[64] Kuch (1996) 218 points at the "Aithiopian" giant with whom Theagenes wrestles as an exception to the rule (e.g., Theagenes' Greek training is contrasted to the Aithiopian's ἄγροικον ἰσχύν, "brute force" 10.31.5). It may be relevant that this giant is brought as a gift by Meroebos who reigns over a vassal state, and is called "Aithiopian" only accidentally (the name of the vassal state is never given, cf. above); for Hydaspes and the Aithiopian spectators, he is clearly an exotic "other" (cf. 10.25.2, 10.30.7).

Why, then, is Charikleia white (except for her black birthmark)?[65] We should first recall that she is no foundling taken up by the black king and queen, but the opposite: she is their natural daughter, white only "by mistake", and exposed because of her colour. So she *is* Aithiopian. The oracle which prefigures the ending in fact seems to suppose that she is even becoming black (2.35.5):

> To the black land of the Sun will they travel,
> where they will reap the reward of those whose lives are passed in virtue:
> a crown of white *on brows turning black* (ἐπὶ κροτάφων ... μελαινομένων).

The "crown of white" is the white mitre, indicating priesthood, which Charikleia finally receives from her mother the queen, and Theagenes simultaneously from the king (10.41.2). The author quotes these lines of the oracle again, but does not interpret them for us. John Morgan may well be right in suggesting that "[w]ith their ordination Theagenes and Charikleia become [Ai]thiopian; the white crown makes their skins metaphorically black",[66] although one would have wished for some confirmation in the text. A less dignified interpretation would be that the white-skinned young couple is now gradually getting darker, truly "scorched-faced", under the Aithiopian sun.

Heliodoros also leaves it to us to speculate why, from the start, he chose to make Charikleia white. In addition to the mythical precedent, the white Andromeda, considerations regarding the Greek readership of the novel may have prevented him from presenting a black heroine; it would have made it less easy for them to identify with her. And, more important still, the whole play with Charikleia's true identity would have been spoiled. As we have seen all along, it was plot construction that decided what material Heliodoros should adopt from his sources and how

---

[65] 10.15.2: μέλανι συνθήματι. This mark seems to have been invented *ad hoc* in the recognition scene, but the author grabs the opportunity to give it an emblematic force: "like a ring of ebony staining the ivory of her arm" (ibid.). Lonis (1992) 237 uses the mark, as a sign of *métissage*, in his attempt to show that Heliodoros has a vision of a "rapprochement des cultures", that of "Delphi" with that of "Meroe".

[66] Morgan (1989) 318. I am less happy with Morgan's expression in his "The *Aithiopika* of Heliodoros: Narrative as Riddle", in: J.R. Morgan and R. Stoneman (eds.), *Greek Fiction: The Greek Novel in Context*, London-New York 1994, 97–113, p. 108, making "honorary [Ai]thiopians" of Th. & Ch. — is she not rather an "honorary Greek"?

he was to manipulate it. It was easier for him to produce and explain a white Aithiopian than to accommodate a black heroine; our question is one that probably never even crossed his mind.

References

Baslez, M.-F., Ph. Hoffmann, and M. Trédé (eds.) 1992: *Le monde du roman grec* (Études de littérature ancienne, 4), Paris.

Bernand, É., A.J. Drewes, and R. Schneider 1991: *Recueil des inscriptions de l'Éthiopie des périodes pré-axoumite et axoumite*, Vol. 1-2, Paris.

Bersina, S.Ya. 1989: "Milanese Papyrus No. 40", *Meroitica* 10, 217-224.

Bowersock, G.W. 1994: *Fiction as History: Nero to Julian*, Berkeley.

Burstein, S.M. 1995: *Graeco-Africana: Studies in the History of Greek Relations with Egypt and Nubia*, New Rochelle, NY-Athens-Moscow.

Chauvin, P. 1990: *Chronique des derniers païens*, Paris.

Colonna, A. (ed.) 1938: Heliodori *Aethiopica*, Roma.

Colonna, A. (ed.) 1990: Eliodoro, *Le Etiopiche* (I Classici greci e latini TEA), Milano.

Conti Rossini, C. 1919-20: "Meroe ed Aksum nel romanzo di Eliodoro", *Rivista degli Studi Orientali* 8, 233-239.

Desanges, J. 1983: "L'Hellénisme dans le royaume de Méroë", *Graeco-Arabica* 2, 275-296.

Desanges, J. 1992: "Bilan des recherches sur les sources grecques et latines de l'histoire de la Nubie antique dans les trentes dernières années", in: Ch. Bonnet (ed.): *Études nubiennes*, Vol. 1, Geneva, 363-378.

Dihle, A. 1984: *Antike und Orient. Gesammelte Aufsätze*, Heidelberg.

Donadoni, S. 1984: "Les inscriptions grecques de Nubie", *Graeco-Arabica* 3, 9-19.

Eide, T. 2000: "The 'Blameless' Aithiopians — A Misunderstanding?", *Graeco-Arabica* 7-8, 123-127.

Feuillatre, E. 1966: *Études sur les Éthiopiques d'Héliodore. Contribution à la connaissance du roman grec*, Paris.

FHN I-III = T. Eide, T. Hägg, R.H. Pierce, and L. Török (eds.): *Fontes Historiae Nubiorum*, Vol. 1: *From the Eighth to the Fifth Century BC*, Bergen 1994; Vol. 2: *From the Fourth to the First Century BC*, Bergen 1996; Vol. 3: *From the First to the Sixth Century AD*, Bergen 1998.

Hägg, T. 1982: "Some Remarks on the Use of Greek in Nubia", in: J.M. Plumley (ed.): *Nubian Studies*, Warminster, 103-107.

Hägg, T. 1984: "A New Axumite Inscription in Greek from Meroe: A Preliminary Report", in: *Meroitistische Forschungen 1980* (Meroitica, 7), Berlin, 436-441.

Hägg, T. 1987: "*Callirhoe* and *Parthenope*: The Beginnings of the Historical Novel", *Classical Antiquity* 6, 184-204 [No. 2 in this volume].

217

Hägg, T. 1990: "Titles and Honorific Epithets in Nubian Greek Texts", *Symbolae Osloenses* 65, 147-177.

Hägg, T. 1991: "Greek Language in Christian Nubia", in: A.S. Atiya (ed.): *The Coptic Encyclopedia*, Vol. 4, New York, 1170-1174.

Kuch, H. 1996: "A Study on the Margin of the Ancient Novel: 'Barbarians' and Others", in: Schmeling (1996) 209-220.

Leclant, J. 1968: Rev. of Feuillatre (1966), *Revue des Études Grecques* 81, 629-632.

Lesky, A. 1959: "Aithiopika", *Hermes* 87, 27-38.

Lonis, R. 1992: "Les Éthiopiens sous le regard d'Héliodore", in: Baslez et al. (eds., 1992) 233-241.

Morgan, J.R. 1982: "History, Romance, and Realism in the Aithiopika of Heliodoros", *Classical Antiquity* 1, 221-265.

Morgan, J.R. 1989: "A Sense of the Ending: The Conclusion of Heliodoros' *Aithiopika*", *Transactions of the American Philological Association* 119, 299-320.

Morgan, J.R. 1994: "The *Aithiopika* of Heliodoros: Narrative as Riddle", in: J.R. Morgan and R. Stoneman (eds.): *Greek Fiction: The Greek Novel in Context*, London-New York 1994, 97-113.

Morgan, J.R. 1996: "Heliodoros", in: Schmeling (ed., 1996) 417-456.

Papanikolaou, A.D. 1973: *Chariton-Studien. Untersuchungen zur Sprache und Chronologie der griechischen Romane* (Hypomnemata, 37), Göttingen.

Pouilloux, J. 1983: "Delphes dans les *Ethiopiques* d'Héliodore: la réalité dans la fiction", *Journal des Savants*, 259-286.

Rattenbury, R.M., T.W. Lumb, and J. Maillon (eds.) 1960: Héliodore, *Les Éthiopiques (Théagène et Chariclée)*, Vol. 1-3, 2nd ed. (Collection des Universités de France), Paris 1960.

Reardon, B.P. (ed.) 1989: *Collected Ancient Greek Novels*, Berkeley.

Reeve, M.D. 1989: "Conceptions", *Proceedings of the Cambridge Philological Society* 215, 81-112.

Rougemont, G. 1992: "Delphes chez Héliodore", in: Baslez et al. (ed., 1992) 93-99.

Saïd, S. 1992: "Les langues du roman grec", in: Baslez et al. (ed., 1992) 169-186.

Sandy, G.N. 1982: *Heliodorus* (Twayne's World Authors Series, 647), Boston.

Schauenberg, K. 1974: "Achilleus als Barbar: ein antikes Mißverständnis", *Antike und Abendland* 20, 88-96.

Schauenberg, K. 1981: "Andromeda I", in: *Lexicon Iconographicum Mythologiae Classicae*, Vol. 1:1, Zürich and München, 774-790.

Schmeling, G. (ed.) 1996: *The Novel in the Ancient World*, Leiden.

Snowden, F.M. 1970: *Blacks in Antiquity: Ethiopians in the Greco-Roman Experience*, Cambridge, MA.

Speidel, M.P. 1988: "Nubia's Roman Garrison", in: *Aufstieg und Niedergang der Römischen Welt* II.10.1, Berlin-New York, 767-798.

Szepessy, T. 1957: "Die Aithiopika des Heliodoros und der griechische sophistische Liebesroman", *Acta Antiqua Academiae Scientiarum Hungaricae* 5, 241-259 (repr.

218

in H. Gärtner (ed.): *Beiträge zur griechischen Liebesroman*, Hildesheim 1984, 432–450).

Török, L. 1989–1990: "Augustus and Meroe", *Orientalia Suecana* 38–39, 171–190.

Török, L. 1997a: *Meroe City: an Ancient African Capital*, Vol. 1–2, London.

Török, L. 1997b: *The Kingdom of Kush: Handbook of the Napatan-Meroitic Civilization* (Handbuch der Orientalistik, 1. Abt., 31), Leiden-New York-Köln.

Vantini, G. 1984: "Greek and Arab Geographers on Nubia ca. 500 B.C.–1500 A.D.", *Graeco-Arabica* 3, 21–51.

Vercoutter, J., J. Leclant, F.M. Snowden, Jr., and J. Desanges 1976: *The Image of the Black in Western Art*, Vol. 1, Cambridge, MA, and London.

Vycichl, W. 1977: "Heliodors *Aithiopika* und die Volksstämme des Reiches Meroë", in: E. Endesfelder, K.-H. Priese, W.-F. Reineke, and S. Wenig (eds.), *Ägypten und Kusch* (Schriften zur Geschichte und Kultur des Alten Orients, 13), Berlin 1977, 447–458.

Warmington, E.H. 1974: *The Commerce between the Roman Empire and India*, 2nd ed. London.

Wenig, S. 1978: *Africa in Antiquity: The Arts of Ancient Nubia and the Sudan*, Vol. 2: *The Catalogue*, New York.

Wildung, D. 1997: "Meroe and Hellenism", in: D. Wildung (ed.), *Sudan: Ancient Kingdoms of the Nile*, Paris-New York, 370–380.

Addendum

Too late to be used for the present article there appeared a valuable collection of essays on the *Aithiopika*: R. Hunter (ed.): *Studies in Heliodorus* (Proceedings of the Cambridge Philological Society, suppl. vol. 21), Cambridge 1998. Of special interest for the present topic are the contributions of J. Hilton, "An Ethiopian paradox: Heliodorus, *Aithiopika* 4.8", T. Whitmarsh, "The birth of a prodigy: Heliodorus and the genealogy of Hellenism" (both discussing Charikleia's birth and whiteness), and D.L. Selden, "*Aithiopika* and Ethiopianism" (the colour issue).

219

From the Afterlife of
Apollonius of Tyana

13

Apollonios of Tyana
— Magician, Philosopher, Counter-Christ
The Metamorphoses of a Life*

[not previously published]

We begin with a description of an historical event that started early in the morning of February 23, AD 303. It took place in Izmit, then called Nicomedia, the capital of the Roman province of Bithynia. The Emperor Diocletian had finally, only two years before his abdication, decided to solve the Christian problem. Lactantius, the church historian, is our witness (*On the Deaths of the Persecutors* [*MP*] 12–13):[1]

> A suitable and auspicious day was sought for carrying the business out, and the festival of the *Terminalia* on February 23 was chosen as best, so that a termination so to speak could be imposed on this religion.
> "That day was the first which was the cause of death,
>   the first which was the cause of ills" (Vergil, *Aen.* 4.169–70)
> – ills which befell both them and the whole world.
> When this day dawned …, suddenly while it was still twilight the prefect came to the church with military leaders, tribunes, and accountants; they forced open the doors and searched for the image of God; they found the scriptures and burnt them; all were granted booty; the scene was one of plunder, panic, and confusion. The rulers themselves from their vantage-point — the church was built on high ground and so was visible from the palace — argued with each other for a long time whether the building ought to be set on fire. Diocletian won the argument by warning that a large fire might cause some part of the city to go up in flames; for the church was surrounded on all sides by a number of large houses. So the praetorians came in formation, bringing axes and other iron tools, and after being ordered in from every direction they levelled the lofty edifice to the ground within a few hours.
> The next day an edict was posted in which warning was given that those who adhered to this religion would be deprived of all official posi-

---

* Revised version (1999) of a paper presented at the conference "The Use and Abuse of the Past: Writers, Historiographers, Holy Men and Women in the Eastern Mediterranean World" at the Swedish Research Institute in Istanbul, November 26–28, 1998.

[1] Trans. Creed 1984, 19ff.

tions and status, and would be subject to torture whatever order or rank
of society they came from, that any legal action brought against them
would be valid in court, while they themselves would be unable to bring
actions for wrongs done to them, for adultery [read: rape], or for theft;
they would in fact lose their freedom and their right of utterance. One
man, admittedly acting wrongly but showing great courage, snatched
this edict down and tore it up … He was immediately arrested; and he
was not merely tortured; after being roasted by due process of law and
enduring this with amazing patience, he was finally burnt to death.

This is the start of the last of the officially sanctioned persecutions of the
Christians in the Roman empire, known as the "Great Persecution".[2] It
continued for some ten years. Why it came about at all at a time when
there were already many Christians in influential positions, also in the
imperial palace and family, is a complicated issue. It certainly came as a
great shock to many Christians. Diocletian himself seems to have been
reluctant; according to Lactantius (*MP* 11, 14), the *Augustus* was more or
less tricked into starting the persecution by his *Caesar*, Galerius; then it
rapidly accelerated and went out of his control.

But Lactantius also points at another individual as the one "who
had instigated and recommended the persecution" (*MP* 16.4 *qui auctor
et consiliarius ad faciendam persecutionem fuit*). This man was a certain
Sossianus Hierocles, apparently at the time of the scene just described
newly appointed governor of Bithynia (*praeses Bithyniae*) and thus immediately responsible for the execution of the imperial edict in Nicomedia.[3] Later we find him persecuting Christian philosophers and virgins in
Alexandria (Eusebios, *Martyrs of Palestine* 5.2–3).[4] But what particularly
interests us here is his role as, apparently, the chief ideologist behind the
Great Persecution.

Lactantius himself gives us more clues in his *Divine Institutes* ([*DI*]
5.2–3).[5] Hierocles, it appears, had written a pamphlet called "A truthful
discourse (directed) to the Christians" (Φιλαλήθης λόγος πρὸς Χριστιανούς) which had circulated in Bithynia on the eve of the Great Persecution.[6] The pamphlet itself is lost, but its general contents may be recon-

---

[2] See Labriolle 1942, 302–315; Frend 1965, 477–535, and 1987; Barnes 1981, 22ff.

[3] On his career, see Barnes 1976 and 1981, 22, 164–167; cf. Moreau 1954, 292–294.

[4] Bardy 1958, 137 with n. 3.

[5] Monat 1973, 134ff.; Eng. trans. in *The Ante-Nicene Fathers*, VII.

[6] On this pamphlet, its title and date, see Hägg 1992. [No. 14 in this volume].

structed; for in addition to what Lactantius says about it, there survives a small treatise generally referred to as *Against Hierocles* [*CH*] and — probably wrongly — attributed to the Greek church historian Eusebios. Its full title seems to have been: "Reply to Philostratos's *Life of Apollonios* occasioned by Hierocles's comparison between him and Christ".[7]

We have now, by the back door, reached the Apollonios figuring in the title of this paper — or at least one of the Apollonios figures of the title, the "Counter-Christ". This is the figure that Hierocles used in his pamphlet in order to demonstrate the falsehood of the Christian faith as founded on the divine status of Christ. Who, then, are the other two? Apollonios the magician and wonder-worker was born in Tyana in Cappadocia, either around 3 BC or around AD 40 and died about 100 or 80 years later; he was thus contemporary with, or (more probably) a generation younger than, Jesus of Nazareth with whom Hierocles compared him. Apollonios the philosopher and Neopythagorean, in turn, is the hero of the *Life of Apollonios of Tyana* [*VA*], a biographical novel composed by the Greek author Philostratos around AD 220.[8]

My point, of course, is that all our three Apollonioses, the magician of the first century, the philosopher of the third, and the counter-Christ of the fourth, are one and the same person — a person with one historical identity, about which we know fairly little, and with two constructed identities that we know all the better. My paper will thus provide an illustration from classical antiquity of the "construction" of an historical person for various uses in later historical situations. In the process, as we shall see, the original identity may be more or less erased from historical memory, while the person in his constructed identities may play a far more important role than he did in his own age and historical context.

Antiquity is well suited for the demonstration of typical historical mechanisms. We can discern the contours more clearly and follow the long lines better than in modern history with its myopic perspective

---

[7] Ed. Forrat and des Places 1986, text and Eng. trans. in Conybeare 1912, II, 483–605. On this treatise, see Hägg 1985 and 1992; on its title, Junod 1988 and Hägg 1992, 139 n. 7; on the question of authorship, Hägg 1992, 144–150 [No. 14 in this volume](cf. T.D. Barnes in *Lexikon für Theologie und Kirche* III (1995), 1009). Frede 1999 seems unaware that the authenticity of this work has been questioned.

[8] Most easily available in the Loeb (Conybeare 1912) and Tusculum (Mumrecht 1983) editions, with facing trans. The Greek text they offer is based on C.L. Kayser's Teubner edition (1870) which is, in turn, an *editio minor* of the same scholar's edition of 1844 (still the sole truly critical edition of this important text).

and often confusing multitude of sources — provided, of course, that we have any distinct sources at all. In our case, the *Life of Apollonios* by Philostratos and the pseudo-Eusebian treatise *Against Hierocles*, in combination with archaeological evidence, allow us to follow the metamorphoses of this fascinating figure stage by stage.[9] And we can check in the answer book of history the results of this double construction through two millennia, in environments very different from the East Anatolian places that Apollonios himself once frequented.

It was Hierocles' polemical use of Apollonios that secured him such an attention through history. The local wonder-worker would have been forgotten and the Pythagorean sage considered harmless, but for this sudden elevation to a counter-Christ, indirectly responsible for such bloody events as those in Nicomedia and the following ten years of persecution. Well into our own century the biography by Philostratos, which does not even mention Christianity, has regularly been edited together with "Eusebios's" refutation, as if it contained some subversive stuff that might threaten Christian readers.[10]

Moreover, historians of religion and critics of Christianity in the late 19th and early 20th centuries adopted Apollonios, as constructed by Hierocles, for their purposes.[11] The quotation of a couple of book titles will show where Apollonios had his modern supporters: *Apollonius of Tyana, the Pagan Christ of the Third Century*, and *Pagan Christs: Studies in Comparative Hierology*.[12] As late as 1977 there appeared in France a book with the title *Apollonius de Tyane et Jésus*,[13] attempting to show that Apollonios of Tyana and Jesus of Nazareth are polar incarnations of the myth of Christ, with the Greek as the aristocratic pole and the Aramaean as the popular one. The balance was lost when Constantine supported Christianity and closed the temples of Apollonios. It is time to rehabilitate Apollonios, the author concludes, and to bring into being "Christian Pythagoreanism". So Apollonios still invites new or modified constructions; he is conveniently resurrected to embody modern religious agendas.

---

[9] Cf. the useful survey in Speyer 1974.

[10] This is still the case in the Loeb Classical Library edition, Conybeare 1912; but the long tradition was broken with Mumprecht 1983.

[11] For a sketch of the earlier "Modern Polemics over Apollonius of Tyana", from the Renaissance to the 19th century, see Dzielska 1986, 193–212.

[12] Réville 1866 and Robertson 1911.

[13] Bernard 1977.

We shall now return to late antiquity and Hierocles, and from there work our way backwards to the historical Apollonios of the first century. But unlike most modern scholars who have studied this figure,[14] my chief aim is not to establish the historical truth about the man Apollonios, but to describe the successive stages in the construction of the figure. The authentic Apollonios is important in this context mainly as a foil to his constructed identities. Yet, it is not unimportant that Apollonios *was* an historical figure. This is the very basis for the use — and abuse — of him. Even if Philostratos's biography is largely fictitious, it derives its substance from history. The invented hero of a novel could never have had the historical impact that Hierocles achieved for Apollonios.

Hierocles was not the first to use Apollonios in antichristian polemics. In his lost work *Against the Christians*, the Neoplatonist Porphyry compared him favourably to St. Paul (frg. 4 Harnack) and perhaps also to Christ (frg. 60, 63 Harnack).[15] But it was Hierocles, in his *Truthful Discourse*, that gave Apollonios the lead and articulated his counter-Christian persona. We shall see, as far as our sources permit, how his Apollonios was characterized.

Hierocles obviously had Philostratos's *Life of Apollonios* as his main source, perhaps his only one, and selected from that biography what suited his immediate purpose. The author of *Against Hierocles* scorns him for his credulity and for having taken Philostratos as a witness to truth. Large parts of this apologetic treatise are devoted to showing the contradictions and implausibilities in Philostratos's image of Apollonios. Apparently, Hierocles had read the biography as an authentic historical report of the life of Apollonios, while our Christian apologist — knowing "construction" before the word — reads it as a literary work: the Apollonios figure it represents must be strictly distinguished from the historical individual.

The apologist is right, of course; and source criticism, in this case, suited his polemical purpose. Hierocles, on the other hand, was not necessarily just credulous. For *his* purpose, it was essential that the biography

---

[14] Bowie 1978 is fundamental. Of later studies, see, in particular, Dzielska 1986 (on which cf. Bowie 1989).

[15] The authenticity of the various alleged fragments of Porphyry's work is disputed. Cf. Barnes 1973, 429f, 1127; Meredith 1980, 1127, 1130; Frend 1987, 12; Frede 1999, 234, 236.

did contain the truth about the historical Apollonios — had he doubted this or started discussing it in his pamphlet, his case would have been lost. A fundamentalist belief in the text as a witness to historical truth was necessary; if he still did construct a new figure, this was achieved through that much less offensive expedient, *selection*.

While the apologist tries to discredit Hierocles's image of Apollonios by pointing to inconsistencies in the *Life*, Hierocles in his turn had wanted to demonstrate that the stories about Jesus in the Gospels are full of internal contradictions. He had accused Paul and Peter and the other disciples of "sowing lies" and spoken of them as "unskilled and unlearned", noting that "some of them made gain by the craft of fishermen" (Lact. *DI* 5.2.17).[16] Ps.-Eusebios provides the following direct quotation from the pamphlet (*CH* 2.24–32):

> And this point is also worth noticing, that whereas the tales of Jesus have been vamped up by Peter and Paul and a few others of the kind — men who were liars and uneducated and wizards (*goêtes*) — the history of Apollonios was written by Maximos of Aigeai, and by Damis the philosopher who lived constantly with him, and by Philostratos of Athens, men of the highest education, who out of respect for the truth and their love of mankind determined to give the publicity they deserved to the actions of a man at once noble and a friend of the gods.

Emphasis is laid on the social status of Apollonios, in contrast to that of Jesus. Those who have written about Apollonios are educated men, philosophers and authors, while the stories about Jesus derive from fishermen and workmen. Hierocles, in his "discourse to the Christians", obviously wanted to impress an intellectual group and show that Apollonios was much more their man. The abuse "wizard" (*goês*) is here directed against Christian wonder-workers, but no mention is made of the passages of the *Life of Apollonios* where Apollonios is defended against the very same accusation. Even the suspicion, however forcefully refuted, must be avoided. Thus the ex-wizard Apollonios, as elevated to sage by Philostratos, is used to knock down the wizard Jesus.

Comparing Apollonios and Jesus as wonder-workers obviously played an important part in the pamphlet. Philostratos had indeed, though probably unwittingly, laid the basis for such a comparison; modern scholars

[16] Trans. *The Ante-Nicene Fathers*, VII, 138.

have pointed to the remarkable similarities between the *Life of Apollo-nios* and the Gospels in this respect.[17] Hierocles, however, is looking for differences. He finds the many miracles performed by Apollonios well certified; they are no tricks of wizardry, but must be attributed to "a divine and mysterious wisdom" (θεία τινὶ καὶ ἀρρήτῳ σοφίᾳ, *CH* 2). The Christians, in contrast, he says (ibid.), "in their anxiety to exalt Jesus, ... run up and down prating of how he made the blind to see and worked certain other miracles of the kind." Against the easy credulity of the Christians he sets (ibid.) "our own accurate and well-established judgement": "For whereas we reckon him who wrought such feats not a god, but only a man favoured by the gods (θεοῖς κεχαρισμένον ἄνδρα), they on the strength of a few miracles proclaim their Jesus a god."

Two main points emerge. First, Hierocles regards the written evidence on Apollonios as much more sophisticated and trustworthy than the corresponding reports about Jesus — a source-critical superiority. Second, he stresses how differently the wonders are interpreted and evaluated by the supporters of each. Apollonios, in spite of his superior record as a miracle-worker, is not considered a god, only a "divine man", a *theios anêr*, someone who enjoys a privileged position in relation to the gods. Hierocles does not make the mistake of replacing the Christian God with a Pythagorean god; he probably left out any reference to Apollonios's ascension and reappearance, as recounted in the last chapters of the *Life*. Both his points are made to appeal to intellectuals, presumably those among the Christians that represented the greatest present threat. He has no use for the other Apollonios, the magician of popular appeal, who did figure in the *Life*, beside the philosopher.

There is not so much more to elicit about Hierocles's image of Apollonios, either from Lactantius who is more interested in refuting than quoting, or from Ps.-Eusebios who soon passes on to criticizing the *Life of Apollonios* itself, without Hierocles serving as a selective intermediary. Reading Philostratos seems to have been what others too did for the rest of the century, though often with different intentions from those of Ps.-Eusebios: Hierocles's pamphlet and the ensuing debate, it appears, led to a renaissance for the biography and for its Apollonios. While one looks in vain for quotations and allusions to the biography in Greek lit-

---

[17] The material is conveniently displayed in Petzke 1970. Cf. the discussion in Smith [1978] 1998, 111–123.

erature before Porphyry and Hierocles, they become quite common in fourth-century writers, both pagan and Christian. The book even appears to have had a Latin version at the end of the century, produced by Nicomachus Flavianus, a leading representative of the pagan reaction in Rome.[18] So-called contorniate medallions were minted in Rome, displaying Apollonios with a long philosopher's beard and a laurel wreath around his head.[19]

Thus, a religious figure was created who represented a more realistic and "modish" alternative to Christ than the gods of the old Greco-Roman Pantheon. St. Augustine for one testifies to this in a letter (138.18–19): though basically negative to Apollonios, he admits that he prefers him as a rival to Christ rather than Jove the violator of virgins. The religion or philosophy, of a mixed Neopythagorean and Neoplatonic brand, that Apollonios was often made to embody in this period, could appeal to the upper strata of society, such as the senatorial aristocracy of Rome and corresponding groups in the provinces. Just as Apollonios was a rival of Jesus, this philosophy shared many ideals and attitudes with contemporary Christianity: asceticism, chastity, the purification of the soul, the study of holy books, the belief in old revelations, and the practice of charity. At the same time, some of the aspects of Christianity that repulsed Hellenic sensibilities, such as the Eucharist and the bodily resurrection, were absent in this more purely spiritual cult. Though history proved it wrong — as Ps.-Eusebios already triumphantly proclaims (*CH* 7) — the expectation that the Hellenic aristocrat Apollonios would outdo Jesus the Jewish peasant was no doubt seriously entertained by Hierocles and his supporters at the imperial court at Nicomedia.

The polemical reuse of Apollonios at the beginning of the fourth century seems to have led to a revival of the more popular and genuine cult in the east as well. An increased activity may be traced at the old cult centres where there had been temples and altars raised for Apollonios since the early second century: at his birth-place Tyana in Cappadocia (mod. Kemarhisar, some 110 kilometres NW of Adana), at Aigeai (Αἰγέαι)[20] in Cilicia (mod. Yumurtalık), at Antioch on the Orontes (mod. Antakya on

---

[18] Sidonius Apollinaris, *Epistulae* 8.3.1. Cf. Dzielska 1986, 153f, 166–172.

[19] See the reproduction in Hägg 1983, 116, Fig. 31.

[20] Like its namesake in Macedonia (mod. Vergina), this city is also known as Aigai (Αἰγαί).

the border to Syria), and even at Ephesos on the west coast where Apollonios was said to have demonstrated his prophetic and magic powers.[21] New inscriptions honouring the miracle-worker and benefactor were put up. Apollonios "talismans" — statues and other artefacts with magic properties — were sold and bought all over Asia Minor (probably with Antioch as the centre of production); and this commerce continued into the Byzantine period. Paradoxically, Apollonios was now even adopted by the Christians as a holy man endowed with special connections to the divine sphere. The capital too was protected by him: talismans he was supposed to have left in Byzantium kept mosquitoes and storks out of the city — the storks that poisoned the water by dropping snakes into the cisterns — while other talismans saved Constantinople from scorpions, kicking horses, and floods.[22]

So, while becoming a venerated symbol of paganism against Christianity in some circles and being denounced as a magician and a false prophet by the Church fathers, Apollonios was also gradually assimilated into popular Christian cults and beliefs in the east. Apollonios the philosopher and Apollonios the magician had divergent careers.

We shall now go back a hundred years from the fatal events of AD 303 to look closer at Philostratos's work and *his* picture of Apollonios. His *Life of Apollonios* — the original Greek title[23] is generally considered to be τὰ ἐς τὸν Τυανέα Ἀπολλώνιον, "On Apollonios of Tyana"[24] — was a commissioned work. In his introduction he writes that the Empress Julia Domna, to whose circle in Rome he belonged, had engaged him

---

[21] Thus Dzielska 1986, Ch. II, "Apollonius and his Cities"; cf. Bowie 1989, 252f, who is more sceptical of the evidence for pre-4th-century cults, as well as to the connection between polemics and revival of cult.

[22] The "Tradition of Apollonius' Magic" is told in detail in Dzielska 1986, Ch. III, to which I refer for sources and other documentation. See also the detailed exposition in Dulière 1970.

[23] See *VA* 8.29 (referring to Damis's memoirs) and *Lives of the Sophists* 570. The title "Life of Apollonios" first appears in Eunapios, *Lives of the Philosophers and Sophists* 454 (but cf. also *VA* 5.39).

[24] Swain 1999, 157 n. 1, translates "the deeds/sayings relating to/in honour of Apollonius of Tyana" and prefers to use the title *In Honour of Apollonius* (as suggested already by Anderson 1986, 121). Bowie 1994, 189 (cf. 1978, 1665) points to parallels in titles of novels and translates *The Stories of Apollonius of Tyana*, thereby (like Swain) backing up his own current agenda ("Philostratus: Writer of Fiction"). Cf. the discussion of genre and title in Anderson 1986, 227–239 (esp. 235 and 238 n. 57).

to write the *Life* (*VA* 1.3). She had handed over the memoirs (*hypomnê-mata*) of Apollonios written by a certain Damis from Nineveh, who had been a disciple of Apollonios, and asked her court sophist to produce a stylistically more accomplished version. Julia Domna (ca. 170–217), the wife of Emperor Septimius Severus and the mother of Caracalla, was of Syrian dynastic offspring and is commonly associated with the increasing Oriental influence in Rome at the beginning of the third century. There was evidently an interest in Apollonios in these court circles.[25] It is uncertain, however, whether it was his Pythagorean philosophy that aroused this interest, or other traits in the traditional picture of the man. In the *Life of Apollonios*, it is the sun-god that Apollonios regularly prays to, and the sun-cult was introduced in Rome from Syria. This devotion may have made Apollonios a suitable object of praise; but it is equally possible that the prayers to Helios rather belong to what Philostratos himself added — if so, perhaps to please Julia Domna.

By saying "added", the implication is that Philostratos had written sources for his work. However, the character and identity of such sources belong to the most intensely discussed questions concerning the *Life*.[26] It is true that the author himself repeatedly refers to and names his sources, but such insistence may belong to his literary apparatus with a view to making the *Life* look authentic. First, the "memoirs" of Damis; most scholars today regard them as pure invention by Philostratos. There is a middle way, however, chosen by a recent contributor to the debate: even if the memoirs of Damis were a fake, Philostratos was not necessarily their fabricator; it may be that he used such a work in the belief that it was genuine.[27] This would save us from supposing that Philostratos deliberately made his royal benefactrix, Julia Domna, his accomplice in a literary fraud.

In addition to the memoirs of Damis, the author states (*VA* 1.3) that he made use of a biography by Maximos of Aigeai and of Apollonios's own will. Though some would place Maximos in the same category as

---

[25] Dio Cassius 78.18.4 reports that Caracalla (emperor 211–217) built a *herôon* to Apollonios. According to the biography in the *Historia Augusta*, Alexander Severus (emperor 222–235) had a private shrine with images of Apollonios, Christ, Abraham and Orpheus (*Alex.* 29.2).

[26] Cf. Palm 1976; Bowie 1978; Anderson 1986, 155–173; Dzielska 1986, 19–49; Koskenniemi 1991, 9–18; Flinterman 1995, 67–88; Swain 1996, 383f.

[27] Flinterman 1995, 79–88 (with refs. in n. 111 to earlier adherents of this theory).

Damis, there are in fact good reasons for believing that the work existed and treated Apollonios's youth.[28] Philostratos also mentions a third work on Apollonios, a biography in four books written by one Moiragenes. Since we have some external evidence for that work as well — a possible fragment and a reference in Origen's *Against Celsus*[29] — we need not doubt its existence. But Philostratos warns against using it because, he claims, its author "was ignorant of many of the circumstances of his life" (1.3). This has sometimes been taken to imply that he depicted Apollonios only as a magician and wizard, being "ignorant" of the philosophical side of his subject that Philostratos himself wants to emphasize.[30] But his manner of discarding off-hand his predecessor and competitor on the book market is well-known from biographical writings of later times too and need not in itself imply any fundamental differences between the two pictures of Apollonios.

In addition to his biographical sources, Philostratos claims to have had access to authentic documents from Apollonios's own hand. The will is one such item, of unknown status. In the course of the *Life* he also quotes a number of letters from Apollonios to emperors, philosophers, and others.[31] The authenticity of these letters has been doubted; and it may well be that some are genuine, some not: the author, inspired by existing letters, may have fabricated others to insert into his narrative (cf. below). By quoting and discussing such a mixture of authentic and fictitious material, biographical texts as well as documents of the object's own hand, the *Life of Apollonios* would be an early example of a "documentary novel".[32]

For our limited purpose, it is enough to conclude that Philostratos had some written material at his disposal, but that it was in his own interest to exaggerate the number and richness of his sources. His references to sources and his discussion of their value and truthfulness right through his work are part of his rhetorical strategy to give the biography an authentic and scholarly character — they are part of his *Beglaubi-*

---

[28] See Graf 1984/85.

[29] *Contra Celsum* 6.41 (referred to as *apomnêmoneumata*), cf. Francis 94f; on the fragment, see Bowie 1978, 1677.

[30] See Bowie 1978, 1673f, who argues against this view, and cf. Swain 1996, 384f.

[31] For discussion of the letters of Apollonios, both those quoted in the *Life* and the collection handed down separately, see Penella 1979.

[32] Thus Palm 1976, 40.

gungsapparat. It was important for him to stress that Apollonios was an historical figure and that he was himself seeking the *true* Apollonios (in explicit contrast to Moiragenes). Those who simply equate the *Life of Apollonios* with contemporary novels fail to observe this fundamental difference in attitude, a difference reflected, as we have seen, in its reception history as well.

In our attempt to find out what message Philostratos wanted to communicate by means of his historical hero, we shall first identify some main components of the story.[33] Its structure is that of a chronological biographical account. It starts with the wonderful omens and signs that surrounded Apollonios's birth in a flowery meadow in Cappadocia and ends with his death (told in several alternative versions), his ascent to heaven, and how he later appeared to a disciple at Tyana to prove the immortality of the soul. His life between these points is filled with travels, both between places in the eastern Mediterranean where he demonstrates his divine powers, to Persia, India, Egypt and Nubia to seek true wisdom, and to Spain and Italy on political missions. Besides the kings and sages he visits in the east, he has a number of meetings or confrontations with rival Greek philosophers and with Roman emperors from Nero to Nerva. He is put in jail in Rome, but manages to escape thanks to his superhuman gifts. Long passages in direct discourse break off the narrative: philosophical and political discussions, and an extensive apology *pro vita sua* (8.7). A number of letters are quoted. While the Anatolian scene forms the background for many of his miracles and acts of charity, the travelogue from the Orient is filled with the kind of paradoxographical stuff that was so popular at this time, descriptions of strange animals, plants, minerals, and natural phenomena.

In all this manifold, it is not easy to see what Philostratos is aiming at. He obviously wanted to write a book full of variety and excitement in keeping with contemporary taste, even if most modern critics have not found that his talent for belles-lettres quite equals his ambitions. The late antique novelist Heliodoros, who borrowed some material from Philostratos, was (in the eyes of posterity) more successful in his attempt at an historical novel, the *Aithiopika*. No doubt Philostratos wanted to be widely read, presumably also by others than those who appreciated his more conventional sophistic production (notably his *Lives of the*

---

[33] For a literary appreciation of the *Life*, see Bowie 1994, 189–196.

Sophists). And, by order of Julia Domna, he wanted to "honour" Apollonios[34] — but which Apollonios?

From the start, he puts great emphasis on the description of Apollonios as a follower of Pythagoras. The first part of his introduction is devoted entirely to Pythagoras himself (1.1), before Apollonios is introduced as a Pythagoras for our times (1.2). From his early years, it is stated later (1.7), he grasped the doctrines of Pythagoras "by some mysterious intelligence".[35] Though his teacher in Aigeai was "too fond of food and sex" to be a good example, the boy still learned the essence, and from the age of fifteen he embarked on the life of a Pythagorean (1.8):

> ... he avoided the meat of animals as something impure that dulled the intelligence, and ate fruit and vegetables, saying that everything was pure which the earth produced of its own accord. Wine, he said, was a pure drink, since it came from a plant that had done such good to men, but it disturbed the balance of the mind by darkening the ether in the soul. After purging his stomach in this way he took to going barefoot (that was 'dressing' to him) and wore clothes of linen, refusing those that were made from animals. He also grew his hair long, and lived in the sanctuary [of Asclepius].

His life is a constant quest for purity and wisdom. In the religious sphere, this makes him a reformer of the various cults that he encounters on his wanderings; he purifies them and argues eloquently against animal sacrifice. The fame of this divine man, *theios anêr*, is spread in wider and wider circles. In the bodily sphere, his striving for purity has another consequence as well (1.13):

> Now though Pythagoras was praised for his statement that a man should not have intercourse with any woman except his wife, Apollonios said that that commandment of Pythagoras applied to others, but he himself was not going to marry or have any sex at all. In this he surpassed the famous saying of Sophocles, who claimed that he had escaped an

---

[34] His professed double aim, honour (τιμή) to Apollonios and profit (ὠφέλεια) to readers thirsting for knowledge, is spelled out at the end of 1.3. In 5.39 he only mentions his aim "to furnish with a life of Apollonios those who were as yet ignorant" (trans. Conybeare); similarly 6.35.

[35] Whenever possible, I use for my quotations the abridged English translation by Christopher Jones in Jones and Bowersock 1970.

uncontrollable and harsh master when he reached old age; for Apollonios's virtue and continence saved him from becoming a prey to that vice even as a boy, so that despite his youth and vigour he overcame sex and became master of the uncontrollable.

His purification of body and soul, in turn, led to the acquisition of prophetic gifts, which naturally enhanced his reputation. But he was not only able to foresee the future, but also to find remedies to forestall threatening disasters and plagues. He became known as a miracle-worker, he cured the sick and raised the dead.

Philostratos narrates all this vividly and with illustrative details, while at the same time making it a *leitmotif* of his work that Apollonios was *not* a *goês*, "wizard", or a charlatan — an accusation raised against him in a satirical work of Lucian (*Alexander the False Prophet* 5) and possibly also in the lost biography by Moiragenes. It is a difficult balancing act that Philostratos attempts: to deny magic and sorcery, but still to save the charismatic wonder-worker. As we have seen, Ps.-Eusebios had no difficulty in finding inconsistencies and contradictions.

Apollonios as a holy man and a second Pythagoras is well characterized in word and deed in the *Life*. Yet one looks in vain for propaganda for any specific religion or cult. Having left his Asclepian home base, he moves in a traditional landscape of ancient cults, but does not seem to favour any one of them, except for his habitual prayers to Helios. The hypothesis that Philostratos actually wrote the biography as a response to the Christian Gospels, therefore finds little support in the text. There is indeed much to remind one of the life of Jesus: the description of the holy man's birth and death, his disciples, his healing wonders, and so on. But these may have been commonplaces of the period. It is probable that Philostratos, as a well-informed and widely-travelled man, knew about Christianity and had met Christians; but he never mentions them, either in his *Life of Apollonios* or in his several other works.

The Finnish scholar Erkki Koskenniemi has recently suggested that Philostratos may simply be characterized as "religiously passive".[36] He personally takes no specific interest in these cults, either to propagate or to denigrate any one of them (he is no Lucian). Moreover, since the Severan dynasty apparently, contrary to what has often been thought,

---

[36] Koskenniemi 1991, 70–79.

conducted no active persecution of the Christians,[37] there is no reason to believe that the empress commissioned a work with a specifically anti-Christian tendency. Ironically, then, it was a religiously rather neutral work by a disinterested author that less than a hundred years later was promoted to a holy text for paganism. Through selective vision anything may be achieved.

But if there is no strong religious tendency in the *Life*, what then was its aim, more than painting an attractive picture of a Pythagorean sage and letting the connoisseurs delight in verbal equilibristics? Neutral biographies are a modern invention. Again, an answer may be sought by comparison with other writings by Philostratos. In his *Lives of the Sophists* he appears as the historian of the Greek cultural movement of the imperial period that he himself styled the Second Sophistic. The heroes are Greek "sophists", accomplished orators and writers, who also played an important political role in the Roman empire, locally as well as in contacts with the Roman state and the emperor himself.[38] They often combined their eloquence with a pronounced moral authority.

Perhaps, as Koskenniemi suggests,[39] it was primarily such a sophist and guardian of morals that Philostratos saw in his Apollonios. His closest model for his hero seems to have been Dion Chryostomos, the celebrated orator of Prusa in Asia Minor (mod. Bursa), who was active in the late first and early second century and is portrayed with admiration in Philostratos's own *Lives of the Sophists* (1.7). The wisdom that Philostratos's Apollonios is seeking throughout his life, is transformed into practical politics in his dealings with Roman emperors. Philostratos constructs his Apollonios as a kind of super-sophist. Emperors like Nero, Vespasian, and Domitian engage themselves in oral or written dialogues with Apollonios. His courageous struggle against the tyrant Domitian, in particular, gives him his heroic status.

The heavy politico-ideological constituents of the *Life of Apollonios* have, in modern times, remained in the shadow of the religious topics — again the legacy of Hierocles and Ps.-Eusebios. It has been easy to dismiss them as unhistorical. There is no external evidence for any contacts between Apollonios and these emperors. The only event of this kind

---

[37] See Koskenniemi 1991, 76f with further refs.

[38] For this movement, see Bowersock 1969; Anderson 1993; Schmitz 1997.

[39] Koskenniemi 1991, 45–57, 80–82; cf. also Anderson 1986, 124–131.

that is confirmed by an historical source (Dio Cassius, *Roman History* 67.18) is the scene in Ephesus in AD 96 when Apollonios in a vision sees Domitian being murdered in Rome and cries out in triumph (*VA* 8.26). Moreover, it would not seem, at first sight, that these long discussions of first-century politics could have been of much interest to readers of the 220s or 230s. Yet, as Koskenniemi points out (reviving an old hypothesis), there are a number of striking coincidences between Philostratos's own time and the historical picture he paints in his biography, with a similar succession of good emperors and tyrants.[40] For contemporary readers, it would not have been difficult to translate the pseudo-historical description into current politics, or take Apollonios's advice to the emperors as the author's own recommendations to the present rulers.

Thus, according to this hypothesis,[41] Philostratos dressed in an historical guise political and moral advice that he regarded as relevant to his own age, he used Apollonios of Tyana as his ideological mouthpiece. The Emperor Vespasian of the *Life* has traits of Septimius Severus (Julia Domna's husband), the tyrant Domitian is Caracalla (their son) in disguise. If this holds true, it is tempting to go one step further and look at the conflicting dates for the lifetime of Apollonios. The Apollonios of the biography seems to have been born about 3 BC and to have died about AD 97, while independent evidence rather makes the historical Apollonios a contemporary of Dion of Prusa (as Philostratos says himself in *Lives of the Sophists* 1.7) who was born ca. AD 40. Dio Cassius (78.18.4) places Apollonios's *akme* under Domitian (emperor AD 81–96).[42] In order to achieve his coincidences, then, with tyrant equalling tyrant, and to be able to include the archetypal Nero as well, Philostratos may have deliberately manipulated the chronology and moved Apollonios's whole lifespan some 40 years back in time. On the other hand, the resulting coincidence with the life of Jesus — which from a modern point of view would appear more significant — probably was of no importance at all

---

[40] For the details, see Koskenniemi 1991, 31–44.

[41] For modification of the hypothesis, see Flinterman 1995, 130–161 (defending the historicity of Philostratos's account) and 217–230 (discussing "The topicality of Apollonius' recommendations"), and Swain 1996, 389f (with n. 53).

[42] For discussion of the evidence concerning Apollonios's date, see Dzielska 1986, 30ff, 185 (but cf. the objections of Bowie 1989, 252). The incident in AD 96 on the occasion of Domitian's death, it should be noted, is possible with both birth dates; but it seems more likely with Apollonios in his prime than as a centenarian.

to Philostratos (if he was even conscious of it); for his hero was a political rather than a religious figure.

This is one attractive modern construction of Philostratos's Apollonios, the sophist dispensing political advice. But recent research has produced several alternative Apollonioses on the basis of the same *Life*, and it may, in our context of construction, be of interest to look into a couple of them. Not only can one historical figure be differently constructed in different historical sources and periods, but a potent and enigmatic literary text like the *Life of Apollonios* may likewise, in the hands of modern scholars, be made to produce quite different portraits of its hero, or "aims" of its author. The rhetoric of scholarship uses for its own constructions of the Philostratean Apollonios more or less the same devices as Hierocles did, in particular, selection and shift of emphasis. It will hardly be necessary to refute these constructions in any detail — to see what concealment the selection implies in each case — since they implicitly perform that task among themselves.

Another variety of the *political* Apollonios is suggested by Simon Swain in his *Hellenism and Empire* (1996).[43] Now it is as a *Greek* sophist, a champion of Hellenism in the Roman world, that Apollonios emerges: "His stance against imperial (Roman) authority in defence of Greek culture is a most important theme in the *Life*."[44] He fights for concord among the Greeks, for the restoration of true Greek culture, and against moral decline. "In sum, reform of Greek cities and advice to Roman kings are part of the same Hellenic programme"; and "the superiority of [Greek religion and culture] is the premiss of the whole work."[45]

In a recent article, "Defending Hellenism: Philostratus, *In Honour of Apollonius*" (1999), Swain articulates this reading further. The (strictly) political agenda is toned down and the global defence of Hellenism — through assertion of its virtues rather than refutation of any specific attacks against it — is declared the author's aim: we listen to "the constant replaying of classical culture that feeds the identity of the Greek élite of his day".[46] The role of Neopythagoreanism, as internalized in the Platonism of the period, is emphasized: what Philostratos

---

[43] Swain 1996, 381–395.

[44] Swain 1996, 387.

[45] Both quotations Swain 1996, 394.

[46] Swain 1999, 193.

celebrates through his Apollonios is "a Hellenism which is defined primarily through a combination of religion and philosophy, rather than through the general cultural and political inheritance".[47] Further, his choice of a Pythagorean in the lead for this "apology" had to do with authority: Pythagoras was the most ancient of Greek sages, with a semi-divine status. The threat to Hellenic cultural dominance that one may have felt coming from the East under the Severans[48] could best be countered by a charismatic figure with Pythagorean credentials and a strictly Pythagorean way of life.

James A. Francis, in turn, in his *Subversive Virtue: Asceticism and Authority in the Second-Century Pagan World* (1995), reads the Philostratean Apollonios as a domesticated ascetic and a religious antiquarian. Philostratos, he contends, is striving to rehabilitate "an ascetic philosopher with a reputation of a *goes*, in this case a Pythagorean, into a model of classical ideals and a defender of the social order".[49] Whereas earlier writers, like Lucian, oppose the second-century ascetics as potentially threatening reformers of society, Philostratos advocates their assimilation. He renders his Apollonios harmless by letting him teach different standards for ordinary people and the holy man: only the latter has to live up to the ideals of purity in food and clothing, of abstention from wine, of celibacy and of radical ascetic poverty. The Apollonios of the *Life* is indeed a reformer of cults and moral, but only within the established framework and in the interest of the "social and cultural authorities of the Roman Empire"[50] (while some of his letters, whether genuine or early fabrications, depict him as more of a revolutionary).

Francis does not overlook the political discussions and the panhellenic spirit of the *Life*; but he sees these ingredients in the light of what he considers its main aim and function, to assimilate the ascetic movement in the Roman social order. Though his study reinstates Philostratos's Apollonios as a religious figure, he is critical of the emphasis placed on Apollonios's miracles in earlier research, no doubt spurred by the ever-present comparison with the New Testament. In fact, these play a very subordinate role in the account, and Philostratos, in his construction of

---

[47] Swain 1999, 158.

[48] Swain 1999, 159f, 195.

[49] Francis 1995, 83–129, quotation p. 83.

[50] Francis 1995, 83.

a Pythagorean sage in place of a simple wonder-worker and necroman-cer, rationalizes them as best he can.[51]

There is, however, in Francis's detailed and well-argued study,[52] no attempt to explain the prominence given in the *Life* to Apollonios's travels outside the confines of the Empire. These descriptions have been much studied earlier — e.g., in a monograph by the Uppsala Indolo-gist Jarl Charpentier on *The Indian Travels of Apollonius of Tyana* (1934) — but then mostly from a factual point of view. The challenge of mak-ing sense of them in a literary and ideological perspective has recently been taken up by John Elsner in his article "Hagiographic Geography: Travel and Allegory in the *Life of Apollonius of Tyana*" (1997). He looks upon the theme of travel as "a masterly rhetorical device on the part of Philostratus by which to establish and demonstrate the superiority of Apollonius".[53]

As a serial visitor to the sanctuaries of the empire Apollonios emerges as an atypical pilgrim who reforms and lectures rather than worships; and "the pilgrimage trope" is reversed once more when Philostratos makes the holy man become himself the goal of pilgrimage from every quarter, "a focus for the sacred topography of the Greek world"[54] — all this symbolizing his complete religious authority. His travels outside the empire to all four extremes of the world present a greater problem to the modern interpreter, cluttered as the description is "with the topoi of ethnography: natural *thaumata* of all kinds, a veritable zoo of exotic animals (actual and fantastic), a highly imaginative geography of weird lands and wonderful sites, a virtual museum of strange objects, relics and fabulous works of art, an anthropology of unusual peoples and their habits."[55] This must all be taken allegorically, Elsner contends:[56] the travels are "a reflection of Apollonius' spiritual progress", and "the very range of ethnographic topoi experienced by the sage suggests the depth and universality of wisdom which he has mastered". His personal qualities, such as courage and cleverness, are displayed in action; and his status as

---

[51] Cf. also Kee 1986, 85f.

[52] The criticism in Swain 1999, 193f, does not touch the essence of Francis's argument.

[53] Elsner 1997, 22.

[54] Elsner 1997, 27.

[55] Elsner 1997, 28f.

[56] Elsner 1997, 29, acknowleging a debt to Romm 1992, 116–119 (on Philostratos's India).

a cultural hero is enhanced by the parallels with Heracles, Dionysus, and Alexander, all travellers and conquerors. He travels to the Brahmans in search of wisdom, but then — another reversal — to Spain and Aithiopia to teach it and be acclaimed for it, a "demonstration of the universal applicability of his wisdom".[57]

So geography stands for philosophy, journeying afar for philosophical discovery. When Apollonios, after a life of pilgrimage and ethnographic travelling, finally arrives — as a second St Paul[58] — at the centre of the world, Rome, to defend his case before the emperor, this is the acme of his travels and constitutes his "supreme philosophical test as holy man to the Roman world".[59] To Elsner, Philostratos's Apollonios is the quintessential divine sage, whose final spiritual victory is built on his gradual mastering of the whole world in all its manifold.

These stimulating, and partly conflicting, new readings — presumably conceived at about the same time independently of each other — combine to show what a rich and complex work of art the *Life of Apollonios* is.[60] At the same time, as already suggested, they demonstrate how modern scholars, seeking answers to current questions about power, asceticism, and sacred geography, return from their forages into the text with different novel constructions of its hero — a phenomenon not dissimilar to the historical mechanisms I have been pursuing in this study of Apollonios's metamorphoses.

In Hierocles we have encountered Apollonios as a counter-Christ and then, in Philostratos, as a politically active sophist, or a defender of Hellenism, or a domesticated ascetic, or a metaphorical traveller. But who was Apollonios of Tyana himself? To get something to hold on to, we must try to bypass Philostratos's biography; but its 350 pages of detailed literary description has practically erased the authentic traits of Apollonios from historical memory. What we have at our disposal are a few references to Apollonios in pre-Philostratean literature, some evi-

---

[57] Elsner 1997, 31.

[58] It is interesting to note that the two most recent contributions, Elsner 1997, 33, 35f, and Swain 1999, 182, 184f, again open the door slightly and quietly to the possibility that Philostratos did intend his work (also) as a counter-Gospel (or counter-Acts).

[59] Elsner 1997, 33.

[60] "*Apollonius* is a work of high literary value", says Swain 1999, 174. It may well be that the *Life* will experience a literary reappraisal similar to that of Heliodoros's *Aithiopika* in recent years.

dence of the early cult, and — perhaps — some genuine fragments of the writings of Apollonios himself.

From Lucian's indirect attack on the charlatan Apollonios (cf. above) we may gather that he had a reputation as a magician and miracle-worker, and that he attracted disciples who regarded him as a man with divine powers. How contemporary society at large judged the quality of these powers we cannot expect to learn from Lucian, for he was a rationalist who suspected all spiritual practice. Dio Cassius's description of Apollonios's clairvoyant performance at Ephesus in AD 96 has no similar taint of contempt, it just records the incident as an historical fact that one would have refused to believe could happen.[61] Some literary as well as archaeological and epigraphic evidence suggests that the four places where the cult of Apollonios flourished in the fourth century (Tyana, Aigeai, Ephesus, and Antioch), had shrines for him originating close to his own lifetime.[62] His healing activities seem sometimes to have been associated with the cult of Asclepius.

Cappadocia and Cilicia were probably his main arenas, with occasional excursions as far west as Ephesus. That he should have extended his travels outside Anatolia — to Greece, Rome, and Spain, and to the far east and south — is not corroborated by any external sources. This international activity and celebrity are most probably the invention of Philostratos or the author of Damis's memoirs, if these really existed. It should be kept in mind, however, that there is no intrinsic improbability about such extensive travelling in itself at this time; and the fantastic character of what Philostratos actually tells about Apollonios's experiences and conversations in the Orient does not exclude the possibility that the historical Apollonios might have visited those countries.[63] It caused a stir when it was recently pointed out that a Sanscrit tradition mentions two yogis by the names of *Apalûnya* and *Damîsha*.[64] But this hardly proves

---

[61] Dio Cassius 67.18. At another place, however, the same historian refers to Apollonios "the Cappadocian" as "a true wizard and magician" (78.18.4).

[62] The evidence is collected in Dzielska 1986, 51–84.

[63] I owe this last observation to Jørgen Christian Meyer. It should be noted that an expert on the commerce between the Roman empire and India, E.H. Warmington (1974), though finding much of the *Life of Apollonios* "mere story-telling" (347), still takes seriously the travel routes of its hero in India, treating it as evidence for conditions in the last part of the first century AD (78, 88). Cf. further Anderson 1986, 199–226.

[64] Cf. Anderson 1986, 173 n. 106; Dzielska 1986, 29; Flinterman 1995, 80 n. 113.

that Apollonios and Damis really visited India, rather that the contents of Philostratos's *Life* somehow penetrated there.

Apollonios's status as a magician, prophet and healer of substantial local fame in Anatolia may thus be considered as historically certified. His writings are a less certain, but no less interesting matter. He is said to have written a biography of Pythagoras that was used by later writers. Some have even suspected that the *Life of Apollonios*, in which he appears as a reincarnated Pythagoras, was partly built on Apollonios's own *Life of Pythagoras*.[65] However that may be, we have no reason to doubt that he did somehow appear as a follower of Pythagoras; only Pythagoreanism was not the same in the first as in the third century. To find out more specifically what his own philosophical tenets were, we must go to the few surviving texts attributed to him.

There is a certain consensus today that at least some of the hundred letters in the collection carrying Apollonios of Tyana's name are genuine. Letters that Philostratos does not seem to know, or that contradict his picture of Apollonios, are perhaps more likely to be genuine than those he quotes; but they may also be fabrications by others who, prior to Philostratos, exploited Apollonios's name to market their own convictions. Letters appearing both in the biography and the collection may be suspected to have been copied from the former into the latter. But, in the end, each letter must be judged on its own inherent merits.[66]

In addition, we possess a fragment from Apollonios's treatise "On Sacrifices" (Περὶ θυσιῶν) which Eusebios quotes in his *Preparation for the Gospel* (4.13). Provided this fragment and a few of his more substantial letters with a philosophical content are genuine, it seems that his Pythagorean philosophy was close to what we today call Middle Platonism.[67] Like Numenios of Apamea (2nd century AD), he would be situated somewhere in the borderland between Platonism and Neopythagoreanism, both of which had at this time developed into philosophical movements with a strong religious bent and partly coalesced.[68] However,

---

[65] See Dzielska 1986, 130–134, and Dillon and Hershbell 1991, 9f. with further refs.

[66] For a succinct discussion of these problems of authenticity, see Penella 1979, 23–29. Cf. also Flinterman 1995, 70–76 (on the relationship between biography and letters), Francis 1995, 95ff (who consistently uses the letters to trace differences between the 1st/2nd-century Apollonios and that of Philostratos), and Swain 1996, 395.

[67] On Apollonios's philosophy, see Dzielska 1986, 129–151.

[68] On this development, see now Swain 1999, 163–178.

not surprisingly, the philosophy we glimpse in the fragment and letters is of a more technical kind than the popular variant that Philostratos's Apollonios embodies.[69]

Things are not, then, quite as simple as the title of my paper would indicate, at least not if taken as indicating a strict succession in time. Philostratos did not transform a simple magician into a philosopher; the historical Apollonios already had both strings to his bow, he seems to have been both a respected holy man and a religious philosopher. But he was not the Dion-style sophist and the international traveller that Philostratos made of him, nor the potential founder of a religion that Hierocles implied by elevating him to a counter-Christ — the construction through which he acquired his greatest historical importance and lasting fame.

References

Anderson, Graham 1986: *Philostratus: Biography and Belles Lettres in the Third Century AD*, Croom Helm, London.

Anderson, Graham 1993: *The Second Sophistic: A Cultural Phenomenon in the Roman Empire*, Routledge, London.

Anderson, Graham 1994: *Sage, Saint and Sophist: Holy Men and their Associates in the Early Roman Empire*, Routledge, London and New York.

Bardy, Gustave (ed. & tr.) 1958: Eusèbe de Césarée, *Histoire ecclésiastique*, III (Sources Chrétiennes, 55), Les Éditions du Cerf, Paris.

Barnes, T.D. 1976: "Sossianus Hierocles and the Antecedents of the 'Great Persecution'", *Harvard Studies in Classical Philology* 80 (1976), 239–252.

Barnes, Timothy D. 1981: *Constantine and Eusebius*, Harvard University Press, Cambridge, MA and London.

Baur, F.Ch. [1876] 1966: *Apollonius von Tyana und Christus. Ein Beitrag zur Religionsgeschichte der ersten Jahrhunderte nach Christus*, repr. Georg Olms Verlagsbuchhandlung, Hildesheim.

Bernard, Jean-Louis 1977: *Apollonius de Tyane et Jésus*, Éditions Robert Laffont, Paris.

---

[69] See Dzielska 1986, 136–151. Bowie 1989, 253, speaks of "*VA*'s superficial and vulgarized Pythagoreanism", a harsh verdict. Swain 1999, 177, more usefully distinguishes between "Pythagorean living" and the "technical-philosophical aspects of Pythagoreanism", the term "Pythagoreanism" covering both aspects; the former, of course, is the topic of *VA*.

Bowersock, G.W. 1969: *Greek Sophists in the Roman Empire*, Clarendon Press, Oxford.

Bowie, Ewen Lyall 1978: "Apollonius of Tyana: Tradition and Reality", in *Aufstieg und Niedergang der römischen Welt* II.16.2, 1652-1699.

Bowie, E.L. 1989: Review of Dzielska 1986, *Journal of Roman Studies* 79 (1989), 252-254.

Bowie, Ewen 1994: "Philostratus: Writer of Fiction", in: J.R. Morgan & R. Stoneman (eds.), *Greek Fiction: The Greek Novel in Context*, Routledge, London and New York, 181-199.

Charpentier, Jarl 1934: *The Indian Travels of Apollonius of Tyana* (Skrifter utgivna av K. Humanistiska Vetenskaps-Samfundet i Uppsala, 29:3), Almqvist & Wiksell and Otto Harrassowitz, Uppsala and Leipzig.

Conybeare, F.C. (ed. & tr.) 1912: Philostratus, *The Life of Apollonius of Tyana*, I–II (Loeb Classical Library), William Heinemann and Harvard University Press, London and Cambridge, MA.

Creed, J.L. (ed. & tr.) 1984: Lactantius, *De mortibus persecutorum* (Oxford Early Christian Texts), Oxford University Press, Oxford.

Dillon, John, and Jackson Hershbell (ed. & tr.) 1991: Iamblichus, *On the Pythagorean Way of Life*, Scholars Press, Atlanta, GA.

Dulière, W.L. 1970: "Protection permanente contre des animaux nuisibles assurée par Apollonius de Tyane dans Byzance et Antioche. Évolution de son mythe", *Byzantinische Zeitschrift* 62 (1970), 247-277.

Dzielska, Maria 1986: *Apollonius of Tyana in Legend and History* (Problemi e ricerche di storia antica, 10), "L'Erma" di Bretschneider, Roma.

Edwards, Mark, Martin Goodman, and Simon Price in association with Christopher Rowland (eds.) 1999: *Apologetics in the Roman Empire: Pagans, Jews, and Christians*, Oxford University Press, Oxford.

Elsner, John 1997: "Hagiographic Geography: Travel and Allegory in the *Life of Apollonius of Tyana*", *Journal of Hellenic Studies* 117 (1997), 22-37.

Flinterman, Jaap-Jan 1995: *Power, Paideia & Pythagoreanism: Greek Identity, Conceptions of the Relationship between Philosophers and Monarchs and Political Ideas in Philostratus' Life of Apollonius*, J.C. Gieben, Amsterdam.

Forrat, M., and É. des Places (ed. & tr.) 1986: Eusèbe de Césarée, *Contre Hiéroclès* (Sources Chrétiennes, 333), Éditions du Cerf, Paris.

Francis, James A. 1995: *Subversive Virtue: Asceticism and Authority in the Second-Century Pagan World*, The Pennsylvania State University Press, University Park, PA.

Frede, Michael 1999: "Eusebius' Apologetic Writings", in Edwards et al. 1999, pp. 223-250.

Frend, W.H.C. 1965: *Martyrdom and Persecution in the Early Church: a Study of a Conflict from the Maccabees to Donatus*, Basil Blackwell, Oxford.

Frend, W.H.C. 1987: "Prelude to the Great Persecution: The Propaganda War", *Journal of Ecclesiastical History* 38 (1987), 1-18.

Graf, Fritz 1984/85: "Maximos von Aigai. Ein Beitrag zur Überlieferung über Apollonios von Tyana", *Jahrbuch für Antike und Christentum* 27/28 (1984/85), 65–73.

Hägg, Tomas 1983: *The Novel in Antiquity*, Basil Blackwell, Oxford.

Hägg, Tomas 1985: "Eusebios vs. Hierokles: En senantik polemik kring Apollonios från Tyana och Jesus från Nasaret", *Religion och Bibel* 44 (1985), 25–35.

Hägg, Tomas 1992: "Hierocles the Lover of Truth and Eusebius the Sophist", *Symbolae Osloenses* 67 (1992), 138–150 [No. **14** in this volume].

Jones, C.P., and G.W. Bowersock (eds.) 1970: Philostratus, *Life of Apollonius*, trans., ed., abridg. and introd., Penguin Books, Harmondsworth.

Junod, Eric 1988: "Polémique chrétienne contre Apollonius de Tyane", *Revue de Théologie et de Philosophie* 120 (1988), 475–482.

Kee, Howard Clark 1986: *Medicine, Miracle and Magic in New Testament Times* (Society for New Testament Studies, 55), Cambridge University Press, Cambridge.

Koskenniemi, Erkki 1991: *Der philostrateische Apollonios* (Commentationes Humanarum Litterarum, 94), Societas Scientiarum Fennica, Helsinki.

Labriolle, P. de 1942: *La réaction païenne. Étude sur la polémique antichrétienne du Ier au VIe siècle*, L'Artisan du livre, Paris.

Mead, G.R.S. [1901] 1980: *Apollonius of Tyana: The Philosopher Explorer and Social Reformer of the First Century AD*, repr. Ares Publishers, Chicago.

Meredith, Anthony 1980: "Porphyry and Julian Against the Christians", in *Aufstieg und Niedergang der römischen Welt* II.23.2, 1119–1149.

Monat, Pierre (ed. & tr.) 1973: Lactance, *Institutions divines, Livre V*, I–II (Sources Chrétiennes, 204–205), Les Éditions du Cerf, Paris.

Moreau, J. (ed. & tr.) 1954: Lactance, *De la mort des persécuteurs*, I–II (Sources Chrétiennes, 39), Les Éditions du Cerf, Paris.

Mumprecht, Vroni (ed. & tr.) 1983: Philostratos, *Das Leben des Apollonios von Tyana* (Tusculum), Artemis Verlag, München & Zürich.

Palm, Jonas 1976: *Om Filostratos och hans Apollonios-biografi* (Studia Graeca Upsaliensia, 10), Almqvist & Wiksell International, Uppsala.

Penella, R.J. 1979: *The Letters of Apollonius of Tyana* (Mnemosyne, Suppl., 56), E.J. Brill, Leiden.

Petzke, G. 1970: *Die Traditionen über Apollonius von Tyana und das Neue Testament* (Studia ad Corpus Hellenisticum Novi Testamenti, 1), E.J. Brill, Leiden.

Réville, Albert 1866: *Apollonius of Tyana, the Pagan Christ of the Third Century*, John Camden Hotten, London.

Robertson, J.M. 1911: *Pagan Christs: Studies in Comparative Hierology*, 2nd ed., London.

Romm, James S. 1992: *The Edges of the Earth in Ancient Thought: Geography, Exploration, and Fiction*, Princeton University Press, Princeton, NJ.

Schmitz, Thomas 1997: *Bildung und Macht. Zur sozialen und politischen Funktion der zweiten Sophistik in der griechischen Welt der Kaiserzeit*, C.H. Beck, München.

Smith, Morton [1978] 1998: *Jesus the Magician: Charlatan or Son of God?* Seastone, Berkeley (originally published: Harper & Row, San Francisco, 1978).

Speyer, Wolfgang 1974: "Zum Bild des Apollonios von Tyana bei Heiden und Christen", *Jahrbuch für Antike und Christentum* 17 (1974), 47–63.

Swain, Simon 1996: *Hellenism and Empire: Language, Classicism, and Power in the Greek World AD 50–250*, Clarendon Press, Oxford.

Swain, Simon 1999: "Defending Hellenism: Philostratus, *In Honour of Apollonius*", in Edwards et al. 1999, pp. 197–221.

Warmington, E.H. 1974: *The Commerce between the Roman Empire and India*, 2nd ed., Curzon Press and Octagon Books, London and New York.

Hierocles the Lover of Truth and Eusebius the Sophist

[originally published in *Symbolae Osloenses* 67, 1992, 138-150]

Among the extant works of Christian apologetics, Eusebius' *Contra Hieroclem* (hereafter: *CH*) has probably been the most neglected. Slim in volume and idiosyncratic in its main concern — detailed polemics against Philostratus' *Vita Apollonii* (*VA*) — it has attracted nothing like the attention given by Patristic scholars to, for instance, Origen's *Contra Celsum*. But neglect, when dealing with literary works of classical antiquity, is of course just a relative concept. Beyond Patristic and Eusebian studies, *CH* has through the centuries been secured life and potential readership as a regular appendix to the editions of *VA*, starting with the Aldina (1501-02) and ending with the Loeb (1912).[1] Recently, the historical interest of the treatise has been explored by Timothy Barnes,[2] and Manfred Kertsch has provided an *Ehrenrettung* for its philosophical-rhetorical contents.[3] It has also been adduced by Eugene Gallagher and Patricia Cox in discussions of the divine man in antiquity.[4] And finally it has been accorded the honour of a critical edition of its own, in the "Sources Chrétiennes",[5] closely followed by a concise lexicon article by Wolfgang Speyer.[6]

139

[1] Philostratus, *The Life of Apollonius of Tyana*, ed. F. C. Conybeare, Vol. ii (1912), with text based on C. L Kayser's Teubner edition of 1870. This pious habit of not letting the pagan saint have the last word, was first broken with V. Mumprecht's Tusculum edition of *VA*, München 1983.

[2] "Sossianus Hierocles and the Antecedents of the 'Great Persecution'", *HSPh* 80, 1976, 239-252, and *Constantine and Eusebius*, Cambridge, Mass. & London 1981, 164-167 (referred to below as Barnes, "Soss. Hier." and *C&E*, respectively).

[3] "Traditionelle Rhetorik and Philosophie in Eusebius' Antirrhetikos gegen Hierokles", *VChr* 34, 1980, 145-171.

[4] E. V. Gallagher, *Divine Man or Magician? Celsus and Origen on Jesus* (SBL Diss. Series, 64), Chico, Cal. 1982, 165-172; P. Cox, *Biography in Late Antiquity. A Quest for the Holy Man*, Berkeley-Los Angeles-London 1983, 73-80.

[5] Eusèbe de Césarée, *Contre Hiéroclès*. Introduction, traduction et notes par M. Forrat, texte grec établi par É. des Places (Sources Chrétiennes, 333), Paris 1986. (Hereafter: Forrat & des Places, or, with reference to introduction and translation only, as Forrat.)

[6] "Hierokles I (Sossianus Hierocles)", *RLAC* Lief. 113, 1989, 103-109 (referred to below as Speyer).

The new critical text is by Édouard des Places, while Marguerite Forrat is responsible for the translation and notes and the greater part of the introduction, which deals extensively and competently with the historical background, the figure of Apollonius, and the contents and character of the treatise itself. In addition, des Places provides some basic information on manuscripts, editions and the constitution of the text. Thus we now possess an excellent tool for further research on *CH*. The following notes are offered as a supplement on some issues which, to my mind, have not been adequately treated in the new edition, or not raised there at all.[7] They will concern both Hierocles' lost pamphlet and Eusebius' answer.[8]

140

I. Hierocles' pamphlet: title, number of books and editions

Hierocles' lost work is known to us through two secondary sources, *CH* and Lactantius' *Divinae Institutiones* (5.2.13-3.26). In the former, it is referred to in such a manner that most scholars assume its title to have been ὁ Φιλαλήθης "The Lover of Truth".[9] Forrat, without discussion, follows this practice, calling the treatise Philalèthès, "l'Ami de la Vérité'", throughout; Speyer (105) likewise translates "der 'Wahrheitsfreund'". Lactantius, on the other hand, says that Hierocles *ausus est libros suos nefarios ac dei hostes* φιλαλήθεις *adnotare* (*Div. Inst.* 5.3.22). Some regard

---

[7] I can dispense with discussing the title of Eusebius' work, since this matter has already been raised in a review article by E. Junod, "Polémique chrétienne contre Apollonius de Tyane", *RThPh* 120, 1988, 475–482. As Junod rightly observes, the conventional title *Contra Hieroclem* both lacks manuscript support (though des Places fails to give the pertinent information) and is misleading as to the character of the work: this is *not* a second *Contra Celsum* — Eusebius does not think Hierocles merits the honour of a refutation, especially because Origen already said what has to be said — but (as the mss. have it) Eusebius' *Reply to Philostratus' Life of Apollonius occasioned by Hierocles' comparison between him and Christ*. (I understand πρός as "in reply to" [LSJ s.v. C.I. 4] rather than "against" [Loeb], "contre" [Forrat, also Junod].) Instead of *Contra Hieroclem* we should consequently speak of Eusebius' *Ad Vitam Apollonii* (or similarly).

[8] Some of the issues were touched upon in my article "Eusebios vs. Hierokles. En senantik polemik kring Apollonios från Tyana och Jesus från Nasaret", *Religion och Bibel* 44, 1985, 25–35. I wish to thank Per Beskow and the Collegium Patristicum Lundense for the opportunity to discuss further these matters in a seminar at Lund University in December, 1988.

[9] E.g., Barnes, *C&E*, 22. In "Soss. Hier.", 242, n. 15, Barnes censures the few exceptions to the rule.

this as the exact title: "Wahrheitsliebende Reden"[10] (or similarly). Our first problem, then, is: Did the author, in the title of his work, refer to himself as a "lover of truth", or did he rather characterize his pamphlet as "truth-loving", "truthful"? (I leave aside a third possibility, apparently favoured by Lampe, *PGD*, s.v. 2, that the title was in the neutre: (τὸ) Φιλάληθες, "Love of Truth".)

The adjective φιλαλήθης of course primarily refers to human beings (thus all the instances registered in LSJ). But it may also be used in a transferred sense, as when Origen (*Cels.* 6.16) speaks of Scripture as αἱ φιλαλήθεις γραφαί. It is precisely this use, I contend, that we encounter in Hierocles' title: he called his pamphlet Φιλαλήθης λόγος (in the singular)[11] — and he did so with clear reference to its forerunner, Celsus' Ἀληθὴς λόγος. Whether he knew Celsus directly or through Origen, we cannot tell; but he probably used Celsus' arguments, perhaps even borrowed his words, as may be inferred from *CH* 1.3–21.[12] It is true that Eusebius here speaks quite generally of Hierocles' shameless robbery of arguments "from others" (7 ἐξ ἑτέρων, 21 ἑτέρωθεν); but his recommendation to the reader to turn to Origen for refutation, makes the inference natural.

But what is the precise meaning of Φιλαλήθης λόγος? It is common to translate Celsus' Ἀληθὴς λόγος as "The True Doctrine", with a Platonic ring, rather than, e.g., "A True Discourse".[13] I am not convinced that this is correct; but what matters here is that Hierocles, at least, obviously did not catch (or bother about) the potential Platonic allusion: his own title, modelled on that of Celsus, must mean simply "A Truth-Loving (or Truthful) Discourse (or Treatise)". A "doctrine" can be "true", but not, I assume, "truth-loving".

[10] Thus R. Hanslik in *Der Kleine Pauly* 2, 1975, 1133.

[11] Earlier Eusebian scholars like E. Schwartz (*loc.cit.* below, n. 19) and G. Bardy (in his ed. of *Hist. Eccl.*, Vol. 4, Paris 1960, 24) without discussion referred to the pamphlet by this name; but now that the incorrect title seems to prevail and risks continuing to do so through the influence of Barnes, Forrat & des Places and Speyer — the reasons for preferring Φιλαλήθης λόγος need to be spelled out.

[12] I quote *CH* by chapter and line in Forrat & des Places.

[13] Lastly in R. J. Hoffmann's translation, Celsus, *On the True Doctrine*, New York-Oxford 1987. J. Quasten (*Patr.* 2, 52), on the other hand, translates "True Discourse". On the debate, see A. Wifstrand, "Kelsos' stridsskrift mot kristendomen", *Svensk teologisk kvartalsskrift* 18, 1942, 1–18, pp. 3 f., and M. Borret in Origène, *Contre Celse*, Vol. 5 (Sources Chrétiennes, 227), Paris 1976, 24–28 (himself voting for "Discours véritable").

Lactantius provides an additional piece of information which seems to confirm the interpretation of λόγος as "discourse" (*Div. Inst.* 5.2.13): *composuit enim* (sc. Hierocles) *libellos duos, non **contra Christianos**, ne inimice insectari videretur, sed **ad Christianos**, ut humane ac benigne consulere putaretur*. In Greek terms, this would be "not κατὰ Χριστιανῶν, but πρὸς Χριστιανούς", and presumably these words were part of the title: Φιλαλήθης λόγος πρὸς Χριστιανούς, "A truthful discourse (directed) to the Christians".[14]

This brings us to the next issue: Does Lactantius' reference to *two* φιλαλήθεις books (*libri, libelli*) mean that he knew of two separate treatises by Hierocles with the same title, as some have thought,[15] or, as others have argued,[16] that he knew only a later (enlarged) edition than the one which Eusebius read, the Φιλαλήθης λόγος? In my opinion, neither conclusion is warranted. The word *liber* is here used in the meaning "volume" (*OLD* s.v. 2.b): the truth-loving λόγος, "discourse", consisted of two λόγοι (LSJ s.v. vi.3.d) or βίβλοι, *libri*, "books".[17] It may well be, as Speyer (107) suggests, that the first book contained the general attack on the Christians, while the second was devoted to the comparison between Jesus and Apollonius; but Eusebius does not say so. He does not find it necessary even to mention that Hierocles' treatise consists of two books; while Lactantius, referring to Hierocles' characterization of his own "books" as φιλαλήθεις, does not intend to give the accurate title of the work.

There is thus no foundation for the idea of two editions of the pamphlet to be found in Eusebius' and Lactantius' different ways of referring to it. Nor is one entitled to draw such a conclusion — as Barnes (*C&E*,

---

[14] Eusebius *CH* 1.4 and 2.32 (quoted below) refers to the book as τὸν **καθ'** ἡμῶν ... λόγον, but I take this as a description of its character rather than a quotation of its title.

[15] See Forrat (18, n. 3) who rightly dismisses this idea.

[16] E.g., Barnes, "Soss. Hier.", 242 f., and *C&E*, 165. Forrat (25) too believes in two editions, but in the reverse order, adding a freely invented reason for the alleged abbreviation: "Hiéroclès publia les deux livres originels en un seul, ce qui leur donnait une force de persuasion beaucoup plus grande" (On this hypothesis, why in ca. 310 should Hierocles still have referred to himself as *vicarius Orientis*, which he obviously does [as Forrat (13) admits] in the version Eusebius read? Cf. below, II (2).) Speyer (105) follows Forrat.

[17] Photius, *Bibl.* cod. 39 (p. 8a26–29) too speaks of Hierocles' "books" in the plural: ... τοὺς ὑπὲρ Ἀπολλωνίου τοῦ Τυανέως Ἱεροκλέους λόγους. But Photius' testimony has no independent value since it was Eusebius' treatise, not that of Hierocles, he read.

165) and others do — from Lactantius' statement that Hierocles' written attack on the Christians was subsequent to the start of the persecution proper (*Div. Inst.* 5.2.12 *quo scelere non contentus, etiam scriptis eos quos afflixerat insecutus est. composuit enim…*), while the reverse — and no doubt historically correct — order is implied by *CH* (see below, II). This is an insignificant (and natural) mistake on the part of Lactantius: he will have taken notice of the treatise only after its author and message had passed from theory to practice. It is also possible that the public recitations of the discourse in Nicomedia, as distinct from readings in private circles (Lact. *Mort. pers.* 16.4 calls Hierocles *auctor et consiliarius ad faciendam persecutionem*), started only after February, 303. This would amount to a kind of "publication", and Lactantius will not have been in a position to know that the treatise had been written (and probably circulated) earlier.[18]

It remains to explain why the title Φιλαλήθης λόγος is not clearly spelled out in *CH*. In a number of instances, it is obvious that Eusebius makes a point of calling Hierocles, ironically, "the lover of truth", just in order to show how ill this designation fits its object (e.g. *CH* 4.2). Thus, for the rhetorical effect, he transfers the adjective from the book to its author. But in four cases, all in the first two chapters, it is his explicit intention to give the *title*. I do not think it is a coincidence that the word λόγος in fact does occur in all four contexts, although only once next to the adjective:

143

CH 1.3 πρὸς μὲν γὰρ τὰ λοιπὰ τῶν ἐν τῷ **Φιλαλήθει**, οὕτω γὰρ εὖ ἔχειν αὐτῷ τὸν καθ᾽ ἡμῶν ἐπιγράφειν ἐδόκει **λόγον**, …

CH 1.11 … ἐν ὅλοις ὀκτὼ συγγράμμασι τοῖς Ὠριγένει γραφεῖσι πρὸς τὸν ἀλαζονικώτερον τοῦ **Φιλαλήθους** ἐπιγεγραμμένον Κέλσου Ἀληθῆ **λόγον**, …

CH 1.18 … φέρε μόνην ἐπὶ τοῦ παρόντος τὴν κατὰ τὸν κύριον ἡμῶν Ἰησοῦν Χριστὸν τοῦ **Φιλαλήθους** τουτουὶ **λόγου** παράθεσιν ἐπισκεψώμεθα, …

CH 2.32 ταῦτα ῥήμασιν αὐτοῖς Ἱεροκλεῖ τῷ τὸν καθ᾽ ἡμῶν ἐπιγεγραφότι **Φιλαλήθη λόγον** εἴρηται.

---

[18] Similarly Forrat, 18–20.

With the highly affected style which characterizes the treatise (see below, II (7)), this kind of hide-and-seek game should come as no surprise. The alternative that Eusebius should have got the title wrong, consequently missing the allusion to Celsus' title, seems less probable, especially in view of the second instance quoted. The third instance may even be interpreted as giving a title that includes the word λόγος. We should thus probably translate it, not (with Forrat) "ce traité, l'Ami de la Verité'" or (with Conybeare, the Loeb translator) "this treatise called the 'Lover of Truth'", but rather "this 'Truthful Discourse'". The same of course applies to the fourth example.

To sum up: There is only evidence for one edition of Hierocles' treatise; it was called Φιλαλήθης λόγος πρὸς Χριστιανοὺς, consisted of two books, and was composed before the start of the persecutions in February, 303.

II. Contra Hieroclem: date and authorship

The date of *CH* is disputed. To start with the most recent estimates, Barnes (*C&E*, 165) places it "shortly before 303, after the army had been purged of Christians but apparently before Diocletian issued persecuting edicts which affected Christian civilians". His main reasons are: Eusebius twice (*CH* 4.39–40; 20.1–2) refers to his adversary "in a way which implies that Hierocles was *vicarius Orientis* at the time of writing" (ibid.), which he was until he, in or shortly before February 303, became governor of Bithynia (Barnes, "Soss. Hier.", 243); there is in *CH* "no hint that Christians are still being or have recently been executed" (ibid., 242); and, more specifically, Eusebius — unlike Lactantius — shows no sign of knowing that in 303 Hierocles the pamphleteer became Hierocles the active persecutor of Christians.

Forrat (20-26), for her part, does not accept Barnes' arguments, but places *CH* after 311. In her opinion, the general tone of the book, esp. Chs. 4 and 48, shows that Christianity has already triumphed over its persecutors. She believes that while it is true that Hierocles' pamphlet was written and distributed before the great persecutions started in 303, it remained unknown to Eusebius, in Palestine, until after Galerius' death in 311, and that he wrote his refutation not long before he prepared for publication his two other, greater apologetical works, the *Praeparatio Evangelica* and *Demonstratio Evangelica*. This, in turn, means that it was probably composed in the same few years as Eusebius also wrote his voluminous refutation of Porphyry's *Adversus Christianos* (Forrat, 23, n.2, 25 f.) and his *De martyribus Palaestinae* and published the first edition of his *Historia Ecclesiastica*.

In dating *CH*, Barnes and Forrat thus take the same opposite positions as Adolf von Harnack and Eduard Schwartz,[19] respectively, did in the beginning of the century.[20] Besides the more subjective or speculative arguments, both sides dispose of what seems to be more objective proof for their respective conclusions. We shall look at the arguments in turn, also bringing in material that has no direct bearing on the question of date, to see whether there is any as yet untried way of solving the contradictions.

(1) The final victory of the Christian faith over paganism is confidently anticipated in *CH*. This may mean composition either before the start of the great persecution (spring 303) or after its end (311 or later, dependent of geographical standpoint). Forrat's argument that the years immediately preceding 303 should not in fact have given rise to such confidence, even if historically correct, does not preclude that some Christians at that time may indeed have felt confident and secure. Hindsight should not make us favour 311+ rather than 303–.

(2) *CH* refers to Hierocles as being *vicarius Orientis*. This does not, as Barnes thinks, exclude a later-than-spring-303 date for *CH*. It is enough that Hierocles in his treatise referred to himself as holding that position and that the author of *CH*, at the time of writing, had no further — external — information about Hierocles' later positions (governor of Bithynia, prefect of Egypt).

(3) *CH* does not — in contrast to Lactantius — indicate with a word that Hierocles also became a prominent practising persecutor of Christians, not just a theorist (and an insignificant one at that). Forrat thinks that Eusebius, from his Palestinian point of observation, need not have had any knowledge of Hierocles' role as a leading persecutor in Bithynia and, later on, in Egypt. This does not seem very credible in itself and is bluntly contradicted by the fact that Eusebius in his *De martyribus Palaestinae* (5.3, only in the longer recension)[21] does mention Hierocles

---

[19] E. Schwartz, "Eusebios von Caesarea", *RE* VI: 1 (1907) 1370–1439, col. 1394.

[20] For the history and bibliography of the debate, see Barnes, "Soss. Hier.", 240.

[21] On the two recensions, cf. Bardy (above, n. 11) 36. According to Barnes, *C&E*, 148–150, and idem, "Some Inconsistencies in Eusebius", *JThS* 35, 1984, 470–475, pp. 470 f., the long recension is the original one, written in the summer or autumn of 311.

by name as personally responsible in Alexandria for the martyrdom, in January 310, of a prominent Palestinian, the philosopher Aedesius. At that place, in turn, Eusebius does not mention that Hierocles had been the author of an anti-Christian pamphlet — to which Eusebius himself had devoted an apologetical work! This is indeed one of the apparently insoluble contradictions: if *CH* was composed first, why is Eusebius in *Mart. Pal.* silent about Hierocles' earlier "merits", and vice versa? Could he really have forgotten all about it since 303–? Advocates of the 311+ date are in a still more difficult position: If the two works were written in about the same time, Eusebius (Forrat [22 f.] proposes) either did not think it proper to go outside his immediate topic — "d'exalter la résistance des martyrs" — in *Mart. Pal.*, or he wanted in *CH* to conduct his argument "sur le seul plan idéologique".

(4) Another crux: It is stated in *CH* (1.22–25) that Hierocles was alone in setting up Apollonius as a rival to Jesus. This is not correct, since Porphyry obviously had done the same.[22] Had Eusebius not yet read Porphyry's *Adv. Christ.* in 303– (Barnes, "Soss. Hier.", 241, *C&E*, 174)? Or did he, in 311+, regard Porphyry's use of the parallel as too insignificant to mention (Forrat, 27, 46–55)? Besides hardly being compatible with the wording in *CH*,[23] the latter suggestion is psychologically not very credible, seeing that Eusebius in these years writes 25 books in refutation of Porphyry's treatise and also, when composing his *Praep. Ev.* and *Dem. Ev.*, all along "demeure obsédé par cet auteur comme Pascal le sera par Montaigne et Voltaire par Pascal", to use J. Sirinelli's words quoted with approval by Forrat (23, n. 2) herself.

The real cruces are thus (3) and (4), both involving incompatibility between *CH* and other works by Eusebius. They evaporate — both as cruces and as dating criteria — if we try the hypothesis that Eusebius of Caesarea is not in fact the author of *CH*. Such a hypothesis, once put forward, would seem to receive support from some other odd facts about *CH*:

---

[22] The fragments in question (Nos. 4, 60, 63 Harnack) are discussed by Forrat (46–48).

[23] Forrat is in fact forced to overinterpret ἐξαίρετος … γέγονεν, "was chosen", in the relevant passage of *CH* (1.22–25) to suit her own explanation: "… seul parmi tous les écrivains qui nous ont jamais attaqués, Hiéroclès a recemment *mis au premier plan* le parallèle et la comparaison entre cet homme et notre Sauveur" (italics mine).

(5) Eusebius never in his voluminous writing refers back to *CH*. It is not only that he does not do so in connection with Hierocles in *Mart. Pal.*, but contrary to his usual practice[24] he never reuses material from *CH* in any other context.[25] For instance, he could easily have incorporated parts of his comments on Philostratus' Neopythagorean hero Apollonius in his *Praep. Ev.* Was *CH* perhaps a work of his youth which he had half forgotten in later years, or regarded as immature?[26] Hardly, in 303 he was already forty (and there are in his later production several "Selbstzitate" from another work more securely dated about 303, the *Chronicle*).[27] Had he lost his copy? Or was *CH* simply not his work?

(6) The Bible is never quoted in *CH*. In Eusebius' *Praep. Ev.* there are more than four hundred biblical quotations or allusions (one on every second or third page), in his *Hist. Eccl.* some six or seven hundred. Is this to be explained just by the fact that *CH* is a rather idiosyncratic specimen of the apologetic genre, an *Ad Vitam Apollonii* rather than a *Contra Hieroclem*?[28]

(7) The style is perhaps the most intriguing aspect of *CH*. Forrat (78 f.) speaks of "une tonalité bien différente de ce qu'on lit habituellement sous la plume de l'apologiste chrétien", and further: "Eusèbe se montre, dans le *Contre Hiéroclès*, preoccupé d'effets stylistiques, …, et ce souci d'élégance dans la critique n'est pas sans conferer à certains passages de cet ouvrage l''agrément' et l''éclat' que lui ont toujours déniés les critiques, qu'ils soient anciens ou modernes." Eduard Schwartz, editor of *Hist. Eccl.*, formulates his impressions of *CH* in the following manner: "Die Form des Werkchens ist von einer bei E[usebius] ungewöhnlichen Affektation, wozu ihn vielleicht die Lektüre Philostrats

[24] Cf. Schwartz (above, n. 19) 1388: "Es gehört zu den Eigentümlichkeiten des E. daß er seine schriftstellerischen Produktionen immer von neuem wieder aufnimmt, ausbaut und überarbeitet."

[25] Thus Forrat, 10.

[26] Thus Barnes, referring also to Harnack, in *JThS* 24, 1973, 440.

[27] See Schwartz (above, n. 19) 1376.

[28] See above, n. 7. P. Maraval, in a review of Forrat & des Places in *RHPhR* 68, 1988, 360–361, notices the absence of biblical quotations, "ce qui est bien le signe qu'il s'adresse ici en priorité aux païens cultivés". But the first lines of the treatise show that the friend to whom it is (or pretends to be) dedicated was a Christian, though in Eusebius' view liable to be influenced by pagan propaganda, and (*pace* Forrat, 69–72) the author's ironic and condescending tone throughout towards pagan beliefs makes it evident that *CH* was intended for internal use.

verführt hat."[29] Édouard des Places, editor also of *Praep. Ev.*, testifies from his point of view (Forrat & des Places, 89 f.): "Le style d'Eusèbe dans le *Contre Hiéroclès* diffère sensiblement de celui des grands traités apologétiques, la *Préparation* et la *Démonstration évangéliques*; ramassé, incisif, il se rapproche de la seconde sophistique dont Philostrate était un des représentants; parfois aussi de Lucien." Friedhelm Winkelmann, in a review of the new edition of *CH*, doubts that the last word has been said about its date, because of, among other things, "zu starke Stilunterschiede zu den nach 311 abgefaßten Werken".[30]

In a separate article entitled "La seconde sophistique au service de l'apologétique chrétienne",[31] des Places exemplifies what he considers as Philostratean (or generally rhetorical) influences in the text of *CH*. He ends by expressing his disagreement with Barnes' judgement of Eusebius, uttered (something des Places forgets to mention) with specific reference to the *Praep. Ev.* (*C& E*, 183): "Nor, either in his own statements or in his treatment of quotations, does [Eusebius] show any interest in style for its own sake; he is completely impervious to the stylistic dictates of the Second Sophistic movement." Barnes, in his turn, refers to another editor of *Praep. Ev.*, Karl Mras, who wrote: "Eusebius ist als Stilist kein Purist. So sehr er gedanklich und sachlich von Clemens abhängig ist, in seinem Stil ist er von diesem (der mit der zweiten Sophistik kokettiert) ganz unbeeinflußt."[32]

149 As we have seen, Schwartz and des Places both ascribe the different stylistic character of *CH* in comparison with Eusebius' other works to a more or less deliberate imitation of Philostratus' style. In my opinion,

---

[29] Schwartz (above, n. 19) 1394. Cf. J. Moreau in *RLAC* 6, 1966, 1067, with a different explanation: "Der Stil der kleinen Schrift ist besonders gepflegt. E. hat sich bemüht, den rhetorisch geschulten Staatsbeamten mit seinen eigenen Waffen zu schlagen." Contrast Barnes, *C&E*, 167: "… an ephemeral work, composed in haste to meet the sudden needs of controversy."

[30] *ThLZ* 113, 1988, 680 f.

[31] *CRAI* 1985, 423–427.

[32] K. Mras in Eusebius, *Werke* 8:1 (*GCS* 43:1), 2. Aufl., Berlin 1982, ix, further substantiated in "Ein Vorwort zur neuen Eusebius-Ausgabe (mit Ausblicken auf die spätere Gräzität)", *RhM* N. F. 92, 1943, 217–236. The dissertation of E. Fritze, *Beiträge zur sprachlich-stilistischen Würdigung des Eusebios* (Borna-Leipzig 1910) does not immediately help us in this matter, since it treats only a selection of Eusebius' works (*Vita Const., Laus Const., Hist. Eccl.*); but of course Fritze's work, esp. his section on rhetorical figures, would provide valuable comparative material for a closer study of the stylistic features of *CH*.

Eusebius' usual stylistic indifference, as defined by Mras, Barnes and others, does not make such a proposition very likely — unless *CH* were some kind of school exercise of his youth, which, however, chronology excludes (Hierocles' treatise, which he answers, cannot be much earlier than 303). If one even believes, with Schwartz, Forrat and des Places, that *CH* was written in the same busy years as Eusebius brought out his great works of apologetics, such an act of stylistic chameleonship seems downright incredible.

(8) In addition to the style proper, the general attitude of the author and the generic peculiarities of the opusculum are untypical of Eusebius. A small sample of recent comments will illustrate this. Pierre-Marie Hombert says that *CH* "nous revèle un aspect moins connu d'Eusèbe: l'ironie mordante d'un polémiste".[33] Des Places, in his most recent contribution to the topic, speaks of "l'originalité du *Contre Hiéroclès* dans l'œuvre d'Eusèbe", of "le ton allègre du pamphlet", and further defines the work "un exemple isolé de la diatribe dans l'œuvre d'Eusèbe" (suggesting, however, that the lost *Contra Porphyrium* might have had a similar character).[34] *CH* thus reveals, still according to des Places, "un aspect méconnu dans la personnalité complexe d'Eusèbe de Césarée". Once we have started questioning the authenticity of *CH*, these positive statements necessarily appear in another light.

The above considerations are of course not enough to prove the inauthenticity of *CH*. Authors do sometimes produce works which are not quite "in character", and there are perhaps other aspects of language or thought to link *CH* with Eusebius and outweigh the differences.[35] The fact that it is unanimously transmitted as a work of Eusebius, and was

150

---

[33] In a review of Forrat & des Places in *MSR* 45, 1988, 111–112.

[34] É. des Places, "Le Contre Hiéroclès d'Eusèbe de Césarée à la lumière d'une édition récente", in E. Livingstone (ed.), *Studia Patristica* 19, Leuven 1989, 37–42.

[35] Kertsch (above, n. 3) does point to some parallels between *CH* Ch. 6 and other works of Eusebius (esp. *Laus Const.*), but their nature of rhetorical-philosophical topoi makes them less useful in a discussion of authorship. Interestingly, however, for our present concern, Kertsch (n. 26) observes that Eusebius, while (according to des Places in *Aegyptus* 32, 1952, 223–231) generally quoting Plato literally, in *CH* 6.2–3 gives a free paraphrase of *Leg.* 715e–716a. If of general application, this difference in quotation technique might support the case for *CH*'s inauthenticity. But the matter obviously needs further investigation (cf., e.g., the almost literal quotation of the same Platonic *locus classicus* in *CH* 47.20–22 and the free one in *Praep. Ev.* 15.5.2!).

known as such to Photius and Arethas, of course carries weight.[36] But our hypothesis has the merit of solving the contradictions concerning the date as well as the paradox of "Eusebius the sophist", and would thus deserve being examined in more detail by Eusebian scholars, in particular by experts on his style. Thanks to des Places, *CH* is now for the first time available in an edition suitable for such a comparative stylistic analysis; in the earlier editions, some of the sophistic peculiarities were hidden through emendation or the acceptance of the more trivial readings of late manuscripts.

If through such a study it should prove possible to show that *CH* was probably not written by Eusebius of Caesarea, the next question will inevitably be: Was it added to the Eusebius corpus just because of its apologetic character, or can it perhaps be attributed to another Eusebius? Not until the question of authorship is settled, one way or other, will it be time to return to the problem of date and historical context. It may have to be resumed on quite a different basis.

---

[36] Photius (*Bibl.* cod. 39) refers to the work as by Εὐσεβίου τοῦ Παμφίλου. So does our oldest ms., the famous apologetics codex *Paris. gr.* 451 copied in 914 for Arethas. On the other hand, it should be noted that *CH* is absent in St. Jerome's catalogue of Eusebius' writings (*De Vir. Ill.* 81); it is true, though, that it may hide under the concluding *multaque alia*.

Photius at Work:
Evidence from the Text of the *Bibliotheca*

[originally published in *Greek, Roman, and Byzantine Studies* 14, 1973, 213–222.]

Several problems are connected with the genesis of Photius' *Bibliotheca*. In particular, the date and place of composition have been much discussed, and the main object of that discussion has been to identify the diplomatic mission to the Arabs in which Photius took part. According to what he himself states in the letter of dedication to his brother Tarasius which precedes the text of the *Bibliotheca*, his setting out on that mission was the chief stimulus for the composition of this huge work. But Photius' own words in the same letter have been the starting point also for the discussion of another question, which will be the subject of the present article: did Photius, as he himself alleges, compose from memory?

In this journal, Nigel G. Wilson recently published a judicious examination of the different theories regarding the external circumstances of composition.[1] When he arrives at the composition proper ("the author's method"), he deliberately takes up a somewhat provocative position: "It is not usual to take seriously his [*scil.* Photius'] assertion that he worked from memory. Instead, the *Bibliotheca* is thought to be the revised and expanded version of notes made during many years of reading. Doubtless he did have notes of this kind, but I think his claim may be substantially true; in other words, I would suppose that his notes were very brief and he relied on his memory for the most part."

In support of this view, Wilson adduces other instances of astonishing feats of memory, from Eustathius to Lord Macaulay.[2] Now, my intention is neither to discuss whether the alleged analogies are relevant at all to a work of this particular kind (a learned compilation of about 270 dif-

---

[1] *GRBS* 9 (1968) 451–55. The standard treatment of the subject is by K. Ziegler in *RE* 20 (1941) 667–737, esp. 684ff. See also P. Lemerle, *Le premier humanisme byzantin* (Paris 1971) 37–42 and 189–96. Quotations of the text of the *Bibliotheca* in the present article are from the edition by R. Henry (Paris 1959–).

[2] Wilson, *op.cit.* (*supra* n.1) 454–55, supplemented in *GRBS* 12 (1971) 559–60.

214 ferent works of literature), nor to give voice only to a general feeling of scepticism, founded on the quantity of the material reproduced, partly literally, in the *Bibliotheca* (the text would amount to about 1,500 printed pages of normal size). This would mean just repeating what has long been a fairly common opinion, and Wilson's remarks should at least make us avoid sweeping statements, implying that our own poorer powers of memory are the standard for all individuals and all times.

To arrive at a more satisfactory answer to the question, I think it is necessary to leave behind the undifferentiated manifestations of disbelief or belief[3] in Photius' words in the dedication and instead to turn to the text of the *Bibliotheca* itself. First, there is need for a more concrete confrontation of the proposed ways of composition with the various kinds of material which make up the *Bibliotheca*: what is really to be expected from someone composing from memory or from notes or with the original books before his eyes, and what is it we have? Are not different methods to be assumed for the composition of the different types of sections or 'codices'? Secondly, it should reasonably be possible to detect small traces of the method left in the text, tool marks, so to say, if only we inspect it closely enough. A suitable basis for such an inspection should be the many, often neglected sections dealing with works that have been transmitted to us also in their original versions, where we may compare Photius' product with the raw material.

The present attempt is based on the examination of a very small fraction of the entire text, namely, the two 'codices' 44 and 241, in which Photius treats of Philostratus' *Vita Apollonii*.[4] The object is not to give an exhaustive documentation of the material but just to point out the different kinds of evidence available, to see what conclusions can be drawn from them and thus to invite further discussion along more specific lines than hitherto.

---

[3] I take Wilson's words about Photius' claim being "substantially" or "largely" true as a concession to the possible existence of brief notes, not as suggesting a differentiation between summaries, excerpts, etc.

[4] The material made use of in this article was collected during my work on an investigation with a wider scope, concerning Photius' methods of compilation in general and conducted with the generous support of the Alexander von Humboldt-Stiftung. Fuller documentation — and the justification for some statements made just in passing here (for instance, concerning the nature of the *VA* manuscript used by Photius) — will be provided in a forthcoming account of this investigation.

As is well known, the *Bibliotheca* is not a homogeneous work. For some of the books he has read, Photius is content to give just the title and perhaps a short personal opinion of the contents; from others he makes extracts of dozens of pages. The *Vita Apollonii* is first summarized in a couple of pages (cod. 44), and later on nearly 30 pages are extracted from it (cod. 241). The extracts are in two series, the first one consisting of fairly long coherent pieces, obviously quoted because Photius was interested in the subject matter, and the second one consisting of about 120 shorter examples of Philostratus' style. Of primary importance to the present discussion is the *order* of the excerpts. A comparison with the preserved original work shows that nearly all are reproduced exactly in their original sequence within each series. As regards the first series, this is perhaps not so remarkable, since many of the excerpts (though not all) are connected by subject matter. A reader of the biography, equipped with a good memory, might be able to attach most of them to the various stages of Apollonius' long journeys (though it seems odd that he should care to commit to memory also which book contained which material within the continuous story).[5]

But what about the 120 stylistic samples? Some of them consist of just a word or two, others of half a sentence torn from its context, yet others of several sentences belonging together. What are we to think of a man who, in giving *from memory* a fair number of examples of an author's phraseology, produces the samples *in their original order* and with a tolerably even distribution all through the work in question (in this case, a text of about 350 pages)? The only possibility, as far as I can see, is that he revived in his memory the text of the *whole* work once more, only to stop at every third 'page' (on the average) to dictate (or write down) a quotation. This is, of course, absurd; the order of the samples, if taken from memory, would be mainly associative, and since the associations would be based on elements of vocabulary and phraseology, not subject matter, in the case of these small scraps, the resulting sequence could never be identical with the original one. No doubt the arrangement which we find in cod. 241 is the typical result of someone turning over once more from the beginning the leaves of a book which he has just read, his eyes falling on a peculiar word or phrase here and there. This picture is not contradicted — it is rather confirmed — by the four

---

[5] *Cf. Bibl.* 328a18–20 and 331a11–24.

216 excerpts out of 120 that are 'misplaced':[6] none of these has been 'moved' more than *one* step, each being so near to the excerpt which has usurped its place in the sequence that the *same* page in the manuscript which Photius was reading could very well have contained them both.

Now if Photius had the original in front of him when he was supplementing his main series of excerpts with these stylistic samples, what would make us think that he had a moment earlier drawn *from memory* those extensive *verbatim* extracts from the very same work? We may also note in passing that there is no fundamental difference between the two series of excerpts as regards their literalness. It is true that the number of summarizing transitional passages is much greater in the first series than in the second. But also among the stylistic excerpts we find whole sentences of Photius' own making, numerous explanatory additions[7] and so on, and when it comes to the pure extracts, the instances of omission or substitution of separate words or variations in word order are largely of the same character in both series. A good illustration of the fact that a stylistic excerpt need not be truer to the original than one in which the emphasis is on the subject matter is provided when Photius happens to quote the same passage from *VA* 2.6 in *both* series: in the stylistic sample (*Bibl.* 332a22), he substitutes ἀνθρώποις for Philostratus' ἀνδράσιν, whereas his earlier quotation of the phrase (*Bibl.* 324b23) exactly reproduces the original wording. In other cases, the relationship is the reverse. Evidently, the method of reproduction was the same in both kinds of excerpts.

The next type of argument has to do precisely with the phenomenon of *literal* quotation. It is more ambiguous than the argument from order. As the alleged analogies adduced by Wilson show, literalness in itself is not decisive, nor, for that matter, are occasional deviations from literalness into freer paraphrase. Both phenomena can be used to support composition from memory as well as dictation directly from the manuscript of the original. But I should like to call attention to a special feature of Photius' literal quotation which I think largely escapes this ambiguity.

---

[6] *Bibl.* 331b6–7, 331b28–29, 332a36–b2 and 334b23–24.

[7] *Cf. Bibl.* 332a28–29, 332a36–b2 and 331b11, 20, 29, etc. Instances like these disprove the suggestion of Lemerle, *op.cit.* (*supra* n.1) 193, that the second series could be "la transcription, faite par un secrétaire, de passages remarquables notés par Photius au cours de sa lecture."

It is possible to demonstrate from a number of common readings that Photius must have used a manuscript of the *Vita Apollonii* which belonged to the branch nowadays labelled the *deterior familia*.[8] Most variants taken over by Photius from this source are unobtrusive and are of no interest in the present context. But the special feature referred to above is the occasional transmission of *textual errors* from the copy of the *Vita Apollonii* which Photius happened to read into the text of the *Bibliotheca*.

When, for instance, Photius makes an extract from *VA* 5.5, he passes on to his readers, among other things, the following description of objects which Apollonius and his followers saw in the Herakleion of Gadeira (*Bibl.* 328b37–40): ἡ Πυγμαλίωνος δὲ ἐλαία ἡ χρυσῆ … ἀξία μέν, ὥς φασι, καὶ τοῦ θαλλοῦ θαυμάζειν ᾧ εἴκασται, θαυμάζεσθαι δ' ἂν ἐπὶ τῷ καρπῷ μᾶλλον· βρύει γὰρ αὐτὸν cμαράγδου λίθου. This is exactly the text which most manuscripts of the *Vita Apollonii* offer. But the best one, π, reads βρύειν, which is clearly required by grammar: αὐτόν, referring to "the fruit" (which "teemed with emeralds"), is left in the air without the infinitive βρύειν, the accusative-and-infinitive construction being due to the implied report by Apollonius and his followers. That Photius himself was acquainted with the verb and its construction is shown, by the way, in *Bibl.* 9b23, where he uses it to characterize Philostratus' style: βρύων γλυκύτητος.

For the proper evaluation of such a feature it is necessary to recall briefly Photius' special qualifications and the character of his work. He was well educated, and he was widely read in Greek literature of all periods. There can be no doubt that he could produce a grammatically correct text in Greek (I leave apart Atticist peculiarities and the like).[9] Both the *Bibliotheca* and his *Lexicon* testify to his philological interests. As regards the *Bibliotheca*, he chose for reproduction passages which particularly attracted his attention because of their contents or style, and the literal quotations are freely mixed with sentences of more or less his own mak-

---

[8] Cf. *supra* n.4. For the classification of the MSS of the *Vita Apollonii*, see the editions by C. L. Kayser (Zürich 1844 and Leipzig 1870).

[9] In his review of Henry's edition (*supra* n.1), vol.5, in *JHS* 90 (1970) 227, K. Tsantsanoglou expresses some doubts concerning Photius' "grammatical efficiency," as it is reflected in his *Lexicon*. But the main charge seems to be that Photius took over errors from his predecessors; the one example given of Photius' "own" mistakes (from the *Amphilochia*) has nothing to do with grammar.

ing, serving as connecting links. The omissions he makes generally do not seriously disturb the coherence of the extract — they would mostly pass unnoticed by a reader who had no access to the original. There is, as a rule, nothing mechanical about his work; it is not the work of a scribe who copies mechanically from the text in front of him.

How, then, should we explain an occasional slip like βρύει, instead of βρύειν? If the mistake appeared for the first time in the text of the *Bibliotheca,* it would be no problem: it would be a *lapsus calami* or *linguae,* possibly committed by Photius himself, or perhaps rather to be dismissed as a later error of transcription due to some scribe. But now we have to do with the mechanical transmission of an elementary blunder from the original. As far as I can see, this could hardly have happened if Photius had been reviving from memory a text which he had read on some earlier occasion, a text, *nota bene,* in his own language, a text which he understood and in which he now and then made skilful manipulations in order to choose the essential and skip the padding. The obvious explanation is that he had, in fact, the original text before him at the moment of dictation; only under such circumstances would it be psychologically understandable that his attention could slacken for a moment, so that his *verbatim* reproduction came to include also the obvious mistakes in the original. The one conceivable alternative, however improbable, would be that he was endowed with a very special kind of eidetic memory, which permitted him to 'read' anew from memory with no greater mental effort than if he were reading from a book. We shall presently see whether there are any traces of such a capacity elsewhere in the *Bibliotheca.*

It is time to turn to a fundamentally distinct kind of reproduction, namely, the résumé, as exemplified by cod. 44. Here, too, the whole of the *Vita Apollonii* is covered, but now the arrangement is not chronological but thematic. Within one of the thematic groups, the separate episodes referred to are given, at least partly, in the same order as in the original work,[10] but generally the subjects follow each other quite freely, apparently just as they presented themselves to the mind of Photius after he had read the book. No one would deny that *this* is a summary made from memory (with or without the help of notes made during the reading). We may even, by a closer examination of the summary, get some hints as to the qualities of the memory at work in this process.

[10] *Bibl.* 10a5–18.

The circumstance that the original sequence of the events is generally not adhered to is, of course, not an indication of a specially bad memory; the summarizer simply had no intention of being true to the original in this respect. The factual information given in the summary is, on the whole, quite accurate. There are, however, one or two misrepresentations of the facts. The most obvious one concerns Philostratus' story of Apollonius meeting a tame lion in Egypt (*VA* 5.42). As Photius correctly observes (*Bibl.* 10a6–9), Apollonius discerns the soul of King Amasis in the lion, but the explanation added — that this is the penalty for the king's deeds during his lifetime — has no foundation in Philostratus' account (where the point is that a lion is a most appropriate place for a king's soul). There is nothing in the formulation itself or in the context to indicate that Photius was aware of his addition. To all appearances, we have to do with a slip of the memory: Photius recalled the main facts of the incident, but he did not have a clear enough remembrance of the details to prevent a confusion with similar episodes which he had read or heard elsewhere.

On another occasion, Photius picks out, in order to illustrate the superstition conveyed by Philostratus in the biography, the description of some Indian means of influencing the weather (*Bibl.* 10a26–29): πίθους γὰρ αὐτοῖς πλήρεις ὄμβρων καὶ ἀνέμων δοὺς ὕειν τὴν χώραν ἀνομβρίας ἐπεχούσης ἐξικμάζειν τε αὖ καταρρηγνυμένων ὄμβρων ταῖς ἐκ πίθων ἀνὰ μέρος χορηγίαις κυρίους ἐκάθισε … As regards the factual information, this summary is quite true to the original (*VA* 3.14), but the wording is to a large extent new. This is not to be explained, as in many other cases, as the natural consequence of the compression of a detailed episode into a short summary nor as a simplification of a complicated text. Of course more details are given in the original, but several words or phrases could have been taken over directly by Photius without making his version longer than it is. Compare, for instance, the following counterparts to Photius' formulations: καὶ διττὼ ἑωρακέναι φασὶ πίθω λίθου μέλανος ὄμβρων τε καὶ ἀνέμων ὄντε. ὁ μὲν δὴ τῶν ὄμβρων, εἰ αὐχμῷ ἡ Ἰνδικὴ πιέζοιτο, ἀνοιχθεὶς νεφέλας ἀναπέμπει καὶ ὑγραίνει τὴν γῆν πᾶσαν, εἰ δὲ ὄμβροι πλεονεκτοῖεν, ἴσχει αὐτοὺς ξυγκλειόμενος … The words for 'jar', 'rain' and 'wind' are identical, but that is all: ἀνομβρία is used by Photius instead of αὐχμός, ὕειν instead of ὑγραίνειν, χώρα instead of γῆ, and so on.

Two possible explanations present themselves. Either Photius made a point of *not* reproducing the original wording, *i.e.* he sought *variatio*, or he remembered the *facts* quite well but did not have the actual *wording* ringing in his ears (or lingering before his eyes). My reasons for preferring the latter explanation are the following. First, *variatio* would be quite pointless in this connection, since the reader of the *Bibliotheca* is not supposed to have read the original nor to have a copy of it at hand. Secondly, Photius both in cod. 44 and in cod. 241 expresses his high opinion of Philostratus' style and in giving examples of the work in cod. 241 he never hesitates at complicated syntactic structures or obsolete words. Why should he deliberately avoid Philostratus' phraseology here? Thirdly, and most important, we have in cod. 241, interspersed among the literal excerpts, some sections of summary which show Photius' method when he really remembered the wording of the original or even had the text before his eyes when summarizing. For instance, he describes the habitation of the naked sages in Ethiopia in the following way (*Bibl.* 330a14–17): οἰκεῖν δὲ τοὺς Γυμνοὺς ὑπαιθρίους φησὶ καὶ ὑπὸ τῷ οὐρανῷ αὐτῷ, ἐπί τινος δὲ γηλόφου ξυμμέτρου, μικρὸν ἀπὸ τῆς ὄχθης τοῦ Νείλου. The constituent parts of this description are fetched from different parts of *VA* 6.6: τοὺς δὲ Γυμνοὺς τούτους οἰκεῖν μὲν ἐπί τινος λόφου, φασί, ξυμμέτρου μικρὸν ἀπὸ τῆς ὄχθης τοῦ Νείλου, and, ten lines further on: ... ζῶντες ὑπαίθριοι καὶ ὑπὸ τῷ οὐρανῷ αὐτῷ. The compound γήλοφος, finally, is used by Philostratus in another sentence between the two passages just quoted. No striving for *variatio* can be discerned.

The faculty of memory displayed by Photius in cod. 44 is, then, of an ordinary and far from superhuman kind. Having read a book, he was able to give a fairly accurate account of the things in it that interested him, but he does not seem to have remembered the exact words of the author. The special kind of memory needed for the literal reproduction of large quantities of text, as in cod. 241, he shows no signs of possessing.

Some intricate problems, however, remain unsolved. There are other codices in which the intermingling of summary and word-for-word quotation is more complicated than in those treated here. Only a minute analysis and comparison with the originals, if preserved, could trace the rôle of memory in their composition. Furthermore, the important question is left, whether those summaries which are wholly — or largely (the notes!) — the products of memory, like cod. 44, were written down or dictated *separately*, only a comparatively short time after the reading, or *all at the same time,* when Photius was about to set out on his mission. If the latter was the case, the composition was, after all, a remarkable feat of memory, measured by our standards, in spite of the exception we have to make as regards the great mass of literal excerpts.

Perhaps the answer to this question might be given by a stylistic analysis of the summaries. If, as has sometimes been argued,[11] Photius unconsciously adopted certain traits of the style of the original work also in summarizing its contents in his own words, this is hardly explicable in any other way — provided that the above characterization of his memory holds good also when confronted with materials from other codices — than as the result of an immediate writing down of his summary when the text was still fresh in his memory and the impression of the style not muddled by the reading of other works. There is a long way to go, however, before the characteristics of Photius' own style or styles are so distinctly worked out that they may be profitably contrasted with the small modifications in style that were possibly due to his momentary reading.

Let us, finally, return to Photius' own words in the dedication and the postscript of the *Bibliotheca*[12] and compare them with the outcome of the present examination. First, we may note that in referring to the constituents of his own work Photius only uses the term ὑποθέϲειϲ. It seems reasonable to believe that in doing so he was thinking, in the first place, of the *summaries* proper (even though he makes no explicit exception of the codices consisting of excerpts). As we have seen, for *their* composition he undeniably had to rely on his memory. Only his claim to have made several of the summaries on a single occasion, after the lapse of some time, is perhaps open to doubt. Secondly, and regardless of the proposed restrictive sense of the term ὑπόθεϲιϲ, we have to consider the *function* of Photius' references to his memory. They are not, as seems to be taken for granted in much of the discussion of the prob-

---

[11] See, for instance, Philostorgius, *Kirchengeschichte,* ed. J. Bidez (Leipzig 1913) xv f, R. Henry in *RBPhil* 13 (1934) 615–27, and Lemerle, *op.cit.* (*supra* n.1) 193 ("par un curieux mimétisme …").

[12] Letter to Tarasius, line 2 Bekker … τὰϲ ὑποθέϲειϲ ἐκείνων τῶν βιβλίων, οἷϲ μὴ παρέτυχεϲ ἀναγινωϲκομένοιϲ, line 7 ὅϲαϲ αὐτῶν ἡ μνήμη διέϲωζε, and esp. lines 12–16 Εἰ δέ ϲοί ποτε κατ᾽ αὐτὰ γενομένῳ τὰ τεύχη καὶ φιλοπονουμένῳ τινὰ ὑποθέϲεων ἐλλιπῶϲ ἢ οὐκ εἰϲ τὸ ἀκριβὲϲ δόξουϲιν ἀπομεμνημονεῦϲθαι, μηδὲν θαυμάϲῃϲ. Μίαν μὲν γὰρ ἑκάϲτην βίβλον ἀναλεγομένῳ τὴν ὑπόθεϲιν ϲυλλαβεῖν καὶ μνήμῃ καὶ γραφῇ παραδοῦναι ἀξιόλογον ἔργον ἐϲτὶ τῷ βουλομένῳ· ὁμοῦ δὲ πλειόνων, καὶ τότε χρόνου μεταξὺ διαρρυέντοϲ, εἰϲ ἀνάμνηϲιν μετὰ τοῦ ἀκριβοῦϲ ἐφικέϲθαι οὐκ οἶμαι ῥᾴδιον εἶναι. The postscript, p.545,13 Bekker, see Wilson, *op.cit.* (supra n.1) 452.

lem, to be regarded as a boast, empty or not, of his enormous powers of memory (nor, of course, as a scholarly declaration of all the stages of his work). The insistence on composition from memory is no more than a formula expressing modesty and intended to forestall possible criticism for mistakes or superficiality[13] — a criticism which could, of course, be directed primarily at the summaries, where Photius' personal contribution was more important than in the case of the excerpts. Considered in this light, Photius' words are not incompatible with a more differentiated view of the composition, which attributes to his memory a restricted but not unimportant rôle in the heterogeneous working process behind the *Bibliotheca*.

---

[13] See O. Immisch in *RhM* 78 (1929) 113-23.

16

Bentley, Philostratus, and the German Printers

[originally published in *Journal of Hellenic Studies* 102, 1982, 214–216]

Referring to a copy of F. Morel's edition of Philostratus (Paris 1608), which contains MS notes by Richard Bentley and bears the shelfmark 679. g.13, the *British Museum General Catalogue of Printed Books* clxxxix (London 1963) Col. 253 states:

> Imperfect; wanting all that in the preceding copy follows the work of Eusebius against Hierocles. The first four leaves are inserted from another edition, and between the fourth and thirteenth page the leaves are wanting.

To the best of my knowledge, the true nature of the inserted leaves has not been noticed hitherto. The reason may be the Catalogue's emphasis on the incomplete state of this copy: readers will naturally have turned, in the first place, to the complete copy which also contains MS notes by Bentley (shelfmark 678.h.8). It must have been the latter (or possibly C.48.1.3, where all Bentley's notes are copied in the more distinct handwriting of C. Burney) that was consulted, e.g., when C. L. Kayser prepared his critical edition of *Vita Apollonii* (Zürich 1844).[1] In the complete copy the marginal notes of Bentley continue — although with great variations in frequency — right through the works of Philostratus, providing MS collations as well as numerous emendations to the text.

But what of the copy first referred to? It contains, indeed, four printed pages (not 'four leaves') from 'another edition'; to be exact, specimen pages for Bentley's *own* critical edition of Philostratus — which never appeared!

That this is so should be evident from the following description. The four pages contain the first three chapters of *Vita Apollonii* (i 1–3, ending with τῷ γὰρ Νινίῳ), the Greek text printed in the outer column, the

---

[1] P. xv with n. 2. *Cf.* also Kayser in his Heidelberg edn of *Vitae Sophistarum* (1838) xxxviii f., and *RE* xx.1 (1941) 174.

Latin version in the inner, and notes at the bottom of the page. Two different founts have been used for both the Greek and the Latin text.[2] The wording of the Latin largely coincides with the corrections to Morel's version which Bentley himself has written between the lines in the complete copy of Philostratus, and the Greek text is also often changed in accordance with the marginal notes in that other copy. Moreover, the format of the critical notes printed at the bottom of the four pages corresponds well to that of the handwritten notes which we find from p. 13 on in our incomplete copy. Incidentally, these notes as well as the revision of the Latin translation and the cancelling of Morel's headings to the chapters are to be found only in a small part of the copy, pp. 13–29 and 37–65, corresponding to *Vita Apollonii* i 8–15 and i 18–ii 4. The rest of this incomplete copy (including its continuation in another volume, shelfmark 679.g.14) contains no notes at all in Bentley's hand.

Obviously, the incomplete copy is identical with the copy intended for the printer of the new edition. Whereas the complete copy contains all Bentley's work on the text through the years, the incomplete one represents — as far as his notes go — the final stage before the edition went to the press. The first twelve pages are missing because they have already been sent to the printer. The four printed pages inserted in their place are what Bentley received back. But is this all that was printed (the twelve missing pages contain four more chapters), and why was the edition never completed?

The first question I shall have to leave open: perhaps some other library or private collector has the answer.[3] The other one I shall discuss more fully. In fact, there occur at different places vague references to specimen pages of a Bentley edition of Philostratus having been cir-

[2] The printer has demonstrated one of his Greek founts on p. 1–2, another on p. 3–4. The first Latin fount has been used on p. 1–3, the second on p. 4 only. The second Greek fount is *without ligatures,* apparently a very early example of its kind. I wish to thank Dr S. Fogelmark (Lund) for discussion and elucidation of this and several other points in the present paper.

[3] The present writer, who is preparing a new critical edition of *Vita Apollonii* for the Bibliotheca Teubneriana (Leipzig), would be grateful to be notified if someone knows of the existence of more pages of Bentley's unfinished edition: Professor Tomas Hägg, Department of Classics, Sydnesplass 9, N–5000, Bergen, Norway. [The preparations for this edition never extended beyond the examination of manuscripts, cf. the introductory essay to the present volume.]

culated,[4] and J. H. Monk, in his large biography of Bentley (2nd edn, London 1833), has his story to tell. In 1691, Bentley had undertaken to edit three authors: Philostratus, Hesychius, and Manilius (i 34). Arriving at the year 1694, Monk resumes (i 57 f.):

> The projected editions of Philostratus and Manilius were now in a state   215
> of readiness for the printer; but the increased expense of paper and printing in England, the consequence of war and new taxes, deterred him
> from publishing books, which from their nature could only meet with a
> limited sale at home, and for the exportation of which the circumstances
> of the time were unfavourable. Accordingly he designed to print his Philostratus at Leipzic, and sent thither the early part of his text and notes
> for that purpose. But when he received the first sheet as a specimen, he
> was disgusted with the meanness of the printing, and resolved that his
> labours should not come forth to the world in so unseemly a dress. Indeed, it may be remarked that Bentley always placed a high value upon
> typographical elegance, and was more fastidious upon this head, than
> might have been expected from one who so well understood the intrinsic merits of a book. After some time he abandoned altogether the view
> of this publication, as Professor Wolf remarks, 'to the joy of Olearius of
> Leipsic, and of nobody else.' To this German, who undertook to publish the two Philostrati, he sent part of his apparatus, the collation of a
> manuscript belonging to New College *De Vitis Sophistarum,* and that of
> a Baroccian manuscript, both which he had made during his residence
> at Oxford. The edition of Olearius, which appeared in 1709, contains
> Bentley's notes as far as p. 11, taken from the first sheet just mentioned
> which had been circulated as a specimen.

This is certainly a good story, but I doubt that it is quite true. There are reasons to believe that Monk has combined the evidence at his disposal wrongly and that his conclusion about Bentley's esteem for 'typographical elegance' having won over his understanding for 'the intrinsic merits of a book' has no real foundation in this case. There were less capricious grounds for abandoning the project.

My reconstruction of the course of events, tentative as it must be, rests partly on the same evidence as Monk used, chiefly the (published) correspondence of Bentley, partly on the contents of the incomplete copy of Morel's Philostratus in the British Library, which Monk does

---

[4] In Olearius' edn of Philostratus (Leipzig 1709) p. x, in Fabricius' *Bibl. Gr. (cf.* below), and in the Bentley Bibliography by A. T. Bartholomew (Cambridge 1908) no. 138.

not seem to have inspected. Already its contents as described above shed new light on the process; but there is still more information to be extracted from that same copy.

First, the four pages inserted into the copy are obviously identical with the specimen pages that, according to Monk and others, were circulated in the learned world and referred to in Olearius' edition. There may have been more pages (*cf.* Monk on Olearius), but these four were certainly part of the lot circulated. But the quality of printing displayed in the four pages, with the two different founts to choose between, does not seem so bad as to provoke the reaction described by Monk; rather the contrary. And it is hard to believe that Bentley should have had a specimen circulated that he himself strongly resented. Monk seems to be wrong in identifying the first specimen from the printer with the one that was circulated.

Second, there are two more leaves inserted before p. 13 of the copy. One is blank. The other one is of a smaller size than the surrounding leaves, is printed on the *recto* only, has no pagina stated, but a column title: PHILOSTRATI DE VITA APOLLONII. It contains an extract from Book viii of *Vita Apollonii,* which reproduces the text and translation of Morel's edition, from the top of p. 393 through to p. 394, line 9, adding only a fair number of misprints. The quality of printing is poor, compared both with Morel and with the four preceding pages of Bentley. This could indeed be the specimen which Bentley rejected. In that case, the printer had simply been asked to choose a page from Morel at random, print it in the typography he suggested for Bentley's edition, and send it as a specimen — with the known result.

Combining the evidence of this page and that of the four others, we must conclude that Bentley did not after all give up his project just because he received an ugly specimen. On the contrary, he managed to achieve a higher standard of printing, and went on. In fact, his reaction in the letter to Graevius in May, 1694, is not quite as categorical as Monk would have it: *Philostrati specimen, quod a Lipsiensibus nuper accepi, non placet: repudio omne edendi consilium, nisi typos elegantiores paraverint.*[5] This rather sounds like the reflection of a threat addressed to the printer, and possibly it had the intended effect. However, I leave it to others, better qualified, to judge whether the same printer pro-

---

[5] Quoted from *The Correspondence of Richard Bentley* i (London 1842) 87.

duced both the first and the second specimen, and who the printer(s) were.[6] As far as publishers are concerned, one may think of Th. Fritsch in Leipzig, who in 1691 had announced another edition-never-to-appear of Philostratus, by H. Muhlius;[7] now, three years later, the latter may well have abandoned his project. Fritsch in 1696 published Kühn's Pausanias and Spanheim's Julian, both of which are mentioned in connection with Bentley's Philostratus in a letter from Graevius to Bentley of 25th December, 1694.

This letter from Graevius, written half a year after Bentley's threat, confirms that Bentley had not given up his plans — at least as far as Graevius knew; he reports how the editions of Julian and Pausanias advance, and then adds: *'In tuo Philostrato quo usque progressi sint* [i.e., the printers in Leipzig] *ex te cognoscemus'.*[8]

The real reason for abandoning the project was surely less capricious, and far more trivial. Upside down, on the *verso* of the rejected specimen leaf, we find in Bentley's handwriting his disposition for the project, with detailed titles of ten different texts, all to be edited by R. B. himself. The edition is to contain not only the whole Corpus Philostrateum: *Vita Apollonii, Epistulae, Heroicus,* both collections of *Imagines, Vitae Sophistarum;* but also the other works that were traditionally connected with it: Eusebius' *Hierocles,* the *Epistulae* of Apollonius, and works of Callistratus and Eunapius. The gigantic enterprise — from which Bentley is obviously not deterred by the ugly printing of the *recto* — is to end with 'Indices Graeci et Latini Accuratissimi et Locupletissimi'! It is true that Bentley's MS notes in the complete copy cover all the texts contained in Morel's edition, but from the incomplete one we now know that the actual work on the huge project never exceeded the first two books of *Vita Apollonii ...*

There is also, as far as I have been able to find out, nothing in Bentley's published correspondence to support Monk's statement that the editions of Philostratus and Manilius were in 1694 'in a state of readiness

216

---

[6] Dr Fogelmark calls attention to the similarity of the Greek fount used on p. 1–2 of the second specimen with that used for the edition of Dionysius of Halicarnassus which appeared with Chr. Günther in Leipzig in 1691.

[7] Eloquently introduced in W. E. Tentzels *Monatliche Unterredungen,* June 1691, 521–6. On Heinrich Muhlius (1666–1733) and his mainly theological career, cf. *Allgemeine Deutsche Biographie* xxii (Leipzig 1885) 481 f.

[8] *Op. cit.* (n. 5) 89.

for the printer'. In 1690, Bentley first mentions 'an Edition of Philostratus, which I shall set out this next year',[9] in 1692 Graevius expresses his delight that Bentley is now fully engaged in the work on the new edition,[10] and in December 1694, as we have seen, Graevius just asks about its progress.

For the same period there is also some — unfortunately rather confusing — information to be had from other sources. With reference to Bentley's Philostratus, Fabricius states in his *Bibliotheca Graeca:* 'Hujus primum folium Lipsiae excusum vidi Anno 1691'.[11] He must be mistaken. The statement cannot be reconciled with the evidence of the letters, and the reference he gives in this connection, to Tentzel's *Monatliche Unterredungen* 1691, p. 521, is also wrong: it refers to the announcement of Muhlius' edition (above n. 7). When, some lines further down, he really wants to refer to Muhlius, his reference (1693, 882 f.) is to Bentley! And at this place Tentzel only says that Bentley's edition, printed in Leipzig, will be welcome when it appears.[12] Thus, Fabricius cannot be adduced as a support for Monk's timetable, and Tentzel's *Monatliche Unterredungen* unfortunately do not mention Bentley's Philostratus again.

The project thus seems to have been abandoned simply because it had not advanced very far at all when, in the later part of the 1690s, other well-known activities increasingly absorbed Bentley's time.[13] It thus shared the fate of many other similar enterprises. There seems to have been a definite decision at some time between December 1694, and the beginning of 1698. Graevius, who constantly tries to push Bentley on, continues in letters of February and June 1698 to ask for the editions of Hesychius and Manilius, but Philostratus he mentions no more.[14] Al-

---

[9] *Op. cit.* (n. 5) 11. The earlier edition of Bentley's letters, *Richardi Bentleii et doctorum virorum epistolae partim mutuae* (Leipzig 1825) 127, reads 'which I shall *send* out this next year', which may have misled Monk.

[10] *Op. cit.* (n. 5) 46.

[11] Vol. iv. 2 (Hamburg 1711) 53. The whole passage is reprinted, without correction, in the 3rd edn, vol. v (Hamburg 1796) 555 f.

[12] November 1693, 882: 'Dannenhero ist kein Zweiffel, der *Philostratus,* so ietzo in Leipzig mit seiner neuen Lateinischen *Version* und *Annotationibus* in Druck kommet, werde bey der gelehrten Welt angenehm und willkommen seyn.'

[13] Cf. *op. cit.* (n. 5) 18 (Feb. 1691?), 164 (15 Feb. 1698), 194 (20 Aug. 1702: 'scias me toto hoc biennio vix unum et alterum diem vacavisse humanioribus literis').

[14] *Op. cit.* (n. 5) 158, 175.

ready in his letter of 6th February, 1697, when quoting Spanheim's laudatory reference to Bentley's projected Philostratus (in his Julian of 1696), Graevius abstains from any remark of his own on this (delicate?) topic — he just wants to elicit from Bentley his comments on a certain locus in *Imagines,* which he also receives in Bentley's reply of 26th March.[15]

On the other hand, this decision, whenever it was made before 1698, does not seem to be connected with another one; namely, to let Olearius take over the job and use Bentley's collations. The young Olearius — 'iste egregius juvenis' — is not mentioned in the correspondence until June 1698, when he is about to set out for London and is introduced to the great man by Graevius: 'Cognosces juvenem integerrimae vitae, et nostrarum artium cupidissimum…'.[16] There is no mention of Philostratus here; possibly Olearius' visit to London was the very occasion when the idea to let him take over was formed. Eleven years later Olearius' edition appeared, in Leipzig, with Fritsch.

Anyway, the German printers are not the ones to blame for the fact that Bentley gave up and the learned world had to wait another 150 years for a decent edition of Philostratus.

[15] *Op. cit.* (n. 5) 138–43.
[16] *Op. cit.* (n. 5) 175 f.

Reviews

17

[Review of]

Xenophontis Ephesii Ephesiacorum libri V de amoribus Anthiae et Abrocomae. Rec. ANTONIUS D. PAPANIKOLAOU. Leipzig: B. G. Teubner 1973. XX, 117 S. (Bibliotheca Scriptorum Graecorum et Romanorum Teubneriana.) 25 M.

[originally published in *Gnomon* 49, 1977, 457–462]

Von den fünf griechischen Romanen nachklassischer Zeit, die vollständig auf uns gekommen sind, hat wohl der des Xenophon von Ephesos bei der Nachwelt die geringste Wertschätzung gefunden. Das Werk blieb mit knapper Not erhalten: nur eine Hs (cod. Laurentianus conv. soppr. 627, 13. Jh.), bisher kein einziger Papyrus (von Charitons Roman besitzen wir schon vier Fragmente). Den Verfasser, der wohl im zweiten nachchristlichen Jh. Schrieb, kennen wir sonst nur durch eine magere Notiz in der *Suda.* Der Patriarch Photios, ein eifriger Romanleser, hat offenbar gerade diesen nicht gelesen. Eine vollständige Übersetzung (ins Italienische, von A.-M. Salvini) erschien erst 1723, die editio princeps (durch A. Cocchi) 1726, fast zwei Jahrhunderte später, als Heliodor seine starke Wirkung zu entfalten begonnen hatte. In den nächsten hundert Jahren entstanden freilich — neben ein paar ausführlich kommentierten Ausgaben (Locella 1796, Peerlkamp 1818) — mindestens ein Dutzend verschiedene Übersetzungen der *Ephesiaka*, und zeitgenössische Beurteiler sprachen sich über die Qualitäten des Romans oft recht positiv aus.[1] Bei späteren Philologen aber, die andere Maßstäbe anlegten, war die Ablehnung um so eindeuti-

---

[1] Xenophon hat z. B. nach dem *Universal-Lexicon aller Wissenschaften und Künste* (Bd. 60, Leipzig und Halle 1749) "in einer sehr schönen Schreibart geschrieben". Einer der ersten Übersetzer (J.-B. Jourdan), zitiert in Moréris *Grand dictionnaire historique* (Bd. 10, Paris 1759), findet Xenophon 'clair et précis dans ses descriptions, aussi noble que simple dans la plus grande partie de son récit'. Ein später Nachfolger dieser Übersetzer und Kritiker ist B. Kytzler, dessen uneingeschränktes Lob für Xenophon – er spricht u. a. vom "sublimen Intellektualismus einer späten, differenzierten und höchst bewußten Prosa" – im Nachwort zu seiner 1968 in Frankfurt a. M. und Berlin erschienenen Übersetzung zu lesen ist. In anderer Hinsicht unterscheidet sich jedoch diese Prachtausgabe, 'Die Waffen des Eros' genannt und mit erotischen Illustrationen (von G. Manzù) versehen, von ihren bescheideneren Vorgängern, die unter Titeln wie 'Der Triumph ehelicher Treue' vorgestellt wurden.

ger. E. Rohde nannte den Ephesier einen "stümperhaften Poeten", durch "beispielloses Ungeschick" der Erfindung und "Dürre des Ausdrucks und der Darstellung" gekennzeichnet (*Der griechische Roman* 398 ff). G. Dalmeyda zeigte sich jedoch in der Einleitung seiner Budé-Ausgabe des Romans (1926) hellhöriger für Xenophons Eigenart: er unterscheide sich von den übrigen Romanschriftstellern durch "un air de conteur populaire". In der Tat dürfte keiner, der z. B. Habrokomes' Begegnung mit dem alten Fischer Aigialeus in Syrakus (V 1) ohne Vorurteile liest, dem Verfasser Erzähltalent absprechen können (von Originalität spreche ich nicht). Sein Register ist jedoch nicht groß, und er hat bei der Anlage des Romans seine Kräfte überfordert. Die im kleinen Format anmutig wirkende Schlichtheit wird leicht zur Monotonie, wenn sie einen ganzen stoffreichen Roman unveränderlich beherrscht.

Die letzte Zeit hat die früheren Versäumnisse der Philologen wiedergutgemacht. H. Gärtner verdanken wir einen gründlichen Artikel zu Xenophon von Ephesos in der *RE* (9 A, 1967, 2055–89); im Vergleich dazu tritt die stiefmütterliche Behandlung der übrigen Romane in derselben Enzyklopädie deutlich zutage. Als erster der Romane erscheint dieser jetzt auch in einer neuen Teubner-Ausgabe, von A. Papanikolaou besorgt und mit Einleitung (VII–XII), Bibliographie (XIII–XIX),[2] kritischem Text mit drei verschiedenen Apparaten (1–71), Namenindex (73–75) und — besonders zu begrüßen — vollständigem Wortindex (77–117) ausgestattet.

In der Einleitung werden die Überlieferungsverhältnisse und die Editionsprinzipien kurz besprochen. Der Bericht über den Laurentianus und die ersten Ausgaben geht über das schon Bekannte nicht hinaus.

---

[2] Unter den Editionen sollte auch der (um zwei weitere Übersetzungen vermehrte) Nachdruck der editio princeps, Lucca 1781, erwähnt werden (er erscheint jetzt nur unter den Versionen); ferner ist die Ausgabe von Mitscherlich trotz des Datums 1794 erst nach der von Locella (1796) erschienen (vgl. Mitscherlich 189 f). – Zur Liste der Übersetzungen sind die französische von Ch.-M. Zévort (Paris 1856) und die neugriechische von X. Ἰ. Καππε (Smyrna 1871) hinzuzufügen. Auch die lateinische Übersetzung von der Schilderung des Artemisfests (I 2,2-5 u. 3,1), die schon 1489 in A. Polizianos *Miscellaneorum centuria prima* (c. 51) veröffentlicht wurde, sollte nicht vergessen werden. Eine unveröffentlichte rumänische Übersetzung von N. Pauletti von 1846 (Bibl. Acad. Rom. 198) wird von M. Marinescu in *Rev. Ist. Rom.* 11-12, 1941-42, 349-357, besprochen. – Zu spät, um unter den textkritischen Beiträgen verzeichnet zu werden, ist wohl A. Borgogno, 'In difesa di alcune lezioni del codice Laurenziano conv. soppr. 627', *Par. del Pass.* 136, 1971, 38-43, erschienen; der Artikel enthält jedoch kaum etwas, das die Textgestaltung P.s beeinflußt hätte.

Neu ist dagegen, was der Hrsg. von der im British Museum befindlichen Hs der *Ephesiaka* (Add. 10378), auf die B. E. Perry aufmerksam gemacht hat (*The Ancient Romances* 345), zu sagen hat. Sie sei nicht vor dem 18. Jh. hergestellt; der Schreiber erwähne nämlich D'Orville und Hemsterhuys und scheine die "editiones Cocchi et Salvini" (= Cocchis Edition und Salvinis Übersetzung?) vor Augen gehabt zu haben. Leider wird die letzte Behauptung nicht weiter begründet, und da wohl nur eine Auswahl der Abweichungen dieser Hs (B) vom Laurentianus (F) im Apparat verzeichnet ist, kann der Leser den Abhängigkeitsverhältnissen zwischen den Hss und den Ausgaben auch nicht selbst nachgehen.[3] Allerdings dürfte als sicher gelten, daß B neben F keinen selbständigen Wert besitzt, sondern bei der Textgestaltung nur als Quelle für Konjekturen in Frage kommt.

Der Hrsg. spricht sich fernerhin in der Einleitung für eine möglichst nahe Anlehnung an die überlieferte Sprachform aus. Es soll nicht, wie in Herchers Teubner-Ausgabe der *Erotici scriptores* (1858–59), durch 'Verbesserungen' der Grammatik der falsche Anschein eines konsequent angebrachten Attizismus gegeben werden. Bereits Dalmeyda setzte sich dieses Ziel: "Noyer sous une prétendue correction des faits de morphologie ou de syntaxe qui marquent l'évolution de la langue, ce n'est, en somme, qu'un jeu de dilettante, et c'est rendre à l'auteur un service hypothétique" (XXXVI). In der Praxis war er jedoch nicht ganz konsequent (vgl. L. Castiglioni, diese Zeitschr. 5, 1929, 321–326, und H. Ljungvik, *Eranos* 28, 1930, 75–82), und P(apanikolaou) will nun den entscheidenden Schritt tun.[4] Er verzeichnet schon in der Einleitung typische 'Koine'-Formen, die früher (jedoch normalerweise nicht bei Dalmeyda) korrigiert wurden. Im Wortindex kann man weitere nützliche Hinweise auf bemerkenswerte Formen und Konstruktionen finden.

Die Textgestaltung zeichnet sich meistenteils durch eine nüchterne Zurückhaltung aus. Dalmeydas Text ist verständlicherweise der Ausgangspunkt gewesen.[5] An etwa 135 Stellen habe ich Abweichungen da-

459

---

[3] Auffällig viele Übereinstimmungen zwischen B und Locella sind im App. verzeichnet.

[4] P. ist selbst mit Untersuchungen zur Sprache und Chronologie der griechischen Romane hervorgetreten: *Chariton-Studien*, Göttingen 1973, erweiterte Fassung seiner Kölner Diss. 'Zur Sprache Charitons' (1963).

[5] Auch als Druckvorlage hat er offenbar gedient; vgl. die falschen Anführungszeichen 21,22 und das versehentlich stehengebliebene Ny ephelkystikon 69,28.

von vermerkt. Die eigenen Konjekturen des Hrsg. sind bescheidener Art und Frequenz,[6] die Wahl zwischen den zahlreichen neuen Vorschlägen anderer Gelehrter, die seit dem Erscheinen der Budé-Ausgabe veröffentlicht worden sind, ist im allgemeinen besonnen. Die Rehabilitierung der Überlieferung ist weniger radikal, als die Einleitung erwarten läßt. In dieser Hinsicht wäre m. E. größere Kühnheit angebracht gewesen; viele alte Änderungen werden immer noch mechanisch mitgeschleppt. Dies gilt weniger von der Grammatik als von mehreren Eingriffen sachlicher und stilistischer Art, die den übertriebenen Forderungen früherer Kritiker an Logik und Ökonomie des Ausdrucks in diesem einfachen Unterhaltungsroman entsprungen sind. Es wird auch manchmal ein übertriebenes Streben spürbar, die bekannte sprachlich-stilistische Stereotypie dieses Autors, die sich jetzt durch den Index noch leichter belegen läßt, durch zusätzliche Eingriffe zu vermehren.

460 Aus guten Gründen ist der Hrsg. z. B. an den folgenden Stellen zur Überlieferung zurückgekehrt: 2, 6–7; 5,16; 5,22 (vgl. 36,29); 6,19; 7,21; 9,5; 12,2; 22,3; 27,9; 28,14; 29,4–5; 33,15; 37,4; 39,2; 46,1; 48,28; 52,22; 53,2; 60,3; 63,12; 64,27; 65,22; 70,29. — Die Namen der Hauptpersonen werden nach der Hs durchgehend Ἀβροκόμης (die aspirierte Form begegnet in der Hs nur vereinzelt) bzw. Ἀνθία (nicht Ἄνθεια) geschrieben. — Auf Blass-Debrunner 283,3 u. 284 verweisend behält der Hrsg. 38,6 αὐτῆς (als possessiven Gen.) bei, statt mit den früheren Editoren das Reflexivum αὑτῆς zu schreiben; warum dann nicht auch 52,14 (und 52,17 nach Präp.?), wenn nun einmal bei solch spröder Materie der Hs Zutrauen geschenkt wird (in der Mehrzahl der Fälle sah P. sich ja doch durch die Stellung des Pronomens gezwungen, in die aspirierte Form zu ändern: 52,18; 57,27; 60,5 usw.)?

Auch an den folgenden Stellen hätte er sich m. E. an die Überlieferung halten sollen: 2,8 (vgl. 13,13 und s. Cataudella); 6,28 (s. Castiglioni und Wifstrand); 8,4 (τοῦ θεοῦ bezieht sich auf Apollon, vgl. Zimmermann, *WüJbb* 4, 1949–50, 261 f); 9,22; 10,2 (πόμα τὸ ἐρωτικόν, zum Art. vgl. Schmid, *Atticismus* III 63 u. 201, IV 67); 10,9 (vgl. Ach. Tat. II 8 u. 37,6–10 und s. Castiglioni); 11,6 ἀγωγὴν 'Fahrt', nicht 'Abfahrt'; die Stelle ist also mit Thuk. IV 29,1 [vgl. dazu Classen-Steup] u. VI 29,3, wo die Mehrzahl der Hss auch ἀγωγήν liest, nicht ganz analog; dagegen ist 11,9 die Änderung besser motiviert und die Erklärung des Fehlers evident); 13,21 (ἐκ τῶν, s. Ljungvik); 13,22 ("adorabant eoque sibi

---

[6] Die wichtigeren findet man in Ἐπιστ. Ἐπετ. τῆς Φιλοσ. Σχ. τοῦ Παν. Ἀθηνῶν 20, 1969-70, 351-362, begründet. Auf diesen Artikel und die übrigen textkritischen Beiträge, die in der 3. Abt. der Bibliographie verzeichnet sind, verweise ich unten nur mit dem Namen des betr. Gelehrten.

propitios reddere conabantur" Ljungvik); 15,8 (s. Castiglioni); 16,20 (s. Ljungvik); 17,5 (unnötige Gleichrichtung); 20,2 (vgl. 23,1); 20,19 (s. Cataudella); 21,15
(vgl. 33,30, Char. II 2,6); 23,8 (ἐγγράφει paßt zu πινακίδα, wie γράφει 22, 17
zu γραμμάτιον); 24,30 (s. Wifstrand); 27,10-11 (s. Ljungvik); 28,10 (ὡς 'ut ...
ita'); 29,6 u. 45,23 (s. Castiglioni); 32,28; 33,28; 34,6; 34,16 u. 71,16 (P. schreibt
Dat. Ὑπεράνθει statt -η oder -ῃ F, auf den Gen. -ους 35,24 hinweisend; aber
der Akk. heißt -ην 33,11 u.ö. [dagegen Μεγαμήδη 38,1], der Vok. -η 35,7); 35,12
(ὀλίγου... παρῆλθον οὐκ εἰπών, vgl. Kühner-Gerth³ I 204,4); 41,21 (das erste
τὴν reicht für beide Begriffe aus, vgl. Kühner-Gerth³ I 611,2); 49,26; 53,26 (die
Form ἀλεία ist bei mehreren Autoren nachklassischer Zeit belegt, vgl. Thes.
Graec. Ling. s. v.); 55,9 (ἡμέρας 'einige Tage', vgl. Char. V 9,6 und Ach. Tat. I
8,10); 64,4 (πεπόνθαμεν, vgl. Cataudellas Parallelen).

Unter den durch Konjekturen verbesserten Stellen erwähne ich: 3,18; 4,30-5,
1; 7,19; 17,9; 50,6; 60,5. An den folgenden Stellen andererseits scheinen mir
die gewählten Lösungen unbefriedigend oder hat der Hrsg. Schwierigkeiten
stillschweigend übergangen: 2,15-16 u. 3,2-3 Jacksons beide miteinander eng
verbundene Umstellungen sind fast unausweichlich (seine scharfsinnige Begründung muß in extenso gelesen werden); vermutlich entstand in demselben
Vorgänger von F (mit Zeilen von etwa 40 Buchstaben) auch die Unordnung
in 14,12-14 (ἐν τούτῳ gehört vor ἐφίσταται), 31,19-20 (ἐκεῖ nach εὐδαίμονες?),
40,15-17 (ἂν) und 58,26-27 (ἅμα gehört zu ἔλεγε προσπεσοῦσα, vgl. 53,19 u.
57,26). — 3,13 ὅπλα ist, wie früher oft bemerkt, undenkbar; eine Randnotiz,
mit Z. 11 ἐσθής korrespondierend, hat das ursprüngliche Attribut verdrängt.
— 7,3 προσεποίουν ist sachlich verdächtig, s. Giangrande (der προσεπεῖπον
vorschlägt). — 7,25 παραστής: s. die berechtigten Einwendungen bei Zimmermann a. O. 258 f. — 9,26 ἠμέλ<λ>ησας Cataudella. — 10,26 χρόνῳ καλῶν
(Hemsterhuys) bedeutet eine kleinere Änderung und ergibt einen besseren Sinn
und eine schönere Satzstruktur als die Konjektur von P.; für χρόνῳ ohne Attr.
vgl. 70,5. — 11,14 <ἐνεβιβάζοντο> paßt, auf Sklaven bezogen, viel besser als
<ἐπέβαινον>; daß das Verb bei X. E. nicht im Pass. belegt ist, ist kein Argu-
ment. — 11,24-25. Die überlieferte Wortfolge ist sicher richtig; möglicherweise
könnte, falls die Brachylogie als zu hart empfunden wird, eine Änderung in τοῖς
(statt τῶν) ἐν τῇ νηὶ συμμιγής (mit einer gewöhnlichen verkürzten Ausdrucks-
weise, vgl. Kühner-Gerth³ II 310 f) erwogen werden; die Korruption war bei
den drei umgebenden τῶν fast unvermeidlich. P.s Universalmittel <καὶ> (vgl.
19,16; 31,26; 55,4; 57,2; 58,17) ist selten befriedigend. — 29,17-18 Cruces sollten
ἄγει ... αἰγιαλὸν umrahmen (Giangrande betrachtet sogar ἄγει bis einschl.
Μαντώ als eine Randbemerkung). — 31,25-26 Salvinis τὸν ἵππον ist inhaltlich
besser als Herchers <καὶ>; es ergibt auch die bei X. E. beliebte Wiederholung
(ἵππον...ἵππος). — 34,17-18 Cruces desperationis! — 41,28 P.s Versuch, diese
korrupte Passage herzustellen, ist denen seiner Vorgänger weit unterlegen. πότου statt τόπου ist evident (vgl. Ach. Tat. II 3,3 τοῦ δὲ πότου προϊόντος ἤδη bzw.
V 23,2 für die banale Verwechslung πότον/τόπον), die Einwände P.s fallen u. a.
durch 43,12 ὑπὸ μέθης weg. Das unmögliche ὁ κύριος durch einen Hinweis auf

461

die vermeintliche Epitomierung zu verteidigen, ist ein billiger Ausweg (vermutlich steckt hinter ὁ κύριος [oder ΟΚ͞Σ?] ein Adverb, wie ἤδη bei Ach. Tat.). Die neue Interpunktion 42,1 ist folglich abzulehnen und καὶ 'auch' beizubehalten. — 44,16–17 καὶ Φοινίκης ὅση παραθαλάσσιος (vgl. Wifstrand) könnte eine Randnotiz sein, die darauf hinweisen wollte, daß die Küstengegend der Phoinike ebenfalls παραλία genannt wurde (von etwa 400 n. Chr. bis zur Eroberung durch die Araber sogar als Name einer eigenen Provinz [s. z. B. Georg. Cypr. 967 Ἐπαρχία Φοινίκης Παραλίας], während das Hinterland Phoinike Libanesia hieß, vgl. RE 12:2, 1925, 2484 und 20:1, 1941, 369). — 50,28 S. Castiglioni; Borgognos Versuch (s. o. Anm. 2), mit Locella ἐν ὀργῇ ἔχειν als 'strafen' zu deuten, überzeugt nicht (vgl. Thuk. II 65,3). — 51,6 Peerlkamps Vorschlag ist sachlich (Kontinuität der Erzählung), stilistisch (die für X. E. typische Parenthese und Wortwiederholung) und paläographisch weit überlegen; zur Nachstellung des zweiten Subjekts vgl. 25,30. — 55,4 Abreschs Vorschlag ist vorzuziehen, vgl. 26,16. — 63,28 Wie versteht der Hrsg. diese Stelle? Locellas <ἰδών> ist wenigstens erwähnenswert. — 68,23 ἔρωτα ist hier Nonsens, die beste Heilung bleibt die von Locella (vgl. 11,17; 36,30; 45,4; 69,18).

Im kritischen Apparat hat der Hrsg., da nur eine Hs heranzuziehen war, zahlreiche Vorschläge zur Verbesserung des Textes verzeichnen können, ohne daß die Übersichtlichkeit gefährdet ist. Während Dalmeyda sich auf die eigenen Abweichungen von der Hs beschränkte, findet man in der neuen Edition nicht nur die wichtigsten Beiträge der fünf dazwischenliegenden Dezennien, sondern auch eine freigebige, in vieler Hinsicht belehrende Auswahl der Leistungen früherer Kritikergenerationen; so lassen sich z. B. die Emendationen Herchers als ein fortlaufender grammatischer Kommentar zum Text lesen. Auch auf die erfolgreiche Verteidigung des überlieferten Wortlauts wird an einigen Stellen hingewiesen, jedoch viel seltener als wünschenswert wäre; die gelehrten Ausführungen der Kenner des nachklassischen Griechisch, die in späterer Zeit am Xenophon-Text gearbeitet haben, verdienen es auch dann erwähnt zu werden, wenn durch Anführung von Parallelen und genaue Interpretation der Textstelle die Überlieferung als einwandfrei ausgewiesen wird (vgl. z. B. Ljungvik a. O. zu I 4,5 ἀντιλέγοντι und zu IV 3,3 λογιζομένη). Bestenfalls verhindert ja eine solche Praxis auch neue vermeintliche Emendationen tatsächlich heiler Stellen.

Zu Dalmeydas Berichterstattung über den Laurentianus war offenbar nicht viel hinzuzufügen. Abgesehen von Akzenten und Spiritus (meistens αὐτοῦ/αὑτοῦ usw.) sind nur die folgenden Stellen zu bemerken: 7,14; 13,2; 31,7; 33,3; 38,18; 50,5. Verdächtig scheint mir die Berichterstattung zu 62,26 und 65,27. — 8,25

u. 8,26 ist Ljungviks Name irrtümlicherweise mit den Konjekturen verbunden worden; er verteidigt in Wirklichkeit beidemal die Überlieferung.

Die zwei zusätzlichen Apparate sind weniger umsichtig zusammengestellt. Der Parallelenapparat verzeichnet ausschließlich Ähnlichkeiten der Motive und Ausdrucksweisen in Charitons Roman (mit Hinweisen nur auf des Hrsg. eigene Ausführungen zur Frage der Abhängigkeit zwischen den beiden Romanen). Eine Erweiterung auf die übrigen Romane (auch die Fragmente) und andere verwandte Literatur, wozu Vorarbeiten nicht fehlen,[7] hätte ein vollständigeres Bild ergeben; die Abhängigkeitsfrage läßt sich ja nicht durch einen isolierten Vergleich zwischen Chariton und Xenophon lösen.

462

Ein besonderer Apparat gibt die Stellen an, an denen nach Ansicht K. Bürgers (*Hermes* 27, 1892, 36–67) der Roman in verkürzter Fassung überliefert worden ist. Auf den Versuch des Rez., die schwachen Grundlagen der Epitomierungstheorie darzulegen (*ClMed* 27, 1966, 118–161 [no. 6 in this volume]), verweist der Hrsg. zwar in der Einleitung (VII), die Hinweise zu Bürger im Apparat aber müssen dem Benutzer des Textes den Eindruck geben, die Epitomierung an sich wäre eine unbestreitbare Tatsache, ja sogar, daß die Stellen, an denen der Epitomator gearbeitet hätte, genau lokalisierbar wären.

Der Wert des mit großer Genauigkeit zusammengestellten Wortindex wurde schon oben hervorgehoben. Unbefriedigend ist jedoch, daß der Index ohne besondere Kennzeichnung auch konjizierte Wörter verzeichnet (z. B. κατευθύς III 11,4 und συγκαθείργομαι IV 6,6), während die entsprechenden überlieferten Lesungen oft fehlen.

Für die künftige Beschäftigung mit Xenophons Roman stellt diese sorgfältige Textausgabe, besonders dank des ausführlichen kritischen Apparates und der vollständigen Namen- und Wortindices, ein vorzügliches Arbeitsinstrument dar.

---

[7] F. Garin, *StudIt* 17, 1909, 423-460. Viel Material auch bei K. Kerényi, *Die griechisch-orientalische Romanliteratur* (2. Aufl. Darmstadt 1962), und R. Söder, *Die apokryphen Apostelgeschichten und die romanhafte Literatur der Antike* (Stuttgart 1932, Nachdr. 1968).

[Review of]

1. R. MERKELBACH, *Die Quellen des griechischen Alexanderromans.*
Zweite, neubearb. Auflage unter Mitwirkung von J. Trumpf.
[Zetemata, 9.] München, C.H. Beck 1977. 285 S. *DM 208,-.*

2. J.TRUMPF, Anonymi Byzantini *Vita Alexandri regis Macedonum.*
[Bibl. script. graec. et roman. Teubneriana.]
Stuttgart, Teubner 1974. XXVI, 205 S.

[originally published in *Byzantinische Zeitschrift* 73, 1980, 54-57]

1. "Die Grundthesen dieses Buches konnten ganz unverändert bleiben"
stellt der Verf. im neuen Vorwort fest. Trotzdem handelt es sich kei-
neswegs um einen bloßen revidierten Nachdruck des erstmals im Jahre
1954 erschienenen Werkes, das in der Erforschung des Alexanderromans
Epoche gemacht hat, sondern tatsächlich um eine Neuauflage, z.T. neu-
geschrieben und beträchtlich erweitert (1. Aufl.: XI+255 S.; 2. Aufl.: 285
S., trotz größeren Satzspiegels). Die wichtigsten Neuheiten beziehen
sich auf die spätere Überlieferung des Romans, die inzwischen unter
der zielbewußten Leitung Merkelbachs von mehreren Gelehrten aufge-
arbeitet worden ist: van Thiel, Bergson, Trumpf u. a. Der letztgenannte
hat auch die Neubearbeitung der betreffenden Teile des vorliegenden
Buches besorgt.

Die unveränderten Hauptthesen sollen hier nicht wieder aufgenommen werden (vgl. H. Dörrie, *Gnomon* 27 [1955] 581-586; F. Pfister, *B.Z.*
53 [1960] 124-126); vielmehr sieht es der Rez. als seine Aufgabe, das Neue
kurz vorzustellen (das Vorwort gibt darüber zu summarische, z. T. nicht
ganz zutreffende Auskunft). Nicht zum wenigsten wird, wer die 1. Aufl.
schon besitzt, an einer solchen Berichterstattung interessiert sein: der
Preis der Neuauflage ist herausfordernd hoch angesetzt.

Die vorbildlich klare Aufteilung auf allgemeinen bzw. besonderen
Teil, Exkurse und Texte im Anhang ist beibehalten. Für das Ganze gilt,
daß die Bibliographie sorgfältig komplettiert und die Hinweise zu Text-
editionen gegebenenfalls modernisiert worden sind. Für diese mühselige
à-jour-Führung des technischen Apparates, von der nicht viele Seiten ganz
unberührt sind, wird jeder Benutzer des Buches dankbar sein. Davon

abgesehen sind aber die wichtigeren Veränderungen oder Zusätze auf
bestimmte Punkte konzentriert.

Allgemeiner Teil. S. 34–45: beträchtlich erweiterte Behandlung
der Gründungsgeschichte von Alexandria, Betonung des ätiologi-
schen Charakters dieses Romanabschnittes, Heranziehung neuerer
Lit. (Welles, Fraser u. a.). S. 51: Hervorhebung echter persischer Re-
densarten in den Briefen des Darius (1. Aufl. S. 35 Anm. 3). S. 58–60:
Neues (nach Gunderson u. a.) zur Deutung des indischen Orakel des
Sonnen- und Mondbaumes. S. 62: Ausführlicheres zum Brief II 23–41
(Land der Finsternis). S. 64–70: Weiteres zu den Wunderbriefen: neue
literarische Parallelen, Heranziehung der Rez. ε, Bemerkungen über
den Wirklichkeitshintergrund der Beschreibungen von Kynokepha-
len usw. (aus den Nachträgen der 1. Aufl S. 252–254), über Alexanders
Trostbrief an Olympias (1. Aufl. S. 111), über ein Motiv manichäischen
Ursprungs in II 36 Rez. β. S. 77–88: über Nektanebos, den vater Alexanders (vgl. 1. Aufl S. 57f.), und über Alexanders Luftfahrt unter besonderer Hervorhebung der (ägyptischen bzw. persischen) rituellen
Hintergründe dieser beiden berühmten Episoden der Alexander-Le-
gende. S. 91: Hinweis auf den Bilderzyklus zum Alexanderroman auf
dem Baalbek-Mosaik.

Besonderer Teil. Im Abschnitt über die Überlieferung (S. 93–108) ist
viel neues Material hinzugefügt, bes. S. 94–100: das neuentdeckte byzantinische Florilegium, die Rez. ε (vgl. unten), die neugriechische Version
"Rimada", Neues zu den armenischen, lateinischen und slawischen Übersetzungen. S. 108: zum Grabepigramm über Alexander aus Alexandria
(vgl. 1. Aufl. S. 96). Sonst ist dieser Abschnitt gar nicht "ganz neu" geschrieben, wie man aus dem Vorwort glauben könnte, und noch weniger
kann man das von der folgenden Analyse des Romans (S. 108–155) sagen:
S. 109 und 116–118 finden sich kleinere Zusätze, aber sonst ist der Text
bis S. 132 aus der 1. Aufl. fast wörtlich übernommen. S. 132–138 ist im
Gegenteil das meiste neu oder neugefaßt: es geht hier um den problem-
reichen letzten Teil von Buch II, wo jetzt der Unterschied zwischen den
verschiedenen Rezensionen viel klarer hervortritt. Auch S. 143–155 sind
weitgehend neugefaßt: Bemerkungen über Palladios' Schrift *De gentibus
Indiae et Bragmanibus*, über den Zusats der syrischen Übersetzung zum
Wunderbrief III 17 (z. T. nach Exkurs IV der 1. Aufl S. 155–161), über
Alexanders Besuch bei Kandake, über die christliche Interpolation in III
29, Heranziehung der "Rimada" für die Rekonstruktion von III 30–33,
Neues zum versifizierten Anhang in der armenischen Übersetzung. (In

der Tabelle S. 150 steht immer noch versehentlich I 33, 1–10 [usw.] statt
III 33, 1–10 [usw.]).

Exkurse. I, III und VIII sind in der Hauptsache unverändert (Zusätze
S. 171 und 223). Zwei Exkurse der 1. Aufl. sind weggefallen: V, "Über den
Wert der Redaktion J des Archipresbyters Leo", und VII, "Der Verfasser des *Itinerarium Alexandri*" (Begründungen im Vorwort). Ihre Plätze
haben eingenommen: V (S. 198–201), "Die Weihe der Sarapis-Statue
im Mailänder Papyrus" ("etwas veränderte Fassung der im *Archiv für
Papyrusforschung* 17 [1961] 108–109 erschienenen Miszelle"), und VII (S.
215–218), "Alexanders Besuch in der äthiopischen Götterhöhle" (Text von
III 24 mit ausführlichem Apparat, unter Heranziehung neuer Textzeugen). Im Exkurs II haben einige Emendationen zu Iulius Valerius (S.
163f.) entsprechendes zur Metzer Epitome ersetzt. Exkurs IV über die
Epistola Alexandri ad Aristotelem ist z. T. neugefaßt (bes. S. 193f.) und
auch kräftig beschnitten (vgl. S. 196 Mitte). Exkurs VI (S. 201–214),
"Die jüngeren Handschriften des griechischen Alexanderromans", ist
größtenteils neu geschrieben und gibt ein eindrucksvolles Zeugnis von
den Fortschritten auf diesem Gebiet seit 1954 (neues Stemma S. 211).
Auch die späteren byzantinischen und neugriechischen Bearbeitungen
werden behandelt, Trumpf selbst bereitet eine kritische Gesamtausgabe
der mittelgriechischen Prosaversion vor (S. 212).

Zusammenfassung und *Schematische Übersicht* über die Abhängigkeits-
verhältnisse (S. 224–226) sind bis auf einige Kleinigkeiten unverändert.
Die "Liste der aus der historischen Quelle genommenen Stücke" (S.
190 der 1. Aufl.) fehlt aber jetzt; ob dies ein stilles Zugeständnis davon
ist, daß die kategorische Aufteilung auf "hist. Qu." bzw. "Ps.-Kall.", die
allerdings im Text der neuen Aufl. meist unmodifiziert stehengeblieben
ist, doch nicht mehr die volle Stütze des Verf. genießt?

Von den beiden *Texten* im Anhang ist der erste — Merkelbachs Rekonstruktion des hellenistischen "Briefromans" — "fast unverändert
geblieben" (einige neue Vorschläge zum Text der Papyri im App., im
Text nur vereinzelte Veränderungen, wie XIV, 4–5), während im Testa-
mentum Alexandri der neue lateinische Text von Thomas den alten von
Wagner ersetzt.

Neue textkritische Beiträge sind über das Buch verstreut; die Verbesserungen zu Iulius Valerius werden S. 164 verzeichnet, man vermißt aber
eine entsprechende Liste der Konjekturen zum griechischen Text des Ps.-
Kallisthenes. Ob in der Zukunft diese mit "Merkelbach" oder "Trumpf"
oder beiden Namen bezeichnet werden sollen, erfährt man nicht.

Im großen und ganzen haben Verf. und Bearbeiter ihre heikle Aufgabe erfolgreich gelöst: es galt ja, ein Buch, das gleichzeitig als Bahnbrecher und Handbuch auftritt, auf den heutigen Stand der Forschung zu bringen, ohne den ursprünglichen Pioniergeist zu ersticken.

2. Was Trumpf vorlegt, ist die editio princeps einer byzantinischen Fassung des Alexanderromans, die in einer einzigen Hs., dem Oxon. Bodl. Barocc. 17 (Q, 13. Jh.), vollständig erhalten ist; sie hat die Bezeichnung "Rezension ε" bekommen. Nur ein Kapitel (5, über das Pferderennen Alexanders beim capitolinischen Agon in Rom!) war früher aus der Hs. Q ediert worden (H. Meusel, 1871), woraus G. Millet im Jahre 1926 auf die Existenz einer weiteren Rez. des Romans schloß. Es handelt sich um eine Nacherzählung der Geschichte mit neuen Worten, die, wie Trumpf bemerkt, sehr an die byzantinischen Heiligenleben erinnert (s. Merkelbach-Trumpf S. 206–208). Trotz der vielen verschiedenen Quellen — neben der zur Rez. α gehörigen Hauptquelle auch Palladios, Ps.-Methodios, die in den *Excerpta Latina Barbari* erhaltene alexandrinische Weltchronik und Alexanders Brief an Aristoteles — hat diese Fassung somit einen eigenen, einheitlichen Ton erhalten; man liest sie gern. Sie wurde nach Trumpf "frühestens Ende des 7., vermutlich eher im 8 Jh." geschrieben.

Das Vorwort der Edition ist dreigeteilt — die Hss. (mit Stemma), die Prinzipien der Ausgabe, die Quellen der Rez. ε — und wird von einer bibliographischen Übersicht der Rezensionen des Romans, der mit dem Alexanderroman verwandten Texte und der Sekundärliteratur begleitet. Neben der Hs. Q (die einige Folia vermißt und am Ende beschädigt ist) hat der Hrsg. auch andere Hss. herangezogen, die verschiedene Teile derselben Fassung aufweisen: Oxon. Bodl. Holkham gr. 99 (H, 15. Jh.; bis III 31 Rez. λ, danach Rez. ε), Mosquensis mus. hist. gr. 436 (K, 14./15. Jh.; hauptsächlich Rez. β, aber mit zahlreichen, verstreuten Zusätzen aus Rez. ε), und schließlich die Hss. der Rez. γ, in erster Linie Oxon. Bodl. Barocc. 20 (R, 14. Jh.); die Rez. γ folgt hauptsächlich der Rez. β, nimmt aber auch viele Abschnitte der Rez. ε auf. Zwei weitere Hss. werden als von H abhängig eliminiert. QH und Kγ bilden zwei Familien, hinter denen ein einziger Archetypus stehen soll, durch mehrere, für alle Hss. gemeinsame Fehler gekennzeichnet. Dies alles wird im ersten Teil des Vorworts sorgfältig beschrieben und begründet (S. VI vermißt man die Feststellung, daß nicht auch H Sonderfehler enthält, S. XII wird das Verhältnis zwischen D und C nicht ganz eindeutig aufgezeigt, auf derselben S. wird zu p. 26, 13 δυνατὸς statt δυντὸς als die Lesart von K, δύσβατος statt -ον als die von Q angegeben).

Neben Berichterstattung über Orthographie, Akzente, Sprachform usw. stellt der Hrsg. im zweiten Teil des Vorworts auch fest, daß die Textzeugen der Rez. ε unter sich weniger abweichen als die der Rezensionen β und λ, was wenigstens teilweise die Rekonstruktion des Texts des Archetypus ermögliche. Der Aufbau des Stemmas spiegelt eine verhältnismäßig einfache Wahl zwischen den Varianten vor. In Wirklichkeit erweist sich dies als eine Illusion, nicht nur weil oft Q der einzige Zeuge ist, sondern auch durch die Zahl und Art der Varianten in denjenigen Abschnitten, wo die Bezeugung reichhaltiger ist: auch was die Überlieferung betrifft, gleicht diese Schrift den Heiligenviten, der kritische Apparat strotzt in diesen Abschnitten von Varianten, zwischen denen die Wahl nur willkürlich sein kann. — Der Gebrauch des mittelgriechischen Prosa-Alexanders (Mgr) als Schiedsrichter zwischen den ε-Hss. wird S. XIV ungenügend begründet: wohin im Stemma gehört denn ihre Vorlage? Auch was S. XIV Anm. 3 über Kontamination gesagt wird, erweckt Bedenken: wenn die Abschreiber den Text der Rez. γ (RDC) "niemals" mit anderen Exemplaren der Rez. ε verglichen haben, wie erklärt man die Übereinstimmungen QD contra RC (z. B. p. 113,6 u. 131,7) oder QC contra RD (z. B. p. 119,10–11 u. 131,8)? Doppellesungen schon in γ, die zur gemeinsamen Quelle von DC als solche weitergegeben wurden? Oder interne Kontamination zwischen den γ-Hss.? Dies hätte ausgeführt werden sollen, weil die Antwort ja für die Richtigkeit der befolgten Regel für die Textkonstitution ("Lectiones recensionis γ verae agnoscuntur vel consensu codicum RDC omnium vel *consensu singulorum cum codicibus QHK*", Sperrung des Rez.) entscheidend ist.

Im dritten Teil des Vorworts über die Quellen werden auch die Begründungen zur Datierung der Rez. ε gegeben: die Verwendung des byzantinischen Zwölfsilbers an mehreren Stellen, die Erwähnung der (nach anderen Quellen) im 7. Jh. im Kaukasus lebenden "Bersiler", und (entscheidend) die Benutzung der syrischen Weissagungen des Ps.-Methodios von Patara in der griechischen Übersetzung aus dem 7. Jh. (vgl. Trumpf, *B. Z.* 64 [1971] 326–328).

Der Text (S. 1–178) erscheint in 46 Kapitel eingeteilt: der Hrsg. sah sich durch die Eigenart dieser Rez., was Stoffauswahl und Disposition betrifft, dazu gezwungen, mit der alten Buch- und Kapitelzählung C. Müllers ganz zu brechen. Diese Entscheidung mag die einzig mögliche gewesen sein; als Kompensation hätte man aber unbedingt eine Konkordanz in Tabellenform sowie auch deutliche Angaben der entsprechenden Kapitelzahlen der anderen Rezensionen auf jeder Seite fordern können; jetzt sind die Angaben im Apparat beim Anfang der neuen Kapitel verborgen. Auch die jeweils benutzten Hss. hätten zu jeder Seite angegeben werden sollen. Sonst sind Text und Apparat technisch gut hergestellt. — Einige Berichtigungen zum Text finden sich bei Merkelbach-Trumpf, S. 96.

Ein Index nominum propriorum, der gleichzeitig einen kurzen Kommentar (mit bibliographischen Angaben) zum Inhalt darstellt, und ein Index verborum notabilium, wo auch sprachliche Notizen untergebracht sind, schließen die verdienstvolle Arbeit ab.

57

19

[Review of]

Chariton. Le roman de Chairéas et Callirhoé. Texte établi et traduit par GEORGES MOLINIÉ. Paris: Belles Lettres 1979. 255 z. T. Doppels. 1 Kte. (Collection des Universités de France.)

[originally published in *Gnomon* 53, 1981, 698–700]

Man hätte gewünscht, diese neue Ausgabe von Charitons Roman vorbehaltlos begrüßen zu können. Die frühere textkritische Edition von W. E. Blake (Oxford 1938) ist seit (wenigstens) zwei Dezennien vergriffen, und in eben dieser Zeit ist gerade dieser Roman — der älteste unter den erhaltenen griechischen Romanen — in den Vordergrund der Forschung gerückt. A. Papanikolaou hat die Sprache und die Datierung des Romans erörtert (1963, 1973), R. Petri hat in der Nachfolge Merkelbachs seine mögliche Verbindung mit den Mysterienkulten untersucht (1963), J. Helms hat die Kunst des Charakterisierens studiert (1966), und K.-H. Gerschmann hat seine "werkimmanenten" Chariton-Interpretationen vorgelegt (1975), um nur die monographischen Darstellungen zu verzeichnen. Außerdem ist Chariton als bisher einziger Vertreter der Gattung von G. L. Schmeling in Twayne's World Authors Series einem größeren Publikum vorgestellt worden (New York 1974), und durch K. Plepelits besitzen wir jetzt eine kommentierte deutsche Übersetzung, die wissenschaftlichen Ansprüchen genügt (vgl. diese Zeitschr. 52, 1980, 492).

An einer neuen Ausgabe hat es aber gefehlt. Der Chariton-Spezialist F. Zimmermann arbeitete jahrelang an einer großen Edition mit Kommentar und Übersetzung; sie ist in einigen Handbüchern mit dem Druckjahr 1960 aufgeführt (A. Lesky, *GGrL²*, 1963, 926; Kröners *Wörterbuch d. Antike⁸*, 1976, 123; E. Schmalzriedt, *Hauptwerke d. ant. Lit.*, 1976, 397), in Wirklichkeit jedoch niemals erschienen. Einige der führenden Textreihen haben seit langem neue Editionen in Aussicht gestellt, doch nur die Collection Budé hat bisher ihr Versprechen auch eingelöst.

Äußerlich betrachtet ist das Buch ansprechend. Eine Einleitung (1–46) berichtet über Autor und Werk, die konstitutiven Elemente des Werkes, die künstlerischen Qualitäten und die Textüberlieferung. Der Text gründet sich auf eine Neukollation des codex unicus (cod. Laurent. Conv. Soppr. 627) und verwertet auch zwei neue Papyri (Oxy. 2948, Michael.

I), die Blake nicht kannte.[1] Die Übersetzung ist mit erklärenden Anmerkungen versehen, und ein ausführlicher 'Index des noms propres et
des principaux thèmes' (205–254) erschließt die Handlung des Romans.
Ein Plan der Mittelmeerwelt, in dem die Reisewege von Chaireas und
Kallirhoe eingezeichnet sind, veranschaulicht die Analyse der Handlung,
die in der Einleitung (14–21) geboten wurde.

Die inneren Qualitäten entsprechen der guten Anlage der Edition jedoch nicht. Die Einleitung enthält zwar wertvolle Einzelheiten, die aber
in der wortreichen und verschwommenen Darstellung fast verschwin-
den. Gerade als Einleitung zu einer Textausgabe ist diese Art Essay wenig
geeignet; man vergleiche etwa die präzise Weise in der Plepelits in der
genannten Übersetzung über die Forschungslage informiert. In bibliographischen Dingen ist M(olinié) offenbar ganz hilflos. Die 'Bibliographie'
(47–48) verzeichnet grundsätzlich *nicht* die wichtigeren Beiträge zur Interpretation und Textkritik, die in der fast 50seitigen Einleitung erwähnt
worden sind. Die muß man also in den Fußnoten suchen, wobei dort
die Titel und Namen nicht selten entstellt sind.[2] Der Gebrauch von 'op.
cit.' und 'ibidem' ist einfach grotesk (z. B. S. 73 Anm. 1).

Die ersten Seiten des Textes enthalten keine textkritischen Notizen,
ohne daß der zufällige Benutzer des Buches durch irgendeinen Hinweis
gewarnt wird. In der Einleitung findet man die Erklärung (45): das "erste" Blatt des Hs (= fol. 48) sei heute "absolument indéchiffrable" (man
erfährt nicht, ob nur auf Mikrofilm oder überhaupt). Deshalb hat sich M.
entschieden, hier Blakes Text (der auf den von Blake selbst überprüften
Lesungen Cobets fußt) einfach nachzudrucken, jedoch ohne Blakes kritischen Apparat auch nur in Auswahl mitzuteilen. Die totale Aporie, die
M. in seiner Begründung ausdrückt, is unberechtigt; Blake hat sorgfältig
angegeben, wo er eine von Cobet und ihm selbst eindeutig ermittelte
Lesung der Hs durch eine Konjektur ersetzt hat, und wenigstens diese
Stellen hätte M. in seinem Apparat unbedingt notieren sollen.

Von diesen ersten Seiten abgesehen, kehrt M. in seiner Textgestaltung
weitgehend zu den Lesungen der Hs oder den Verbesserungen der ersten

---

[1] Unnötigerweise sind die Sigla verändert worden: *L* statt *F* für die Florentiner Hs, und
ganz unschön "codex Wilckanus", *W*, für den bekannten, von U. Wilcken in Luxor er-
worbenen und später durch Brand zerstörten "codex Thebanus deperditus".

[2] Zur Liste der Übersetzungen ist hinzuzufügen: die 2. Aufl. des Sammelwerks 'Il romanzo classico', unter dem Titel 'Il romanzo antico greco e latino' (Firenze 1973) erschienen, und die spanische Übersetzung von J. Mendoza (Biblioteca Clásica Gredos
16, Madrid 1979).

Herausgeber und Kritiker (bes. Reiske, D'Orville, Cobet und Hercher) zurück. Das ist im Prinzip berechtigt und bedeutet eine willkommene Ernüchterung nach Blakes textkritischen Ausschweifungen. Das Ergebnis ist trotzdem m. E. gar nicht befriedigend, weil der Hrsg. infolge mangelnder Analyse des Kontextes und mangelnder Kenntnis der Sprache und Gattung zu oft eine wenig überzeugende Wahl zwischen den Konjekturen bzw. zwischen Konjekturen und Überlieferung getroffen hat. Ich werde das durch Besprechung der Stellen, an denen der Hrsg. eigene Textverbesserungen vorgeschlagen hat, zu demonstrieren versuchen.

Zwei von M.s Konjekturen finde ich durchaus erwägenswert (V 10, 8 und VI 3, 1). Zwei andere stammen in Wirklichkeit nicht von M., sondern finden sich schon in Blakes Apparat (I 10, 5 und VI 3, 4); die zweite von ihnen (ursprünglich von Blake vorgeschlagen) ist die akzeptable Ergänzung einer Lakune, die erste dagegen (von D'Orville/Cobet) erübrigt sich ('Wiederherstellung' eines indirekten Reflexivums). Gleichfalls verfehlt ist M.s eigene Augmentierung eines augmentlosen Plusquamperfekts in IV 5, 5.

Ich bespreche etwas ausführlicher einige der restlichen neun Konjekturen von M.s Hand. I 3, 2 κρύφα δὲ καὶ ἀδήλως ἐπελθόντες σημεῖα κώμου ἦσαν καὶ κατέλιπον L, εἶσαν M. Es ist aber eher ein Verbum für 'bringen' (wie D'Orvilles <ἐκόμ>ισαν erforderlich; was man konkret mit den verschiedenen Arten von 'Zeichen' tut, wird nachher erzählt (u. a. δᾷδας ἔρριψαν, was M.s Vorschlag unmöglich macht). — III 9, 11 καθάπερ οὖν νέφος ἢ σκότος ἀπεκάλυψε τῆς ψυχῆς Διονύσιον καὶ περιπτυξάμενος Φωκᾶν 'σύ' φησιν '...' L, ...νέφος ἔσχατον ἀνεκάλυψε τῆς ψυχῆς Δ-ιος... Blake, ...τὴν ψυχὴν Δ-ίου... M. Es gibt auch eine Reihe älterer Versuche, diese offenbar korrupte Stelle zu heilen. Blakes Text ist, wie so oft, eine Mischung des Guten (Δ-ιος, schon von Reiske vorgeschlagen), des nicht Notwendigen (ἀν-) und des ganz Willkürlichen (ἔσχ.). M.s Vorschlag finde ich noch schlechter: der harte Subjektswechsel ist nicht beseitigt, und diese Bedeutung von ἀποκαλύπτω ("qui *cessèrent d'assombrir* l'esprit de D."), mit der Wolke und dem Dunkel als Subjekt, ist wohl kaum möglich. Notwendig scheint mir nur die leichte Änderung Δ-ιος zu sein; auch bei Ach. Tat. kommt ἀποκαλύπτω in der Bedeutung 'entfernen, abwerfen' zweimal vor (VI 16, 4 und VIII 10, 8; vgl. O'Sullivan, *Lex. to Ach. Tat.*, s. v. I 2 "cast off"). — V 8, 2 φράσοι L, φράσαι M. Blakes φράσῃ ist wegen der exakten Parallele in VIII 1, 14 und 4, 1 vorzuziehen. — VI 4, 10: Wo ist das Wort προϋπηρεσία belegt, und woher stammt die Bedeutung "importante mission"?

Im kritischen Apparat werden nur diejenigen Konjekturen verzeichnet, die in den Text aufgenommen sind. Der Benutzer der Edition ist dadurch dem Urteilsvermögen des Hrsg. ganz ausgeliefert, was in diesem Fall bedeutet, daß Blakes Ausgabe mit ihrem vollen kritischen Apparat immer noch unentbehrlich ist. Eine besonnene Auswahl der früheren Konjekturen hätte M.s Apparat nicht überlastet, aber die Brauchbarkeit seiner Edition wesentlich erhöht.

In den Anmerkungen zur Übersetzung begründet der Hrsg. einige seiner textkritischen Entscheidungen. Darüber hinaus werden, allerdings sehr sparsam, Erklärungen von Namen und Sachen gegeben. Die Auswahl scheint recht zufällig zu sein, und die Sekundärliteratur zu Chariton wird nicht verwertet. Es wird z. B. zu I 1, 2 ἐθνῶν τῶν ἐν ἠπείρῳ (übersetzt: "peuplades de l'intérieur") nur vermerkt: "Il doit s'agir des régions méridionales d'Europe". Kein Wort über das (von Zimmermann u. a. vermutete) Wortspiel mit dem vorhergehenden Ἠπείρου, Epirus, kein hinweis auf die früheren Erklärungen von ἠπείρῳ: Kleinasien (Zimmermann, Blake), Griechenland (Perry), Italien nördlich des heutigen Kalabrien (Plepelits). Einiges von dem was man in den Anmerkungen vermißt, wurde (ohne irgendeinen Hinweis) schon in der Einleitung berührt (z. B. die juristischen Aspekte von Kallirhoes Verkauf in I 12 ff, s. S. 9), aber zu viel wird sowohl dort als auch in den Anmerkungen zu flüchtig (z. B. 80, 187) oder gar nicht kommentiert. Daß es sich um einen Roman handelt, bedeutet nicht, daß die sachliche Erklärung uninteressant ist.

Die Parallelen aus den späteren Romanen hat M. überhaupt nicht verzeichnet, und andere literarische Reminiszenzen bei Chariton als die Homer-Zitate werden nur unvollständig notiert. So wird auf die Menander-Entlehnungen in I 4, 2 und II 1, 5 hingewiesen, aber die entsprechenden Hinweise fehlen zu I 4, 3 (fr. 542 Koerte-Thierfelder) und I 7, 1 (fr. 59, 4). Sappho wird als Parallele zur Heiratsschilderung in I 1, 11–16 angeführt, Soph. *Aias* 550 f zu III 8, 8 andererseits nicht. Das auch von Demosthenes gebrauchte Sprichwort in III 9, 3 und VI 5, 1 wird richtig notiert, während in I 3, 1 (vgl. auch IV 7, 3 und VIII 1, 5) die Travestierung einer berühmten Passage der Kranzrede (§ 169, vgl. Ps.-Longinos 10,7 mit Russells Anmerkung) und in V 2, 4 die wörtliche Entlehnung aus der Pantheia-Geschichte der Kyrupädie (VI 4, 3) unbemerkt passieren.

Die stilistische Qualitäten der französischen Übersetzung zu beurteilen, überlasse ich anderen. Was das sachliche anbelangt, haben meine Stichproben keine gröberen Versehen aufgedeckt, obwohl hier und da die

700

Übersetzung hätte präziser sein können (z. B. I 7, 3 "changeur", VIII 3, 7 "nos retrouvailles") oder m. E. nicht ganz das Richtige getroffen hat (z. B. II 8, 7 "au lieu de", "assez facile", III 3, 4 "qui restait immobile", VIII 1, 11 "unique au monde", 2, 4 "les prisonniers", 2, 5 "pour le rejoindre"). In I 10, 8 scheint mir Zimmermanns Deutung von ἐπιψηφίζω "genehmigen, billigen, beipflichten" (*Studi in onore di A. Calderini e R. Paribeni*, Bd. II, Milano 1957, S. 138) evident richtig zu sein.

Möge das Erscheinen dieser Ausgabe, die in vielen Hinsichten ein Monument der ungenutzten Möglichkeiten darstellt, der Verwirklichung der anderen geplanten Editionen nicht im Wege stehen. Blake ist noch nicht ersetzt.

20

[Review of]

BARTSCH (S.) *Decoding the ancient novel: the reader and the role of description in Heliodorus and Achilles Tatius.* Princeton: Princeton University Press, 1989. Pp. x + 201. $29.50.

[originally published in *Journal of Hellenic Studies* 112, 1992, 192–93]

It is a pity when authors (or publishers) fall for the temptation to give their products attractive rather than accurate titles. 'Decoding the ancient novel' creates expectations which this short book cannot meet. What it does, and mostly does well, is — as the subtitle indicates — scrutinize one particular (admittedly important) feature in two of the 'sophistic' Greek novels. And this feature, 'an apparently inexplicable appetite for discursions and descriptive passages of every sort' (4), is something that sets these two novels apart from the genre at large, as the author herself admits (4, 36 f.).

As a background Bartsch surveys the role of *ecphrasis* in Second Sophistic theory and practice. The exegetical (Philostratus) and allegorical (Cebes, Lucian) modes of describing painting are well distinguished and the habitual coupling of description with interpretation well exemplified. One misses, however, a retrospect on the use of descriptions of works of art in Greek literature from Achilles' shield in *Il.* xviii onwards (Downey in *RAC* is conspicuously absent from the bibliography). B.'s account sometimes creates the impression that the precepts of the *progymnasmata* came first and the literary application followed. The fact that *ecphrases* of works of art (as distinct from those of places, personages, circumstances etc.) are not even mentioned by rhetorical theorists until Nicolaus (fifth century), while they dominate in imperial literature, should be sufficient warning in this respect.

Having thus tried to form an idea of 'what the reader in the Second Sophistic might expect' (36) when encountering an *ecphrasis,* B. proceeds to the famous pictorial descriptions in Achilles Tatius. To what extent do they have a literary use as 'Mittel thematischer Vorschau' (Sedelmeier) or as 'proleptic similes' (Harlan), to what extent are they 'only' rhetorical showpieces? Like other interpreters who, since Friedländer's pioneer study (1912), have attempted this game, B. is more successful in some demonstrations than in others. Her explanation of the garden description within the Europa *ecphrasis* (Ach. Tat. 1.1) is attractive, while her ingenious attempt to make the details of the Andromeda-Prometheus diptych (3.6–8) foreshadow the fake-sacrifice of Leucippe (3.15) failed to convince the present reviewer. 'It is here that Achilles Tatius plays most skilfully with the reader's expectations and with their notions of how to read the work. For when the events that have been foreshadowed finally occur, they are recognized at once, marked clearly as they are by the correspondence of details that Achilles Tatius has cleverly inserted into both accounts' (58). Clearly, indeed? The reader's 'inferential walk' (Eco, quoted on p. 44) through Achilles Tatius will have been among the most frustrating experiences imaginable if B. should be right. When it comes to her exegesis of the Philomela painting (5.3–5, cf. esp. 68–76), I am tempted to quote Perry's laconic comment on Merkelbach's *Roman und Mysterium:* 'This is all nonsense to me.'

The next topic, dreams and oracles, is much more straightforward and B.'s interpretation correspondingly less controversial. She demonstrates that in Achilles Tatius not only Pantheia's dream (2.23) but also that of Clitophon (1.3) allows of double interpretations, one immediate and one disclosed only with hindsight (to speak of 'misinterpretation and later enlightenment' [87], however, is not quite to the point); and there is an illuminating discussion of the twin dreams in 4.1. Heliodorus's novel exhibits a more variegated use of dreams and oracles; among them, B. pays particular attention to Thyamis's oracular dream (1.18), analyzing the author's repeated 'play upon the hermeneutic process' (98) until its true fulfilment with Thisbe's substitute death (2.8). The analysis of other dreams in the *Aethiopica* is less rewarding, a fact for which the interpreter is not to blame.

Heliodorus's forte lies elsewhere, as becomes clear when our attention is turned to the next topic, the description of spectacles. His visualizing power and theatrical obsession have often been noted. B., always trying to relate the stylistic features to the reading process, emphasizes the role of the spectators in the novel. Their reactions to what is displayed are meant to guide the reader's interpretation and emotional response; e.g. the brigands in the introductory scene 'act as proleptic models for the extratextual viewers' (120), Cnemon represents the reader in the description of the procession at Delphi, and the Ethiopian spectators show how the author wants us to react to the grand finale.

The last chapter before the conclusion is rather a mixed bag. Among 'other descriptions' we find paradoxographical digressions, 'protreptic' descriptions (a fine name for a banal function), and geographic or ethnographic descriptions which are there to give the fiction an authentic-looking framework: 'the unexpected is made to occur within a world that is real and that the readers accept as such' (163). There are many acute observations here, but also instances of over-interpretation. E.g., the grapes changing from immature to ripe (Ach. Tat. 2.3.2) are thought to 'foreshadow the entire progression of Clitophon and Leucippe's love affair' (147), and the bare mention of an embroidery depicting the battle of Lapiths and Centaurs (Hld. 3.3.5) is supposed to linger in the reader's mind until, in 10.29.1, Theagenes (a Thessalian, like the Lapiths) is 'doing battle not with a man-horse (centaur) but with a bull-horse (hippotaur)' (148) — but he does, in fact, nothing of the sort, for the hippo-part of this 'hippotaur' is the horse he is riding! The critical standards B. uses in dismissing the fancies of others (149 n.1) might well have been applied to her own.

This is an intelligent and illuminating study, even though the author's judgement does not always seem to match her ingenuity. It is well-written, generally accurate (but the *Vita Apollonii* is placed in the second century on p. 7, and Agatharchides among Second Sophistic writers on p. 160), and handsomely produced.

[Review of]

Xenophon's Imperial Fiction: On "The Education of Cyrus." By James Tatum. Princeton: Princeton University Press, 1989. Pp. xix + 301; 6 ills. in text. $32.50.

The "Cyropaedia": Xenophon's Aims and Methods. By Bodil Due. Aarhus: Aarhus University Press, 1989. Pp. 264.

[originally published in *Classical Philology* 86, 1991, 147–152]

H. J. Rose, in his influential *Handbook of Greek Literature*, passed a devastating judgment upon Xenophon: "In him, a mind which it would be flattery to call second-rate and a character hide-bound with convention attain somehow to very respectable literary expression and are presented with at least two subjects on which it is nearly impossible to be wholly dull" (4th ed. [London, 1950], p. 305). The education of Cyrus was not one of these, we understand some pages later: "Unfortunately, he felt impelled to embody his ideals of royalty in a work of the imagination, a sort of composition for which he was singularly unfitted. The *Cyropaedia* ... has the distinction of being the first historical novel and the first moral romance that has come down to us. It is further distinguished by being one of the dullest writings in any tongue .... An extraordinary fact is the popularity of the *Cyropaedia* among men otherwise of good taste ..." (pp. 307–8).

Now two scholars, both no doubt "of good taste," simultaneously and independently have tried to redress the balance and explain the paradox alluded to at the end of my quotation. Not that Rose's verdict (or that of his contemporaries, for he was not alone) has remained unchallenged: on the contrary, even if his well-turned phrases still echo in the minds of many and the writings of some, Xenophon has regained respect and the *Cyropaedia* some of its esteem, if not its readership. But there are still differences of opinion, partly determined by nationality, as a check of some of Rose's modern counterparts confirms. While the French (Flacelière and de Romilly) and some Germans (notably Schmalzriedt in *Kindlers Literaturlexikon*)[1] pay the work detailed and positive attention, Dover

[1] Reprinted in E. Schmalzriedt, ed., *Hauptwerke der antiken Literaturen* (Munich, 1976), pp. 126-27.

(in *Ancient Greek Literature*) is rather noncommittal, and the Cambridge *History of Classical Literature* chooses (or happens?) to pass over the *Cyropaedia* in almost complete silence.

Yet, expressing esteem (or the opposite) is one thing, laying the scholarly foundation for a balanced estimation of the aesthetic and historical value of a literary work is another, and in the latter respect the *Cyropaedia* has suffered nearly complete neglect (even H. R. Breitenbach's treatment in Pauly-Wissowa is disappointing). So, what Breitenbach did for the *Hellenica*, Olof Gigon for the *Memorabilia*, Leo Strauss for some of the *opuscula*, is now at last attempted for the *Cyropaedia*. In spite of the common motive of *Ehrenrettung*, the two books under review are very different, and are best discussed separately.

James Tatum's main object is to study "the way Xenophon intertwined the fictional and the political in a single text" (p. xiii). He chooses to start with the *Nachleben*, an approach rather fashionable in this kind of semi-popular account, but not so easy to handle; among other things, one has to describe the reception of a work before one's reader is properly acquainted with the work received. Under the heading "The Classic as Footnote," T. presents a kaleidoscopic view of the fate of the *Cyropaedia*, with a number of brilliant pieces, but with no clear pattern emerging. Perhaps it is too much to expect such a pattern: probing the history of a classical work's reception is one of the more demanding tasks one may undertake, especially since there is little in the way of systematic *Vorarbeiten* to rely on. But T.'s chosen leitmotiv — the reasons for the gradual decline of interest in the *Cyropaedia* among people seeking political instruction and among those "just looking for a good read" (p. 18) — probably could have produced more coherence and structure, if only chronology had not too often been sacrificed for the sake of an impressionistic to-and-fro. But we are indeed served plenty of appetizing material in this chapter.

The next chapter, "The Rise of a Novel," already shows the skill of presentation and sensibility in literary interpretation we may expect from the author of *Apuleius and the Golden Ass*. Searching for "the forces within Xenophon that led him to undertake such a project" (p. 37), T. rightly emphasizes Xenophon's own words in the prologue as the best starting-point (as Due does in her book), and he presents a close and enlightening reading of this text. But he also takes us on a guided tour through Xenophon's earlier writings, showing how the *Cyropaedia* is the culmination of a life-long struggle, in theory and practice, with problems of leadership. The approach owes something to W. Higgins' reading of Xenophon,[2] and that is no bad model. My only serious quarrel is with T.'s easy-going dismissal of generic questions (e.g., p. 57: "Like any prose writer, he was engaged in the invention of his own genre as he went along" — though not everyone in his scribbling happens to invent, or prefigure, two genres as successful as novel and biography).

Thus we are prepared for the analysis of the *Cyropaedia* proper, which fills chapters 3 through 9 and is formally arranged as a scrutiny of the secondary characters of the work: family, foes, and friends. "Formally," since each chapter also, and more importantly, examines one particular aspect of Xenophon's art or object. "The curious return of Cambyses" (8. 5), with its commonplace and seemingly unmotivated fatherly advice, is Xenophon's reminder that paternal authority is absolute and that ruling and obeying, ἄρχειν and ἄρχεσθαι, are inseparable faculties. Even Cyrus is "being ruled," as long as his father is alive; it is as much part of his training for kingship as are his exercises in ruling. This should demonstrate that the title Κύρου παιδεία covers practically the whole work and not, as is still often maintained, just Book 1; his "education" — like that of any crown prince — ends only on the day he formally mounts the throne. But I do not think it is right to put such emphasis on the word παῖς in 8. 5. 22 (pp. 78, 80) to prove the point; it is certainly not necessary. It is hardly correct to say that "Cyrus remains a *pais* until his sudden transformation into an old man at the end of Book 8" (p. 91): a παῖς, "son," he remains only to his own parents (as we all do); to others he ceased being a child already in 1. 5. 1 (p. 90), and it is only his παιδεία, not his childhood, that continues up to 8. 7. 1. T. shares with some contemporaries an obsession with words and their etymology — rather than their actual meaning — and this is not the only time that he permits himself to be carried away on that wave (cf. also, e.g., pp. 134–35, where the notes hide some of the reservations that should have been in the text).

We are then taken on the long journey from the child Cyrus' manipulation of his grandparents (chap. 4) to the mature king's management of his empire (chap. 9). On the way, a dense chapter (5) is devoted to the invented uncle Cyaxares, who is created to serve as a foil to Cyrus

149

---

[2] *Xenophon the Athenian: The Problem of the Individual and the Society of the "Polis"* (Albany, 1977).

himself; the next two chapters are given over to the sophistically trained Armenian Tigranes (6) and to Croesus (7). As regards the story of the beautiful Panthea and her husband Abradatas (chap. 8), T. interestingly supplements the usual "sentimental reading" with an analysis that brings out "its essentially political purpose" (p. 171). At all times, Cyrus is at the center: "there are as many Cyruses as the sum of the people he meets" (p. 190).

This is all done with much ingenuity and skill, and is (on the whole) persuasively presented. Our understanding of how the *Cyropaedia* works takes an important step forward. Yet I must admit that I have my doubts about certain aspects of this modern reading of the *Cyropaedia*: it brilliantly explores the potentials of the text, but it does not critically examine where Xenophon ends and the modern reader begins. Without discussion, it takes for granted a consistent and sustained characterization that, as far as I am aware, neither drama nor the novel achieved in antiquity. Much is read between the lines; feelings, thoughts, and intentions that are not in the text are ascribed to the characters as if they were alive and available for psychological scrutiny independently of their author. If this is what T. means by saying that he will "make the *Cyropaedia* a twentieth-century text rather than a remote historical document" (p. xiii), I can only state my disagreement. One simple example will have to suffice. After Abradatas has been killed in battle, Cyrus and Panthea meet; and Panthea accuses both herself and Cyrus of being responsible for her husband's death (7. 3. 10). After quoting her speech, T. continues (pp. 184–85): "Cyrus weeps for some time in silence. He cannot reply to this charge. When he finally does speak, he is once again intensely conventional [Cyrus' answer, at 7. 3. 11, is quoted]. Cyrus cannot afford to answer what Panthea has said. Hence his turn to the conventional consolations for the survivors of dead heroes." Between the two speeches, Xenophon in fact only reports that Cyrus wept for some time in silence before speaking. There is no hint that Xenophon intends Cyrus' short silence to indicate that he cannot find an answer or does not consider his subsequent speech of consolation an answer ("But ... ") or means it to be conventional in any negative sense. It is the modern reader who may find it conventional (as T. often does find Xenophon's rhetoric) — with the result that some find him dull, while others ascribe to him subtleties of characterization far beyond his intentions and means (cf. also pp. 78, 139, 141, 158, 194). A middle course would no doubt recommend itself: a historically based reading (heroic death and the promise

150

of a monument, sacrifices, and free escort are a consolation, however commonplace) and a dose of "Tychoism" in dealing with the rhetoric (each scene fully exploits its rhetorical potential).

The last chapter, "Revision," deals both with the authenticity of *Cyropaedia* 8. 8 (which T. defends, without adding new evidence) and with Plato's criticism of Xenophon's educational concept in the *Laws*. We are thus back with the reception of the work, and the circle is closed. This is typical of T.'s book: its style and disposition are worked out with minute care and refinement. Well-chosen mottoes abound, and an intelligent use is made of illustrations (of the fifteenth through seventeenth centuries). The notes contain numerous valuable discussions of a philological nature, which have not been permitted to break the flow of the main narrative.

Bodil Due's book is altogether more straightforward, less occupied with its own rhetoric (for better and for worse). True to its subtitle, it treats Xenophon's "aims and methods," though in reverse order: its first part is devoted to "Structure and Narrative Technique," its second to "Meaning and Message." The introduction presents a picture of allegedly common negative attitudes to Xenophon and the *Cyropaedia* (cf. also p. 230 on the "disdain" for Xenophon among scholars) that seems exaggerated or at least dated. It then reports on the state of research with regard to genre and title, the authenticity of the final chapter, and Xenophon's reason for choosing Cyrus the Great as his ideal ruler. The most substantial part is the discussion of what D. prefers to call the "epilogue" — thus anticipating her own conclusion, that 8. 8 is an organic part of the *Cyropaedia*, corresponding to 1. 1, its "prologue." This conclusion is based on a close comparison of the wording of the two chapters (though the change from 1st pers. plur. in the prologue to 1st pers. sing. in the epilogue is never discussed). The author repeatedly returns to the same issue (pp. 30–31, 33–38, with refutation of S. Hirsch's recent arguments against authenticity),[3] since Xenophon's deliberate planning of his work is one of her main tenets.

In the chapter "Framework and Form," the most interesting observations are made in the section entitled "Time" (pp. 42–52). It is demonstrated how Xenophon almost imperceptibly makes the narration of particular scenes pass into the description of typical behavior over an

[3] *The Friendship of the Barbarians: Xenophon and the Persian Empire* (Hanover and London, 1985), pp. 91-97.

extended period of time (termed "narrative shortening" by D., p. 102; T., p. 85, speaks of "emblematic scenes"). Xenophon thus subtly combines concreteness and a narrow focus in the scenes we are made to witness with an impression of generality and the passage of time. For authors of biographies, this is a technique still worth studying. Another sensible discussion concerns the problematic dating of the events narrated in 2–8. 6, i.e., the events between Cyrus' youth and his old age and death. The conclusion — that all these events took place in one year, while the second half of Cyrus' life occupies only a couple of pages! — is probably correct. The fact that this does not agree with the general reader's impression should perhaps have caused D. to qualify her overall admiration for Xenophon's skill as an author.

There are other things in the same chapter that I find rather less convincing. Observing that the author makes very few remarks in the first person, D. (pp. 31–33) chooses for discussion two occurrences of (the parenthetic) οἶμαι (3. 3. 59, 8. 2. 6) and one of οὐκ οἶδα (8. 2. 12). Though it is certainly true that such items "contribute to making the style of the work resemble that of historical writing" (p. 33; a reference here to J. Morgan's analysis of "the historiographical pose" in Heliodorus would have been appropriate),[4] I firmly disagree with the second part of the conclusion: "But they also stress points of special interest and importance" and "serve the function of calling attention to the present time" (ibid.). Rather, they are of a purely phraseological nature, bearing only a formal resemblance to genuine authorial intrusions into the narrative. I am also hesitant about the section entitled "Anachronistic Ideas" (pp. 38–42): the term "anachronism" is misleading, since displacement in time is not the essential thing here (why not try the rare term "anachorism"?), and most instances are to be explained, I believe, by the simple fact that Xenophon has to use his own language in describing things Persian. Why single out ἐρώμενος / ἐραστής and σοφιστής as "anachronisms," but not (e.g.) ἔφηβος (1. 2. 4), ἱκέτης (4. 6. 2), and κωμάζω (7. 5. 25)? It would perhaps be wisest, *pace* Hirsch, to call the whole of the *Cyropaedia* one great anachorism — following the definition from the Penguin *Dictionary of Literary Terms*: "Action, scene or character placed where it does not belong …."

---

[4] "History, Romance, and Realism in the *Aithiopika* of Heliodoros," *CA* 1 (1982): 221-65, esp. pp. 227-34.

In the following two chapters, "People around Cyrus" and "Recurrent Themes," D. emphasizes the unifying function of the recurrent secondary characters such as Cyaxares and of themes such as strategic devices and religious customs. I believe the main thesis to be exaggerated; after all, secondary characters, invented or historical, are necessary ingredients of any story, and authors, not least Xenophon, do have their hobby-horses, which may recur without deliberate artistic intention. Nevertheless, these chapters contain much valuable material pertaining to Xenophon's art of characterization and to his paradigmatic technique, as well as an excellent treatment of the Panthea story and its integration into the main narrative (pp. 79–83).

Much of what D. does in this first part dealing with narrative technique is pioneer work: surprisingly little has been studied systematically before, probably because of the misconception that simplicity means artlessness. In her second part, she covers more familiar ground. Among Xenophon's "Sources and Models," most space is naturally given to Herodotus, without a quite proportional return. Antisthenes' importance is minimized, and the discussion of possible influence from Persian sources largely concentrates on the death-scene, which is considered more Socratic than Persian. On the whole, there is in this chapter an understandable but dangerous tendency to equate Xenophon's sources with those at our disposal, and to analyze Xenophon's version in terms of "deviations" from the surviving "models." 152

The three remaining chapters are united by a common theme, Xenophon's ideology of leadership. Particularly noteworthy in the treatment of Cyrus as the embodiment of the ideal leader is the detailed analysis of φιλανθρωπία and ἐγκράτεια. The horizon is also widened to include the other ideal leaders in Xenophon's writings: Jason of Pherae in the *Hellenica*, Agesilaus, Socrates (!), and the heroes of the *Anabasis*, Cyrus the Younger and "Xenophon the officer" (thus covering much of the same ground as T. in his chap. 2, but very differently). It is all done with diligence and circumspection, and these chapters should be read by everyone with an interest in fourth-century political ideology and morality. I end by quoting from the conclusion (p. 237), on the message of the *Cyropaedia*:

> What [Xenophon] wants to stress is the absolute necessity of moral strength in life as in politics. Without the highest possible moral standards in the leader — and a leader there must be in a state, as well as in

an army or a family — there is no hope of success or stability and thus no hope of improving the sad and confused conditions of human life.

It is reassuring to note that both books under review, for all their differences in approach, agree in viewing this as Xenophon's legacy, conveyed most impressively through his last great work. They also agree, of course, in their high appreciation of Xenophon as a political thinker and an author. To a large extent, they manage to penetrate his deceptive simplicity (of mind and style alike) and demonstrate his true qualities — though T., I suspect, makes him seem rather more subtle and sophisticated than he was, D., more artistic and premeditating. In so doing, they admirably succeed in explaining why the *Cyropaedia* was so favorably received for so long, but hardly why it has more recently been considered so uncommonly dull.

[Review of]

TATUM (J.) Ed. *The search for the ancient novel.* Baltimore: Johns Hopkins, 1994. PP. xiii + 46.3. £54 (£20.50, paper).

MORGAN (J.R.) and STONEMAN (R.) Ed. *Greek fiction: the Greek novel in context.* London: Routledge. 1994. Pp. x + 290. £40 (£ 12.99, paper).

[originally published in *Journal of Hellenic Studies* 115, 1995, 201-202]

Modern study of the ancient novel came of age, it has been aptly re-marked, with the international conference which Bryan Reardon con-vened in Bangor in 1976 (nowadays conveniently referred to as 'ICAN I'). Now, less than twenty years later, it is rapidly approaching its acme, at least if we are to judge by the quality of many of the contributions to the two books under review. The first one is a selection of high-class articles based on contributions to ICAN II, arranged at Dartmouth in 1989 (the whole range of subjects actually treated at that conference was already displayed in J. Tatum & G.M. Vernazza [eds.], *The Ancient Novel: Classical Paradigms and Modern Perspectives* [1990]). The second book is a multi-author survey of the Greek novel and its literary context. Since at least one more such collective enterprise is under way, there may well be a general feeling that the happy days are gone when a single scholar could be expected to cover adequately the whole field. The first book contains twenty-four contributions, the second sixteen; only six contribu-tors appear in both, which is again an indication of the large number of well-qualified scholars working in the field or on its fringes.

Although the editor of *The Search for the Ancient Novel*, James Tatum, has made a brave effort to arrange the contributions in eight topical categories, it is obvious that the quality of each piece rather than any wish to create an internally coherent collection has (rightly) guided his choice. Each article might as well have appeared, separated from the rest, in a periodical; but it is of course practical to have them collected in one volume. The editorial work deserves the highest praise; one only misses a subject index to give easier access to the book's riches.

The topics cover everything from genre theory to the European *Nachleben*, from Trimalchio's underworld to the *Alexander Romance* in Arab writings, from aretalogy to twentieth-century Greek prose fiction. Rather than using up my space listing all the authors and titles, I have chosen to discuss a selection of articles, in accordance with the focus of this journal as well as my own qualifications. (I also pass over articles which summarize studies already published separately, or explicitly coincide with parts of books in press.) It should at this point be emphasized that among those omitted in my review are half-a-dozen contributions to the early modern reception of Greek and Roman novels; anyone interested in that underdeveloped area of study is well advised to turn to this volume.

The collection begins with two papers on theory. The late Jack Winkler's 'The invention of romance' is a slightly revised reprint of an article published in 1982, i.e. pre-*Auctor & Actor*. Daniel Selden's 'Genre of genre' is of more actual interest, looking with healthily critical eyes on the generic concepts which, from Huet onwards, underlie our study of the texts we habitually group together as 'ancient novels'. It is suggested that *syllepsis* is the 'master trope' of ancient fiction; and we are offered (pp. 50 f.) somewhat unexpectedly, a learned discussion of Ach. Tat. 1.4.3 (Σελήνην/Εὐρώπην).

Three papers on Longus elucidate this rich text from very different angles. One, Froma Zeitlin's on the description of three 'gardens of desire', has been published elsewhere in a still more detailed form. Bryan Reardon, reflectively meandering through Longus' story and between different readings of it, finds the ambivalence, the irony, the light touch to be its distinction — and its defence against Rohde's accusation of superficiality and speculation, against Chalk's attempt at a theologizing reading. Geoffrey Arnott combines a fine sense for the literary qualities of the text with a natural scientist's precision in his contribution on animals (especially birds) and plants in Longus. He shows convincingly (partly in opposition to Vieillefond in the recent Budé edition) that Longus' degree of accuracy, particularly in ornithological matters, is surprisingly high — he must have been 'essentially a countryman', Arnott concludes, not the urban armchair escapist many have envisaged.

The topic of realism in the Greek novels is continued with Suzanne Saïd on the city and Brigitte Egger on women and marriage. Particularly interesting in both contributions is how careful historical research — on the city's institutions (the agora, the gymnasium. etc.) or on marital law — can be used to illuminate, with a high degree of precision, the novelists' balancing between contemporary and classicizing elements. At the same time, the differences between the novels are well brought out against the historical foil; e.g., Saïd accurately observes how Chariton 'creates an economical setting for a novel located in the past by a process of abstraction', whereas Heliodorus the antiquarian, confronted with the same challenge, stages 'a montage of political and cultural references' (226 f.).

The occurrence of aretalogical themes and structures in ancient novels is the subject of a concise contribution by Reinhold Merkelbach. In another, Judith Perkins reads the *Acts of Peter* as a text which combines its religious message with a more hidden agenda for social and political reform. Suzanne MacAlister, applying Bakhtin's concept of 'alien speech' to the Byzantine 12th-century novels, finds that these take over the revelatory-dream motif from their ancient models but systematically sabotage its conventional function.

'Who read ancient novels?', asks Susan Stephens, and using mainly papyrological evidence she answers: only a few, and they belonged to the same 'high culture' public who also read Demosthenes and Thucydides. 'No evidence currently available allows us to construct another set of readers for ancient novels' (p. 415). Except the evidence provided by the novels themselves, perhaps, one is tempted to rejoin. No, says Ewen Bowie in his parallel study of their readership, based mostly on internal or other literary evidence and arriving at similar conclusions. Both studies are well argued (except for Stephens' use of statistics) and contain much material which will be of value for the continued debate on this elusive topic; but I find the conclusions largely unconvincing (for reasons I have set out in detail in R. Eriksen [ed.], *Contexts of Pre-Novel Narrative* [1994] 47-81) [no. 4 in this volume].

Greek fiction: the Greek novel in context is a composite title which well covers the book's contents, including its questionable aspects. It does treat the five ideal Greek novels (here labelled 'The love romances'), with one short contribution on each, focusing on a particular aspect of importance, different for each author: women in Chariton, love in Longus, ego-narrative in Achilles Tatius, etc. So this is not an introduction to the Greek novel, since none of the extant specimens is presented in full. But an introduction it is, and a good one, to the novel's context-but only the Greek context (and the Egyptian), while the Roman novels are conspicuously missing (*cf.* the title's '*Greek* fiction'), with all the light

202

they might shed, by contrast or contiguity, on their Greek contemporaries (other regrettable omissions for reasons of space are conceded in the introduction, pp. 8 f.). So the question arises (and is not adequately answered in the introduction) to whom this collection is addressed. Not to newcomers, surely (they would need a better coverage of the main texts): presumably, then, to people with a basic knowledge, but without the context? But the boast on the cover (and less loudly in the introduction, pp. 1 f.) that 'this volume extends the boundaries of the subject beyond the "canon" of the romances properly called' etc., misrepresents the situation. One may raise much justified criticism against each of the existing introductions to the subject, from Helm onwards, but they certainly do not ignore the 'fringe' texts.

It would have been better to stress quality and insight: here, at last, experts on the various texts or literatures have been asked to give concise and readable presentations of their specialties, and the result is excellent, a notable advance on what we previously had in the same format. James Tatum writes pleasantly and authoritatively on the *Cyropaedia,* sometimes adding fresh viewpoints also of interest to those who read his monograph. Richard Stoneman gives a new, better informed and more closely argued version of his attractive reading of the *Alexander Romance,* which he first presented in the introduction to his Penguin translation. Gerald Sandy, who translated the novel fragments for Reardon's collection, is here given the chance to discuss them. Ewen Bowie, knowledgeable and circumspect as always, looks at Apollonius of Tyana and other writings by Philostratus as works of fiction. Richard Pervo delights us with an overview of the apocryphic acts of the apostles, changing perspective but not attitude from his study of the canonical Acts.

Other contributors are less well known to students of the Greek novel. Patricia Rosenmeyer, after a rather crammed survey of letters and letter collections in ancient literature, proceeds to an informed analysis of *Chion of Heraclea,* 'our prime surviving example of the ancient epistolary novel' (p. 152). Its special features of 'epistolarity' are well brought out while one misses comparisons with the other ego-narratives and historical novels; and it was her misfortune that Niklas Holzberg's *Der griechische Briefroman* (1994) appeared too late to be used. Simon Swain's chapter on Dio (the *Euboicus*) and Lucian is informative, but somewhat unfocused, and his use of the term 'novelistic' (p. 170 f.) puzzling, as is the surrounding discussion. Perhaps the most valuable piece in the whole collection is John Tait's 'Egyptian Fiction in Demotic and Greek', concise and clarifying, supplemented with an excellent bibliography. There is also much for a classicist to learn from Lawrence Wills' well-written chapter on Jewish novellas and from that of Judith Perkins on saints' lives; she stresses the new ideals (suffering, poverty) which hagiography represents, in contrast to its generic cognate and historical predecessor, pagan romance. Suzanne MacAlister on the Byzantine 'learned' novels shows how these can be read on several planes (pagan/Christian, sexual/spiritual etc.); but her contribution is all too short to give more than tantalizing (and not always convincing) glimpses.

On the 'love romances' proper, the contributions of experts like David Konstan, John Morgan and Bryan Reardon need no specific comment: they do not disappoint (except that Morgan's piece on Heliodorus, with its eccentric point of view, highlights the problem of the book's intended readership raised above). But I was particularly impressed by Brigitte Egger's reading of Chariton, focusing on the representation of the heroine, but also skilfully casting light on other important aspects of the narrative; it is easily the most balanced discussion of women's roles in the novels I have come across.

The generally high level of the contributions, in style and argument, shows that the editors have taken their task seriously, not only picking the right people, but also working actively to make them achieve their very best. And the bibliographies alone, judicious and up-to-date, are worth the book's (pbk) price.

[Review of]

R. Hunter (ed.): *Studies in Heliodorus.* Proceedings of the
Cambridge Philological Society, suppl. vol. 21. Pp. 232. Cambridge:
Cambridge Philological Society, 1998. Pbk. ISBN: 0–906014–19–0.

[originally published in *The Classical Review* N.S. 49, 1999, 380–381]

With a title as unassuming as its pale covers, this book brings together
nine new essays on the *Aithiopika*, all but one first presented to a Cambridge 'Laurence Seminar' in 1996. The diversity of approaches appears
from the three main headings under which they are sorted, 'Narrative
technique', 'The construction of culture', and 'Reception'.

'In her left hand carrying the flame of a lighted torch (*lampadion*),
and in her other hand holding out a shoot of palm (*phoinix*)' — these
two symbolic items in Charikleia's hands at Delphi (4.1.2) constitute
hitherto unnoticed leitmotifs in the novel, according to Ewen Bowie
('Phoenician games in Heliodorus' *Aithiopika*'). In particular, he sets
out to uncover the 'Phoenician' novelist's intricate play on the various
meanings of the word *phoenix*. Philip Hardie ('A reading of Heliodorus,
Aithiopika 3.4.1–5.2'), under the headings 'Digression', '*Enargeia*', and
'*Ekphrasis*', demonstrates important characteristics of Heliodorus' narrative style by analysing part of Kalasiris' narration to Knemon about the
Pythian spectacle. Knemon's simple account of his Athenian misfortunes,
in turn, is used by Richard Hunter ('The *Aithiopika* of Heliodorus: beyond interpretation?') to illuminate, by contrast, the sophistication of
the other narrators, Kalasiris and 'Heliodorus'; Chariton's novel provides
another foil, to good effect. John Morgan ('Narrative doublets in Heliodorus' *Aithiopika*', 60–78) compares recurrences of similar motifs or
structures in the course of the narrative, arguing that such 'repetitions,
in Heliodorus' case at least, are meaningful and deliberate' (64); consequently, the second of such 'doublets' may be fully appreciated only if
its mate is recognized and remembered in some detail.

All four pay tribute to Jack Winkler's seminal study of 1982 on 'The
Mendacity of Kalasiris', and have obviously greatly enjoyed this particular
game, letting their imagination loose and happily leaving it to the reader
to distinguish between the credible and the fanciful. Hunter, perhaps

the soberest among them, still does not let the doubt intimated in his title and first paragraph prevail over the temptation to join the game. The danger, of cause, does not lie in what this star quartet is presenting us with — their learning, ingenuity, and rhetorical brilliance vouch for much entertainment and considerable enlightment — but in what kind of scholarly model they are setting up for others in the profession.

The two contributors to the middle section are newcomers to the field, each with a recent dissertation on the *Aithiopika* among his credentials. John Hilton ('An Ethiopian paradox: Heliodorus, *Aithiopika* 4.8') takes the narrative of Charikleia's birth that her mother embroidered on the baby's swaddling band as his point of departure for a study of 'the central paradox' of the novel, the heroine's white skin. There is much of interest here; but the insistence on albinism as an explanation seems misconceived (this is no African legend), and it is curiously denied (86) that her whiteness is in fact essential for most of the construction of the plot. Tim Whitmarsh ('The birth of a prodigy: Heliodorus and the genealogy of Hellenism') likewise discusses Charikleia's birth: she is the 'prodigy' of the title, or rather one of them, for the novel itself is also — it is argued more forcefully than convincingly — a wonder and a hybrid in its author's eyes, because it 'violates the canons of art with its bold generic cross-contaminations' (118). This, however, is just one strand in the article which also provides important and persuasive treatment of Heliodorus' 'foreignness' vs. his 'Hellenism', of his intertextual dialogue with the *Odyssey* and of the rôle played by his 'Egyptian' Homer. Bakhtin's 'heteroglossia' concept is fruitfully applied, but one of his several false generalizations concerning the Greek novels rightly condemned ('almost exactly wrong', 95 n. 8).

Finally, we are offered three (very different) examples of the 'creative reception' (157) of Heliodorus' novel. Panagiotis Agapitos ('Narrative, Rhetoric, and "Drama" Rediscovered: Scholars and Poets in Byzantium Interpret Heliodorus') shows what may be gained, in terms of precision and novel perspectives, when a trained Byzantinist tackles the complexities of reception and revival. Starting with Photius' and Psellos' comments on Heliodorus, Agapitos discusses the true significance of their and later Byzantine writers' theatrical vocabulary (*drama, tragôdia* etc.) in a theatreless society. The article culminates in a deft analysis of the twelfth-century 'Heliodoran' verse novels of Prodromos and Eugeneianos, demonstrating the latter's dual use of Heliodorus and Prodromos and the shift from narrative fiction to rhetoricized drama that characterizes

381

both. Clotilde Bertoni and Massimo Fusillo ('Heliodorus Parthenopaeus: The *Aithiopika* in Baroque Naples') open another window: alongside Byzantium's 'Charikleia' there now appears 'Teagene', 'a martial and passionate hero of melodrama' (168) as depicted in Giambattista Basile's (1565–1632) huge epic poem by that name. It follows the novel closely, but exhibits various kinds of amplification and interpolation that are analysed here with exemplary clarity and ample illustration. The 'complex dialectic between epic and novel' (181), with the *eros* of the model 'corroding' the heroic demands of epic canons, is subtly displayed. The last contributor, Daniel Selden ('*Aithiopika* and Ethiopianism'), takes us to nineteenth- and twentieth-century United States and presents a vivid and dedicated account of the historical development of Ethiopianism and Afrocentrism and the part that the *Aithiopika*, on and off, has played in that process.

Hunter and his sub-editor, Mary Whitby, deserve full credit for an expeditious and diligent job. The book ends with a common bibliography, but there is regrettably no index.

Editors' Postscript

Editors' postscript

Good humanistic scholarship, as Tomas Hägg has hinted in writing and in conversation, depends on striking the right balance between learning, ideas, and sound judgement. Without the latter, the attraction of new ideas will often lead the learning astray; without learning, ideas and sound judgement tend to solve irrelevant problems; without ideas, learning and sound judgement make for repetitive and dull scholarship.

Apart from providing a wealth of new insights into ancient Greek fiction the present selection of Tomas Hägg's studies offers as many lessons in striking that balance. Just as we have been inspired by Tomas Hägg's writings it is our hope that his articles will be read beyond the circle of specialists by historical, literary, and philological scholars for their sheer model value.

Although the author, in the scholarly memoir we asked him to write as introduction, eloquently casts himself as a victim tossed around by Tyche on the sea of academic topics and institutions, we are not fooled. His scholarly results would never have come about without meticulous preparation nor without his extraordinary interest in other people's work. Add to this his social habitus that has won him so many friends within and without his own fields and institutions. His innate ability to contact people and to listen to them has certainly created ideal conditions for his own as well as collective scholarly projects.

It has also, in administrative matters, landed him the position as the *genius loci* and *almus pater* of our department, something we personally have benefitted enormously from throughout, respectively, twenty-six and twelve years. In fact his social habitus too can be circumscribed within the triangle of learning, ideas, and sound judgement.

Learning, in social terms, would match Tomas Hägg's interest in and knowledge of classical institutions in the Nordic countries, their *Schwerpunkte*, their institutional setup, and their scholars — established as well as younger ones. It has been a huge benefit for the small department at the University of Bergen to have a professor who has kept a lively contact with his own country, Sweden, and who is often invited to various places in Denmark and Norway as well. His academic network has furthermore constantly been enriched by shorter and longer sojourns in England, Germany, France, Greece, the USA and a number of other countries. We need not dwell further on the international network as it is amply documented in this book.

In collegial fora Tomas Hägg is a powerhouse of constructive ideas, ranging from planting the seed for large interdisciplinary scholarly projects, through ingenious departmental squaring of the circle of faculty demands in teaching programmes, to the ways of getting a guest lecturer to Bergen within the budget — because he happens to know both the same lecturer's Swedish schedule as well as the relevant cheap flights to Norway.

Much of Tomas Hägg's energy has been invested in bringing people together. His basic social tenet, it would seem, is inclusion: it is important to get as many relevant people as possible to join a meeting, to contribute to *Symbolae Osloenses*, to study at the Norwegian Institute in Athens, to follow this course, to join that research group etc. A sound judgement of the combination of activities and persons has been instrumental for his success in arranging numerous gatherings and finishing large projects. He does not belong to those who are quick to raise the voice, but his quiet authority always makes people listen. Matters great and small, practical as well as personal, have his attention, just as he regards the teaching of elementary Greek for beginners as much his province as giving seminars for advanced students and aspiring scholars. On an individual level we are convinced that numerous students and colleagues, like ourselves, have left a conversation with Tomas Hägg with their priorities much clearer on account of his sound judgement.

By editing *Parthenope* we wish to pay tribute to our long-time colleague and friend. In putting together the book we incurred various pleasant debts. For a first correction of some of the scanned files we would like to thank Christian Høgel and Richard Holton Pierce. The latter has furthermore been generous in correcting the English style in the freshly written or translated pieces. The Faculty of Humanities at the University of Bergen gave a grant for producing the book and so did the 'Construction of Christian identity'-project under the Research Council to which prof. Jostein Børtnes directed our attention. When the costs of the production rose beyond the expected, Nordea Danmark Fonden was kind to give extra financial support. We are most grateful to all of them.

Museum Tusculanum Press and its director, Marianne Alenius, accepted our proposal and encouraged us on our way. It is fitting that MTP has taken on this book, because it was an infant MTP that in the late 1970s represented the first reception of Tomas Hägg's studies outside of Sweden (see publications A7 & A8).

Highly successful colleagues may, we suppose, sometimes be a mixed blessing if they have little care for their immediate environment, but in Tomas Hägg's case it is as pure as a heroine of a Greek novel because he always applies his learning, ideas, and sound judgement to facilitate the success of others. In that spirit we would like to offer this small token of gratitude to a most generous colleague.

Lars Boje Mortensen & Tormod Eide
Bergen, December 2003

Publication acknowledgements

1. "A Professor and his Slave: Conventions and Values in the *Life of Aesop*", in P. Bilde et al. (eds.), *Conventional Values of the Hellenistic Greeks* (Studies in Hellenistic Civilization, 8), Aarhus University Press, Aarhus, 1997, pp. 177-203.

2. "*Callirhoe* and *Parthenope*: The Beginnings of the Historical Novel", in *Classical Antiquity* 6, University of California Press, Berkeley, 1987, pp. 184-204.

3. "Some Technical Aspects of the Characterization in Chariton's Romance", in *Studi classici in onore di Q. Cataudella*, vol. 2, Università di Catania, Catania, 1972 (pr. 1975), pp. 545-556.

4. "Orality, Literacy, and the 'Readership' of the Early Greek Novel", in R. Eriksen (ed.), *Contexts of Pre-Novel Narrative: The European Tradition*, Mouton de Gruyter, Berlin, 1994, pp. 47-81.

5. "Epiphany in the Greek Novels: The Emplotment of a Metaphor", in *Eranos* 100, Uppsala Universitet, Uppsala, 2002, pp. 51-61.

6. "Die *Ephesiaka* des Xenophon Ephesios – Original oder Epitome?", in *Classica et Mediaevalia* 27, Museum Tusculanum Press, Copenhagen, 1966, (pr. 1969) pp. 118-121.

7. "The Naming of the Characters in the Romance of Xenophon Ephesius", in *Eranos* 69, Uppsala Universitet, Uppsala, 1971, pp. 25-59.

8. "The *Parthenope Romance* Decapitated?", in *Symbolae Osloenses* 59, Taylor & Francis, Oslo, 1984, pp. 61-91.

9. "Metiochus at Polycrates' Court", in *Eranos* 83, Uppsala Universitet, Uppsala, 1985, pp. 92-102.

10. "The Oriental Reception of Greek Novels: A Survey with Some Preliminary Considerations", in *Symbolae Osloenses* 61, Taylor & Francis, Oslo, 1986, pp. 99-131.

11. "Hermes and the Invention of the Lyre: An Unorthodox Version", in *Symbolae Osloenses* 64, Taylor & Francis, Oslo, 1989, pp. 36-73.

12. "The Black Land of the Sun: Meroe in Heliodoros's Romantic Fiction", in V. Christides & Th. Papadopoullos (eds.), *Proceedings of the Sixth International Congress of Graeco-Oriental and African Studies, Nicosia 30 April – 5 May 1996*, Archbishop Makarios III Cultural Centre, Bureau of the History of Cyprus, Nicosia, 2000 (= *Graeco-Arabia* 7-8, 2000), pp. 195-220.

13. "Apollonios of Tyana – Magician, Philosopher, Counter-Christ: The Metamorphoses of a Life", previously unpublished.

14. "Hierocles the Lover of Truth and Eusebius the Sophist", in *Symbolae Osloenses* 67, Taylor & Francis, Oslo, 1992, pp. 138-150.

15. "Photius at Work: Evidence from the Taxt of the *Bibliotheca*", in *Greek, Roman, and Byzantine Studies* 14, Duke University, Durham, 1973, pp. 213-222.

16. "Bentley, Philostratus, and the German Printers", in *Journal of Hellenic Studies* 102, The Society for the Promotion of Hellenic Studies, London, 1982, pp. 214-216.

17. [Rev.] A.D. Papanikolaou (ed., 1973), *Xenophontis Ephesii Ephesiacorum libri V de amoribus Anthiae et Abrocomae*, in *Gnomon* 49, Verlag C. H. Beck, München, 1977, pp. 457-462.

18. [Rev.] R. Merkelbach (1977), *Die Quellen des griechischen Alexanderromans* 2. Aufl. & J. Trumpf (ed., 1974), *Vita Alexandri regis Macedonum*, in *Byzantinische Zeitschrift* 73, Verlag C. H. Beck, München, 1980, pp. 54-57.

19. [Rev.] G. Molinié (ed., 1979), *Chariton, Le roman de Chairéas et Callirhoé*, in *Gnomon* 53, Verlag C. H. Beck, München, 1981, pp. 698-700.

20. [Rev.] S. Bartsch (1989), *Decoding the Ancient Novel: The Reader and the Role of Description in Heliodorus and Schilles Tatius*, in *Journal of Hellenic Studies* 112, The Society for the Promotion of Hellenic Studies, London, 1992, pp. 192-193.

21. [Rev.] J. Tatum (1989), *Xenophon's Imperial Fiction: On "The Education of Cyrus"* & B. Due (1989), *The "Cyropaedia": Xenophon's Aims and Method*, in *Classical Philology* 86, University of Chicago Press, Chicago, 1991, pp. 147-152.

22. [Rev.] J. Tatum (ed., 1994), *The Search for the Ancient Novel* & J.R. Morgan & R. Stoneman (eds., 1994), *Greek Fiction: the Greek Novel in Context*, in *Journal of Hellenic Studies* 115, The Society for the Promotion of Hellenic Studies, London, 1995, pp. 201-202.

23. [Rev.] R. Hunter (ed., 1998), *Studies in Heliodorus*, in *The Classical Review* N.S. 49, Oxford University Press, Oxford, 1999, pp. 380-381.

Index

The index comprises authors, anonymous texts, and a selection of mainly literary concepts. When available, names are given in their traditional Latin or English form (Herodotus, Plutarch etc.).